LOVE'S SURRENDER

"Please," she cried, trying to draw away. But he only clasped her closer, kissing her neck, her cheeks, her lips, until she felt faint with the unaccustomed surge of feeling that coursed through her. Dimly, she was aware of his hands, searching, insistent, undoing buttons. He drew her down into the tall grass, murmuring endearments, his voice thick and imploring.

Again, she made a move to free herself. But it was too late, and the emotion gripped him, overpowered her. At last, with a cry, she reached for him, giving herself up entirely to the dizzying sensations that he aroused in her...

Avon Books are available at special quantity discounts for bulk purchases for sales promotions, premiums, fund raising or educational use. Special books, or book excerpts, can also be created to fit specific needs.

For details write or telephone the office of the Director of Special Markets, Avon Books, Dept. FP, 1790 Broadway, New York, New York 10019, 212-399-1357.

A GALLANT PASSION

HELENE LEHR

AVON
PUBLISHERS OF BARD, CAMELOT, DISCUS AND FLARE BOOKS

A GALLANT PASSION is an original publication of Avon Books. This work has never before appeared in book form.

AVON BOOKS
A division of
The Hearst Corporation
1790 Broadway
New York, New York 10019

Copyright © 1984 by Helene Lehr
Published by arrangement with the author
Library of Congress Catalog Card Number: 83-91192
ISBN: 0-380-86074-0

All rights reserved, which includes the right to reproduce this book or portions thereof in any form whatsoever except as provided by the U. S. Copyright Law. For information address Kidde, Hoyt and Picard, 335 East 51 Street, New York, New York 10022

First Avon Printing, February 1984

AVON TRADEMARK REG. U. S. PAT. OFF. AND IN OTHER COUNTRIES, MARCA REGISTRADA, HECHO EN U. S. A.

Printed in the U. S. A.

WFH   10 9 8 7 6 5 4 3 2 1

TO KENNETH
*for his love, his support,
and his understanding*

A GALLANT PASSION

BOOK ONE

Chapter 1

When the coach rolled into Whitlow, Massachusetts, on that January day in 1823, the snow had stopped, but under the lowering pewter clouds the air was just as dank and cold as before. Indeed, the dark gray afternoon sky that hung over the New England countryside gave the illusion that dusk had already fallen, although it was a good hour before it should have.

The passengers, nine in all, alit in various stages of weariness, their bodies stiff and cramped from the seven-hour ride. Within moments, all but two of them had gone their various ways, and only a young girl and a small boy remained standing in the snow-covered street outside the Golden Eagle Inn.

Relieved of his burden of passengers and baggage, the driver of the coach quickly secured the horses and made for the inn, anxious for the warmth and congeniality that awaited him.

"Please, sir..."

The girl's voice halted him, and, annoyed by this interruption, he looked down at the slight figure that had followed him.

"Could you kindly tell me where the mill is?" she asked. She stood quietly now, eyeing him in an almost deferential manner.

"It's about a mile outside of town," he responded, pointing. "Right on the river. But you'll have to walk, I ain't about to drive you there."

The girl nodded, accepting this without question, her expression placid in the face of his gruffness and all too obvious impatience. "And a boardinghouse? Could you recommend such a place?"

"I've no knowledge of that," he replied irritably, his mind on a steaming bowl of meat broth and a tankard of ale. Without further words, he turned away and made for the warm, welcoming light that beckoned so invitingly.

As the driver reached the door of the inn, it opened, and a young man with a shock of red-gold hair emerged, stepping aside to let the older man enter.

"Good evening to you, Mr. Poole," said the young man, nodding affably.

The driver peered. "Evening, Christian," he said, hurrying inside.

Christian hunched his shoulders against the piercing cold and plunged his hands into the depths of his pockets. He was so lost in thought that he almost collided with the girl, causing her to stumble and nearly fall. Quickly his hands shot out, steadying her.

"Oh, I'm sorry," he exclaimed. "Are you all right?"

"Yes," she replied in a somewhat breathless voice. Then, in a subtle movement, she drew back, and seeing this, his hands dropped to his sides again and he smiled tentatively.

"Did you just get off the coach?" he inquired pleasantly.

She nodded, her gaze direct and solemn, appearing to judge his worth. He was not much older than her own fifteen years but, being almost six feet tall, he towered over her by a good six inches. His hands when he had grasped hold of her were steady and firm, indicating a strength that was confirmed by broad, muscular shoulders. His eyes were blue, a pretty color, she thought, neither light nor dark; neither were they so vivid as to detract from his features as a whole. It was a nice face; compassionate, but with a hint of gentle humor.

The young man was regarding her quizzically. She was dressed plainly, he noted, but not shoddily, and her woolen garments and dark-blue shawl seemed to have been made with a loving hand. "Do you need help?" he asked impulsively.

Gray, deep-lashed eyes stared at him steadily. "No, no, I'm fine," she replied, taking another step away. "But I thank you for your concern," she added politely. A vague feeling of wrongdoing descended upon her, for she was perfectly aware that it was improper for her to be standing here, alone with a stranger.

He hesitated, still uncertain, but Jena was waiting, and her temper, should he be late, would be spirited. He and Jena were not yet engaged, but he hoped it would come about soon. With that in mind, he shrugged his shoulders and again plunged his hands in his pockets. "Well, I'm off then," he said with a smile. "Goodbye."

The girl watched him go, and then, with a sigh, returned to where her brother was standing. Bending over, she picked up the small cloth valise and, grasping hold of the boy's hand, began to walk in the direction of the mill.

"I'm hungry, Sarah," the boy said in protest, casting a backward glance at the inn. "Why can't we eat first?"

"We can't eat until we're settled, Aleceon," she said firmly. "If there is no work for us here, we'll have to move on. There's not that much money to be wasted. The coach fare took four dollars, and we've only about three left."

"We should have gone to Boston." The tone of voice was petulant, but he fell in step beside her.

"We couldn't pay the fare that far," she reminded him in a patient voice. "Now come on, walk faster, it'll keep you warm." She adjusted the scarf around his neck, pulling it up slightly so that it covered the lower part of his thin face. Then she drew her own shawl closer about her slender frame.

She tried not to think of the past few weeks, of the fire in which her mother, her father, and her older brother had perished, together with the house, the barn, and all they had possessed. But her efforts were less than successful; the image blazed as brightly as had the flames that had destroyed everything. If her mother hadn't awakened, hadn't gotten her and Aleceon out in time...Sarah turned her mind away from that. Best to look ahead, to get on with the more immediate problem of survival.

She glanced down at her brother. There had been those in Brockton who had wanted to send Aleceon to the Massachusetts State Orphanage, for he was barely eleven years old. She herself, at fifteen, was too old, but since the Panic some eight months ago, there were more people than jobs. It was, they clucked sadly, the almshouse for her.

But Sarah Edgewood was not about to let either of those things happen. What the neighbors had not known about, and what she prudently had not told them about, was the tin box buried not far from the back door. It had contained only seven dollars, but it had been enough for her and her brother to get passage on the next coach out of town. As Aleceon had said, Boston would offer them a greater chance of employment, but their money simply would not carry them that far.

She had stayed in Brockton only long enough to see her parents and Davie decently buried, availing herself of neighbors' generosity to do that properly, and taking temporary refuge in a neighbor's house. Then, with the few clothes she had managed to salvage, and with her brother in tow, she had left Brockton.

Now all her hopes were pinned on the mill. She knew that they hired only girls and young boys, and she said a quick prayer that there would be a job for them both, at least for a few months, anyway. If they could save enough, they might make it to Boston after all.

Along the side streets that angled out from the broad main avenue were the residential houses, which now, in the dusk and snow, seemed all alike, right down to the neat picket fences that stood like dwarfed sentries protectively enclosing each plot of ground. Everywhere, bare branched trees etched a tortuous pattern against the dimming sky, swaying now and then when prodded by the intermittent wind.

As they passed the Emporium, the door opened, and a woman, heavily bundled up, called a laughing good-bye to the unseen proprietor. The door closed again, emitting the muted sound of a bell and a brief odor of spices and food that made Sarah's stomach lurch. Unconsciously, she wet her lips and swallowed hard. She had not dared spend any of their small cache for food when the coach had stopped for the midday meal. Neither she nor Aleceon had eaten since 5:30 that morning, almost twelve hours ago.

Taking a deep breath, she resolutely turned her attention to the matter at hand and away from the enticing thoughts of food. The streets this late in the day were almost deserted, and only a few hardy pedestrians hurried along, anxious to conclude their business and return to the comfort of their fires.

"It's almost dark, Sarah," the boy complained, his voice muffled behind his scarf. "They'll be closed by the time we get there."

"No, no," she assured him. "It's not as late as it appears. It's the weather that makes it seem so. Look, there's the Common. It can't be much farther to the edge of town, and the driver said that it was only a mile away."

A sigh greeted these words, but Aleceon made no further comment.

She hurried along, glancing down to see that the boy was keeping pace, and beneath her woolen cap, her face was etched with a concern that sat uneasily on her youthful features. What to do if there was no work here? her mind questioned uneasily. Where else could they go?

Ahead, she could now see the snow-covered fields, the bare-branched trees casting streaks of dark purple ribbons across the white expanse. Here and there, patches of ice picked up the faint remaining light, glistening like a sugar crust on a freshly baked cake.

It was dark by the time they reached their destination. She could see the workers, almost all of whom were girls, as they streamed from the building, and she quickened her step, praying that they would not lock up before she got there.

Two-storied, with a bell tower perched atop the roof, the mill seemed to extend into the river itself. Its garish red façade, even now after dark, was clearly visible against the white snow, which seemed to create a luminous light of its own.

Studying it, Sarah thought it impressive; above all, it offered hope. She would not allow herself to think past the next few minutes. Aleceon, she knew, was exhausted to the point of barely being able to walk, and even if they did secure work, there was the long trek back into town ahead of them, a prospect she did not let herself dwell upon.

The girls were beginning to pass her now, most of them as though she were invisible. But one of them, a plump girl who appeared about seventeen, stopped.

"Are yer looking for a place at the mill?" she asked, regarding Sarah. She tilted her head, and from under the starched brown bonnet her bright blue eyes stared steadily.

"Yes, I am," Sarah responded, halting before her. "For me, and for my brother as well."

The girl laughed, and the sound, while coarse and harsh, was not unfriendly. "Yer in luck, then," she offered. "We've had four girls leave this week. Three of them got married, and one's too sick ter come back."

"Thank you for the information," Sarah said quickly, casting an anxious look toward the front door. "Is someone there now?"

The girl shrugged, the movement barely visible beneath her heavy shawl. "Maybe. Master Enright leaves early, but Master Jonathan usually stays around and locks up. If yer gonna get hired, it's one of them yer'll have ter see." She began to walk away. "Good luck," she called, running now to catch up with her friends.

Sarah watched her only briefly and then, prodding Aleceon with a firm hand, quickly moved forward again.

Inside the rather small room that served as an office, she paused uncertainly, peering about her. It was empty, and so she just stood there, clutching Aleceon's small, mittened hand. The one narrow, curtainless window emitted a desolate, dim light, producing a cheerless ambience in the sparsely furnished room.

"What is this place?" the boy inquired, wrinkling his nose. He didn't look up at her; instead, he surveyed his surroundings with a critical eye.

"It's a yarn mill, Aleceon," she replied quietly. "This is where they separate the wool so that it can be spun into yarn," she went on. "You've seen me do it at home by hand. Here they do it with machines." The sound of footsteps made her fall silent, and when a young man entered, she regarded him gravely, without speaking.

"Yes, what is it?" he asked in some surprise as he caught sight of her.

Sarah swallowed, suddenly shy, realizing that this must be Jonathan Enright, the mill owner's son. She had never seen anyone dressed so grand. He had a lean, handsome face, framed by black hair that was thick and wavy, but she thought his dark eyes far too brooding for a man of his years. She guessed him to be in his late twenties, yet there was a deliberateness in the way he moved and spoke that seemed better suited for a man twice his age.

"Are you looking for work?" he prompted, and, going behind the cluttered desk, sat down.

"Yes, sir," she murmured, nodding her head slightly. "And for my brother as well," she added quickly before he could speak. "We're together."

"I can see that," he replied with a brief smile. "What can you do?"

"Anything, sir," she responded. "I have had schooling," she added in hopeful tones with a lift of her brows.

He laughed, showing white, even teeth, but the expression did not reach his dark eyes, which remained somber and thoughtful. "There's nothing here that requires schooling," he said at last. Then he regarded Aleceon with a doubtful look. The boy, he saw, was small-boned, with a delicate cast to his finely etched features, not at all like the robust lads he was wont to hire. "That's your brother, you say?"

"Yes, sir."

"He looks sickly to me," was the dour comment.

"Oh, no," Sarah said in a rush. "He's small for his age, but strong. My father always said he didn't know what he would do without Aleceon during harvest."

The man nodded, then passed a hand across his brow in a tired gesture. It had been a long day and he was bone-weary. Girls he needed, especially now that they were shorthanded. But the boy..."Does your family live around here?" he inquired.

She looked at the floor. "They were killed. In a fire," she added in a barely audible voice.

He sighed and fell silent for a moment. "There is a

job for you," he said at last. "But there is nothing for the boy. I'm sorry."

Sarah's hopes fell. They would both have to get work if they were to survive. There would be rent, food, and, before too long, clothes. She could make do, but Aleceon would soon grow out of his shoes. Nor did she want to be separated from her brother all day long; she wanted him around where she could keep an eye on him. He was all she had left.

"Sir," she murmured, seeing his expression and wondering frantically what they would do if the grandly dressed young man turned them away. The long journey and the endless hours without food combined to produce an unutterable weariness, and she swayed slightly, still gripping Aleceon's hand as if for support. "I cannot stay unless we both have a place. We need the work, both of us," she whispered, her gaze attentive and compelling.

Again the man sighed, this time more deeply, annoyed by the unaccustomed feeling of sympathy he felt for the young girl. She looked like a waif with those gray, solemn eyes that stared at him so piercingly. Just enough of her hair was visible under the close-fitting cap so that he could see that it was chestnut brown and very fine in texture. By contrast, the boy's hair was lighter, a dark blond in color, and his eyes were a dark, smoky blue. They certainly didn't look like brother and sister, he thought. Even the expression was different. The girl's intelligent, intent; the boy's petulant and sullen. He would be trouble, that one, Jonathan Enright decided, and with the schedule they had to meet in the coming months, he could ill afford lazy help.

Enright's Mill, while not the largest in the area, was one of the most profitable. Their mill wheel was of the latest design, as were their carders and skein-winders. Four dormitories housed over one hundred employees, mostly female, and all of them worked diligently and efficiently at their assigned tasks.

Jonathan was still viewing the boy with doubt. It almost surprised him, therefore, when he heard himself say: "All right. You can both start tomorrow. The pay's a dollar and eighty cents a week for you; after three months, two dollars and fifteen cents. For the boy," he added reluctantly, "one dollar and fifteen cents."

She wet her lips. It was much less than she had hoped for, and she was doubtful that it would even cover rent and food. But it was a job, a paying job, and that was all that mattered.

He took out his watch and, noting the time, stood up. "Do you know where the dormitories are?" he asked.

"Dormitories?"

"About a quarter of a mile down the road, there is a narrow pathway. Just a few hundred feet along it are the dormitories where our employees live. There are four separate buildings. Go to number three and speak to Mrs. Dietz. You both can eat there tonight; tell her I said so. Your brother can then go to the men's dormitory. It's just across the way." Seeing that she was still regarding him with uncertain eyes, he added: "Two dollars and fifty cents a week will pay for your room and your board, for the both of you."

Sarah now calculated. Her arithmetic was not as good as her reading and writing, and so it took a few moments. There would be forty-five cents a week left over!

"Thank you, sir," she said gratefully and, for the first time, smiled. "What time shall we report?"

Now he laughed in genuine amusement, noticing how her smile lighted up her face, replacing solemnity with spirited animation. "You'll hear the bell," he said gently. "There's none in Whitlow that don't."

Sarah bobbed her head and, gripping Aleceon's hand, murmured her thanks as she backed out of the room.

Thinking the office a bit dimmer now that she had left it, Jonathan Enright watched her go. Then he thought of his father, and wearily his mind recoiled from yet another scene. They disagreed on so many things, it seemed, and he was certain that his father would be furious when he learned that two had been hired where one would have served. Still, they had agreed that the hiring or dismissal of employees was within his sphere of control; and with that thought in mind, Jonathan prepared to return home.

Chapter 2

Outside, the cold seemed even more pronounced, and bundling Aleceon as best she could, Sarah started out for the dormitories.

"You said you would take care of us, Sarah," the boy muttered after a few steps, his voice holding a note of condemnation.

"And so I shall," she retorted in a mild voice, refusing to be baited. Aleceon, despite his age and slender build, had a violent temper that when aroused bordered on viciousness. She had no idea where he had gotten such a trait. Neither her mother, father, nor Davie had ever shown such inclinations and, like herself, were quite bewildered when Aleceon went into one of his tantrums. There was, she knew, a dark side to her brother, a side she never permitted herself to look upon for too long a time.

But she loved him, fiercely and protectively, as if he were her own child. And in a way, he was. On the night that he had been born, she and her mother had been alone in the house. The child was not due for another two weeks, and her father and Davie had gone into town. The birth, thankfully, had been a swift and easy one. Even now, years later, she still remembered the thrill, the overpowering feeling of love she had experienced when she first held the infant Aleceon in her arms. Her mother had never been truly well after that, and the day-to-day care of her baby brother had fallen to her.

Sarah could see the dormitories now. Turning to Aleceon, she repeated: "I've said that I would take care of us, and I will. You need have no fear."

"I'm not afraid," he told her in a calm voice that still managed to convey disapproval. "I just don't want to work in a mill...."

She patted his shoulder as they approached the front door. "It won't be long, I promise," she said, trying to mask her desperation with a cheerful smile. How did she know how long it would be? she wondered, lifting the brass knocker. And even if they did get to Boston, five miles away, what would she do there? She was aware of her brother's irritation, but chose to ignore it. He always seemed provoked when she wouldn't do just what he wanted her to do. He expected so much from her that Sarah wondered how she would ever be able to live up to his expectations.

The evening meal was almost over, but after Sarah related her message, Mrs. Dietz, a dour woman in her late forties, who acted as housekeeper, shuffled her and Aleceon right into the dining room. "You can unpack your belongings later," she announced, ushering them into the room. "Sit down and eat first."

Gratefully, Sarah and Aleceon headed for two empty seats at the end of the long trestle table. The food was simple enough, a hearty mutton soup, thick slabs of brown bread, cheese, and cider, but it looked like a banquet, and they ate with appetite.

"Yer got a place, I see."

Startled, Sarah looked up to see the girl she had met on her way to the mill. "We did, both of us," she affirmed with a smile.

"Well, it's better than the streets. I'm Betsy O'Connor," she said, nodding as Sarah gave her name.

Betsy then glanced at Aleceon, ready to offer a friendly word, but the boy looked away. Strange little bugger, she thought. He looked out of place, somehow. The two of them were obviously without means, as who wasn't? But he gave the impression that he was looking down on them all. Physically, he looked to be about eight, but the expression of cynicism and boredom that seemed to be carved on his youthful features would have looked out of place on a person twice that age.

"Yer live around here?" Betsy went on, now studying Sarah with unconcealed curiosity.

"No," Sarah replied, taking another mouthful before continuing. "We come from Brockton."

The other girl nodded as if this was quite ordinary. And indeed, few of the girls were from Whitlow.

After the meal, Betsy went along as Mrs. Dietz took Sarah to the sleeping quarters. Aleceon, it appeared, would sleep in a separate building.

"Mrs. Dietz," Betsy said as they entered the comfortable-sized room, "how about letting her bunk next ter me? There's an empty bed."

The older woman made an impatient gesture at the suggestion. "It makes no difference to me," she retorted briskly, leaving the room.

Sarah put her valise on the narrow bed. The mattress was of straw; the sheets, however, were clean and the quilt appeared warm enough. She glanced at the two small windows that were spaced at intervals along each wall, but right now they were opaque with lacy tracings of frost, concealing any view they might have to offer.

There was only one fireplace, set about midway along one wall; while laid out, it was not yet lit. A few of the other girls now drifted in, and one of them saw to this task. Expertly wielding the bellows, the girl soon coaxed the flames into existence. While it did little to alleviate the chill, the sight of the small blaze was nonetheless comforting.

"Not much, is it?" Betsy noted wryly. Then she grinned impishly, her plump cheeks dimpling, her Irish ancestry quite evident in her fair skin and bright blue eyes. "But we each got our own bed, such as it is. Some places put two, and even three girls in a bed. I wouldn't like that, I can tell yer."

Despite its plainness, Sarah eyed the mean accommodations almost avidly, as if she were viewing a warm and safe haven. "It's fine," she responded, sitting on the bed. She was conscious of a soothing feeling of relief, as though, at least for the moment, her problems were solved. They had eaten, they had a place to sleep, and they had work. For the present, it was enough.

Betsy peered with interest as Sarah now unpacked her pitifully meager belongings. "I hope yer have an apron in there," she remarked as Sarah hung her one spare dress on a peg. At the look on Sarah's face, Betsy shook her head slightly. "I didn't think so." She got down on her knees and pulled a box out from under her bed. Rummaging through it, she produced an apron, high-necked and long. Shaking it out, she handed it to Sarah. "Here, use this till yer get one. If the lint gets into yer clothes, it'll be there ter stay."

"Thank you," Sarah said, quite overwhelmed by this act of kindness.

"Yer got a family?" Betsy inquired, sitting on her own bed.

Sarah shook her head. "Not anymore," she replied, explaining about the fire.

"Too bad," Betsy commiserated, undressing. "I lost me folks a long time ago," she went on, her voice slightly muffled as her head briefly disappeared beneath her woolen dress. "I used ter live with me sister and her husband in Salem, but I had ter leave."

"They wouldn't take care of you?" Sarah exclaimed, shocked.

Betsy hung her clothes on the wooden peg beside the bed before she answered. "Oh, they were doing that, to be sure. And I expect our Amy would have kept me, except for..." She laughed that harsh laugh again and cast a glance at Sarah. "Certainly her husband would have. Our Amy caught him paying me too much attention one night, and so I had ter leave."

Betsy's face remained impassive as she thought of her leave-taking, although the experience had been a painful one. From the time her body had begun to mature, the swell of her breasts especially noticeable on her then thin body, her brother-in-law's eyes had followed her about, at first surreptitiously, and then with an avidness he had made little effort to conceal.

The night he had drunkenly entered her small bedchamber in the attic, murmuring incoherently and ripping at her flannel nightclothes with clumsy, rough hands, was the last night that she had spent in the house of her sister. The decision had been her sister's. Amy had been furious, not with her husband, but with her thirteen-year-old sister!

These morose thoughts were interrupted as Sarah asked: "How long did you live in Salem?"

"Three years. Before that I lived in Yorkshire with me mam."

"England?" Sarah murmured in some surprise.

"Aye, England. I was born in Dublin, but me dad died before I was a year old, and me mam, who came from Yorkshire, took me and our Amy back home."

"Then you came here?"

"Not right off. Our Amy came first. She's nine years older than me," Betsy explained. "When she married, her husband brought her here ter America, and they settled in Salem. When me mam died, our Amy sent for me."

"And how long have you been here, at the mill?" Sarah asked.

"Four years. It's not so bad, really. Enright's is not like some of them. We work only twelve hours a day. Sunday's our own. But yer have ter go into town ter church," she added as an afterthought. "Mrs. Dietz is especially strict about that."

Sarah thought of the neat, white-steepled church she had passed on her way to the mill. "Do you attend the First Congregational?" she asked tentatively, thinking that, come the Sabbath, they could attend meeting together, but Betsy shook her head, and Sarah fell silent.

Seeing her expression, Betsy's brow deepened into a frown of censure. "Gawd almighty, I'm no papist, if that's what yer thinking."

Sarah flushed. "No, I only meant—" she began, but the other girl continued, interrupting her.

"I'm a Protestant. It's the Presbyterian church I attend; that's clear on the north side of town. And quite a hike it is, too," she grumbled.

In her nightclothes now, Betsy crawled beneath the quilted covers. Suddenly overcome with weariness, Sarah hurriedly undressed and did the same.

Chapter 3

The next day dawned just as cold and gray as its predecessor. A few white flakes straggled down from the overhead gloom in a halfhearted attempt to relieve the clouds of their heavy burden, but then, as if the effort were too much, the snow again ceased.

As usual, Jonathan made his rounds early to see that all was running smoothly. Despite his father's protestations that it was unnecessary, he tried to be here each day at six o'clock, when work began. It was because of his own singular determination that the mill was one of the most profitable in all of New England, though he doubted that his father gave him credit for that state of affairs.

Entering the carding room, Jonathan paused a moment. Two sides of the spacious room hosted tall, fairly wide windows in an effort to capture as much light as possible. Even so, on dark, gloomy days such as this, it was necessary to resort to oil lamps despite the discomfort produced by the smoke, which had a tendency to make eyes smart and water, not to mention the ever-present danger of fire that was created. This early in the day, the lamps were lit, and Jonathan blinked his eyes as he came into the room.

Walking about, he observed the girls at their work. And, regardless of his father's assessment, his gaze was critical. They hired only girls as operatives, as did most of the yarn mills, because girls worked for less—as was only right—and because they created no problems with rowdiness or drunkenness.

The turnover, of course, was high. Most of them were married and gone within five years or so; even the boys averaged not much longer.

He paused now, watching the new girl for a few moments; then he nodded in satisfaction. She was working quickly, smoothly.

His eyes scanned the room until he noticed the new boy. It would be his job to walk up and down the aisles, sprinkling water on the floor. The added moisture lessened the tendency of the cotton threads to snap and break as they were wont to do when dry and brittle. This the boy was now doing, although his movements were desultory and haphazard. There were other young boys about, some carrying boxes of raw material, and some feeding the machines while the girls operated them.

"Mornin', Master Jonathan," Jed Peach said, approaching.

Jonathan turned to the foreman, then frowned. "Peach, I've told you that I do not want to see that in such evidence," he said, pointing to the cat-o'-nine-tails held by the man.

Peach looked affronted. He was of medium build, wiry, and his face sported a perpetual scowl even when he laughed. "Look here, Jonathan," he said in a cajoling manner. "I've worked for your father for more than sixteen years now, and he never objected. Why, I've hardly used it more than once or twice in all this time," he added in a gross understatement. Although his words took exception, Peach's attitude was one of careful respect. He did not like the younger Enright, who was a far more complicated individual than was his father.

Jonathan gave a sound of disgust. Once or twice! he thought, trying to control his anger. Daily would have been more truthful. The mere fact of chastising the girls did not in itself upset him. But fear, he had noticed, made them careless, tense; in turn, their productivity dropped.

"Master Enright never disapproved, nor does he now," Peach went on righteously, and in truth he could not understand this young man's attitude. "Besides, all the little trollops have to do is see it, and they knows enough not to slack off. Can't run a place without discipline," he argued earnestly.

Jonathan's mouth tightened, but he knew that in this his father would endorse the foreman. "Look,

Peach," he said in clipped tones, "I know that it is common practice elsewhere, but if I catch you beating any of my help, I'll string you up!"

The foreman relaxed, feeling as if he had won a victory. "Only for show, Master Jonathan," he soothed. "Only for show."

Jonathan grunted. "Are all the machines in operation now?" he asked. They had twenty-five on the first floor; fifteen carded wool, nine carded cotton, and one, called a *mule*, produced a fragile cotton thread. On the second floor were the skein-winders. This was the finished product. Most of their sales were to the farmers in the surrounding area who brought their raw material to the mill and paid a fee to have the work done. Occasionally, Jonathan would buy the raw material outright; the finished product would then be sold mostly to the townsfolk.

"We're short a girl on one of the cotton carders," Peach replied, relieved by the change of subject. He didn't doubt Jonathan's words for a moment. The younger Enright had a temper both swift and deadly, all the more dangerous because it was a cold anger instead of a heated one.

Jonathan's brow creased in thought. Most of the girls were already operating two machines, except for the new one. "Bring one of the girls down from upstairs," he instructed, and with another searching glance about the room, he turned and walked back into his office.

Standing in front of a cotton carder, Sarah had glanced only briefly at Jonathan Enright as he stood talking to the foreman, and then diligently returned her attention to the sharp-toothed contrivance that whirled and clattered. The machine was not difficult to operate, but one did have to take care not to get one's fingers too close to the iron teeth that combed and cleaned the mass of tangled wool that passed through it.

Now she looked quickly at Peach. The foreman terrified her; he had already given her a cursory blow with the evil little whip he carried, and her shoulder still stung from it. She also didn't like the way he looked at her, nor the way he smelled. He had put his mouth close to her ear as he explained the working of the carder. At first she had thought he did this because the room was so noisy that it was almost impossible to hear when one talked normally, but then she had felt the wet tongue as he nuzzled her neck, and with a shudder she had drawn away. That was when she had received the blow, together with an angry command to get working.

She watched him cautiously for the rest of the morning, trembling when he approached her, but aside from a critical scrutiny of her work at intervals, he paid her no mind.

Returning to the dormitories at noon for dinner, Sarah questioned Betsy about Jed Peach.

The girl laughed stridently. "Pay him no mind," she advised, biting into a bannock cake and viewing Sarah with something like amusement. "He does that all the time."

Again Sarah shuddered, remembering the foul breath and unwashed smell. Seeing her reaction, Betsy's face grew somber and leaned closer. "Look here, lass," she said quietly. "Yer need this job, or don't yer?"

"I do, but—"

"Then don't rile Peach," she interrupted. Noting Sarah's dismay, she reached over and patted her hand. "He don't mean no harm, but he can cause trouble. He's a mean bugger when he wants ter be." She resumed eating, for their thirty minutes were almost up and there were long hours ahead before they could return for supper. Although they were given these thirty minutes for dinner, at least ten of them were consumed in racing back to the dormitory and, afterward, back to the mill again.

"I seen him foul up a girl's machine when she spoke up against him," Betsy went on. Taking another piece of bread, she stuffed it in her apron pocket to be consumed on her way back.

"What happened?"

Betsy shrugged and wiped her mouth with the back of her hand. "She got fired, that she did."

Sarah put down her spoon, her appetite suddenly

gone, and then the bell rang, summoning them to the machines once more.

Even with the bitter cold outside, the carding room was oppressively hot, with a closed-in, musty odor that incorporated body heat, damp woolen clothing, and acrid lint. At times throughout the endless afternoon, Sarah glanced longingly at the windows, knowing that just beyond them the air was crisp and cold and clean.

"It's the humidity, lass," Betsy explained when Sarah later questioned her as to the mystery of the forever-closed windows. "As damp as yer might think it is out there, it needs ter be more so in here."

Sarah thought of Aleceon walking up and down the aisles all day long, sprinkling water about, and she wondered just how much humidity was needed! And then she thought of the coming summer with no little trepidation. If it was hot now, what would it be like then!

During the weeks that followed, Sarah's days sunk into numbing monotony, aching feet, and a curious sense of time gone astray. Peach kept his distance as if sensing her repugnance, but his voice and manner were gruff each time he had occasion to address her. Tardiness, or trying to speak to one's neighbor—no easy thing over the constant nerve-racking clattering of the machinery—was inviting a blow with the cat-o'-nine-tails, which was promptly delivered by the foreman. Sarah noticed that Peach never used his whip when Jonathan Enright was on the floor; but delivery of the chastisement was only delayed, never forgotten.

Dinner, served at noon, was the only break in the long day, except for privy calls. Since there was only one relief girl—and she divided her time between the two floors—there were not many of those, either. Breakfast and supper were served before the work day began and at its end.

After the first week, Sarah's body began to adapt to the new strains placed upon it, and she found that she could join the other girls in the parlor for an hour or so after supper, joining their sociable gossip and singing and sewing. On Sundays, after she and Aleceon attended two church services, she would meet Betsy and together they would stroll by the river, weather permitting, or would just sit in the parlor eating lemon cake and talking.

February was well on its way when Aleceon got sick. He'd been coughing for days, and when she saw the blood, Sarah insisted that he stay in bed. She pleaded with Mrs. Dietz, and finally a doctor was summoned.

Standing by Aleceon's bed, Sarah watched with fearful eyes as the examination progressed.

At last, the doctor, a portly man well into his sixties, closed the black leather bag with a snap and then, adjusting his steel spectacles, viewed Sarah with disinterest.

"Consumption," he announced curtly, ignoring her gasp of fright.

"You will do something?" she pleaded, her heart thudding against her ribs. "He will get well?"

He made a vague gesture, not too pleased with having been summoned out to the mill in the first place. Every time it happened it seemed he went unpaid, although they were good enough at making promises. And from the look of this one, he thought, viewing Sarah, it would be the same old story all over again. "Not much to be done, girl," he said gruffly, picking up his bag. "They either get well, or they die. Rest would help, lots of it." Momentarily, he gave thought to prescribing a tonic, but it was, really, a waste of time. The boy was frail to begin with; he could not possibly survive.

With his words, Sarah nodded, clinging to the small bit of hope he offered. Rest, the doctor had said; and rest was what he would have, she vowed, looking at Aleceon's flushed face. She suddenly realized how utterly alone she was; their welfare, and perhaps even their lives, rested solely upon her own wits. There was no one, no one to whom she could turn for help.

For one moment, she raged against the feeling of abandonment that crept over her; it was a leaden weight in the pit of her stomach. Then, with a tremendous effort of will, she controlled herself so that once again she appeared placid and calm.

But Aleceon, glancing up at his sister, was not deceived. He sensed rather than saw her momentary lack of confidence. It did not unduly alarm or disturb him, any more than had the doctor's diagnosis, for he knew his sister's strength and resourcefulness. It had surrounded him all his life, like a protective shell. He closed his eyes and quite coolly and unemotionally reflected that, if only one member of his family had to survive the devastating fire besides himself, he was fortunate that it had been Sarah.

Thinking him asleep, Sarah turned and left the room. Much to the doctor's surprise, she carefully counted out two dollars in coin for his payment.

That night she could think of nothing except the advice of the doctor. Rest, he had said. But that was easier said than done. Aleceon had been in bed for the past week now. That was bad enough, but now that he wasn't getting paid and she was paying for his room and board as well as her own, their little reserve of money was dwindling at an alarming rate. Another week, two at the most, and they'd be in debt. Aleceon's job was not difficult, but he was cold and wet for a good part of the day, and Sarah knew that if he returned, it would only worsen his condition.

"Talk ter Master Jonathan," Betsy counseled when she learned of Sarah's plight. "But make sure yer talk only ter him," she stressed. "Old Master Enright ain't about ter be moved by any problem that we might have."

So Sarah watched and waited for the opportunity to speak to Jonathan Enright alone. But each time she saw him, he was in the company of his father or Jed Peach and, mindful of Betsy's words, she was afraid to approach him.

It was the last day in February, and coincidentally her sixteenth birthday, when the temperature dipped far enough at night to freeze the river.

"Gawd, each time it happens, I don't know whether ter be happy or sad," Betsy exclaimed as they all stood outside.

"I don't understand," Sarah commented. Drawing her shawl tighter, she shivered in the raw air.

"The wheel's stuck. Yer see?" Betsy pointed to the massive wheel in the river, now immobile, captive to a force greater than its own. "If it don't turn, the machines won't run. No machines, no work. Either a day off, or a day without pay. Take yer pick."

"Without pay?" Sarah's voice held such dismay that Betsy was instantly contrite.

"Aw, I'm sorry, Sarah. I forgot." She turned and her face brightened. "Look, there's Master Jonathan." She observed the young man, who was carrying an ax and walking with purposeful steps to the river's edge. "Lord almighty," she murmured. "He's gonna try and free the wheel!" She looked at Sarah, wide-eyed. "Last time someone did that, the ice split and he fell in. Was weeks afore they found him. Not until all the ice broke. Master Enright must not be here this morning." She shook her head. "He'd never let his son go out there. He usually sends one of the boys. They're lighter, and there's less chance of the ice cavin' in under them."

With the rest of the girls, they watched with absorbed attention as Jonathan walked out upon the frozen river and headed for the captive wheel.

Although only half of it protruded, it was taller than he was and he looked dwarfed as he stood beside it. Carefully he walked around it, stopping now and then as if to test his footing. At last he chose his position. Raising the ax high, he began to chop at the ice. The second stroke broke through and a chunk of the white stuff disappeared into the black water. Again and again the ax fell as Jonathan worked his way around the wheel.

He had almost completed the huge half-arc when there was a tremendous crunching noise and the ice split in all directions. A moment later Jonathan gave a short cry and rapidly sunk from view in an almost graceful motion.

"Oh, my Gawd, there he goes!" Betsy shouted. "Just like the other one."

Sarah ran to the edge of the river with the others. Jed Peach, with a few of the men who were wagon drivers for the mill, grabbed some rope and began to heave it out across the frozen expanse. Only Jonathan's head and shoulders were visible as he frantically gripped at the slippery ice in an effort to stay afloat.

Time and again the rope fell short. Without thinking, Sarah grabbed the end from the startled Peach. "I'll take it out to him," she said, and before anyone could protest, she gingerly walked toward Jonathan, rope in hand. As she neared, he saw her.

"Get down!" he shouted to her. "Spread your weight evenly. Crawl...." His voice was momentarily lost as he renewed his effort. By now his clothing was a leaden, dragging weight, and he needed all his strength just to keep afloat.

She did as she was told, dropping first to her knees, and then, putting her gloved hands down, she inched her way forward.

It seemed a long time, but was in fact only moments before she was close enough to throw the rope to him. On the second try he caught it, and wrapping it around his arm and wrist, and holding on with his other hand, he shouted to the men to pull.

Quite easily now, Jonathan was drawn up; he slid across the ice as they drew him to the bank.

Everyone seemed to have forgotten all about Sarah as they clamored about Jonathan. Only Betsy was waiting to help Sarah to her feet.

"That was a brave thing yer did," Betsy said, viewing her with a new respect and admiration. "If that ice didn't hold, yer'd be long since gone and none the wiser."

She put an arm about Sarah, who was now visibly shivering with cold. Wherever she had come in contact with the ice, her clothing was damp and beginning to stiffen in the cold. Her teeth began to chatter and her slim body was racked by uncontrollable shivers that threatened to rend her bones apart.

"There now, lass," Betsy consoled, and the mere sound of her voice was soothing, out of all proportion to her words; gratefully, Sarah listened to the droning comfort of it. It seemed so long, she thought irrationally, since someone had spoken to her like that; so long since someone, anyone, had taken charge. She felt drained, exhausted, despairing. "Come along, luv," Betsy went on, leading her gently. "What yer need is tea, hot and bracing like. It'll do yer a world of good, it will that."

They returned to the dormitories, and later that morning they heard the bell, summoning them back to the machines. Jed Peach had sent one of the boys out to finish the job that Jonathan had begun. They were all, of course, docked for those hours during which the machines had stood idle.

Later, they learned that Jonathan had returned home to change his clothing, and impatiently Sarah waited all that day for his return.

But she waited in vain.

Chapter 4

Returning home that morning, Jonathan had barely enough time to change into dry clothes before his mother, followed by his sister, Elizabeth, who was carrying extra blankets, entered his room.

"Jonathan!" Rachel exclaimed, seeing that he was again dressed. "Surely you do not plan on going out again? You are chilled to the bone!"

"I'm fine now that I've gotten out of those wet clothes," he assured her, somewhat amused by her concern. Normally his mother seldom questioned his comings and goings any more than she did those of his father.

"Mother is right, Jon," Elizabeth insisted, gently propelling him into the deep chair by the fireplace. As soon as he was settled, and ignoring his protestations, she arranged the blankets, one on his lap and one around his shoulders.

"Mrs. Bowe is on her way up with something hot," Rachel said, still eyeing him sternly.

"Mother," Jonathan began, and then sighed, only half in annoyance as they continued to fuss about him. In spite of his resolve, he felt incredibly weary.

"Why didn't you send one of the boys out?" his mother asked in exasperation.

"Had I done that, someone might have died," he answered firmly. "I want none of that on my conscience."

Her mouth compressed into a thin line. "As if the world would miss one less ragamuffin," she declared, unmoved.

He made no reply to this, and instead said, "I really should go back." He gave his mother a quick look. "I suppose that Father has already left?"

She nodded curtly. "Your father left for Boston this morning as planned. And I might add, Jonathan, that had he been around, none of this would have happened!"

She viewed her son in an almost accusing manner, as if this disruption in the normal routine of her day had been deliberately planned.

"Mr. Peach will see to things, Jon," Elizabeth said soothingly. She put a hand to his brow and he motioned irritably.

"All right, all right," he said to his sister, putting his head back. "I *am* a bit tired, I suppose." He heard the door close and was just beginning to doze off when he again heard someone enter. Seeing Charity Bowe, he smiled. He had been only fifteen when his father, over the sincere objections of Rachel, hired the cook. Rachel's objection had not so much to do with Mrs. Bowe, as with her daughter, Lottie, whose mentality was severely deficient.

Her eyes sharp upon him, Charity's plump and kindly face was filled with concern. "Are you feeling all right, Master Jonathan?" she asked, placing the tray on the glimmering oaken surface of the bedside table. She continued to search his face as if she could find the answer to her own question.

"There's nothing wrong with me," Jonathan responded blithely, amused by all this unusual concern for his welfare.

"I've brought you some hot broth," she stated, unconvinced, and then, pointing to a small cup, added: "And you drink that medicine there, too; I brewed it myself." She wagged a finger at him as if he were still a child. "Drink it all up, you hear? We can't have you taking chill."

He tried not to grimace. If it was anything at all like her usual medicinal brews, he was not looking forward to it, chill or no. "I'll drink it all, Charity," he assured her. "I promise." He smiled again, fondly.

But when she left the room, he quickly emptied the contents of the cup into the fireplace, causing the flames to momentarily sputter and protest at this assault. Then he drank the broth, and now truly weary, he crawled into bed. He thought about the girl who had so bravely come to his rescue. Just before sleep claimed him, he promised himself that he would raise her wages in the morning. It was the least he could do.

* * *

It was dark when Charity again climbed the stairs, her organdy apron rustling softly with each step, another tray clutched firmly in her strong, capable hands.

Outside Jonathan's door, she placed the salver on the small hall table; then she tapped lightly on the door. Receiving no response, she opened it, peering inside. For a moment, she just stared. Then her scream, high and rapier sharp, cut through the evening's stillness with a suddenness that momentarily paralyzed all those who heard it.

Mrs. Reddy, the housekeeper, was first on the scene, her usually staid expression replaced by one of outraged shock at this untoward intrusion into the normally serene household.

Elizabeth appeared almost simultaneously and, with a startled, frightened cry, was the first to recover her wits.

By the time Rachel appeared only moments later, Elizabeth had already sent for the doctor and was cradling her brother's head in her lap.

He lay sprawled on the floor between the bed and the fireplace, unconscious, his breathing rapid and shallow.

It was some hours later when the doctor, having pronounced pneumonia as Jonathan's malady, took Rachel aside. He was the same portly, bespectacled man who had not a week past attended Aleceon, but now his manner was grave and concerned.

"I understand that Mr. Enright has gone to Boston," he said to Rachel as they stood in the hallway outside Jonathan's bedroom.

"Yes," she confirmed. "He left this morning."

Doctor Waite hesitated. He disliked dealing with women in any kind of emergency. They were so unpredictable, flighty, given to hysterics when calmness was needed. "I do not want to unduly alarm you, Mrs. Enright," he said slowly, "but I think that you ought to send for him."

Her breath stilled in her momentarily as the ominous meaning of his statement took hold. "He's not going to..." She stopped, unable to even speak the word, and put a hand to her lips.

The doctor frowned at this display of agitation, yet he knew that he had to impress upon her the urgency of sending for her husband. "It is very serious," he replied in even tones. "Jonathan is young, and that is in his favor. But he is having great difficulty in breathing. I've done all I can to alleviate the problem, but the next twenty-four hours will be crucial."

Rachel clasped her hands tightly to keep them from trembling. "I will send for Mr. Enright at once," she said.

It was almost dawn when Edward, riding in the sleigh that had been sent to fetch him, reached the outskirts of Whitlow. Neither the cold nor the freezing temperatures had abated, although the sky had at last cleared and the stars shone with icy brightness in a final defiance of the approaching morning. A pale, waning moon cast a feeble light on the iced branches of trees, and they sparkled like grotesque jewels.

For once, Edward was glad of the snow-covered ground; had the trip been made in a carriage, progress would have been considerably slower. As it was, the iron runners slid swiftly and smoothly over the well-traveled road.

Since he had been awakened so abruptly some hours before, Edward's normally well-organized mind had produced a jumble of incoherent, fragmented thoughts and images.

The thought of Jonathan being seriously ill was an idea that he had never before contemplated; his mind touched upon and drew away from the dreadful consequences should his only son die.

He took a deep breath and the cold air struck his lungs with a force that was almost painful. Shifting his weight, he ran a hand across his chest; he was by now almost used to the sharp, searing pains that occasionally gripped him when he was angry or upset, although normally they dissipated after a short period of time. With conscious effort, he turned his mind away from his own problem and again thought of Jonathan.

"Pneumonia" Tully, the coachman, had said, and had shaken his head regretfully when Edward questioned him for further information. He had reported, however, Jonathan's reckless actions of the previous morning. Edward was torn between anger and dismay at the foolhardiness of his son.

And if Jonathan died? What then? In the brightening light his face looked haggard at the thought. Had he, Edward, worked for so long, only to have some stranger reap the benefits of his labor?

With a mixture of dread and relief he saw that they were at last home, and without waiting for Tully to open the door, Edward hurriedly alit from the sleigh and ran up the front steps, his breath coming in quick, short spurts.

Both Rachel and the doctor were waiting for him in the front hallway and after hastily removing his heavy cloak, Edward said: "How is he?"

Rachel looked away, and the doctor took a step forward. "He is about the same, Mr. Enright," he advised.

Edward frowned. "What does that mean?" he demanded, and began to climb the stairs. "Speak plainly!"

The doctor fell in step. "Your son is alternating between delirium and unconsciousness; his breathing is very labored, and his fever is now at a dangerous level."

They were outside the bedroom door when Edward again spoke. "Is he going through the crisis now?"

The doctor shook his head slightly. "I do not believe so," he murmured. "I believe the worst is yet to come. In these situations, the crisis can appear as late as the fifth day. Unfortunately, the longer it takes, the weaker the body becomes."

Edward opened the door and entered the room. Elizabeth was seated beside the bed, but did not get up as her father entered. Her face looked tired, and her eyes were red and swollen from weeping. Edward's entrance produced fresh tears and she put her face in her hands, weeping softly.

Approaching the bed, Edward stood there looking down at his son. A sound of raspy breathing filled the room as Jonathan seemed to strain for each breath. He was unconscious, his face bright with fever.

Suddenly, with no warning, Jonathan's body grew rigid, and the awful sound of labored breathing momentarily ceased. In horror, Edward watched as the flushed face grew pale and white, a thin bluish line rimming the lips.

The doctor acted swiftly, placing a tongue depressor horizontally in Jonathan's mouth; simultaneously the young man began to gasp for air, his body moving in tortuous spasms.

"Hold him down!" the doctor ordered, placing his own hands on Jonathan's shoulder and thigh. "He is having a convulsion. Hold him down!" the doctor said in stronger tones as Edward hesitated.

Jolted from his numbed state, Edward quickly responded. And then, with his son's heaving body beneath his hands, Edward was gripped by overwhelming emotion. The intense feeling that he had always had for Jonathan presented itself in a flash of brittle clarity. Pride, he had always named it; but now he knew it for what it was: love. He almost sobbed with the realization of it, with the realization that it might now be too late to let Jonathan know.

After minutes that seemed like hours, Jonathan quieted and lay still, the color returning to his face and, as before, brightening into an unnatural crimson.

"It's over," the doctor said, relieved, and removed the slender piece of wood from Jonathan's mouth. He wiped his brow. Glancing at Edward, he started. "Mr. Enright!" he shouted. "What is it?"

Although he moved quickly, the doctor was not in time to reach Edward as he pitched forward, his body half on the bed, half on the floor. He paid no mind to Elizabeth's sharp cry as he deftly examined the stricken man. Straightening, he faced Elizabeth and Rachel, who now stood in the doorway. For a moment he stared at the white, shocked faces. Then he averted his gaze.

By the end of the week, Sarah was desperate. Money was needed and she did not have it, even with this week's pay. For the past four days she had hoped and prayed that Master Jonathan would recover sufficiently to return to the mill, but he still remained seriously ill.

The day after the incident on the ice, Mrs. Dietz had addressed the girls during the midday meal and somberly reported the death of Edward Enright, who, hurriedly summoned from Boston to attend to his son, had suffered a heart attack. Gloom hung over everyone at the twin disaster, but to Sarah, the worst disaster of all was that Jed Peach, ill-tempered as ever, was still in charge.

Having little recourse, she at last appeared before the foreman, but her pleas fell upon deaf, uncaring ears. Aleceon, she was informed curtly, was discharged due to his extended absenteeism. If she wanted to stay, fine.

"But I cannot pay for us both," she explained, close to tears.

Peach's eyes narrowed in satisfaction as he watched her. He knew her type, all right. Thought she was better than anyone else; he'd recognized that from the start. Each time he came near her, she looked at him as if he was something that had crawled out from under a rock.

Fear he could have tolerated, indeed he relished it; but the disgust she had displayed enraged him. He'd like to throw her on the floor right now and let her have it good. He toyed with the idea for a bit, all the while watching her tear-stained face, completely unmoved by the sound of a soft sob that escaped her lips. Conscious of a tightening in his loins, he got to his feet and, with slow, measured steps, walked toward her.

Sarah had neither the experience nor the sophistication to even suspect his thoughts. She therefore felt no fear, her whole being still immersed in the dreadful, more pressing problem of mere survival. Unbidden, the image of the almshouse flashed across her mind, and she knew that, for Aleceon, death lurked in its shadowed corners.

"Mr. Peach!" Betsy's voice boomed at him from the open doorway. "One of the machines broke down. Yer'd best come and have a look."

The foreman glared at her, but Betsy regarded him with a half smile, making no move to leave. She did not fear the likes of Jed Peach.

He made an exasperated sound and again retreated behind his desk. "I'll be right there," he growled to

Betsy, and then fixed Sarah with a hard look. "Well, you don't expect us to pay for your brother's keep, do you?" he said to her. "If we was to make exceptions, why, in no time we'd have everyone's sick brother or sick sister here! The boy's got to go. If you can't let him go by himself, then you go with him. Understand?" He thrust his chin out for emphasis.

"Yes, sir." All sorts of thoughts crowded her mind as Sarah backed from the room. There was no money left at all. If she finished out the day, there would be only enough to cover the past week's rent and board. Momentarily, she gave thought to collecting her wages and running, without paying. But that would be akin to stealing. Besides, Aleceon was in no condition to run.

As they walked back to their respective machines, Betsy said, "I'm sorry, Sarah. I hope I didn't mess things up by angering him." She glanced sideways, wondering if Sarah knew what Peach's intentions had been. Just a quick look into the office and she'd seen the bulge in his breeches. It was then that she had jammed her own machine and intruded upon them. But a look at Sarah's face told her that the girl suspected nothing; she had either not noticed or not understood. Betsy shook her head. How was such an innocent to survive?

"I'm certain that he would have said the same thing, whether you were there or not," Sarah said dully, her voice barely audible over the noise.

She resumed her work, her hands moving automatically while her thoughts became even more despondent.

Mrs. Dietz, while sympathetic, could offer no aid. "There's the gristmill," she said that night. "But they won't take the likes of you, Sarah. Besides, they don't have a place for their workers. Most come in from the farms and go home at night." She felt a twinge of compassion, which she sternly repressed. "Look, I'll give you some food. It's the best I can do. I got my own job to think of."

With Betsy's supporting arm about her, Sarah made her way upstairs to gather her meager belongings. But then, in despair, she sat down on the edge of the bed.

"I cannot send Aleceon to the orphanage," she cried

out. "Nor can I take him to the almshouse. He will die! I don't care for myself; I can always get work of some sort. I could even hire out. But who will take Aleceon with me?"

Betsy took her hand. "If I had any money, I'd gladly give it ter you," she said sincerely. "I've not more than seventy-five cents put away, but yer're welcome ter it, Sarah."

Sarah shook her head sadly. "You're a good friend, Betsy," she said slowly. "But that wouldn't even get us to Boston."

Betsy pursed her lips, her mind working with its usual agility. "Look, Sarah, there's one way. But..."

She looked up. "What is it? Please, tell me."

"Well, termorrow afternoon there's ter be a vendu at the town hall."

Sarah frowned in perplexity. "Vendu? You mean an auction? Like for the slaves?"

Betsy laughed in amusement. "Hardly. Only the South sells people. No, it's a Pauper Auction. It's not the highest, but the lowest bid that wins."

Sarah's perplexity deepened, and Betsy continued. "Yer see," she said with an almost apologetic glance, "the town is able to care for yer, that is, for the needy, those that can't support themselves. But it costs money, and they don't like it. So once a month they hold a vendu. If a man bids, say, ten dollars for a person, why then the Town pays *him;* he don't pay the ten dollars, he gets it!"

"But what do they do with the people? Where do they go?"

"Well, that's the chance yer take. Mostly it's farmers wanting extra hands. They get paid money for taking yer, and in turn they give yer food and shelter. Yer work at what they say, and after a while, I hear, they even pay a wage. Some of them do," she qualified. "But yer gotta be careful, especially with yer brother," she went on. "There's captains come down from Boston and other harbor cities. They take the young boys, and from what I've heard tell, their lot's a hard one."

Sarah's face hardened. "I'll not let them take him away from me. We won't be separated." Then she glanced at Betsy, her face at once hopeful and anxious. "Would they take us both?"

Betsy shrugged. "No harm in asking," she pointed out logically.

Sarah looked undecided, and seeing her expression, Betsy said, "Look, I'll see ter the boy. Go on down ter the Town Hall and talk ter Matthew Benson; he's the deputy, and sort of runs things."

Chapter 5

The sky, which for days now had entertained snow-filled clouds, finally cleared and turned a dazzling blue that not even the golden sun could pale. Luminous color reflected off the snow, producing a brilliant clarity that, despite its beauty, was too painful to look upon for any extended length of time.

Against this glare the draperies in Jonathan's room were partially drawn; nevertheless, a lustrous ambience pervaded, warming wood and brass to burnished hues.

Restlessly, Jonathan moved his body slightly beneath the downy quilt, awareness slowly returning as he awakened. He remembered that when he had returned to the house, wet to the skin, Rachel had insisted that he stay home, seated before the fire, wrapped in blankets. They had tried to dose him with a foul-smelling brew that Charity had concocted and swore would keep him from catching a chill. This, he recalled, he had thrown into the fire as soon as he was alone in his room.

But now, opening his eyes, he realized he should have taken it. That he'd been ill, he knew, because at brief times clarity had returned, only to be snatched away in the force of feverish delirium.

Cautiously, conscious that his slightest movement caused his very bones to ache, he turned and looked at Elizabeth, who was sitting on a chair close by the bed. Her black dress, long-sleeved and high-necked, seemed particularly severe for daytime, he thought hazily, and with one part of his mind he wondered why she had chosen such an outfit. She was regarding him doubtfully; then, after a moment, she spoke, her voice tentative and uncertain.

"Jon?" She leaned forward slightly, regarding him attentively now.

He grinned weakly. "I think so."

Her smile was wide, relieved, and she reached over and took his hand. "Thank God. I wasn't certain that you were really awake. For days now you have just talked gibberish each time I spoke to you."

"Days?" he said, incredulous. "How long..."

She patted his hand. "This is the sixth day, Jon. You've been very ill. We've been frantic..." She broke off, biting her lip, finding it impossible to tell him more.

He tried to sit up, but weakly fell back again, coughing, and grimaced at the painful rumble that came with this effort.

"Please, Jon, don't move. Are you hungry?" she asked, and at his nod of affirmation, hurried from the room.

He had nodded, but was in fact uncertain. The only thing he felt with any certainty was exhaustion. Never in his life could he remember being so tired. He'd been all right when he had gone to bed that afternoon, but then he'd awoken feeling chilled and shivering beneath the downy quilt.

He had gotten up, intending to stoke the fire.... That was the last thing he remembered. Once he thought he saw his father, but that could not have been real, because his father was in Boston making preparatory arrangements for buying a new carder. He had planned on spending the whole week there, and Jonathan wondered now whether he had returned.

Of course, he thought ruefully, his father would be furious when he learned of all this. Although Edward supported Jed Peach as foreman, Jonathan knew that his father did not trust the man to actually run the mill.

Stupid, he chided himself. Not only was it common practice to send one of the boys out when the ice froze, it was just plain common sense, he now realized. He promised himself that he would never again act so foolishly.

He looked toward the door as Rachel, followed by Elizabeth and a servant who was carrying a tray, entered. His mother's face was pale, and her manner, even for her, subdued. She, too, was dressed in somber fashion, and the thought struck him that perhaps they had thought that he would die.

Approaching the bed, Rachel placed a hand upon his brow. "Thank heavens the fever's gone," she murmured. "Set the tray over there," she instructed the servant, pointing to the bedside table.

Again Jonathan made the effort to rise, and Elizabeth hastily said, "Don't, Jon. I'll feed you." Picking up the steaming bowl of broth, she dipped a spoon into the liquid, then brought it to his mouth.

After only a few spoonfuls, he pushed her hand away. "Enough." He sighed deeply and, leaning back, closed his eyes a moment. Then, as if a thought suddenly came to him, he opened them again. "The girl...," he said to Elizabeth. "How did she fare?"

Elizabeth looked puzzled, then alarmed. Was his mind wandering again?

"There was a girl!" he insisted, shaking his head slightly, annoyed by the overwhelming lethargy that seemed to grip him, making even speech a chore.

"She's fine," Elizabeth said quickly, wondering who he was talking about. "I assure you, Jonathan, she's just fine."

Again he fell back, closing his eyes. The slight effort had caused his head to pound with a throbbing intensity.

"Let him rest," Rachel advised. "Come along, Elizabeth." In the hall, she faced her daughter. "Did you tell him?"

Elizabeth shook her head. "I couldn't. He still seems so weak."

"It's just as well." She looked away, sighing deeply. "There's nothing he can do now."

"Mother," Elizabeth said as Rachel began to walk away. "I think it would be a good idea for Justin to see to things at the mill until Jon gets on his feet again."

Rachel regarded her daughter with doubtful eyes. "He knows nothing of running a mill," she said. "And I don't think your father would have approved," she added.

About them, the hallway bore traces of the deathly

sweet scent of the funeral flowers that wafted up from the parlor below. It was so insistent, that smell, Elizabeth thought tiredly, never allowing one to forget, even for a moment, that death had visited this house.

"But someone has to see to things," she protested, annoyed with her mother's indecision. Ever since her father died five days before, her mother had been walking about as if in a trance. "You know that Father didn't trust Jed Peach," she went on in a softer tone. "It's true that Justin doesn't know much about the operation, but it's not necessary that he know. Someone should be there to keep an eye on things. And it will only be for a week or so, until Jon feels better."

Rachel shook her head slightly, defeated by her daughter's insistence. "If you feel that would be the right thing, then do it," she said noncommittally as she slowly descended the steps.

Downstairs, she walked toward the parlor, halting before the closed door. For a moment she stood there, her hand on the knob; then she opened it.

The room was cold and dim. No fire burned in the grate, and behind the tightly drawn draperies, the windows were opened. As was common, Edward's body waited here, among his own family, before being moved to its final resting place.

At the far end of the room, candles burned on either side of the coffin, which rested on a makeshift platform, draped heavily in black.

There was no one in the room now, although during the past days, people had come and gone, paying their last respects. This would be the last night that Edward would rest in his own home; tomorrow was the funeral.

Slowly, she moved forward until she stood before the bier. He looked to be asleep, the lines of age and of worry and of pain miraculously washed away by the hand of death that had so unexpectedly clutched him.

Has it been only days? she wondered. She felt bereft, as if she had been alone, abandoned, for a very long time.

She reached out a hand and touched his cheek. It was cold, rigid; it was not Edward. Edward had left her days ago.

She did not weep, because she could not believe. She could not even remember her last glimpse of him as he fell; strangely, all she could remember was the stricken look upon the face of the doctor as he glanced up at her. He spoke the words that pronounced death, but she couldn't remember them.

She shivered in the cold room. She should have worn her shawl, she thought absently. The air was as cold as Edward, as cold as death.

The next day, Saturday, Whitlow hosted two events. In the morning, Edward Enright was laid to rest in the town's only cemetery, and in the afternoon, the town hall hosted its monthly Pauper Auction; both events were well attended.

After the funeral, Justin Lansing went straight to the mill. With Edward gone, he felt as if an obstacle had been removed from his path. It was Jonathan who would now control everything. They had told Jonathan only this morning about his father's death, and after making a valiant attempt to get out of bed, he had suffered a relapse. But when Jonathan did recover, no doubt he would be pleased—and grateful—to see how his future brother-in-law had stepped in to take charge during this most trying of times.

The employees had been given time off to attend the funeral, but when Justin arrived just after the noon hour, everyone was again at work.

Facing Jed Peach with an air of importance, Justin announced that he would be in charge until Jonathan Enright was well enough to return.

Skeptically, Peach viewed the thin elegance of the man who stood before him, and almost grinned at the way in which he was dressed, as if on his way to a grand ball. He had heard that Lansing was a minister, but to Peach he looked more like a dandy in his fawn-colored waistcoat and silk cravat. Above the wide collar his sandy-colored hair was of fashionable length, curling just below his ears, his sideburns perhaps a trifle conservative. Standing there, leaning heavily on his ebony-tipped cane, his ruffled shirt gleaming whitely, he appeared quite elegant. It was only when he moved that the limp was noticeable and one became aware that the cane was not an affectation but a necessity.

Observing the doubtful expression upon the foreman's face, Justin raised a brow and his green eyes focused with a granite intensity.

On anyone else this air of prodigious dignity would have appeared slightly ludicrous, but on Justin Lansing it appeared natural and unassumed. It was difficult for anyone who knew the man ever to visualize him as a child. One would have thought that he sprang from the womb by some mysterious metamorphosis, fully dignified and fully matured.

Such, of course, was not the case; and as a child, Justin had been sickly, born with a withered left foot that might have been utterly useless had it not been for his mother's selfless devotion and attention to her only son. His father, a minister of the Second Congregational Church of Boston, had been a stern, unbending sort of individual who had quite early incurred the hatred and contempt of his son.

In one way, the supposition about Justin's childhood would have been correct; it had been brief to the point of being nonexistent, and when his mother had died when he was four years old, his own compassion and humor had been laid to rest with her.

There was never any question as to what he would be; his father gave him no choice. From the time he was four, the gospels and scriptures had been pounded into him, more often than not with the aid of his father's heavy hand. That man's death a short three years ago, while Justin was still in Harvard Divinity Seminary, had moved him not at all. And at the end of his study, some six months after that, he had sold everything and moved to Whitlow. The choice of Whitlow had been most casual; any place would have served his purpose, which was to leave Boston and memories contained there, for good.

He had met Elizabeth, quite unsurprisingly, at church. It had been at the very first service he had attended, his purpose having been to introduce himself to the resident minister, a dry, humorless man named Alvin Carpenter, and to make known his own availability as visiting minister, a good stepping-stone to beginning his career.

He had noticed the Enrights immediately, not only because they were seated in the first pew, but because Edward Enright had an air of superiority, of success, about him that was almost tangible. It was evident, even to the casual eye, that the Enrights were wealthy; it was also evident that their daughter was unmarried, and available.

A few, select words in the ear of the Reverend Carpenter had effected an introduction. That had been a mere six months ago. Justin had known from the start that Elizabeth would make him a suitable wife. She was a trifle spirited, but that could be dealt with after they were married. Initially, Justin had detected some resistance with regard to his courtship. This came not from Elizabeth but from Edward Enright, who had a tendency to view with suspicion any man who approached his daughter. Therefore, before three months had passed, Justin made certain that Edward Enright knew that his intentions were of the honorable sort. Actually, Justin's appraisal of Elizabeth was cool and detached. Love didn't enter into it, although he was intelligent enough to realize that Elizabeth would marry only for love. In retrospect, it hadn't been too difficult. It was, he realized, easier for a man to gain a woman's love when his own emotions were not involved.

Still observing Peach, Justin now said, "It would greatly facilitate matters if you would show me about."

Shrugging, Peach led the way into the noisy room. Justin, leaning on his cane, followed.

"This here's a carding machine," Peach remarked as they entered. "The raw wool gets fed in there," he pointed. "It passes through the iron teeth and comes out here, clean and untangled."

"Remarkable," Justin commented, somewhat impressed by the mechanics of it all.

"Over here's a cotton carder," Peach went on, raising his voice. "Fibers are much more fragile than the wool," he explained, "so we use only experienced girls as operatives. See there," he pointed again. "When the cotton comes out, it gets wound on those bobbins, same as the wool."

"Then where does it go?" Justin asked, curious in spite of himself.

"It gets taken over there, to the spinning frames, and from there it goes upstairs to the skein-winders. That's our finished product."

Justin glanced about him. Noting one unusual machine, exceptional for its clattering sound, he asked, "What is that one?" As they moved closer, Betsy viewed the elegant visitor with interested eyes.

"It's called a *mule,*" Peach explained, beginning to enjoy himself. He didn't often get the opportunity to show off his expertise. "This is the only machine that takes a bit of real skill."

"And that's what I've got, eh, Mr. Peach?" Betsy grinned impishly at the foreman and he gave her a playful slap on the rump with his cat-o'-nine-tails.

Appalled by this display of frivolity, Justin's brow creased in censure, but all he said was, "Why is more dexterity needed here?"

For a moment, Peach regarded him blankly, then he said, "Because the cotton is spun into such a fine thread that the least bit of overpressure would snap it. It needs a cautious hand, one that knows exactly when to stop the stretching."

"Hmm." They moved away again, and as they neared the door to the office, Justin regarded the small, thonged whip Peach held so loosely. "You need that often?"

Peach made a vague gesture. "Sometimes the girls get to dawdling, especially toward the end of the day." He lifted the cat-o'-nine-tails and viewed it almost with affection. "This wakes 'em up, you might say." He grinned. "'Course, Jonathan don't like me to use it, but old Master Enright didn't mind overly much."

"Well, while I am in charge, Mr. Peach," Justin stated somewhat pontifically, "I suggest that you make good and heavy use of it. There will be no slacking off, at any time, do you understand?"

For the first time, Peach grinned enthusiastically, viewing Justin Lansing with new respect. "Yes, sir," he replied smartly.

Glancing across the room, Justin's eyes narrowed. "And I suggest that you begin with that bit of baggage that's operating your...mule. I will not tolerate back talk or familiarity." He glared at Peach. "Do it now!"

Peach hesitated. Betsy O'Connor was their highest paid and most skillful operative. Smart-mouthed she might be, but she was a good worker. And Peach, for all his faults, felt he displayed his heavy hand only when justified. Now, under Justin Lansing's darkening countenance, he reluctantly went to carry out his orders.

Approaching Betsy, he brought the whip down on her back smartly, but without much leverage, and to her wide-eyed outrage said loudly: "Mr. Lansing is in charge now, and he don't want no back talk!" He glared at all the girls. "You all understand that?" He stood there, hands on his hips, but, except for the noise of the clanking machinery, there was silence.

Having observed his first order carried out, Justin nodded once, and then entered the office. When the door closed, Peach again turned to Betsy, who, tight-lipped, refused to look at him. Now his expression was almost conciliatory.

"I couldn't help that," he said in a voice barely audible over the machines. "It was orders."

"And yer sure enough carried them out, didn't yer?" Betsy retorted scathingly.

"Look, it didn't hurt none," he protested. "I know; it merely tapped you. I was careful."

She glanced at him sideways, still angry at the undeserved chastisement. "I'd like for it ter merely 'tap yer,' Jed Peach!"

He moved closer, running a hand along her thigh as he did so. "I wouldn't hurt you, Betsy; you know that," he said softly. "Haven't I always treated you right?"

She viewed him with a cynical expression, but made no move to draw away from the hand that now frankly moved exploringly about her body. Then she sighed deeply. A girl had to protect herself, she thought resignedly. If it took a few liberties to keep Jed Peach on her side, so be it.

Chapter 6

The sleigh slipped along the snow-covered road at an easy pace, the horse only gently prodded by the man who held the reins. His name was Samuel Hockings, and beside him was his eldest son, Christian, aged nineteen.

Samuel Hockings owned the Golden Eagle, Whitlow's oldest inn and taproom; and, although the Town Hall was only a short distance away, the weather had precipitated the decision to take the sleigh. After only a one-day interlude of clear skies, the snow, now mixed with hail, had begun again that morning. It was now descending with a frenzy, making even walking a battle against the elements.

For a time, father and son had ridden in silence and at last Christian, without looking at his father, said, "It's not right, Pa."

This was not the first time he'd said that, and the elder Hockings displayed little surprise or even interest upon hearing it again. "It's not a question of right, son. Only necessity."

"Buying people! It's just like they do in the South. You said time and again how wrong that is."

Samuel nodded. "I did. And I still believe it. But we're not 'buying' anyone," he pointed out, tugging on his hat. Even with the adjustment, the snow and hail pelted his face and neck, already lined and weather-beaten from his forty-seven years of exposure to the harsh New England climate. "The town's paying us to take a needy pauper off its hands," he said, turning to glance at his son. "Would you rather they forced them into the almshouse? A person could get trapped in there till the day they died. Besides, they're free enough to come and go." Samuel was answered by a stony silence from his son. In a gentler tone, he added, "Your ma's ailing, boy. She needs help. The Lord's seen fit to bless us with three healthy sons, but there's no girls to help out. We all done our best through the winter, but now spring's coming fast and you know that with the warmer weather we get busy."

If this sounded ludicrous to Christian, watching the swirling snow about him, he made no comment. And in truth, spring was only weeks away, despite the capricious March weather.

"Now your ma's been in bed these past two weeks, ever since the birthing," Samuel went on. "You were there when the doctor came. Woman trouble, he says, and there's not much to be done about it. We're gonna get a girl to help out, and that's all there is to it. Anyway, it's our Christian duty to help those who need it."

The young man just glanced at his father, but made no comment. Besides, he'd said it all before. Why couldn't they just hire someone instead of attending the vendu? Of course, he knew the answer. Hiring meant paying steady wages. A pauper need only be fed, clothed, and housed. If he didn't like the arrangement, he could always move on. If he got sick, he was sent back to the town constable.

When they arrived, numerous horses, wagons, and sleighs were hitched around the Common. The town held the vendu only once a month, sometimes not even that, depending on the number of destitutes around. There always seemed to be more of them during the winter months.

Samuel and Christian edged their way to the front of the milling crowd in the large room that was the town hall.

"Samuel!" a man called out, heading in their direction. He was tall and thin to the point of being gaunt. This was John Choate, owner of Whitlow's only weekly newspaper, the *Bellringer*. "How's the missus feeling?" he asked, approaching them.

Samuel gripped the outstretched hand. "Still ailing, John."

"Sorry to hear that," the other man responded. "Here for the vendu?"

Samuel nodded. "Hoping for a girl to help Ella."

Choate frowned. "There's only one young girl," he offered. "In fact, there's only about ten people in all. There's a woman with five young ones, but I think they'll split them up, at least the older ones. But the girl's got a young boy with her, her brother. Matt tells me the lad is sickly," he added, referring to Matthew Benson, the deputy in charge of the vendu.

"I got no use for a sick boy," Samuel declared firmly, eyeing his friend.

"Well, looks like you're out of luck then. He's going to offer them as a pair. The girl refuses to leave her brother. 'Course, there's always the woman with one or two young ones."

Samuel shook his head at this suggestion. "Women with babes is more concerned about them than their chores. How old's the girl?"

"Don't rightly know," Choate replied. "Appears to be about fifteen, sixteen. The boy is about ten, maybe eleven."

"How sick is he?" Samuel inquired.

The other tilted his head and gave a short laugh. "Sick enough to be lying down and coughing a lot."

Christian, standing to the side of his father, listened as the older men exchanged pleasantries and gossip, and after a moment, he began to walk aimlessly about the large room, stopping now and then to greet an acquaintance or neighbor. To the far side of the room, he paused before an open door, and, peering inside, he saw a group of people seated on benches. A glance at their expression and dress told him that these were the paupers.

It was not difficult to recognize the girl that John had spoken of; she was the only young girl in the group. The boy, presumably her brother, lay stretched out on the bench, his head in her lap. Save for the fretful cry of the baby the other woman held in her arms, the room was silent. They sat, all of them, still as statues, not looking at each other, not speaking, not communicating in their evident misery.

He was about to turn away when the girl looked up and saw him, and in that moment he blinked in astonishment. It was the girl who had gotten off the coach that night not three months past! At first, her eyes held fright, and Christian likened them to the look of a deer he had once shot, in that split second when the animal caught sight of him just before he fired. But then, seeing that he wasn't Matt Benson, she seemed to relax slightly, watching him with wary eyes, evidently not recognizing him.

She was seated close to the door. Without thinking, Christian took a step into the room and stood before her.

"Are you frightened?" he asked quietly, and with the sound of his voice, he saw her eyes widen in recognition. But she made no reply, and so he went on, "Don't be. It'll be my pa who bids for you. He's a good man, well respected by all." He regarded her with an anxious expression, wondering why it was so important to him that she be comforted. And with his spoken words he knew that if his father would not bid, he, Christian, must persuade him to do so.

She wet her lips slightly and as the boy in her lap stirred, she absently patted the thin shoulder, all the while regarding Christian in a solemn manner. There was, he decided, a dignity about her that somehow appeared right—not out of place. The others looked beaten and crestfallen by their fate, but not she. She looked guarded, suspicious, but not beaten. She nodded now as if accepting his words as gospel truth.

"I don't even know your name," she murmured, still regarding him in some wonderment.

"It's Christian. Christian Hockings," he said. He stood there, uncomfortably aware that the woman with the baby was now staring at him intently. Her eyes were wild-looking and she appeared as if she would scream at any moment. The rest of her children stood grouped about her, looking, in turn, bewildered and resentful.

Christian again looked at Sarah and nodded his head at the boy in her lap. "Is he bad?"

"No, no," she assured him, drawing Aleceon closer. "He has a cough, a bad cold. He'll be well once he's warm and dry." She felt little compunction at the lie. If that's what it would take to see Aleceon safe and warm, then so be it.

Christian was about to speak further when Matt Benson entered, regarding him with some surprise. "Checking out the merchandise, Christian?" the deputy asked, laughing. His face reddening, Christian Hockings hastily retreated to his father, who was, for the moment, alone.

"Where have you been?" Samuel asked. "They're about to begin."

"I know." Christian came closer. "I've seen her. The girl John Choate spoke of. She'd be perfect, Pa."

Samuel's brows knitted in curiosity as he regarded his son. "Perfect! Not long ago you were telling me how wrong this is." He took off his cap and scratched his head. "You may be right, too. I've been thinking on it. Wouldn't take all that much to hire out a girl...."

"No!" Christian said quickly, alarmed by this development. "I was wrong," he explained weakly, seeing his father's sharp eyes upon him. "Like you said, it would be helping them." He wondered if his words sounded as hollow to his father as they did to his own ears. Samuel opened his mouth to speak, but Christian grabbed his arm. "Look, there's Matt. They're starting now."

Samuel continued to regard his oldest son in perplexity for a moment and then with a rueful shake of his head turned his attention to the proceedings. John Choate returned and was about to speak, but at the sharp retort of a gavel, both men fell silent.

Matt gave his usual speech about the needy and how it would help all, the town, the person, the bidder, if they could be removed.

The first was an old woman. "In her seventies, she is," Matt called out. "But good at spinning, carding, and cooking. Do I hear a bid?"

There was silence, and Matt boomed: "Come now. You won't have to worry about feeding her much. And she's quiet, too!"

"Twenty-five dollars," someone called out, and Matt looked affronted.

"You trying to break the town, George? Be reasonable!" There was much laughter, although the old woman did not join in. She stood there, eyes downcast, thin shoulders slumped forward, her dry lips seeming to move in a silent prayer.

"You'd have to pay me more than that to take her!" someone else called out, and the laughter gained momentum.

"There's a bad one for you," John Choate whispered to Samuel. "He's here at every vendu. Bids high for the worst of the lot. That old lady won't last a month; he'll work her hide off." He breathed deeply as if to wash away the sour taste of the words he had just uttered.

There were, however, no other bids, and realizing it, Matt grudgingly paid out the twenty-five dollars.

The woman and her five children were next. A burly man whom Samuel recognized as a ship captain bid low enough, one dollar for each, to secure the services of the three oldest boys, leaving a young lad of about four standing beside the woman. The child she held in her arms, Matt reported, was a girl.

Fifteen dollars was bid for the boy, and seventeen dollars for the woman and the infant.

Two men followed next, one old, one crippled. Neither was bid upon, and reluctantly, Matt returned them to the constable. They would have to remain wards of the town.

Then the girl and her brother mounted the platform. Christian watched them with attentive eyes. The boy was standing on his own two feet, but leaning heavily against his sister who had an arm about him.

"These two must be bid upon as one," Matt informed the assemblage. "The lad is sick now, but he'll work good enough when he's recovered."

"Looks like trouble to me, Matt," someone called out. "But I bid twenty-five for them both."

Christian turned from the girl and looked at his father. "Are you going to bid, Pa?" he asked, suddenly fearful for her welfare.

"Twenty-four!" Samuel called out.

"Twenty-two!" was the return bid.

"Twenty-one!" Samuel replied, raising his hand.

"Seventeen!"

Samuel hesitated, and Christian grabbed his arm. "Please, Pa!"

With a sigh, Samuel called out: "Ten dollars," and at that the room fell silent.

"It's a good bid!" Matt sang out. "It's yours, Samuel."

Sometime later, back on the snow-covered street, Christian helped Aleceon into the back of the sleigh, while Samuel flung the small valise in.

"We've only a short ride, girl," Samuel said. "There's a blanket back there. Best cover the boy. You can sit up here with us if you like—less bouncy."

He fell silent as he climbed up onto the seat and, with a slight snap of the reins, moved the horses forward. The wind had abated, but the wet snow, still mingled with icy bits of hail, fell steadily.

Samuel was wondering what Ella would say about all this. About the boy. Yet, the only alternative was to wait another month, and then there would be no guarantee that a suitable girl would be offered. At least this one looked strong and healthy enough. And the boy's condition could improve.

"Where you from, girl?" he asked. He searched his mind for the name Matt had given him; Sarah. Sarah Edgewood.

"Brockton, sir."

Beside her, Christian cleared his throat. "How...how did you come to be at the vendu?"

Haltingly, Sarah explained about the fire and the subsequent job at the mill and the reason for her departure. She made no mention of the incident on the ice, and indeed it had gone from her thoughts, crushed under the pressing need for mere survival.

"Then you lived on a farm?" Samuel asked when she was through, and at the murmur of affirmation, said, "That's good. You know all that needs doing?"

"Oh, yes, sir."

"Mrs. Hockings is ailing," he said. "The chores will be yours to do. You understand?"

"Yes, sir."

"About the boy," he went on. "He can bed down in the loft. It's warm enough when there's a fire. He can rest until he's on his feet again."

Sarah blinked back the tears of gratitude. "I'll work hard, Mr. Hockings. I promise you, you will have no regrets. And when Aleceon's on his feet again, he'll do his share. Until then, I'll do for both of us."

Samuel nodded, pleased. Perhaps he hadn't made such a bad bargain after all. He stopped the sleigh at the front door of the Golden Eagle and, alighting, they entered.

The taproom was almost deserted except for an old man who sat at one of the tables, desultorily viewing a half-filled pewter mug in front of him. Behind the counter, a young man glanced up as they entered, but offered no greeting as Samuel led the way to the rear.

Stepping around chairs and tables, Sarah was aware of a curious intermingling of odors: stale beer and beeswax; burning logs; and beans and molasses.

When they entered the living quarters to the rear, she saw that the main or common room for eating and living was large and spacious, the fireplace, with its heavy oaken lintel, fully ten feet in length. It was, in fact, the same size as the one in the taproom.

A woman was sitting in a rocker, a shawl about her thin shoulders and another about her legs. Sarah assumed this must be Mrs. Hockings, and she could see how lines of weariness and illness were deeply etched in her face. She greeted her husband with only a trace of a welcoming smile.

"This here's Sarah," Samuel said to his wife. Removing his heavy jacket, he hung it on a peg by the door.

The young man had followed them from the taproom, and now a boy appeared, and they all stared at Sarah with undisguised curiosity.

Politely, she nodded as Samuel introduced his youngest son, Will, who was eleven years old. The young man who had been in the taproom was also the son of Samuel Hockings. Lucas was introduced by his father with somewhat less enthusiasm. Christian, at nineteen, was the oldest of the boys. Sarah noticed that all three sons of Samuel Hockings had blond hair although, unlike Christian's reddish-gold hair, Will, the youngest, could be described as a towhead.

Lucas Hockings, at eighteen, was even taller than Christian and, for that matter, his father, with the same light hair and blue eyes. But there the resemblance ended. His eyes were close set, narrow, his brows perpetually drawn down as if in speculation. Nor were they kind eyes, Sarah thought, repressing a shiver of apprehension. While the others spoke, almost casually, of her welfare, Lucas Hockings viewed her in cool silence, his eyes traveling from her soft brown hair to her small feet, now encased in badly worn, damp shoes. Again the eyes worked their way up, now locking hers in an unblinking stare.

Then Mrs. Hockings noticed Aleceon, who was standing uncertainly just inside the doorway, his face flushed and eyes overbright. He was so tired that he could barely stand and he stood there mute, not looking at anyone.

The woman frowned. "You were only supposed to bring the girl, Samuel."

"It's her brother."

She peered closer. "He looks puny. Is he sick?"

"He's ailing somewhat," her husband admitted.

A soft sigh greeted these words. "It won't do," she protested. "Send him back."

"Please, ma'am," Sarah spoke up for the first time. "He won't be any bother. I'll see to him myself."

"Nursing him won't leave you time to do nothing else," she noted in a toneless, almost disinterested voice.

"He doesn't take care at all," Sarah said in a rush. "All he needs is rest. I will do his share until he's up and about."

Lucas Hockings had been staring at Sarah. Now his eyes darted toward Christian, who, oblivious of this new watchfulness, was gazing at Sarah in a kindly, reassuring manner.

"I don't think it would be a good idea—" Ella began, but then Lucas interrupted.

"She's right, Pa. We've no use for a sickly pauper." He regarded Aleceon unblinkingly, his blue eyes narrowing. "Look at him! He's about to drop in his tracks. He'll be no help, only another mouth to feed."

While Samuel had gazed upon his wife in a conciliatory manner, he now turned to his son, eyes blazing. "And there's none who've asked you!"

Lucas's eyes turned flinty as he regarded his father,

but he made no retort. Instead, he again looked at Sarah, who nervously sought the reassurance of Christian.

And it was there. He was smiling, although she noticed how grim and intense were his eyes. With a flash of insight, Sarah realized that Lucas had not been trying to thwart his father, but his brother! The enmity between them shimmered, and she was astonished that no one else saw it.

"We have no choice, Ma," Christian said quietly. "You need help, and you need it now. We can't wait another month..Sarah'll do just fine, I'm sure of it."

Ella hesitated. "Can you cook?" she asked Sarah.

"I can," Sarah replied quickly. "And make butter, cheese, and soap, too. I can do milking, spinning..."

Ella gave a scanty laugh at the girl's exuberance. "There's no milking to be done here," she observed flatly. "And we buy our soap and butter at the Emporium." She peered closely, affronted by the girl's complexion, which had the delicate sheen of fine porcelain, and wavered, torn between indecision and weariness. "Well, it's too late now to do anything," she conceded with a deep sigh. "We'll try it for a while."

At this, Christian cast a relieved look at Sarah, whose eyes were still riveted upon the woman who suddenly seemed to hold her fate in her worn hands.

"There's rooms upstairs," Ella went on, "which we rent out. There's no one there now, but come spring we get busy. It'll be your job to keep them clean. And guests or no, the rooms get dusted and swept up. You can do this after you make breakfast. Understand?"

Sarah nodded, afraid to speak lest the woman again change her mind.

"We serve food at the Eagle," she continued. "That'll be your job, too. Leastways until I get on my feet again." She scowled at Aleceon. "The boy can keep the place swept up, haul the ashes out, and bring the wood in."

Again Sarah nodded, making a mental note to add these three chores to her list.

"Well, you can get started," Ella said, getting to her feet in tired motions. "Now that the vendu's over, there'll be those who will be stopping by before they go home."

Quickly, Sarah removed her shawl and mittens, and

without further words went to the fireplace. As always, one of the heavy iron pots held water. A quick glance to her right showed her the pantry, and, entering it, she easily located the cornmeal for tomorrow's breakfast. Returning, she took another pot off its hook, filled it with some of the water, then added the cornmeal. Strewing a bit of salt in the pot, she slowly stirred it with a wooden pudding stick.

"Come on, boy; I'll show you where to bed down." Samuel was leading Aleceon to the sturdy wooden ladder that led to the loft. "Christian, bank the fire, then get some blankets. We'll make the lad a straw mattress in the morning. Will, you take Sarah's valise and put it in the small bedroom upstairs." He turned to Sarah. "Our rooms are on the third floor," he explained to her. "Yours is the first on the right. All the rooms on the second floor are for guests."

At the command from his father, Will hurried forward, and, picking up the small grip, flashed Sarah a shy smile. He was the same age as Aleceon, but sturdy, and was several inches taller. She returned the smile and, turning, said to Samuel, "I can bank the fire, sir. I know how."

He nodded. "All right." He looked at his sons. "Get outside now. Customers will be coming and there won't be anybody to serve them."

A few minutes later, Sarah checked to see that Aleceon was comfortable and warm, and noted with some relief that he had already fallen asleep. Descending the ladder, she stood there a moment, taking note of her surroundings.

The loft, reached by the wooden ladder, ran almost the whole width of the common room itself, which appeared to be an addition to the main three-storied structure. There was no source of heat in the loft, and the roof was sloped, so one could stand upright only in the center, but its close proximity to the large fireplace made it not too uncomfortable.

The ceiling of the large room was of oak beams, darkened with age and smoke and soot. Entering the pantry again, she saw it was quite large, with barrels along one wall, some filled with molasses, some with rice, and some with brown sugar, as well as a smaller barrel of loaf sugar. There were several wheels of cheese, and both salted and fresh meat. From the ceiling beams, strips of dried apples and pumpkin hung down like bedraggled ribbons.

There was even a buttery, though it appeared long out of use. The wooden churn sat in a corner, solitary, bereft of its intended use; on the shelf, the milk keelers, too, sat forlorn and forgotten.

She nodded, satisfied, and then walked to the center of the common room. The table had drop leaves on both ends. These she raised. Then she located the trenchers and set the wooden bowls on the table so that they would be ready for the morning meal.

Soon the pudding was bubbling gently on the trivet. The brick oven, she could see, had not been swept clean of ashes and was not hot; there had been no bread baked this day.

Elsewhere, too, there were signs that a woman's hand had been lacking for days. The pewter dishes stacked neatly enough in the cupboard were dull and without shine; the hooked rug by the back door was covered with grime and had obviously not been beaten in days.

She went back into the pantry, shivering in the unheated room; locating the beef and potatoes, she brought them back into the kitchen. Then she began to prepare a stew.

An hour later, Christian entered. "Are you finding everything you need?" he asked kindly.

"I am," she replied. "The food will be ready shortly."

"Don't worry," he soothed. "Not much traffic tonight, after all. The weather's keeping everyone indoors." He started for the door and turned. "When you get done, go on up to bed. You look tired and we're about ready to close up." He smiled again and was gone.

Returning to the hearth, she raked the ashes around the hot coals, covering them with a perforated copper lid that would assure that the coals would not go out at night. Then she stirred the pudding once more. By morning it would be ready for breakfast, needing only a bit of molasses and perhaps some milk. A hasty pudding, her mother used to call it, although the name certainly didn't seem to fit the hours of cooking it took.

Before she left the kitchen, she made certain that she knew where the bacon and coffee were stored.

With a final glance about her, Sarah went upstairs and entered the small bedroom, closing the door behind her.

The room was indeed small; there was a trundle bed and a narrow table with a washbasin and a lamp, which was unlit. However, a small fire had been laid in the grate and provided her with enough light to undress.

As she lay in bed she tried to assess her situation. The Hockingses seemed like decent folk, and for this she said a quick prayer of thanks. Only now, hours later, did she begin to relax after the ordeal of the vendu. Her fright had abated, but she was still sick at heart over their humiliation. Sitting in that room all afternoon, torn by the uncertainty of their fate, had left her trembling with apprehension. Work, she didn't mind; in fact, she welcomed it, for it took her mind off things. But she knew well enough what would be the plight of some of those poor unfortunates with whom she had shared those hours.

Matt Benson, after she had spoken to him, pleaded with him, had reluctantly agreed to offer them as a pair. "But only for one time," he emphasized sternly. If it didn't work, then they would be auctioned off separately; the other choice was to leave town.

Never would she forget the humiliation of the vendu, the callous disregard of those in charge that had rendered her so dismayed and defenseless. On her own, she might have sought another avenue of escape, but with Aleceon ill, she had had no other thought than to have him safely sheltered somewhere, whatever the cost to her.

She would work hard, she decided. All they needed was time; time for Aleceon to get on his feet again, time for winter to pass. With the warmer weather, she could walk to Boston if need be. There were plenty of berries and fruit trees along the way.

The next morning, Ella Hockings awoke, shifting her

body wearily with returning awareness. She could hear Samuel as he moved about their bedroom, dressing. It was still dark. With a deep sigh, she sat up.

"No need for you to get up, Ella," Samuel said quickly. "The girl's fixing breakfast. You just stay there and rest, like the doctor said."

With another sigh, she sank back, pulling the covers up under her chin. In all her forty-one years she never remembered ever lying in bed like this, except right after a birthing. She closed her eyes as Samuel left the room.

But in a way, she thought, that's just what this was. She had lost the child she had been carrying, and wistfully, she thought of the daughter she would never have. But her body refused to spring back like the other times. Of course, four days of labor would wear out even a young woman, she thought tiredly. The child had been in a bad position, and at last, on the third day, Samuel had sent for the doctor, his trust in the midwife shattered by his wife's alarmingly weakened condition. By the time he had arrived, the child was dead and the labor stopped. He had had to cut, and the subsequent infection had almost cost Ella her life.

When she again opened her eyes, the sun was streaming in the window. Carefully she sat up, and placing her feet over the side of the bed, eased them into the waiting slippers. Donning a woolen robe, she went down to the kitchen, her hair still in its thick, nighttime braid.

The boy was apparently still asleep in the loft, but the girl was nowhere to be seen.

Blinking, she looked about the large room. It was spotlessly clean; even the tabletop had been scrubbed with a wire brush and now gleamed white in the slanting rays of the sun that streamed in through the back window, showering the wooden floor with golden dust that swirled lazily in its descent.

On the trivets, iron pots and kettles issued forth enticing aromas, and from the brick oven there came the yeasty smell of baking bread. Two pies, both made of dried apples, were resting upon the tabletop, shimmering with cinnamon and sugar and spices where the flaky crust had split.

The back door opened and the girl, carrying an armful of wood, entered. She laid the wood on the hearth, and, straightening, wiped her hands on her apron. Then she spied Ella.

"Oh," Sarah said, "I'd no idea that you were up." She pulled out a chair by the table and then walked toward Ella. "Come on now. You sit down and I'll fix you some food."

Somewhat astonished, Ella allowed herself to be led to the chair.

"I've fixed a caudle," Sarah was saying as she spooned some of the leftover pudding into a wooden bowl. She poured a bit of fresh milk over it, then added a liberal portion of sweetening. "As soon as you've finished this, I'll get it for you. My mother always said that a caudle's good for what ails you."

Without replying, Ella raised the spoon to her lips and ate.

Will opened the door and stuck his head in. "Need another plate of stew," he called out.

"I'll bring it out," Sarah replied, hastily filling a pewter dish with a generous helping of food. She smiled once at Ella Hockings and left the room.

Alone again, Ella continued to eat almost absently as her eyes scanned her kitchen. The pewter had been polished, along with just about everything else.

By the time she finished the pudding, the girl had returned. Still too astonished to speak, Ella watched as the girl began to beat eggs in a bowl, adding a dollop of wine. A few spices joined the mixture and then she poured the frothy liquid into a mug.

"Here, ma'am. You drink this up, and then you just rest yourself."

Later that afternoon, with Mrs. Hockings again asleep and Aleceon resting comfortably, Sarah sat on a wooden stool just outside the door, peeling potatoes. The day was clear and bright and calm, and the mid-March sun shone with an unexpected warmth, turning the new snow soft and shimmery as it melted.

She glanced up, seeing Christian approach, his arms laden with wood, and she smiled.

And seeing that smile, Christian was conscious of an odd sensation in his chest. "No need for you to haul wood," he said awkwardly, dumping his burden on the ground. He straightened. "How's the boy?"

"He's sleeping again," she replied. "He'll be all right," she said with a grim determination.

"I'm sure he will be," Christian agreed quickly.

"He's all I have," she added, as if that explained everything.

He nodded. "You've no other family at all? I mean, aunts, uncles?"

She shook her head, her hands moving quick and sure at their peeling. "No one; just me and Aleceon."

"How...How did the fire come about?"

She shrugged. "I was asleep. I'm really not sure how it started. It was in the kitchen, that much I know. The first I knew of it was my mother screaming at me to grab Aleceon and get out."

"And did you?" he asked.

"Yes." She paused a moment, then went on. "We all got out, at first. Then Pa and my brother Davie went back in. They threw some clothes and things out of the window, but the heat got too bad and they had to come out. By then, the wind had carried the flames to the barn and they ran in to try and put it out."

Again she paused, as if unwilling to view the final scene of the tragedy, but then she continued. "From where we stood, we could see the roof. It was white hot and getting ready to cave in. My mother called and shouted, but Pa and Davie didn't hear. So she ran in, and..."

He put a hand on her slim shoulder. "I'm sorry," he said simply.

She regarded him gravely. "Seems like it happened such a long time ago," she mused wonderingly, her hands falling idle in her lap. "Three months. That's all it's been. Three months."

During the days that followed, Sarah relaxed somewhat, feeling the acceptance about her. Even Ella's attitude warmed noticeably and, although she still addressed Sarah in a brusque manner, there was an occasional wondering expression in her eyes as she gazed upon this young girl who had so suddenly been deposited within their midst.

Only Lucas caused a discordant note, and she was uncomfortably aware of his eyes as they followed her about.

Twice in the first week she was at the Eagle, Christian and Lucas fell into an argument. The second time, they almost came to blows, and only Samuel's exasperated intervention prevented them from physically assaulting one another. Lucas, it seemed, got along with no one, and Sarah finally surmised that the fact that one day the inn would belong to Christian, as eldest son, was a primary source of irritation to Lucas. He rarely spoke to her, and when he did, his voice was gruff, almost accusing. She diligently applied herself to her chores, averting her eyes from that gaze as much as possible.

Chapter 7

"Until death do you part," the minister intoned, and Elizabeth raised her face to Justin, secure in the knowledge that at last he would have to kiss her lips, a thing he had never done before. It was, however, a short, unsatisfactory gesture, unlike what she had been expecting.

She turned then and, smiling, her eyes holding only a hint of a shadow, received the congratulations of the guests that had gathered in the lavishly decorated Enright ballroom to witness her wedding.

Jonathan approached her, and kissed her lightly on the brow. As soon as he moved away, the smile left his lips. He had given his sister away, but had it not been for the fact that his father had already given his consent, Jonathan was not entirely certain that he would have gone through with it. He disliked Justin Lansing intensely, and considered him a poor choice for a husband.

Not that he begrudged a man his calling, Jonathan thought, still observing his sister; it was just that the man's faith was cloaked in a Calvinism of the worst sort. For him, everything boiled down to death and damnation, and for one as spirited and alive as Elizabeth, Jonathan thought the match ill-conceived.

It was a mere eight weeks since Edward's death. Although Jonathan had objected to going through with the wedding, his mother, surprisingly, had insisted. And quite strongly. "Your father gave his consent, as you know," she said to him. "Elizabeth's gown is completed, and arrangements have been made."

He had been shocked, but the aura of glacial dignity with which Rachel had surrounded herself ever since the death of her husband was like a solid, impenetrable wall. The feeling was so strong that Jonathan dared not even extend his hand toward his mother, certain that it would be blocked by an unseen force before it reached its destination.

If she had wept, shed even one tear, Jonathan had not seen it, and yet, paradoxically, he thought his mother most affected of them all by what had happened.

He could not, however, term the effect grief. Whatever else Rachel was feeling, it was not grief, thought Jonathan, viewing his mother as she mingled with the guests, urging refreshments, accepting congratulations and condolences with the same fixed smile.

Feeling oppressed, he left the ballroom and went into the library. There he stood by the window staring pensively at the gray gloom that it framed.

God, how could his life have gone awry in only a few short days! It was incredible when he thought of it, and he tried not to, but today it was especially vivid.

Might it all not have happened, as his mother icily contended, had he not impulsively gone out onto the ice that day? Certainly he would not have fallen ill; perhaps his father would not have died, although Doctor Waite had assured him that the elder Enright's heart was in a severe state. "It could have happened anytime," he had said.

And the girl. His mind, over these past weeks, had returned to her repeatedly. What had happened to her?

Peach didn't know. He had questioned the foreman, at first sorely irritated by the dismissal, although he had to reluctantly agree that under the circumstances the foreman had acted correctly. Peach insisted that Sarah Edgewood, together with her ailing brother, had left Whitlow. Maybe headed for Boston, although he did not know for certain.

Over the past weeks Jonathan had made several trips into Boston. Tentative inquiries had been made, but it was an impossible task. A girl, destitute and alone, was a nonentity in that thriving city.

And Edward. God, how he missed his father. And how strange it was in view of the fact that they had seemed to quarrel constantly. Jonathan's shock, when at last he was told, had been indescribable.

"Jon!"

He turned and made a special effort to smile at his sister. In the gray gloom she appeared like a vivid flash of color. Elizabeth had the fine, chiseled beauty of the patrician; he noted approvingly how her black hair, parted in the center and coiled in ringlets about her ears, effectively contrasted with her flawless skin.

"Are you almost ready to leave?" he asked, taking hold of her gloved hand as she approached. Her pelisse, snug at the bodice and fashionably cut, was the color of honey.

"Oh, yes," she replied, breathless. And then she made a pert frown. "I certainly hope that the weather in Saratoga is more pleasant. How dreadful to have rain and fog for my wedding day."

He raised her hand and brushed his lips across the smooth satin of her glove. "Surely you don't believe in old wives' tales, my dear," he said chidingly, thinking how lovely she looked.

She gave a small laugh. "No, I suppose not." Then she sighed. "Doubtless the roads will be a mire, though."

"Perhaps it would be wise to leave tomorrow," he suggested.

"No, no. I have no intention of delaying my honeymoon. We shall leave as planned."

She began to walk away. Following her into the hall, Jonathan impulsively said, "Will you write to me?"

She paused and turned around. "Of course," she said brightly. "And you, Jon? Will you give some thought to what we have discussed?"

"Yes, I will." He would not allow himself to frown. The trip to Saratoga had been his wedding gift to Elizabeth and Justin. His brother-in-law, however, had had the temerity to request, instead, the financing of a church. Had it not been for Elizabeth, who was so looking forward to three weeks in Saratoga, he would have complied. Now, it appeared, they wanted both. Justin, of course, promised to repay Jonathan eventually.

As Elizabeth went up the stairs, Jonathan returned to the library. He had no wish to join the guests, and uncharitably wished that they would soon take their leave.

Perhaps a church would be a good idea, he reflected,

returning his gaze to the colorless scene outside. But not at the mill, at least not at this one.

Within his mind during these past weeks, he had had an idea, one which refused to leave him. It was, as yet, a nucleus, and he spoke of it to no one. Perhaps when Justin returned, he would once again consent to going to the mill each day for a while, in return for which he, Jonathan, would build him his church.

Because he was certain now that the answers to his questions—which had to be resolved before he could even speak of his idea—would be found in England. And when Justin and Elizabeth returned, he now suddenly made up his mind, he would go.

Behind him, in the hallway, he could hear voices; the guests were getting ready to leave. He knew that he should at least make an appearance, but he had no desire to do so.

A terrible feeling of oppression gripped him. This should have been a happy day; perhaps, if his father had been here, it would have been.

But his father was gone and would never return. Why did we pass each other like strangers? he wondered, and in the moisture-laden panes saw the reflection of his own tears.

Chapter 8

Knowing that her and Aleceon's survival depended upon the charitable inclinations of Mr. and Mrs. Hockings, Sarah worked; she worked harder than at any other time in her life. She was up before first light and was the last one to lay her head down at night, settling into her new life with the resilience peculiar to youth, and bringing to it her own dignity and determination to do well.

Her days were an endless round of sweeping, polishing, dusting, stoking fires, black-leading grates and, when guests arrived, making beds, and washing and ironing linens. This was all in addition to the cooking, time-consuming in itself. There was little time for brooding or reminiscing, and Sarah wasted no effort in either.

Only Sundays offered some respite, and that time was spent in church. On some days she thought she would collapse with the unrelenting fatigue that pressed down upon her like a leaden weight, leaving her light-headed and trembling.

Of them all, only Christian tried to alleviate her overwhelming responsibilities. But he was, for the most part, too busy himself to help out each day. If she gave idle consideration to leaving, these musings were soon and irrevocably dispelled when she thought of Aleceon and her responsibility to him. She would sternly reprove herself for being lazy and ungrateful to the family that had taken them both in.

Spring came at last, chasing frost and snow into hiding, and then blossomed into summer. As though to make up for the starkness of the lengthy winter, the land turned lush with heavy foliage and with berries, fruits, and vegetables. Wildflowers dotted fields and meadows, and for a time their scent almost overcame the pungent smell of salt and sea that wafted inland from the not-too-distant ocean.

In the fields, men plowed, coaxing the earth for yet one more crop, and the young boys, after hurriedly completing chores, fished or swam in the streams and ponds that dotted the verdant land like silver jewels in an emerald setting.

As suddenly as it came, summer melted into the flame of autumn, with showers of golden leaves that crackled underfoot. Color appeared everywhere; maples glowed with red, and birches preened in yellow; apples blushed with a rosy tint, and the air was vivid with a winy tang.

Sarah thought there was no place on God's green earth that could compare with the magnificent riot of color that swept the countryside of New England in autumn. Nothing was hesitant or timid; neither the blazing reds, warm browns, nor bright yellows held back their glory. And not to be outdone, a cerulean sky added its intensity, creating a perfect harmony of color.

And in Sarah, too, a flame was lit—for Christian. Her body seemed to become aware of him even before her mind did. At first there was merely a restlessness within her, leaving her perplexed and confused. Her body was changing, too, the curve of her breast and hips becoming more pronounced beneath her muslin frock.

By the time winter again locked the land in ice and snow, Sarah expected almost daily to be told that she and Aleceon would have to leave. Ella had recovered most of her strength, and except for a nap in the afternoons, began to take an active hand in the chores, lightening Sarah's prodigious burden. Aleceon, too, had almost fully recovered his health, although he had a tendency to tire easily.

In view of these developments, Sarah waited to be informed that she and her brother were no longer needed. But no one spoke the words.

Only once during this time had she seen Betsy O'Connor, since, for both of them, only Sundays offered a change in their routine.

"Lord luv yer, lass," Betsy had exclaimed, catching

sight of her one frosty November Sunday. She had hugged Sarah, and then searched her face carefully. "Yer looking well. How's yer brother?"

Sarah explained that he was improving. "And you, Betsy? How are things at the mill?"

Betsy's normally cheerful expression turned sour, and she sighed heavily. "Not too well, lass. Since Master Jonathan's gone, it's the devil himself who's in charge."

"Mr. Peach?"

Betsy shook her head. "It's Master Lansing I'm speaking of. He's Master Jonathan's brother-in-law."

Sarah looked confused. "But where is Master Jonathan?"

"In England, would yer believe that? He's been gone for months now." She shook her head again. "Poor man, he took the death of his father hard, he did that."

"Isn't he coming back?" Sarah asked. Although she had expressed interest, it was only superficial. That part of her life seemed far behind her.

"He won't be back till summer, they say. But I'll not be around then," Betsy went on. Then, almost shyly, she added: "I'll be getting married soon."

"How wonderful!" Sarah exclaimed, taking her hand. "I'm so happy for you, Betsy. Who is the man so fortunate as to be getting you for a wife?"

"His name's Thomas. Right now, he's a wagon driver at the mill, but he's had an offer ter work as apprentice to a shipwright, so we're both going ter Boston."

Sarah was dismayed to hear that Betsy would be leaving Whitlow, but she continued to smile brightly. "And when is the wedding?"

For the first time, a shadow crossed Betsy's merry face. "It'll be soon, lass." Her face brightened again. "I don't know exactly, but it'll be soon."

They exchanged good-byes and promises to stay in touch that each felt they would not be able to keep, then, with a wave of her hand, Betsy continued on to the north end of the town to her own church.

The days continued to pass, until, one morning in late March, Sarah realized with a start that she had been at the Eagle for one whole year.

She was now seventeen. The fresh air and good and

plentiful food had put a glow in her flawless complexion and had given a shine to her chestnut-brown hair. But if Christian noticed any of these changes that had occurred in her within the past year, it was not apparent in his attitude toward her, which remained, as always, kind, considerate, gentle. In church he sat not with his family or with her, but with a girl named Jena Witcomb—an act that was tantamount to announcing an engagement.

Again the weather warmed, cloaking the land in a deceptive fragility that belied the rigid, resistive soil that lay just beyond the thin mantle of delicate new leaves and buds. Sap was gathered from maple trees, sheep were shorn, crops were planted. The subsequent plowing unearthed yet more rocks, and these were dutifully added to the walls that delineated the fields.

One day toward the end of April, a basket over her arm and a light shawl loosely draped about her shoulders, Sarah was carefully picking the plump blackberries that grew in abundance, almost casually, like weeds about the area. The air was rich with the scent of buttercups and clover, and so engrossed was she in her pleasant task that she never heard Christian approach, and was therefore somewhat startled when he spoke.

"Do you need an extra hand?" he said, grinning at her surprised expression.

"Basket's almost full," she replied, smiling.

"Well, I'd best keep my hand in," he commented cheerfully. "I don't want to lose my touch now that I'm not going to be working at the Eagle anymore."

Surprise returned, tinged now with dismay at this unexpected announcement. "What do you mean?"

He plucked a few berries, half of which he ate, before he replied. "I'm going to work for Amos Witcomb, at the smithy. I start next week. He's going to teach me a trade. Amos doesn't have any sons, and now that business is picking up, he needs someone to help out."

"What does your father say about all this?" Sarah questioned, her thoughts on Jena Witcomb. She was dumbfounded that Christian would even think of leaving.

He made a face, not looking at her. "He wasn't too

happy about it," he admitted. "But the inn is not for me." His eyes returned to her. "Can't make money at it, and when Pa's gone, there will be Lucas and Will. Split three ways, there'll be nothing for any of us."

Was money the only reason? Sarah wondered. Or did it have to do with Jena? The thought was an agonizing one. "Is money important to you?" she asked finally, conscious of his nearness. His short sleeves were rolled up and she could see the play of muscle in his arms as he moved.

"I aim to be something," he said slowly, his gaze turning intent and thoughtful. "Not just an innkeeper, either."

She wet her lips. "Are you going to be staying at the smithy, then?"

"No, no. The shop is only about a mile away."

"I wish you luck," Sarah said in an attempt at casualness. Her basket now full, she began to head back toward the inn. For a time they walked in silence, and then she spoke. "I've never thanked you proper."

Surprised by this, he looked down at her. A few tendrils of her fine brown hair had loosened from her cap and these moved wispily in the gentle breeze. "Thank me? For what?" he asked, genuinely puzzled.

Shyly, she glanced up at him. "For that day at the town hall. When you spoke to me kindly."

He gave a sound of denial. "I didn't do anything." He laughed a bit, remembering his first sight of her, and she was startled to see his eyes dance mischievously, his manner become teasing. But over it all lay a patina of tenderness and her heart ached with a sweet longing that was almost painful. "You looked out of place," he said. "Like you didn't belong with the rest of them." He grinned broadly. "And scared, too."

Her laughter was soft. "Guess I was. Scared, I mean. I wouldn't have minded so much if it hadn't been for Aleceon."

"Well, it turned out all right, didn't it? Ma's really pleased with you. I think she likes you more than she lets on." He didn't mention Aleceon, because no one was pleased with him. He was sullen and he was lazy. "In fact," Christian went on, his voice holding a note of enthusiasm, "she told Pa that by the end of the summer you were to get a wage."

At this news, Sarah flushed with pleasure. "Your folks have been good to me, Christian. I don't know what would have happened to us if they hadn't come along."

Watching her, Christian thought, unexpectedly, that the slight figure who walked beside him had somewhere along the way turned into a young woman. With a shock, he realized that Sarah was not the little girl he had first seen outside the Eagle a year and a half ago. And she was fine-looking, too, he thought, bemused. Almost beautiful...

He was about to reply, but they were now in sight of the inn. Glancing ahead, he spied the buggy in front. "There's Amos," he exclaimed. "And...hey!" He waved and began to run as he caught sight of the girl standing just outside the door.

Sarah halted, and her heart constricted painfully as Christian ran to the girl's side.

The men shook hands, and Christian's smile was wide as he greeted Jena, who casually, possessively, placed a hand on his arm. A moment later they entered the inn.

Sarah waited until they were lost from view, then she went around to the rear and headed for the summer kitchen. This was little more than an outside porch with a low wall enclosing the area that held a wood-burning stove and a table and a few stools placed randomly. It was cooler and more pleasant to do the cooking here in the warm months.

Absently, she placed the basket of berries on the table. Why had she thought that Christian would notice her? she wondered desultorily. And yet somehow she had thought that her feeling, grown so intense over these last months, had at least been observed, if not shared by Christian.

Apparently not. Certainly he would not have rushed forward so enthusiastically to join Jena Witcomb if he had had the slightest feeling for *her*.

The sound of laughter and voices emanated from the common room. One laugh in particular assaulted her ears—the high, penetrating sound made by Jena Witcomb. Even though Sarah had seen her at least once a week, mostly at church services, Jena Witcomb had never deigned to speak to her. She had eyes for no one but Christian, and did little to hide that fact. She was, Sarah had grudgingly to admit, a pretty girl. But in unguarded moments, Sarah saw the gleam of malice and discontent that lit her eyes when she thought herself unobserved. She was a year younger than Christian, nineteen, and her body was full and ripe in its first flush of maturity.

Lacklusterly, Sarah now sat down on a low stool.

"What are you doing?"

Startled, she looked up to see Aleceon. "Just sitting," she replied.

He sat down on the low wall, kicking his heels against the stone with monotonous regularity. She frowned at him. Almost thirteen now, Aleceon was still slight of build, and at first glance appeared younger than his years. His face, however, had an older and wiser look to it than it should have had.

"Why aren't you about your chores?" she asked with mild annoyance, wanting to be alone. "Have you seen to the wood?"

He grimaced. "There's enough," he replied sullenly. "I'm tired of choppin' and splittin' and sweepin'. Besides, I don't feel so good." He peered at her slyly, knowing that this always won her sympathy, but she appeared not to have heard him; at least she was paying him no mind, so he relaxed. "How long are we going to stay here?" he said at last. The words were laced with reproach.

He remembered, so clearly, the night after the fire when she had shown him the money she had taken from the tin box. "With it, we will make a new start," she had assured him.

He had never doubted her. He knew she could do it if she put her mind to it. Sarah was resourceful; and she had the capacity to cope, he thought.

"I don't know. For a while yet." Sarah regarded him, annoyance growing. "You should be grateful for the kindness these people have shown us."

He snorted. "Grateful! They get free work from us," he observed scathingly, astounded by his sister's stupidity. "What's so kind about that?" Even he could see that Ella Hockings could not do without her. But Sarah would never ask for a wage, he thought contemptuously. She was too grateful for a roof and a meal. There were people like that, grateful for anything, like dumb animals. It distressed him to realize that his sister was apparently one of them.

"You have chores to do," she reminded him in a tight voice. "Be about them!"

"You're just sitting," he noted sarcastically, making no move to get up.

"I don't want to intrude while they are entertaining guests," she replied, glaring at him.

Even through her annoyance, Sarah felt a profound relief as she looked at her brother. She had come so close to losing him that it would be unthinkable of her to feel anger at anything he said or did. Indeed, she was ashamed of the annoyance she now felt. It's because of Christian, she thought, contrite, becoming acutely aware that she was venting her own unhappiness on Aleceon.

Jena's laughter again shrilled, and Sarah stiffened at the sound of it.

A thought came to Aleceon, and he viewed it with horror. Little snatches of conversation, fleeting images of expression upon the face of his sister now came to him, solidifying like the pieces of a puzzle.

She couldn't! Damn her soul to hell, he thought, watching her. She couldn't be in love with Christian Hockings! The thought rose up in his throat, choking him with its implications. He would be stuck here forever! Christian was leaving the inn, he had overheard them talk of it. The fool was going to work at the smithy. Then what? He was not against his sister marrying; after all, what else was there for a woman to do? But he was dead set against her marrying a nobody, a smith's apprentice. God, how could she care so little about us both, he wondered.

"We ought to be moving on," he said stubbornly, willing her to understand. "Mrs. Hockings is back on her feet now. How long do you think they are going to let us stay here?" She made no immediate response, and his voice fell into a cajoling whine. "You promised to take care of us, Sarah. We don't have any more than when we left Brockton. Even less!"

"Aleceon!" She fell silent as the voices grew louder and she knew that they were now outside.

After they were all gone, Sarah picked up the basket of berries and made for the kitchen. "Bring the wood in," she said to Aleceon in a low voice. "Then get back to your chores."

Seeing only Lucas in the common room, Sarah faltered in the doorway, her step hesitant. From the look in his eyes as he sat at the table, a tankard of ale before him, she could see that he was angry. The word *angry,* however, when applied to Lucas, Sarah thought, did not adequately describe his emotion. It was as if he were filled with a rage that threatened to devour him.

He stared at her in a brooding manner as she placed the basket on the table then quietly set about making the dinner meal.

For a time there was silence, but it was an uncomfortable, threatening quiet, deadly with unspoken words that Sarah did not wish to hear.

"The bloody bastard's gone and done it!" Lucas said at last, his tone low and grating. Sarah turned her head slightly, but made no response; after a moment, a long moment during which she could feel his eyes blazing at her, he continued in the same voice. "Don't pretend you don't hear me, Sarah girl. You hear everything, don't you? Quiet as a mouse, you are, but you don't fool me."

She walked back to the table, picked up the basket, and looked at him. "I don't know what you're talking about, Lucas," she said.

Suddenly, with a swift movement, he grabbed her wrist, upsetting the basket and spilling the berries about. "You're just like the rest of them, aren't you? It's Christian this, and Christian that. Fine Christian. Kind Christian."

She pulled away from him, rubbing her wrist and

viewing the devastated fruit. "Look what you've done," she said in exasperation. "Half of them are on the floor!"

He leaned forward, his nostrils white and pinched. "It's true, isn't it!" he demanded.

"I don't see what you are so upset about," she said at last, and in an attempt to salvage the berries, scooped those that were strewn about the tabletop back into the basket. "You're always going on about how the inn should be yours. Now, with Christian leaving, it will be. I should think that that would make you deliriously happy." Try as she might, Sarah could not conceal the note of sarcasm that crept into her voice, and at the sound of it, Lucas stood up and regarded her contemptuously.

"The inn!" His voice contorted into a grimace of disgust. "What the devil do I care about the inn! Christian's always had it easy. Everything is handed to him like he deserved it!"

Astonished by the outburst, she just stared at him. "You never wanted the inn at all, did you?" she breathed. "It's just your brother. You want everything that he has...."

"It wouldn't surprise me in the least if he marries Jena and gets Witcomb's business to boot." He brought his face closer. "How'd you like that, Sarah girl?" He gave an unpleasant laugh. "Had your cap set for him, didn't you? Oh, don't deny it," he said quickly as she began to speak. "I've seen how you watch his every move. You can't take your eyes off him." He paused, hearing voices. He gave Sarah a look that filled her with uneasiness. "You would be better off with me, you know," he said quietly. Abruptly, he turned and made for the door, stepping aside as his mother entered.

Lucas did not stay in the taproom, but left by the front door. He walked aimlessly, his mind a seething, tormented thing, raging in his head.

Always, it seemed, he had hated Christian. Hated and envied him, for looking at his brother was like looking into a distorted mirror; and in that reflection Lucas saw all the things he wanted to be and was not, and never could be. Christian was the eldest, the handsomest, and from his tongue poured forth the silver voice of reason. Christian was seldom angry, and when he was, it was a cool, logical emotion, a contradiction in terms to Lucas, who had the predator's instinct, a sheer animal-like fury embedded in self-preservation.

To Christian had gone his father's love and pride. To Christian had gone his mother's dependence, for in times of trouble she always looked to Christian for the answers. And he could see, today, the dismay that was stronger in her than in his father at Christian's decision to leave. She didn't think that he, Lucas, was capable of handling the inn should his father die.

Even Will, insipid and nondescript, doted upon his eldest brother with an admiration that shone like a beacon on a dark night.

Worst of all, what was now eating at him was the realization that Christian had, in part, made this decision because of him. He had stepped aside because he thought that in so doing he was giving Lucas the one thing that he really wanted.

As he walked, Lucas gave a cry of rage at this latest selfless act of his hated brother.

And Sarah. His step slowed as he absently regarded the approaching twilight that covered the far hills in soft purples and crimson. He had been attracted to her from the very first night that she had come to them, small and soft and vulnerable. And to whom had she turned? Who was it that received her soft glances? Once again, the answer was Christian.

The sky was dimming fast now, and the chirping sounds of night made a first, tentative appearance.

In the quiet softness of the evening, Lucas's face grew thoughtful. Sarah. Perhaps here was one way for him to best Christian, he thought, slowly smiling one of his rare smiles.

Chapter 9

Sun slanted in the window, opened now to take advantage of the warm and sweet-scented day.

Sarah was alone in the kitchen, Ella taking her afternoon nap upstairs; the men were in the taproom, which was in the throes of its usual noontime flurry of activity.

She hummed a fragment of a tune as she worked. She liked kneading dough; it was almost comforting, and after the news of yesterday, and the knowledge of Christian's impending departure, Sarah was grateful for any diversion, however small it might be.

Her hands worked in a rhythmic manner, and she was so engrossed in her task that she never heard Lucas enter. Beneath her palms the dough was now smooth and elastic. Satisfied, she laid it aside, raising a hand to her damp brow, glad of the faint breeze that wafted in from the river through the open window.

She was so startled when the arms went about her waist that the scream of fright died in her throat. Standing behind her, Lucas clasped her close, his hands clutching her breasts, his mouth working its way along her neck and up to her ear, which he none too gently bit.

She struggled but the grip tightened.

"Don't fight me, Sarah," he murmured in a thick voice that she hardly recognized. "You've no need to fear. I mean you no harm."

"Let go of me," she whispered urgently, trying to remain calm. What was the matter with him? she thought frantically. Didn't he know that on the other side of the door the room was filled with people? Didn't he care?

She winced as his hands tightened their grip, squeezing her breasts painfully; then, abruptly, he released her, spinning her around to face him. She opened her mouth to call out, but in a quick movement, his mouth covered hers. She felt the wet, probing tongue, and again began to struggle, but he pulled her closer. Drawing his head back, he put a hand over her mouth, still holding her in a firm grip.

"Don't cry out," he muttered through clenched teeth. "If you do, you'll regret it, I promise you. I'll see to it that you and your precious brother are sent packing." Almost cautiously he removed his hand.

Terror momentarily paralyzed Sarah; she felt that she had not even the strength to tremble. No one had ever before touched her. She knew, or thought she knew, what happened between a man and a woman. She had lived most of her life on a farm, had seen the animals rut.

"Let me go, Lucas. Please," she urged in a low voice. His face, above all, frightened her. It was darkly fused with color, his nostrils pinched and white, his mouth slack as he breathed heavily.

"Lay down," he ordered. "On the floor." Placing both hands on her slim shoulders, he pressed hard, and Sarah, now feeling faint, almost collapsed.

In a moment he was on her. Pushing up her cumbersome skirt, he swore softly. The pain of his thrusting fingers made her cry out involuntarily and quickly he covered her mouth with his. She clenched her teeth but he bore down harder and then she felt the warm salty taste of her own blood as his teeth cut sharply into her lip. He thrust harder, and again she involuntarily opened her mouth.

The fingers abruptly halted their assault and she was aware that he was fumbling with his clothing. She struggled, but his weight was ponderous as he slid between her legs. With his mouth still firmly pressed upon hers, his hand slid down her back and, clutching her buttocks, he drew her body roughly up to meet his.

With a moan he began to force himself upon her. She felt a roaring in her ears as her senses threatened to desert her. She again tried to draw away from him, and he lunged viciously. Once more there was pain as he met the resistance within her.

Suddenly, the insufferable weight left her body, producing a curious, airy feeling. She could breathe again, and cautiously Sarah opened her eyes.

Christian, holding Lucas's collar in his fist, was gazing at his brother in rigid anger, his mouth white and compressed as he tightened his grip, causing Lucas to gasp for air as the collar choked him.

"You bastard," he spat in a low, menacing voice. "What do you think you're doing!"

"Take your hands off me," Lucas said, his own voice thick with fury. "What business is it of yours? She was asking for it. I saw the way she was looking at me." He slapped at the hand and almost absently, Christian released him, looking down at Sarah.

One look told him that the girl was terrified. A small trickle of blood rolled down her chin, and her lips were already swollen and bruised. She looked as if she had been struck in the face. Her skirt was still up about her waist, revealing long, shapely legs, the swell of her thigh, and... Quickly he averted his gaze, again glaring at Lucas. Rage swept through him, leaving him weak with its potency, accelerating his breath into short, sharp spurts. He actually took a step backward, afraid of what he might do to his brother.

"If I ever catch you near her again, I'll kill you," he said, his voice harsh, filled with loathing and the truth. "You're no better than an animal."

"Listen, you..." Lucas's voice halted in mid-sentence as Ella, standing in the doorway, regarded her sons with perplexity. Sarah, hidden by the table and still on the floor, went unnoticed.

"What's wrong?" she asked. "Is it your father?"

"No, no, Ma," Christian said consolingly. Walking toward her, he put an arm about her. Gently, he turned her around and led her back to the foot of the stairs. "Nothing's wrong with Pa. Nothing's wrong at all," he said. "Sarah tripped and fell and hit her face on the hearth. We were just trying to help her."

"Clumsy girl," Ella muttered, allowing Christian to prod her forward. "Don't pamper her," she said, her foot on the bottom step. "She's a sturdy girl."

"I won't, Ma," Christian said. Leaving her side, he returned to the kitchen.

Lucas was still standing there, now adjusting his rumpled collar. When he caught sight of Christian, he scowled, and turning, went outside, slamming the back door behind him.

With his departure, Sarah got to her feet. Her terror had subsided but she was visibly trembling with the remembered force of it. "It seems I'm always thanking you, Christian," she said softly, smoothing her skirt.

"Are you hurt?" he asked solicitously, approaching her.

"I don't think so." She touched her mouth gently. "Is my face marked?"

"A bit," he admitted, "but not bad. I've told Ma that you fell, so no one will question it." He regarded her seriously. "Did he..."

"I'm not sure." Suddenly embarrassed, Sarah turned away. "Please, let's not talk about it."

He moved uneasily, wanting to leave, yet held in place by a desperate urgency that he did not understand. He wanted to comfort her, to put his arms about her, but he dared not touch her. "He won't do it again, I promise you, Sarah. I'll see to it. And if he does bother you in any way, I want you to tell me. You hear?"

She nodded, wishing he would go. Her trembling increased as the full import of what had happened suddenly hit her.

For a moment Christian made no move, but sensing that she wanted to be left alone, returned slowly to the taproom.

Sarah stood there, breathing deeply, trying to overcome the fear that still wended its way through her body. It had all been so unexpected! She had seen him watching her all these months; it seemed that every time she looked at him, Lucas was looking at her with those eyes that were expressionless and malevolent at the same time. But she had thought only that he resented her and Aleceon, resented their being here.

Almost fearfully, as if Lucas were still there, hiding, waiting, she glanced about the sun-drenched kitchen, which, despite its cheerful ambience, now appeared sinister to her.

She walked toward the ladder, conscious of the soreness of her body. Each time she took a breath her breasts, against the restraining coarse muslin of her gown, ached anew.

Slowly she climbed the ladder; that, too, produced unpleasant sensations. In the loft, she went behind the screen and almost hesitantly began to remove her clothing. With great care she searched the material. There was no blood. Her body, too, came under minute scrutiny; bruises, but no telltale stain of crimson.

With a great sigh of relief that ended in a sob, she hurriedly dressed again. Descending the ladder, she wondered morbidly if a man could tell whether a woman had or had not been with a man. Was she now still to be considered untouched, pure? Men, she knew, were very particular about that in a wife. Although under other circumstances, she reflected wryly, they didn't seem much to care about it at all.

That night at supper, Sarah kept her eyes down, unwilling to look at either Christian or Lucas, although for different reasons. She wondered whether Christian's opinion of her had changed, and her heart ached with the thought that it had. She realized furiously that Lucas had done what he had done, not because he wanted her, but because he wanted, as always, to thwart Christian.

But why? she wondered. Christian didn't want her, he wanted Jena. Obviously Lucas must have misconstrued his brother's kindness toward her, mistaking it for something other than what it was.

Chapter 10

True to her word, Ella Hockings began to pay Sarah a wage. It was only two dollars a week; but since she had neither room nor board to pay, Sarah felt that it was a windfall. No mention of a wage was made for Aleceon, which only made him more sullen and uncooperative.

The first thing she did with the welcome money was to buy Aleceon new clothes and shoes; he had been wearing Will's castoffs, a situation he grumbled about constantly to his sister.

By the first of June, Sarah had saved enough to buy herself some material for new clothes. Today, in delicious anticipation of that event, she headed for the Emporium.

She had already selected two bolts and had turned her attention to the wide display of ribbons offered, when Jena Witcomb, accompanied by another girl, approached her.

"You're Sarah Edgewood, aren't you?" she asked, her manner stiff and unfriendly. Her dress, made of fine lawn, was a shade of pink that did little to complement her red hair and high coloring. Nevertheless, she displayed a haughty attractiveness, accented by the level look in her hazel eyes, which were now fastened upon Sarah with a directness that was disconcerting.

Somewhat surprised, Sarah only nodded. It was the first time that Jena had ever addressed her, or even acknowledged her presence in the past fifteen months.

"I'm Jena Witcomb, and this is my friend, Maryann Choate." Jena waited for the nod of acknowledgment, then continued in the same curt manner. "You work at the Eagle, don't you?" she asked, as if she had just discovered this fact.

"Yes..." Sarah was acutely aware of the twin forces of hostility and mockery that glittered like an aura about the young woman, who was observing her in an oddly intent manner, as if assessing her worth, and finding her lacking.

Jena arched a brow, held Sarah's gaze for a moment longer, then turned toward her friend. "Sarah's a pauper," she informed Maryann Choate. "Both she and her brother would have wound up in the poorhouse if it hadn't been for Mr. Hockings taking them in."

The other girl looked at Sarah with an almost avid expression that did little to enhance her plain features. "What is it like to be in a vendu?" She shivered, and before Sarah could reply, said: "I think I'd do just about anything to avoid that!"

"I would have preferred to avoid it, too," Sarah replied smoothly, realizing that she was being baited. She smiled grimly, absently rubbing her fingertips across the velvet smoothness of the material that lay on the counter beside her. It was far too expensive for her meager savings but she couldn't resist examining it. With a glance at both girls, she added: "However, in my case, I was most fortunate."

"I'll say. Free room and board. I'd be ashamed to take a handout like that!" Jena smiled coldly, and Sarah was genuinely puzzled by the dislike she saw, a dislike that Jena made absolutely no effort to conceal.

"I work for my keep," Sarah said quietly, ignoring their laughter. She sensed that several of the customers had turned to look at them curiously, and could not prevent the flush that came to her cheeks.

"You don't look like you're working today," Jena pointed out, then turned in annoyance as Maryann nudged her arm.

"Look, Jena. There's Jonathan Enright! I'd heard that he just returned from England. And, oh, good heavens, he's walking in our direction!" Maryann's face turned a bright crimson under her flowered bonnet as the well-dressed man neared.

Tossing her red hair, Jena preened prettily as Jonathan approached. He bowed slightly in their direction, sending them into paroxysms of giggles that produced a wry look of amusement on his handsome face. Then he turned toward Sarah, who was regarding him with somber eyes, wondering how she could graciously take her leave without appearing foolish.

"Miss Edgewood," he said, again bowing slightly.

Heat flamed her cheeks, flushing her pale face with color as she acknowledged his greeting, quite astonished to learn that he remembered her name.

He smiled slightly, lightening his usually somber countenance. Despite, or perhaps because of, his intensity, he was a most appealing man. She realized that he was quite handsome, the veneer of confidence and authority upon his lean, even-featured face giving him an air of unequalled refinement.

"You look surprised," he said, watching her. "But you did save my life, after all. They say if you save a man's life, you are responsible for him thereafter."

Sarah frowned. "I don't recall hearing that said. But, at any rate, I hardly saved your life, Mr. Enright."

His brooding look returned. "I think you did. No one else would walk out on the ice. I've never thanked you properly. I wish to do so now."

"No thanks are necessary, Mr. Enright." She glanced at the two girls still standing close by, and could not help but be delighted by their gaping mouths as they listened to this exchange. Jena in particular displayed a slack-mouthed astonishment, giving her pretty face a somewhat vacuous expression.

Jonathan, too, looked at them, appearing surprised by their continued presence. "Ladies, would you excuse us?" He smiled engagingly. "I suspect you must be angry with me," he said to Sarah when the girls at last departed. "And I do not blame you. Not a bit."

"I?" she said, genuinely puzzled. "Why on earth would I be angry with you?"

"Well," he chuckled softly, momentarily regarding the tips of his highly polished shoes, "you did do me a great service, and you must think me positively brutish for ignoring your own plight."

"I have never given it a thought," she murmured truthfully. "I couldn't imagine that you would concern yourself with me or my affairs."

"Nevertheless, I have, as you can see." To her raised

brows, he added: "I am here today only because I knew that you would be."

"And how did you know that?" She tilted her head slightly as she gazed up at him.

"Why, I made an inquiry or two," he stated, as if it were the most natural thing in the world to do.

She was silent a moment, digesting this bit of news. She found it quite incredible that Jonathan Enright would give her a second thought, much less ask about her.

"I was more distressed than I can say," he went on, "when I learned that you and your brother were actually forced into the vendu." He lowered his voice, and for this she was grateful. "When I learned that you had left the mill, I quite naturally assumed that you had left Whitlow. I've been abroad for a good part of this past year or I would have learned all that happened by now." He paused a moment as a woman approached, rummaging with a gloved hand through the assortment of displayed materials. He gave the woman a quick glance and then, placing a hand on Sarah's elbow, gently guided her to a more secluded spot.

"I do not visit the Eagle often, as you probably know," he said, halting. About them, the air was pungent with the smell of pickled meats, cucumbers, and tomatoes. His thoughts shifted. "If I had been at the vendu that day, none of this would have happened. I want you to know that."

She lowered her eyes and colored deeply, embarrassed that he would know of that degrading episode. But then, she thought in resignation, it seemed that everyone knew of it.

"I'm so sorry for what happened," he went on, apparently unaware of her distress. "I did inquire from Mr. Peach as to your whereabouts, but he did not seem to know where you had gone. This past week I finally learned everything, quite by accident. I went to the Eagle today, and Mrs. Hockings was kind enough to tell me that you would be here."

"I haven't fared so badly," Sarah now said. A swift glance out of the front window showed her that Jena and her friend were still staring. Sarah raised her chin and smiled brightly at Jonathan Enright, as if it were a common occurrence for her to be standing here, exchanging pleasantries with the richest man in Whitlow.

"Perhaps you would like to come back," he was asking her. "There will always be a job for you."

"Thank you," she replied, "but I'll stay where I am. The Hockingses have been good to me and Aleceon."

He nodded. "I understand. Samuel's a good man."

"I was sorry to hear about your father. It must have been a shock," she said quietly, recalling Betsy's words.

"It was," he affirmed. "I was the one who was sick—and he was the one who died." He spoke in a low tone, and although his words could be described as flippant, Sarah knew he was concealing an emotion too painful to be allowed to surface again. "Sometimes I feel as if it were my fault," he mused.

"Don't think like that!" she said quickly, her gray eyes attentive and searching. "It was God's will, after all."

"Yes. Yes, I guess it was. It doesn't lessen the grief, though."

"Nor is it supposed to. It just helps to understand the whys of it. I know how you feel. I experienced the same sort of doubts and guilt when my parents and brother died."

"That's right," he said softly, remembering. "I'd forgotten. You have had loss enough to understand how I feel." He looked at her, and, unexpectedly, his mind's eye suddenly saw the young woman before him gowned and coiffed in the most fashionable manner. The image quite stunned him.

He stared, quite oblivious that he did so, enchanted by the trick of his imagination. She was as beautiful in her quiet way as was Elizabeth in her flamboyancy. It had been more than a year since he had last seen Sarah Edgewood, and in the interim, she had become a woman.

He became aware that she was regarding him curiously, her expression at once bemused and wondering. What a dolt she must think him, he thought, chagrined. He flushed slightly and became even more disconcerted that a mere chit of a girl could so affect him.

"My apologies, Miss Edgewood. I did not mean to stare," he stammered, even more unsettled by the glint of amusement that lit those incredible gray eyes. "Do you ever have a day off?" he said impulsively, hardly daring to think of the consequences of such an innocent statement.

For the moment she regarded him blankly. "We don't do chores on the Sabbath," she replied, wondering at the unusual question.

Delight softened his expression. "No, I don't expect you would; but I mean, you must have some free time."

Her laughter was quick and light, producing a sound so pleasant to his ears that he irrationally wished that it would continue. "Miss Edgewood," he said, in control of himself once more. "This Friday night there will be a reception at my house. My sister, it seems, has invited half of Boston to celebrate her first wedding anniversary. It would be my pleasure if you would allow me to escort you."

Sarah colored deeply, astonished by what she had just heard. One look at his face, though, told her that he had spoken in the utmost seriousness. "I don't know," she said, almost at a loss for words. "I do not even know your sister...."

This was received with a gentle laugh. "Then it is time that you met her," he replied blithely. "You will like Elizabeth."

"But I have nothing to wear...."

"Don't concern yourself with that," he said quickly. "I'll take care of it." He studied her for a moment. "You're about the same size as Elizabeth, and she has two wardrobes filled with dresses."

She began to protest, her excuses sounding lame even to her own ears, but he would have none of it. Before she even knew what had happened, he was gone, promising to come for her the following Friday.

"I'll be in touch before then," he assured her, and with a short bow, headed for the front door.

That evening, it being Saturday, Sarah was far too busy to think of Jonathan's invitation and any consequences it might have for her. But the following afternoon, after church, offered the few hours of leisure that she could call her own, and her thoughts returned time and again to the coming event. She was torn between excitement and incredulity. She had never been to a splendid affair before, and delightful visions teased her imagination. The whole thing had a touch of unreality about it, and her thoughts dissolved into daydreams.

Through Monday and Tuesday, she waited, applying herself dutifully to the tasks at hand. However, she could not help but notice that the hours passed, one after the other, with no further word from Jonathan Enright.

By the time Wednesday evening came, and five days had passed since she had spoken to Jonathan, Sarah reasoned that he had forgotten all about his invitation. Her feelings were ambivalent. Disappointment was mingled with sharp relief. He had, she decided, spoken impulsively, and had no intention of taking her anywhere, certainly not to a grand party. He had merely been amusing himself, at her expense.

Then, the next morning, Thursday, a carriage pulled up at the rear door of the Eagle, looking ludicrously out of place, and a young, dark-haired woman got out. She stood there, apparently surveying her surroundings, while the coachman, reaching into the carriage, brought forth a small valise.

Sarah opened the door before she could knock, and just stood there, staring. The young woman was about nineteen, small-boned and with delicate features. Sarah thought her the most beautiful woman she had ever seen.

"Are you Sarah?" she asked in a low voice, tilting her head.

"Yes, I am." Sarah bobbed her head, resisting the impulse to curtsy.

The laughter was a silver sound. "My name is Elizabeth Enright Lansing. May I come in?"

"Oh, yes, indeed." Sarah stepped aside and held the door open.

Only Ella was present, the men being in the taproom, and she stood there, her hands folded in her apron as if she couldn't believe the vision that graced her kitchen.

The driver, or servant, whatever he was, placed the

valise upon the table and then stepped back to the doorway, where he stood in respectful silence.

Elizabeth had this while been studying Sarah. She had insisted upon coming here herself, determined to view this paragon that had prompted her brother's unusual action. Jonathan was not given to fanciful behavior, especially where women were concerned. Although this was hardly a woman, she mused. The girl could be no more than seventeen. But she was a beauty, all right, Elizabeth thought, with those gray eyes and chestnut-brown hair. There was a look of breeding, of refinement about her face; even her carriage was erect and graceful, without affectation.

"I understand that you will be joining us tomorrow evening," Elizabeth said at last. She could not repress a feeling of delight, thinking how shocked her mother would be, not to mention her friends. As for Justin... her eyes clouded momentarily. He was displeased enough by the mere thought of the reception, and would most likely have forbidden the frivolous display, had he been able. But the simple fact of the matter was that the house in which he lived belonged to Jonathan Enright. Even the very food Justin consumed belonged to his brother-in-law. He had, therefore, reluctantly agreed, and in a cloud of audible disapproval, had secreted himself in the study to work on a sermon, refusing to have any part in the preparations for the coming festivities.

"Mrs. Lansing..." Sarah was gripped by nervous apprehension. This could not be happening, she thought wildly. Not to her!

Again there was the lilting, not unkind, laughter. "Please, call me Elizabeth." She was unfastening the straps of the valise. "I was unsure of your coloring," she remarked conversationally, and if she noticed Sarah's agitation, chose to ignore it. "So I brought along two dresses. You may choose either one you wish." She drew forth a vivid blue satin, and shook it out, holding it up against Sarah.

Sarah just stared. She had never in her whole life seen such a splendid dress. Suddenly, fear joined apprehension. She could never wear anything so grand.

Unable to help herself, she took a step back, afraid of even touching the gown, lest she inadvertently soil it.

Elizabeth would not be put off. She held the shimmering dress before Sarah, tilting her head left and right, then she frowned. "No. I think the pale green would be better." Carelessly, she laid the gown aside and took the other one out. "Ah, yes." For the first time she turned to Ella Hockings. "Do you agree?" she asked pleasantly.

"It's... fine," was all Ella could manage.

"Good. Then it is settled. I'm afraid that it will have to be pressed." She rummaged through the valise again while Sarah watched in bewilderment. "Here are the gloves, and a pair of shoes, although I daresay they may be a bit large for you."

Released from her trancelike state, Sarah protested: "I couldn't! You've done too much already. I..." She gestured, helpless, and at a loss for words. Things were moving too swiftly.

She was ignored. Elizabeth merely motioned to the coachman, who immediately stepped forward and collected the valise and the discarded blue gown.

Then Elizabeth turned, regarding Sarah with a critical eye and tapping her lips with a tapered, well-manicured finger. "I'm afraid," she mused, "that we must do something about your hair. I'll send someone tomorrow who will help you to dress." Walking toward the door, she again smiled. "I look forward to seeing you tomorrow night," she said graciously.

When the door closed, Sarah and Ella exchanged glances that contained both bewilderment and excitement. Then they burst out laughing and for the first time in their association, put their arms about each other in a fierce embrace. Ella felt like crying. Had she had a daughter she could not have been more moved.

Sarah was certain that she would never be able to sleep that night, but surprisingly she drifted off as soon as her head was upon her pillow. The next morning, she was downstairs early. By the time Ella appeared, breakfast was ready.

"I couldn't sleep," she explained, placing a steaming

platter of ham on the table. "I was too excited." Quickly she stepped toward the oven to check on the biscuits.

Ella nodded, understanding. "After the men eat, I'll iron the dress," she offered. "And we'll put hot water on for a bath. A real one. Can't have the Enrights thinking we don't treat you right." She glanced up at the loft, barely suppressing a sound of disgust. "Aleceon! Get yourself down here and bring in the wood!" Her voice was curt and she ignored the pleading look that Sarah cast in her direction. She went to the cupboard, opened a drawer, and drew forth a small bundle. Carefully, she removed the cloth. "It's white soap. The scented kind."

Sarah viewed the pitifully small sliver. "I couldn't take it," she protested, overcome by the generous gesture. "Truly, I couldn't."

"Nonsense! It's been sitting there for years, and I've no use for it." Ella turned away, suddenly embarrassed by the unaccustomed intimacy.

After breakfast, Ella announced in a firm voice that Sarah would be bathing. "And none of you come back here till dinner, hear?"

It took many trips to the well to fill the tub with water, a chore, Ella noted with surprise, that Aleceon did without so much as a grumble. She could not, of course, know about the elation that had filled him since learning of Jonathan Enright's interest in his sister.

Many more minutes were consumed while the kettles rested over the flames, but at last the water was ready, and a bit shyly Sarah removed her clothing and stepped into the tub. She could sit if she drew her knees up, and with the precious piece of soap, she washed herself. Ella carefully pressed the satin gown. She had refused to admit to her growing fondness for Sarah during these past months, but now it burst upon her, flooding her with tenderness.

"It's gonna be a grand party," she mused, smiling at Sarah. "And you'll be the prettiest one there."

Sarah had to laugh. "You've seen what Mrs. Lansing looked like in her everyday clothes!" she remarked. Leaning over, she picked up a towel that had been resting on a chair, and wound it about her wet hair. "I can just imagine what she'll look like in one of her party gowns."

"No matter," said a determined Ella, laying the flatiron aside. "Everyone will have seen her before. No one will have seen you." She held the gown up. "There. My, that's the prettiest dress I've ever seen. They must not come any fancier."

The dishes were hardly cleared away from the midday meal when the carriage again pulled up to the rear door. The driver was the same, but instead of Elizabeth, a plainly dressed woman in her early fifties got out. This time the driver stayed where he was, and the woman, carrying a small bundle, walked up to the porch.

Opening the door, Sarah let her in.

"My name's Polly Ingram, and I've come to do your hair," she announced brusquely. Reaching out, she took hold of a tress and rubbed it between her fingers, paying no mind to Sarah's startled look. Then she gave a nod of satisfaction. "Good. It's fine, and has just a bit of a wave in it." She looked about her. "Well, let's get to it," she said, pointing to a chair. "I must get back to do Mrs. Lansing. This is a big night for her."

Obediently, Sarah sat down on the settle by the hearth. And her hands for once idle, Ella, too, sat, fascinated by the procedure. First the woman took the curling irons and placed them on the hearth close to the fire to heat. Then she neatly arranged brush, comb, and pins within easy reach.

Although Sarah could not see what was happening, she could tell by Ella's expression that quite a change was taking place. Whether it was for the good or bad, she did not know, and she feared to ask lest she offend Polly Ingram.

It took the better part of an hour, but at last the woman stepped back and viewed her handiwork. Then she nodded, apparently pleased with the result. "It will do," she said, gathering her things. "You have nice hair. Don't ever cut it," she advised emphatically.

With that, she was gone, and Sarah just sat there, afraid to move her head for fear that she would undo what had been done.

Questioningly, she looked at Ella, who just shook

her head in bemused wonder. "I never would have believed it if I didn't see it with my own eyes," she declared, truly astonished.

"But how do I look?" said an exasperated Sarah.

Again Ella shook her head. Then, getting up, she went to fetch a looking glass. Returning, she held it before Sarah. "You look like a lady," she said with wonderment in her voice. "And none finer I've ever seen."

Sarah stared at her reflection as if she had never seen herself before. Indeed, the face that stared back, framed by artificially contrived curls, cleverly woven with a dark-green velvet ribbon, was one she was hard pressed to recognize. Gently, she touched a curl, sure that its fragile structure would fall apart.

"Now don't you do anything!" Ella ordered. "I'll see to supper. You just sit there until it's time to dress."

"I'm too excited to eat," Sarah said tremulously.

"'Course you are," Ella agreed, putting the bread in the oven. "No matter. There will be lots to eat at the reception. But mind," she turned now and faced Sarah. "If they offer you wine, you just hold it, and don't drink any!"

Still viewing her reflection, Sarah solemnly nodded.

When the men appeared for their evening meal, they, too, stared at the transformation. Will, with an open, delighted grin; Aleceon, quizzically, as if not believing his eyes; Samuel, with a broad grin that somehow was prideful; and Lucas, with a black, enigmatic smile.

When, a short time later, Christian returned, he viewed her with a scowl that conveyed utter displeasure. "Makes your head look big," he said disparagingly. He had learned of this business only the night before. He disapproved, but could offer no explanation, even to himself, for his feelings. He saw Sarah's dismayed expression at his assessment, but he felt no desire to temper it.

"I think she looks like a princess," Will declared, walking around her chair and studying the intricate coif.

"Where'd you ever see a princess?" Lucas retorted with a snort.

His younger brother glared at him. "In a book Mr. Goodman has in the store. I seen it!"

"It looks nice, Sarah," Samuel said, motioning his younger son to the table. He noticed that there was no plate for her. "You'd best get some food in you," he advised, sitting down.

"No, no," she said with a laugh, trying to mask the doubt that suddenly assailed her at Christian's words. "I couldn't eat, I really couldn't. Besides," she said, getting up, "it's time for me to dress."

"I'll help," Ella offered, following her upstairs. "There's a mighty passel of buttons to do."

Three petticoats went under the dress and, carefully, so as not to damage the hairdo, Ella helped Sarah put them on. The gown itself she stepped into. It had only the barest sleeve and was worn off the shoulder.

Glancing down, Sarah gasped, putting a hand to her partially exposed bosom.

Behind her, Ella was busily attending to the tiny pearl buttons. Then she placed the kid slippers before her. With one hand on Ella's shoulders, Sarah put her feet into them. They were, as Elizabeth had warned, just a trifle too large, and Ella very cleverly balled two pieces of woolen yarn into the toes to take up the slack. Then she laced the ribbons, which wound, sandal fashion, up the ankle. Sarah pulled on the long matching gloves and picked up the lacy fan that Elizabeth had thoughtfully provided.

"You look beautiful, Sarah," Ella said, viewing the finished ensemble. The pale green was most flattering to Sarah's coloring, and the band of dark-green velvet ribbon that ran from each shoulder to the front of the bodice made her waist appear even smaller than it was. "I never saw it before, but you are beautiful. Come down and let everyone take a look at you."

In the common room again, there was a stunned silence as the men looked at her; even Christian could find nothing to say about the awesome sight. He felt uneasy and didn't know why; he knew only that he approved of none of it. Sarah was regarding him gravely as if seeking his approval, and Christian was struck anew by that exquisite face. Almost avidly, his eyes swept along the angles and contours of her features as if with some part of him he knew that he would have to memorize them and so hold her image before him always. But he did not speak.

Sarah, reassured by their expressions, laughed delightedly. "Oh, I wish you all were coming with me."

Ella laughed a little sadly at this. "That would be a fine mess," she noted acidly. "I can just see the expressions if me and Samuel were to enter the Enrights' house."

Sarah was about to comment when there was a knock at the door. Nervousness returned, and she realized uneasily that, until this moment, she had been playing a game, delighting in dressing up; now the game had ceased.

It was Christian who opened the door, and he stood there, scowling at Jonathan Enright.

"Ask Mr. Enright to come in!" Samuel said sharply, annoyed by this unusual display of rudeness on the part of his normally courteous son.

"Good evening," Jonathan said with a nod of his head, and when he saw Sarah, he broke into a wide smile. "You look grand, Sarah!"

"Thanks to your gracious sister," she murmured softly. She could see that he was genuinely pleased with her appearance, but it only slightly calmed her tension. It took all her effort to resist the urge to run from the room... from this incredible situation she found herself in.

"We'd best go," Jonathan now said. "We don't want to be late." He held the door open for her, and Sarah realized that the time for running was past.

"You'll bring her home at a decent hour?" Christian demanded, still scowling.

Surprised, Jonathan looked at him as if noticing him for the first time. Controlling his annoyance, he replied: "I assure you, Mr. Hockings, Sarah will be in the best of care."

And then Sarah and Jonathan left.

Chapter 11

Sarah felt as if she would be ill. What was she doing here? she wondered frantically, only half listening to Jonathan's gay chatter as he sat beside her in the coach. She didn't belong here, in this fine carriage, in this fine gown, with this fancy hairdo. She would make a fool of herself.

By the time they reached the Enright house on the outskirts of town, she was trembling so badly she was afraid to stand up lest her legs collapse beneath the weight of her fear. And the sight of all the grand carriages lining the drive, with their fancy equipage and liveried coachmen, did little to relieve her feeling of inadequacy.

It was a fine, mellow evening, with only an occasional gentle breeze to disturb the serenity, but Sarah felt chilled as they entered.

Wealth and all it could buy were evident in the Enright house; but more, there was a sense of importance, of authority, that was almost casually displayed. In spite of herself, Sarah felt a twinge of excitement as she looked about her.

"Come along," Jonathan was saying as they walked through the large entry hall. "I promised my mother that I would present you in private before we join the others." He led her into the library. The lilting sounds of music, so easily discernible in the hallway, were less distinct here.

The rich oak floor was covered by the subdued elegance of a gray and rose-colored rug, which was in perfect harmony with the dark paneled walls. The chairs were of rosewood and covered in a pale yellow brocade, the texture of which Sarah could not help but marvel at.

As Jonathan presented her, Sarah was relieved to

see that Elizabeth was in the room. And the smile she flashed was friendly, welcoming.

Sarah noted that the older woman still bore traces of the beauty that she had passed on to her daughter, but it had been corrupted by time, or perhaps by life itself. There were no traces of the warmth that Elizabeth's beauty radiated; the fineness, the delicacy of the features were buried under what Sarah guessed was a permanently discontented expression.

Rachel was smiling graciously, but her eyes were speculative as she regarded Sarah.

"We are pleased that you could join us, Miss Edgewood," she said coolly, nodding her head slightly. Seating herself in a comfortable chair, Rachel indicated that Sarah should sit on the settee beside Elizabeth. Imperceptibly, she raised a hand, and a liveried servant stepped forward, deftly filling the waiting wineglasses.

"Do you drink wine, Miss Edgewood?" inquired Rachel.

"No," replied Sarah with some regret, mindful of the advice she had so recently received.

Rachel smiled thinly. "Then perhaps some champagne?" she suggested, again motioning to the servant.

Was champagne the same as wine? Sarah wondered. But she had not the courage to refuse again and made no protest when her glass was filled with the sparkling concoction.

"You look lovely, Sarah," Elizabeth was saying. Sensing the girl's discomfort, she continued to speak lightly, casually discussing the weather and the latest fashions with equal aplomb.

But Rachel did not appear at all charmed by the innocent, unsophisticated manner of the girl her son had so inexplicably brought home. She flashed Jonathan an annoyed look, but he was laughing at some foolish witticism of Elizabeth's and did not notice.

At last he stood up and, extending his hand toward Sarah, said: "Enough. Now I would like all our guests to meet you."

In the arched doorway of the ballroom, Sarah paused to take in the gracefully twirling dancers. If outward appearances were any indication, the evening promised to be a glittering success.

It had been some time since she had last danced; it seemed a lifetime ago. Many dances and festivities were held at the close of harvest, but surely never in a setting as elegant as this. Conscious of Jonathan's hand upon her elbow, Sarah allowed him to lead her into the swirl of movement.

It was easier than she thought it would be, and after a faltering start, she easily followed his lead.

Standing in the entryway, Rachel Enright watched them with a brooding gaze. Something in the look upon her son's face caused a tightening in her chest. He was gazing down at the girl with something like... like admiration. Yes, that was it. Admiration. But what could he possibly find to admire in such a piece of baggage? she wondered, irritated.

Then she started, surprised by the woman who approached her. She turned to see Abegail Tremont, who, with her husband, Fenster, a prominent Boston solicitor, had made the trip down from the city just for the evening's festivities.

Abegail's brown eyes glinted in malicious amusement. "Who is the charming grirl Jonathan is so engrossed in?" she asked. At the sight of Rachel's reddening face, her laughter trilled. "Oh, my dear, don't be so upset. Really, it is the most amusing thing that has happened in ages. The whole room is abuzz." Her voice lowered. "Tell me, is it true?"

"Is what true?" Rachel managed to ask.

"Why, that Jonathan is planning to marry a servant, a pauper!"

"I cannot imagine where you heard such a thing," Rachel said, more than a bit annoyed.

"I must say," Abegail went on, enjoying herself, "the girl certainly does not dress like a servant. Why, she is outfitted as well as Elizabeth!" She was still laughing softly when, as the present dance ended, Fenster Tremont approached Jonathan and Sarah. After a few cordial words, Abegail was horrified to see her husband dance off with the girl. For a moment she was speechless, her fan working in time to her agitation. Then with a look that could only be termed a glare, she moved away from Rachel, her mind already forming the words of censure she would pour upon the head of her unsuspecting husband.

Jonathan went to Rachel's side. "It's a grand party, Mother," he said, smiling broadly.

She viewed him with grim eyes. "I would hardly have used that term," she noted sourly, and at the lift of his brow, related the gossip that was currently circulating among her guests.

He laughed, but to her attentive ear it seemed forced, spurious. "Ridiculous," he said at last, his eyes moving away from hers. "I merely like her, that's all. I admire Sarah; she is an unusual girl."

Admire! Rachel thought, dismayed. The word she herself had chosen. Under what circumstances did a man admire a woman? She knew of very few. "Listen to me, Jonathan," she said, drawing him aside. "I do not mind if you amuse yourself with this girl, but remember, the circles in which we move are not hers. They are worlds apart."

"Not all that far apart, Mother," he remarked, his face concealing his annoyance. "If we lived in England, quite possibly that view would be valid. But here in America, a man is not held to the station in which he was born. Nor a woman," he added in such low tones that Rachel had to bend forward to hear him.

"Nonsense!" she exclaimed, irritated and not a little alarmed by her son's words. "Oh, I agree that a man, a man of intellect, of ambition, can go far in this country. But he must be exceptional, and even that does not qualify him for entrance into Society." She sniffed. "As for a woman, the only way she can rise above her station is to..." She broke off, appalled by what she had been about to say. "We will discuss this at another time, Jonathan," she said tersely and quickly moved away to rejoin her guests.

The evening was almost at an end when Elizabeth drew Sarah aside.

"I do hope that you have enjoyed yourself as much as we have enjoyed having you," she remarked, smiling sweetly. "And I also hope that this will be the first of many visits." She spoke sincerely, for she had taken a liking to Sarah.

"I've never had such a wonderful time," Sarah said simply and truthfully. She hesitated, then said: "But as for again visiting, I don't think..." She colored, visibly embarrassed. "I mean—surely you must be aware that I am without means."

"What rubbish!" Elizabeth stated irreverently. She quickly sobered at the sight of Sarah's expression. "Was it dreadful?" she asked in quiet tones. "That vendu business, I mean."

"Yes," she replied slowly, sensing that Jonathan's sister spoke with sincere interest and not with any malicious intent. "It was dreadful. Perhaps the worst thing of all was the uncertainty, the fact that, in a sense, someone else held your life in his hands."

"Forgive me," Elizabeth said softly. "I should never have mentioned it." She brightened. "But it all turned out for the best, didn't it? You might not be here now if it weren't for those circumstances. I must admit," she went on after a moment, "that I could not have acted as bravely as you did. On your own, you could have stayed on at the mill."

"I had no choice," Sarah said. "Aleceon would have had to be sent away. That was something I could not have let happen, regardless of the consequences. I really did not act bravely at all."

Elizabeth arched her brows at this assessment. "That is an opinion I do not share. You see, I know what you did for Jon. He told me. Of course, the first time he mentioned you, I had no idea of what he was talking about, much less who." She peered intently at Sarah. "Did you know that he tried for months to find you? Imagine his surprise when he discovered that you were still in Whitlow."

Sarah smiled at Jonathan's sister, thinking that his surprise certainly couldn't have matched her own, in light of the past week's events.

Rachel joined them at that moment, and despite her stiffly cordial manner, Sarah was certain that Jonathan's mother would be glad to see her go.

In the carriage again, Sarah had a buoyant feeling,

although whether it was from the excitement of the evening, or the champagne, she couldn't tell.

In some surprise she saw that Jonathan was leading the horse, not back to the Golden Eagle Inn, but over a little-used road that led to a rise overlooking the town.

At last he halted the animal and, extending his hand, helped her out of the carriage.

Below, the town sparkled and glittered like a handful of carelessly strewn jewels upon a carpet of black velvet. The whole evening had glittered, Sarah thought happily.

Watching her delicate profile, Jonathan smiled, lost in the splendor of the vision presented by the young girl at his side. The first tentative stirrings of desire nudged him, and he moved closer, putting an arm about her shoulders.

Startled, she looked up at him, eyes wide and questioning.

"Did you have a good time?" he asked softly, toying with a wayward curl. Her hair was soft and silky beneath his touch. The stirrings grew stronger, and he could feel his breath quicken.

"It was marvelous," she said, wondering at the breathless tone in her voice. His nearness disturbed her, but she couldn't bring herself to move away from him. His fingertips traced her cheek and neck, leaving a path of warmth in their wake, and Sarah was grateful for the darkness, for she could feel her skin flush hotly. His eyes gazed into hers with an intensity that mesmerized her, and she found that she could not look away.

"You are so beautiful," he murmured, almost to himself. "Tonight I was the envy of every man."

Her flush deepened until her ears tingled with the force of it. She had never thought herself beautiful, and wondered if he was being kind.

Something in those gray, solemn eyes gave Jonathan pause. His own hesitancy irked him. By now, this far into the evening, he would have had his way with any other girl. And expected her to be grateful for his attentions. Then why the hesitation? What was it about this girl that made him act this way? From the time he had seen her at the Emporium, he'd been doing foolish things. And here he was, about to do another.

Taking her hand, he led her back to the carriage.

"I meant what I said," he said softly, as they headed back to town. He glanced at her. "You really are beautiful."

"Thank you," she whispered, still unsettled. Her thoughts were in a whirl, and she was at a loss to explain how she felt. "I suspect it's the gown your sister was kind enough to give me."

His laughter rang out through the moon-dappled night, leaving Sarah even more confused by this strange young man, whose presence she found exciting and mysterious.

Over the ensuing weeks, despite his mother's objections, Jonathan squired Sarah, often taking her on the five-mile drive into Boston. Although neither Ella nor Samuel took exception to Sarah's absence of a Friday evening or Saturday afternoon—indeed, Ella seemed to view the situation with a certain amount of pride—Sarah always took care to rise an hour or two earlier in order to assure that her chores would be finished before she left.

Jonathan showed her the sights of Boston, taking her to the theater and restaurants of that flourishing city. They attended lyceums and concerts, and Sarah was introduced to a whole new world, one that she had until now only dreamed about. Clothes had, at first, been a dreadful problem, and Sarah had refused to let Jonathan purchase anything for her. Once again, Elizabeth solved that problem; after she and Justin had been married, she had ordered a whole new wardrobe, "one fitting for her new role as wife of a minister," she had laughingly explained, insisting that Sarah take a goodly portion of the castoff dresses that had hung unused in her wardrobe this past year. A bit of needlework, and they were as good as new.

If Rachel viewed it all with cold despair, two other people observed this courtship with a more interested eye than did the two principals. One was Christian, who grew more and more dismayed, and was at a loss to explain his feelings, even to himself. The other was Aleceon, who grew more and more ecstatic as it appeared that Jonathan Enright's attention showed no signs of dissipating. At last, he thought in glee, his sister was about to keep her promise. She would take care of them both.

One day in late June, some three weeks after the party, Sarah, her chores completed, was waiting for Jonathan, who was coming to fetch her. They were going into Boston for a concert, and she was looking forward to it. Dressed for the evening, she entered the common room to find Christian staring at her in an oddly intent manner.

"You are seeing rather a lot of Mr. Enright," he blurted out, helpless to control the unwarranted anger that shot through him at the sight of her.

Sarah glanced quickly at him, her face awash with surprise at the tone of his voice, so used was she by now to his gentle manner. He was staring intently, as if his answer would be found in her compelling gray eyes rather than from her rosy lips.

She murmured something in affirmation, but her words flew past him without cognizance, for in that moment, he knew what was causing his own emotional upheaval. He was jealous! The thought quite astounded him, and for the moment, he was ashamed. What right did he have to be jealous of Enright's attention to Sarah? She was free. He had no claim on her.

Walking to the hearth, he began to stoke the fire, his movements tense and abrupt. A shower of sparks flew up in protest, glowing redly in indignation before subsiding again. "I don't see why you have to see him every week," he muttered, watching the blaze he had created. "I should think you've more important things to do; things around here," he waved a hand at the spotlessly clean kitchen.

Sarah blinked, confused by this churlish display of ill temper. "Your mother has no objections," she noted in a small voice. "You know I wouldn't leave if it would cause her any hardship." Why was he acting this way? she wondered, upset. Surely he must know that she took care to see that everything was done before she went out.

An indecipherable growl greeted those words. Putting his hands in his pockets, Christian paced about the room, casting annoyed looks in her direction. "I'll bet you think he's in love with you," he said sarcastically, after a while. "Can't you see that he's only amusing himself?"

She bit her lip, feeling close to tears. "I never thought that," she protested, wondering at the unfairness of his accusation. "Mr. Enright is only being kind, I realize that. But I may never again get the chance to—"

"Get the chance for what?" he interrupted, stopping before her. "The chance to marry the richest man in town?" He fell silent at the sight of her pale face, her tear-glazed eyes. He was appalled by his behavior, thoroughly ashamed of himself. His face flushing, he turned away from her. God, what was the matter with him? He had no right to speak to Sarah this way. Chances were, that Jonathan Enright *was* in love with her. After all, a man could easily fall in love with Sarah.... His breath caught in his throat.

Sarah had begun to speak again, but he did not hear her. Within him, anger fled as if it had never existed. The realization was one that he didn't want to face, but could not deny.

"Christian? Christian! You've not heard a word I've said," Sarah complained.

"Please forgive me, Sarah," he said brusquely. "It was rude of me to interfere. I have no business questioning your comings and goings. They're none of my affair."

But they could be! her mind cried out to him. Yet his face was so cold and bleak she dared not speak the presumptuous words.

Once more he looked at her, torn by anguish at the vision of her youthful loveliness and dignity; then, with great effort, he turned and walked from the room.

He needed time to think. He knew with a quiet but deep certainty that he had to have this girl, or be damned to a life without fulfillment of his love.

Chapter 12

Jena Witcomb stood before the wood-burning stove in the kitchen of the seven-room house in which she and her father had lived alone since her mother had died some years before. She stared, unseeing, at the ragout bubbling in the iron pot. Absently, she stirred it once with a wooden spoon and continued with her thoughts, thoughts that had of late become an obsession.

All of her thoughts revolved around Christian, as they had since the first day she met him. She had been nine and he had been ten at the time, and many years were to pass before he returned her obvious interest. She had been certain that when he came to work in her father's shop the proximity would bring them closer; and it had, for a while.

Lately, however, Christian seemed unaware of her. Her mouth tightened now and her eyes narrowed. She knew exactly why Christian's attentions were wandering.

She walked over to the table and began to cut slices of cold beef from a roast. These she arranged on thick slabs of bread. The shop was only a few hundred feet from the house, and each day at this time she brought dinner to her father and Christian.

Oh, yes, she knew, she thought. Carefully wrapping the sandwiches in linen cloths, she laid them in the waiting basket. She knew exactly where Christian's attentions were: on that stupid little pauper. A servant in his own house!

She had watched him these past two weeks at Sunday meeting. Normally the girl sat next to Mrs. Hockings, and this past Sunday had been no exception. What *had* been different was the fact that Christian had managed to position himself beside her.

Even during the interlude between the two services,

when they had all availed themselves of the lemonade and cake provided by the wife of Reverend Carpenter, Christian had spoken only a few perfunctory words to her. Jena's face flamed as she thought of that mortification.

But she would not give him up without a fight, she decided grimly, adding bannock cakes to the basket. She would not give him up at all! Bad enough that the wretched little pauper had managed, in some unbelievable way, to capture the attention of Jonathan Enright. She wasn't content with that. No, she wanted Christian as well.

Jena covered the top of the basket with a clean towel and set out for the shop, her mind working as quickly as her short, rapid steps upon the cobbled street.

It was the third of July and the day was bright and shimmery with heat. Glancing up the street, she could see a group of women and young boys busy with decorations for the celebrations that would be held tomorrow. Bertha Beasley was in charge of the committee this year, and was determined that the festivities would be the best ever. From the sale of cakes and bakery goods over the past six months, enough money had been raised to hire a band from Boston, a feather in Bertha's cap: No one had ever been able to accomplish that before. Lanterns were already strung up about the Common. The gala Independence Day events were scheduled to begin promptly at eight o'clock in the morning and would continue past dusk.

Jena paused, watching the activity for a moment, her mouth pursed in contemplation; then, rearranging her face into its usual beguiling expression, she entered the smithy.

Christian was hammering out a piece of metal that glowed white under the pounding; so intent was he that he did not immediately notice her. For a time she watched the play of muscle in his arms and shoulders with avid interest. At last, becoming aware of her intent gaze, he looked up.

"Ah, food," he said, grinning. Picking up the metal with a pair of tongs, he plunged it into a nearby tub of water. There was a sudden swish of steam, rising in a small cloud of grayish white.

Jena watched in satisfaction as Christian and her father began to eat.

"Aren't you gonna join us, honey?" Amos Witcomb asked, biting appreciatively into the sandwich. His tanned, lined face regarded her questioningly.

"No, Pa," she replied, still watching Christian. "I've already eaten." She turned as if to go, then again faced her father as if she'd just had a thought. "Pa, I think it would be a good idea if you were to invite Christian to stay over tonight. There's no need for him to go all the way home and come back tomorrow."

Christian grinned at her. "I do that every day, Jena," he pointed out. Finishing the last of the sandwich, he reached for another. He was uncomfortable in her presence, knowing that sooner or later he would have to tell her that his feelings had changed. It was a prospect he was not looking forward to.

"But the festivities will begin early," she said, pouting. "And you did promise that you would take me."

Dismayed, he looked up at her. He had promised, but that was before he had fallen in love with Sarah!

Amos chuckled and clapped him on the back. "She's right, Christian. You can bed down in the shop; there's plenty of room. Can't understand why you don't stay over, anyways. All that traipsing back and forth."

Christian opened his mouth to speak and closed it again. He had no intention of telling them why he felt it necessary to return to the Eagle each night, even though it would be more convenient to move into the back room. But the combined insistence of Jena and Amos, whom he greatly respected, prevailed, and he reluctantly agreed. As long as his father was home, Lucas wouldn't do anything foolish, and it was, after all, for only one night.

That night as he lay on the pile of blankets hastily arranged in a corner, Christian thought of Sarah. Hands clasped behind his head, he stared up into the dimness and smiled. The fact that Jena wanted him to accompany her tomorrow night might turn out to his benefit.

He could tell her then that it was all over between them and that he planned to ask Sarah to marry him.

Just the thought of Sarah caused his heart to beat faster. She was so beautiful, he thought dreamily. And one day when he was successful—and rich—he planned to give her everything that money could buy. He did not, and would not, dwell upon Jonathan Enright, nor any feeling that Sarah might have for that man.

He drifted into a half doze, and was almost asleep when he felt soft arms go about him. In that almost drugged state, he quickly responded to the warm, moist mouth that covered his, and involuntarily his arms clasped the naked female body close to him. He was wearing only breeches and made little protest when he felt the buttons being undone.

He moaned once as a soft hand began to stroke him, easily producing a throbbing arousal. Drawing his breath in sharply, wide awake now, he sat up so quickly that he almost unbalanced Jena.

"What the devil!" He glared at her in the dim light, but instead of moving away, she pressed her body closer. Against his bare chest he could feel her nipples grow taut and turgid as her hands busily worked about him.

She murmured his name, her voice all but unrecognizable. "Don't send me away, Christian. I want you to make love to me. Please."

Trying to control his own breath, he grasped her wrists in a rough gesture. "Damnit, Jena, stop it! What's come over you?" He was quite shocked by her actions. She ignored him. In a sudden motion, she pressed her weight against him, causing him to fall backward, still holding her wrists. She straddled him quickly, lowering herself upon his rigidness.

Involuntarily, his hands went about her plump buttocks. For only a moment he wanted to push her away, but the rapid movement of her body caused his muscles to tighten and instead he grasped her closer, thrusting upward to meet her. He squeezed her flesh tightly, knowing that he was hurting her and not caring. Still clutching her in a tight grip, he raised himself up and flung her down on her back, their bodies locked.

In only moments her body went rigid, arching beneath his and seconds later, his own body went taut.

Afterward, still resting within her, he raised himself up on an elbow and stared down at her face, dimly outlined in the dull red of the glowing embers in the forge. Her eyes were closed and her mouth flaccid as if ecstasy had robbed her muscles of usefulness.

In disgust, he withdrew himself, sitting up again. Christ, he thought, running his hand through his red-gold hair. To think there was a time he'd thought himself in love with her! My God, he reflected, suddenly relieved, I might even have married her!

He glanced down at her. She seemed to be asleep. Her legs were still sprawled out at an awkward angle and he could see the thin trickle of blood that stained her thighs and the blanket beneath her. Guiltily, he looked away. She had been a virgin. Somehow in the frenzy of their coupling he'd not noticed.

Leaning over, he shook her arm roughly. "Jena! Jena! Get up. Get dressed."

She opened her eyes, regarding him almost dreamily. "You are mine, Christian," she whispered, stroking his back.

He recoiled from her touch and stood up, hastily buttoning his breeches. "Get up!" he hissed angrily. "Get up before your father discovers you're gone." At the thought of Amos he felt worse than ever, and he fought the sudden impulse to reach out and strike Jena for putting him in this situation.

Stretching her body languidly, she rolled over. "He's sound asleep," she observed carelessly. "Once he's asleep, he never wakes up till morning." She stared at him intently. "I love you, Christian," she said softly. "There's nothing I wouldn't do for you."

The admission meant nothing to him because Jena meant nothing to him. "Then go back to the house," he stated quietly, barely able to contain his disgust. "That is what I want you to do."

She got up and dressed, confident that with her actions she had forever removed Sarah Edgewood from Christian's heart.

But the next day she watched in agony as he squired

Sarah about town, parading her before everyone, virtually announcing his intentions. Then her agony turned to anger.

"What's the matter, honey?" Amos inquired solicitously. "Did you and Christian have a fight?" At the sight of her stricken face, he patted her shoulder. "It'll be all right. Don't you worry none." He glanced toward the strolling Sarah and Christian. "A man likes to sow his wild oats," he murmured awkwardly. "He'll come back to you, you'll see."

He will come back to me, all right, Jena vowed silently, not replying to her father. I'll see to that.

"You look very pretty, Sarah," Christian was saying as they walked. She was wearing a dress of yellow lawn, the full skirt of which artfully incorporated ribbons of a deeper shade of the sunny color. He wondered, as he looked at her, whether she had agreed to join him today because Enright was in Boston, or because she actually wanted to be with him.

"You have been looking at me for almost two years, Christian," she murmured, glancing demurely at him from under a wide-brimmed, ribbon-bedecked hat. "I haven't changed any." Despite her protestation, she could not help the flush that swept across her face; even her ears tingled with the force of it.

"Oh, but you have," he said quickly. "And for the better, I might add."

She made no reply to this, and for a time they walked in silence. It seemed that most of the town's five thousand-odd inhabitants—which included those employees from the mills, the tannery, and the outlying farms—had turned out for the celebration of the Fourth. People and children thronged the broad streets, the picnic grounds, and along the banks of the river. The day was fine, clear and sunny and calm, and the air smelled of flowers and pastries and homemade candies.

"How are things going at the shop?" Sarah asked at last, in an effort to fill the silence that had fallen between them. She was still gripped by the happy emotion that had flooded her that morning when Christian had unexpectedly invited her to join him today.

"Fine," he responded quickly. "Mr. Witcomb's letting me do more and more. Raised my wage, too!"

"That's wonderful," she said, truly pleased.

He hesitated, and another small silence descended. Thoughts of the previous night's events kept intruding upon him, but he remembered them with no pleasure. Instead, a great feeling of shame enveloped him and he fervently hoped that his face did not reveal it. After a while, in a voice so low that Sarah could barely hear him, he said: "Do you think you could care for me, Sarah?"

Surprised, she glanced up at him, wondering as to the meaning of his words. In the past week or so, Christian had been acting oddly; angry and distant by turns, and then suddenly attentive. "Of course I care for you, Christian," she said slowly. "You are like...family to me." She averted her face, afraid that he would see her true thoughts, see the love that she felt for him.

He frowned at this. "We're not family," he said curtly. "And somehow I think you know what I mean."

Again she flushed. "Yes...I care for you," she said slowly, cautiously, afraid to allow herself to hope, to think that after all this time, Christian would turn from Jena to her.

"Have you ever thought about your future?" he asked abruptly, as if discussing business.

"My future?" The words were repeated wonderingly as if she had never before spoken them and was uncertain as to their meaning. "Why, I suspect the future will come a little at a time, day by day, just as it always does."

"But surely you plan on, well, marrying someday?"

"I guess all girls think of that, Christian," she replied. And then she was conscious of a stab of resentment. She stole a glance at him, wondering if she was interpreting his words correctly. "Why are you speaking to me like this?" she demanded, suddenly upset. "What about Jena?"

He motioned irritably. "A man has to, well, look around, before he decides upon someone he wants to spend his whole life with." He took a breath. "There was a time when I thought that it was Jena, but..."

She halted and faced him squarely. "Does she know how you feel now?"

He shook his head. "There was never a right time...." he began lamely.

"Well, I think you had better find a right time. You should see to that before you speak to me, Christian Hockings!" Her demure, fine-featured face was stern and his heart swelled at the sight of it.

She was right, of course, he thought, ashamed. "I will speak to her," he promised, his voice husky, and again there was quiet between them. "I won't always be an apprentice, you know," he then said. "I mean to go far, to make something of myself. Pa is always saying that here in America anything's possible. And I believe it! Of course, he wants to stay with the inn, but that's not the way."

"And what is?" she asked, amused now by his simple conviction.

"I'm not sure yet. But this land's growing. Day by day, almost hour by hour. I was talking to John Choate one night, and he says that we import most things from England and France. Just think of what it would be like to make it here! Not to be dependent on other countries. The mills are coming up all over, Sarah," he said enthusiastically. "Gristmills, carding mills. One of them even turns out nails for a couple of pennies a pound! That's eating into Witcomb's business. John predicted that. He says we will be astounded at what will take place over the next ten years."

"You speak highly of Mr. Choate," Sarah noted.

"He's a friend. John is a man whose word can always be counted upon."

She nodded solemnly at this. "If you cannot count on a person's word, then you cannot count on the person at all."

"You can always count on my word, Sarah," he said quietly, and was delighted by the glow that lit those usually solemn gray eyes.

"I never thought otherwise, Christian."

They had reached a grassy knoll on the outskirts of the picnic grounds, and quite naturally they sat down in the sweet-smelling grass. They could hear the pleasant hum of happy conversation and the occasionally shrill laughter of the children as they romped and played and, very faintly, the sound of the band as it played in the Common. Above them, great leafy boughs shaded the hot sun, allowing only dappled bits of fluttering gold to penetrate.

All this went unnoticed by the two young people, who were preoccupied only with each other.

"What about Jonathan Enright?" Christian suddenly asked her. "Do you care for him, too?"

She looked away, watching a large bumblebee as it lazily circled about a flower. "Jonathan is just a friend." She looked at him now, seeing how the patches of sunlight accented the gold in his hair. "That's all he is, Christian. That's all he ever was."

He took hold of her hand. It seemed very small and very white as it lay within his. "Sarah..." A choked cry escaped from him as he reached for her. His kiss was tender at first, then more insistent as her nearness overwhelmed him. If he had any doubts, they fled his mind in this instant, never to return.

It was her first kiss, and Sarah was astonished at the depth of emotion it created within her. Unthinkingly, her arms went about his neck and she clung to him. All her pent-up hopes and feelings for this man culminated in a shock of desire that only momentarily shamed her, then she relaxed, giving in to the exquisite flush of joy that flooded her body.

When he at last drew away, they gazed at each other in utter wonder, as if their discovery of love was unique in mankind's history.

Again Christian sought those soft lips. Moving gently, he pressed Sarah back until she lay on the grass. Her body was pliant against his, and he could feel the quickening beat of her heart beneath his own. In the deepest part of himself, Christian knew that this was how it should be. All else was a farce, a sham. He had thought he knew what love was about. Now he knew that glory was yet to come.

Without volition, his caresses became more insistent as a wave of desire crested over him, producing an aching need that he could no longer control. Her breasts were soft and firm beneath his touch and he moved his hand to undo the buttons on her bodice.

He sensed, rather than saw, her sudden resistance, for he was attuned to every nuance of her movements. He paused, then his arms went about her, and he just lay there holding her, his cheek against the sweet softness of her hair.

For a long time they lay thus, oblivious of their surroundings, conscious only of each other and their nearness.

Finally, Christian drew away and, sitting up, regarded Sarah with a serious expression. Jena. The thought came unbidden, unwanted. He didn't even want to think of last night.

"Sarah," he said at last, running a hand through his hair. "Just give me a few days to get things straightened away. Then..."

She sat up, putting a fingertip to his lips, silencing him. "We will speak of it then," she said, with a soft smile.

He grasped her hand, holding it tightly. "No. We will speak of it now. I love you, Sarah. I will never love anyone else but you. I want to marry you, to be with you, always." He searched her lovely face for the answer that would give meaning to his own life.

Sarah struggled with happy tears, knowing that no moment of her life would ever produce the joy of this one. "I've loved you for such a long time," she murmured. "I would be honored to be your wife."

A great sigh escaped his lips, as if he had been holding his breath. He kissed the hand he still held, then released it.

Leaning back, he stretched his long body out comfortably on the grass. Staring at the clear blue sky above him, his mind busily worked with plans for the future; his and Sarah's future.

That very night, however, something happened that was to delay those plans.

Amos Witcomb, having imbibed too heavily of the refreshments offered on this Fourth of July, drunkenly stepped in front of a horse-drawn carriage and, seriously injured, was carried to his home.

Chapter 13

It was mid-August, and the weather had turned unusually hot and humid, the heat pressing down with a force that made the very air seem heavy. People and horses alike moved sluggishly through the muggy atmosphere, which seemed invaded by a saturating dampness that caused clothing to cling and skin to itch.

Sarah had seen little of Christian in these past weeks, which, she thought morosely, was to be expected. Poor Mr. Witcomb had suffered a broken back, and what the doctor vaguely termed injury to his internal parts.

The brunt of the work, therefore, fell upon Christian, who all but lived at the shop, trying desperately to keep up with orders all by himself. He stayed there each night, opening up at first light, and continuing until after dark. There had been no chance for them to talk, and more than once, Sarah wondered whether he had spoken to Jena.

She thought it unlikely under the circumstances. While she was sorry for what had happened to Mr. Witcomb, Sarah couldn't repress her happiness. She loved Christian with an almost unbearable devotion, and longed for the day when they would be together always. The memory of his kiss still burned on her lips, and she thought often of that day when they had discovered their love. She knew that the memory of those sweet hours would never leave her.

And so, during these weeks, she waited patiently, daydreaming at times of the day when she and Christian would be married.

On a hot Saturday afternoon, with only the incessant buzzing of insects to break the stillness, Jonathan returned from Boston, where he had spent the past weeks on business.

"If you can get away, I'd like you to come for a drive

with me," he said, appearing at the back door soon after the midday meal.

"Go on, Sarah," Ella encouraged her before she could speak. "I'll see to things here." She smiled and nodded affably at Jonathan, and after only a small hesitation, Sarah removed her apron. If Christian was to speak to Jena, it was only right that she tell Jonathan that she could no longer receive him. With that in mind, Sarah followed Jonathan outside and, with his assistance, stepped into the waiting carriage.

For a while they rode in silence as Jonathan, the reins held loosely in his hands, guided the horse on the path that led to the river.

Even after he had halted the carriage and they began to walk along the bank, Jonathan remained silent. Sarah pondered on the cause of this behavior, but could find no explanation that might account for it.

At last she gave it up, her mind groping for words to tell Jonathan what had happened between her and Christian. But each time she was about to speak, one look at Jonathan's brooding countenance effectively silenced her.

Shyly, she glanced up at his partially averted face, thinking again what a grand-looking man he was. And then she sighed, because she was truly, deeply, fond of him. But she loved Christian, and that would never change.

Abruptly, he halted by an old oak tree, so large that its branches drooped over the water's edge. The river here was slow-moving and deep, its surface shimmering with slashes of gold and white.

"Is anything wrong?" she finally asked him.

He hesitated a moment before replying. "Not unless my being in love with you is wrong," he said softly, taking hold of her hand.

Speechless, Sarah just stared at him. At the sight of her surprised look, he said, chidingly, as though she were a child: "How could you not have known of my feelings? I haven't been able to get you out of my mind." He released her and, plunging his hands into his pockets, stared moodily at the sluggish water. "I've stayed away these past weeks deliberately," he said quietly, then again looked at her.

After a moment, he moved closer. Placing his hands on her shoulders, he bent down and gently kissed her on the lips.

It was the first time that he had done that, and she was too startled to move away.

The kiss was pleasant enough, but Sarah could not help but notice the difference in her response when Christian had kissed her. Now there was no feeling of that almost unbearable pleasure that had invaded every corner of her body, producing sensations that she had never known existed. No feeling of joy, of warmth, of longing, gripped her, and she stood quiet and passive beneath the embrace.

His lips were now upon the softness of her neck as he murmured her name over and over, still holding her tightly against him. She felt the warmth of his hand leave her back and fumble with her bodice. With the intimate contact, her body stiffened and she placed her palms against his chest in an effort to push him away.

For a moment he didn't respond, his touch becoming more insistent, demanding, until she uttered a small cry of alarm.

At the sound, he immediately released her, his breath a long, wavering sigh as he fought for control.

A moment passed, then he placed the palms of his hands on either side of her face as he gazed intently into her eyes.

"Please forgive me, Sarah," he whispered huskily. "It's just that I want you so badly."

She opened her mouth to speak, but he put his fingertips to her lips.

"No. Don't say anything," he said quickly. "Just listen. These past weeks have convinced me. I want you to be with me, to come away with me." Again he took hold of her hand, his dark, brooding appearance enhanced by the attentive look in his eyes. "I'm asking you to marry me, Sarah. I want you to be my wife."

"Jonathan..." The feeling of dismay was so strong that she trembled with the force of it. *Now*, her mind told her. Now was the time to tell him. Her feelings for this man were profound, but it was not, and never could be, love.

"No," he stopped her. "Don't give me an answer just yet. Think on it."

"You don't understand," she tried to explain, feeling close to tears. She had never, never expected this. Jonathan, she had thought, was being kind to her, found her amusing, enjoyed her wide-eyed delight at all the wondrous sights he had shown her. Never by word nor by deed had he ever indicated that there was more.

"Don't give me your answer now," he repeated, leading her back toward the carriage. "It's too important a decision for you to make hastily. Too important to my future, and to yours."

Future, Sarah thought distractedly, settling herself beside him. There was that word again. But her future was with Christian, for that was to whom her heart belonged.

"I must go to New York," he now said. "I'll be away four or five weeks. I would like you to think about what I have said while I am gone. When I return," he glanced over at her, still unsmiling, "you can give me your answer."

They spoke no more and his parting words were stiff and formal as he took his leave, his kiss on her cheek dry and chaste.

That afternoon, Christian came home long enough to collect clean clothes, leaving his soiled ones for his mother to launder. There had been no time for him and Sarah to speak alone, but Christian had taken her hand and pressed it tightly to his lips before departing for the smithy. And Aleceon, seeing the gesture, scowled, his eyes narrowing with condemnation.

He bided his time and, later, in the dusky hot twilight, as Sarah sat alone on the back porch, he approached her. She glanced at him only once, then returned her attention to the bowl of beans in her lap.

"Why do you waste your time with Christian Hockings?" he demanded, an angry expression on his face.

"What a strange way to put it," she said, amused by her brother's choice of words.

"You know what I mean," Aleceon said harshly, sitting down beside her.

For the moment they did not speak and the only sound was the sharp snap of the beans as Sarah broke them in half.

"What about Mr. Enright?" Aleceon pressed. "Has he declared himself?"

"If he has, I do not think that it is any of your concern," she said mildly.

"Oh, isn't it! What about me?" He waved a hand. "You're the one responsible for my being stuck here. They're rich," he said of the Enrights. "And we'd be rich if you married him."

She let her hands fall idle as she regarded her brother. "Aleceon! I have done the best for us that I could."

"You have not," he insisted. "The best would be for you to marry Mr. Enright." He gave her a piercing glance. "He's asked you, hasn't he! I can see it by your expression." In a sudden surge, petulance turned to anger. "Did you dare turn him down?" Reaching out, he grasped hold of her arm, squeezing it fiercely, ignoring her wince of pain. "Did you, Sarah?" He brought his face closer until she could feel his warm breath upon her cheek. "Did you forfeit our future because you're sweet on that dolt!"

"Aleceon!" she protested, alarmed by his behavior.

Abruptly, he released her, getting to his feet, his eyes still bright with anger. "I shall never forgive you, Sarah!"

She shook her head, watching him walk away. Ah, but he was young, she reflected, rubbing her bruised arm. He did not realize that one did not marry a man for money. In time, Aleceon would come to see that she was doing the right thing.

Christian had seen little of Jena during these past weeks. Most of the time she stayed in the house, nursing her father. Once a day she would bring him food, but he was too busy to speak with her, and she would hurry back to her father's side, truly distressed over Amos's condition.

September came. Amos Witcomb's condition had not

improved greatly, and Christian was still in charge at the smithy.

One Saturday afternoon, Jena unexpectedly appeared, her face grim and white. Christian paused at what he was doing, certain that she brought bad news about Amos.

She glanced about, making certain they were alone. Then she fixed Christian with a hard stare. "We've got to get married," she blurted.

He dropped the tongs and just stared at her, dumbfounded by this announcement. "What are you talking about?" he demanded, irritated. "I am not going to marry you! I don't even love you!" There, it was out, and despite his abruptness, he was glad that it was said.

She looked at him sharply, eyes narrowed. "I'm not talking about love, Christian," she replied softly. "I'm talking about the baby I'm going to have. Your baby." Beneath the starched bonnet, her face was implacable. Involuntarily, his gaze darted to her waist, noting how the brown-faced cloth fell smoothly, snugly, about her body.

"Now look here, Jena," he protested. "What sort of a joke is this? I've not hardly seen you these past months, much less..." He took a breath. "If it's a baby you're having, it's not mine!"

"Oh, yes it is." She regarded his shocked face unsmilingly. "Don't tell me whose baby it is. I've been with no other than you. It's true!" she said fiercely. Even his veiled accusation did not lessen her obsessive love for him. Once they were married, all thoughts of the little pauper would leave his mind. She would see to it.

His hands clenched into fists, and for the moment he could not speak. He felt curiously weak and defeated. "Are you sure?" he said at last.

She lifted her chin. "Oh, I'm sure all right. And we've got to get married right away!"

"Why have you waited this long?" he asked her in a cold voice.

"I wanted to be certain," she answered. "Well, I know for sure now." Suddenly upset by his aloof, uncaring expression, she exclaimed: "If you don't marry me, I'll tell Pa! He'll make you do the right thing...."

"I don't need anyone to make me do the right thing," he stated flatly. "If it's my child that you're carrying..." He could not finish, so overcome with dismay was he. The feeling was so powerful that it left him feeling drained and ill.

Her attitude softened, and she relaxed. "It is, Christian," she said earnestly, her eyes searching his. "I swear it. And I'll make you a good wife. You'll see, you won't regret it."

He turned away. But I regret it already, he thought with a deep sigh.

Returning home that night to tell his parents his plans, Christian barely responded to Sarah's greeting, and she could offer herself no acceptable explanation for the sudden feeling of disquiet that coursed through her.

In a halting voice he told his parents that he and Jena Witcomb were to be married. Although Samuel and Ella seemed surprised by the sudden announcement, they made little comment. But Sarah, standing by the hearth, went white at the news, oblivious to the anguish in Christian's eyes as he looked at her.

She felt mortally ill as she heard his words, spoken in an oddly unemotional manner, and unbidden, the acid sting of tears smarted her lids. Had she imagined that day? she wondered distractedly. Perhaps she had dreamed it all: their closeness, his hesitant, probing questions about her future, his sweet kisses, the tightly reined tremor of his desire.

Her eyes blazed with a hurt that she could not conceal, a pain that gnawed at her insides like some omnivorous beast, and her body moved with a quick desperation as she returned to her chores.

After the dinner dishes were done and the room swept clean, Sarah went outside. Aimlessly, she walked toward the river, lost in thought. A snapping twig made her turn around in startled fright, and as she saw Christian, she quickened her step away from him.

"Wait! Sarah, wait!" he called, running until he was

by her side. The sun had already set and the sky was pink and luminous in defiance of approaching dusk.

She kept on walking in silence and for a time he, too, was quiet. Finally he reached out, and taking hold of her arm, effectively halted her progress. "Look at me, Sarah," he pleaded. "I know what you're thinking, and it isn't so."

"It is not so that you are marrying Jena Witcomb?" she asked coolly, moistening lips suddenly gone dry and parched.

A pained expression crossed his face. "Yes, it's so," he admitted. "I didn't tell them why, though, but I want you to know. There's to be a child...."

Her eyes went wide and then she tried to break away, but he held her fast.

She stared at him for a long moment, aware that somewhere close by, a bird chattered noisily, that somewhere a small animal scurried along, secure in the cover of the tall river grass. Within her was only hollow silence.

"It happened months ago, before I...we...Oh, my God, Sarah, please understand. It's you that I love! It's you that I will always love. But I cannot turn my back on her. It is as much my fault as hers."

She felt her body relax, more in resignation than anything else. But she couldn't speak because of the sob that was in her throat.

"Sarah," he murmured, touching her cheek tenderly. "I think I have always loved you. From that first day you came to us. But I didn't know what the feeling was." He searched her face in the dimming light. "Now I know, and it's too late." His voice ended on a note of anguish and with a deep moan, he grabbed her to him and kissed her.

"Please," she cried, trying to draw away. But he only clasped her tighter, kissing her neck, her cheeks, her lips, until she felt faint with the unaccustomed surge of feeling that coursed through her. Dimly, she was aware of his hands, searching, insistent, undoing buttons. He drew her down into the tall grass.

"Sarah," he murmured, his voice thick and imploring. "Don't turn away from me, from our love. You're more precious to me than life itself."

Her bodice was open, revealing the pure curve of her bosom, her skin damp and shining with a silver luminosity, and she could feel the warmth of his hands course through her body, producing a delicious weakness that she fought vainly to resist.

"No," he whispered, his lips in the hollow of her breast. "Don't fight me. For this one night, let me love you. You are now, and always will be, the only one I love."

Once more, she made a move to free herself. But it was too late, and the emotion that gripped him, overpowered her. At last, with a cry, she reached for him, giving herself up entirely to the dizzying sensations that he aroused in her.

He continued to caress her for long moments, ignoring her whimpering, breathless cries, and then helped her to undress.

The grass felt soft and cool against her back, and when she looked up into his eyes, Sarah knew that this was right, knew that the memory of this night would have to last a lifetime.

"Christian," she said softly, holding her arms out to him. Gone were thoughts of resisting, and she surrendered completely to the one person who had her heart, now and for always.

He moved gently at first and her small cry of pain was quickly followed by a gasp of pleasure as she pulled him closer to her.

So engrossed in each other were they, that they thought themselves alone and unobserved. There was nothing for them but feeling, sensation, and Sarah thought that paradise itself could offer no more pleasure than she experienced in Christian's embrace.

But their extreme emotions clouded their senses, because neither one saw, nor heard, the figure that crept surreptitiously to the cover of the large elm tree not too distant from where they lay in the tall grass.

Reaching up, Lucas easily grabbed hold of a branch and hoisted himself into the leafy covering. Settled in complete seclusion, he watched, his mouth twisted into a sardonic smile. The moon had risen, full and pale, bathing the naked lovers in its soft white glow, and from his vantage point, Lucas saw them clearly.

The little bitch, he thought contemptuously. He studied the heaving bodies with interest, feeling no arousal at the sight, only a deep hatred for them both. She had rejected him, and for that, one day, she would pay, he vowed. As for his brother—the pious, upstanding, mealymouthed Christian—all his high-sounding words had been false. He'd only meant to tumble her himself, first chance he got.

Lucas almost laughed aloud as he watched Sarah's white arms grip Christian in a frenzy as their passion at last expended itself. Even then, Christian did not move himself from his warm haven; he merely raised himself up on his elbows and regarded Sarah with a moonstruck expression, murmuring words that he, Lucas, could not hear. But they were words, he was sure, that would greatly amuse him. Betrothed to Jena, not a bad piece, really, and lying in the grass with the hired help. That was Christian!

Sarah's face was hidden by the grass that trembled slightly in the night breeze as if quivering to an ecstasy of its own, caught in the thrall of the Indian summer evening. But, having observed her flailing arms and heaving thighs, he would bet her face reflected the same passion-spent satisfaction as his brother's.

With the lovers apparently engrossed in each other, Lucas took the opportunity to drop to the ground, and then with quiet steps he returned to the inn, a deep brooding look upon his face.

The following Sunday, Christian Hockings and Jena Witcomb were married, and the celebration lasted all day. Sarah, pleading illness, did not attend.

The next morning, Sarah wrote to Jonathan Enright and accepted his proposal of marriage. The wedding was set for January, some three months hence.

But long before that, Sarah knew that she carried Christian's child.

BOOK TWO

Chapter 14

Fenster Tremont, the Enrights' attorney, ate appreciatively, nodding his nearly bald head with its fringed sideburns now and again as Jonathan outlined his plans.

Outside, the Friday April evening offered a chilly rain, but the dining room was warm and cheery under the invisible embrace of a merrily crackling fire and brightly lit brass lamps. The servants moved quietly, unobtrusively removing empty soup bowls, filling wineglasses, and passing plates piled high with ham or beef or delicately seasoned squab.

About the table, Jonathan's idea was being received with varying degrees of enthusiasm.

Justin, with what Sarah referred to as his stern, ministerial expression, looked decidedly unconvinced. This somber expression was punctuated by the severe look of the black cloth suit that now graced his lean, elegant frame, enhancing his sharp features and giving his eyes a peculiar crystalline light. By his side, Elizabeth looked enthusiastic as she always did at any suggestion made by her brother. At the far end of the table, Rachel's face, as usual, was hard to read. She seemed neither to approve nor disapprove.

Because of their age, neither Benjamin nor Caroline joined them at the table for any meal other than breakfast. If it had been up to Sarah, she would have welcomed her son and daughter at the table, but their fidgeting—particularly Caroline's—and high, occasionally shrill voices, severely distracted both Rachel and Justin, the latter of whom seemed to have no patience with children and was forever extolling the virtue of those who were seen, but unheard.

Fenster chewed, swallowed, and then wiped his mouth on the serviette before he spoke. "It will require a great deal of money, Jonathan," he remarked with some skepticism as the younger man concluded.

"I'm aware of that," Jonathan responded quickly. His face darkened. "Although I've been unable to secure the investors that I had hoped to interest in this venture, I believe there's another way. I, personally, will put up half the money that will be needed."

"Even if you do," Fenster noted, "there still remains the problem of the machinery."

Now Jonathan smiled. "That, at least, will be no problem. When Sarah and I were in Manchester last year, I spent several weeks touring their factories, as I did when I first went there some years ago. I found their working conditions deplorable, but I was impressed with their machinery. They are, as you know, loath to sell them, but I have seen enough to make my own specifications; and I have already made arrangements to have them built. Best of all, Fenster, is the cylinder. With it, cloth can be printed!"

"How did you get your hands on that, my boy?" Fenster asked him, also smiling now.

Jonathan's answer was a laugh. "Come now, Fenster. I shall not reveal all my secrets to you. Suffice to say that greed is a widespread sin; it can be found anywhere." He turned toward Sarah and gave her a small, conspiratorial wink.

"Nothing like this has ever been done before, Jonathan," Fenster pointed out. "Certainly not to the extent you describe." However, it was only a cursory remark, and Sarah, smiling to herself, could see that his eyes were filled with muted excitement. Jonathan had long ago told her of his plan, but tonight was the first time that he had unveiled it for the others.

"Think of it," Jonathan went on with enthusiasm. "A mill where the entire process is self-contained. From raw cotton to the finished cloth, all in one mill! It works in England. It can work here."

"I don't question that it works. But the capital, Jonathan." Fenster made a small shake of his head. "You would need better than a hundred thousand dollars for such an operation. Where would you get it? And where would you build? Certainly not in Whitlow. There's not enough room for an operation such as you are describing. And the water. We'd need the water rights," he emphasized.

"We'll sell stock for the balance that will be needed," Jonathan advised, unperturbed. "And I know just the site. The old Mason farm along the Taunton. There's better than five hundred acres, and with Louis Mason gone these many years, I'll bet his widow would be more than interested in a bid for her land. She owns the water rights, too. I've checked."

"Jonathan may be right," Rachel put in at last. "At least about Marian Mason. She has been ailing of late, and the farm is very run down since Louis died. They've never had any children, you know, and she is quite alone."

The solicitor regarded her in silence for a moment. "It is a bit out of the way, though," he commented. "Where would you get the workers?"

"That's the beauty of it," Jonathan replied. "We'll not only build the mill, we'll provide housing as well, for the workers to live in. It will be a self-contained community!"

"Oh, now, wait a minute," Fenster laughed indulgently. "A new mill is one thing. But you're talking about a whole town!" He was quite astonished by the scope of it all.

"Yes, I am," Jonathan affirmed quickly and seriously. "We will even open our own stores. That way, when the workers spend their wages, they will be paying it back to us!"

Thoughtfully, Fenster rubbed his chin. It might work, he was thinking. They could process all the fiber, spin, and weave, all under one roof. Right now, each mill did its own section and sent it on to the next.

"I'd like you to see to the paperwork, Fenster," Jonathan said.

"Of course. Can you come into the office on Monday morning?"

Jonathan frowned slightly. He had wasted too much time already, and was not inclined to waste any more. "I would like to get at it right now, if you don't mind."

With only a small sigh, Fenster viewed the remaining repast before him. Since his wife had died a year ago, it was seldom that a well-rounded meal such as this one graced his table.

"Very well," he said at last, getting to his feet. "I should have known that you did not summon me from Boston just for supper." He gave Jonathan a wry, affectionate look.

"You have not finished eating, Jonathan," Rachel said as he walked over to her and planted a kiss on her dry cheek.

"I can always eat, Mother," he said softly. "Right now, I am going to build a city." Passing by Sarah's chair, he briefly touched her shoulder in a tender gesture. "I'll see you later, darling," he murmured.

Later, in the drawing room, Justin sipped a glass of dry sherry, slightly annoyed that he had not been included in the family discussion. Just because he was in God's employ did not exclude him from being a part of the family, he thought, disgruntled. Jonathan seemed to think that he, Justin, would not be interested. But he was, very much so. Because here, at last, would be the church that he had waited so long for; the church that Jonathan had been promising. All well and good to be known as the most sought-after guest minister in the area, but even that could not compare to having a church of his very own.

And, of course, Elizabeth hadn't spoken up. He eyed her with something like distaste. She always took the side of her brother. Never his.

At that moment, Mrs. Markham, the children's nurse, appeared, holding the four-year-old Benjamin by one hand, and three-year-old Caroline by her other hand. Immediately, Sarah got up and went to her son to kiss him goodnight. Then she hugged her daughter close, kissing the petal-smooth cheek lovingly.

Touching, Justin thought sourly, his mood becoming more despondent. Everyone had children but him. And Sarah was again pregnant. Three times in five years of marriage!

But not so Elizabeth. Elizabeth went on, month after month, as barren as the one before. He finished his drink and dolorously poured himself another, hoping that the children would leave quickly. The very sight of them set his nerves on edge.

Rachel, too, looked upon her daughter-in-law and grandchildren with affection as they hugged each other goodnight; then the children ran toward her. Caroline laughingly won the small race; it was a game they played each night, and Rachel strongly suspected that Benjamin allowed his sister to win periodically.

"It is not seemly for young ladies to run, Caroline," she chided, but kissed her granddaughter with true love. The little girl bore a startling resemblance to Sarah, except for her expression, which was quite animated, and seldom if ever somber.

Then the boy came to her, holding his face up for his goodnight kiss. She could not repress a smile but, viewing that little face, again felt the stirrings of unease. He was sturdy, had been from the day that he was born. Unusual for a child born so prematurely. And then there were his eyes: they were blue. Blue as cornflowers in the springtime. Jonathan's eyes were dark brown; Sarah's eyes, gray.

She kissed the upturned cheek and patted the blond head. And whence that hair? she wondered as she had so many times before. As fine and as soft as a fragile gold thread. Not like Jonathan's black, thick, and wavy hair; not like Sarah's chestnut-brown and almost wavy hair.

Sarah claimed that her son resembled her father; and that might be true, Rachel mused as she watched the children depart with their nurse. But if so, then Sarah looked nothing at all like her father. On the other hand, Benjamin's coloring *was* similar to Aleceon's.

With the thought of that vagrant little troublemaker, Rachel glanced at the banjo clock. After eight, and he was not yet home! It wasn't unusual for him to miss supper. Lord only knew where he spent his time; she didn't want to. She only hoped that he would be sober when he returned. Jonathan had, she grudgingly admitted, gotten a good wife in Sarah, who was unfailingly attentive and obedient. But his young brother-in-law almost negated that gain, in her opinion.

Jonathan had sent him to a private school, but Aleceon had been so disruptive and unruly that he had been dismissed. Another school had been tried, with the same result. Now, almost nineteen, Aleceon just came and went as the mood struck him.

"I think that Jon's idea is marvelous," Elizabeth was saying, as Sarah again settled her heavy bulk on the settee.

"So do I," Sarah replied with a smile, and in truth, she was proud of her husband. During these past five years, she had learned to respect Jonathan, and though his brooding, intense ways occasionally troubled her, he was always kind and thoughtful. He was very ambitious, but she couldn't fault him for that. They were wealthy, very wealthy, and Sarah was pleased to know that her children's futures were secure. Jonathan periodically chided her for her prudent ways, but the years of privation had taken their toll, and her conservativism remained.

The child moved within her, and Sarah placed a hand on her abdomen, comforted by the life thriving there. How different from that first time, she mused, still smiling at Elizabeth as she continued to extol her brother's virtues. For weeks after she had discovered that she was pregnant with Benjamin, she had walked about in a daze. For night after endless night, she had paced within the small confines of her room, pondering her fate.

And that, perhaps, had been the crux of the matter. It was not just her fate; it was Aleceon's—and her unborn child's—welfare that had rendered her sleepless with indecision. What, after all, could she have done on her own, with a baby and Aleceon dependent upon her? They needed a home, care, an education, none of which she had been in a position to supply.

Even so, Sarah had almost told Jonathan about Benjamin when the boy was born, but she could never bring herself to do so. Never bring herself to destroy his obvious adoration and pride in his son. And with Christian lost to her forever, it seemed a pointless course to pursue. Christian and Jena had been married, and then Amos had taken a turn for the worse and died. Only months after that, Christian had inexplicably sold the smithy and, with Jena, left Whitlow. Some said he went to Boston, others said he went to New York.

Sarah didn't know where he was. Her love for him had not dimmed, had not been tarnished in these five years. The pain of losing him had been compensated for somewhat by her children, although at times she would look at Benjamin and feel an agonizing wrench in her heart. Christian had never written, never tried to contact her in any way. And for that she was grateful. Even now, occasionally, she was prodded by the temptation to learn his whereabouts, to know how he fared. And, yes, to know whether he still loved her.

But in spite of it all, Sarah considered herself fortunate. Her husband loved her and the children, and if she sometimes secretly acknowledged that there was a void in her existence—where true love and passion should have been—Sarah firmly pushed such thoughts aside.

The only thorn in her otherwise serene days was her mother-in-law. For the first two years of her marriage, Sarah had despaired of ever coming to terms with Rachel. The woman was unbending and rigid in her attitude toward her daughter-in-law, and on more than one occasion had let Sarah know in no uncertain terms that she considered it an irrefutable fact that her son had married beneath himself.

The children had helped. Rachel was sincerely devoted to both Benjamin and Caroline. She fussed over and spoiled them, as much as her reserved character would allow.

After Caroline was born, Rachel appeared resigned to her son's marriage, and suddenly set about making Sarah "presentable." Tutors appeared from nowhere, followed by music teachers, and regular lessons in deportment—this last furnished by Rachel herself. Jonathan found all this amusing, and made no effort to interfere.

Sarah smiled to herself. She had obviously passed all of Rachel's tests, for it was only rarely now that her mother-in-law took exception to anything she did. She turned her attention back to the present, aware that Elizabeth was still speaking to her.

She noted that her sister-in-law looked lovely in a hyacinth-blue gown that so admirably set off the color of her eyes, but Sarah suddenly realized that she was viewing a brittle sort of beauty. Elizabeth had lost considerable weight in this past year and, slender to begin with, now possessed a fragility that was quite alarming.

Suddenly, while his wife was in the midst of a sentence, Justin stood up, appearing agitated, and taking hold of his cane, leaned heavily upon it. "It is time to retire, Elizabeth!" he announced abruptly, and bidding his mother-in-law a curt goodnight, limped from the room. He neither spoke to Sarah nor glanced in her direction. This behavior on the part of her brother-in-law did not unduly disturb Sarah, who had long since grown used to it. She did not even take it personally, for Justin's attitude toward women was as intolerant and rude as it was toward children. Only Rachel received a grudging respect.

With only a small hesitation and an apologetic smile, Elizabeth immediately stood up and followed her husband out.

Their apartments were on the second floor, comprising a sitting room and a bedroom; the rooms were at the rear of the large, three-storied house. Ahead of Elizabeth, on the landing, a large portrait of Edward Enright hung on the cream-colored wall. As she always did, Elizabeth now stared at it intently, half expecting the painted figure to extend a hand toward her in solace.

At the top of the steps, she halted, the knuckles of her hand whitening as she gripped the balustrade. With a sickening realization that tore at her heart, Elizabeth now saw what her father had seen, knew what he had tried to convey. But, of course, he could not have known about it all; it had been mere instinct that had guided him when he had voiced his doubts about her marriage to Justin.

Still, why hadn't *she* seen it? Elizabeth thought despairingly, still staring at the portrait. How could she have mistaken fanaticism and intolerance for love and strength?

She turned and saw that the door to their bedroom was ajar, spilling warm lamplight onto the polished wood floor. The sight chilled her.

Bracing herself against the coming ordeal, Elizabeth slowly entered the room, closing the door behind her. She made an effort to remain calm, but as she viewed her husband, the coldness within her increased. Justin had propped his cane against the night table beside the canopied bed and, with motions that were deliberate and unhurried, was removing his clothing.

She made no movement, but stood very still, watching him.

"Why are you standing there?" he demanded harshly.

A great sense of weariness enveloped her. "Justin, I..." She bit her lip, her face pale even in the warm glow of the lamplight. For a moment she continued to stand there, her attitude helpless, and then, as if she had to call upon a hidden reserve within herself, she said: "There will be no child this month."

Silence.

Justin regarded her with obvious disgust. "Behold!" he muttered. "'Your house is left unto you desolate.'" In horrified fascination, Elizabeth watched as he took a halting step toward her and began to tear at her gown. In only moments the flimsy stuff hung about her waist in tatters.

Her face white, she covered her bare breasts with her arms. "Justin...please, no!" She stared at him pleadingly, trying to quell the rising fear that surged through her, making her legs tremble. All day long she had been dreading this moment, hoping that night would never come.

"You are like the barren fig tree, Elizabeth," he said in an oddly stiff voice that was at once glacial and condemning. "'And if it bear fruit, well,'" he intoned. "'And if not...cut it down!'" In a quick motion, he grabbed her arm and flung her across the bed, where she lay rigid and unmoving with a fear that now bordered upon terror.

Then he picked up his cane and struck her bare back.

She gasped in pain and buried her head in the pillow to stifle her cry. Even expecting it, she was, somehow, never prepared for it.

Picking up the Bible on the bedside table, Justin opened it, thrusting it at her. "Read!" he commanded.

With a trembling hand, she took the proffered book, which he had opened to Corinthians. "'The wife hath not power of her own body, but the husband...'" Again the cane descended. "Justin, please!" she cried out, raising a hand in supplication.

Ignoring her, he reached over and flipped the pages. "Read!"

With eyes blurred by tears of pain, her voice strained and breathless, she read: "'For the husband is the head of the wife, even as Christ is the head of the Church; and he is the savior of her body....'"

Again the cane fell and Elizabeth bit hard on the pillow. At last he flung it aside and stood there, viewing her, panting from his exertion.

"I shall, as always, sleep in the other room until this affliction, this evidence of God's displeasure upon you, ceases." He bent over slightly. "And pray, Elizabeth! Pray that in the coming weeks, He sees fit to end your barrenness!"

With that, he picked up his cane and, limping, went into the adjoining room, closing the door firmly behind him.

Elizabeth glanced once at the Bible she still held clutched in her hands. Then, in a quick motion, she flung it from her. She lay there, her back on fire, trembling violently, too anguished for tears.

At last she got up, her movements agonizing, and went to the mirror. Her skin was red and wealed, but unbroken. He was always careful about that. Each month about this time he acted violently. At least for the past year he had. Each night he shared her bed, and each night he did his duty. She could not term it lovemaking, for it was not endearments he whispered to her, but scriptures. At this time of the month, however, he would not share her bed, for she was, he said, unclean.

You fool! she silently told her reflection, and the

image offered no argument. The man she thought she had loved did not exist, had never existed. She had been in love with an idea; a phantom clothed in the elegance of Justin Lansing.

I shall tell Jonathan.

And what would that accomplish?

He will put a stop to it.

At what risk to himself?

She turned away from the looking glass. She knew her brother better than anyone else did, including Sarah. Knew that under that gentle-appearing façade—which was not in itself false—ran an undercurrent of cold, implacable anger. Like a mountain spring, it ran hidden, indiscernible to the casual eye. Jonathan seldom lost his temper, but when he did, he was capable of violent extremes.

Finally, wearily, she removed what was left of her clothing and put on her nightdress. Even the soft, silky material felt hot and rough against her back. Then she lay down on the bed on her stomach.

But, despite Justin's exhortations, she could not pray.

In her own room, sitting at her dressing table, Sarah carefully removed pins and ribbons from her hair, then began brushing it. Jonathan was still closeted with Fenster Tremont, and when she heard the faint sound of a knock on the door, she frowned. Putting down the brush, she got up and went into the sitting room that adjoined her bedroom.

"Come in," she called, crossing the room in graceful movements. As the door opened, she halted, her frown deepening. "Aleceon! Where have you been? This is the third time this week that you have missed supper."

"I'm certain that I was missed," he remarked sarcastically, sprawling upon the divan, not bothering to close the door. By the look of him she could see that he had been drinking again. His gray silk cravat was askew, and the pearl stickpin that she had given him on his last birthday was conspicuous by its absence.

"Where have you been?" she repeated, trying to control her anger as she closed the door.

He shrugged. "Boston," he replied vaguely, studying

the wallpaper with its bloated roses. For a moment he regarded it with absorbed interest, then looked away.

Slowly, Sarah walked to a chair and sat down, all the while viewing her brother with a stern expression. "Aleceon," she said quietly, "you must start acting responsibly."

"Oh, for God's sake," he growled, raising a hand in an impatient gesture as if to fend off her words. "Don't start preaching to me again! You can leave that to your sanctimonious brother-in-law."

"I did not mean to preach." She took a deep breath and looked down at her hands, which were clasped tightly in her lap. "I assume that you did not come to visit me just to say goodnight." She looked up at him again. "What is it this time?"

He shifted uncomfortably, his eyes not meeting hers. "I...need a loan."

"I just gave you fifty dollars, not two days ago!"

Now he did look at her, his expression angry, accusing. "What of it! You've more than enough. What am I supposed to do? Do you think that I like crawling to you each time I need a few dollars?"

"You could get a job," she suggested mildly, cringing as the force of his voice reached her.

"Doing what?" he spat at her. "What does the brother-in-law of Jonathan Enright do?" His voice became harsh and brittle. "And why should he need to do anything?" The question was delivered with rapier sharpness, but Sarah didn't answer, because this argument was not new.

All at once his voice became cajoling as he leaned forward, hands resting on his knees. "Look here, Sarah, it's only a loan. I'll pay you back."

Her expression as she viewed him was doubtful. Since he had never paid back any of the money she had given him, there was no reason to suppose that he would begin now. "I know perfectly well that you gamble it away," she said softly, ignoring the closed look that settled upon his face. Involuntarily, her eyes darted to his cravat, realizing, without being told, where the missing stickpin had gone.

"Well, what of it?" he replied, again vexed. Few people had the power to enrage him as much as did his own sister, he thought gloomily. "I've had a run of bad luck, that's all."

"Ah, Aleceon," she said despairingly, feeling close to tears.

He got to his feet, moving impatiently. "I'm only asking you for twenty dollars, Sarah. You needn't act as though I were taking your last penny. I know how generous Jonathan is with you." Again, with lightning swiftness, his mood changed. Going to her, he got down on one knee, and taking hold of her hand, smiled engagingly. A lock of dark blond hair fell across his forehead and she resisted the urge to push it back into place. "Just give me a little time," he pleaded, eyeing her intently. "For so long we have scrimped and scraped; don't begrudge me a little fun. A man needs to sow a few wild oats."

In spite of herself, Sarah smiled, and giving in to her inclinations, raised a white hand to his brow, smoothing back his hair. It was a gesture he abhorred, but he continued to smile at her in his most charming manner.

"Will you lend me the money, darling?" He lifted her hand and pressed it against his cheek.

She looked deep into his eyes, but her own were so blinded by love that she could see no duplicity. Instead, she saw his handsomeness, his charm, his beguiling ways. Then, with a small, sad laugh, she got to her feet. "Don't I always?" she said. As she walked into the bedroom, she didn't notice how the smile upon his lips hardened into triumph.

When Jonathan finally came in, Sarah was already in bed. She laid aside the book she had been reading, and smiled at him.

"Are the children asleep?" he asked, extinguishing the lamp.

"Yes, for hours," she replied.

"Benjamin will be angry with me," he remarked. He removed his vest, dropping it carelessly on a chair. "I promised I'd look in on him before he went to sleep." As he undressed, he told her of his conversation with Fenster. "Just think of it, Sarah," he said, getting into bed. "In another year, two at the most, we'll have the beginnings of the finest mill city in all of New England." He arranged the covers about them and took her in his arms, kissing her forehead.

"Do you think the cylinders will work?" she asked him, trying to settle comfortably within the circle of his arms.

"I'm convinced they will." He turned to her in the darkness. "It's all for you, you know," he whispered, his lips against her throat. "For you and for Benjamin. And," he added, patting her stomach, "perhaps another son as well?"

She laughed softly. "And Caroline? What of your daughter?"

"Caroline will one day marry. A worthless fellow, I'm sure," he said with a sigh. He continued to caress her stomach, pausing now and again as he felt the child move beneath his touch.

"Are you so certain it will be a son?" she asked, teasing.

"Quite certain," he declared. His lips moved from the hollow of her throat to the swell of her breast above the soft cotton of her nightgown. "And I can't wait for him to make an appearance, so I can have you all to myself again." He raised himself up on an elbow and peered at her in the dimness. "I don't like sharing you," he said seriously. "I want you all to myself."

Sarah repressed a sigh as he again lay down, his arms about her, his body pressed close to hers. He had shown the same signs of restlessness and impatience near the end of her other two pregnancies. In itself, not odd, perhaps. But beneath that, she detected an undercurrent of another emotion, a darker one. She hesitated to term it jealousy; yet the parallel disturbed her. Fortunately, once born, he adored his children.

Jonathan's hold tightened, and Sarah hoped he would fall asleep soon. The closeness and restricted movement on her part produced acute discomfort. She knew from experience that if she lay very still, he would soon go to sleep. Then she could move away to her side of the bed and rest, undisturbed.

How strange, she thought, lying there in the darkness. When Christian had held her close to him, she had not felt the need to be free of the restriction of his arms. But although she felt a deep fondness for Jonathan, his embrace suffocated her. He aroused no passion in her; but Sarah held him blameless for that, knowing the deficiency was within herself.

At last she became aware of Jonathan's heavy, evenly spaced breathing. She waited a few more moments, then gently loosened his hold on her and eased herself away.

Chapter 15

The following day dawned gray, with wet skies that shed a cold, insistent drizzle. The far hills were a dark, smoky green, their outlines blurred.

In the kitchen, Charity Bowe moved about with sure steps. There was no wasted motion. Despite the outside gloom, the large, well-appointed kitchen was warm and pleasant, basking in the light provided by the fireplace and a brass lamp placed on a sturdy wooden table. Charity ambled to the wood-burning stove and, with the aid of a handful of dry chips, coaxed the fire into flaming existence for another day.

She had been the cook for the Enright family for almost twenty years now, and as none of the other servants—not Phillips, the butler, nor Mrs. Reddy, the housekeeper, had more seniority, Charity Bowe answered to no one save the mistress herself.

Technically speaking, of course, there were three mistresses in the Enright house, but Elizabeth rarely concerned herself with the staff, and as for the other one... Charity Bowe sniffed disdainfully at the thought of Sarah Enright. That one was little better than a scullery maid when all was said and done. As if fine clothes and jewels and a tutor—a tutor, no less—could make her what she wasn't. For two straight years she had had instruction of one sort or another; Mrs. Enright had seen to that. She had been taught how to speak like a lady, how to dress like a lady, how to conduct herself like a lady. Even how to play the piano!

As if it all made any difference. Ladies didn't speak to the staff like that one did, pleasant like, as if they were all equals.

Even though her mind worked in one direction, Charity's hands acted independently, kneading and shaping the dough into that day's bread and rolls. She glanced across the room at the girl who sat at the other end of the wooden table, peeling potatoes.

"You about done, Lottie?" she asked, not for the first time deploring the girl's dilatory manner. If it had been any other than her own daughter who helped out in the kitchen, Charity would have seen to it that she had long since been sent packing. But then, the girl was a bit slow-witted, and allowances had to be made. "Did you hear me, Lottie? Are you about done?"

The girl, who was nineteen but looked no more than fifteen, glanced up, and then looked down at the bowl of potatoes as if assessing the question.

"There's more to be peeled," she said finally in a nasal tone, and turned her attention to her work again.

Charity shook her head. Placing the neatly shaped rolls in a pan, she put it into the oven. Lottie was slow, but meticulous about any task she was given. Apples and potatoes were shaved with the thinnest of peelings, porridge was stirred until creamy and entirely without lumps, and pots were scoured until they shone as brightly as the silverware.

A tap on the back door interrupted her mental wanderings. Wiping her hands on her apron, she opened the door, her huge frame almost filling the space. She had expected the grocery delivery boy, not the young woman she was now staring at, a young woman obviously pregnant.

"If you're looking for work, we ain't got any," she said curtly. "And if you're looking for a handout, we ain't got any of that, neither." She was about to close the door when the woman spoke.

"Please, I want ter see Mrs. Enright."

Charity snorted at this presumption. "What would she be wanting to see the likes of you for?"

"I'm... a friend."

Now Charity laughed out loud. "Mrs. Enright's friends call at the front door," she pointed out acidly, hands on hips.

"No," the woman said quickly. "I mean Sarah; Sarah Enright."

Charity made no immediate response, but continued to regard the intruder with a wary eye.

"Please," the young woman persisted. "Will yer tell her that I'm here? Me name's Betsy. Betsy O'Connor."

Charity finally moved aside. "Well, come on in," she muttered in grudging tones. "And wipe your feet!" She pointed to the braided rug. "I don't want my kitchen muddied up."

Betsy entered the warm kitchen and after carefully wiping her shoes as she had been instructed, stood by the door, nervously clutching the small reticule she held in her hands. Her brown woolen shawl was damp and dappled with silver drops that glittered in the firelight like small gems.

Charity turned to her daughter, whose attention, despite the sudden appearance of a stranger, was still riveted upon the potato in her hands. "Lottie. Lottie!" The girl looked up, surprised. "Go and get Mrs. Reddy," Charity instructed. "Go on!"

With great care, the girl laid the half-peeled potato on the well-scrubbed table and, just as carefully, placed the small knife beside it. Then she got up and without a word left the room.

"Girl's a bit addle-brained," Charity explained, returning to her work. "But she's a good girl." This last was offered with a pointed look at Betsy's swollen stomach.

Betsy, however, did not rise to the bait, but merely nodded courteously, watching as Charity began rolling out a pie dough.

A few minutes later, Lottie returned, followed by a tall woman with a gaunt face and a severe manner that was reinforced by the black bombazine dress she wore. Her eyes as she viewed Betsy were unfriendly, condemning.

"What do you want here?" she inquired without preamble in a voice that matched her demeanor.

Betsy wet her lips nervously. "I want ter see Mrs. Enright. Mrs. Sarah Enright."

"And is she expecting you?" Mrs. Reddy asked, not bothering to hide her distaste for the shabby, bedraggled, and pregnant creature standing before her.

"No, ma'am," Betsy admitted. "But I'm sure she'll see me if yer tell her I'm here." She wondered if that were true. It had been more than five years; maybe

Sarah wouldn't even remember her. At the thought, she paled slightly and shifted uneasily.

Charity and Mrs. Reddy were exchanging deep, knowing looks. Neither one of them doubted for a moment that the trollop who stood in their kitchen was indeed a friend of Sarah Enright. Many times, in the privacy of the kitchen, over tea, they had speculated with no little amazement on their master's choice of a wife. Any one of a number of suitable ladies would have fallen at his feet, given half a chance.

At last Mrs. Reddy emitted a deep sigh, her expression leaving no doubt as to what a bother this all was, and she said: "Very well. I will inquire if she will see you. You may wait here."

After Mrs. Reddy left, Charity glanced at her daughter. "Finish the potatoes, Lottie," she said, and then cast a look at Betsy, her curiosity whetted. "You from around here?"

"Aye."

"I've never seen you before."

"I...don't actually live in town," Betsy explained. She still stood by the back door, her chapped fingers playing with the narrow strap of the reticule, conscious of the weariness that pressed down upon her. She had spent all but a few dollars of her meager savings on the fare from Boston to Whitlow and had spent the previous night in the station waiting for the five o'clock coach. She had not slept at all, wondering whether she was making the right move or not. Thomas was gone these many months, having signed on with a ship going God knew where. He had left as soon as he had learned of her condition. Until the past week, she had been employed in a factory, but her pregnancy was so obvious they would no longer allow her to work.

"You live with your family?" Charity probed, placing the dough in the pie pan.

"I have no family," was the quiet reply.

Nor husband, I'll bet, Charity thought.

The door opened then, and Mrs. Reddy beckoned. "Come along with me," she said to Betsy, her manner stiff and disapproving. Without looking to see if she were being obeyed, she turned and walked along the hall.

Quickly, drawing her shawl closer, Betsy followed, trembling now with her own audacity.

A bit awed, her eyes took in the rich hangings and polished woods and shining tile. So engrossed in her surroundings was she that she almost bumped into the housekeeper when the woman abruptly halted before a door.

"In here," Mrs. Reddy directed curtly, opening it. Inside, she faced Sarah, who was standing by the window. "This is the young woman who claims to be a friend of yours, madam."

Sarah regarded the housekeeper coolly and Betsy was immediately aware of the change in the girl she had once worked with. "And so she is, Mrs. Reddy. You may leave us. Please close the door on your way out."

With only a slight tightening of her thin mouth, Mrs. Reddy did as she was told. When the door closed, Sarah broke into a delighted smile. Coming forward, she embraced Betsy warmly. "How good it is to see you again," she said, sincerely delighted to see the young Irishwoman.

Relieved, Betsy returned the embrace. "I should never have come," she murmured, suddenly contrite. "I wouldn't have, if I didn't need help so bad."

Noticing Betsy's condition, Sarah laughed softly, patting her own stomach. "I see that we are both about to add to our family. Come, sit down." She led the way to the settee. The room, furnished in a stiffly formal manner, greatly impressed Betsy, who had never before seen the likes of it. Her eyes took in the black-and-white-tiled hearth with its cheerily blazing fire, the exquisite silver-gilt clock that rested upon the mantle, the two oval-shaped mirrors on either side with their intricately carved frames, and she sighed deeply. People actually live like this, she thought wonderingly touching the plush velvet of the couch she was sitting on.

"Now," Sarah said, when they were settled. "Tell me what's wrong. Is it money you need?"

"Oh, no," replied Betsy, truly shocked. "I wouldn't have come ter yer for money, Sarah! My, yer sure do look grand," she said, momentarily diverted by the smart, fashionable outfit that Sarah was wearing. She radiated a quiet elegance that bespoke wealth and security, but Betsy felt no envy, only a sort of awe.

"Thank you. It's been a long time, Betsy. I've thought of you often, even thought of trying to find you in Boston. But," she smiled wryly, "the doctor advises me not to travel until the baby is born. After Caroline was born, Jonathan and I spent some time in England, and when I returned, we discovered that I was again to have a child." She bent forward slightly, and Betsy caught the faint scent of lavender. "Are you still living in Boston?"

Betsy shook her head. "I had a job at a factory, but they won't allow a girl ter work when she's pregnant; leastways not after she's showing."

"I'll speak to Jonathan...."

"No, no," Betsy said quickly. "Please, it's the rule, and I know it."

"And your husband?" Sarah inquired tentatively.

Flushing violently, Betsy looked down at her hands in her lap. "I'm not married, Sarah," she admitted in a low voice.

"I see. Then who...?"

But Betsy shook her head in a quick motion. "No sense in mentioning names. He can't help me. He's married." Although, she thought bitterly, that was something she hadn't known about Thomas until it was too late. Nobody at the mill had thought of him as having a wife; he lived alone. But it turned out that he did have one; one who had run away from him, Betsy thought, just as she ought to have done. A hot feeling of resentment shot through her, not for her predicament, but because she had been so gullible, so believing. He had said they would be married, and right up to the time she had told him she was to have a child, he kept telling her so.

Sarah's gaze turned thoughtful, and she sighed. "So you have no job, no family, and no husband. Have you contacted your sister?"

"Lord, she'd be the last one, Sarah. She kicked me out once, and she ain't about ter let me in her house again!" Not, she thought glumly, that she would want to return. But now, with the advantage of years behind her, Betsy added: "I don't blame her, yer know. Leastways, not anymore. I think I'd probably have done the same, meself."

Sarah thought this a great improbability, but she made no comment. "And money?" she prompted.

"Some. But not enough ter last till this is all over." She looked at Sarah earnestly. "All I need is a place ter stay until the baby's born, then I can go back ter the factory. I'll work at whatever's needed. Yer don't have ter pay me—" She broke off, close to tears as Sarah put her arms about her.

"Nonsense! Of course you shall be paid. Nor will you return to the factory. What would you do with the child while you worked?" She fell silent a moment, frowning slightly as she thought. Her mother-in-law would not be pleased at what she was about to do, but Sarah, for once, gave that only momentary consideration. Right now, this was more important, more immediate. In her present condition, Betsy could not possibly work in the main part of the house, and the second floor was fully staffed. That left only the kitchen. Surely Charity could use another hand. Abruptly, she stood up and pulled on the bell cord, smiling reassuringly at Betsy, who was regarding her in a bemused fashion.

When, a moment later, Mrs. Reddy appeared, Sarah turned. "Mrs. O'Connor will be joining the kitchen staff," Sarah stated, ignoring the sudden, insolent look of skepticism. "She has recently lost her husband and is now expecting her first child. Therefore, please instruct Mrs. Bowe to assign Mrs. O'Connor light chores until after the child is born. She is to be paid seven dollars a week. Please see to her quarters and inform Mrs. Bowe. I will send her in directly."

Nodding stiffly, Mrs. Reddy withdrew, but not before she cast a black look in Betsy's direction.

Ignoring that look, Betsy stood up and turned toward Sarah. "I don't know how ter thank yer, Sarah—Mrs. Enright," she amended quickly.

"Sarah is fine, when we're alone. And it's a kindness I owe you," Sarah replied gently, and again putting her arm about Betsy, led her to the door. "After the child is born, I want you to stay on. In a few months' time, Jonathan and I and the children will be moving into a house of our own. When that happens, I would be so pleased to have you come with me. And the child, of course. And you won't have to stay in the kitchen." She looked at her friend with an almost apologetic expression. "You *do* understand that this house belongs to my mother-in-law. I don't have much say." She opened the door. "Don't let Charity Bowe get you down," she advised with a broad smile that lit up her face. "She has a sharp tongue, but she's a good sort, really." She kissed Betsy's brow with true affection. "I've got to go now. If you need anything, let me know."

"I won't forget this," Betsy said fervently. "I'll be with yer as long as yer want me, Sarah." She hurried along the hall back to the warm kitchen, bracing herself for Charity Bowe's reaction, which she was certain would be outrage.

Watching her go, Sarah's smile turned sad. Betsy had seemed so grateful; yet who was she to cast a stone? Sarah wondered silently. There, but for the grace of God, went she. How strange, she thought. At times in our life we do an act of casual kindness, never realizing that at some time in the future it could be repaid from the most unexpected quarter. She remembered so clearly the day she had arrived at the mill; Betsy had been the only one who had taken the time to speak with her, to offer a kind voice and a bit of advice.

Standing there, Sarah was suddenly struck by the injustice of it all. Why did women have to suffer so? Their lives began, existed, and ended, all under the heavy hand of society and convention. And we ourselves perpetuate it, she thought unhappily. But there were movements afoot, instigated by her own sex, to correct some of these circumstances; mere whispers yet, but they were nonetheless being received with shock and outrage. Perhaps one day, Sarah reflected, if their spirits remained uncrushed, changes would be brought about. Perhaps.

"Sarah!"

She turned and faced her mother-in-law. One look told her that Rachel had already been informed of the day's events.

"Mrs. Reddy tells me you have hired a girl, a friend of yours, to work in the kitchen!"

Sarah nodded and walked back into the parlor in an attempt to prevent the sound of their voices carrying into the kitchen. Rachel seldom raised her voice; she did not do so now, but she had the knack of speaking, when she so chose, with a ringing clarity of tone.

"I did," she responded at last. "I hope that it won't present any problems."

Rachel, who thought that her daughter-in-law had acted with the utmost presumption, said: "I do think, Sarah, that you could have checked with me." Her expression settled into grimness.

"You're perfectly right," Sarah quickly agreed. "And I apologize for acting in such a forward manner. But the girl really is an old friend of mine, and is in desperate need of work."

The explanation left Rachel unmoved. "I understand that she is to have a child... and that she is unmarried," she stated coldly.

"I believe that Mrs. Reddy has her facts only half correct," replied Sarah calmly. "Mrs. O'Connor is widowed; and, yes, she is to have a child." She made a mental note to enlist the aid of Jonathan in this small deception, confident that he would grant her wish.

A raised brow was the only comment to this declaration, but Rachel decided not to take exception. "She is Irish," she stated, as if that would convince Sarah that she had made a terrible mistake.

"Yes, I know."

Exasperated, Rachel went on, her voice strained and accusing. "Surely you cannot expect us to have a... a papist in the house!" She was truly appalled and could mentally envision Justin's heated response to such an unacceptable situation. Of course, he would be right.

A small smile touched the corners of Sarah's mouth. "Betsy is not Catholic, Mother Enright," she corrected quietly. "She is a Protestant. I believe that she attends the Presbyterian Church."

Much relieved, but still annoyed that Sarah had taken it upon herself to do this thing, Rachel sighed. "Very well, Sarah. We will leave things as they are, for the time being. But in the future, I do wish that you would leave staff matters in my hands."

"Thank you, Mother Enright," Sarah said, wishing fervently for the time when she would have her own house. "And I promise you that I shall do no more hiring without first consulting you," she added meekly.

Sarah's third child, another boy, whom she named Nicholas, was born two months later. Only two weeks after that, Peggy, one of the second-floor maids, tentatively, and with no little trepidation, awoke her mistress just before dawn.

"It's Betsy, ma'am," she whispered, still fearful of her temerity. She glanced once at the still sleeping Jonathan Enright and hastily looked away. "She's in a bad way. Mrs. Bowe said I was to tell you."

Throwing the coverings aside, Sarah quickly got out of bed and donned a robe.

In the hall, Peggy murmured, "I'm sorry I woke you, ma'am."

Sarah absently patted the girl's shoulder. "You did the right thing," she assured her, and with Peggy holding the lamp high, the two made their way to the servants' quarters on the third floor.

Entering the small chamber, she saw Betsy on the narrow bed, her face a chalky white. Charity Bowe was murmuring in a low voice, now and again patting Betsy's hand in a comforting manner. Another woman, whom Sarah didn't recognize, was also there, and in her arms she held a small bundle. There was no movement, no cry, and it seemed like nothing more than a crumpled blanket.

Quickly, Sarah approached the trundle bed. "What's wrong?" she demanded, pressing down her fear. "Why haven't you called me before this!"

"Everything seemed to be all right, Mrs. Enright," Charity explained, with a short glance in her direction. Despite her first impression, she had grown very fond of Betsy over the past two months. The young Irishwoman even managed to make Lottie smile with her antics and lively manner. Charity motioned toward the other woman. "Mrs. Baker is a midwife, and she came right away when the pains started."

"Why didn't you call a doctor?"

Charity Bowe looked affronted. "Never had no need for other than a midwife myself," she replied defensively.

Sarah bit back a retort, but before she could speak, the midwife said, "Doctor wouldn't have done any good. The child was dead before it came out. Tore her up a bit, though," she went on flatly. "She's bleeding bad."

Furious now, Sarah turned to Charity Bowe. "Get a doctor immediately. Go!" With a short, sullen glance, the cook got up. "Where is Mrs. Reddy?" Sarah asked as Charity reached the door.

"Sleeping," was the reply. "She wouldn't have took kindly to being woke up just because one of the servants was giving birth."

"Get the doctor," Sarah again ordered, and, turning, went to Betsy's side. Placing a hand on the young woman's brow, she was relieved that it was cool, if damp. Then she took hold of a hand. "Betsy? I'm sorry about the child, but you'll be all right. I promise you."

Betsy opened her eyes, for the moment not seeming to recognize Sarah. Then she smiled weakly. "I'm nothing but trouble, lass. Soon as I'm on me feet, I'll get out of yer way."

"You'll do no such thing!" Sarah exclaimed quickly. She was growing alarmed by the look of Betsy, who now seemed unable even to focus her eyes. "When the new house is completed, we shall do just as we have planned," she insisted. "You will come and stay with me." She gripped the cold hand. "I need someone."

"Like a personal maid?" A small smile appeared on the white lips. "I'd like that."

Sarah bit her lip, sternly repressing threatening tears. "Others may call you that," she whispered, gripping the hand tighter. "But to me, you will be what you have always been. A friend." She sat there, holding Betsy's hand, until the doctor arrived. Then she stepped outside to wait.

Thirty minutes later the doctor emerged, wiping his hands on a towel. "She'll be all right," he said offhandedly. "Three, maybe four weeks, and she'll be on her feet again."

"The child?" Sarah inquired, faintly annoyed by his condescending manner.

He shook his head and pursed his fleshy lips. "Nothing I can do about that."

Despite her ordeal, in only two weeks' time Betsy was well, helping Charity in the kitchen. Sarah was helpless to correct the situation, but when, the following April, the new house was at last completed, she made certain that Betsy had a suitable room near her own.

Jonathan promptly named their new residence Somerset Hall; the mill town, now about two-thirds completed, he christened Taunset.

The house in Whitlow was sold, and Rachel Enright, together with the staff, moved into the newly completed house, a grand structure built along classical lines and boasting twenty-two rooms on three stories.

Temporarily, until their own house could be constructed next to the church, Justin and Elizabeth also moved into Somerset Hall.

The months that followed were a whirlwind of decorating and furnishing, and Sarah thought that she had never been so happy in her whole life. Her children were healthy and robust, and now that Benjamin was going on seven, Jonathan insisted upon taking the boy with him to inspect the progress at the mill. His adoration for Benjamin was so marked that Sarah laughingly accused him of spoiling the boy. But Jonathan would only clasp Benjamin to him in a fierce embrace, his love so evident that Sarah did not have the heart to pursue her complaint. At those times, her conscience would nag at her, and she couldn't help but wonder if Jonathan would still love Benjamin if he knew that the boy was not his own. It was a thought that she could not face squarely, the one thing that continued to trouble her, marring the total contentment that would otherwise be hers.

But she refused to let it dampen her happiness, pushing those thoughts ever deeper within her, in the hopes that, one day, they would vanish forever.

Chapter 16

From the depths of the comfortably upholstered carriage, Aleceon stared moodily out of the window on this September evening, and in the passing lamplight his face appeared even more drawn, more tired than usual.

He could smell the sea now, and he leaned forward in anticipation as the carriage threaded its way along the waterfront.

At last they reached their destination, and Aleceon quickly got out. The building was ordinary enough, indistinguishable from any warehouse along the Boston wharf. It was ugly, square, its exterior weather-beaten under the constant assault of dampness and salty air.

There was nothing outside to indicate that it served any other purpose than the one for which it had been originally intended. Bales and boxes were piled haphazardly against the walls, and coils of rope and a few canvases were strewn about; only the most discerning eye would have noticed that the position of it all never changed. Certainly Aleceon would not have noticed. He had learned of this place quite by accident only six weeks before.

"Will you be spending the night, sir?" Tully asked, looking down at him from his perch atop the wooden seat. He kept his expression bland and respectful, but like the rest of the household he disapproved of Aleceon Edgewood.

"Yes, yes," Aleceon replied, impatience lacing his tone. Fumbling in his pockets, he threw a few coins at Tully. "Stay in town. Come for me about noon." With that he turned, and hurried through the darkness to the front door.

Inside, the decor changed dramatically. There was a small entry hall with a staircase that led to the second floor. Off this entry was a large room, garishly done in defiant reds and golds. Since the windows were boarded up, the lamps burned twenty-four hours a day. The walls were obscured by heavy brocade hangings. The floors, too, were thickly carpeted, and, as a result, although the room now held more than forty people, sounds were muted.

The occupants were for the most part men. A few stood at the bar, talking to the flamboyantly dressed girls who smiled brightly and always seemed to be captivated by the words spoken to them, but most were seated at card tables. Although the ceiling was a good twenty feet high, the large room was smoky, the odor stale, neither of which seemed to bother anyone.

"Ah, Mr. Edgewood."

The woman who advanced toward him was in her fifties, with dark, lusterless hair that was piled in tortuous ringlets about her fleshy face. To call Rose obese would have been to understate the mountain of flesh that covered her five-foot frame. Her skin was almost ghostly in its whiteness, as though she had never been outdoors in her life.

"I suppose you would like to see Kitty," she said amiably, fanning herself gently with the yellow lace fan she carried in her mitted hand. "She is...otherwise occupied at present. Why don't you sit down at one of the tables while you wait?"

Aleceon allowed himself to be led to a vacant chair. The other men merely nodded and turned their attention once more to the cards.

A glass of whiskey was placed before him, and Rose stayed only long enough to see Aleceon produce his gold coins.

Lovely color, gold, she thought in satisfaction as she moved away. The drinks—only whiskey and rum were served—were complimentary here at Rose's, she having long since learned that a man played less inhibitedly and less skillfully when relaxed by liquor. Glancing toward the arched entry, she saw a young woman about to enter and she scowled, motioning slightly with her fan. The young woman immediately stepped back into the hall again.

Rose approached her. "He's waiting for you," she said,

seeing Kitty's eyes rest questioningly upon Aleceon. "But I don't want him interrupted for a while." The girl nodded as Rose continued. "How many times has he been here now?"

Kitty wrinkled her pretty brow while she mentally calculated. She was sixteen, with dark auburn hair and with the fair, creamy skin that usually went with such coloring. "Five," she said. "Not counting tonight."

At this, Rose inclined her head. "It's time, then," she said, and walked back into the large room.

Kitty returned to her room on the second floor. It was empty now, her previous customer having been removed upstairs to sleep it off. This chore was performed by Seth, a massively built deaf-mute who was, in fact, Rose's brother.

Downstairs, after having drunk four whiskies, Aleceon was losing. But, as everyone knew, luck changed. A bad run of cards could only be followed by a good run; with this in mind, Aleceon pushed the last of his money to the center of the table.

Luck was apparently not ready to change direction, and this money, too, was lost. In dismay, Aleceon leaned back in his chair, and almost simultaneously Rose was by his side, lightly resting her plump hand on his shoulder.

"Ah, your luck will change," she observed with a small laugh. "You must give it a chance. Nothing pleases me more than to have a guest win."

Aleceon regarded her with a lopsided smile and shrugged. "That's all I've brought with me, Rose," he said, starting to get up. But her hand, with surprising strength, detained him.

"Among friends we do not speak of money," she chided, and with a look at the dealer, said: "This gentleman's credit is good. Accept any marker he presents." Then she tapped Aleceon lightly with her fan and, bending over, whispered: "Kitty will be free shortly. Amuse yourself for a while, then I shall send you to her." Still smiling, she walked away, her little black eyes critically scanning the other tables to see that all was in order.

By the time Aleceon left the table and stumbled up the stairs, he was in debt for more than six hundred dollars. An exorbitant sum, and one that he had no idea how he was going to repay.

Inside the small bedroom, he fell upon the rumpled bed. Immediately Kitty was beside him.

"I lost it," he mumbled, only half aware of her presence. His eyes took in the cluttered room with its fringed red-velvet draperies and gilt-framed mirror, and a sense of oppression gripped him. Despite the coolness of the September evening, the room was hot, the air sultry and stale.

"Ah, we all have bad turns, lovey," she murmured, deftly undoing his cravat. "Come on, now, it's not all that terrible." With practiced movements, she undressed him, pulling the silken quilt over him. This he immediately threw aside, not even noticing as she slipped out of her vivid red gown. Then she crawled onto the bed and took Aleceon in her arms.

The drinks had dulled his senses, and it was long moments before her skillful hands and lips could arouse a response from him.

At last he raised himself up on an elbow and stared down at her. "You're a good girl, Kitty," he mumbled. Then he rolled over on top of her, heedless of his weight upon her soft, warm flesh.

For a short time the pain of losing and the problem of money receded as he thrust himself into the young, eager body beneath him. But Kitty's expertise was such that in only a few minutes he again lay beside her, spent.

When his breath calmed, the misery of his indebtedness returned, and he groaned with a feeling of hopelessness. Fifty dollars, maybe even one hundred, he could get from his sister. But six hundred!

"Poor lovey," Kitty sympathized, stroking his brow. Her hips moved against him inquisitively, but she could sense that he was, for the time being, completely uninterested. She got out of bed and, walking toward her dressing table, opened a drawer and took out a small vial. Pouring the liquid contents into a small glass, she returned to Aleceon's side and, kneeling on the carpeted floor, held the glass out to him.

"What is it?" he asked, viewing the glass doubtfully.

"Only a bit of laudanum. Calms the nerves, it does. I use it all the time." This was not true, because Rose was very strict about opium. Not from any moral standpoint; she just didn't want her girls walking around in a stupor when there was work to be done. But laudanum, at least initially, was given to their customers free of charge. Just like the whiskey and rum. Unlike the liquor, however, it did not remain free for long.

There was a third floor to Rose's lucrative establishment. It was not anywhere near as sumptuously furnished as the first floor, nor as comfortably decked out as the second. The third floor was no more than a series of small cubicles, each of which held only a straw pallet and a blanket. Seth was in charge here, and Rose seldom set foot on the third floor.

Gambling, prostitution, and the dispensing of opium in the form of laudanum were all highly profitable; and, for the privilege of operating undisturbed, Rose paid the authorities handsomely.

There was a fourth operation, however, of which even the authorities were unaware, and it was this last one that had made Rose so enormously wealthy. She could have retired long ago except for the boredom inherent in such a move.

For this last operation, she had to be selective. Only a few men met the requirements for involvement. Money was not a factor. In fact, it was better if it were in short supply. And a certain weakness of character. Too, there had to be a ruthlessness and a complete lack of sentimentality. These traits she had immediately recognized in Aleceon Edgewood. When he repeatedly asked for the same girl, she almost thought that she had erred; but Kitty assured her that whatever Aleceon Edgewood found attractive about her, love or even affection played no part in it.

Having drunk the harmless-looking liquid, Aleceon now seemed half unconscious. But inside, his mind and senses were soaring. Almost objectively, as if he were two different entities, he marveled at the lightness of spirit he felt.

What had he been worried about? he wondered as

he mentally advanced into the maze of glorious color and sensations that claimed him.

Still naked, Kitty stood at the foot of the bed, watching Aleceon with almost clinical detachment. She had given him a small dose, rightly figuring that he had never before taken any. Three, perhaps four times, and he would thence have a craving for it. They all did, sooner or later.

Kitty turned as Rose entered, followed by Seth.

Rose, too, observed the young man for a long moment, then turned to her brother. Seeing his eyes fastened avidly upon Kitty, she turned in a swift motion to the girl. "Get some clothes on!" she ordered angrily, and just as irritably addressed her brother. "Put him in another room. Don't take him upstairs yet. Let him sleep it off. But keep an eye on him, it's his first time."

Seth, who could read his sister's lips, nodded. With only a quick glance at Kitty, who was stepping into her gown with deliberate slowness, he easily picked Aleceon up and carried him from the room.

"Take his clothes to him," Rose instructed Kitty, heading for the door. "And stay away from Seth!"

Stay away from Seth, Kitty thought, making a face at Rose's receding bulk. That was a laugh. Sooner or later, the oaf had his way with them all. She shivered at the prospect, remembering the heavy hands and ungentle touch. Only once had a girl refused Seth, and the next day she had been found at the bottom of the stairs, her neck broken from an accidental fall.

At the door to her room, Kitty hesitated, Aleceon's clothing in her arms. Only when she heard Seth's heavy tred as he made his way to the third floor, did she venture out into the hallway.

Chapter 17

When Betsy entered Sarah's room, her face was flushed with muted excitement and concern, but when she saw Aleceon, her expression fell into a scowl. With motions that were short and abrupt, she straightened the frilled organdy apron that fell smoothly over the long black woolen dress she wore, and absently adjusted her white cap.

It was only two days before Thanksgiving, and the whole house bore traces of the festive occasion, the rooms smelling of pine, cinnamon, and the rich dark molasses that would go into the pumpkin pies. Just beyond the security and warmth of the house, the November air howled and raged, breathing powdered snow like some invisible, enraged beast.

Trying not to show her disapproval, Betsy listened to Aleceon's latest request for money. She busied herself as unobtrusively as possible, flicking imaginary dust from the dainty, embroidered chairs, straightening the heavy walnut frames of already perfectly situated pictures.

Achieving unobtrusiveness was not difficult, because as far as Aleceon was concerned, she could have been a part of the furniture. He never spoke to her, rarely even glanced in her direction. He did not do so now.

Betsy thought how much she disliked and distrusted the young man; honey in his mouth, and vinegar in his heart, she mused, pursing her lips. There was something terrible, something dreadful, about Aleceon, and although she chided herself for this nebulous feeling that would occasionally grip her, Betsy nevertheless could never entirely rid herself of the unease.

She remembered the boy that Aleceon used to be. She had thought him inept, lazy, and, at times, churlish. But now that he was grown, she detected a furtive, almost sinister quality in him. No one else seemed to notice it, though, certainly not Sarah, who could see little wrong with her brother except for his distressing propensity toward gambling and idleness.

When he had at last removed his tedious and sullen presence from the otherwise cheerful room, Betsy breathed deeply, and went over to Sarah.

"I'm not the one ter carry tales, lass, and yer knows that for a fact. But there's something going on in this house that yer ought to know about."

"Has Mrs. Reddy been sending food home to her sister again?" Sarah asked, with a slight smile.

"I wish it were no more, that I do," Betsy said with a slight shake of her head. "Yer've always told me how kind Mrs. Lansing has been ter yer, and how fond yer are of her. If it weren't for that..."

"Elizabeth?" Sarah straightened, her attention caught at last. "Is something wrong with Elizabeth?"

Betsy took a step nearer, her voice dropping to the barest whisper, although they were quite alone in the room. "It was Peggy who told me, and she swears that it's true. Seen it with her own eyes, she did."

A flicker of annoyance crossed Sarah's face. "Seen what? Betsy, what are you talking about?"

"The marks, lass. Mrs. Lansing's back is striped with weals, like she's been beaten—bad."

Sarah's face paled and she started violently. Intently, she searched Betsy's eyes, but in their clear depths she could see only seriousness and a lack of guile. "Beaten! My God, what are you saying?"

"It's true," Betsy insisted. "Peggy's seen the marks when she helps Mrs. Lansing ter dress, even though she tries ter hide it. Peggy thinks it's *him* what's doing it." Nor, Betsy thought, did she herself doubt that for a moment. If there was one person in this house that she was afraid of, it was the reverend. Man of God or no, Betsy swore she saw the glint of Satan himself in those green eyes.

"That's absurd," Sarah exclaimed, truly shocked. She had never really liked Justin, but this she could not believe. The thought made her shudder with revulsion. "Have you spoken of this to anyone else?"

Betsy shook her head in denial. "Yer knows I keep me own counsel," she stated emphatically. "And if it was anyone else, I probably wouldn't even speak of it ter yer."

Sarah got to her feet, checking the time as she did so. The tall cherry clock in the corner informed her that it was not yet nine. Jonathan, who had gone to Boston, was planning to stay over at Fenster's house. The new mill was scheduled to begin operations as soon as the holidays were over, and they were attending to the last-minute details.

But could she speak of this to Jonathan? Sarah wondered, her thoughts returning to Elizabeth. Certainly not without proof. While she was certain that Betsy's report was accurate, there still remained Peggy. Flighty and imaginative, the girl easily could have misconstrued what she had seen.

Even if she could speak to her husband, did she have the right? If this monstrous tale were true, then why hadn't Elizabeth herself spoken out?

"I will speak to Mrs. Lansing," Sarah said at last. But after a few steps across the pale green carpet, she halted. Justin would, of course, be in their apartment. How could she possibly speak with Elizabeth while he was in the room!

Seeing that hesitation, Betsy suggested in a tentative voice: "I could ask Mrs. Lansing ter come here. What with Mr. Jonathan gone, what more natural thing could there be than ter say that yer're lonesome and in need of company?"

Sarah threw her a grateful look. "You do that, Betsy. I want to get this matter straightened out as quickly as possible."

While Betsy went to get Elizabeth, Sarah paced the floor of her sitting room, restless from the sudden uneasiness that gripped her.

For months now she had been aware of a change in Elizabeth. She of the silver laugh, seemed now to laugh but rarely, and when she did, it was a sad, almost apologetic sound, as though laughter were a thing that she did not deserve. And her eyes, too, Sarah thought with growing awareness. They had always shone with exuberance, with a sheer delight at life itself. Lately, those eyes had dulled, giving the impression that she had looked upon life and found it lacking.

Less than ten minutes had gone by when there was a soft knock upon the door; a moment later, Elizabeth, clad in a mauve silken robe, entered.

"Oh," Sarah said, looking at her sister-in-law. "You were ready for bed, and I've disturbed you."

"No, no," Elizabeth said, coming into the room. "I was just reading. I...wasn't very tired. Really, I was glad when Betsy said that you wanted company."

She sat down on the settee, her fine hands with their tapered fingers clasped loosely on her knees. She looked much younger than her twenty-five years with her black hair, unbound now, hanging freely about her graceful shoulders.

But she was so painfully thin! So fragile! Elizabeth, Sarah thought with a sudden glow of clarity, was like a rare plant in a conservatory. It could only survive, produce its splendid flower, if all conditions were favorable. Exposed to cold, uncared for, it would wither and die, its leaves turning arid and crumbling like dust.

"I...was lonely," Sarah said inanely, seating herself in a small, upright chair that faced the settee. Suddenly she was nervous, unsure; how did one broach a subject of this delicate nature? And was it her place to even try?

Watching her, a frown creased Elizabeth's normally smooth brow, and her eyes filled with concern. "There's something wrong, isn't there?" She leaned forward. "What is it, Sarah?" she asked, viewing the unusual agitation of her normally placid sister-in-law. "You're not ill, are you? Shall I send for the doctor?"

"No, no," Sarah protested with a small laugh that caught in her throat. "It's...been so long since we've talked..."

Relaxing again, Elizabeth leaned back. "Of course it has been, and I'm to blame. The days slip by and we think our own thoughts, never realizing that others may need us..." She smiled that sad smile that had of late hovered about her lips as if it had found a permanent resting place. "I'm here, Sarah," she said quietly. "If you need to talk, I'm here."

The acid sting of hot tears closed Sarah's eyes, and for the moment, she could not speak. Her forehead felt damp, despite the chilled night, and she brushed her brow with a trembling hand. "It seems that Peggy has told Betsy the most ridiculous tale. I ought not credit it, but," she paused, and seeing Elizabeth's expression, which had become wary and alert, felt a stab of horror. "My God, it's true...," she said, the words emerging in a horror-filled whisper.

Elizabeth abruptly got to her feet and, walking toward the window, held the draperies aside with one hand while she seemed to study the brittle night. "I should have known better than to let Peggy help me dress," she mused, almost to herself. "But time has a way of making one careless."

Sarah stood up, but made no move to approach Elizabeth. "Time? What do you mean by that, Elizabeth? How long has this been going on?"

"Almost a year," she replied in a dead tone, turning to face Sarah. She was standing very still, and Sarah was again struck by Elizabeth's incredible beauty. Nature must have made only a few of these creatures, she thought, for Elizabeth defied time and convention. And a brutal husband. She would have been exquisite in any time, any place, for such was the perfection of her face and form that nothing about her bore the slightest imperfection.

Except that now, having lived about half of her lifetime, Elizabeth's eyes were haunted, reflecting an agony that her delicate loveliness should never have been forced to endure.

Sarah took a deep breath. "Surely he does not actually, I mean, he doesn't..."

A cynical look hardened Elizabeth's delicate features. "Doesn't beat me?" she said; then, in a quick movement, she opened her robe, dropping it to her waist, and turned. At the sight of her back, Sarah gave a short cry and put her hands to her lips while, calmly, Elizabeth again adjusted her robe.

"But why!" Sarah said when she could again speak. "Why would he do such a thing?"

Elizabeth raised a finely arched brow, returned to the settee, and sat down, her movements languid and unhurried. "There have been only two things that Justin has required of me. One was his church—that has already been accomplished, as you know. The other is a child. He blames me for our childlessness." She looked away while Sarah regarded her with quiet astonishment. "Each month, he reminds me of my derelict duty."

Feeling quite weak now, Sarah, too, sat down. And then anger replaced shock. Some men, she knew, did beat their wives. Old Mr. Potter, their nearest neighbor in Brockton, did so regularly, and his wife had been hard pressed to conceal the fact. But Justin? He was a minister, a man of God!

"But this is beastly!" Sarah exclaimed in outrage. She ached with compassion and an overwhelming sense of helplessness. She longed to offer comfort, solace; yet what had she to offer? She put an arm about Elizabeth. "It cannot go on," she stated firmly. "I will speak to Jonathan...."

"No!" The answer was swift, emphatic; startled, Sarah withdrew her arm. "Jonathan would probably kill him, and while I would not act the bereaved widow," Elizabeth said, "what it would do to my brother is something that I could not live with."

At this assessment of Jonathan's reaction, Sarah's eyes widened in disbelief. "Jonathan would never react violently," she protested. "Certainly he would be angry, and certainly he would speak to Justin in strong terms but—"

"Jonathan must not know," Elizabeth broke in, her tone carrying a conviction that could not be violated.

Sarah waved a hand in a helpless gesture. "Well, something must be done! What about your mother?"

Elizabeth's laugh was caustic, a mere ghost of its silver sound, and, puzzled, Sarah just waited. "Oh, my dear Sarah," she said at last. "I have already made that mistake." The laughter ended, sounding more like a sob.

"Rachel knows?"

"Oh, indeed. She said that I had made my choice, and it was mine to live with. She reminded me that my husband was within his rights, and cautioned me to never again approach her with my personal problems."

Again Elizabeth issued that wretched laugh. "Don't concern yourself with me, my dear Sarah. It will all be over soon."

"What do you mean?" Sarah said, alarmed.

Turning toward her, Elizabeth slowly smiled. "I am to have a child, probably in April," she said quietly. "Justin doesn't know yet, but he will. In due time, he will."

Sarah put her arms about the slender body and hugged her. "I'm so glad for you." She drew away. "You *do* want the child, don't you?"

Elizabeth patted her hand as if it were Sarah who needed reassurance. "Of course I do." She got up. "I must go now. I'm sure that my husband is waiting up for me."

The following evening as they all gathered in the drawing room before supper, Sarah found it difficult to speak with any degree of civility to Justin. It had taken all her willpower to keep Elizabeth's confidence, to say nothing to Jonathan of the beastly way in which his sister was being treated.

Quite dispassionately, she observed Justin as he and Jonathan shared a drink before supper, but even to her newly observant eye, she could discern no evidence of his behavior in his demeanor. Indeed, he appeared cold to her, lacking even the rudimentary fire necessary to produce such heated emotions. Even his sermons, she reflected, while filled with threats of dire damnation, lacked a basic intensity, so that at times he appeared to be merely shouting, rather than speaking from conviction.

And now, her gaze shifting to Jonathan, she saw that her husband was growing restless under Justin's steady barrage of words.

"Have you seen this yet?" Justin was asking Jonathan as he handed him a copy of the weekly *Genuis*.

Taking the small tabloid offered him, Jonathan

scanned the story headlined on the first sheet. "It doesn't surprise me," he commented, putting the newspaper on a table. "As you know, I agree with Mr. Garrison, up to a point," he said. "However, he is far too radical in his ideas."

"How can you agree with him at all?" Justin put in dryly. "His ideas on Abolition are insane! He is fortunate that Francis Todd has merely instigated a libel suit. What Mr. Garrison really deserves is a sound thrashing!"

"I agree that Mr. Garrison is a bit enthusiastic in his campaign for Abolition," Jonathan remarked mildly, but Sarah could sense that he was trying to control the usual stab of annoyance that gripped him whenever Justin spoke. "Even you must agree, though," he went on, "that the man is entitled to his opinion. And to express that opinion in his own newspaper."

"Oh, I doubt sincerely that he will have the newspaper much longer," Justin remarked, his tone leaving no doubt that he was delighted with that possibility. "A lawsuit of this magnitude is bound to break him."

"If Mr. Garrison loses his paper, I'm certain that he'll try again."

"I really don't understand your attitude, Jonathan." Justin stared accusingly. "The very cotton you use in the mill comes from the South! What do you suppose will happen if that supply is shut off?"

"Why would it be?"

"If Abolition becomes a fact, who do you think will work in the fields? The cotton will lie there, rotting, and your supply will be cut off!"

A deep sigh met that assessment. "The cotton will not rot," Jonathan replied tiredly. "The workers I employ are paid a wage. There's no reason why the plantation owners can't do the same."

This attitude particularly incensed Justin, whose normally pale face flushed with indignation. Jonathan had to be the only manufacturer of cotton cloth in the North, perhaps the whole country, who viewed Garrison with something that approached tolerance. It would serve him right, Justin thought now, if the slaves *were* freed, for that would surely stop the flow of cotton and, subsequently, shut down the mills and factories. Only a fool could not see the consequences of William Lloyd Garrison's idiotic proposals.

Again Jonathan picked up the paper, purposefully blocking out Justin's answering retort. The trial, he read, was not scheduled to begin until March. Early this month, at the beginning of November, a man named Francis Todd had transported, by ship, seventy-five Negroes who were then consigned to slavery in the South. The vessel had departed from Boston, and this had so incensed William Lloyd Garrison—that outspoken foe of slavery—that he had begun a vicious editorial campaign against Todd, for which he was now being sued for libel.

With relief, Jonathan now heard Phillips announce supper, and he stepped forward to help Sarah to her feet. When they were at last seated at the table, Justin bowed his head and, in stentorian tones, said grace.

They were halfway through the meal when Elizabeth, an enigmatic smile upon her lips, informed them all of the coming child.

It was hard to tell who was more surprised: Justin, Jonathan, or Rachel. Aleceon, as usual, had not come home for the evening meal.

With a small gasp of surprise, Sarah realized that Elizabeth had not told her husband about the event until this very moment.

Rachel's sharp eye flew from her daughter to Justin, and back again. She and Jonathan began to speak at once, their congratulations both sincere and assiduous, although Rachel's felicitations seemed to be tinged with relief, Sarah noticed.

Sarah herself was probably the only one who noticed the frankly disbelieving look that Justin cast in his wife's direction. But when Jonathan turned toward him, Justin seemed to gain control of himself, coolly acknowledging the proffered well-wishes and murmuring something that Sarah could not hear.

Sarah found the balance of the meal a strain, anxiously glancing first at Elizabeth, then at Justin, and fervently hoping that the coming child would ease the situation between them.

Jonathan tried to persuade his sister to remain at Somerset Hall until the baby was born, but, surprisingly, both Justin and Elizabeth were in agreement on that point. Their house was completed; and they would move the following week as planned.

Chapter 18

Disconsolate, his attitude that of a defeated man, Aleceon sat down at an unoccupied table and ordered a drink.

At an adjoining table, two men were discussing the news of Mr. Garrison's conviction, arguing, at times heatedly, as to the justification of his sentencing. But Aleceon's thoughts were turned so far inward that he did not even hear their words.

How was it possible? he was thinking with true disbelief. He had almost done it. In the past six months, he had recovered more than four of the six hundred dollars he owed, helped, at times, by Sarah's paltry contributions.

But now, tonight, luck had once again turned on him, leaving him with a debt in excess of five hundred dollars. Although Rose had not as yet pressed him for payment, he knew that that happy circumstance would not go on forever.

He had, only a short time before, left Kitty, and while she had been generous enough with her personal favors, she had sadly refused him the benefits of the little glass vial. This deprivation now added a restless nervousness to his cheerless state of mind, and he kept clenching and unclenching his fists in an effort to control the shaking of his hands. He felt physically ill; even the relative dimness of his surroundings seemed fused with a brilliant glare that pained his eyes.

In a convulsive movement, his hand clutched the glass and in one swallow he downed the whiskey. A devastating feeling of impotence swept over him and his heart pounded wildly, giving his face a flushed and feverish look.

Another drink was placed before him and he eagerly

consumed it, grateful for the raw warmth that seemed momentarily to calm him.

"Aleceon? My God, is it you?"

Startled, he looked up, and recognizing the well-dressed man who had spoken, blinked and exclaimed: "Lucas!" Automatically, he gripped the outstretched hand, and without waiting for an invitation, Lucas Hockings sat down. Viewing the fawn-colored frock coat and yellow silk vest with its small pearl buttons, Aleceon observed: "You must be doing well."

A short, mirthless laugh greeted this statement as Lucas ordered a drink for himself. "It's not I but Christian who is doing well." The words were laced with bitterness. "You've heard of Hockings Metals?" As Aleceon nodded in affirmation, he went on. "Christian owns it; started it three years ago."

"My God, you must be rich!" Aleceon blurted out, with no little envy. Although he had heard of the name before, he had no reason to suppose that the flourishing enterprise belonged to the same Hockings he had known. Who would have thought that that dolt Christian could have become so successful? He was stunned.

Again there was that laugh. "Not I, my friend, not I. I work for Christian, that's all." He regarded Aleceon with sardonic amusement.

"And your brother, Will?"

Lucas shook his head. "He loves the inn too much to leave. Besides, my father passed away last year and now Will runs it all. Christian wanted to bring him and my mother to Boston, but they want to stay where they are, for the time being, anyway." He looked about him with avid eyes, then returned his attention to Aleceon. "How long have you been coming here?"

"A while," Aleceon replied noncommittally, dejection returning in full force.

They sat and drank, and it was close to dawn when Aleceon, his speech slurring noticeably, related his predicament and the horrendous debt he had incurred.

Lucas listened attentively and then shook his head when Aleceon was through. "I wish I could help you," he said with liquor-induced generosity. "But, like you, I live on the charitable inclinations of others." He grunted, shifting in the chair, his close-set blue eyes narrowing beneath heavy brows. "Here we are, the Enrights and the Hockingses," his hand swept in an arc as he pointed first to Aleceon and then to himself. "And neither of us has a dollar we can call our own." He slammed his fist down on the table. "That's not right, Aleceon! We should take steps to correct our unfortunate circumstances. We should take what is rightfully ours." He looked at his old acquaintance with a sharp intensity. "And since yours is the most pressing problem, we shall begin with the Enrights."

Lucas smiled wickedly, thinking that at last he would have his revenge on both Sarah and his brother. He was due payment from them both, and it was time to collect.

In the library, at Somerset Hall, Sarah listened to the late March wind as it howled and raged, sweeping across the land from the sea with a vengeance.

The weather had been threatening all day, and she had canceled the one social call she had planned for this Tuesday, sending Phillips with a message of regret. She wondered whether the storm would continue through tomorrow. Wednesday was the day she usually rode the seven miles into Boston, to shop, to visit with friends, to return a social call.

She frowned, thinking of her trip the week before. The social tea, given by the wife of a prominent Boston publisher, had at first been boring. Sarah usually attended these functions with an eye more to duty than to pleasure. A great many of the women were wives of the customers who patronized the mill, and Sarah felt duty-bound to attend.

But her boredom hadn't lasted long. Her hostess, a petite woman whose hands were in constant motion, had gushingly reported on Boston's newest member of Society.

"And he is so handsome," she trilled, unaware of Sarah's wandering attention. "He owns Hockings Metals," she went on. "But he has just purchased a small publishing company. I've invited Mrs. Hockings to join our next gathering. I'm certain that the two of you will have something in common. I understand that she's from Whitlow. Didn't you once tell me that you and Mr. Enright used to live there?"

Sarah was grateful that she had been seated during this outpouring, since she could manage no more than an inane smile, which she hoped approximated interest.

How she managed until three o'clock, when the tea was over, she didn't know. She did know that she would never attend a gathering if Jena were to be there. It would reopen a wound that might never heal.

Christian was in Boston. Over the past week, the thought came unbidden throughout the course of her day. Even the Book Committee for the School of Taunset, of which she was chairwoman, and in which she felt a vital interest, could not claim her attention.

It was six years since she had last seen him. Why, then, was his face still so vivid? She had only to close her eyes to see him, see the shock of red-gold hair, the blue eyes, the lean, well-muscled body. The image had taunted her on more than one sleepless night throughout these years.

He had made no effort to contact her. Did that mean he no longer loved her? Had forgotten her?

She gave a small moan of despair and, sitting down, reached for her embroidery, which she attacked with dogged determination, while, outside, the wind grew stronger.

The torrential rain came just before midnight, and along the shores the waves pounded viciously at the impediment of rocks that blocked their passage farther inland.

"Sounds like a nor'easter," Jonathan commented, entering the library. "I've told Phillips to secure all shutters, and batten down as best as possible."

His words were punctuated by a great gust of air that roared down the chimney just at that moment, and in dismay Sarah watched the spray of gray ash that powdered the polished wood floor about the hearth.

"I've never seen the weather so fierce," she remarked as Jonathan poured himself a drink from the glass decanter on the rosewood table.

"Don't be alarmed, darling," he said, coming to sit

beside her. "The house is sturdy. I've made certain of that." Gently, his hand touched the smoothness of her cheek.

She was about to reply when Phillips entered, followed by Peggy, who was standing in the doorway, dripping with rain, her face flushed. The maid was the only one of the staff who had accompanied Elizabeth when she and Justin had moved into their new house some months before.

"Peggy, what are you doing out in weather like this? And at this hour!" Sarah exclaimed, getting up. "Come closer to the fire, you're wet through!"

"I can't do that, ma'am," the girl protested earnestly. "I have to get back right away. It's Mrs. Lansing. Her time's come."

"Oh, my God," Jonathan said, rising. He put the glass down and advanced toward them, his face etched with rigid concern. "It'll be impossible to get the doctor out here in this weather." He frowned at Peggy in an accusatory manner. "The child isn't due for another two weeks!"

"I know that, sir," Peggy said, close to tears, "but it's comin' anyways."

"When did it begin?" Sarah asked quickly, trying to mask her dismay.

"About four hours ago," Peggy replied, and hastily took a step backward as Jonathan shouted at her.

"Four hours! My God, why did you wait this long!"

"It wasn't me, sir," Peggy hastened to explain, truly upset. Her tears now joined and mingled with the wetness on her cheeks. "The reverend said no doctor was necessary, that a woman having a baby was no more than God's natural order of things." Now she broke out in audible sobs. If Master Jonathan was angry with her, she could just imagine how the reverend would act when he learned that she had disobeyed him. "But I can't help her," she said in a choked voice. "I don't know what to do!"

"Is Reverend Lansing with her now?" asked Sarah, appalled by this latest evidence of Justin's disregard for his wife.

"Yes, ma'am. He hasn't left her side since it started. He's... he's praying."

Jonathan stared at the wet and terrified face before him, his expression helpless and angry by turns while Sarah turned to the butler.

"Phillips, get Mrs. Bowe," she instructed. "Hurry!" Then she turned to her husband. "Don't worry, darling. Everything will be all right. With Mrs. Bowe's assistance, I can see to Elizabeth."

At this, Peggy's face crumpled into relief, so glad was she that someone else would now take charge. But she remarked in a doubtful voice, "I'm not sure the reverend will let you in her room."

"He'll let us in," Jonathan stated grimly.

Phillips returned, carrying Sarah's wraps and Jonathan's cloak. Mrs. Bowe, heavily shawled, plodded with her heavy steps right behind him.

"Don't bother to awaken my mother," Jonathan instructed Phillips, taking the cloak. "There's no reason for her to be needlessly upset." At the front door, he halted, swearing softly. "We can't take the carriage, not in this wind!"

"It's only a mile or so," Sarah said. "We can walk."

"That'll take too long," Jonathan pointed out. "Can you ride a horse?"

"If I have to," said a determined Sarah, but Charity Bowe's face blanched at the suggestion.

"Master Jonathan, I ain't never been on a horse!" She was about to protest further, but Jonathan took hold of her plump arm.

"Then it's about time you were," he said brusquely. "You can ride with me. There will be nothing for you to do but hang on." He looked at Peggy. "You ride with Mrs. Enright. Come on, we're wasting time, and the weather will only get worse before it gets better."

A short while later, the two horses, each carrying their burden of two people, cautiously picked their way through the howling blackness, instinct alone keeping them on the roadway.

Jonathan, in the lead, allowed his horse no more than a brisk walk in spite of the urgency of the situation; he was too conscious of the slick mud underfoot and Sarah's inexperienced hand on the reins of her mare to attempt a faster gait. Seated in front of him, her bulk taking up most of the saddle, Mrs. Bowe trembled and whimpered, hanging onto the pommel, her eyes closed tightly against wind, rain, and fright.

It could not have been more than fifteen minutes, although it seemed like an eternity, before he at last saw the lighted windows glowing like beacons ahead of them. At last, with a sigh of relief that was disdainfully flung aside by the wind, he dismounted and helped the others to do the same.

Jonathan went into the library to wait, having issued strict orders to Sarah that if Justin refused her entrance to Elizabeth's bedroom, or tried to prevent her from doing what needed to be done, she should call him immediately.

Surprisingly, however, Justin said nothing when they entered. He was kneeling by the bed, hands clasped and eyes closed, his thin dry lips moving in barely audible prayer. At the sight of him, Sarah felt a surge of revulsion. Could God listen to one so sick in spirit? she wondered distractedly.

"Justin," she said quietly, trying to quell the flood of anger that flared through her. "Please, go downstairs and wait with Jonathan. Mrs. Bowe and I will attend to Elizabeth."

His eyes opened and stared at her for a moment, and in his pale face they seemed like bits of green ice. He seemed about to protest, but just then Elizabeth's scream rent the stillness, vying with the raging wind and blending with it. He studied his wife for some moments, his expression cold and unsympathetic; at last he got to his feet.

"I will wait in the adjoining room," he announced. With a censorious glance at the woman upon the bed, and with no words of comfort for her, he left.

"Sarah," Elizabeth gasped, reaching out a hand. "Thank God you've come." She wet her lips and panted with the abnormal exertion required of her frail body.

"Everything will be all right," Sarah soothed, stroking the damp forehead. "Mrs. Bowe and I will see to everything. Set your mind at ease, darling."

The hours went by with only Elizabeth's screams, punctuated by the continuing wind, to mark the passing time.

It was dawn by the clock, although the darkness had not abated, when the child's cry announced an end to Elizabeth's travail. Close on that sound, Justin entered the room.

Her eyes blinded by tears, Sarah put the child in Elizabeth's arms, then wearily stepped aside as Justin, leaning on his cane, approached the canopied bed.

The baby was a girl, a tiny creature whose face held the promise of its mother's beauty, perfect in every way—save one. Its left foot was twisted inward, withered and useless.

Justin, viewing his infant daughter for the first time, blanched. He glared with undisguised loathing at Elizabeth, who was regarding him placidly, her face lighted by a strange glow of satisfaction.

"It is God's judgment upon you!" he choked at last.

She smiled coldly, disdainfully. "No, Justin," she answered quietly, ignoring the flush of rage that crept up his throat, covering the pale skin with crimson. "It is God's judgment upon you. You insisted upon a child. Insisted that I pray for one." She paused, seeing the pounding and pulsing at his temples, seeing the distress and anxiety in his eyes. And she was unmoved. "God has answered my prayers, Justin," she commented softly. "You have a child." Carefully, she removed the blanket that partially covered the infant. "Don't you think that she resembles you?" she asked maliciously. "Look upon her, Justin. See what God has granted you."

"You blasphemous strumpet!" He paused, breathing heavily, his rage so great that he felt mortally threatened by it. "Thou foul beast!" Then he raised his cane, and Sarah's hand flew to her throat as she gasped in horror. She was about to step forward. Elizabeth, holding the child in her arms, made no move to defend herself, but the look in her eyes halted his movement. There was something terrible in that look, something so powerful that it caused Justin to take a step backward.

"I will never again share your bed," he announced

in a thick voice that was hardly recognizable. "You've birthed a cripple! It is all the family you'll get from me!"

Turning, he limped from the room, looking at neither Sarah nor Mrs. Bowe, who was viewing him with a stunned look upon her kindly face.

Sarah rushed to Elizabeth's side, but before she could speak, Elizabeth said: "Isn't she beautiful? Isn't she, Sarah? Isn't my daughter just beautiful?"

Sarah, her eyes filled with tears, leaned over and kissed Elizabeth's brow. "That she is," she whispered. Reaching out, she took hold of the infant's tiny hands.

And Sarah saw that the child *was* beautiful. The skin was the color of pale cream and glowed with a roseate tint in the light of the bedside lamp. She was neither red nor wrinkled, and her pale gilt hair shone like a silver halo about her small, well-shaped head. "What will her name be?" Sarah asked.

Still viewing her daughter with adoring eyes, her face reflecting unutterable tenderness, Elizabeth said simply: "Hannah. She shall be called Hannah." And in those few brief moments, her faith in God returned, stronger than ever before. For here, in her arms, was living proof of His existence. Only God could have created this beautiful, wonderful, precious child she now held so close to her breast.

It was midmorning before Jonathan and Sarah, accompanied by Mrs. Bowe, returned to Somerset Hall. This time, they rode in the carriage, which Phillips had driven over earlier. The two horses were roped to the rear, dutifully following.

The rain had stopped, and the fierceness of the wind had diminished, but it was still blowing briskly with a bite in it that was both chilling and uncomfortable. Overhead, the heavy black clouds parted now and again, allowing a golden sun to fan out across the countryside, then capriciously closed ranks once more, withholding the promise of a clear day.

When they arrived, Rachel and Aleceon were waiting. Together they sat down to a late breakfast, simply and hastily prepared by Betsy with the aid of Lottie.

Sarah noticed that Aleceon was looking haggard, as if he had not slept the night before, but she was so weary from her long night's vigil that she had neither the strength nor the inclination to comment upon it. Caroline and Benjamin entered the room, and although they had already eaten, Sarah permitted the children to join them.

Adding milk and sugar to the hot rich tea, Jonathan haltingly told his mother of the birth of her latest grandchild.

For a moment, Rachel was silent, viewing the beefsteak and eggs before her without appetite. Then she said: "I will go to her later today. No doubt she is resting now." She regarded Jonathan thoughtfully. "Perhaps it would be wise if I were to stay with her for a while."

Jonathan was relieved that the suggestion came from his mother. He had had the same thought. There was something sorely amiss in the house of his sister. He did not know what it was; perhaps it was better that he not know. His feelings for Justin were such that he could have cheerfully throttled the man with no provocation at all. But Elizabeth never complained, so she must be reasonably content.

"That's a good idea," he told Rachel. "I'm sure Elizabeth would appreciate having you with her. I've told Phillips to send for the doctor. I think both Elizabeth and the child should be properly examined."

"Can I go with Grandmama?" Caroline spoke up, looking from her father to Rachel. "I would love to see Aunt Elizabeth's new baby." Her gray eyes danced with excitement at the prospect.

"I don't think so, dear," Sarah interjected. "Perhaps next week..." The child began to protest, and Aleceon, who had this while been sitting in silent boredom engrossed with his own problems, at last spoke.

"Don't fuss, Caro." He rumpled her chestnut-brown curls. "If you like, you can come to Boston with me today. We will look at the ships, and if you behave yourself, you can look in the shop windows to your heart's content."

"And eat in a restaurant?" Caroline wanted to know, gazing upon her uncle with shining eyes.

"That, too."

Sarah threw her brother a grateful look. For all his failings, Aleceon seemed genuinely fond of Caroline, or perhaps it was because the child so idolized her young uncle. Occasionally, when she cajoled him, Aleceon would take Caroline on an outing, but this was the first time that he had volunteered to do so.

Chapter 19

Carefully, his hand wet with perspiration despite the coolness of the April evening, Aleceon turned the dial on the safe. The picture that had hitherto concealed the safe—a dreary watercolor of some unknown, inane countryside—had been tossed carelessly on one of the two wing chairs in the room.

In only a moment he would know whether his observations during the past weeks had been correct. Most days when he returned home, Jonathan went directly into the study and deposited any money paid to him at the mill into this safe. The mill had been in operation for the past three months, but because the housing was only partially completed, and the quota of employees not quite at maximum strength, they were not yet in full production.

Each day, Aleceon had contrived to be in this room, hidden by the folds of the heavy, plum-colored draperies. It had taken many days before he was certain of the safe's combination because, at times, Jonathan's body hid the manipulations of his hand as he whirled the dial first right, then left, then right again.

Aleceon did not hurry. At this hour, everyone would be having supper. His absence, he knew, would go unquestioned, since there was nothing unusual about his missing the evening meal.

By his side, Lucas Hockings was watching the proceedings with interest. Only moments before, Aleceon had opened the window to the study, and Lucas, waiting outside, had climbed through it into the room. A single lamp on the desk was lit. It now flickered uneasily in the draft from the opened window, throwing moving shadows across Aleceon's back as he studiously applied himself to his task.

So intent were they that they never heard the door

open, even though young Benjamin, unaware that the room was occupied, had made no effort to be quiet. He had, earlier in the day, left one of his wooden soldiers on his father's desk. It was now his intention to retrieve it, in spite of the fact that he had already been summoned to the table.

For the moment, Benjamin just stood there, his mind not quite taking in the scene his eyes were viewing. He blinked, more in surprise than concern, at the sight of the two men.

"What are you doing?" the boy said at last, coming closer, his head tilted in curiosity.

Both men spun around, startled; Aleceon was the first to recover. "Get out of here!" he hissed to his nephew.

"You're... you're trying to get at Father's safe!" Benjamin exclaimed, realization dawning. He was perfectly aware that no one, not even the servants, was permitted near the wall safe. Not even his mother had ever dared to touch it.

"You little bastard," Lucas said harshly, lunging at the small figure. In a moment his hands were about Benjamin's neck.

Taken aback by this frenzied reaction, Aleceon quickly intervened. The noise of the ensuing scuffle brought Jonathan, Betsy—who had been on her way to fetch Benjamin—and Sarah into the room.

"What the devil's going on here!" Jonathan demanded, his eyes darting from his son to his brother-in-law. Lucas was on the floor where he had fallen in his altercation with Aleceon. Jonathan did not at first recognize him, although he saw him lying there. Quickly he walked to the desk and took out a pistol from a drawer.

At first he thought that Aleceon had surprised an intruder, but as Benjamin, his voice tearful, explained what had taken place, Jonathan's expression traveled the gamut from bewilderment to disbelief to utter fury.

"This is the end, Aleceon!" he said grimly, ignoring Sarah's pleading look. "I have put up with your irresponsibility long enough. A scoundrel I can abide, but a thief I will not have in my house!" A wave of loathing washed over him, but his hand, as he held the pistol, was steady. "You have exactly one hour to collect your belongings and get out. If I even so much as see you or your colleague there in Taunset again, I will have you both arrested."

Sarah hastily instructed the gaping servants to leave and take Benjamin with them. Then she put her hand on her husband's arm. "Please, Jonathan. I'm certain that this can all be explained...."

He shook her off, his face implacable, unrelenting. There was an air of ruthlessness about him, of deadly determination, that was reflected in his tightly compressed lips.

"No!" he said, his gaze still fixed upon Aleceon, who was watching him with sullen resentment. "I've had enough. I've been patient for too long. I will not have this sort of example around to influence my son."

Lucas now got to his feet and Sarah was engulfed with confusion at the sight of this man who had suddenly, so inexplicably, appeared in her life once again. She simply could not imagine what he was doing here, in her own home!

He was trembling with rage and frustration. "Your son!" Lucas spat, baring his teeth in an ugly grimace. He glared at Sarah, then at Jonathan. "That's not your son, you fool!" He began to laugh hysterically, immensely enjoying the sight of Sarah's suddenly ashen face.

"Lucas, for the love of God, stop it! You don't know what you're saying," she cried out to him.

Confused, Jonathan looked curiously at his wife. "You know this man?"

"It's Lucas Hockings," she said in a voice that was barely a whisper.

Jonathan's gaze traveled back to Lucas, whom he only vaguely remembered, and who had, in the intervening years, grown sideburns and a mustache that altered his face considerably. Slowly, Jonathan walked around the desk and stood before Lucas, the pistol still held firmly in his hand. "What are you talking about?" He glared now at Aleceon. "Is this another one of your tricks?"

His face defiant, Lucas responded with another ugly

laugh, and, at the sound, Sarah felt cold and numb. She could not speak, could not move. She could only stand there and listen in growing horror to the words that were like stabs in her heart.

"I don't know about your other brats," Lucas said, his chin thrust forward belligerently, "but Benjamin is my brother's son."

Jonathan stared at him blankly, and this only enraged Lucas further. He had needed only one look at Benjamin to see the face of his hated brother. There could be no mistake. "Go on, ask her!" he shouted, pointing at Sarah, who appeared as still as if she had been carved from marble. "Ask her why your son was born a scant seven months after you were married." A shot in the dark, but one that, he saw with satisfaction, had found its mark. "Look at him, you fool! Look and see the son of Christian Hockings!"

Slowly, very slowly, Jonathan faced Sarah. At the sight of her white face and parted lips, he could not form the question. A black cloud of anguish descended upon him, causing a roaring in his ears, and he knew the answer.

Lucas's laughter was the only sound in the room; even Aleceon seemed bewildered by this turn of events.

Suddenly that sound became too much for Jonathan to bear, and raising the gun slightly, he fired.

The laughter ceased immediately as Lucas Hockings fell, a bright stain of crimson quickly darkening his white shirt. Jonathan opened his mouth to speak—and then pitched forward onto the floor.

Jolted from her trancelike state, Sarah screamed, bringing the servants rushing into the room. Phillips moved forward quickly and, with the aid of the others, picked Jonathan up and placed him on the sofa. His eyes were open but unseeing, and his mouth was slack. Only the rise and fall of his chest indicated life.

"The doctor!" Sarah said shrilly, hysteria descending upon her like a miasmic fog. "Run, fetch him!" She turned toward Aleceon, her eyes bright with loathing. "Get out," she ordered, her voice ragged with grief and fear and hatred. It was her own brother who had brought this serpent into her house. "I never want to see you again."

He gave a shaky laugh, unsettled by all that had so unexpectedly happened. "My being deprived of your tedious company does not faze me in the least, my dearest sister," he muttered with more bravado than he was feeling. Unsteadily, as if drunk, Aleceon moved from the room, almost stumbling over Caroline as she stood half concealed by the door frame, viewing the scene with fright and confusion. Angrily, he pushed the small figure aside.

At the foot of the stairs he paused, and, with thoughtful eyes, turned to look at his sister as she stood in the doorway, comforting her weeping daughter. And she had dared to preach to him! She with her bastard son. He watched a moment longer, then, with an ugly half-smile upon his lips, he ascended the stairs to pack.

For the next hour or so there was a flurry of activity as Jonathan was moved to his room and made as comfortable as possible. The doctor arrived and, after a brief examination, told Sarah what she already knew. Jonathan had suffered a massive stroke.

The constable, too, arrived. Forcing herself to bear a semblance of calmness, Sarah related that Lucas Hockings had been shot when caught in the act of robbery. Of Aleceon's presence she said nothing; Betsy, by her side, fully corroborated her words.

It was after midnight when Sarah finally went to the bedroom across the hall from the room she normally shared with her husband.

Too numb and exhausted even to undress, she collapsed in a chair, her mind in limbo. The tears should have been there, but they weren't; she felt nothing. Even the images and thoughts of her brother that paraded before her unwilling mind brought no real grief, only a detached sadness.

When she opened her eyes the next morning, Sarah saw that dawn had just begun to lighten the sky.

She hadn't slept long. When she sat up, still in her clothes from the evening before, she was conscious of the leaden fatigue that pressed down on her with relentless force. She knew she should lie down again, but she also knew that she wouldn't be able to recapture the luxury of sleep.

She got up, wavering, steadying herself by placing a hand on the post of the canopied bed, until the room righted itself once more.

Then, with a quick, light step, she walked across the hall to check on Jonathan, praying that there had been an improvement, praying that he would get well again.

He was sleeping. His face in repose looked almost normal, but he was still lying in the same position as the night before.

Guilt tore at her at the sight of him. She almost cried out, and placed a palm across her mouth to still her emotions. He looked so helpless. He, with his strength, his pride, his ambition. And his dream.

Did he hate her now? More important, did he hate Benjamin? She realized that from this day forward, her marriage would never be the same. The relationship that had remained constant all these years was shifting beneath her like wet sand before the oncoming tide.

"Jonathan," she whispered, her voice ending on a sob. She longed to go to him, to comfort him, to tell him how sorry she was. But at last she turned and left the room.

She returned to the bedroom across the hall to find Betsy waiting, her face reflecting her concern as she viewed Sarah's weary movements.

Sarah was grateful for the woman's presence. Betsy was the one person with whom she could relax. There was no need of pretense, nor did Betsy now ask for any explanation. She alone of all the servants had remained in the room last night, and she knew exactly what had happened, and why.

She began to bustle about, murmuring soft admonishments, while she poured hot water, carried up from the kitchen, into a cast-iron tub.

"Yer should have stayed in bed," she grumbled, helping Sarah out of her clothes.

The bath relaxed the aching tension in her limbs, and by the time she was dressed and had eaten a light breakfast, Sarah was ready to face the doctor again. He had returned earlier, with a colleague from Boston to aid him in his examination of Jonathan.

The prognosis was the same. Little hope was offered for any change in Jonathan's condition.

The words left Sarah numb; she could absorb no more guilt than that which already had such a hold on her.

She spent the rest of the morning in the library, trying to focus her thoughts, to calm her chaotic nerves. It was almost noon when the butler announced the gentleman caller, and Sarah looked up to see Christian standing in the doorway.

She made no immediate movement, her shock too great for even a welcoming smile.

There, beneath the hat, which he quickly removed, was the shock of red-gold hair, the eyes warm and luminous and something else now, harder, it seemed. He had filled out, the promise of his masculine strength now fulfilled in the breadth of his shoulders, the muscular outline of his thighs. An eternity of time had passed, yet no time, really. So much had changed, yet so much remained the same. For in that first glance, she knew that she still loved him, would always love him.

"Sarah." He pronounced the name as if it were a benediction.

She saw how he had changed in these past eight years. Almost twenty-eight, he had lost the look of youthful anticipation in his eyes. He was now cloaked with a patina of self-assurance that gave him a commanding air. There was an undeniable aura of sophistication about him that added to the charisma he exuded.

She closed her eyes, then opened them again, trying to force her thoughts into an organized channel. "Come in, Christian," she said quietly. Then, turning to Phillips, said: "Bring whiskey for Mr. Hockings; a sherry for me." Again she regarded Christian. "You're looking well," she remarked, her voice seeming to tremble in her ears. Sitting down on the settee, she arranged her pale-blue silk gown with ice-cold fingers. "I can't tell you how sorry I am...," she began, but he halted her words with his own.

"Don't, Sarah. I know that none of this was your fault."

But it's all my fault, she thought in anguish. They were silent while the butler brought refreshments, and only after he left did Christian again speak.

"I can't say that I'm happy about what has happened; yet you must know that there was little love lost between Lucas and me."

"He was your brother," she whispered.

"He was," he agreed calmly. "And for that reason alone, I mourn him." He drank his whiskey, then stared at her in a brooding manner. "Lucas was fated to meet the end that he did," he observed solemnly. "If it hadn't been your husband, it would have been one of a score of others. He swaggered through life, making enemies with each step."

Uncomforted, she turned away. Seeing that face, so lovely even in sorrow, Christian longed to take this woman in his arms, to kiss away that expression of regret and remorse.

For a moment, he was tempted. But, steeling himself, he said: "Don't blame yourself, Sarah. Men merely follow their destiny; they are powerless to do otherwise."

An awkward silence fell with the conclusion of his words. Sarah nervously twisted her hands in her lap. She moistened her parched lips. "I...I understand that you're doing well," she said at last. She didn't look at him; she feared looking at him. He had sat down beside her on the settee, and she could feel the warmth of his body reaching out to her, taunting her with its nearness.

"As well as can be expected," he answered.

She thought of moving, but her limbs wouldn't respond. Her body and her mind worked at odds with one another, and she clasped her hands even tighter, afraid they would reach for him of their own accord. "When you sold the smithy, I wasn't sure where you had gone." Why did her voice sound so strange? she wondered. She cleared her throat in an effort to rid herself of the wavering sound.

"I was in New York for a while." He fell silent; then,

as if unable to help himself, he reached out and took her hands in his.

The physical contact sent a shock through her whole body. She had no desire, no will to pull away.

"Sarah," he said, his voice a mere whisper. "We can't continue to throw away our lives like this...."

That voice, she thought helplessly. She could turn away from him, away from that face that was as familiar to her as her own. But she couldn't turn away from that voice. It invaded her senses like a physical caress.

"God forgive me," he went on. "I'm almost grateful for what has happened. Grateful for the chance to see you again."

She wanted to speak, to tell him it was wrong to think such thoughts, but the words remained locked inside her, unborn beneath the weight of more pressing emotions.

"Sarah?"

The voice was cajoling, hypnotizing her with a longing that matched her own.

"These years I have stayed away from you, have not been of my choosing," he whispered. "I can't tell you of the countless times when I wanted to see you, to come to you." He placed his hands on her shoulders, turning her toward him. "Do you think that having found you again, I will let you go?"

Sarah looked into his dear face. From deep within her, she found the strength to meet his gaze with steady eyes. "It's too late, Christian," she said slowly, her voice barely audible over the beating of her heart. "It's too late."

His hands fell away and he clenched them into fists. "It's not too late," he said to her. "It will never be too late. I love you as much today as when I last saw you."

She could listen to no more. Her throat ached with the pressure of keeping her thoughts confined, and she knew that if he did not leave, and soon, she would reach for him. And she would never let him go.

Sarah stood up, and immediately Christian got to his feet. He stared at her but she would not meet his eye. She could not.

At last he emitted a deep sigh and, picking up his hat, walked toward the door. "I know about Jonathan," he said quietly, turning to look at her again. "If ever you need help, please come to me."

He opened the door and stopped abruptly as he saw the two children. He noticed the girl first, and his heart twisted within him. No need to ask if this was Sarah's daughter. It was all there; the hair, the eyes—no, that was not quite right. They were the same color, that was all. Here, in this child, he saw an impishness that was alien to Sarah. These eyes had never known want, hunger, distress. They had known only love and acceptance.

Briefly, he regarded the small, serious face of Benjamin Enright as the boy looked up at him. "Excuse me," said Christian, stepping aside.

Benjamin looked past this stranger at his mother. "I'm sorry, Mama," he said to her. "I didn't know that you had company."

Sarah paled, but her voice was steady. "It's all right, children. Come in. Mr. Hockings was just leaving."

Christian watched as the children scampered into the room. The young girl threw him a shy smile as she passed by him, hurrying to catch up with her brother. Christian watched a moment longer; then, with a sad smile, he turned and was gone.

Bereft, Sarah clutched her son to her in a fierce embrace. Then she wept, overcome with a sense of loss and regret for what might have been.

"Mama?"

Sarah took a deep breath, brushing her cheek with the back of her hand. She smiled tremulously at the concerned expression on her son's face. The boy looked as if he were about to cry, and she hugged him. "It's all right, Benjamin," she said softly. "I'm all right now."

He regarded her doubtfully, and she patted his cheek. "Run along now. It's almost time for dinner." She kissed him, and then Caroline, who was staring at her, wide-eyed. She'd never seen her mother cry before, and was greatly unsettled at the sight.

Sarah kept the smile in place until the children left, then the feeling of weariness returned, stronger now.

Walking into the hall, she began slowly to climb the

stairs. It was time she looked in on Jonathan, to see if he was comfortable, to make certain that he lacked for nothing.

She ran her fingertips across her face to make certain that no trace of her tears remained. Outwardly, they were gone; inwardly, her heart wept. My love, my love, she whispered to herself as Christian's image pervaded her mind.

Why had she sent him away? she thought frantically. Having found him after all these years, how could she have let him go? "We can't continue to throw away our lives," Christian had said. But wasn't that just what she'd done?

She mustn't think of such things, she told herself. To do so was to invite madness.

"Lass? Are yer all right?"

Sarah started, having been unaware of Betsy's approach. "I'm fine," she managed.

"Dinner's about ready," Betsy said to her, frowning. "And afterward, yer'd better take a nap. Yer look all done in."

Sarah nodded. "I'll be right down. I want to look in on Jonathan first."

Turning, Sarah walked the few steps to the bedroom door. Her hand on the cool smoothness of the knob, she hesitated a moment to gather the vestiges of her waning strength. Then she entered, her turmoil carefully concealed.

Chapter 20

On the way back to his house on Beacon Street, Christian stared moodily out of the carriage as it ambled along Charles Street, with its wooden piles that fended off the high tides of the Bay.

In the insistent, monotonous clopping of the horses' hooves, he seemed to hear Sarah's name repeated, over and over. But then, many things over the years had provoked her name, her image, her glorious eyes, to appear before him. He wouldn't have thought it possible, but she had grown more lovely, more desirable, with the passing years. At times, his longing had almost defeated him; how often he had wanted to throw caution to the winds and race to her side. But, he would always wonder, did he have the right to destroy the fabric of her life? He had thought not.

Now he wasn't so sure. He tried to recapture his pleasure at seeing her again. But their parting had left him with only the bitter ashes of longing.

And yet, through it all, he knew her feelings had not changed, any more than his had. Time was a feeble enemy against their love. He was convinced of that now. Though it gave him small measure of comfort, he clung to that thought, desperately.

Sighing deeply, Christian peered out of the window. He would soon be home. Home to Jena, and home to his daughter, Rebecca.

His brow creased as he thought of his little girl. Rebecca should have been born some seven months after he and Jena married.

But she hadn't been. She was born almost a year afterward. Rebecca hadn't been born sooner for the simple reason that Jena had not been pregnant when they married. He didn't discover that bit of deception until two months after they had wed, when Jena learned she was truly pregnant—for the first time.

God, how he had hated her when he learned of her trickery. He could have killed her; knowing that, he had buried himself in his work, sleeping in the shop more often than not. When they moved to New York, he opened a new business, leasing the facilities initially, using the money from the sale of the smithy. Then he returned to Boston. He told himself that this was where he would have the greatest chance for success. But in his heart, he knew otherwise. It was Boston's proximity to Taunset that drew him back. Here only seven miles separated him from Sarah. Here there was a chance that, one day, they could meet, even by accident.

Regardless of his reasons, the move had been beneficial. He had experimented, at first with ornamental ironwork, which brought in a much greater profit than the more utilitarian contrivances such as nails, pots, and shovels. From there, he had gone on to small machines, and finally, to making machine parts. It was far easier and cheaper to replace a broken part than to purchase a whole new piece of machinery. Later, he added the larger machinery. At last, he had enough capital to expand, with the eventual result being Hockings Metals.

When Rebecca was born, his rage and anger subsided somewhat. He loved his daughter fiercely, protectively; and, while he had no further use for Jena, she was, if nothing else, a satisfactory mother.

There had been one other child, a boy, who was stillborn. The birth had been particularly difficult, and Jena had almost lost her life. The doctor had advised no more children. With that last link broken, their own relationship had dissolved, at least the physical side of it.

Christian looked out of the window as the carriage passed an establishment identified by a neat plaque as Hockings Publishing Co. He had acquired the small firm some six months before, after Nathaniel Wilson, an idealist with a genius for ineptitude, had gone bankrupt.

Christian had made many changes, the first of which

had been to discard the hopelessly outdated wooden flatbeds, which were cumbersome and unreliable, replacing them with modern presses boasting cast-iron frames. Instead of importing them from London, he had had them made in his own factory. He had, however, kept the employees. There were only twelve, with two apprentices; in addition, he had installed Porter Quincy as manager, luring him from a New York publishing company by drastically raising his wage.

Now, after only six months in operation under the firm hand of Quincy, the small company was at last showing a profit.

The carriage rumbled along the cobbled streets, and Christian again thought of Sarah. Was she happy? Did she live her life with a never-ending ache as he did? He often had wondered, over the years, whether he had worked so hard to make a success of himself for her, knowing that somehow, someday they would be together again; knowing, too, when that day came, he had to be on her level. The Enrights' level.

Arriving at his imposing gray-stoned house, Christian entered to hear Rebecca's sharp cry. Taking the steps two at a time, he raced to his daughter's room.

The girl stood, hand against her flaming cheek as Jena reviled her in a shrill voice.

The child had inherited the best of both Christian's and Jena's physical qualities. Her long, thick hair was a dazzling copper color with burnished highlights that shone like threads of pure gold. Her eyes were a somewhat darker shade of blue than Christian's, and her fair skin was pale and translucent, except that now, under Jena's heavy hand, one side of her face was scarlet. She was a sweet child, fragile and quiet and demure. She was, however, given to daydreaming, and this, at times, produced a carelessness that enraged her mother.

"This is the second time this week that you have dirtied your frock!" Jena screamed, delivering another blow. "I will not have it! You are almost eight years old, time that you began to behave like a lady! Why can't you act more like Mary Simpson?"

"Be damned to Mary Simpson!" Christian interrupted curtly, entering the room. Startled, Jena turned around. He saw her face, distorted with anger, and was struck anew at how unlovely she was, a state of affairs that had nothing at all to do with her features. She was still slim and, he supposed, attractive, but the illusion was destroyed by the lines of constant ill temper.

"My daughter need emulate no one," he went on, quietly fixing his wife with a hard look.

Jena's eyes narrowed at his tone. "Your daughter!" she spat. "She is mine as well. And I do not propose to have her raised as a...pauper!" She thrust her chin out, delighted to see the stiffening in his body. "You may find them appealing, Christian, but I do not!" Beneath her elaborately coiffed hair, her features were hard and unrelenting as she viewed her husband with obvious scorn. She knew perfectly well where he had been, and the thought enraged her. After all these years, to have that little guttersnipe again enter her life! It was unthinkable. To Lucas and his unexpected demise, she gave no thought at all. He had been a fool, a parasite, and she considered his death most fortunate.

Christian opened his mouth to deliver a sharp retort, but then, seeing the anguish in Rebecca's eyes, he swallowed his words of recrimination. If he took his daughter's side, he knew that eventually Jena would have her revenge. Better that he talk to his wife in private, he decided and, turning, left the room.

That evening after supper, he joined Jena in the drawing room, which he seldom did, preferring instead the solitude of his own study. It was a pleasant, expensively furnished room, with only the finest woods and the most luxurious of carpets in evidence. The fireplace was of Italian marble, and even the tall vases that stood in the corners were of imported malachite.

After a small silence, he said: "I don't think you should punish Rebecca for soiling her dress." With effort he kept his voice mild, not wishing to start another argument, yet determined to make his feelings known on the subject.

Jena arched a brow, her manner unruffled. "Surely, Christian, you will leave the disciplining of our daughter to her mother. I want only what is best for her." She paused a moment before continuing, her expression unreadable. As soon as she had learned that Sarah, however fleetingly, had again entered her life, she had decided upon a course of action. Christian had to be bound to her, securely and forever. And there was only one way.

"If we ever have a son," she went on, "I promise you that I shall leave his upbringing to you." She watched in satisfaction as her words had the desired effect. Christian, she knew, yearned for a son. She was aware of how wistfully he watched his men friends when they spoke with pride of their sons. "Of course," she continued blithely, gesturing with a ringed hand, "it may be that we will never have a son. And for that, you can only blame yourself, Christian." She sat in rigid disapproval, daring him to speak.

As usual, Christian said nothing, unwilling to admit even to himself that he could no longer sleep with his wife. There was no amount of persuasion, no amount of seduction, no amount of cajoling that could arouse him enough to perform an act of love with a woman he abhorred. His mind, his body, his being, longed for the one woman he could not have.

Jena was not stupid. She had no idea of trying to seduce her husband, at least not physically. Emotionally, however...

Her voice grew soft as she walked toward him, her honey-colored gown rustling softly as she moved across the carpeted floor and knelt beside him. "Christian," she whispered, "you mustn't shut me out this way. I love you. All I have ever done, I did because I love you."

"Please, Jena," he said, about to turn away, but her hand on his arm held fast, fingers clutching.

"You've always wanted a son." Her eyes were bright as she studied him intently. "You need a son! Who is to benefit from all you've accomplished?"

Unconvinced, he looked down at her. "You know what the doctor said...."

Her grip tightened. "I don't care what he said. He's a fool!"

She watched him closely, instinctively knowing that if she asked him to share her bed for personal reasons, he would refuse. But a child! A son! She almost smiled at his expression of longing. There were ways, she knew, of preventing conception. She had no qualms whatsoever about using them. Once she got him back into her bed, she was confident she could keep him there—at least until a child was born. Since there would, of course, be no child, he would be returning to her bed for a long, long time.

"Christian," she murmured softly. "I, too, want a son. Your son..." With that, she released him, and walking from the room, did not turn around.

For long moments he stared into the fire with unseeing eyes. His marriage was no more than a mockery. Yet whose fault was that? Could he in all honesty blame Jena? He had done little, if anything, to make it work.

With a deep, despairing sigh, and slow steps, he followed his wife to her room.

Sarah allowed Tully to help her out of the carriage and onto the sunlit street in the midst of Boston's most prestigious group of shops. The May afternoon was pleasantly warm, with only a gentle breeze that was filled with the scent of apple blossoms.

"I expect that I'll be at least an hour," she told him.

"You just take your time with your shopping, Mrs. Enright," Tully said respectfully, his lined face showing each of his sixty years. "I'll wait for you right here."

"Thank you—" She fell silent, hearing her name called, and turned to see Christian.

He was smiling as he approached, well dressed in a bottle-green frock coat and pale yellow vest, across which a gold chain glinted in the sunlight.

"What are you doing in the city?" he inquired pleasantly, his delight at seeing her again quite evident in his blue eyes.

"I had planned to do some shopping," she replied, feeling flustered by his sudden appearance. She put a gloved hand to her hair as the gentle breeze loosened a tendril from under her wide-brimmed hat.

"Is it anything that you can't postpone for an hour or so?" he asked, smiling down at her. "I'd be delighted if you would have tea with me."

"I don't want to detain you," she faltered. "I'm sure you have more important matters to attend to."

"Nothing is more important to me than you," he murmured. Then he smiled. "As a matter of fact, I've been doing some shopping of my own. "Next week is my daughter's birthday." He fumbled in a pocket, then drew forth a small box. Opening it, he showed Sarah a small, exquisitely carved cameo. "Do you think she'll like it?"

"It's beautiful," Sarah exclaimed, examining the brooch.

He put the box back in his pocket. "Then it's settled. You'll join me?"

"I...," she began, but taking her arm firmly; Christian would not allow her to protest.

"There's a new restaurant just down the block. Come along, you can do your shopping afterward." He gave her no chance to refuse, and still holding her arm firmly, propelled her along the street. Only minutes later, they entered the elegantly appointed establishment.

"I'll order if you like," Christian offered when they were seated.

"Yes, please do," Sarah murmured, listening as he spoke to the waiter. Watching him, she was again struck by his manner. His eyes still held a look of gentleness and reassurance when he looked at her, but at other moments, she could see a cold, appraising look that he obviously presented to others. This was a much more confident man than the one she had known. She was drawn to his strength, felt almost helpless in the face of it.

At last he turned toward her, giving her his full attention. It was three weeks since he'd last seen her, and her face had lost the drawn, pale look she'd had the morning after the accident. She now appeared rested, and to him, as lovely as he had ever seen her. Her pelisse of gray-faced cloth was fashionably cut, with a full circular skirt and tight-fitting bodice that now, unbuttoned, revealed just a bit of the rose-colored dress she wore beneath.

"You're looking splendid, Sarah," he said softly, his admiration open. Her hair, he saw, was swept up in a loose pompadour beneath her hat, and secured with pins. He noted approvingly that she wore small pearl earrings. Jena was given to ostentation and, he thought, constantly overdid the accessories that she wore.

"I was thinking the same thing about you, Christian," Sarah admitted with a soft smile.

He chuckled easily. "I guess we've both changed," he acknowledged, leaning back slightly as the waiter placed their first course before them. As the aroma of the clear consommé wafted about, Sarah realized that she was indeed hungry.

"How is Jonathan?" Christian asked as they ate.

"He's about the same," she replied quietly.

He frowned, annoyed with himself for bringing up Jonathan's name. "I'm sorry," he said. "For everything."

"You have nothing to be sorry for," she said. "What happened was through no fault of yours."

Slowly, he put down his spoon and regarded her attentively. "I have never forgotten you, Sarah." As he spoke, his eyes never left her face. "Nor have my feelings for you changed in any way." He sighed deeply, toying with the spoon. "And it was all for nothing," he muttered, almost to himself.

"What do you mean?"

He was silent a moment, then, as if making a decision, he continued. "When I married Jena, I thought that she was carrying my child." His voice was so low that she bent forward slightly, studying him with care. "She wasn't," he admitted bitterly. "Rebecca was born almost a year after we married."

Sarah's face went white with shock, and for a moment she couldn't speak.

"It's true," he said, seeing her expression. Leaning forward, he took hold of her hand. It lay within his, cold and unmoving, as she continued to stare at him.

When she spoke, her voice sounded strange even to her own ears. "You mean Jena lost the child?" She felt lightheaded, disembodied; a curious sense of being outside herself, watching and listening to the words that Christian spoke, but unable to accept their reality.

"I mean she was never pregnant," he said bluntly. "Oh, God, Sarah. It's you I loved, you I *still* love." His jaw tightened. "I should have followed my heart and married you, which was what I wanted more than anything else." He gave a mirthless laugh, releasing her hand. "But then, I wouldn't have Rebecca. And you—you wouldn't have your son and your lovely daughter."

Sarah took a sip of water. "I have two sons," she managed to say. "But Nicholas is just a baby. It was...Benjamin that you saw."

He smiled. "He's a fine lad. How I wish that I had a son," he added wistfully.

Sarah suddenly felt all her appetite disappear, and Christian noted her ashen face with concern. "Is anything wrong?"

She felt as if the breath had been squeezed from her body; the room began to sway in an alarming manner. "I'm...just not very hungry," she whispered.

Quickly, he motioned to the waiter, instructing him to clear the table and cancel the balance of their order. "Just bring us some hot tea, right away," he said.

The tea was placed before her, and Sarah sipped gratefully at the hot liquid. It seemed to revive her, and slowly the color returned to her pale cheeks. But her mind still reeled with the thought of Jena's treachery. The woman had destroyed not only Sarah's and Christian's lives, but in a sense Benjamin's and Jonathan's as well. Sarah couldn't conceive, much less understand, the mind that had caused such devastation.

Reassured that she was feeling better, Christian relaxed. "I've missed you so, Sarah," he said. "The only reason I returned to Boston was to be near you. I couldn't stay away any longer." His blue eyes darkened. "Sarah, I love you so very much," he whispered. Reaching over, he placed his hand on top of hers. "You said it was too late. But it isn't. Not unless you've stopped loving me." The pressure of his hand increased. "Is that it, Sarah? Have you stopped loving me?"

Her gray eyes shone with tears. "My love for you will never change," she admitted tremulously.

"Then there's nothing more to be said." He spoke firmly, in command of himself once more. "Tomorrow I will make arrangements for the purchase of a house. I know of just the property. It's about a mile outside of the city. Small, but very discreetly located. We can meet there once a week. We can finally begin our lives, Sarah."

For a long moment, Sarah made no response, but continued to look at him, an expression of exquisite sadness upon her face. When she spoke, her voice was low and steady, hiding the torment she was now feeling. "If you love me, Christian, you must not ask this of me," she said simply.

If she had spoken any other words, given him excuses, refused, Christian would have insisted, would have gone ahead with his plans, carried her off if necessary.

But she had said the one thing that defeated him. He withdrew his hand, his jaw working against the feeling of futility that engulfed him.

"I understand," he said at last, but the bitterness tinged his voice with despair.

Do you, my darling? Sarah wondered silently. If I agreed to see you, even occasionally, sooner or later the truth would emerge about Benjamin. Our son. And that must never happen. Never. She would not have her son branded illegitimate, wouldn't be responsible for saddling him with such an iron weight to carry around with him for a lifetime. Right now, only she and Betsy knew for sure. And that was the way she intended to keep it. As for Alecon, and even Jonathan, they might have suspicions, but it was, after all, her word against that of Lucas Hockings, who was now dead and could never speak his foul words again.

How had he known? she suddenly wondered. How odd that she hadn't wondered about that before. But, she decided, even Lucas had only guessed. He couldn't possibly have known for certain.

And, of course, there was Jonathan himself. She owed him something, and the only thing she had to give was herself, her fidelity. She couldn't give him her love, for that had been claimed a long time ago.

Chapter 21

From the first-floor parlor of Somerset Hall, Fenster Tremont stared pensively out of the bow window, his gaze only superficially on the exquisite side garden that now, in mid-June, was fully in bloom. It was a lovely area, styled formally with neatly trimmed hedges and shrubs lined out in a geometric pattern. By comparison, the rear gardens, bordered by poplars, hosted a profusion of casually appointed lilacs, anemones, pansies, and even violets and wild roses.

Raising his eyes, he could see the shimmer of water through the trees. The house was set a good mile from the Taunton, but because it sat on a rise, the river was easily discernible.

Ordinarily, he delighted in the view, which had a calming effect upon him; but today he was too preoccupied. He was thinking about Jonathan, whom he had known for many years. When he first became Edward Enright's solicitor, Jonathan was merely a boy. Now the boy was a man, a man in a state better suited to a vegetable than a human being.

With a sigh, he turned from the window and made for the decanter of brandy so thoughtfully provided by Phillips. Fenster poured himself a generous helping of the amber liquid while he waited for Sarah to join him. She was still in Jonathan's room. That was where he had been until a few moments ago. But the sight of Jonathan so depressed him that Fenster managed only a few, awkward words before hastily taking his leave.

He wondered, as he had often since the event, what had precipitated the devastating stroke some six weeks before. There had been a row, that much he knew, and Lucas Hockings had been shot and killed. Attempted robbery, Sarah had said. Betsy O'Connor, and even the other servants, had verified it. There had, under the circumstances, been no charges filed against Jonathan Enright.

But what the devil had Lucas Hockings been doing here? What need would he have had to rob anyone? His brother was one of the wealthiest men in Boston!

Few people were aware of it, but for the past two years, Christian Hockings had quietly and without much ado been buying land on the perimeter of the city, particularly the west end. Since the city was moving in that direction, his holdings had increased in value tenfold.

There were those, Fenster knew, who termed Christian Hockings ruthless in his drive for power and wealth, but Fenster also knew that these traits were a necessary evil for a man of ambition. And Hockings was certainly ambitious. Fortunately, he was also endowed with resourcefulness and a cool logic that made him a formidable adversary, as those very people who had termed him ruthless had discovered.

And the brother of this immensely successful man had been shot while trying to rob a safe! It made no sense.

Sarah then entered the room, and Fenster smiled at her. She was dressed in a gray silk dress that matched those incredible eyes of hers. "I thought we should have a talk," he said, seating himself in a comfortable chair. He placed the brandy glass on the table, eyeing her with appreciation. She was, he thought, one of the loveliest women he had ever met. He had thought so the first time he saw her, and the intervening years seemed only to enhance her grace, imparting a glorious maturity to her well-defined features and high cheekbones. There were those who questioned Jonathan's choice of a wife; Fenster himself had never done so.

"I understand that there is little chance of Jonathan regaining his health," he said slowly.

She nodded, sitting in a chair across from him. Except for a slight mobility in his right hand, Jonathan was completely paralyzed; he could not even speak. Only his eyes followed her about, and in their depths she saw, or thought she saw, a love that had turned to hate.

Her own overwhelming sense of remorse and guilt weighed on her heavily each time she looked at him.

The physician, a specialist called in from New York, offered no encouragement. There was little chance, he had told her, that Jonathan's condition would change.

"The doctor offers little hope," she related quietly. "Still, I pray he's wrong."

"They have been known to be," Fenster commented. "But even if Jonathan does regain his faculties, it will take time. A lot of it." He leaned forward, observing her with serious eyes. "In the meantime, Sarah, what do you propose to do?"

"About what?"

He smiled gently. "The mill, Sarah. Someone has to take charge. You have to hire a competent supervisor. A foreman is well and good, but too many administrative details have been piling up in these past weeks; orders have been accepted and have gone unfilled; employees have been on half pay...."

Her gray eyes went wide. "But that's dreadful!" she exclaimed, suddenly angry with herself for not giving thought to all this sooner. "You must see to it immediately!" she insisted.

"I will," he assured her. "But my intervention will be merely a stopgap. Someone must see to these things full-time." He took a sip of his brandy. "Jed Peach, I suppose, is doing his best, but he drives the operatives viciously. They'll accept it—as long as the money is there." He regarded her with level eyes. "Do you have anyone in mind?"

She bit her lip, her thoughts whirling. With Aleceon gone, Jonathan incapacitated, Justin impossible, and Benjamin too young, there was no one. Except... "Why must I hire anyone?" she mused in a barely audible voice. The thought took hold, and grew. Fenster was watching her with a bemused look, but she ignored him as her mind began to explore the possibilities.

Some of the larger mills, she knew, hired agents; but as yet Taunset had no need for such individuals. Besides, those mills that did employ agents did not usually have one owner but, rather a multitude of shareholders. Happily, fully 67 percent of the stock in Taunset was in the name of Enright. She need therefore answer to no one.

It could be done. *She* could do it. The time and effort involved was just what she needed. There would be no time to think of anything else, no time to dwell upon Christian, who seemed to invade her every waking hour. She hadn't gone into Boston often in these past six weeks, but on those occasions when she did, she couldn't help looking about, hoping and dreading at the same time to catch a glimpse of him.

In a way, the mill was an answer to her prayers. She could, at least in part, atone for all that had happened by helping Jonathan while he could not act on his own.

Sarah now regarded Fenster with steady eyes. "I'm not going to hire anyone," she said at last. "I will do it myself."

He laughed, genuinely amused. "But my dear Sarah, you couldn't possibly handle the running of a mill."

"Must I remind you, Fenster," she replied in a cool voice, "that I once worked at Enright's? I know the operation as well as anyone, and since my marriage, I am also well versed in the administrative end of it."

Seeing that she was in earnest, his laughter ceased. How absurd, he thought, too polite to voice his thoughts aloud. "You're a woman," he said, as if that explained it all. "Women do not run mills."

Smiling now, Sarah reached over and patted his hand lightly. "This one will." She got to her feet; automatically, Fenster stood up. "And if there is anything that I don't understand, I'm certain you'll come to my assistance admirably."

Fenster was shaking his head, still too dumbfounded to take it all in. He opened his mouth to protest again, but found himself, instead, saying: "By God, if anyone can do it, you can." He paused a moment, as doubt once again prodded him. "But surely you can't be thinking of going ahead with the original plan?" he said, a note of incredulity creeping into his voice. "Things would be much simpler if you would produce a plain cloth."

"I have every intention of carrying out Jonathan's plan in its entirety," Sarah stated emphatically. Her thoughts were tumbling about now, as her determination solidified. "Enright's will produce a cloth that, until now, has only been produced in Europe," she went on in a firm voice. Restless and excited, she walked by Fenster's side as they left the room.

At the front door, Fenster Tremont paused, his face sobering again. "There's Jonathan to consider, Sarah," he reminded her gently. "Will he approve of all this?" As soon as the words were out, he regretted them, and at the sight of her clouded face, patted her arm. "I'm sorry. Of course, we cannot know that."

"I will be at the mill in the morning," she stated, her eyes focusing on the future.

That same afternoon, Sarah summoned the carriage and went to visit Elizabeth.

Although the outside of the structure greatly resembled her own house, on a smaller scale, there was something oddly austere and bitter within the house of Justin and Elizabeth.

Here the dark, highly polished wood floors glimmered like a malevolent mirror; the paneled walls, too, were dim, without the life or warmth inherent in most woods. Draperies were heavy, and almost always closed against the sunlight, as if that bit of light would be a heresy against the relentless gloom. Even the fire, red and snapping, did little to alleviate the foreboding atmosphere.

Rachel was still staying at the parish house—a circumstance for which, in light of recent events, Sarah was grateful—and a nurse had been hired to see to Hannah. Following the doctor's advice, the infant was subjected to daily exercise and massage of her tiny foot, for short periods of time now, to increase as she grew older.

Sarah found Rachel and Elizabeth in the front parlor, the tea table before them set with small delicacies and a freshly baked cake.

"I'm glad you came, Sarah," Elizabeth greeted her.

Sarah seated herself, and sighed deeply as Elizabeth poured tea, her mind still on her sudden decision of that morning. Now that she had thought it through, she wondered whether she was doing the right thing.

"Is Jon worse?" Elizabeth asked as she noted Sarah's somber expression.

"No, no," Sarah quickly replied, accepting the porcelain cup. "His condition is unchanged."

"I'll be moving back to Somerset Hall," Rachel announced suddenly. "Elizabeth is fully recovered, and Hannah is receiving excellent care. I would feel more comfortable being close to Jonathan at this time."

"Of course, Mother Enright," Sarah agreed. "We'll both be pleased to have you come home." She was, in fact, relieved by Rachel's decision, in light of her own. If she were to be gone from the house for a goodly portion of each day as she planned to be, she would feel easier with the household under Rachel's watchful eye. She turned to Elizabeth. "How is Hannah?"

"Doing splendidly!" was the enthusiastic reply. "I'm certain that she already knows who I am. And the doctor's reports have been most encouraging. He assures me that she'll be able to walk...."

"Of course the child will walk!" Rachel snapped, clasping her hands in her lap. "But do not delude yourself, Elizabeth. The doctor is most likely correct in his further evaluation that the child will have a limp."

Elizabeth's eyes flashed with a hint of her old stubbornness. "I will not have her walk with the aid of a cane! Hannah will walk, and she will walk in a normal manner!"

Rachel's mouth contorted into a moue of exasperation, but she made no further comment. Instead, she got to her feet and with a great sigh that raised her ample bosom, said to Sarah: "I'll see that my things are put in the carriage, as I'll return with you."

With Rachel's departure, Sarah again viewed Elizabeth, who said, with a tinge of bitterness: "She just doesn't understand."

"I'm sure she does," Sarah replied softly and with a smile. "I think she just doesn't want you to be disappointed."

"I won't be," Elizabeth responded. "Oh, Sarah, she's so beautiful. You must see her before you leave."

Sarah's laugh was indulgent, affectionate. "Of course. You don't think that I came just to see you?" she teased.

"I wouldn't miss the opportunity of visiting with my godchild."

Immediately, as if she couldn't wait, Elizabeth stood up, and Sarah followed her upstairs to the nursery.

Here, at least, was lightness and joy, reflected in bright colors and gay ruffles. Amidst it all, the child smiled sweetly, grasping the air with pudgy white fingers, wriggling her small body in pleasure at the attention suddenly bestowed upon her.

Elizabeth's face was luminous as she gazed upon her daughter. "She has made it all worthwhile," she murmured, and Sarah looked at her attentively, searchingly.

"The child has...eased the situation for you?" she asked tentatively, her voice low.

"Justin no longer raises his hand to me, if that's what you mean." She smiled enigmatically, playing with the baby's fingers. "I doubt that he ever will again."

Sarah was conscious of a great relief at the words. "Is he happy with the child?"

The dark blue eyes regarded her thoughtfully for a moment. "That is not a word one applies to Justin," Elizabeth observed, again looking upon her daughter. "He rarely visits here," she went on, her voice holding no regret or sadness. "When he does, he simply stands before the child's bed, silently staring at her. He has never held his daughter in his arms, much less bestowed a kiss upon her."

Sarah was appalled at these cool words, but Elizabeth's face held only satisfaction, and trace of—triumph?

The nurse, who had this while been seated at the far end of the room, diligently hemming a piece of linen, now approached them and said: "It's time for the child's exercise, Mrs. Lansing."

"Of course." Elizabeth turned to Sarah. "Let's go back downstairs. I hope you can stay awhile longer. Your visits mean so much to me."

"I think you should know of a decision that I made this morning," Sarah said. They were back in the parlor, the tea things having been cleared away in their brief absence. "I have decided personally to take over the management of the mill until Jonathan is able to do so."

Stunned, Elizabeth just stared at her. "You, Sarah?" she breathed. "But what on earth do you know about running a mill?"

Amused, Sarah smiled at her sister-in-law. "Quite a lot, actually. Have you forgotten that I was once employed by one?"

"No, I haven't forgotten. But..." Elizabeth shook her head in amazement. "But that was just a yarn mill, Sarah. This one produces whole cloth!"

"I realize that, and I won't pretend it'll be easy. But the mill has been in operation for months now. The workers are experienced, and in a short while, I will be, too. Besides, I won't actually be doing the process physically, you know."

Elizabeth thought of her husband, and smiled slightly; she didn't have to guess what his reaction would be when he learned of this. To Justin—as to most of the clergy—a woman's mind was exiguous. She did not really possess one in the true sense of the word. He taught, insisted upon, obedience: wife to husband, mill worker to mill owner, man to God. Slight variations of this theme ran through each of his sermons. Lately, he had added slave to master, for he was radical in his anti-Abolition cause.

A thought came to her as she listened to Sarah, and she did not question in her own mind that it might be disloyal or even heresy; it was a fact, a truth, indisputable, therefore unarguable.

It was the Church that kept the masses, the workers, at bay. It was the Church—and men like Justin—that taught the people to accept their lot—be content, for a better life will follow. Obey, suffer, accept.

But it was not true! she suddenly realized; it was not true at all. Why should the poor accept their lot without trying to better themselves? Her own father had refused to accept. He had made his fortune by defying the odds, flouting convention, and in so doing had achieved success.

And so would Sarah. Sarah would prevail, and succeed.

"There is no real reason why a woman cannot run such an operation," Sarah was saying to her. "No practical reason, that is."

Still listening intently, Elizabeth realized an even more startling conception, one that truly shocked her with its seducing simplicity. The worst enemy of women was—women! It was women, in the form of mothers, elder sisters, and even teachers, who taught the obedience that forever shackled the female, made her so dependent upon the male. Even when grown, a woman had an aversion, a horror, of being "unladylike." From the richest to the meanest, a woman had to be, think, and act with acceptable propriety—or she was shunned by her sisters as being unworthy, shunned by men who considered her indecent, and doomed to that outcast throng of spinsterhood—in itself the ultimate failure.

We perpetuate our own imprisonment, she realized, astounded.

And then, comforting her, came the thought that among their numbers, there were those few who would not conform, who would fight—not subtly, as she had done with Justin, a silent battle of wills—but openly, defiantly.

And, like Sarah, they, too, would succeed.

Sarah, watching the play of emotion on Elizabeth's face and not knowing what to make of it, now reached out and took hold of her hand.

"Please tell me you approve. I should hate to think that you didn't."

"Approve! Good heavens, Sarah, I most certainly do approve." Unable to contain her enthusiasm, she gripped Sarah's hand tightly. "I think it's marvelous. Jon will be so proud of you...." With the mention of her brother, the light left her face. Releasing Sarah's hand, she sighed. "I do so hope that he recovers."

"We all hope that, my dear," Sarah said quietly, getting to her feet as Rachel strode into the room with the abrupt proclamation that she was ready to depart.

On the way home, Sarah told her mother-in-law what she intended to do. Rachel's reply utterly astounded her.

"I think that's a splendid idea, Sarah," Rachel commented simply and without question. She had long ago discovered the strength within her daughter-in-law, and was more than willing to turn matters over to her capable hands.

The reaction at the mill, when Sarah arrived the following day and stated her intention of taking over, was mixed, particularly among the wagon drivers. These burly, hardworking men who delivered the finished products to the customers, viewed a woman employer as nothing short of sacrilege. A few resigned immediately, and Sarah did nothing to change their decision. But her no-nonsense air and fair-minded attitude eventually won over the rest.

Knowing that she could never work with him, Sarah dismissed Jed Peach that first day, and in his place, installed one of the drivers, Corbin Blackwell. With Peach went the cat-o'-nine-tails, and all it represented. She had never understood why Jonathan, feeling as he did, had continued to employ Peach after his father died.

Despite her high resolve, the first shock Sarah received when she studied the account books was that, in its six months of operation, the mill had shown a steady loss! Fully 27 percent of the stock was still outstanding, and the machinery itself was heavily mortgaged.

Laying aside the books until she could consult with Fenster, Sarah toured the mill that afternoon. Before too long, each of the rooms contained within the four-story edifice would need an overseer, but, although eventually the mill would employ better than a thousand operatives, right now there were considerably fewer than that number.

Though she had seen it many times during construction, Sarah had not visited the mill since it went into production. Now, viewing the looms, with their swiftly moving brass-tipped shuttles, she realized that she had long since forgotten the incredible noise. Memories flooded her mind as she thought of the days when she had stood in front of those machines, and she promised herself that, if it were at all possible, she would make things easier for these girls than it had been for her.

She spent the balance of that day familiarizing herself with the complete operation. At the end of that time, she was convinced that she could handle the job.

In the days that followed, Sarah acquainted herself with administrative details, taking orders, introducing herself to customers, getting to know, and gain, the trust and respect of her employees.

Then, one afternoon two weeks later, she had occasion to check on an order that her records showed was almost a week overdue.

For a while, she stood among the clanging machinery and watched; her eyes narrowed as she viewed the emerging cloth.

Turning abruptly, she made her way downstairs and headed for the cloth-room. Here she viewed the finished material with a sense of shock. It was plain cotton cloth!

"Why isn't it printed?" she demanded of Corbin Blackwell, unwinding the offending bolt on a long table and sternly regarding her foreman.

"It's the cylinder, Mrs. Enright," he explained, raising his voice above the unceasing din. He was a tall man with a homely, obliging face that was saved from plainness by the intelligence and perception that lighted his brown eyes. "We only had two, and they both broke the first day in use."

"Do we still have the mold?"

He nodded. "Yes, ma'am. I think it's around here somewhere."

"Where were they manufactured?" She listened as he mentioned a factory in Philadelphia. A long way, she thought, frowning. More time wasted. Surely there must be a place in Boston where the cylinders could be rebuilt.

Hockings Metals. She bit her lip. Was this an excuse on her part, she wondered, to contact Christian? To see him again? But the time involved in shipping the molds to Philadelphia, having them rebuilt, and returned, would be weeks, perhaps months, of lost time.

At last she addressed her foreman, who had this while been waiting in respectful silence. "See to it that at least two more are made. And Mr. Blackwell," she said as the foreman turned to go. "This time, take the mold to Hockings Metals." After a moment's thought, she added: "If you still have them, take the broken cylinders with you. Speak to Mr. Hockings himself. Tell him I sent you. I'm certain that he will be able to determine the weakness and correct it."

She returned to her office, telling herself that she had done the right thing, that Christian played no part in her decision. And by the time her long day was over, Sarah had almost convinced herself that it was so.

Chapter 22

The window was open, for the late June evening was mild, and the gentle breeze was sweet-scented and pleasant. The curtain billowed slightly, playing with the warm air before allowing it to enter the bedroom.

In the soft light of the single burning lamp by his bedside, Jonathan turned his eyes cautiously and viewed the sleeping form sprawled out on the couch, snoring with a sound that was both monotonous and regular in cadence. It was annoying, that noise, but he could do little about it. Sarah had assigned the footman, a sturdy Irishman named Patrick Ahern, to stay with him at night and to lift him into and out of his wheelchair during the day.

At first, it had enraged him that the man who was supposed to be caring for him, slept. The light, too, was a damned nuisance, but that was another thing he was helpless to correct.

However, since he had discovered a few weeks ago that he could wiggle his toes, he used these night hours to exercise, and he had only yesterday decided that the light was a blessing in disguise. He could see the movement, and it heartened him. Of course, he didn't dare exercise during the day, for he was never certain when his mother or one of the servants would enter his room.

Jonathan concentrated, straining his muscles, turning all his efforts, mental and physical, into the movement of his feet. His right hand was now quite mobile; his left hand, too, was beginning to respond.

It was a powerful feeling of determination that drove him, to what end he didn't fully know. There was no time to think on that now. He needed all his concerted willpower to force his recalcitrant muscles into even a modicum of movement.

He was driven not only by determination, but by

hate. Raw and uncontrollable, it dominated his every waking moment.

In the beginning, this hate had spewed out in all directions, even at the Fates who had so unceremoniously used him. But at last it had solidified, converged, and now rested where it belonged: on the one person who was the cause of it all—Sarah.

He would kill her, he knew that. What he did not know was when, or how. Answers to those questions would come. He had little to do during the day but think.

He could have forgiven her for her infidelity—he thought of it as that, even though it had happened before their marriage. He could even forgive her for taking over the mill. From her tedious evening reports, it was apparently beginning to flourish. What he could not, and never would forgive, was Benjamin.

Benjamin, the son he loved above all else, was not his son at all! For that, Sarah would pay. And she would pay with her life.

God, how he would make her suffer, he vowed. She would wish she were dead long before she was.

The thought comforted him, and as the first light of dawn brightened the sky, he slept, exhausted with the night's endless effort.

Chapter 23

Fenster Tremont stood at the window of his office, absently noting the traffic on the street below. From his second-story vantage point, he could see in both directions. Carriages and lorries and wagons all lent their various noises, which occasionally were overcome by the shrill cry of a peddler hawking his wares.

The July morning was warm and overcast, promising rain. The weather had been this way for three days now, and the threatened moisture had not yet materialized. Fenster hoped that it would rain; the muggy heat set his bones to aching.

At last he saw what he had been looking for, and with great interest he watched the fine-looking carriage as it rolled up to the entrance below and stopped.

Agilely, the driver leapt down and opened the door, standing aside in a respectful manner as a tall, well-dressed man emerged. From this height, Fenster could see only the top of his black hat and the shoulders of the light-brown frock coat. But he did not need to see any more because he knew who it was.

The message he had received yesterday advising that Christian Hockings would call promptly at nine o'clock had been quite a surprise to him; and now, taking his watch out, Fenster saw that it was exactly that hour.

By the time his secretary announced his caller, Fenster was calmly seated behind his polished desk, a gracious smile planted on his face.

"Mr. Hockings." He stood up, extending his hand, which Christian firmly shook before seating himself in the large leather chair nearby. "It is a bit early for a drink," Fenster noted, again sitting down. "But may I offer you coffee? Or perhaps tea?"

"Nothing, thank you," Christian replied. "I won't be taking up too much of your time."

Fenster spread his hands out. "Take as much as you like, Mr. Hockings," he said sincerely. "If I can assist you in any way, it would be my pleasure to do so."

Christian smiled thinly. "I understand that Mrs. Enright is now running the mill at Taunset."

Fenster blinked, then quickly recovered. "You heard correctly, Mr. Hockings," he replied, surprised at the other's interest in such a matter. For the moment, he wondered uneasily whether Christian Hockings was seeking revenge for the death of his brother. If so, he'd have no part in it, Fenster decided. Not even to snare the Hockings Metals account, which he had initially hoped was the reason for this unexpected visit.

"Is that legal?" Christian inquired, his expression bland. He looked as though he had asked about the weather.

"Legal?"

"For a woman to handle such matters," Christian patiently enlarged. Nothing about him revealed the overwhelming astonishment he had experienced when he had first learned what Sarah was doing. His first inkling had been when Corbin Blackwell brought the cylinders to him. Christian had easily found the defect and corrected it. "It is my understanding," he went on, "that a woman cannot own a business."

"Oh, it's perfectly legal, Mr. Hockings," Fenster assured him. "Naturally, Mrs. Enright does not *own* the business, per se. It belongs to her husband. Upon his death, it will belong to their eldest son." He leaned back in his chair, elbows on the armrests, making a tent of his fingertips as he continued. "I understand what you're getting at," he mused, still wondering about the other man's interest. "When a woman marries, anything she owns automatically becomes the property of her husband. She could not own a business, or any real estate for that matter, solely in her own name. However, we have a unique situation here. Jonathan Enright is not dead; on the other hand, he's quite incapable at this time of running his business or even making decisions. And Benjamin is too young to do either. What Mrs. Enright is doing is unusual, to say the least, but it is perfectly legal."

Christian inclined his head thoughtfully. "There's been some resistance, has there not?"

Fenster shrugged. "Initially. But that's beginning to die down."

Christian's eyes were unwavering as he viewed the solicitor. "Are you certain of that?" he persisted. "My sources have informed me that Taunset is in a bit of financial difficulty."

Unwilling to answer this, Fenster frowned. Seeing that, Christian seemed to relax. "I am happy to see that you have Mrs. Enright's welfare in mind," he observed amiably. "But actually, no affirmation is necessary. I've looked into the matter myself quite thoroughly."

"And what have you found?" Fenster inquired in a cold voice that was not lost upon his visitor.

Christian smiled, even more pleased with the solicitor's attitude. Since going into business for himself, he had found solicitors, as a whole, a group not to be trusted. He had fired two of them in the last four years when he had discovered his accounts mishandled and mismanaged. One had been a fool, his mistakes sheer carelessness; the other had been a rogue, intent upon getting rich by bilking his clients. Happily, Fenster Tremont seemed not to fall into either of these categories.

"How would you like to handle the account of Hockings Metals?" Christian suddenly asked. Removing a cigar from his vest pocket, he lit it, and then leaned back, viewing the solicitor through a cloud of blue-gray smoke.

Fenster blinked, quite startled by the man's change of mood. "Naturally, I would be pleased," he replied carefully. But he was, despite this affirmation, uncertain. If Hockings had come here today to give him his account, then why the devil was the man so interested in Taunset?

"Fine," said Christian in a brisk voice. "Then it's settled. I'll send our files to you this afternoon. Meanwhile, you can have the papers drawn up." He viewed Fenster with open-eyed candor.

"Very well." But as he saw Christian's expression harden, his own sense of caution increased.

"Now that that is settled, I would like to hear more

about the financial difficulties at Taunset." Christian studied the solicitor intently, unsmilingly.

For a long moment Fenster Tremont regarded his visitor; then slowly, he got to his feet, all traces of amiability gone.

"Mr. Hockings," he said quietly, and with great deliberation, "I do not, under any circumstances, discuss one of my clients with another. Nor with anyone else, for that matter," he added pointedly. "I think perhaps that our association would be ill-advised, and I must ask you to leave." He watched in some confusion as Christian, instead of showing signs of anger, or even of getting to his feet as requested, broke out in a delighted grin. More confused than ever, Fenster just stood there, feeling a bit foolish. He was beginning to understand the success of Christian Hockings.

Casually, as if he had all day to spare, Christian leaned over and extinguished his cigar in the large amber-colored ashtray. Then, just as casually, he rose. "I think that our association will work out just fine," he remarked softly, extending his hand. Automatically, Fenster responded, and found his hand gripped tightly and firmly.

"Now," Christian continued in his brusque tone, "let's get down to business." Hands in his pockets, he ambled about the room, stopping by the window that only thirty minutes before had framed Fenster Tremont. It had at last begun to rain, and narrow rivulets coursed down the panes in an irregular manner, distorting the view beyond.

"Contrary to what you may think," Christian said, "it is my intention to invest, and invest heavily in Taunset." He turned and faced the solicitor, whose brows lifted at this sudden announcement. "In fact, I wish to invest seventy-five thousand dollars." Ignoring Fenster's look of shock, he went on. "If my information is correct, this sum will adequately alleviate any financial distress at Taunset."

"Are you serious?" Fenster sat down heavily, quite astounded by this turn of events. He wondered if this was the normal manner in which Christian conducted his business relationships; if so, he must have left a trail of confounded people in his wake.

Christian was frowning slightly. "You will find that I am seldom otherwise when it comes to business, Mr. Tremont."

"How...?"

"Offer top price for the stock in existence that may be up for sale, and purchase any outstanding stock at current market value. One thing!" he cautioned, returning to his seat. "I do not wish my name to be used in any way. I do not want it known, not even to Mrs. Enright, that I am putting up this money."

"But why? She will be relieved...."

"Those are my terms!" Christian stated emphatically, fixing Tremont with a hard look. "I presume that it can be done?"

Fenster nodded his head. "Of course. A dummy corporation..."

"Then do it." As usual, when he had the right man for the right job, Christian stepped aside, unwilling to bog himself down in details that were, at any rate, better left in more experienced hands. Getting to his feet, he drew forth a gold watch from his vest pocket. "I'll be in touch," he said. Heading for the door, he left a thoroughly bewildered Fenster Tremont staring after him.

Sarah did not question Fenster's explanation of a French businessman by the name of Henri Valois who, through his Boston solicitor, had unaccountably purchased the 27 percent of the issued stock in Taunset Enterprises.

It was a windfall; it was marvelous! And she set about inaugurating plans that, since Jonathan had first told her of his mill city, had grown and flourished in her imagination.

One dormitory was already built, and this she allowed to stand. But the rest of the living accommodations she insisted be regular houses. They were small, four-room structures, but built sturdily, with one large common room for living and eating. Window boxes were installed, and these, courtesy of Taunset, were planted with gaily colored flowers.

Trees were planted amidst grassed areas and stone walkways. The mill itself, four stories high and facing on the Taunton River, was made of brick. The church, Justin's domain, rested on a hill somewhat toward the center of the two hundred or so houses. From the vantage point of the rise, the small cottages created a neat patchwork effect, bordered as they were by hedgerows, each enclosing a smaller patch of green grass.

More workers came, girls and young boys at first, but then women, and finally men, who were needed to drive the wagons.

At one point, Fenster tried to convince Sarah that the workers should be paid in scrip—standard procedure in a lot of the mills. Sarah emphatically overruled this suggestion, insisting that the operatives be paid in hard coin, to save or spend as they desired.

Although she did not confide this as yet to the solicitor, when things were running smoothly, she planned to reduce the work hours to ten. She thought it wise to keep that idea to herself for a while. Only a few years back, carpenters in Boston had struck, demanding the ten-hour day. The year before that, the women weavers in Pawtauket had gone on strike, protesting the increased hours thrust upon them. Both situations had appalled Jonathan and Fenster Tremont, who had exclaimed: "Damned unionists! They'd destroy a way of life for their own gain."

Sarah, having worked the long, aching hours, knew that the day would have to be shortened eventually. Better to do it on her own than to have her employees force her hand. Improved working conditions would not mean a decrease in profits, either; she'd see to that.

Profits were essential, and to the shareholders, of paramount importance—the only consideration, in fact. The profits would be there, but not so much from the sweat of the workers as from the product itself. She would charge more, and aim for the so-called carriage trade. Regular cotton cloth would be produced—it was, after all, the bread and butter of cotton manufacturers. But there would also be the elegance of the finer, patterned cloths. For these she planned to charge substantially more, always making certain that she undercut by a few cents the imported cloth of the same quality.

The printed cloth sold rapidly. Initially, there was

some resistance from a few of their customers, all men, who were reluctant to do business with a woman, however charming she might be. But the fact that Enright's was the most accessible mill in the area interjected a note of practicality, and soon, even in Boston, tongues wagged and gossips buzzed about "that woman who runs the Taunset mill."

As the months passed, Sarah Edgewood Enright, formerly acceptable by Boston's inner Society, was shunned by the women of that illustrious group. But neither her schedule nor her inclination permitted her to feel this "loss."

Not content with a single color on white cloth, she began to experiment, and now, six months after assuming control, Sarah was filled with a sense of satisfaction. She knew that nowhere in the country, not even in the fabulous Lowell's, was such a multicolored cloth being offered.

After working a twelve-hour day, just like her employees, Sarah returned home. After supper, which she usually ate alone in the study while going over her papers and accounts, Sarah visited Jonathan, and for twenty or thirty minutes, spoke at length of the day's events.

Whether he understood or not, she was unable to determine, for he still stared at her in the same expressionless manner, only his eyes alive and, to her, accusing. She was meticulous about imparting each and every facet of the day's happenings. And the fact that the mill's operation was producing a greater profit than ever before was reported by her with no little pride.

But did he approve? Disapprove? Forgive? She didn't know the answer, and it tormented her constantly.

At night she fell wearily upon her bed, her body relaxing under the skillful ministrations of Betsy's sturdy hands as she massaged muscles and tendons.

Then she would lie alone in the darkness and think, her mind too wound up to relax. More and more in these past months she found her thoughts straying to Christian. She hadn't seen him since that day they had met in Boston, almost eight months ago.

And these thoughts too, seemed a further betrayal

of Jonathan. But God, how she loved him still. Was there never to be an end to her yearning? She couldn't stop herself from wondering how different her life would have been if she had married Christian. Right now, this very moment, he would be beside her; she would be safe, and contented, within his arms.

She emitted a small cry of despair and buried her head in her pillow. She tried to hold back the tears, but they came, hot and scalding, and she wept, feeling a loss so profound that she felt crushed beneath the weight of it.

Some miles away, on this bitterly cold December evening, Jena tossed upon her bed, her once soft hair now matted and tangled with perspiration. Beneath her, the sheet felt damp and uncomfortable.

Again the pain came. She opened her mouth to scream, but only a weak, mewling cry emerged. She panted and tried to focus her eyes upon the doctor who stood at the foot of her bed. She couldn't see him well, because her legs were drawn up and a sheet draped over her knees. But he was there; she could feel his hands as they tried to coax the infant from her body.

She hated it, this unborn thing inside her that was tearing her to pieces. Between agonizing pains, she fantasized, mentally visualizing its death; dreamed of killing it, beating it breathless with her bare hands.

She saw Christian's face as he periodically entered her room, only to be sternly banished by the doctor. Her husband's face looked pale and concerned. But was it her welfare or the child's that produced such solicitation? She didn't know. Didn't want to know. She hated him, too. He was the one responsible for it all.

Jena did not blame herself for her predicament; she had, after all, only tried to be a good wife. These last months had passed in heavy lethargy, her mind refusing to dwell upon what lay ahead. She had been ill for a great deal of her confinement and had rarely left her room.

And now, the time was here.

She struggled, fighting for breath, fighting against pain. And death.

Another spasm tore at her, erasing any coherent thought from her mind. As if in the distance, she heard her own voice, thin and wailing, as it rose and ebbed with unceasing anguish.

No one had been more surprised than she by her pregnancy. She had done all the things her friends had told her about. Ironically, in only one month's time, she had been caught. At first, even though her annoyance and fear had been great, the look in Christian's eyes had made it all worthwhile. But nothing was worth this! her mind screamed.

Downstairs, the firelight cast a warm amber color about the tastefully furnished study, dusting wood and glass alike until they glowed with a burnished hue. A tall, richly carved grandfather clock issued its dolorous, monotonous ticking, occasionally punctuated by the sonorous announcement of the passing quarter hour; otherwise the room was silent.

With a start, Christian heard the clock toll four. It was almost morning, and with a definite sense of unease he realized that eighteen hours had passed. Eighteen hours since Jena's first pain began. He remembered his mother's protracted labor, spanning four days and resulting in a dead child; not to mention her own brush with death.

A light tap on the door brought him quickly out of the chair, but it was only Mrs. Macky, his housekeeper.

"I thought you would like some coffee, sir," she said.

"Yes, thank you," he responded, sitting down again. He watched absently as she poured the coffee and set a plate of thinly sliced cake beside it. Then she straightened, viewing him through steel spectacles, her ruddy face filled with concern.

"Is there any news about Mrs. Hockings?" she asked.

He shook his head and, reaching for the cup, sighed. "I haven't been upstairs for the past three hours."

"I'm sure everything will be all right," she said solicitously. "Sometimes these things can't be hurried along, no matter what." Then she left, closing the door quietly behind her.

No matter what, he mused desultorily. He was suddenly angry with himself. The doctor had been explicit after the last child was stillborn. Another baby would be dangerous to Jena, he'd said.

Damnit, Christian thought, running a hand through his reddish-gold hair, why did I let her talk me into it! And yet, she had seemed genuinely sincere in her desire for another child. The doctor could have been wrong. Still might be wrong.

And the baby; what of it? He realized that, till now, he had given little thought to it, so concerned was he with Jena's welfare and his own sense of guilt. That guilt sharpened considerably when he admitted to himself that he did not love Jena. But, love or no, he did not desire her death.

If she did die, and the child with her... Christian put his head in his hands and made a conscious effort to turn his mind away from such morbid thoughts. Of one thing he was certain. However this business turned out, there would be no more children. He would see to that!

He leaned his head back, and was unaware that he had dozed until the clock struck six. Then, quickly, he was awake. Getting up, he went into the hall and was halfway up the stairs when he saw the doctor emerge from Jena's room. Suddenly, he was aware of the silence. No screams, no sound of a child's cry.

On legs that felt leaden, Christian approached the doctor, who was regarding him solemnly. Although his mouth opened, Christian could not speak.

"I'm sorry, Mr. Hockings," the doctor said quietly. "Your wife is dead. I did all I could, but it was not enough to thwart nature." His lips tightened primly as he noticed Christian's stricken face.

"Oh, my God," murmured Christian, white-faced. He stood very still, making no effort to enter Jena's room. Then the doctor reached out and put a heavy hand on his shoulder.

"I don't know whether this will alleviate your loss, but the child is alive, though weak."

Christian looked at him as if he were trying to make sense of the words. "The child?" he repeated inanely.

The doctor nodded. "You have a son, Mr. Hockings."

Chapter 24

There were times, Rose thought, glancing about her office, when men were such fools. She was glad that she had never married one of them, glad that she had long ago chosen to go her own way, alone and unencumbered. Of course, she reflected, she hadn't had that many choices. Her father was no more than a dim, blurred shape in her mind; and after Seth was born, he disappeared completely. Her mother had stayed around a bit longer, until Rose turned fourteen.

They had lived, her mother, Seth, and herself, in a one-room flat, of which Rose now remembered little except its distressing lack of heat. She did, however, recall clearly the cold and bleak day that she had awakened to find her mother gone. She hadn't realized that right away, of course. It had taken three days for that truth to make itself known. Three days, during which she and Seth had shared one loaf of bread between them. When the food was gone, she knew that their survival depended upon her.

The choices were narrow, the most obvious being marriage. She sighed now, again relieved that she had escaped that trap. Oh, there had been one occasion when she had almost been caught. It had happened a year after her mother deserted them, a year during which she had worked at every menial job she could find, a year during which she had managed to put aside a few dollars for emergencies. In retrospect, she considered herself fortunate that the man had been a scoundrel. Rose never needed to learn a lesson twice. He had not only relieved her of her virginity, but had absconded with her small savings as well.

Seth, of course, had been useless. He was younger than she by five years; that, and his handicap, had precluded his ever being her provider.

A survivor at heart, Rose had therefore taken the only course left open to her: the streets—or, more properly in this case, the waterfront.

Once her decision was made, she refused to work for anyone, recognizing from the start that she would never make money if she had to turn over even a portion of her earnings to others. In this, Seth *had* been helpful. One look at his massive frame had stopped anyone from arguing with her independence.

She hated the work, but she did do it well; so well, in fact, that in only four years she had been able to open her own establishment. Begun on a small scale, with only three girls, it had, over a twenty-five-year period, expanded to today's lucrative enterprise. She viewed her accomplishment with no sense of shame, but rather a great deal of satisfaction.

She had not, in these intervening years, changed her opinion of men, and now, as she viewed Aleceon Edgewood's dispirited face and trembling form, it was stoutly reinforced.

"Five thousand dollars is a lot of money, Mr. Edgewood," she mused softly, seeing him wince. They were alone in her office, except for Seth, who stood by the door, arms folded across his broad chest. Rose knew that her brother, staring intently at her lips, was able to understand each word she spoke. Indeed, such was the rapport between them that occasionally words were not even necessary for their communication.

"I'll get the money," Aleceon insisted, uncomfortably aware of the giant of a man who watched him with unblinking intensity. He both hated and feared Seth. There was, he had often thought, something inhuman about him. He was like a predatory cat, silent, deadly, sinister. "I just need time, that's all." He ran nervous fingers through his dark blond hair, conscious that his hand was shaking uncontrollably. He looked at Rose with what he hoped was a calm expression. "We all have a run of bad luck, you know that." He tried to smile, and gave it up.

"You've had an extended run of bad luck, Mr. Edgewood," she noted casually. "I'm afraid that I must ask you to honor your markers. Naturally, I cannot allow you to use our...other facilities until your debt is clear."

He moistened his dry lips. He could forego Kitty, but the vials of clear liquid that she dispensed—those he could not do without. "I'll get it," he insisted again, trying to control the note of desperation that crept into his voice.

She allowed a cold smile to play about her mouth. "Where?" She raised a brow, studying him.

He thought of Sarah. God, she would never go for this sum! It was difficult enough just to get fifty dollars out of her. In any event, he had not seen her in almost a year now. He had been making do with loans from Kitty. There, too, a bit of subterfuge had been necessary. He had convinced her that he was in love with her, had promised to marry her—as soon as his debt was cleared.

Over these past months, he had tried frantically to make good on his markers, but in so doing, had run his debt up to the astronomical sum of five thousand dollars! Even now he was uncertain as to how he could have done such a thing.

"I'll think of something," he said at last, refusing to give in to the anxiety that tore at him.

Pursing her lips, Rose continued to watch him. "Perhaps I know of a way," she suggested thoughtfully, as if the idea had just come to her. "If you were to perform a small service for me, I could easily be persuaded to destroy these," she said, again tapping the papers.

He regarded her with wary eyes, suddenly alert. Rose, he knew, could never be called generous, and when she extended a favor, she expected one in return. "What do you want me to do?" he asked carefully.

As she explained, his face turned ashen. The words rolled over him, their sounds just as ominous and as menacing as thunder on the distant hills.

For a long moment, after she had concluded, he was silent, conscious of a sickening feeling of nausea that was like a blow to his stomach. His trembling increased, and his mouth felt caked with bile.

"I can't do that!" he protested, when he again found

his voice. "I...don't even know of anyone. I...," he floundered, for once truly shocked.

"Come now, Mr. Edgewood," Rose interjected, her manner both stern and cajoling. "Surely you know of a suitable girl." She glanced at him sideways. "Perhaps there is even one close to home," she suggested.

Almost stumbling, Aleceon got to his feet, rubbing his hand across his mouth. He went to the door, but Seth made no move to step aside. His progress effectively halted, Aleceon faced Rose. "I said that I'll get the money, and I will! I don't want to discuss this any more!"

"Very well, Mr. Edgewood," Rose said calmly in the face of his anger. "I am not an unreasonable woman. Today is the twenty-seventh of April. I will give you thirty days. Payment must be made, in one form or another, at the end of that time. If it is not," she glanced briefly at her brother, "then I am afraid that you will have to deal with Seth." Her laugh was disquieting as her eyes returned to Aleceon. "I assure you that he is not as amiable to deal with as I am." She nodded at Seth, who now stepped aside, allowing Aleceon to leave.

Downstairs in the main room, Aleceon sat down at a small table in a quiet corner and ordered a whiskey. Quickly downing it, he ordered another. He wanted to leave, but his legs felt weak and his hands were shaking badly.

White slavery! He'd heard of it, of course, but never in his wildest imagination had he supposed Rose to be a part of it. Between five and ten years old, she had said. That was what had truly shocked him. Why, his niece Caroline was seven, just a child! He downed another drink, motioning with his free hand for still one more.

Goddamn his sister, he thought, flushing with hot rage. If it were not for her, he wouldn't be in this predicament. Her and her bastard son! She had her nerve, throwing him out of the house, living a life of luxury, refusing to share it with her own brother.

It was all her fault.

* * *

"Will there be anything else yer'll be needing me for?" Betsy asked Sarah.

Glancing up from the book in her lap, Sarah replied, "No. Thank you, Betsy." She shifted her weight to a more comfortable position in the large, canopied bed, and Betsy immediately stepped forward to plump up the pillows.

"It's getting late, lass, and yer have ter be up early tomorrow, so don't yer stay up too late." Straightening, Betsy glanced down at the half-filled cup on the night table. "Yer tea's cold...," she began, but Sarah smiled and, reaching out, patted Betsy's plump arm.

"Go on, now," she said softly. "I don't want any more tea. I'll read for a while and then go to sleep." Betsy reluctantly left for her own room, which adjoined this one. Sarah adored Betsy, but the woman had a tendency to fuss over her constantly.

Alone, Sarah tried to concentrate on her book, but the words on the page drifted across her mind without leaving their meaning. Had she done the right thing? she wondered.

She had released Patrick Ahern from his nightly vigil, but only because Jonathan had indicated that this was what he wanted. He had done this by blinking and glancing toward Ahern; after questioning him at length, she had determined that he preferred to be alone at night.

Naturally she had acted in accordance with his wishes, but she was still unsettled by the thought that he was alone and unattended. What if he became ill during the night? There was no way he could call out. Of course, his room was just across the hall from hers, but the wooden doors and partitions were of solid oak, and she could hear little of what went on in the hall, much less in the rooms across from hers.

She sighed deeply and again shifted her weight. Her restlessness seemed to be increasing lately. Betsy believed this was caused by her long hours of work, and was forever urging her to slow down. But she couldn't; Jonathan's condition weighed too heavily on her mind. She had to keep things going, for his sake. Perhaps she should not have moved out of their bedroom in the first place, she mused. Yet the doctor had felt that it was for the best, allowing Jonathan to rest undisturbed. Still, his solitude bothered her.

Leaning her head back, Sarah closed her eyes. Immediately she saw Christian's face, and the sudden longing that gripped her almost made her cry out.

With a deep sigh, she sat up, trying to gain control of herself. After a moment, she opened a drawer in the bedside table and reached for the letter concealed within the pages of a book.

The letter was from Christian. Sarah stared at it for long moments, but she didn't read it. She knew the words by heart, but its physical presence was like a part of him, and she put the letter to her lips, tears streaming silently down her cheeks. It was the first and only letter she had ever received from him. His expressions of love were like a soothing balm to her heart, and she cherished each word.

With another sigh, she returned the letter to its resting place, then lay down again. Christian had written more than words of love; he had told her of Jena's death, and how she had died giving birth to his son, David.

Jena was dead, Christian was free.

But she was not, and never would be. She was tied to Jonathan, irrevocably and forever, tied with a sense of guilt that was more binding than any marriage vow could be. If Christian wanted her now, today, Sarah knew she could not go to him.

And that was the devilish part of it all. It could be done so easily. No one, least of all Jonathan, would ever know.

But she couldn't do it; her own conscience wouldn't permit it, no matter how her body cried out its need. Jonathan was where he was now because of her, and if it took the rest of her life, she would try and make it up to him. She owed him that much.

A slight noise roused her, and Sarah opened her eyes. For a moment, she lay quiet, listening.

There it was again, a faint scratching sound at the door. She tilted her head, drawing her brows together. Were her eyes playing tricks upon her? For a moment she thought she saw the doorknob turn. She stared at it steadily, but it remained motionless.

Ruefully, she shook her head, amused at herself. Certainly she was too old to begin hearing goblins and ghosts at her bedroom door. Glancing at the clock, she was astonished to see that it was 2:30 in the morning!

"Well," she murmured aloud to herself, amusement increasing. "That's what you get for dozing off." She put the book on the table and, reaching over, extinguished the lamp. The draperies were only slightly ajar, but a thin stream of pearly white moonlight traced a delicate line across the carpeted floor.

Her eyes had already closed when she heard the sound again. This time, she sat bolt upright, peering across the darkened room. Despite her earlier amusement, her heart was pounding against the thin material of her nightdress, and she put a hand to her breast in an effort to calm herself.

"Betsy!" she called out, annoyed by her quavering voice. "Betsy, is that you?"

A moment later, the door that led to Betsy's room opened, emitting a wavering yellow glow from a hastily lighted candle that met and merged with the moonlight.

"What is it?" Betsy asked breathlessly, coming closer to the bed. Sarah could see that her face was etched with concern. "Are yer sick, lass?"

In some confusion, Sarah stared at her, and then directed her eyes toward the still closed door that led to the hall.

"I...I thought that you were at that door," she said weakly, pointing.

Betsy glanced in that direction. "Now what would I be doing in the hall at this hour?" she asked, somewhat irritated at being unnecessarily frightened. With a determined step, she walked toward the door and flung it open.

Beyond, Sarah could see the dimly lit hall, empty and silent. With a sniff that adequately conveyed her feelings, Betsy firmly closed the door again.

She returned to the bed, viewing Sarah sternly. "Yer've been dreaming, lass. Now yer just settle yerself down there and get some sleep." She bustled about, smoothing the sheets and straightening the covers; gratefully, Sarah again rested her head on the soft pillow.

Jonathan closed his door and leaned against it heavily, feeling weak and dizzy.

The effort had taken far more exertion than he had anticipated. For long moments after he had reached her door, he had had to steady himself, one hand on the doorframe and the other on the knob.

Around him, the hall had seemed to tilt and sway dangerously, and he had clung to consciousness only with the greatest willpower. Of course, the long hours in bed each day didn't help, but he tried to make up for that at night, after everyone was asleep. Now that he had at last gotten rid of Ahern, he walked the floor of his room from wall to wall, back and forth, in an effort to strengthen his muscles. He was still weak, though, and his left leg had the distressing tendency to buckle unexpectedly.

Tonight was the first time that he had attempted to venture beyond his room. The need for stealth and quiet had proved too much for him. He needed more time, more exercise.

The day would come soon when he would be ready, of that he was convinced. Day by day, he felt strength returning to him.

With slow, measured steps, he walked toward the window, his thoughts upon his wife, feeling the all too familiar rush of bitterness. I loved her, his mind shouted in silent anguish. I loved her! And all she had offered in return was a crushing treachery.

For a moment he rested his head against the cold pane of glass in the window. It felt like a soothing cloth, calming him against an onrushing illness.

Then he turned away, in control of himself once more. Heading toward the nearest chair, he sat down and smiled, although it appeared more of a grimace; his facial muscles were still stiff and unresponsive.

He had had no intention of entering Sarah's room; not tonight, at any rate. Tonight had been only practice.

He had heard her call out, and knew that, next time, he would have to move with much more care.

Breathing deeply, Jonathan willed his body to relax, to cease its trembling, and gradually he calmed, his breath coming easier.

He still hadn't completely formulated his plan; he knew only that Sarah must die. She had been unfaithful to him. The thought of Benjamin was like a knife-thrust in his heart. Betsy seldom brought the children in to visit him, but when she did, he couldn't bear to look at Benjamin, for the rage swelled and pounded within him, threatening his carefully guarded self-control.

Sarah thought him helpless, thought she was now free to pursue her own inclinations.

But he would never let her go. Never. In death, she would remain his, forever.

Cautiously, Jonathan got to his feet again, grateful for the moonlight that poured in through his window. He could see everything quite clearly. Some nights he had to walk with his arms outstretched before him, for he dared not turn on a lamp.

It was not yet four o'clock. He had rested long enough. There were a good two hours yet before the household would come to life.

He would put the time to good use.

Chapter 25

Betsy hummed as she dusted Sarah's sitting room, paying particular mind to the delicate porcelain figurines that graced the mantel. Sunday afternoon was perhaps not the best time to do this sort of thing, she supposed, it being the Sabbath and all. But, having returned from church an hour or so ago, she had discovered that Sarah had gone out; and it was, after all, a good opportunity to get the work done.

Passing by the window with its white, ruffled curtains, Betsy glanced outside to see if the weather had cleared. She was not really surprised to see that it had not.

"Looks more like a day in January than May," she grumbled to herself.

Then, her brow furrowing into deep lines, Betsy stepped closer to the window, peering down into the front driveway, her eyes straining against the gray fog that all but obliterated the landscape. Mixed with the fog was a light rain that had been falling now for the past week, almost without a break.

What she saw, through the small, diamond-shaped panes, was Aleceon, holding Caroline by the hand, walking toward the front gate!

Now why would he be taking the girl out on a day like this? she wondered. Surely he was not planning on a drive! The roads were bogged down in mud from the past week's unremitting rain. And what's he doing back here, anyway? she mused silently, watching.

She was further mystified when, once outside the gate, Aleceon lifted Caroline into a waiting carriage.

Her annoyance mounted at the sight. Cheeky little bugger, she thought angrily. No doubt he thought he could get back in Sarah's good graces by suddenly paying attention to his niece. That was a laugh. He cared as much about Caroline as he did about anyone else—which was to say, very little.

Putting the dust rag down on a table, Betsy hurried to Caroline's room just down the hall, her mind already forming the angry words she planned to hurl at Mrs. Markham for allowing the girl to go out in weather like this.

At the sight that greeted her eyes, she felt the first shiver of apprehension, as if someone had run a cold, wet finger up the back of her neck. Sprawled in a chair, head thrown back and mouth open, was Mrs. Markham, snoring gently.

Approaching her, Betsy shook the woman once or twice in a none too gentle manner, invoking little response. Picking up the empty glass on the table, she sniffed it.

Wine. But... She sniffed again. There was another, more subtle odor. Her suspicions that Mrs. Markham had been drugged were confirmed a moment later when she located the bottle of wine. It was almost full; there had been only one drink poured from it. Certainly not enough to render a person unconscious.

Thoroughly alarmed now, and not knowing why, Betsy ran into the hall. Cornering a footman, she all but shouted at him.

"Miss Sarah! Where is she?"

"Why, both Mrs. Enright and her mother-in-law went to call on Mrs. Lansing," the man informed her. They would both be returning soon, he added, viewing her stricken face with curiosity.

"What time did she say she would be back?" Betsy demanded.

"They should be back in an hour or so," was the reply.

No time! she thought frantically. She wasn't certain why she felt such a premonition of danger, but the force of it took her breath away.

"Get the carriage," she said, running toward her room to get her shawl.

"But..."

"Do it!"

Some of the urgency she was feeling must have

transmitted itself to the man, because he turned and ran down the stairs to do as he had been told.

Within minutes, Betsy was seated beside him on the driver's bench, clutching her shawl tightly about her, her mind numb with a heavy fear that felt colder by far than the chilly mist.

"Where are we going?" the footman asked, prodding the horses forward through the fog and rain.

"I don't know," she answered shortly. "When we get ter the road, turn right."

And, please God, she prayed, let them find the other carriage.

When Captain Joshua Fielding entered Rose's establishment on this dreary May day, it was past noon. Outside, the fog still swirled, adding to the gray mist that blended with the sea, completely obliterating the horizon.

The captain was a short man, with a fringe of graying hair around his otherwise bald pate. He was totally unprepossessing, certainly not the sort of individual that one would have guessed commanded a vessel of the likes of the *Lucinda*, which was easily the largest cargo ship in the bay.

Nevertheless, he did. Twice a year he put into Boston harbor, and twice a year, after his cargo was unloaded, he visited Rose. Twenty-four hours was as long as the *Lucinda* anchored; it was more than enough time to conclude his business here.

He was not always successful. Nor did he expect to be; the nature of his business was far too delicate and uncertain to warrant such happy circumstances.

Upon entering, he was immediately shown to Rose's private quarters at the rear of the second floor. Once the door had closed, he was struck anew—as he always was—by the disparity between these private apartments and the rest of the premises.

He never ceased to marvel at it. There was no flamboyance here, no garish colors, no effort at exotic ostentation. The room that he knew to be her sitting room was elegantly and tastefully furnished in pastels;

only the finest material, only the richest woods, only the latest in wall coverings met the eye.

Even Rose herself seemed to relax, to discard the stiff, ever watchful mien she presented to her guests— not that he could be called a guest in the broad sense of the term.

Still, she was a hard and calculating woman, Fielding knew, as he accepted the drink she handed him. It would never do to underestimate Rose. A man, or a woman for that matter, did so at their own peril.

"How was your trip?" she inquired cordially, as she poured her own drink.

"Well enough." He eyed the brandy appreciatively before he tasted it.

"No trouble with the authorities?"

"None."

She relaxed as she sipped her drink. "I have a cargo for you this time." She ignored the gleam in his eyes and continued. "It will cost you double, though."

"What?" said Fielding slowly, frowning. "You know the price. Five thousand a head, no more, no less." Brandy forgotten, he stared at her with pale, unblinking eyes.

Unruffled by his refusal, Rose smiled briefly. "I also have an idea of what you sell them for." She raised a hand as he began to protest. "But that's not the reason," she went on to explain. "This one happens to be special. A real beauty. Not the waifs and ragamuffins you usually pick up. I'll wager this one will fetch more than you normally get."

Fielding drank, his expression clearly indicating that he was unconvinced. He did not want to argue with Rose; neither did he want to set a precedent. Right now, she was his only source. This business, he reflected dourly, was not like opium; everybody, it seemed, had a hand in that.

"All right," he said at last, but was secretly prepared for heavy bargaining. "Let's see her. But mind!" he stressed, following her into the next room. "I make no promises."

"Only right," she agreed, and then, placing a finger to her lips, cautioned him to silence.

The room they entered was small, no more than five feet by seven feet, and held only a small bed and a table with a candle on it. The candle was lit and cast a feeble, wavering light upon the small figure on the bed, who had not so much as moved with their entrance.

In spite of himself, Fielding caught his breath. She was lovely; she was beautiful! He had never seen such a face. Clouds of chestnut-brown hair fanned the pillow, the pure curve of her cheek traced clearly in the honey-colored light. He could not see her eyes. They were closed, because she was drugged.

He did not question that. They tended to cry and carry on, until it liked to try a man's patience. All men, that is, except those who tended to pay a high price for her likes. In the East, where she would eventually be sent, she would bring a fortune.

His mouth went dry at the sight of the treasure, and he sincerely hoped that his voice did not reflect his excitement as he asked: "How old is she?"

His eagerness had not gone unnoticed, but Rose did not permit herself to smile. She knew Joshua Fielding quite well. Like most men of small stature, he was prideful; at times, arrogant. It would not help her cause to put him on the defensive. "Not quite eight," she replied.

He took a deep breath, his nostrils flaring. Perfect! The buyers liked them to be between five and ten years old. Up to twelve was acceptable, but they brought less money, for there was a period of training involved, sometimes as much as three years, before they were turned over to their masters. Obviously, the older they were, the less tractable they were.

Fielding had few qualms about his white-slavery operation. He had neither wife nor children, for he was a sensible man, and sensible men do not so encumber themselves.

Again his eyes sought the slight figure on the bed. Most of the young girls that Rose turned over to him were little more than destitutes, orphans who would eventually perish on Boston's grimmer side. When he delivered his cargo in London, they would be sold to buyers representing Eastern potentates, and would thence live their lives in unparalleled richness. No doubt their master would bother them only once or twice before he lost interest, and then they would merely languish in luxury.

Or so he reasoned, when he gave it any thought at all.

"How much?" he now asked.

"I told you. Double the usual. Ten thousand."

"My God! I never expected you to rob me!" he exclaimed in genuine outrage.

At this, Rose laughed softly. "Oh, come now, Joshua," she chided him. "We both know that you make twice that, and more." She turned and began to walk away, but his voice halted her.

"How do I know that she's not deformed in some way? Addled in the wits, perhaps."

The smile broadened. "Would it really matter?" she asked. She fixed him with a hard look. "If you want to inspect her physically, do so. As for her mind, I assure you it's sound."

He bit his lip. Rose was to be trusted, he knew that; but ten thousand dollars! He approached the bed, carefully raising the white shift, which was the only garment the child wore. As Rose had said, she was perfectly formed. There wasn't a mark on her body. This was no orphan, no street child, he mused.

Pulling the shift down again, he stared at Rose, his eyes hardening. "This one looks like trouble. Where did you get her?"

Rose appeared unconcerned by his scrutiny. "The usual places; you need not concern yourself with that." She turned away. "Of course, if you don't want her...."

"All right, all right!" he said ungraciously. "But don't think that I'm about to make a habit of it." The money still rankled.

Her smile returned. "Come, Joshua. Have some food before you leave. Then Seth will help you get the girl aboard when you're ready to leave."

Sarah had been quiet on the relatively short trip home from Elizabeth's house. The weekly visits depressed her, and the steady, monotonous rain of the past week did little to lighten her mood. Elizabeth was so obviously unhappy, although she tried desperately to hide that fact, to be bright and cheerful. Sarah's heart ached for her friend.

Sometimes she wished that she could keep Sunday afternoons for herself, but Elizabeth always seemed so upset when she sent word that she would be unable to visit.

Today had been particularly trying because Justin had taken it upon himself to join them. Usually he occupied himself in his study, writing his sermons or lengthy essays in which he denounced Abolition and Mr. Garrison, who was now revealing his thoughts in the *Liberator*, with equal fervor.

This afternoon, however, he had inexplicably decided to take tea with them, and the result had been a most unpleasant, strained visit.

Ever since that day when Sarah had discovered Justin's true self, she had felt uncomfortable in his presence, her dislike degenerating by degrees into true antipathy.

Nor did his countenance ever lend itself to pleasantness. She was struck by the thought that in the years she had known Justin Lansing, she had never—not once—heard him laugh. The man was entirely without humor.

Poor Elizabeth, she thought, bracing herself as the carriage plowed through the mud. That one such as she should be tied to a man like that for life. Sarah supposed that, at one time, Elizabeth must have loved him. But in all honesty, she had to admit that the charm of the man, however nebulous, escaped her.

She had so hoped that with the birth of Hannah, Elizabeth's life would return to at least a modicum of normalcy. Unhappily, the child, so precious and so lovely, with that silver-gilt hair of hers—a tremendous refinement of Justin's own sandy-colored hair—seemed to have only exacerbated matters in that dreary household.

Still, Justin was apparently no longer mistreating Elizabeth, and that thought at least offered comfort.

As the carriage approached the driveway to Somerset Hall, Sarah leaned forward, catching sight of Betsy's plump figure, a hastily thrown shawl about her shoulders to stave off the continuing drizzly mist. Rachel, sitting beside Sarah, made a comment about the odd sight of her standing in the rain, but Sarah made no answer, for her heart had begun to pound heavily.

It was Jonathan, she thought, catching her breath. Something had happened to him! She knew she shouldn't have left him alone.

As the carriage drew to a halt, Betsy ran forward, and spoke before Sarah could alight.

"It's Caroline," she said in a rush. Ignoring Sarah's suddenly white face, she hurriedly explained what had taken place. "I seen where he took her, but it makes no sense ter me. It's just a warehouse!"

By now, Tully had opened the carriage door and was assisting Rachel to step down. Turning, Rachel said to Sarah, "Summon the authorities at once!"

But Sarah, still in the carriage, hesitated. "No. No, I'll go there myself." She leaned forward. "Betsy, come with me and show us the way." In spite of her first fear, she could not really believe that Aleceon would harm Caroline. This was his way of getting back at her, she decided. He was trying to upset and frighten her. That was all.

"Mrs. Enright..."

Surprised, Sarah viewed Tully, whose face had turned ashen. He looked miserable and seemed unable to bring himself to speak.

"If yer knows owt, speak up, yer bugger!" Betsy exclaimed heatedly, impatient with the man.

"Hold your tongue, young woman!" Rachel commanded, viewing Betsy with undisguised disapproval. "Do you know anything about this matter, Tully?" she then asked.

"Yes, ma'am," Tully replied in a barely audible voice. "That is, no ma'am," he hastily amended, anguish apparent on his face. "I don't know about Miss Caroline being taken away, but I know of the place you're talking about." He threw Betsy a quick glance. "It's...not a warehouse."

"Well, what is it, man?" Sarah was overcome by exasperation. "For heaven's sake, tell us what you know!"

He did. But could not bring himself to look at Rachel's shocked face, or at Sarah's wide and frightened eyes. Even Betsy, speechless for once, could not utter a word and just stared at him, dumbfounded.

"Why on earth would he take her to a place like that?" Sarah wondered aloud. Surely Aleceon could not actually be living in such a place!

"Sarah, I insist that you summon the authorities!" Rachel repeated, annoyed with her daughter-in-law's continued reluctance to act.

Sarah shook her head firmly. She knew that her mother-in-law thought it was because of Aleceon's welfare that she refused to do this. It wasn't that at all. Until she knew just what was going on, the authorities could not only confuse the matter but, more important, they could create a dangerous situation for Caroline. Obviously, Aleceon wanted money, and had taken this despicable method of extorting it from her.

A constable, she vowed, settling back into the carriage and motioning for Betsy to join her, would be called as soon as she had her daughter safely back.

And then, she further promised herself, she herself would see to it that Aleceon was arrested.

Rachel stood there, rigid and disapproving, as the carriage pulled away. Turning back to the house, she glanced upward, and frowned in perplexity. Strange; she thought she had seen the curtain move in Jonathan's room. One of the servants must have left the window open, she thought, mounting the steps. And on a day like today! Jonathan would catch a chill.

Sarah's thoughts were awhirl; a mixture of anger, fear, confusion, and resentment flooded her being. With only half an ear, she listened to Betsy's encouraging and supportive words, but she rode in silence until they reached the outskirts of Boston, not trusting herself to speak.

Approaching the wharf, Sarah was suddenly stricken with doubts, and for the first time was uncertain that she was doing the right thing. How could she possibly walk up to the front door and demand the return of her daughter? What if they refused her entrance? Or worse, denied that Caroline was even there?

"Oh, my God," she murmured, distraught now.

"Aw, lass, we'll get her back, that we will," Betsy said quickly, taking hold of her cold hand. "I'll break down the door meself, if need be. I know she's there, I seen him take her in." And that was a good three hours ago, she thought worriedly, but refused to impart this newest concern to Sarah. Cheeky little bastard, she thought of Aleceon, mentally consigning him to hell's lowest, blackest spot forever. Even that, she decided, was too good for the likes of him.

Sarah leaned forward so suddenly that Betsy reached for her, thinking that she had fainted. But Sarah pushed the helping hand away, her eyes fastened on the tall figure standing on the pier. Leaning out of the window, she shouted: "Christian! Christian! Tully, stop the carriage."

Frantically, she waved a hand at him. "Christian!"

He turned then, his face at first questioning. Recognition followed immediately, and then surprise. He hesitated only a second, then began to run toward her, the delivery of his new machinery, which even now was being unloaded, forgotten.

Before he reached the carriage, she was out. Sobbing now, she quickly told him what had happened. "He's taken her, Christian. I must get her out of there!"

His face blank with shock, Christian just listened, his hands placed upon Sarah's shoulders. Anger made his eyes hard and implacable, but his voice was controlled as he spoke.

"Get back into the carriage, Sarah. Go home. I'll take care of this." Christian's eyes searched her pale face anxiously, for he could see that she was near hysteria. "You can do nothing here," he said gently.

"No, no," she cried out. "I can't go home! Not without Caroline."

"Do as I say!" He tightened his grip, his fingers pressing deep into her shoulders beneath the soft wool of her shawl. "Please go home, Sarah. I give you my word, I'll bring your daughter to you."

Still she hesitated, but deep inside, she was conscious of the soothing feeling of peace that calmed her ragged nerves. Had it been any other than the man who stood before her now, she would have resisted. But this was Christian, her mind told her. Christian, who always seemed to take care of everything. Christian, the man she loved; the man who would never harm her.

She nodded slowly, and allowed him to help her back into the carriage. When she was settled, he closed the door firmly, and for a long moment, just looked at her. Then, abruptly, he turned, heading for the front door of the innocuous-looking warehouse.

Sarah, watching him, took a deep breath. Finally, in a faint voice, she ordered Tully to return to Somerset Hall.

Jonathan lay very still in his bed; it was not much of an effort after all this while. In fact, after his continuous nightly exercises, it was, in a sense, a relief. What he really had to be careful about was falling asleep. For in that uncontrollable state, he could easily turn over or move.

Now he watched his mother as she bustled about the room, grumbling about open windows. Satisfying herself that they were closed, she came over to the bed, staring down at her son solicitously. "Is there anything you need, Jonathan?" she asked.

He moved his eyes slowly until they rested upon her. He was, he knew, supposed to blink. One for yes; two for no. How many, he wondered, for get out!

He blinked twice.

She regarded him with some doubt for a moment longer. "Very well," she said, patting his shoulder. "I'm going to change into some dry clothes, and then I'll read to you awhile before supper."

Watching her go, Jonathan's lip curled with sardonic amusement. Read to him. As if he were mentally incompetent and incapable of reading on his own.

Where had Sarah gone? he wondered. It was almost time for supper, and Betsy was with her, so it was doubtful that she had gone to visit her lover. Her big, raw-boned, son-of-an-innkeeper lover.

His mouth curled with the thought of Sarah in another man's arms, receiving his kisses, caresses. Where did they meet? he wondered. Where did they hold their trysts?

With very little effort, his mind's eye projected the imagined scenes of their illicit passion. He knew Sarah's body intimately, every curve, every swell, every secret place. Did she compare him with her lover? Jonathan ground his teeth viciously at the thought, clenching his hands into fists.

All these years! his mind raged. His breath came faster, and his heart thudded and rocked as his fury built up to swelling, thunderous waves of emotion. All these years, he had thought that Sarah was his, and his alone.

And all these years, he had been sharing her with another man.

Sarah, he mused, toying with the name upon his lips. She was never far from his thoughts, had never been, from the first time that he had seen her at the Emporium that day. He thought of her constantly.

He lay here now because of her; he lived, and breathed, and moved, because of her.

"Ah, my darling Sarah," he murmured in the silence of his room, his thoughts twisting into cold fury. She still had the power to invoke great feeling within him. Hate, after all, was just as powerful an emotion as love.

One might even say, Jonathan thought grimly, that he lived only for Sarah.

Only for her death.

Chapter 26

Christian walked with long, slow strides toward the warehouse.

As he moved forward, the mist and fog enclosed him, and he could feel the biting dampness upon his face. He was grateful for the icy feel of it, for it calmed his raging anger. He knew that he would need a cool head in the moments to come. He also knew that, should he meet Aleceon face to face, he would not be responsible for his actions.

He knew all about Rose's establishment, although he had never set foot inside. Christian had learned of it soon after Lucas began to come here. He had made inquiries, at first merely disgusted with his brother's latest peccadilloes, and then appalled as he learned, quite by accident, of Rose's nefarious operations. He doubted that even the authorities knew about those, although most certainly they were aware of the drugs, gambling, and prostitution.

A flashing sense of dread had swept through him, settling in the pit of his stomach when Sarah told him about her daughter. He knew there could be only one reason that Caroline was brought here.

But then, he rationalized, he could be mistaken. Even Aleceon could not be so foul. Perhaps it was as Sarah thought; her brother had taken Caroline, and would return her when Sarah paid him enough money.

Yet, somehow, knowing Aleceon as he did, this rationalization did little to calm him as he reached the front door. He knocked only once and was immediately admitted by a man who gave him no more than a cursory glance.

Christian refused the polite offer to check his hat and cloak; instead he said: "Tell Rose that I wish to see her."

The man blinked, but otherwise his pale face revealed little expression. "I'm afraid, sir, that she is having her supper. With a guest," he added firmly, as if that precluded further argument.

Christian's eyes glittered like polished steel. "I think she'll see me," he said softly, presenting his card. "My name is Christian Hockings."

The man briefly inclined his head, but if the name meant anything to him it was not apparent in his face. "If you will wait here, sir," he said, "I will present your card." With steps no louder than the encroaching fog, the man mounted the steps and was lost from view.

Christian waited, his outwardly calm manner revealing little of his agitated thoughts. Coolly, he surveyed the main room and with a disinterested eye noted the solemn players at the tables. They seemed engrossed, humorless, each afflicted with a deadly earnestness that seemed to lighten or deepen with each fall of the cards.

Momentarily diverted, Christian watched them, wondering why they would so waste their time. Gambling was, to him, a foolish pastime. Lucas had been addicted to it, playing every chance he got. Fortunately, he had been able to pass up the laudanum; it was one of the few vices he had declined.

A young woman dressed in a magenta lace gown approached Christian. One look at his eyes, and the welcoming words died upon her red lips. With a tentative, almost apologetic smile, she drifted away into the smoky haze.

Less than five minutes had passed before the man returned, but to Christian's taut nerves it seemed much longer.

"This way, Mr. Hockings," he said without preamble and, turning, led Christian up the stairs and down the long, deeply carpeted, and dimly lit hallway. They met no one save a short, unprepossessing man who passed them quickly, eyes averted.

When Christian entered Rose's private apartments, he found it difficult to conceal his surprise at the elegant ambience of the graciously furnished room. But his attention was only momentarily captured.

She was seated in a large, deep-cushioned chair. Her garish gown, with its frills and ribbons and yards of lace, was completely at odds with her surroundings. Her little black eyes viewed him harshly for a moment, then she smiled and motioned with her fan, directing Christian to a chair.

"Please be seated, Mr. Hockings," she said in a voice that was both calm and assured. "We have never met before; however, I am pleased to personally welcome you here."

Obviously she knew who he was, and that could make his mission that much simpler, he thought. Money was, after all, the crux of the matter. And that he had in plentiful supply.

Ignoring her invitation to sit, he merely removed his hat and cloak, laying them on a small, straight-backed chair. He faced her, hands clasped behind his back. "I am here not on pleasure but on business, Miss Kendall."

A finely painted brow drew upward. Few of her customers knew her full name. She continued to smile serenely, but her little black eyes hardened noticeably. "Business is my first love, Mr. Hockings," she noted easily. "Surely you have time for a drink, at least?"

He nodded. Laying her fan aside, Rose got to her feet with surprisingly little effort for one of her size. Then she walked toward the sideboard. As she poured the brandy into two crystal glasses, her movements were calm and unhurried, but her mind was working with its usual agility. When she had read the card that Franz handed to her, a small alarm had sounded within her. She had an instinct for that sort of thing. Besides, few of the men who came here presented calling cards. They much preferred anonymity.

The fact that Christian Hockings knew her full name indicated that he had made some inquiries, although for what purpose she could not fathom. That he knew of her establishment was not in the least surprising to her. After all, his brother had been here. She recalled hearing that Lucas Hockings had been shot. She wondered if that had anything to do with this unexpected visit.

Not plausible, her mind told her as she handed him

one of the glasses. Then she remembered where Lucas Hockings had been killed. A tremor of wariness suddenly shot through her.

What, she mused, was the connection between the Hockingses and the Enrights?

With keen perception, Christian noted her subtly altered expression, and smiled to himself. At least the woman, gross as she appeared, had intelligence.

"Perhaps I should have come here sooner," he mentioned casually, regarding his glass. "You serve a brandy of fine merit, and I understand from mutual friends that your other services are also of high quality."

"Do we have mutual friends, Mr. Hockings?"

"Oh, indeed, Miss Kendall."

She placed her half-empty glass on the small table beside her chair. Her expression remained bland as Christian casually mentioned the dinner party that he had attended only the week before. An occasion, he smilingly reported, that had included the mayor and the chief constable, among other dignitaries.

At last she regarded him squarely, all vestiges of her welcoming manner erased from her fleshy face. "What exactly is it that you want, Mr. Hockings?" she inquired curtly.

"A girl," he replied smoothly, and could not repress a short, mirthless laugh at the surprised expression that flitted across her painted face. "Oh, not just any girl," he continued in a soft voice. He shook his head slightly, regarding her with an almost amused expression that somehow failed to reach his eyes. "No. What I want is a special girl."

"Special? I'm certain that I can fulfill any need you have, Mr. Hockings," she said warily.

"Splendid!" Christian paced about aimlessly, apparently lost in thought. There were, he saw, no windows in the room; it seemed completely cut off from the outside world. No sounds, either, from downstairs or the adjoining rooms penetrated the silence; only the ticking of the fragile silver clock that dominated one corner of the desk intruded upon the stillness.

"Somehow I knew that you could accommodate me," Christian said, a brief smile playing about his lips. He halted before her, staring into her eyes, and for the moment their gazes locked.

Then she looked away. A slight pallor crept over her face, but she was otherwise in control of herself.

"I shall describe her to you," Christian was saying in so quiet a tone that his voice barely disturbed the tranquillity. "She is about three feet tall, and weighs not much more than forty pounds."

Her eyes returned to his, widened slightly, but she made no comment.

One part of Christian was astounded by this woman who viewed him with icy aloofness, her black eyes cold and unreadable; yet he was also aware of the rage building within him, threatening to destroy his own composure.

"Her hair is chestnut brown, very fine in texture. And her eyes..." He paused, and Rose was startled to see the momentary flash of pain that drifted across his face and was gone in an instant. "Her eyes are gray."

Now his face grew rigid and taut and his gaze became stony. "She is seven and a half years old," he concluded.

For the moment, the silence hung between them like a palpable thing, and when Rose at last opened her mouth to speak, Christian quickly demanded: "Shall I give you her name?"

Rose moistened her lips, her mind working furiously as all the pieces suddenly fell together. Automatically, she glanced at the silver clock, a motion that did not escape Christian, whose blood chilled at the thought that perhaps he was too late.

But no, he could see by her compressed lips and the slight flush that stained her sallow skin that the child was still here, somewhere. And Aleceon? Where was that blackguard? he wondered.

Suddenly Rose's expression crumpled into resignation, as if she had reached a decision, albeit a reluctant one. There would be other times, and it would be foolish, she decided, to jeopardize all for the sake of one little chit.

"There is no need for her name, Mr. Hockings," she said smoothly, again getting to her feet. "The girl you mention is indeed here. Temporarily, you understand," she added firmly. A quick look flashed between them, and it was as if they had both agreed upon playing this charade, each for his own reasons. "Mr. Edgewood merely left the child in my care while he did some errands. He said that he would return for her shortly."

"And where is Mr. Edgewood?" Christian asked coldly.

Again her mouth tightened, this time in annoyance. "I don't know that, Mr. Hockings," she said truthfully.

He took a breath. Aleceon could be dealt with at a later time, he decided. Right now, Caroline was the important thing. "Bring the child to me," he said in the same tone. "Now!"

She hesitated only a moment; then, walking to the bell cord, gave it a vicious tug. A moment later the same man who had admitted Christian entered, merely nodding his head when Rose, in curt tones, instructed him to bring Caroline to her.

She waited until he left, then turned to Christian. "The child is...asleep," she said. "You do understand?"

Hearing that subtle admission that Caroline had been drugged, Christian's face hardened, and he clenched his fists to keep from striking Rose. "If she has been harmed...," he began in a strained voice.

"She has not," Rose interjected quickly, raising a ringed hand. "I've told you, she's asleep. That's all."

Christian donned his hat and cloak. They spoke no more, until some time later when the door again opened, and the man, followed by Seth, who carried the now fully dressed Caroline in his arms, entered.

Quickly, Christian stepped forward and took the child in his own arms. She murmured and sighed deeply, but did not awaken, and Christian was filled with relief as he saw that she was, to all outward appearances, unharmed. But then, he reflected bitterly, why would she be harmed? An injured child would be damaged merchandise. There would be little profit in that.

"It has been a pleasure to do business with you, Mr. Hockings," Rose stated acidly.

His glance was brief as he walked toward the door. "Should you see Mr. Edgewood," he said curtly, ignoring her sarcasm, "you might tell him that I am looking forward to renewing our acquaintance." He gave Seth a hard, piercing look as he passed him and entered the hall.

Rose only nodded, then, with an impatient wave of her hand, indicated that Seth and Franz should also go.

When she was alone again, she gave a rueful laugh, entirely devoid of mirth. She knew that she would never again see Aleceon Edgewood. Nor, for that matter, Kitty. That ungrateful girl had run off with him. More fool she, Rose thought, disgruntled. Doubtless they had both left Boston for good.

She walked back to the sideboard and poured herself another drink. Good riddance to them both, she silently toasted, briefly lifting the glass.

To add insult to injury, she thought, truly annoyed, she was out five thousand dollars, having returned Aleceon's markers to him when he had delivered Caroline.

Her brow furrowed in concentration as her mind sought for the words of explanation that she would have to give Joshua Fielding. No doubt he would be most irritated and disappointed by what had happened here tonight.

But then, she reflected, raising the glass to her red lips, business was like gambling. Sometimes you win, and sometimes you lose.

Chapter 27

Having returned to Somerset Hall, Sarah now stood by the bow window in the front parlor, her eyes locked upon the curving driveway and the muddied road just beyond it.

With unusual curtness, she had dismissed her mother-in-law's probing questions upon her return, and Rachel had gone directly upstairs in a huff.

Although her eyes strained, Sarah could see little but unrelieved blackness outside. Still, she could not tear herself away from her vigil. Betsy waited by her side.

"It'll be all right, lass," she said, as she had countless times in these past hours. "He'll bring her back, I know it."

Sarah seemed not to hear, as she frantically waited for her first glimpse of Christian's carriage, her thoughts riveted upon Aleceon. How could he have done such a thing? her mind raged in hurt confusion. That he was weak and irresponsible she had finally come to accept, difficult as that had been for her.

But that he would strike at her very heart, that was what hurt so. She had loved him, cared for him, since he had been born. And, until now, despite their harsh words when last they parted, she had thought that he returned at least a part of that feeling.

They were brother and sister, yet Sarah now thought of him as a stranger. The Aleceon she knew and loved would never have done this. Why hadn't he come to her if he needed money—and he must have, desperately, to have acted as he had.

There was one other source of uneasiness, and Sarah refused even to think upon it, for it was too horrible to contemplate. Why hadn't Aleceon contacted her for the money by now? Why was he making her wait, stretching her agony to unendurable lengths? Surely he knew that she would pay him immediately. Unless something else had happened to Caroline...

Unconsciously, her white, dry lips moved in a prayer as she implored God to keep her little girl safe. Safe and unaware. She would not be physically harmed, not intentionally; that much confidence she still had in Aleceon. But she would never forgive her brother for this. Never!

"Can I get yer something, lass?" Betsy asked. "A bit of tea, perhaps? Or maybe some hot chocolate?" At the sound of Sarah's vehement denial, Betsy sighed deeply, returning her gaze to the window. For some moments she viewed the tiny rivulets that threaded the pane, then her eyes sharpened as she caught a brief glimpse of light that was gone as quickly as it had appeared.

Reaching out a hand, she rubbed at the glass. Again the light flickered, teasing her eye with its momentary brightness. "That looks like Mr. Hockings's carriage now!" exclaimed Betsy.

Without even bothering to verify the sighting, Sarah immediately hurried to the front porch, Betsy close on her heels. Together they descended the steps and stood in the gravel driveway, peering anxiously.

Behind them, in the open doorway, Phillips and Mrs. Bowe stood side by side, their faces reflecting the same anxiety. Mrs. Markham, only now recovering her senses, was resting upstairs. Rachel, exhausted by the day's events, slept soundly.

Before the carriage had come to a full stop, Sarah could see Christian's smile of reassurance. How many times, she thought wildly, had she counted on that smile? She could not imagine having to live the rest of her life without it. A moment later, she saw Caroline, held protectively within the circle of his arms. The girl looked sleepy, but managed a small smile as they drove up to the steps.

Seconds later, Sarah clasped her daughter close, relief flooding her limbs with weakness. Her throat ached with tears, and she could not speak, contenting herself with just holding the child, assuring herself that she was safe.

"Are you all right, darling?" she managed to ask at last, striving to keep her voice calm. She smoothed the child's hair, which was tumbled and disarrayed, aware that her heart pounded so fiercely that her chest hurt with each breath she took.

"I fell asleep," Caroline said, yawning. "Uncle Aleceon took me to visit a lady, and she gave me cake and cider. Then I fell asleep and woke up in the carriage." She smiled sweetly at her mother, wondering why her lips were trembling. "Mr. Hockings said he was taking me home, and that Uncle Aleceon had to stay on in Boston because of business," she further explained, hoping that her mother would not scold her.

"That's right, darling," Sarah was saying, and now allowed Betsy to take Caroline.

"Come on, luv," Betsy said, her usually gay voice strangely husky. "Let's get yer inside where it's warm and cozy."

Sarah watched them go, then turned to Christian, her eyes bright with tears of love and a gratitude so profound that she could barely speak.

"I have thanked you before," she said, gazing up into his dear face. "But never as I do now...." Her voice caught, and she could find no further words.

He regarded her for a moment, solemnly and without speaking. He had given a great deal of thought as to whether or not she should be told of all that had happened. At last he realized that, for her own safety, she must know. He had an idea that, henceforth, Aleceon would keep his distance; yet there was always the chance that one day he would return.

"Sarah," he said quietly, "you must never again allow Aleceon near you or your children." He put his hands on her slim shoulders and, viewing her with the utmost seriousness, told her what Aleceon had planned for her daughter.

From the window of his second-floor bedroom, Jonathan gazed down upon his wife and Christian Hockings.

It was dark, but apparently the front door was still open, because a shaft of light pierced the dimness, giving a golden hue to the swirling fog, providing enough light so that he could see them quite clearly.

He had, only moments before, gotten out of his bed. It was now ten o'clock, and he knew that his mother would be asleep. She had not looked in on him tonight, as she usually did, and for that he was grateful. He found her presence tedious and trying, for he could never relax when she was in the room. Always fussing about him, adjusting covers, reading to him in her monotonous voice.

He regarded the two figures below. Sarah seemed greatly agitated, he noted with interest, although her distraught state left him unmoved. Standing very quietly, Jonathan watched as Sarah's arms went about Christian's neck and he clasped her close to him.

Jonathan's eyes narrowed. He had seen the carriage drive up, and had seen Caroline emerge from within its upholstered depths.

So his daughter was also Christian's, he thought. Only of Nicholas was he certain, for he and Sarah had been in England when she conceived his younger son.

His only son, Jonathan mentally corrected himself. But he had not changed his plan. Benjamin was his; if not by blood, then by right.

Anger swelled within him, almost choking him as he continued to watch. A sickening pang of bitterness assaulted him, like the return of an old illness he thought he had long since conquered. Betrayal. Even the sound of the word was acrid and unpalatable upon the tongue. His hands clutched the windowsill for support, as if the sight before him was unbearable; but he could not look away.

She was sobbing now as Christian tried to comfort her. And for what reason did she weep? But, of course, he knew the answer to that. She wept for her lover, and for their imminent parting.

Straightening, Jonathan smiled coldly. She would weep all the harder if she could but know that this would be their final parting. The time had come.

Letting the drapery fall back into place, Jonathan made his way back to his bed, his steps slow and careful. Now would not be the time to stumble and fall. Grasping hold of his pillows, he arranged them beneath the covers. A casual glance into the room would reveal what appeared to be himself, sleeping soundly.

Then, with the same studied care, Jonathan walked to the door, which he opened just a crack.

The hallway was empty, but he could hear Betsy and Mrs. Markham as they fussed over Caroline, their voices cooing and coaxing as they urged her to eat. He did not take the time to wonder why they would be doing that at this time of night. Caroline was spoiled, he decided, as he stepped into the hall. That would change, later. He would see to it.

Cautiously, he made his way to Sarah's door and, opening it, entered her bedroom. As quietly as he was able, he closed the door.

A single lamp was lit on the bedside table and the fire was burning. His eyes swept around the neat, femininely furnished room. Only the tall mahogany wardrobe offered concealment, he saw. It was not quite flush with the corner of the wall, and there was a space of about two feet between its side and the parallel wall.

Thoughtfully, he viewed the door on the far side of the room and after a moment he walked across the soft carpet and studied it. The key was on this side. Turning it, he pocketed it. Now he walked to the wardrobe and secreted himself within the shadows, leaning against the wall in an effort to conserve his strength.

Then he waited.

Five minutes passed, then another five. Finally, she came into the room.

She closed the door and leaned against it wearily. Her face, even in the warm glow of lamplight, was ashen and drawn. She looked incredibly weary and frail, but the sight aroused no compassion within him. Instead, he was filled with exultation. After all his humiliation, he was about to be revenged. No longer did he begrudge the endless hours he had spent in strengthening his body and once-useless muscles. This moment made it all worthwhile. She had thought herself to be clever; she was about to learn that he was more so.

Sarah walked toward the canopied bed, and with a deep sigh that was quite audible to Jonathan, she sat down. She glanced at the book lying unopened beside the lamp, and then looked away again, as if the prospect of reading was too exhausting to contemplate.

Slowly, unaware that she was being watched, she began to undo the buttons on her bodice. Her mind was still numb from what Christian had related to her regarding Alecoen's intentions. It had so shocked her that she could not even feel hate for her brother, only a sort of detached wonderment that such a man could exist, and that such a man could be her own brother. Christian seemed to think that he might return one day, and Sarah fervently hoped that this was not so; she had no desire to view her brother ever again.

In the shadows, Jonathan's eyes never left her. Grateful that her back was to him, he stealthily stepped out from his hiding place. His mind was curiously empty; he moved on emotion alone.

He was almost beside her when she turned, startled. For the moment she stared at him blankly, almost as if she didn't recognize him.

Then her eyes widened incredulously and her mouth parted slightly. Raising a white hand to her throat, she drew in her breath sharply.

"Jonathan!" She sat there as if sculpted in marble, an alabaster sheen to her flawless skin. Even hating her, Jonathan saw her beauty; and he despised it.

"You mustn't be so surprised," he said, his eyes glowing as if lit from within. "Is it so unusual that your husband pays you a visit of an evening?"

As if moving in a dream, Sarah got to her feet. Shock and surprise faded, and her face was flooded with something akin to relief. "How wonderful," she breathed, standing before him. "But why didn't you let me know? How long...?"

"How long have I been able to speak, to move?" He seemed to consider this, and then his smile widened. "Oh, for months, my darling Sarah. For months." He chuckled softly, seeing her expression fall into confusion. "I've been waiting for the appropriate moment to reveal my recovery to you."

Almost carelessly, he placed his hands about her slim neck, absently noting the throbbing pulse at the base of her throat. Gently he moved his thumbs across it, feeling its soft rhythm beneath the smooth, satiny skin.

Watching his eyes, Sarah experienced a start of fear, as yet unformed because it was so unreasonable. Resisting the impulse to recoil, she stood very still, hardly daring to breathe as he seemed to study her with care. Her gaze moved and rested upon the door that adjoined her bedroom with Betsy's, and she relaxed somewhat. Betsy must be in her room by now. They had both left Caroline, tucked in and under the watchful eye of the now-recovered Mrs. Markham, at the same time. Truly exhausted from all that had taken place, Sarah had bid Betsy goodnight in the hall, urging her to return directly to her own room without coming in here to turn down the bed as she normally did.

And, because of the late hour, she had never thought of entering Jonathan's room, thinking him to be asleep—thinking him to be paralyzed and incapable of movement or speech!

"My darling Sarah," he was murmuring, unaware of her drifting attention. "Has there ever been a man who so loved his wife as I did? You were everything to me," he went on in an unnaturally soft voice, and it was that softness that struck real fear in Sarah's heart.

As if he knew that, or could feel the increased throb in her pulse, he resumed the caressing movement with his thumbs, which were still at the base of her throat. She forced herself to remain quiet, to make no sudden movement. This was her husband, she told herself; she had nothing to fear from him.

"Everything I've done has been for you. And for Benjamin," he added, almost as an afterthought. "My son will be the beneficiary of it all," he informed her seriously. He gazed intently into her wide, gray eyes. *"My* son, Sarah," he whispered, tightening his grip slightly.

Despite her resolve, she gasped, and put her hands up, grasping hold of his wrists. She became aware that his hands were tightening with a slow, even pressure. She opened her mouth to scream, but only a feeble sound came out.

"Ah," he whispered, observing her reaction with

pleased eyes. "Now you know, my darling Sarah. Now you know the price of your treachery."

The grip tightened. Thoroughly terrified, Sarah began to struggle, digging her nails into his wrists, trying desperately to pull away from him. She was astounded by his strength.

Yet while strength had returned to an almost normal degree in Jonathan's hands, his legs, particularly the left one, still had a tendency to weakness. As she began to struggle violently, he lost his balance; still gripping her neck firmly, he fell, pulling them both sideways onto the small bedside table.

The book and the lamp pitched to the floor. In only seconds, the lighted oil caught the pages, sending spurts of little flames into the air. The carpet, now oil-soaked, burst into flames.

Twisting her body in a sudden movement, Sarah completely unbalanced Jonathan, who had to release his hold in an effort to break his fall.

Her screams were hysterical and rent the night, shredding the quiet with their abrupt assault. Moments later, Betsy was pounding on the door.

"Sarah! Sarah, lass, for Gawd's sakes, what is it? Open the door!" She continued the pounding, rattling the knob at intervals.

But Sarah, her hand on her bruised throat, was frantically trying to crawl away from the spreading flames that now threatened to engulf the entire room, all the while keeping a wary eye on Jonathan, who, she was now certain, meant to kill her.

She had almost reached the door to the hallway when he lunged at her. His arms clasped firmly about her waist, he dragged her back toward the flames, heedless of her desperate, pleading cries.

Chapter 28

Christian threw his cigar out of the carriage window and pensively gazed into the foggy night. He pulled his cloak closer about him in an effort to stave off the penetrating chill, and thought longingly of the blazing fire and brandy that awaited him when he at last reached home.

It had been a long day, and an unsettling one. Thank God it had turned out as it had. It could have ended in disaster.

Something would have to be done about Rose, he decided. Going over the details in his mind, he realized that she was shrewd, and dangerous. He sincerely doubted that any feelings of sentimentality or morality were ever allowed to color her decisions, which, he was firmly convinced, were based solely on her own welfare. The fact that she was intelligent, Christian reasoned, made her doubly dangerous.

Yes, most assuredly, something would have to be done. A few words in the right ear and it could be settled. There would probably be some initial resistance, for the very men he planned to speak to no doubt patronized her establishment. But he was certain that they were unaware of her involvement with white slavery. Almost all of the men had daughters; it would take little on his part to convince them to shut down her operations. At least in Boston.

As for Aleceon, even now, after it was all over, Christian had to shake his head in disbelief. He had all of Rose's qualities, without her intelligence. What could be done with a man like that? When all was said and done, Christian had to acknowledge to himself that he had no proof, none whatsoever. Rose had admitted only that the girl had been left in her care for a few hours.

Unadmirable, perhaps, in view of who and what she was, but certainly not illegal.

Someday, he mused grimly, his thoughts tumultuous and savage. Someday, Aleceon would be found. And when he was, Christian promised himself, he would be dealt with on his own level. Above all, Aleceon must never again be allowed to cause Sarah the anguish and torment she had suffered on this night. No one would hurt her again. No one.

In the blackness, Christian nodded to himself, as if making a solemn vow.

The carriage was moving at an easy pace, almost lackadaisically. There was really no reason for haste, after all. Rebecca and his little son, David, were most likely asleep. Only his empty, quiet room awaited him. As for the unclaimed machinery, it would wait till morning.

With a sigh, he leaned his head back, closing his eyes. Sarah's image was immediately projected in the darkness of his mind. He never had to conjure up her likeness; it was always there, complete and vibrant.

God, how he loved her. How was it possible after so many years? How was it possible that his heart had never rid itself of her? Quite easily, he could recall the very first time he had seen her, standing in the snow-covered street, looking lost and alone. How strange, in light of events to come, that he had felt nothing, only curiosity and bemusement at the sight of her. Even afterward, when he at last realized how he felt, he had still, foolishly, hesitated.

There was no one to blame but himself, Christian thought miserably. If only he had spoken out sooner, if only he had revealed his feelings sooner, if only he had ignored Jena and her false claims, if only...

But then, he reflected, he would not have Rebecca. Next to Sarah, she was the most precious thing in his life. Even his infant son, David, weak and frail, aroused only compassion within him. How ironic, he mused wretchedly, to have longed for a son for so many years, only to be given one that he could not seem to love.

He gave a small, wry laugh, chiding himself for his melancholy thoughts of what might have been. That was a path chosen by fools. Straightening, he opened his eyes to the fog-filled night.

A few seconds passed before his eyes conveyed the meaning of what he was looking at. The fog, he saw, seemed suddenly golden, lighted by an unnatural glow. For a long moment, he stared at it, perplexed.

He turned, peering out of the small rear window, his eyes widening at the sight that met his incredulous gaze. In a voice that was strained and hoarse with anxiety, he shouted at the driver to turn about, urging him to speed their return to Somerset Hall, trying to fight down the overwhelming feeling of unease that tensed his body.

Less than a half mile away, Christian saw the flames thrusting defiantly into the night.

Moments later, he could see the house quite clearly. Flames were pouring out of one of the windows on the second floor. A bedroom. Jonathan's? Sarah's? Christian cried out her name in an anguished voice. Suddenly he saw the front door open.

There was Betsy, holding Caroline in her arms and prodding Benjamin ahead of her as they quickly descended the wide front steps. Close on her heels was Mrs. Markham, clutching Nicholas firmly to her breast. The rest of the servants, some coughing and some with handkerchiefs across their faces, began to run out of the house.

Jumping out of the carriage before it came to a full stop, Christian ran forward in an effort to reach Betsy, who was again entering the house.

"Wait!" he shouted, catching up with her at the front door. She was in her nightdress, without so much as a robe over it, her feet bare, and her hair braided in one long plait down her back.

She glanced up at him, her eyes wide and frantic. "Yer don't understand!" she said in a shrill voice. "She's in there! That maniac's got her trapped!" She struggled in Christian's firm grip, trying to break away from him.

But he would not release her. "Sarah?" he said in a rush, wondering who the "maniac" was. Had Aleceon returned? If so, he would kill him. "Where is she?" he demanded, shaking her.

"In her room. It's the first door ter the left of the landing...." She wanted to say more, to tell him about Jonathan, but Christian interrupted her.

"Stay here!" he commanded. "See to the children." Christian ran into the hallway, groping his way toward the stairs.

Close to tears, Betsy watched him disappear into the smoke, then went to where Mrs. Markham was standing, the children grouped about her.

"Mother is still in there!" Benjamin cried out to her as she neared. By his side, Caroline was weeping in a loud voice, and for the moment, Benjamin wished that he could do the same. But he was too old for tears and would not allow himself this luxury. Still, it was very difficult, for the expression on Betsy's face frightened him. He'd never seen her look other than cheerful and composed.

Sensing that, Betsy put an arm about his sturdy shoulder. "She'll be all right, luv," she soothed. "Don't yer fret about her."

"And Father?" the boy asked, looking up at her.

She looked away, but tightened her hold. "Him, too," she murmured, facing the house again. Certainly he can walk out, if he has a mind to, she thought bitterly. His sickness must have reached his brain, for surely it was a madman she had seen clutching at Sarah, trying to hold her down. Having found the door that adjoined her room with Sarah's locked, Betsy had finally gone into the hall and entered Sarah's room from the corridor. Her heart had frozen in her breast at the sight of the two of them. When Betsy approached, Jonathan struck her. She had been about to come closer anyway, when Sarah shouted to her to get the children out of the house.

Uneasily, Betsy now glanced up at Sarah's window, at the flames dancing crazily in a hot, crimson stream. If Sarah was still in that room...Feeling physically sick, Betsy tore her gaze away from the horror, unable to bear the thought that Sarah might not have escaped. Beside her, Benjamin began to whimper; grateful for the diversion, Betsy gave him her complete attention.

Inside, Christian covered his lower face with his

handkerchief, and dropped to his knees, crawling up the stairs one at a time. There were no flames that he could see, and he surmised that the fire was as yet contained on the upper floors.

About midway, he came upon Rachel, sprawled across two steps, her arms clinging to the balustrade as if it were a lifeline. Prying her hands loose, Christian dragged her down the stairs. Leaving her just outside the front door, he again made his way back to the stairs, hurrying now with a sense of impending doom.

As his head came even with the landing, he saw them. He didn't take time to wonder at the sight of an apparently recovered Jonathan Enright, who now had a firm grip on Sarah's wrist. She was alive, and Christian clung to that thought.

They were both on the floor, half in and half out of a bedroom. Sarah was struggling feebly, and even as he watched, her slender body crumpled as she gasped for air in the smoke-filled hallway.

And then she lay still.

Briefly, Jonathan raised his head and stared at Christian. There was no surprise upon his face, and Christian could not help but recoil from that look, which startled him even as it confused him. It was savage, a naked expression of hate and fury. Was it, he wondered, directed at himself? That made no sense. Sarah, then. But why? What could she have possibly done to provoke such demonic loathing? For love to turn to hate, a powerful catalyst had to be present, real or imagined.

Christian dropped the handkerchief, and moved forward, reaching for Sarah. Jonathan flung Christian's hand aside in a vicious motion. To Christian's horror, he grabbed one of Sarah's wrists, and began to drag her back into the bedroom, which was now completely ablaze. Jonathan's face had a maddened look about it, a curious intermingling of rage and determination.

In a moment, Christian was upon him, his fist landing upon Jonathan's jaw with sickening impact that landed him flat. Although it was getting more and more difficult to breathe, Christian again reached for Sarah. Picking her up, he put her over his shoulder. Then, bending over, he grasped hold of Jonathan's arm, attempting to drag the unconscious man from the blaze-filled room.

Suddenly, with a tremendous retort, the floor of the bedroom sank from view and crashed into the parlor below.

Christian sprang back, unable to drag Jonathan after him. Knowing that there was nothing more he could do for the man, Christian raced down the stairs, Sarah clutched in his arms.

Moments later, he stood outside, breathing deeply and gratefully of the cool night air.

Somewhat unsteady on his feet, he walked a distance away, gently laying Sarah down on the wet grass. Betsy rushed forward and, dropping to her knees, cradled Sarah's head in her arms.

"Lass, lass," she murmured in a choked voice, seeing Sarah's eyelids flutter. "Yer had me scared out of me wits."

"The children?" Sarah whispered, only momentarily wondering how she had gotten out of there alive. Then her eyes fell upon Christian, and she knew.

"Don't yer trouble yerself there, luv," said Betsy quickly. "They're all safe and sound; nary a scratch ter share between them." Sarah smiled weakly, trying to convey her gratitude, but Betsy would have none of it.

Briefly, Betsy wondered about Master Jonathan, but her practical mind told her that if he was not out by now, he would never be. Apparently Rachel, too, had by now realized that Jonathan had not gotten out, because she began to cry out his name in a high, thin voice that bordered on hysteria.

"Go to her," Sarah urged Betsy. "Comfort her, if you can."

"I'll do that, lass," Betsy responded, patting Sarah's hand. She got to her feet. "Yer just stay here and rest. I'll see ter her."

Shakily, Sarah got up, welcoming Christian's arm as it encircled her in the familiar protective manner. She did not even question in her own mind how he had come to her in her hour of need. He always had; somehow she knew that he always would.

After a moment, she managed to ask: "Jonathan?"

He looked down at her, his blue eyes steady and caring. "I'm sorry, Sarah. I couldn't save him." He didn't ask her what had happened. There would be time enough for that later.

Together they stood and watched. The rain, now heavier, was at last having an impact. The house would be gutted, but the foundation would stand.

"Are you all right?" Christian asked. Her lovely hair, tousled and unbound, smelled faintly of smoke, and her face was smudged with soot. Yet she looked more beautiful than ever.

She only nodded, feeling his love wash over her, warm and comforting. A resounding noise made her start. Horrified, she watched as a section of the roof caved in, sending a shower of sparks into the air.

Feeling drained, she rested her head on Christian's chest, her bruised throat throbbing painfully. The pressure of his arms tightened about her, and Sarah tilted her head back to look up at him, feeling the coolness of the rain upon her face. Her tears mingled with it, and were washed away.

"If I had lost you—" he began, but his voice broke with emotion.

A smile lighted her face, and her gray eyes shone with the love that no longer had to be repressed. "You will never lose me again, Christian," she whispered.

Epilogue

About them, the late September air was pure and sweet and mild. In the surrounding hills, trees only whispered of autumn, daintily rustling crimson and yellow leaves in the silver haze of Indian summer. Even the more sedate browns and faded greens took on a dignity, a last defiance against the encroaching starkness that waited, silently, to envelop the land in yet one more sleep of winter.

Christian and Sarah walked, hand in hand, along the riverbank, stopping now and again to kiss, or to simply look into each other's eyes as if they couldn't resist contact for more than moments at a time.

At one point, Sarah paused, looking in the direction of Somerset Hall. They were too far away to see it, but she knew that reconstruction was going on. A lot of work had been accomplished in these past four months. It still looked skeletal and forlorn, but it was taking shape, assuming a recognizable form.

"It will soon be whole again," Christian said, watching her.

She turned to him, and his arms went around her. "Do you mind very much?" she asked, looking up at him. "Coming to live at Somerset Hall?"

He smiled as he kissed the tip of her nose. "I would move to the ends of the earth to be with you," he said honestly. "Hockings Metals will move here, to Taunset, just as we've planned."

She rested her head against his chest, feeling a deep sense of contentment. Soon, she told herself. Soon she would have this feeling always. Of necessity, she and Christian met several times a week, in out-of-the-way places, to talk, to make love, to discuss their future. They planned to marry in November. He hadn't wanted to wait, but she had convinced him that they must observe a decent interval of mourning. It had been difficult enough to explain to Rachel that she was planning to remarry at all, and Sarah had taken great pains to ease Jonathan's mother into acceptance.

During these past four months, Sarah had been staying with Elizabeth, as were Rachel and the children. Living in close proximity with Justin and his ponderous rhetoric placed a strain upon them all, and Sarah would be glad to be out of that house, and back home again. Rachel planned to stay with Elizabeth and Justin, although Betsy, Charity and her daughter, Phillips, and Tully, would return with her and the children when Somerset Hall was livable. Mrs. Reddy had chosen to stay with Rachel, and Sarah wasn't too unhappy about that.

Rachel had taken the death of her son hard. Even after four months, she would suddenly break into tears whenever his name was mentioned. Elizabeth, too, was grieved, but her daughter's welfare was paramount in her thoughts, leaving little time for anything else, and therefore blunting her grief.

Sarah had told none of them what had happened on the night of the fire. Sarah thought it kinder to allow Rachel to remember her son as he had been. Christian knew some of it, and Betsy knew all of it; Sarah planned to keep it that way, not wanting unduly to tarnish the memory of Jonathan Enright.

Jonathan, she thought, with deep sadness. She hadn't loved him, but there had been feeling there. A very real, intense feeling. He had died unforgiving and hating; and that was a guilt that she would bear for the rest of her life.

As for the mill, she would continue with that. In spite of it all, that was a part of Jonathan that deserved to grow and prosper. It had to; it was her children's heritage.

"We shall have a full life, regardless of where we live," Christian was saying to her, touching her cheek. "And we will never be parted again." With great tenderness he kissed her, then regarded those solemn, gray eyes. "I give you my word, Sarah," he whispered.

She smiled, thinking of the first time he had said

that to her, thinking that now, at last, her life would begin.

They walked a bit farther, the river accompanying them on its lazy, downstream journey, glittering now and again with the intrusion of sunlight upon its surface. A rabbit pranced by, halting in consternation at the sight of them, then quickly fled to a safer haven.

"Why didn't you tell me that it was you who bought the outstanding shares in the mill?" she asked, after a while. A small smile tilted her lips. It was only after Jonathan's death, when the estate had to be settled, that Fenster had divulged what Christian had done.

Christian cleared his throat, appearing almost embarrassed. "I...didn't want you to think I was interfering," he offered lamely.

Her laughter rang clear and silver. "Oh, my darling Christian." Merriment captured her, lighting her gray eyes until they sparkled. "From the day I met you, you have interfered in my life." When he turned to her, dismayed, she added: "Nor would I have it any other way."

Halting, he sat on the grassy bank, the surroundings devoid of people, nature their only companion. He pulled her down beside him. "I don't want to think of the past," he said. "From this day forward, it will be just you and me, for always," he murmured, nuzzling the warm hollow of her throat.

She couldn't repress a small laugh of amusement. "Just you and me, and five children," she reminded him.

"And I shall love them all," he said quietly, with a grin. "Even those that are still to come. The children that will be yours and mine." He felt free and light and wonderful. Even his infant son, David, was beginning to delight him, and he realized how much he loved him. He looked down at Sarah, his grin disappearing at the sight of her somber expression. "What is it?" he asked, concerned. "If something's troubling you, you must tell me."

She straightened and, drawing her knees up, hugged her legs.

"Sarah?" He reached over and cupped her chin, turning her face toward him.

For a long moment, she stared at him. She had told him most of what had happened between her and Jonathan. Now, she knew, he would have to be told the rest. "We already have a child," she said softly.

Startled, he blinked. "What do you mean?" he stammered. "Are you to have another child?" If so, he was thinking, they would have to marry right away.

"No, my dear," Sarah replied, taking hold of his hand. "Benjamin is ours. He is your son."

He was dumbfounded. "But..."

Gently, she told him, watching the play of emotions on his face: incredulity, shock, bewilderment, and, at last, realization of the truth.

"Oh, my God." He reached for her, holding her close to him, murmuring her name, over and over. "My poor darling," he said huskily. "My poor, sweet darling. When I think of all you've had to bear..."

She drew away, searching his face intently. "I have no regrets," she said. "Certainly not about Benjamin. There are many things in my life that I would change, and doubtless there'll be many more to come. But not Benjamin. Not our son."

For the first time in his adult life, Christian felt hot tears smart in his eyes. But he wasn't ashamed of them. "I love you so very much," he said, his voice unsteady.

For long moments, they clung to each other, drawing strength, a sense of purpose, a sense of sharing from within the very depths of themselves.

"Have you told him?" he asked finally. "Does he know?"

She raised her face to look at him. "No," she whispered. "Not yet. But one day, he will. One day."

Christian accepted this. Benjamin was barely nine. After he and Sarah were married, after he had had time to gain the boy's love and respect, then Benjamin could be told. "I look forward to that day, Sarah," he said fervently. "Oh, God, how I look forward to that day."

They kissed again, lying down in the soft, emerald grass.

"Do you remember the first time we made love?" he whispered, his lips against her ear.

His warm breath sent a shudder through her. "I remember," she said softly, offering no resistance as he undid buttons and ribbons. He removed the pins from her hair, delighted by the shimmering tresses as they tumbled in appealing disarray.

At last they lay, unclothed, beneath the warmth of the sun. Christian marveled at the perfection before him, certain that he would never tire of the sight. His hands moved against the cool softness of her skin, now bathed in gold. His lips traced the path of his hands, and with a small cry of pleasure, Sarah reached for him, drawing him down upon her. As he entered, Sarah felt the sweetness flood her body, and knew it would be like this always. He moved gently at first, then more insistently, as his desire reached a peak of unutterable pleasure. But only when he felt her body tense beneath him did he allow himself the final joy.

They clung to each other then, each unwilling to let the other go.

For a while they lay in silence, pressed against each other, savoring the warm contact of flesh against flesh.

"Oh, my darling, we will have a life together, you and I," Christian whispered, after a while. "It will be envied by all."

And it would be, she thought happily. There was work; there were the children; and, most of all, there was love.

The years were ahead of them, each one glittering with the promise of things to come, of happiness shared. And as she again drew Christian to her, Sarah vowed to fill each one of those days with love.

This is the special design logo that will call your attention to new Avon authors who show exceptional promise in the romance area. Each month a new novel—either historical or contemporary—will be featured.

THE AVON ROMANCE

A GALLANT PASSION Helene M. Lehr
Coming in February   86074-0/$2.95
The spellbinding story, set in New England in the mid-1800's, of a striking young woman who is torn between her yearning for the golden-haired man she loves—and her promise to the darkly handsome man who can give her wealth and social position.

CHINA ROSE Marsha Canham
Coming in March   85985-8/$2.95
In the England of 1825, eighteen-year-old beauty China Grant comes to Braydon Hall, promised in marriage to the eldest Cross brother, Sir Ranulf, who is only interested in her inheritance. Her love is won by his brother Justin, however, and the two must overcome deceit, lies and the threat of death before they can be united.

HEART SONGS Laurel Winslow
Coming in April   85365-5/$2.50
Set against the breathtaking beauty of the canyons and deserts of Arizona, this is the passionate story of a young gallery owner who agrees to pose for a world-famous artist to find that he captures not only her portrait but her heart.

WILDSTAR Linda Ladd
Coming in May   87171-8/$2.75
The majestic Rockies and the old West of the 1800's are the setting for this sizzling story of a beautiful white girl raised by Indians and the virile frontiersman who kidnaps her back from the Cheyenne.

BOLD CONQUEST Virginia Henley   84830-9/$2.95
FOREVER, MY LOVE Jean Nash   84780-9/$2.95
NOW COMES THE SPRING Andrea Edwards 83329-8/$2.95
RANSOMED HEART Sparky Ascani   83287-9/$2.95

Look for THE AVON ROMANCE wherever paperbacks are sold, or order directly from the publisher. Include $1.00 per copy for postage and handling: allow 6-8 weeks for delivery. Avon Books, Dept BP Box 767, Rte 2, Dresden, TN 38225.

Avon Rom 2-84

This is the special design logo that will call your attention to new Avon authors *THE AVON ROMANCE* who show exceptional promise in the romance area. Each month a new novel—either historical or contemporary—will be featured.

BOLD CONQUEST   84830-9/$2.95 US
Virginia Henley   85076-1/$3.50 Canada
This is the story of a passionate red-haired beauty and the gallant Norman warrior who conquers her land—but must fight to capture her heart.

FOREVER, MY LOVE Jean Nash   84780-9/$2.95
Amidst the opulence of nineteenth-century New York and Newport society, a beautiful young woman is wed to a wealthy oil tycoon whose rivalry with his son may tear the marriage apart—before the lovers can admit their true passions.

NOW COMES THE SPRING Andrea Edwards   83329-8/$2.95
Newspaper photographer Tracy Monroe poses as the fiancee of tough-talking star reporter Josh Rettinger, but their role-playing becomes a passion that brings the warmth of spring.

RANSOMED HEART Sparky Ascani   83287-9/$2.95
A lovely young woman offers to sell her jewelry to pay her father's gambling debts but the buyer, a dashing jewelry designer, will accept nothing less than the most precious jewel of all—Analisa!

WHEN LOVE REMAINS Victoria Pade   82610-0/$2.95
DARK SOLDIER Katherine Myers   82214-8/$2.95
ADMIT DESIRE Catherine Lanigan   81810-8/$2.95
LOVE'S CHOICE Rosie Thomas   61713-7/$2.95
DEFIANT DESTINY Nancy Moulton   81430-7/$2.95
CAPTIVE OF THE HEART Kate Douglas   81125-1/$2.75

Look for THE AVON ROMANCE wherever paperbacks are sold, or order directly from the publisher. Include $1.00 per copy for postage and handling: allow 6-8 weeks for delivery. Avon Books, Dept BP Box 767, Rte 2, Dresden, TN 38225.

Avon Rom 11-83

Dear Reader:

If you enjoyed this book, and would like information about future books by this author and other Avon authors, we would be delighted to put you on the mailing list for our ROMANCE NEWSLETTER.

Simply *print* your name and address and send to Avon Books, Room 1210, 1790 Broadway, N.Y., N.Y. 10019.

We hope to bring you many hours of pleasurable reading!

Sara Reynolds, Editor
Romance Newsletter

Book orders and checks should *only* be sent to Avon Books, Dept. BP Box 767, Rte 2, Dresden, TN 38225.

IT'S A NEW AVON ROMANCE LOVE IT!

HEART OF THUNDER
85118-0/$3.95
Johanna Lindsey

Set in the untamed West of the 1870's, HEART OF THUNDER is the story of a headstrong beauty and of the arrogant outlaw who vows to possess her father's land—and her heart.

WILD BELLS TO THE WILD SKY
84343-9/$6.95
Laurie McBain   Trade Paperback

This is the spellbinding story of a ravishing young beauty and a sun-bronzed sea captain who are drawn into perilous adventure and intrigue in the court of Queen Elizabeth I.

FOR HONOR'S LADY
85480-5/$3.95
Rosanne Kohake

As the sounds of the Revolutionary War echo throughout the colonies, the beautiful, feisty daughter of a British loyalist and a bold American patriot must overcome danger and treachery before they are gloriously united in love.

DECEIVE NOT MY HEART
86033-3/$3.95
Shirlee Busbee

In New Orleans at the onset of the 19th century, a beautiful young heiress is tricked into marrying a dashing Mississippi planter's look-alike cousin—a rakish fortune hunter. But deceipt cannot separate the two who are destined to be together, and their love triumphs over all obstacles.

Buy these books at your local bookstore or use this coupon for ordering:

Avon Books, Dept BP, Box 767, Rte 2, Dresden, TN 38225
Please send me the book(s) I have checked above. I am enclosing $_____
(please add $1.00 to cover postage and handling for each book ordered to a maximum of three dollars). *Send check or money order*—no cash or C.O.D.'s please. Prices and numbers are subject to change without notice. Please allow six to eight weeks for delivery.

Name _____

Address _____

City _____ State/Zip _____

Love It! 2-84

ROYAL SERVICE
Stephen P. Barry

"Irresistible...the inside scoop on England's Royal Family."
San Francisco Chronicle

For the millions curious about the truth behind the fairy-tale romance of Prince Charles and Lady Diana comes ROYAL SERVICE. Author Stephen P. Barry, Prince Charles' personal valet for twelve years, reveals in this fascinating, candid book—a book banned in Great Britain—what *really* goes on upstairs at the Royal Palace. With sixteen pages of exclusive photographs.

Replete with personal anecdotes and intimate revelations about Britain's royal household, ROYAL SERVICE discloses:
- What does Charles really think of his royal mom?
- How does Prince Andrew get away with being so rude?
- Who were the women Charles loved but could never marry?
- How did he manage to see his ladyfriends in private?
- What was it like for Lady Diana to be courted by a future king?

Here's the story, as only an insider could tell it, of the Prince's search for a bride, the celebrated romance, and the royal honeymoon cruise, when the fairy-tale couple sailed off on the *Britannia*...alone at last.

67397-5/$3.50 US

Ro 2-84

Buy these books at your local bookstore or use this coupon for ordering:

Avon Books, Dept BP, Box 767, Rte 2, Dresden, TN 38225
Please send me the book(s) I have checked above. I am enclosing $_____
(please add $1.00 to cover postage and handling for each book ordered to a maximum of three dollars). *Send check or money order*—no cash or C.O.D.'s please. Prices and numbers are subject to change without notice. Please allow six to eight weeks for delivery.

Name _____

Address _____

City _____ State/Zip _____

AN UNSPOKEN INVITATION

Drew inhaled sharply. "God, Layla."

Cupping his hand on her face, she moved her cheek against his palm letting his fingers caress her cheek. Slowly she slid his palm across her cheeks, down her throat, her chest, until his hand rested on her breast.

With a gentle squeeze, he cupped her breast, his fingers toying with her nipple.

"Are you sure?" he said, his breathing heavy, understanding her unspoken invitation.

She didn't reply. Still holding his hand, she drew him into her room and quietly shut the door.

The moment the door closed behind him, Drew pulled her into his arms. His mouth covered hers, gently at first, then more firmly until she parted her lips slightly, tasting the fine brandy on his breath.

The need to live and feel alive in Drew's embrace urged her on, as his warm mouth caressed hers. She could feel her lips opening farther to receive his kiss, her body surrendering to his . . .

Also by Sylvia McDaniel

THE PRICE OF MOONLIGHT

SUNLIGHT ON JOSEPHINE STREET

THE MARSHAL TAKES A WIFE

THE OUTLAW TAKES A WIFE

THE RANCHER TAKES A WIFE

A SCARLET BRIDE

Starlight Surrender

Sylvia McDaniel

ZEBRA BOOKS
Kensington Publishing Corp.
http://www.kensingtonbooks.com

ZEBRA BOOKS are published by

Kensington Publishing Corp.
850 Third Avenue
New York, NY 10022

Copyright © 2004 by Sylvia McDaniel

All rights reserved. No part of this book may be reproduced in any form or by any means without the prior written consent of the Publisher, excepting brief quotes used in reviews.

If you purchased this book without a cover you should be aware that this book is stolen property. It was reported as "unsold and destroyed" to the Publisher and neither the Author nor the Publisher has received any payment for this "stripped book."

All Kensington titles, imprints and distributed lines are available at special quantity discounts for bulk purchases for sales promotion, premiums, fund-raising, educational or institutional use.

Special book excerpts or customized printings can also be created to fit specific needs. For details, write or phone the office of the Kensington Special Sales Manager: Kensington Publishing Corp., 850 Third Avenue, New York, NY 10022. Attn. Special Sales Department. Phone: 1-800-221-2647.

Zebra and the Z logo Reg. U.S. Pat. & TM Off.

First Printing: February 2004
10 9 8 7 6 5 4 3 2 1

Printed in the United States of America

To Dennis and Connie McDaniel, who create beautiful music, are funny, happy, and are meant for one another. May love fill all your days together.

To Austin McDaniel: Congratulations on your graduation from college. We're proud of you and know you'll do well in life.

To Melissa: Congratulations on your marriage. May the two of you find happiness that lasts forever.

To Michelle, who's all grown up and in college. Study and play hard, for the days will soon slip away and you'll have to get a real job.

And last but not least to Mallory: I guess you're too big to sit in my lap any longer. Drive safely this summer.

One

New Orleans, 1895

Sunlight glittered through the windows of the St. Louis Hotel, casting bizarre shadows over the dead body of Jean Cuvier. A sparrow trilled a happy song in the courtyard outside the posh hotel suite, the sound eerie and disturbing. Layla Cuvier stared at the corpse of her husband lying on the floor and knew that from this day forward, her life would forever be changed.

No longer will I have to endure his touch.

Her eyes confirmed what Colette, her servant, had told her. Jean lay sprawled on the floor, his brown robe wrapped around him, his face a peculiar shade of pink. Needing the confirmation of what seemed so obvious, she reached down and touched his hand. The feel of cool flesh beneath her fingers sent a shudder through her and she recoiled in revulsion.

"Mrs. Cuvier, a doctor is on his way and the hotel manager has sent for the police," said Colette, wringing her hands in an anxious manner.

Layla felt numb as she stared at the man she had shared a house with for the last year. As his wife, she should feel sorrow at his death, but relief and a sense of peace filled her. She had barely tolerated Jean's presence.

She rose and nodded to her servant and friend. "Please help me dress before the doctor arrives."

"Of course," the maid said, but glanced at her hesitantly.

"Did Mr. Cuvier say anything about feeling ill?" Layla asked, gazing at her husband's still form.

"No. But I went to bed before you retired," the maid said. "Did you hear him call out?"

"After I shut my bedroom door, I heard nothing last night," Layla said, knowing the sleeping draught had ended her insomnia. The draught created a dream world filled with people and color, and a world so different from reality. Yet she would have heeded Jean's call if she had heard his cry for help. "So many nights he slept in the chair."

And Layla loved the nights he left her alone.

"It's so sudden. How do you think he died?" Colette asked.

"I don't know. He hasn't been ill." Layla gave Jean one last glance, stunned at his death. Their last conversation was an ugly reminder of his evil ways and she couldn't help but wonder if his heart could have failed him. Though their marriage had been a farce, she had never expected him to die. "Let's hurry. I'd rather greet the authorities fully dressed."

"Are you all right?" Colette asked gazing at her worriedly as they entered Layla's bedroom. "You seem so composed."

Layla gave the woman a quick glance as she shed her nightgown. "I'm a little shaken, yet I feel strangely calm."

Calm and relieved, she hoped that now his ugly secrets would die with him and she could escape this farce of a marriage and return to her home.

Hurriedly Layla chose a black dress appropriate for a widow. She had barely gotten her ebony hair swept up off her neck in a coiffure that left wisps of curls swirling around her face when Colette opened the door to the police. They swarmed into the suite, covering the rooms like a bevy of ants.

Layla stepped out of her bedroom, and into the doorway of Jean's bedroom to watch with interest as a uniformed policeman leaned over Jean's prostrate body lying on the floor.

The voices of the officers seemed distant and removed and the scene before her surreal, like a colorful nightmare.

A short ugly little man dressed in a shabby brown suit separated from the others and walked toward Layla.

"Mrs. Cuvier?" he asked, his intimidating eyes focused on her.

"Yes?" She felt as if he stared deeply into her soul, but she had nothing to hide and met his gaze, undaunted by his beady eyes.

"Detective Dunegan of the New Orleans Police."

They walked the short distance to the lavishly decorated parlor of the suite.

"Please sit." She pointed to a chair in the small sitting area as she sat across from him.

"How did your husband die?" he asked. He took out a notepad and a pencil from his tattered coat pocket.

"I don't know. My maid awakened me this morning with the news that she'd found Mr. Cuvier lying on the floor of his bedroom. I hurried into his room, where I found him lying there, his body already cold," she said, clenching her hands in her lap. "I have no idea how long he has been dead."

Layla glanced toward the bedroom, half expecting Jean to walk through the door, laughing that he had fooled them all.

"When did you last see him alive?" the detective asked.

She thought back to the night before. They had fought fiercely and she had been determined to return home to Baton Rouge this morning. She had intended to meet with an attorney to see what kind of legal recourse was available to her, but miraculously nature had taken care of things.

Now she prayed the ugly truth would die with Jean and she could return to her previous life. She licked her lips nervously.

"The last time I saw Mr. Cuvier was around midnight," she said, remembering how she had left him in the parlor asleep in the very chair the detective occupied.

A man stood in the doorway to Jean's room with a stethoscope hanging around his neck. "Detective Dunegan, can I speak with you a moment?"

Through the open window, she could hear laughter in the courtyard of the hotel, the sound incongruous with the atmosphere in the suite.

The two men disappeared into the bedroom. Their muffled voices held an excited undertone, though she could not understand what they said. As the minutes passed, she sat feeling more nervous, wondering whom she should contact regarding Jean's death.

"Now where were we?" he asked. "Oh, that's right. You said the last time you saw the deceased was around midnight." He paused and frowned at her. "Did you and Mr. Cuvier sleep in separate rooms?"

"Yes. My husband kept odd hours, and I have trouble sleeping and don't like to be disturbed."

"So, you heard nothing in the night? He didn't call out to you for help or assistance?"

"No, I took a dose of a sleeping draught not long after he came home." She gave the detective a puzzled glance. "Do you always ask these kinds of questions when a man dies?"

"I'm just doing my job, Mrs. Cuvier," he said matter-of-factly.

Layla glanced around and noticed that more and more policemen seemed to be filling the hotel suite. They stood around in little clusters talking, occasionally glancing in her direction. A few of the officers seemed to be combing the room as if they were looking for something.

"What are they doing?" she asked alarmed. She had never heard of the police doing this when someone died.

The atmosphere seemed charged with some ominous foreboding that she didn't understand.

He ignored her question. "How would you describe your marriage to Mr. Cuvier?"

"Why are you asking me these questions? How could my relationship to my husband be any of your business?" she asked, distressed. "He's dead! Shouldn't you be calling the coroner?"

"Ma'am, the coroner is with your husband. Now please, Mrs. Cuvier, just answer the question."

She gazed at the detective, feeling suddenly uneasy.

"Our marriage was fine. My husband traveled frequently and we seldom saw one another," she said, a cold chill going down her spine. She glanced back to see a policeman coming out of her room holding her vial of laudanum in his hand. "Where is he taking my medicine?"

"Don't worry, Mrs. Cuvier, it will be returned to you in good time," the detective said, not looking at her, but nodding to the policeman.

Uneasiness filled her every breath and she didn't understand why the police seemed so engrossed with Jean's death. "How did my husband die?"

"I'm asking the questions, Mrs. Cuvier," the detective

said, ignoring her query. "Did you and your husband have an argument last night?"

She paused looking at the man, uncertain how to answer the question. "We had a slight disagreement."

You selfish bastard! The words she had yelled at Jean reverberated through her mind and she knew she could never tell them the whole truth about their quarrel. Otherwise they would think she had been involved in his death.

"What was the fight about?"

"It was such a minor disagreement, I scarcely recall," she lied. "I think I've told you enough. You need to tell me why you're asking all these questions."

The detective gazed at her, his eyes cold. The room became silent and she felt like hundreds of eyes were focused on her. A creeping sensation started along the base of her spine and suddenly she felt afraid. Everyone stared at her as if she had done something horrible.

Even the bird that chirped noisily through the window had ceased its singing and all sound was suspended in uncanny silence.

"How did my husband die?" she insisted, her voice rising. The detective watched her, his beady eyes intent. "Tell me!"

"According to Doctor Benson, your husband was poisoned."

The room seemed to fade as Layla felt her body go numb. Poisoned? "Oh—Oh my. No. It couldn't be, that's impossible."

As soon as she uttered the words, she knew a whole host of people who would like to see her husband dead. And before the day was over, there would probably be even more who cheered at the news.

"Oh, God!" she said, realizing the depth of trouble that would soon surround her.

"Can you tell me what your husband ate or drank last night?"

Uneasy, Layla swallowed. "I don't know what he had for supper, since he wasn't here. I gave him his usual cup of tea before he went to bed."

She knew she had put laudanum in his drink, as she often did, but she had not intentionally killed him, and she had definitely not poisoned him.

Could she have given him too much?

A shiver ran through her. Did she accidentally kill Jean with her antidote for passion? The detective stared at her, waiting.

He leaned in close, his voice demanding. "Did you poison your husband, Mrs. Cuvier?"

Her heart pounded in her chest. They would think that she killed Jean if they found out what she had learned last night, the reason for their fight, the fact that her marriage was a complete farce.

"Of course not! I would *never* kill anyone," she said emphatically.

"You're extremely calm and cool, considering your husband just died. You haven't shed a tear."

Layla couldn't help but realize what he said was true. She didn't feel any grief or remorse that Jean was dead, only a sense of relief at being free, but that didn't mean she had killed him.

"My father arranged my marriage to Jean. Ours was more a marriage of convenience. But I would never poison him. That would be a sin."

Silence echoed in the room filled with people eager to hear her every word. She closed her eyes, hoping that when she opened them, she would awake and realize this was just a nightmare, not reality.

"You said you gave your husband a cup of tea. Did you put anything in his tea last night, Mrs. Cuvier?"

She glanced away, wanting to lie, knowing whatever

she said would incriminate her even though she was innocent.

"I didn't kill Jean!" she said gazing at him.

"Answer the question, Mrs. Cuvier," he said, his voice harsh and forceful. "Did you put anything in Mr. Cuvier's tea?"

She swallowed nervous, knowing no one would believe her innocent. "I—I put a touch of laudanum in his tea."

A gasp sounded in the room.

She responded quickly. "To help him sleep. He didn't sleep well. I did it all the time and he's never had a reaction before." She clenched her fists. "I didn't kill Jean."

The detective tensed, but said nothing. His pencil scratched noisily against his notepad as he hurriedly wrote her comments.

When he looked up, his face was expressionless, his eyes intense, like a hunter closing in on its prey.

"Mrs. Cuvier, I need to interview your servants. Could I ask you to wait in your bedroom? When I'm ready to continue our interview, I'll let you know."

"You want me to just sit in my room and wait for you?"

He raised his bushy brows. "Yes, ma'am."

Layla stared at him in shock. How could he think she killed Jean? Sure, she hated him, but she could never harm him or anyone else, for that matter. This was crazy. Everything seemed to be spinning out of control. Since yesterday her life had disintegrated into shambles.

"I didn't kill my husband," she said one more time as she rose from her chair. She walked toward her bedroom, her head held high, wanting to pack her suitcase, knowing instinctively that it would be the wrong thing to do. She sat down in a chair by the window and stared out at the courtyard below. How could this be happening?

She hated Jean, but to the world they had presented the image of a happily married couple, keeping their problems behind the closed doors of her bedroom. But to physically harm him would damn her forever, and even Jean wasn't worth spending eternity in hell. She had prayed her life would change, but never this drastically. And never like this.

For what seemed like forever, though probably less than an hour, Layla sat looking out the window, watching the birds flitter about the courtyard as they flew from one tree to another. Caged and restless, she wished she could fly away so easily. Finally, the door opened and the detective walked in followed by two women. Layla refused to acknowledge them, fear gripping her insides with a tightening hook.

"Ma'am," the detective said, releasing a young blonde woman who had come in with him. "Tell these women how the man you're suspected of killing was related to you."

What? They hadn't officially charged her with anything. Was this some kind of trick? She turned toward the door and gazed at the detective, trying not to react to his words and contain a cool composure. "I told you I did not kill my husband."

The blonde woman with eyes red-rimmed from crying moaned. "What are you saying? No! You lie. You can't be married to Jean."

Layla knew in that instant who the two women were and she didn't know how to respond. She felt so ashamed, yet she had done nothing wrong. Jean had duped her just like the others.

"Did you marry Jean Cuvier?" the older distinguished-looking woman asked, her expression calm, though her green eyes shimmered with tears.

"Yes," Layla responded, a slight quiver to her voice.

"That can't be. He married me. He's my husband," the blonde woman said, her voice rising, her pain and hurt audible in the bedroom.

Layla resisted the urge to tell her she could have Jean. She had never wanted him.

"And mine," the other woman said quietly, as she sank down onto a nearby chair. "I'm Marian Cuvier. I married Jean twelve years ago at Saint Anne's Cathedral."

The blonde turned abruptly and stared at her in disbelief. "No. That's impossible." She paused, her face twisted into a mask of disbelief. "No. We were married four years ago. I don't understand. He would never do something so horrible."

"And I married him a year ago," Layla whispered, painfully aware of how they had been deceived and how the world would soon know of Jean's deceit.

"Impossible. Jean loved me. That's . . . that's bigamy!" the blonde woman said, shaking her head from side to side.

"Yes, it is bigamy. We were all married to the same man," Marian replied. Her voice sounded hollow and she appeared to be in shock. "And now we're all Jean's widows. The Cuvier Widows."

Layla stared at Jean's wives and knew that though she had only found out about her husband's perfidy twenty-four hours earlier, she would never reveal she knew beforehand of Jean's terrible deeds. For if the detective found out, he would surely believe that she had killed Jean in response to learning of his deceit. And though she hated him for his lies, she could never have killed him.

Layla stood in the reception area of the attorney's office, feeling out of place as she presented her back to

Nicole, Jean's second wife. An air of suspicion and hostility emanated from the woman, making Layla want to return to the hotel. A week of suspicion and distrust had passed since Jean's death.

The only reason she had come to the reading of the will was the hope that somehow she would be able to get her home in Baton Rouge back and maybe even her father's business. The business seemed doubtful, since Cuvier Shipping had absorbed her father's smaller company, her birthright. She only wanted the cash from the sale, if possible.

As if she hadn't suffered more than enough shocks this week, when she had received the notice from Jean's attorney to attend the reading of the will, the name had jumped out at her like a bad dream. Drew Soulier, a boy she had known a short time in school, though she doubted he would remember her. Children of riverboat owners seldom associated with judge's children. And like his father, Drew was now a lawyer. Jean's crooked lawyer, the very man she had recently learned had drawn up the contract between Jean and her father.

If she had been more involved with her husband's life, she would have known that his lawyer was someone she knew, but she had avoided Jean and his business as much as possible. Especially in the days since her father's death, when it became clear that Jean had lied to her father and absorbed his shipping company. Gone was her inheritance and now she stood in Drew Soulier's office, her husband's shyster lawyer, embroiled in a humiliating bigamy scandal.

A door slammed in the reception area, snapping her attention back to the present. Mr. Fournet, Jean's business partner, followed Marian Cuvier. "I'm locking the door, Drew," he called. "The press knows we're here."

Oh, God, the press. Tension emanated from Layla,

for the last week she had hid from newspapermen, seldom leaving the hotel, avoiding even answering her suite door.

"Quick thinking, Louis," Drew replied.

Tall, dark, and imposing, Drew had changed very little in the years since she had last seen him. Certainly he had grown more handsome with his sparkling, emerald eyes, straight nose and strong jaw giving Drew the appearance of a serious attorney. But Layla couldn't help but remember the way Drew helped swindle her father.

"Mrs. Cuvier, how are you?" Drew asked. He took hold of Marian's hand and turned his charm on the woman who would pay his fees, Jean's first and legal wife.

"I'm fine, Mr. Soulier," the cool, sophisticated woman replied as she glanced around the room taking in the other participants.

Layla stood opposite the second widow, Nicole, hoping Drew wouldn't speak to her. What could she say to the man who had helped ruin her father and now herself in a room full of strangers? Nothing that polite society would accept.

Drew whispered to the legal Mrs. Cuvier something that Layla could not hear. His eyes turned and gazed in Nicole and Layla's direction, and she felt certain he whispered about her.

"No," Marian said quickly. "Let us all hear Jean's wishes at the same time," she said loud enough to make Layla realize they weren't speaking of her personally.

"All right. As you wish," Drew replied and turned toward the other women. "Ladies, tea and refreshments are in my office. Please, go inside so we can get started."

He motioned for them to proceed ahead of him.

Marian entered first, followed by Nicole, and finally Layla entered the dark paneled room with two walls of bookshelves. This hierarchy seemed to apply to them even in the reading of the will.

Layla entered, her eyes downcast, hoping she could get through this without having Drew acknowledge her. She only wanted her home back. She longed to return to the city the French had named after the red stick that impaled the heads of bear and fish the Indians used as a boundary marker for the two tribes. Baton Rouge had always called to her heart.

Drew shut the door, enclosing them all together in the cramped room. Like a fine perfume, anxiety seemed to emanate from the women.

Nicole inclined her head in Marian's direction. "Mrs. Cuvier."

Marian returned her nod. Layla, stood with her back straight, her eyes fixed on a distant object, though she could feel Marian Cuvier's interest. She needed to say something to the lady, to tell her she had never meant to intentionally hurt her or her children. In fact, Layla hated Jean even more for the terrible position he had put them all in.

Tension spun around the three women like a fine cloak, wrapping them in its arms, spurring Layla to act.

"Mrs. Cuv . . ." Layla stumbled over the name.

"I think it would be so much easier, if we dropped the formalities and called each other by our given names," Marian said, glancing at each woman.

Layla nodded. "Please; I intend to assume my maiden name again."

"I think that's wise," Marian said crisply.

A taut silence seemed to hang suspended in the air. Marian walked around the desk until she faced the other wives.

"This is an extremely awkward situation we find ourselves in. The press is outside just waiting for us to succumb to arguing over whatever crumb Jean tossed our way." She sighed and stared at them, her expression resigned. "Ladies, I have no desire to come to blows over a man who deceived me like my . . . our dead husband. I only wish to take care of my children and live in peace without them being tarnished by their father's scandal."

Marian paused and gazed at each woman. "Keep in mind, I shall certainly do what I must to protect my babies."

Layla let out a long sigh. "I understand. But Jean lied to me as well."

Nicole removed her hat from her blonde hair and laid the bonnet on a nearby table. "Excuse me, but *I* loved Jean very much. Though I can't help but wonder why he didn't tell me the truth." She took out her handkerchief and dabbed her eyes. "It's so unfair that he died knowing all the reasons he did this but keeping the reasons from us. Surely there's an explanation."

Marian glanced at Nicole as if she were speaking to a child.

"I'm sure he could give you one, but why do you care? He lied to all of us. If he were alive, he wouldn't tell you the truth. He would just invent some new excuse to protect himself," Marian said, her voice kind but resolute.

Nicole shook her head in disagreement. "But I loved him."

"We all did at some time in our life," Marian said, her voice heavy with sarcasm.

"I hated him," Layla stated, her voice quivering with emotion.

Everyone stared at her in stunned silence and she knew she should have remained quiet, but the words had spilled uncensored from her lips, her eyes teary at the thought of how he had deceived them all and taken everything she loved from her.

She closed her eyes, wishing that this would just go away, fearing the coming days could only get worse.

"Ladies, we need to get started," Drew said, standing beside the door, ending their impromptu confessions. "Why don't you all take a seat?"

Layla watched as Drew seated the three women in chairs placed strategically apart, while Louis Fournet stood at the back of the room his arms folded across his chest. When Drew glanced at her, she saw no sign of recognition in his gaze.

Drew cleared his throat. "Before I read the will, I want to acknowledge some facts and let you all know why I invited Louis Fournet. He is co-owner of Cuvier Shipping and for that reason I requested his presence here today." He paused, looking at each of them. "I must clarify my position in this difficult situation. If I had known of Jean entering into any act of marriage with more than one woman, I would have advised against such an unlawful arrangement. I knew nothing of your supposed marriages."

Layla bit her lip to keep from retorting to his blatant lie. How could he not have known that Jean had married her after he had arranged the contract that bought her father's business?

Drew glanced down at the will he held in his hands holding them all in suspense. "According to Louisiana law the only legal marriage the state recognizes is the first one to Marian Cuvier. I'm sorry to say, Nicole, that your marriage and Layla's are not binding. Unless he names you specifically in the will, you receive nothing. If you had been his mistress and he had named you in the will, then you would inherit. But as an illegal spouse, you receive nothing unless you're named in the will."

A tense stillness filled the room.

He cleared his throat and turned to Layla. "Jean

wrote this will four years ago." He paused his gaze lingering sympathetically on Layla, as her stomach clenched with the realization. "I'm sorry, but the will was written before your marriage."

Cold reality washed over Layla, and she trembled in fear as she realized the extent of her loss. A gasp escaped as she opened her mouth, the words seeming to hang suspended, before she managed to speak. "I have nothing?" she asked, perplexed. "What will I do? Where will I go?"

She stood, feeling as if she moved in slow motion. "You don't understand! Jean bankrupted my father's business. My father made me marry him, just so that I would be taken care of. Our shipping company had been the family business for three generations before it was taken over by Cuvier Shipping. Now I have no means of support. I have nothing!"

Drew shook his head. "I'm sorry, Layla. Legally, everything belongs to Jean's estate including the house and the business."

Layla swallowed the knot that seemed to swell inside her throat. She glanced around the room in disbelief. "I have to leave my home?"

"Yes, it's in Jean's name."

Tears pooled in her eyes as she tried to absorb this startling revelation.

"How long before I have to leave the house?" Layla asked, visibly trembling.

"Jean appointed me executor of his will. I'll give you thirty days to find another residence. Is that agreeable, Marian?" Drew asked.

"Yes, please give her all the time she needs to find another place to live," Marian said, her voice filled with understanding.

"Thank you." Layla stood, her knees shook, but she couldn't stand another moment here in this office with these women and especially Drew. "I have to leave . . . I can't stay . . . I have to think about what I'm going to do. I must get out of here."

Flinging open the door to Drew's office, she ran out into the entryway. A sob echoed in the hall as she fumbled with the lock, then yanked open the outside portal and hurried out, letting the door slam behind her. Jean and his ruthless lawyer had taken everything that she loved and left her with nothing but broken dreams and scandal.

Layla walked the length of the suite, wringing her hands, her heart pounding inside her chest, like the warnings echoing in her ears.

With no home, no money, and only the clothes on her back considered her own, she had lost everything. The law deemed everything Jean's property. A mistress could have received more than she.

The suite seemed sinister since Jean's death and with the reading of the will she determined to leave as soon as possible and return to Baton Rouge. She didn't want to stay here with the constant memory of Jean's body lying prostrate on the floor.

Frustration at the drastic changes in her life this last week made Layla want to lash out at anyone within hearing distance. When she had returned to the hotel, she had immediately released the servants, though Colette refused to leave her side. They had been together only a short time, but the woman insisted that Jean had paid her salary in advance and promised to stay until Layla was settled.

For the first time in her life Layla had no ties. No family, no friends, not even a relative living within a hundred miles. Her father and Jean had been her entire life and now both of them were dead. Alone and broke, she felt desperate.

Her only recourse seemed to be to return to the school where she had taught before she married Jean. There at least, room and board would be provided, though she received only a pittance of a salary. With the newspapers filled with stories of the three women, it was doubtful anyone would hire her, including the nuns at the Sacred Heart, but she had no choice but to try.

"Ma'am," Colette said, gazing at her anxiously.

"Yes?" She halted in front of the servant.

"The hotel manager left this note while you were out today." Colette handed her the crisp linen paper.

Anxious Layla broke the wax seal and quickly scanned the missive. "Holy Mother, protect us!"

She glanced up at Colette. "Mr. Sharp has sent me an itemized statement of the charges for our suite. He's also inquiring as to when we'll be checking out. I never realized how much it cost to stay here."

"Surely Mr. Cuvier wanted the expenses charged to Cuvier Shipping," Colette said.

"Maybe so. But I have no ties to that company any longer, and I doubt they would continue to pay my expenditures." Her heart sank, feeling as if the weight of the world pressed her down.

"Talk to Mr. Cuvier's attorney. He can find a way to pay the hotel bill. After all, Mr. Cuvier brought us here."

Layla felt a moment of unease, yet what choice did she have? With no money to pay the bill her only other alternative was to sneak out in the middle of the night. She had never done anything so scandalous in all her life, but the thought of facing Drew again seemed even tougher.

"I don't think I can face him again and be civil. I ran

out of his office today," she said, remembering the young law clerk who chased after her and had seen her safely to the hotel. "We may have no choice but to leave in the middle of the night."

Colette shook her head. "You can't! Reporters are crawling all over this hotel. Two have taken a room on this very floor. Plus, I noticed a policeman down in the lobby. They're watching you. They'll think you're running."

Layla swallowed, pushing down the bile that threatened to rise in her throat. Colette was right. Running away would do no good. Drew owed her at least this small request considering the impact Jean had on her life, not to mention his own.

An overwhelming sense of anger filled her at her changing circumstances. She had hoped the news Frank, her godfather, had given her the night of Jean's death would change her life for the better, not cause her to cringe in fear. But now she must keep his news a secret for she feared the police using it against her.

"All right. I'll send Mr. Soulier the bill."

Two

Drew stood in front of the door of Layla's hotel suite, gripping the note he'd received from her. He had been shocked to discover that the very girl who had filled his adolescent fantasies was Jean's supposed third wife. The prime suspect in his client's murder.

Tall and gangly like a young colt, she had been on the verge of beauty then. Today her quiet sophistication and sultry good looks drew the attention of many men.

Seeing Layla, he had been shocked to learn that she was one of the Cuvier Widows. Why would she marry the man who had taken her father's company? Legalized stealing could only describe how Jean Cuvier had obtained DuChampe Shipping.

So why had Layla married him, unless she intended to regain her father's company with the aid of poison and then learned she wasn't the only Cuvier widow.

If this case went to trial, the whole city would be watching and Drew couldn't think of a better opportunity to show his skills and talents as a lawyer. Winning such a notorious trial could make his firm one of the most sought after in the state, not to mention further his political aspirations with the ward bosses of New Orleans. Once and for all he could prove to the people in his profession that his savvy with the law was more than just a matter of heritage.

Yet the memory of his last murder trial still rankled. He didn't like losing to anyone, but especially not Paul Finnie, the District Attorney of New Orleans.

Closing that train of thought, Drew rapped his knuckles against the door, anxious to meet Layla.

Drew heard a door open behind him and glanced around. He saw a man he recognized as a reporter for the *Daily Picayune* watching him. Another door down the hall opened and a man stared. Though Drew didn't know him, something about the man screamed detective. Layla DuChampe couldn't make a move or have a visitor without either a reporter or a detective documenting her every move.

He realized how his presence in Layla's hotel suite would appear, but the lobby downstairs did not seem to be an appropriate place for them to talk and her servants would be there to chaperone them.

An older woman cracked open the portal just enough to see him.

"Yes?" she asked, peeking through the barely opened door, her eyes suspicious.

"I'm here to see Mrs. Cuvier."

"Who may I say is calling?" she said blocking his view into the hotel suite.

"Drew Soulier."

Her face brightened. "She's been expecting you."

The door swung open and Drew stepped into the lavishly decorated suite of rooms with their rich mahogany moldings and golden sconces. Jean had always liked extravagant living and beautiful women.

And Drew couldn't help but wonder, *Which one got him in the end?*

As soon as the door closed, Layla stepped out of a room, shutting the door quietly behind her. Their eyes met across the small space and he couldn't help the way his palms sweated at the sight of her tall and graceful form standing in the doorway.

She nervously brushed a curl of hair away from her high cheekbones.

"How are you?" he asked. His voice dropped low, his throat tight and dry. She looked even lovelier than she had the day of the reading of Jean's will in his office.

She nodded, her dark curls caressing her long, slender white neck. "I'm fine. Please have a seat."

"Thank you." He gazed at her, feeling like that awkward kid once again. "I'm sorry I didn't acknowledge you the other day in the office, but I didn't think it appropriate."

Her brows raised in surprise. "I hoped you wouldn't recognize me."

"Why?" he asked, perplexed.

She gave him a disdainful look, her dark blue eyes regarding him coolly. And he wondered at the animosity he sensed coming from her. "It's been years, and we were hardly friends."

They sat down across from one another. Her ankles were demurely crossed to the side, her posture regal. She looked more like an angel than a murderer. And even if she had killed Jean, Drew couldn't imagine a jury convicting her.

"You have changed since I saw you last at Lee Grammar School."

"Twelve years have passed. You're no longer a skinny boy either," she said, her voice smooth as silk, brushing over him.

He smiled. "No, I'm not."

"And you've become a lawyer."

He shrugged. "Family occupation. When your father is a judge, your family expects you to follow the tradition."

She gave him a wry smile. He could almost feel the distrust and anger in her gaze and wondered at the cause.

"Last I heard, you were teaching at the Sacred Heart Convent."

She folded her hands in her lap and slowly clenched them, then stretched her fingers. "Yes, until my father insisted I marry Jean. Now, I hope to return to Sacred Heart and teach again."

He shook his head. "I hope you don't have plans to join the convent. It would be a crime for a woman with your beauty to take the veil."

Her brows raised, her gaze questioning. "Why do you say that?"

Drew couldn't help but smile. She'd been the only girl in school with the curves of a young woman. He remembered lying awake at night wondering what she looked like beneath her dresses.

"Let's just say that the sisters I've been around had a homely appearance, different from what you've been blessed with," he said, his thoughts centering on the way her dress accentuated her slender waist and rounded hips. And those breasts! Lord, not much had changed since school except that she was lovelier than he remembered and, instead of a boy's fantasy, his thoughts were a man's.

She could star in his dreams any day. He took a deep breath to cool his errant thoughts. She didn't respond to his comments on her looks, only gave him one of her cool gazes that could put frost on a pumpkin.

The silence made him nervous. "I came to tell you that as the executor to Jean's estate your hotel bill will be paid by Cuvier Shipping. Given the expense of this establishment, I would suggest you not linger here for too many days."

"Don't worry, we'll be leaving just as soon as I can

arrange transportation to Baton Rouge. As you well know, Jean didn't leave me very well prepared financially," she responded icily.

"If it's any consolation, I'm sorry for what happened. I'll even pay for you and your servant to return to Baton Rouge," he said, wondering why he offered, other than the fact he felt sorry for Layla.

She grimaced. "Thank you. Tell Mrs. Cuvier that I'll be out of my home within thirty days."

He nodded, watching her closely, knowing with certainty that something was not right. "Of all the wives, I think your funds were misappropriated the worst by Jean."

Before she could reply, a knock sounded at the door of the lavish hotel suite. He frowned. "Are you expecting anyone?"

She shook her head, "No."

The maid had gone downstairs to get them tea. Drew stood and approached the door. He opened the portal only to be greeted by Detective Dunegan who was accompanied by two burly policemen.

"Mr. Soulier, good to see you."

"Detective Dunegan. What can I do for you?"

The man held up a piece of paper. "We have a search warrant."

Drew scowled. "May I see it?"

He handed the official looking document to Drew.

"Who is it?" Layla asked, coming up behind him.

"Detective Dunegan," he replied, stepping aside so she could see the detective.

"Hello, Mrs. Cuvier," he said, his face showing no expression.

"Detective, how nice to see you today," she responded her voice changing to a syrupy kindness that Drew knew wasn't real.

Drew turned to Layla. "Detective Dunegan has a

search warrant and it appears to be in order. They're going to search your hotel suite."

Layla shrugged and turned away. "Detective, I've told you before that I have nothing to hide."

"So you've said," he replied.

The policeman brushed past them and entered the hotel suite. Layla returned to the settee where she watched the police rummage through the drawers of the desk in the parlor. She sat stoically appearing unaffected by the men going through her things.

Detective Dunegan strolled into the sitting room and stood looking down at Layla.

"We seem to be chatting every day, Detective," Layla said, a flirtatious expression on her face as Drew watched her play the detective.

Obviously charmed, the detective laughed. "True. I have a few more questions to ask you while they're searching the rooms."

"Anything," Layla said.

Drew frowned. "Excuse me, Detective, but I think Mrs. Cuvier needs to have her legal counsel present before she answers any questions."

The detective shrugged. "That's her choice."

Drew turned to Layla. "I would suggest that you not speak again with the police until your lawyer is present."

Layla raised her dark brows at him. "Thank you for your advice, but that won't be necessary. I'm trying to help Detective Dunegan find Jean's killer. I don't need legal representation, as I have nothing to hide."

God, how many of his clients had uttered that phrase? Half of them he knew for a fact had committed crimes.

"It doesn't matter whether you're innocent. Your lawyer needs to advise you on what questions to answer," he said, wondering how anyone who looked so demure could be so stubborn.

She gave him one of her cool expressions. "I want to help Detective Dunegan find the person responsible for Jean's death."

The detective smiled at Drew, a cocky grin that made him realize he would never win this battle. Drew watched him pull his notebook out of his pocket and face Layla. "Mrs. Cuvier."

"Please, Detective, call me Miss DuChampe," she said, a smile creating a small dimple in her cheek. "I'm returning to my maiden name."

Sorrow filled her southern voice, making Drew cringe, though her expression remained stoic. Did she think she could charm the detective out of accusing her of murder?

"When did you marry Mr. Cuvier?" the detective asked.

She gave him a sad look, her lids heavy. For a moment she said nothing as she gazed at him. "As I said before, I married Jean at my father's insistence. We were married on January twenty-fourth, 1894, by a justice of the peace Jean knew. Our marriage was an arranged one that my father promised me would help retain the family business." She paused and glanced at Drew, her blue eyes dark with fury. "Jean dissolved our shipping company as soon as my father passed away."

"When did you learn that your marriage was not valid?" he asked.

She smiled sweetly at the policeman, her voice full of concern. "Detective Dunegan, do you keep losing your notebook, or are these the only questions you have?"

Again she played the detective and the man seemed to actually be enjoying their game of cat and mouse.

The short man smiled at her. "Just answer the question."

"They're trying to trip you up," Drew advised.

"Thank you, Mr. Soulier, for that brilliant piece of advice," she said sarcastically. "I prefer to think Detective Dunegan just enjoys talking with me. Let me answer you again, Detective." She paused. "*You* told me about Jean's other wives."

The detective ignored her comment.

"What did you and Jean fight about the night before he died?"

"I told him I intended to return to Baton Rouge and he didn't want me to leave. He wanted me to stay here."

"But you lived in Baton Rouge. The two of you shared a home there."

"Yes, and my husband came home only every two weeks."

Drew watched Layla, and a small flicker of her eyelids suggested that she lied, but he wasn't certain. He glanced at the detective to see if he had noticed, but the man seemed more interested in his notes.

"When did you realize that Jean was dead?" the detective asked.

She sighed. "Again, Detective, when Colette awoke me, she told me that she'd found Mr. Cuvier lying on the floor of his bedroom. When I went into his room and touched him, his skin was cold and I knew he was dead."

A uniformed policeman came to the door of the parlor area. "Detective, we found this."

He held up a small vial of Bromo Seltzer, his face blank.

The detective took it from his hand. "What is it?"

"Jean often took that for headaches," Layla said.

The detective glanced at her. "Did you ever put this in your husband's drink, Miss DuChampe?"

"Don't answer that question, Layla," Drew quickly interjected feeling the need to protect her.

She gazed at him, a frown marring her beautiful forehead.

"Mr. Soulier, I would ask that you not interfere with my interview," the detective insisted angrily.

"I'm advising her in place of her attorney, whoever he is, not to answer that question," Drew said, fear for her making his voice firm.

"She doesn't have an attorney."

"Don't answer the question, Layla," Drew said, ignoring the detective.

"You are not my attorney, Drew," she asserted and then returned her attention to the detective. She smiled at the man. "No, Detective, I've never put Bromo Seltzer in Jean's drink."

The detective glanced at the policeman. "Officer, please take all of the medications you find. I want them all analyzed."

"Yes, sir," the man said, turning back into Jean's room.

"Miss DuChampe, we're going to be taking that bottle with us. Doctor Benson's test concludes that Mr. Cuvier died of poisoning."

"Mr. Dunegan, why would I kill the man who took care of me? Now he's gone and I'm penniless. Why would any woman put herself in this situation?" she admonished.

"Maybe you found out you weren't really his wife," the detective said.

She smiled and shook her head. "There would have been no reason to kill him, if that were the case. I could simply leave. After all we weren't married."

"So how would you have killed him?" the detective asked.

"Don't say anything else!" Drew insisted. "You've said too much already."

She gave Drew a look that clearly told him to mind

his own business and turned her cool blue eyes back on the detective. "Killing is a sin that would damn me to hell for eternity. I could never kill him or anyone else."

"But you thought about killing your husband?" the detective asked, trying to trip her up.

She paused, frowning. "No. I simply wished him out of my life."

The detective gazed at her for a moment and closed his notebook with a snap. The police had finished searching the rooms and held a bag of things they had taken from the two bedrooms.

"I think that will be all for today," he said.

"So shall I expect you to call again tomorrow?" she asked. "I'm beginning to actually enjoy our little chats, Detective. I just wish you would be a little more forthcoming with information and we didn't spend the entire time talking about me."

Detective Dunegan smiled at her. "I get the feeling we'll soon be spending lots of time together."

She made a clucking noise with her tongue. "I'm sorry, Detective, though your company is delightful, I truly think we've spent more than enough time together already."

They started toward the door when Layla noticed the bag of items they were carrying.

"What have you got there?" she asked, jumping off the settee and hurrying after the detective.

Drew wondered at her sudden reaction. Could she have poisoned Jean and the police have found the source?

The detective stopped and slowly turned toward her. "Items I hope will help with our investigation. In the meantime, Miss DuChampe, don't leave town. There may be more questions later."

The portal closed behind the officers with a resounding thud, leaving Drew and her in the parlor staring at one another.

Drew took a deep breath, resisting the urge to yell in frustration at her. "I would advise you to get an attorney."

"And who do you know that takes clients without pay?" she said, her voice calm, yet stubborn as steel.

"I don't think you understand how serious this situation is. You are the police's number one suspect. You sat right there and answered their questions and even gave them more ammunition when you admitted to wishing Jean out of your life."

God, how could he get past that cool exterior of hers and make her realize the danger she had just placed herself in?

"I'm sure the police will soon find Jean's real killer. Since I did not kill the man, I have nothing to worry about," she said. "When they compile their evidence, they'll realize that many people wanted Jean dead."

"It won't matter. You're the most likely suspect. You had opportunity and motive. You were the last person to see Jean that night." He took a deep breath. "The police are known for focusing on one person and you, Layla, are their target."

She stood and walked over to the door, opening it with a snap that made the door rattle. "Thank you for the offer to pay my hotel bill. From what the detective just said, I won't be leaving anytime soon. Since you don't believe in my innocence there's no need for any further discussion on the subject. Therefore, our interview is over."

Drew picked up his hat that he had placed on a Louis XVI table. He walked to the door, but stopped when he reached her side. She stood there, holding the door open for him, anger shimmering from her blue eyes. Yet, he had the most incredible urge to reach down and kiss her vulnerable lips, until they were soft and pliant beneath his own.

"I didn't say you weren't innocent," he said softly, still uncertain about her guilt or innocence.

Her eyes glistened with fury, though she somehow remained dignified. "No, but you think I'm going to be charged. I did not kill Jean. The police will soon come to that realization."

He wanted to help her. She didn't understand the magnitude of the situation. "You're naïve to think that they're going to look for someone else. No matter how much you try to charm the detective, you're in serious trouble. The New Orleans police are notoriously lazy and crooked."

"Crooked?" she said in exasperation. "You are talking to me about dishonesty?"

He paused at her obvious irritation, wondering at her attitude, but he felt compelled to help her. She had no one. "Look, you have no lawyer. No legal representation. I'm offering you my services."

She tilted her chin farther to gaze directly into his eyes. "You think that I would let you defend me, after the contract you drew up ruined my father? The one that gave him my father's shipping company and eventually forced me to marry a man who unbeknownst to me already had two wives? Think again, Mr. Soulier, I have no need for your services. I will be exonerated."

Stunned, he stared at her red face, as she tossed back her hair, her blue eyes flashing with fury. Did she blame him for her father's inept business practices and her own bad judgment regarding Jean?

"I did not . . ." he stopped. He could tell from her facial expression there was no reaching her. She had made up her mind regarding his part in Jean's treachery. But she would need him or the overworked bloke who took the public defender's cases.

He put his hat on his head. "When the police arrest you, have your servant send for me. I'll get you out of jail. Good-bye, Miss DuChampe. I'll see you at the courthouse."

Layla shut the door behind him and resisted the urge to scream. The arrogance of the man to think she would ever trust him to do any legal work for her. Amazing how twelve years could pass and not only had his body filled out, but also his ego. Now instead of schoolboy pranks, his deceit knew no bounds.

Even when she had riled him by deliberately refusing his offer of help, he had reacted like a man accustomed to getting his way. Well, she didn't need a lawyer because they would soon discover the real person who had so conveniently taken care of Jean. Then Mr. Soulier, attorney-at-law, could take his arrogant attitude, handsome good looks, along with his bossiness, and disappear from her life forever.

For she would be happily ensconced in the Sacred Heart Convent, teaching young women how to read and write, living her life in the safety of the convent walls. Which was a much better occupation than writing wills for men like Jean, swindling aging men out of their business, and hiding clients' devious, deceitful behavior from their victims.

Yet, Drew had agreed that Cuvier Shipping would pay for her hotel room and even offered to pay her passage back to Baton Rouge. She had no idea why. Kindness? Guilt? Or hope for a reward of some kind? And though she had hated the fact, she had no choice but to accept his help.

She sighed. Oh, how she longed to return home. But until Detective Dunegan released her, there would be no paddleboat ride back to the cozy house on the river.

STARLIGHT SURRENDER

And while she sat in this lonely hotel suite, all she could think about was how her last days in the home where her family resided were quickly slipping away. She wanted to go home so desperately that she had accepted Drew Soulier's offer to have Cuvier Shipping pay her way. But not even that was enough to get her past this latest obstacle.

Now she had another worry. Despite her calm assurances to the contrary, Layla couldn't help but fret: Was Drew right? Could she be arrested?

Three

Drew finished reading the newspaper article that told the world of Jean Cuvier's bigamous relationships. He lay the paper down in disgust and wondered for the hundredth time how his dead client could have led such a secret life without his knowledge.

From the time Drew graduated from law school, a fresh young lawyer still naïve in the workings of the law, Jean had been his client. Maybe that was why Jean used him to oversee his will and many of his business dealings. While Drew disapproved of duplicity, he could not deny the man's business helped establish his firm without the aid of his father.

Eric, his law clerk, stuck his head in the door. "Excuse me, sir. A Mr. Bryon Sycamore here to see you."

"Thank you," Drew said, wondering what kind of legal problem this new client would bring. "Show him in."

A large man with dark bushy eyebrows and short curly black hair walked into his office. Dressed like a gentleman planter in his light-colored pants with a blue shirt and gray hat, the over-large man seemed to fill Drew's office.

"Bryon Sycamore," he said in a deep baritone voice as he gripped Drew's hand in a firm handshake.

"Drew Soulier. Please have a seat," Drew pointed to

the chair across from him, closest to the wall fitted with shelves of law books.

"You were recommended to me by Joseph Hoffman." The planter pursed his mouth nervously.

Mr. Hoffman, a ward boss in the fourth district of New Orleans, was a close acquaintance of his father. He oversaw the politics in his area of the city and had promised to help Drew get into city government.

"How can I help you, Mr. Sycamore?"

The man took a deep breath and released it slowly, his forehead wrinkling as his bushy brows drew together in a frown.

"My wife wants a divorce. She moved out of our home into her mother's. She got herself some fancy lawyer and filed for something called a bed-and-board divorce," he said, his large hands shaking nervously. "I don't want a divorce."

Drew didn't respond to his client's confession. He sat listening, trying to absorb all the information this new client disclosed to him, trying to figure out what he wasn't revealing. Most clients told him only what they wanted him to know. Part of his job was to uncover what they weren't telling.

"I'm familiar with bed-and-board divorces," Drew said, jotting down notes. "You remain married, but you're no longer living together. After two years, the court can change it into a regular divorce if the parties have not reconciled. What prompted your wife to take such action?"

The big man rested his large burly hands on his knees. "I have a modest plantation outside of town. I work long hours supervising the men in the fields. She says that my children don't know me because they seldom see me. But if we don't have money, we won't eat, so I have to make sure the field hands don't cheat us."

He shook his head sadly. "She's the mother of my children. I don't want her to leave and take them with her."

"I understand, Mr. Sycamore," Drew said, watching the way the man's face tensed when he spoke of his wife.

"There will be no divorce stigma attached to my children," the brawny man insisted. "I want my family back. You do whatever it takes to make her come home."

Drew understood the man's tough stance, but Mr. Sycamore was in the beginning stages of the long, arduous journey of fighting a divorce. Many times Drew had seen his clients soften and wither with the long months of waiting.

"Let's talk a little more about your wife and why she left," Drew said, trying to relate to his client as he continued taking notes.

The planter's black eyes narrowed suspiciously. "What do you keep writing?"

"I'm taking notes so that after you leave, I will remember what we've discussed. These notes are only seen by me and my law clerk," Drew reassured him. Mr. Sycamore popped his knuckles, which could have been intimidating if Drew had let the daunting sound affect him. Instead he glanced up to see his client's annoyed gaze.

Frustration that his wife had dared to leave him vibrated from him, yet Drew couldn't help but wonder: Wouldn't any man feel this way?

"Make sure that those notes stay between us and no one else," he insisted.

Drew tried to reassure his client. "Everything you tell me will be kept in the strictest confidence."

"It better."

Drew ignored his remark. "So your wife feels that you spend too much time in the fields working. Is this the only reason she would put your family through the scandal of a divorce?"

STARLIGHT SURRENDER

Mr. Sycamore picked up his hat and slapped the brim against his leg in a steady rhythm. "No."

"Tell me what caused her to move to her mother's."

He sighed, the sound heavy in the silence of the room. "We had an argument. She got mad and left."

"What did you argue about?" Drew asked, thinking the man fluctuated between embarrassment and anger at his wife's actions.

"I seen her talking to a man in the plantation store. He's a traveling peddler who comes by the house to sell his goods. I caught him at the house twice." A growling noise emanated from the back of his throat. "She dresses up when he comes around. She smiles at him and once I even caught them laughing together. That peddler has no business coming to my house while I'm out in the fields."

"Do you think there's something between your wife and this peddler?" Drew questioned, thinking that maybe they had gotten down to the real reason his wife moved to her mother's.

"I don't know," the man said crossing his burly arms across his chest. "She's been acting different. Something ain't right."

"Do you have any proof that your wife and this man are anything besides acquaintances?" Drew asked, knowing the man's response could be sharp.

"No," he yelled. "I can't prove anything and that's what maddens me the most. I told her how it looked and she got mad and left."

"What did you say?" Drew asked.

"I told her no wife of mine would be committing adultery."

The lead in Drew's pencil scratched against paper as he hurriedly made notes. Drew imagined the fight must have been ugly, with accusations flying.

"I need to ask you some personal questions. The

more information you can give me, the faster I'll be able to bring your case to a happy conclusion."

The man sat back and for the first time since he had entered the office seemed to relax.

"Many times couples get into an argument and in the heat of the moment, people say things they don't mean and even separate. Later, they come to their senses and realize they don't want their marriage to end. Could this be the case with you and your wife, Mr. Sycamore?"

He shrugged, raising his brows. "Like I said, we argued about her peddling man coming around to the house the night she left." He paused, shaking his head. "She's been mad before, but never stayed away this long and she's never filed for divorce before."

He sighed. "I've given that woman more chances than she deserves. And look at the way she's repaid me. She's moved in with her mother and taken my kids with her."

"How many children do you have, Mr. Sycamore?"

"Only two. After the second one was born, she told me never to come to her bed again, that her childbearing days were over."

Drew said nothing. "What is your wife's name?"

"Teresa."

"And she's at her mother's?" he asked.

"Yes."

"Where does her mother live?"

"In Vacherie."

Drew glanced up from writing. "You told me at the beginning of our conversation that your wife was seeking a bed-and-board divorce. Do you know the name of her lawyer?"

"Joseph Leisson. I went to see him and he refused to talk to me," he said, his brows drawing together in a frown. "Why do you need to talk to him?"

Drew recognized the name. He had done business with the lawyer before. "In case we have to go to trial."

"There will be no divorce!" Mr. Sycamore once again insisted, raising his voice. "So we won't be discussing a trial."

"Let's hope not," Drew responded calmly to the man's emotional outburst. "Is there anything else I need to know, Mr. Sycamore? You've told me everything that happened that night between you and your wife?"

"Of course."

He responded very quickly, heightening Drew's suspicions. Something didn't feel right, and Drew could not help but think the man probably lied, but then again most of his clients fabricated a story to their own advantage.

"So what would you like me to do?" Drew asked. "What if she refuses to reconcile?"

"You tell her I said to get home."

Drew felt a moment of pity for the man. He wanted his wife back and had yet to face the realty she might never return. Or this could be a very simple case of two people who had had a huge misunderstanding that escalated out of control.

Maybe not.

"All right, Mr. Sycamore, I'm going to start by visiting your wife to see if there's a possibility of reconciliation. In the meantime, please don't have any contact with her until after we've spoken."

"She's pouted long enough and caused enough trouble. She needs to come home."

Drew smiled and stood, signaling an end to their meeting. "I'll see what I can do."

"Mr. Hoffman told me about your father's run for congress and how he was defeated. With the scandal of Mayor Fitzpatrick and the impeachment trial, we're actively searching for a new candidate for mayor. The Democratic Club needs young men like you, unassociated with the last corrupt group."

Surprised by the man's turn of conversation, Drew nodded his head. "Yes, I know Mr. Hoffman quite well through my father. He knows of my interest in becoming mayor. After all the indictments and the impeachment proceedings against Mayor Fitzpatrick, this is the year I intend to enter politics."

"Come to one of the meetings with me. I'll introduce you to some of the other men who could be contributors to your campaign."

For a moment, Drew was stunned at the change in his attitude. His uncertainty regarding his newest client disappeared. Bryon could help him on his road to the mayor's office. "I'd appreciate any help you can give me. Thanks for coming in, Mr. Sycamore. I'll let you know how the meeting goes with your wife."

"Any time you want to attend one of the Democratic Club's meetings, I'll meet you there and introduce you to the other members." Bryon Sycamore released his hand and walked out the door.

A client with contacts in the prestigious Democratic Club, Bryon Sycamore could help him establish himself among New Orleans ward bosses and the ruling political club.

Drew sighed. How could a woman tear her family apart and separate her children from her husband? He shrugged. Most of the time, lawyers were presented with the seamier sides of life. His client seemed brusque, but that didn't mean he felt no love for his wife and children.

Eric stuck his head in the door. "Huh, I didn't want to interrupt your meeting with Mr. Sycamore, but you received a message from Colette Malone. Layla DuChampe has been arrested for the murder of Jean Cuvier."

Drew cursed, rising up from his chair. The image of Layla locked behind bars with the prostitutes and other deviant ladies of New Orleans spurred him into action. He had tried to warn her, but deep inside, he had hoped she was right, that the police would never charge her with murder. Unfortunately, he had known when the police had gone to the trouble to obtain a search warrant that something made them believe they had enough evidence to convict her.

"I'm on my way," he said, grabbing his hat off the rack as he walked through his office door.

Would she be happy to see him, when he arrived at the jail? She blamed him for everything bad that had happened to her since Jean had him draw up the contract for the sale of Anthony DuChampe's business.

And Drew did feel a certain amount of guilt over the outcome, but he had never intentionally hurt anyone. And it wasn't his fault that her father had signed a lousy deal or that she had married Jean. He hadn't even known about her marriage until his client died.

Now the girl of his adolescent fantasies hated him and needed him at the same time. God, no matter what, he would never have wished this on her.

Layla paced the length of the cell she shared with the prostitutes, pickpockets, and assorted criminals. The smell of unwashed bodies and desperation filled the cell and she shuddered to think how long she would be detained here.

Despite Drew's warnings, she had never believed the police would consider her guilty and arrest her. No matter how much she had hated Jean and no matter how many times she wished him dead, she could never have killed him.

Often she had felt guilty longing for his death, but

she could never have poisoned him. At least not deliberately.

And if the police arrested her on the little evidence they had now, what would they do if they found out about the other, more incriminating facts?

She glanced around at the women who lounged on the cots and the floor, waiting for someone to rescue them from this filth. The cell provided no privacy, no time alone and yet she had never felt more isolated and deserted in all her life.

Had God forsaken her, to let her be accused of such a heinous crime?

She paced the floor, her arms crossed over her chest, unable to look at the women for any length of time, due to the scandalous clothing they wore.

"Hey, fancy dress. What are you in for?" a small hard-looking woman called to her. At one time, she must have been pretty, but now her painted face looked cracked and her beauty faded. From the time the uniformed officer shoved Layla inside the cell, the prostitute had watched Layla with a vicious glare.

"Me?" Layla asked, wishing someone would get her out of this cell. Right now, even Drew's smirking face would be a welcome sight.

"Who'd you think I was talking to? So what did you do? Serve the wrong dessert at your tea party?"

The women in the cell laughed and gathered behind the stout little woman, like an advancing army. She wore a low-cut scarlet dress that showed flashes of a black taffeta petticoat as she made her way to Layla.

Layla swallowed, fear filling her, as the women approached her. The whore stopped within three feet of Layla, her hands on her hips. She reached out and touched the silk of Layla's dress.

"Mighty fancy dress you have on. I don't have no

pretty party dress." Her fingers stroked the fabric. "And I like yours. I wonder how it would look on me?"

The women snickered.

"So what did you do?" she asked again, her fingers lingering on the fabric of Layla's dress.

Layla glanced down at the prostitute's hand. She took a deep breath and returned her gaze to the woman. "I'm accused of murder." She paused briefly, staring hard into the woman's eyes. "Now kindly remove your hand from my dress."

The urge to sit down and cry almost overwhelmed Layla, but she braced her shoulders and lifted her chin higher, determined not to show any weakness.

The woman raised her brows, her lips turned up in a slow smile as she casually removed her hand as Layla requested. "For a lady, you've got spunk. So who did you kill?"

Layla considered the woman and decided she did not want to discuss the murder of Jean with anyone, but especially not women she shared a cell with.

"Leave me alone."

She turned and walked away from the prisoners and gazed with longing from her cell at the door that led to the outside world. She felt tainted by the ugly stain of Jean's death as she stood inside the tiny room with its iron bars and concrete walls. Cobwebs hung from the ceiling and Layla watched a brown spider spin a cocoon around a moth trapped in its web.

Though she had spiked his tea with laudanum, the night Jean died and many nights before that, she had never meant to hurt him. Yet, what if she had killed him accidentally?

She shook her head refusing to believe that she could possibly have murdered Jean. But she could not deny that she had given him laudanum and too much of the drug could act like a poison.

Cold fear swept through her and she wrapped her fingers around the iron bars of the cell, gripping them tightly.

Where was Drew? He had promised to get her out if they arrested her. No matter how much she blamed him for her situation, no matter how much she detested him, she would give just about anything to see his conceited face right now.

She swallowed, trying to beat down the panic that swelled and threatened to overwhelm her. The police thought she was a murderer. She could die, for a murder she wanted to commit, but did not.

Drew stood in the bleak little room outside the jail with all the other lawyers and family members who waited patiently for their loved ones to appear. Normally he arranged bail and left the family to await their kin in the stuffy room, but not this time. Certainly he had picked up clients before, but never a woman accused of murder. Never a woman he felt attracted to and knew personally.

An air of desperation stifled the room and he longed to escape back to his town house. Yet the thought of Layla kept him firmly in place. While there seemed to be a quiet strength that held Layla together, he couldn't help but wonder how she would handle being locked in a cell with women from the lowest walks of life. Would she be as angry and defiant with him when they released her?

As soon as he received the message of Layla's arrest he had come straight here. But it took time to arrange her bail, set up her release and then wait while they processed the papers so that she could leave. So he sat in this waiting room, checking his pocket watch yet again, waiting, and wondering if things could get any worse.

Could she have killed Jean? The police reports showed he had been poisoned, but would Layla be so vicious as to poison his tea? She admitted putting laudanum in his cup, but if she were guilty, why would she admit even this much since they would suspect her of murder?

Drew reached in his pocket and pulled out his watch, checking the time again. Layla's release seemed to take forever or could it be sitting here worrying about her was making him feel crazy.

The judge had granted bail only after Drew accepted her into his custody and posted bond. He guaranteed she would show up for the preliminary hearing and trial. Though a date for the trial would not be determined until after the hearing.

The door opened and prosecuting attorney, Paul Finnie, stepped into the room. "Soulier. Rumors are flying that you're going to be working the Cuvier case."

"Finnie, you're still a district attorney here?" Drew asked in exaggerated surprise. "I thought you'd done the city a favor and given up practicing law," he added sarcastically.

The air crackled with animosity between the men.

Paul turned his cool, sophisticated look on Drew and ignored his insult. "Soulier, we haven't worked together since the Peterson murder trial. You remember that case, don't you? The one you lost."

Drew bristled at the reminder of the case that, to this day, he smoldered about.

"I'm looking forward to winning this case too," the district attorney said, his dark eyes taunting Drew.

"Well, if you win this one, that would make two cases you've won. I guess I'd be doing you a favor."

Drew watched as Paul Finnie's explosive, Irish temper seethed as he pulled himself up to appear taller. "I'm not going to respond to that comment."

"Oh come on, Finnie, you and I both know that eventually you'll win more cases, but not until I go into politics," Drew said, knowingly pushing the attorney. "And there is the mayoral election coming up next spring. It might be the right time for me to take over the running of this city. You know, clean up city hall."

"The people in this city are smart enough never to elect you mayor. And as for winning this case, it seems pretty cut and dried. Layla Cuvier poisoned the man she knew to be her husband. I've got motive and also evidence." His mouth turned up in a smile that made Drew want to plant his fist in Paul's curling lips.

"That's your problem, Finnie, you never look below the surface. Things that appear cut and dried seldom are. I'm going to enjoy exonerating my client while the whole city watches," Drew said.

"You can't be so dense as to believe your client is innocent, Soulier. She's admitted that she gave Mr. Cuvier laudanum. And we all know she had every reason to kill him."

"My job is to defend her and no one is going to believe a nice Catholic girl could commit murder. I don't think you can find twelve people who believe she murdered her husband."

The district attorney smiled. "She may not believe in murder, but her bigamist husband is dead and she liked to spike his tea with laudanum. Only this time, she put a little cyanide in with his laudanum, putting him out permanently. All I have to do is tell the jury the truth, they'll figure out the rest on their own."

Drew smiled, trying not to let the man see how much this new information disturbed him. Had Layla really put cyanide in Jean's tea? "I guess we'll let the jury decide."

The man smiled. "If the case makes it to the jury."

"Oh, it will," Drew said.

"I have enough to send this woman to the gallows and that's exactly what I'm going to be asking for," he said, his smile vicious. "The sight of her neck swinging on the end of a rope will prove to the citizens of New Orleans that I'm ridding their city of criminals. Maybe I'll run for mayor."

Drew carefully guarded his expression, scoffing at the district attorney. "She's not a criminal. You're fooling yourself if you think that a jury is going to send a nice Catholic girl who was deceived by her bastard of a husband to the gallows."

"I don't care if she's President Grover Cleveland's daughter. Murder is still against the law. And I can prove she killed her husband," he said patiently.

Drew shrugged. "I guess we'll see who is more convincing when we get to court."

"Yes, we will. Now excuse me, but I have a job to do. I look forward to debating with you in court."

Drew watched Paul as he went through the door, wanting to smash his fist into the nearest wall. Of the two district attorneys in New Orleans, why did he have to get Paul? The man would sell his soul or anyone else's to win.

A disturbed hush fraught with misfortune descended over the room, the other occupants glancing in his direction. He stood against the wall waiting while, one by one, everyone departed until Drew remained alone.

Finally the door opened and Layla entered the room haltingly. She paused just inside the door, her face white, her blue eyes filled with shadows as she glanced around. She saw him and took a cautious step forward. He met her halfway across the room, his arms slipping around her of their own accord, intending to give her a brief hug. She looked like she needed someone to hold her up.

She clung to him, the stagnant smell of the jail and the stench of unwashed bodies overshadowing the sweet smell of lavender.

"Get me out of here," she whispered against his shoulder.

He pulled her into the protection of his arms and hurried her through the door and out on the street, where he hailed the first cab. He helped her into the darkened interior and gave the driver the address of her hotel. Then he sat back and cradled her in his arms.

"Are you all right?" he asked, anxious as he felt her trembling against him. His breathing seemed to stop as she clung to him.

God, he had never thought of how he would feel with her in his arms. Never imagined the sensation of her curves pressed against him. Never thought of the softness of her skin or the way she seemed so small, cradled against his body.

She tried to speak, but her voice broke on a sob. She buried her face into his chest and the silkiness of her hair brushed against his chin. A fierce sense of protectiveness overwhelmed him and an urgent need to safeguard her, completely foreign to him, left him wondering at these feelings.

He didn't understand this urge to shelter and watch over a suspected murderer who blamed him for her troubles. He had gone mad. He fought the impulse, yet the allure of holding her in his arms was strong.

Layla leaned back and looked up at him, tears shimmering on her lashes. "You tried to warn me."

He couldn't speak. Her lips, soft and full, tempted him and turned his brain to mush. Yet the sight of her tears felt like someone had reached inside and yanked his heart out of his chest. God, he would like to spare her the coming days so badly. "Yes . . . but I never thought it would be this soon."

She stared up at him with soft blue eyes, and he ached to ease the pain he saw shadowed there. "I hurried to you as soon as I heard."

She nodded, tears brimming once again. "Drew—"

Layla appeared so vulnerable, so defenseless, unlike the image of strength she had been before. Now she appeared lost and confused, and he was more compelled than ever to help her.

His mouth lowered to her face and he could feel her breath whisper soft against his lips. He needed to feel her lips beneath his. The carriage jostled as they turned a corner, but somehow he didn't move. Her soft mouth beckoned him. He had to kiss her. He couldn't forego tasting her tempting mouth another moment. With a moan he gave up all pretense of trying to resist.

"Hush . . ." he whispered and his mouth lowered over hers. He kissed her tenderly at first, his lips sweeping over hers with gentleness. She didn't refuse his kiss but leaned into his body, her shoulder rested against his chest, her hip against his thigh, her breasts brushing his upper body, in the enclosed carriage.

Desire raced like a firestorm through his body, tightening his loins until he thought he would burst with need.

He only wanted to comfort her, offer her solace, to taste her, satisfy the dreams that continually haunted him at night. Her hands gripped his arm and she pulled back slightly.

Slowly she opened her eyes and stared at him in surprise in the darkened carriage.

God, was he crazy? He had let his lust overcome him

with his newest client. A client wanted for the murder of a man she believed was her husband!

He had never acted so idiotically! He had never longed to kiss someone so much.

This was hardly the place or the way to convince her to let him represent her. Especially when the news he would soon give her left her little choice.

"I'm sorry. I don't know why I did that," he said moving away from her, putting distance between them in the enclosed carriage. He trembled with the effort it took not to touch her again.

Her fingers reached up and touched her silky mouth. "It's been an emotional day. We both forgot ourselves for the moment."

"Yes," he said, latching on to her ready excuse. He had let his desire override his thinking and a lawyer should always be in control. But somehow she had managed to make him forget all his training and focus only on his need to wrap his arms around her.

And even now he wanted to lay her back against the seat and taste her full lips until she begged him for release. He took a deep breath and tried to clear his mind and focus on the necessary details.

"We need to talk about the trial," he said, trying to focus on anything but her mouth and the way she tasted.

The carriage pulled to a halt and he glanced out the window to see the hotel entrance. A doorman opened the carriage door.

"Let's talk in your room."

She put her hand against his chest. "Thank you for getting me out of jail, but I would rather be alone tonight. I need to spend some time reflecting on what I'm going to do."

Layla stepped out of the open carriage door, and Drew hurried after her, his boots slapping the brick sidewalk in front of the hotel. There was no time for reflection. She needed to understand how he had gotten her released into his custody and paid her bail. He had promised the court that she would appear for the preliminary arraignment and the trial. He couldn't risk taking a chance on her running away, his reputation being shredded, and all his hopes and dreams of political aspirations ending because of one miscalculation.

"We've got to talk tonight," he insisted, touching her elbow to halt her.

She stopped and glanced at him. "I appreciate your offer of help. I'm grateful that you came and got me out of jail, but I'm exhausted. Any bad news you have will have to wait until tomorrow."

His fingers squeezed her elbow. "I don't think you understand what I did for you tonight."

Her eyes showed in surprise at the pressure he exerted on her elbow, halting her entrance into the hotel.

"Your bail was twenty-five thousand dollars," he said.

Her eyes widened and she gasped.

"And then the court released you into *my* custody with the promise that you would be here for the preliminary arraignment and trial. I guaranteed you wouldn't run."

She stared at him, stunned.

"I know it's late, but we need to talk about me representing you."

She took a deep breath and then with surprise he watched as her blue eyes flashed in anger and her body stiffened. "I didn't ask for your help. I didn't ask for you to get me out of jail. You may have paid for my release, but until I say so, you are not my lawyer."

She pulled her elbow out of his grasp, her bottom lip trembled and he felt his heart crumble at the sight of fresh tears brimming on her lids.

"I can't do this tonight," she insisted.

He could see the angry words had sapped every ounce of strength she had left. He had pushed her too far and too fast, yet he feared her running away when she realized just how vulnerable her situation was. He had taken a chance that his reputation would be lost if she weren't here to stand trial.

Though he was crazy to leave her at this point, how could he force her when she appeared ready to collapse?

"All right, it's late. I'll give you tonight. But don't even think about running away, because I will hunt you down and when I find you it won't be pretty."

"Don't worry, your bail money is safe. I hardly have the strength left to climb the stairs to my room and I'm sure you'll be around in the morning to discuss representing me."

"Early."

"Sleep well, Drew," she said sarcastically.

Drew watched as she turned and climbed the stairs to the St. Louis Hotel until she disappeared inside. He crawled back into the cab and slammed the door shut.

Yes, he wanted to help her, but he would be damned if she was going to make a fool out of him by disappearing before the trial. He couldn't take the chance, but he had been unable to intimidate her tonight, when she appeared so vulnerable.

As the carriage pulled away, he stared at the door to the hotel where Layla had passed. Tomorrow would find her playing by his rules or going back to jail. Her choice.

Four

Layla opened the door to the hotel and gazed across the hotel lobby, deep in her own thoughts, her nerves raw, her mind buzzing from the noise of the lobby. A crowd of people milled about the open area, some standing in small groups talking. She prayed no reporters lurked waiting for her return and knew she only wanted to reach her room as quickly as possible.

As she crossed the hotel lobby, she noticed Colette speaking to a tall, burly gentleman whose back was to her. His dark hair was peppered with gray, his arms crossed across his chest.

Stunned to see her maid talking animatedly to the stranger, Layla noticed Colette's face seemed softer, prettier than before. Could he be a policeman? A reporter? Though why would she appear so relaxed talking to such a man.

At that moment, Colette turned, facing Layla, their eyes meeting across the room. Colette's eyes widened in surprise, her mouth moving as Layla watched her say something to the stranger.

Layla started toward Colette, curious who this man was. She had never mentioned a man in the short time they had been together.

Within seconds, the tall older man vanished into the

crowd of people and Layla could no longer see him. Colette hurried toward Layla.

Colette approached, shaking her head. "Oh my, I'm so relieved to see you. I didn't expect you to return for quite some time. Are you all right? I notified Mr. Soulier as soon as the police took you away. Let me get you upstairs. You look so pale and tired."

"Who were you talking to?" Layla asked, ignoring Colette's sympathy.

"Oh, him? He asked for directions," she said. "Let me get you up to the room and I'll come back down and get us both something to eat."

Tiredly, Layla nodded. The day's events were clouding her judgment, making her suspicious of everything, even questioning Colette.

"It's late. I don't want anything," Layla said, exhaustion overwhelming her. She needed to get to her room before she collapsed.

"I've been busy trying to scrape enough money together to get you out of jail."

Layla slid her hand onto Colette's arm. "Thank you, but Mr. Soulier took care of my bail. Just help me upstairs. I fear I'm too tired to climb the stairs."

Colette turned and gazed at Layla, her forehead wrinkling into a frown. "Of course you are, the terrible ordeal you've been through. How thoughtless of me to stand here talking your ear off."

They began to climb the stairs, Layla leaning on her maid for strength.

"Colette, do you remember the night that Jean died? Did you hear the argument Jean and I had that night?"

"Yes," Colette said, her gaze questioning.

"What did you tell the police?" Layla asked, suddenly needing to know.

"That you often argued late at night."

"Did you hear what we said to each other that night?" Layla asked.

"Very little."

Layla felt a sense of relief, but somehow she didn't trust her feelings. How could the servants not hear what they'd said to one another? Their voices raised in anger must have echoed through the suite, their words hateful and spiteful. "Did you hear anything that the police would find interesting?"

Colette swallowed. "No, Miss DuChampe. Nothing that they need to know."

Layla nodded her head, recognizing that Colette would not tell what she heard.

Colette inserted the key in the lock, and with a twist of the doorknob pushed open the door. Layla walked into the suite, the air stale and pungent from the closed windows. She leaned her back against a nearby wall, needing support for her shaking knees. Though the smell of death was no longer present, it lingered in her mind, an unwelcome reminder of Jean's murder each time she came through that door.

A quick glance around the room let her sigh with relief. Even this small hotel suite appeared a welcome sight to her tired eyes after the New Orleans jail.

She had never been more terrified when the doors of that cell clanged shut and she had suddenly feared the loss of her freedom, or worse, the loss of her life.

Layla stepped forward and pulled the lace shawl from around her shoulders and handed it to her servant. "I'm exhausted."

"Sit down. Let me at least fix you a hot cup of tea," Colette said, fussing over her as if she had been gone for months instead of hours.

Layla shook her head, she knew exactly what she needed and tea wasn't it. "No, I want a bath and a glass of wine or sherry and my sleeping draught. Please tell me you bought me more medicine."

"Of course, ma'am. I knew you'd be needing your sleeping medicine." Colette clenched her hands and shook her head. "The shame of them taking a fine lady like yourself and putting you behind bars. You don't deserve to be treated that way, with everything else that's happened to you. I was here, I know you didn't kill that man."

A sigh of relief escaped Layla to think she would be getting her sleeping medicine tonight. She heard Colette rambling, but her mind refused to focus on anything more than the fact that tonight her dreams would be filled with happiness and not the sorrow of her everyday life.

"I'm sorry, ma'am," Colette paused as if she were going to say more and then changed her mind.

"Thank you, Colette," Layla managed to mumble.

"I'll send an order down to the kitchen for hot water for your bath."

Layla collapsed onto the settee, her thoughts drifting back to Drew. She touched her lips, the memory of his strong arms wrapping her securely in his protective embrace. For just a moment, she had felt that nothing could harm her, that this man who smelled of sandalwood and tobacco would keep her safe. And oh, how she enjoyed the luxury of that feeling.

Yet she couldn't let his kisses lull her into forgetting for even one moment how Drew had helped that bastard Jean and together the two of them ruined her father. Even tonight he had tried to soothe her in the carriage, kissing her, until she had alighted from the carriage and he had been forced to be honest with her. Then he had shown his real intentions, to force her to choose him as her lawyer.

How could anyone pay twenty-five thousand dollars

in bail? Even a small percentage of that sum was more than she could ever expect to earn or repay. Drew was forcing her to choose him as her attorney and she didn't like his tactics for one second.

But what else could she do?

Confusion swirled through her mind, overwhelming her, leaving her drained. From the boy who had always belonged to a higher level of society than her family, to the man who had rescued her from jail, she did not know what to think of Drew Soulier. And when he had leaned down and kissed her, she had been shocked by her response.

A tingle of awareness she couldn't remember feeling, when she had been kissed before, had rippled through her. Even now she wondered at the effect.

As he held her in his arms, so safe and secure, she actually wanted his lips to touch hers, anticipated the feel of his mouth moving against hers. Touching and kissing were things she had never craved from Jean, but with Drew . . . she had enjoyed the experience.

Yet she felt angry and hurt at his ultimatum. He had paid her bail and now she knew he would demand to be her lawyer. How could she trust him to save her life, when he'd tricked her father?

Better yet, how could her father have been so gullible, to believe Jean when he had made the offer to keep their family business going? How long after the ink dried had Jean offered to take her hand in marriage, to ensure she was cared for? And how could Drew say he knew nothing about the Cuvier Widows, when he had been Jean's lawyer?

She put her forehead in her hands, trying to ease the tension gathered like a storm inside her, howling to be released. The indignity of it all! To be arrested, handcuffed, and paraded through the lobby of the hotel on her way to jail. How many reporters had witnessed her humiliation and would write about the scene they'd observed in tomorrow's paper?

Didn't they realize she was a Christian woman who didn't believe in killing? How could anyone who knew her think she had murdered Jean? Yet it appeared she would go to trial. She could likely die if she were convicted. And now Drew appeared to have trapped her, forcing her to appoint him as her lawyer.

And though she knew his skills were good for writing bad contracts and wills, what did she know of his ability to handle a murder trial? Specifically, the trial that would determine whether she lived or died?

Her hands shook and fear roared through her like a rumble of thunder. She took a deep breath, pushing down the storm surge to a manageable level. It would do no good to panic.

Drew Soulier, attorney-at-law. Tall and muscular, his image swam before her eyes and she tried to resist, shutting her mind against it. She didn't want to place her life in the hands of a man she couldn't completely trust. A showy, arrogant bastard who had written her dead husband's will.

She took a deep breath. No, Jean had never been her husband and she needed to remind herself of that fact.

Drew said he knew nothing of Jean's other women, but how could she believe him? How could she trust him? Yet, Drew had paid her bail. Who else would have gotten her out of jail paying such an extravagant sum of money?

She shook her head, feeling her options were limited and knowing she had little choice in the matter. But worst of all, she felt a powerful attraction to Drew. An attraction she didn't know what to do with and wanted no part of.

Jean had cured her of men for all time and though her mind fought against the allure, her body was very aware of just how attractive the dapper Mr. Soulier could be and the power he seemed to exude. And though she feared losing her life more than anything, Drew roused her curiosity and left her hungry for his kiss.

Yet she needed a powerful lawyer who would take control and persuade the jury of her innocence. And Drew Soulier could probably talk his grandmother out of her last gold coin. Could he do the same with a jury?

Colette entered the parlor. "I've brought your wine and your sleeping draught."

"Thank you," Layla said, her hands shaking. She needed the liquor to dull the fear bubbling inside her and the draught to let her sleep.

"Your bath should be ready soon and I've laid out your nightgown for you."

Layla gazed up at her servant. "Thank you, Colette, I'm sure you must be tired."

"I'm fine, ma'am," the woman said, gazing at her, clearly worried. Since Layla had returned Colette seemed jumpy.

"Who do you think killed Jean, Colette? After all, it *was* just the four of us in the suite that night," Layla asked the question that had crossed her mind in the weeks since Jean's death, but until today she had never really voiced. Somehow she did not believe the police would think her capable of murder. Now she knew differently.

Twisting the cork out of the bottle of wine, Colette glanced up, her expression one of surprise. "I've wondered about that myself, ma'am. Being such a fine, upstanding woman, you could not have killed Mr. Cuvier. I didn't kill him. So that only leaves George, Jean's valet, unless someone came in during the night."

In the soft glow of the lamplight, the shadows

seemed larger than Layla remembered in the suite and she felt her heart beat rapidly in her chest.

"Yes, I've wondered if that was possible, but I didn't hear anything," she responded, the thought of someone coming in and killing Jean frightening.

"Me either. I woke up that morning and it was just like the devil had come for him," Colette said, her gaze staring off, unseeing. She sighed and glanced back at Layla. "Excuse me for being blunt, but Mr. Cuvier was an evil man to have married you and those other women under false pretenses. It was not any angel that came for him that night."

Layla glanced at her, noticing the scowl that formed between her maid's eyes as she struggled with the cork. "Evil man. I like the sound of that. Why is it, then, the police don't believe me?"

The cork popped, causing Layla to jump. She felt so on edge tonight.

Colette calmly poured the wine into the glass and handed it to Layla. "Jean died here, so you are a convenient suspect. But I'm sure the jury will see that you're innocent."

Layla took a sip and let the cool wine slide down her throat. Still, fear curled ready to pounce inside her. She sighed, trying to relax. "Drew tried to warn me, but I didn't believe him. I thought the police would see that I'm blameless. That I would never do someone else harm. If I can't convince the police, why should a jury believe me?"

"Ma'am, the police are corrupt and believe that even the good go bad. But ordinary people will see your sweet angelic face and know that you could never poison anyone. You'll be acquitted."

Layla sighed. "No one deserves to die at the hand of another person, especially a loved one."

"Nor should our loved ones suffer from the abuse

of another person. Mr. Cuvier did the wrong person harm and someone took care of him," Colette said with certainty.

"But it wasn't me and I'm frightened that I'll go to prison or hang for a murder I didn't commit." The fear threatened to overwhelm her again and she gulped her wine. Or could she have put too much laudanum in his drink that night and overdosed him?

That thought could drive a person mad.

Colette touched her arm. "I've heard that Mr. Soulier is a good lawyer." She paused. "And he seems concerned about you."

"Where did you hear he was a good lawyer?" Layla asked, needing to hear something that would convince her she could trust Drew.

The maid's hands trembled as she corked the wine bottle. "One of the maids at the hotel told me that last year Mr. Soulier took on the case of a young boy accused of stealing. The kid was a street orphan and he not only got the boy acquitted, he even managed to put the child into an orphanage. He seems to care about people, and I think if you'll let him help you, he'll get you acquitted."

So Drew had a soft heart and helped street kids. That did not sound like the boy she had gone to school with, the attention-seeking kid who'd always been arrogant and a show-off. Had he used the case of the boy to advance his career, or had it been a selfless act for the kid?

"Ma'am, you're going to need a good lawyer. Not one of those appointed by the court who has to take you regardless of whether they want to handle your case or not."

Layla laid her head back against the sofa and took another sip. The wine warmed her through and through. Drew had limited her choices, but she wasn't ready to concede defeat. She closed her eyes, wishing she were home in Baton Rouge. Tonight she only wanted to drink her wine, take a bath, and say her prayers before she fell into a colorful sleep aided by her medicine.

A sudden rap at the door startled both of the women and they glanced at each other. Layla felt her heart pounding in her chest.

"Are you expecting anyone, ma'am?" Colette asked.

"No, it's late. Not unless that's Drew returning," she said getting up from the settee to walk to the door, ready to let him experience the fullness of her wrath.

"Who is it?" she called.

"Mr. Krause, manager of the hotel. Please open the door," he said.

Layla frowned at Colette and then opened the door. Mr. Krause swept past Layla and entered the suite, not waiting for an invitation. He glanced around the room, and his gaze returned to her. His brows drew together in a frown.

"I'm sorry to inform you that the St. Louis can no longer accommodate you. Your presence here with the police and newspapermen hanging around is disturbing to the other guests. I must ask you to leave tomorrow morning."

Layla stared at him in complete shock. "But . . . I have no place to go. You must give me time to find other accommodations."

"I suggest you try one of the smaller, less renowned hotels in the city. I'll expect you to be out no later than noon tomorrow."

He turned to leave, his task completed.

"Wait!" Layla said suddenly realizing her desperate situation. "At least give me until five in the afternoon."

The man clicked his heels together in an annoying manner. "Fine, I'll give you until five tomorrow afternoon, but then I expect you to leave our hotel."

He walked through the open door and shut it behind him.

Layla threw her wineglass at the closed door. The sound of glass shattering echoed in the suite as she watched red wine run down the closed door, hoping that the alcohol left a stain.

She sank to the floor, great gulping sobs coming from deep within her. Where would she go with no money and no chance of leaving town?

Early the next morning, Drew sat in his office going over the notes he had begun to assimilate since the day of Jean's murder. He added comments from the day before and last night, his mind evaluating the question of Layla's innocence. After all, she had openly admitted she hated her late husband and no one could have blamed her, if she had known about the other wives in advance. But she learned of the other wives at the same time as Nicole and Marian. Yet Jean was dead and Drew had a trial to prepare for.

Eric knocked on his door. "Mr. Soulier, I have the police reports on Mr. Cuvier's murder."

"Thanks," Drew said, taking them from his hand. He flipped through the pages. "Did you read these?"

"Yes, sir," he said.

"What do you think? Did Miss DuChampe kill Jean Cuvier?"

"I don't have enough of the evidence to form an opinion on that, sir," he said.

"Good answer, Eric. But what do your instincts tell you?"

The young man paused for a moment. "So far what little evidence I've seen indicates that she is the murderer. But when I met her the day of the reading of Mr.

Cuvier's will, it was hard to imagine her poisoning her husband."

Drew glanced up and smiled at his clerk. "You can't judge your clients on their looks and behavior. You must take into consideration their actions, but sometimes that can be deceiving, so always try to keep an open mind and dig deeper. Investigate every possibility."

"Yes, Mr. Soulier. Do *you* think she killed her husband?"

Drew thought for a moment. He wanted desperately to believe that Layla was innocent, but everything pointed to her guilt and even his instincts said she killed him.

He sighed. "Most likely she's our killer."

"But if you think she's guilty, why are you defending her?"

"She hasn't hired me yet, but she will. And as her defense counselor it is going to be my job to defend her to the best of my ability, regardless of my opinion."

"Surely, they won't hang her even if she's convicted," Eric said. "She's a woman and what Jean did was both legally and morally wrong."

"Why not? Does she deserve special treatment just because she's a woman? A man is dead."

"Well . . ."

"If you start giving women special treatment, then a lot of husbands aren't going to be sleeping very well at night."

"No, I guess you're right. But it doesn't seem fair to hang her after everything her dead husband did," Eric said, slumping against a wall.

"No, it doesn't, but you know Finnie is not going to back down from seeing her hang. He is after me and her case just happens to be the one that he thinks will ruin my chances of being elected mayor."

Eric nodded. "Does Miss DuChampe know that you think she is guilty?"

Drew gave a chuckle. "Of course not. She would be very upset if she thought for an instant that I didn't believe in her innocence."

"But don't you think that is unfair to her? I mean you're telling her one thing and yet you believe another."

"I have pursued her case strictly for the amount of exposure it will give this law firm. By the end of this case the citizens of New Orleans will be very familiar with my name. If we win, they will see me as a hero for defending a poor woman whose husband betrayed her. That could never hurt my election chances."

"How is that going to affect Miss DuChampe's case?"

"It should help her case if I do it correctly," he said, amazed that this kid didn't quite understand. "If I can build enough public sympathy for her, then those twelve men sitting on the jury are going to think twice before sending her to the gallows." He took a deep breath. "Cases like this don't come along every day and you need to learn to reach out and grab opportunities when you can."

"But I thought that she didn't have any money. How is she going to pay you?"

Drew smiled. "I'm going to take her case for nothing."

"Nothing? Won't she be suspicious?" Eric asked.

"I intend to use her case for all the free publicity I can get. After this trial, my name should be well known in all parts of this city. So when I announce my candidacy for mayor, everyone will know my name and if I get her off, I'll be the hero who saved the poor, innocent, Catholic girl from hanging. As I said, look for opportunities, Eric."

"Are you going to tell her you're running for mayor?"

Drew shook his head. "Not unless she finds out."

"And she's going to believe that you will take her case for nothing?" Eric said astounded. "I wouldn't believe it."

"No, I'm going to tell her I'm writing a book about her case. Maybe I will, maybe I won't."

Drew stood and grabbed his hat from the rack. "Now, I have to go see if Miss DuChampe remained at the hotel during the night and has made her decision. And since I'm sure she doesn't want to return to jail, I'm positive she'll agree to let me handle her case. Get ready Eric, we're going to be defending the most publicized trial of the century, I dare say."

Five

The knock on the door of her hotel suite made Layla cringe over her breakfast. Only one person would call on her this early and that lawyer had a personal interest in finding out whether or not she had left during the night.

The morning sun burned away the dreams of homelessness and murder of the night before and chased away the shadows in the small suite that had become her prison. After breaking down last night, Layla once again felt confident and determined to control her destiny.

Colette answered the door and within moments Layla saw him standing in front of her.

"As you can see, I'm still here," she said, with as much sarcasm as she could muster this early in the morning.

He smiled. "I know that you're a smart woman. I had no doubt that you'd be here."

"Liar."

Drew dropped the *Daily Picayune* newspaper on the table. The headlines were no surprise: *CUVIER WIDOW ARRESTED AND CHARGED WITH MURDER.*

She glanced at him, trying to appear unruffled by the headlines. "You interrupt my breakfast."

"So I do. You appear rested after yesterday's ordeal."

"I'm rested," she said. "Please sit down and help yourself to a croissant."

"Thanks." Drew pulled out a chair at the small table and picked up a croissant and lavished it with butter. Colette poured him a cup of coffee and quietly disappeared.

Though Layla had slept most of the night, she still felt sluggish, with little energy to face the trials today would bring. Last night's dreams of clanging cell doors had awakened her, but the memory of Drew's lips caressing hers had soothed her back into sleep with erotic dreams of the two of them entwined together. And finally in the predawn hours when she dreamed that she stood before the jury, convicted and sentenced to die, she had bolted straight up in bed, refusing to close her eyes another minute.

At that point, she gave up on sleep and instead watched the sun rise over the courtyard, while she pondered her next step.

Now, she sat across the table from the one man she never wanted to depend on, fearing she had no choice but to put her life in his hands.

"Are you all right?" Drew asked, his brow furrowed with concern, his eyes warm and questioning. "You seem a little preoccupied this morning."

"That's only because I am," she replied.

Drew wiped his hands on a napkin that lay on the small table. "Have you made your decision regarding your defense attorney?"

She gave him her best contemptuous smile. "I'm still considering my options," she said her voice honey sweet. "Tell me, besides the bail money, why should I let you defend my life?"

He relaxed and eased back in his chair. "Because I'm the best attorney in this city."

She rolled her eyes.

"It's true. I've won over ninety percent of the cases I've tried. Another five percent have never even made it to trial," he said with a nod of his head.

"And those numbers are suppose to persuade me to forget the past and depend on the man who helped Jean cheat my father?"

He leaned forward, his palms resting on top of the table, his emerald eyes stared intently at her. "You know we can very easily cancel the bail money situation. I can take you back to the courthouse. You can go back to jail and I'll get my money back."

Nothing subtle about Drew's blackmail, but she refused to give in. "I'll take that into consideration when I make my decision. That being said, you still have not answered why I should let you, the man who helped Jean steal my inheritance, defend me."

"As for your father's situation, you can blame me all you want, but I only drew up the papers. Your father made the deal with Jean, not me."

"That's easy for you to say, because they're both dead. Do you have any idea what I've lost?"

He took a deep breath and sighed. "You've lost a lot, but if you don't have a good attorney, you could lose your life."

"So I'm supposed to put my life in the hands of the man who drafted the document that all but gave Jean my father's business, and indirectly, his daughter." She paused and glared at him. "Tell me. How could you not know that Jean married me? You were his lawyer."

"Honestly, I didn't know or I would have stopped him or I would have told you or your father."

"Just like you're going to keep a jury from convicting me of murder."

"I couldn't stop your father from signing that contract. I can't stop a jury from convicting you, but I can present a damn good case of why they shouldn't. Your case is going to be a notorious trial that I have no intentions of losing," he said with conviction.

The sound of a door slamming down the hall and the chatter of people laughing as they made their way to the stairs filled the silence as she thought of his words. Could they be true?

"Do lawyers ever intend to lose?" she asked.

"Not I," he replied. "If you hire me, I'll do everything I can to get you acquitted. All I ask is that after the trial, instead of payment, you allow me to write a book about this case."

Layla swallowed. She had no money to pay him or anyone else she chose to be her lawyer. And what other lawyer in town would take her case for nothing?

"Why do you want to write a book about my case?"

He smiled. "People will find your story interesting and it's good exposure for me."

"For your law practice," she questioned.

"Yes," he replied.

She contemplated the handsome lawyer, still uncertain as to what she should do. No other lawyer would take her case without a fee. Yet, how could she entrust her life to a man she had no faith in, who was once her dead husband's manipulative lawyer and who had cheated her father?

"Tell me, do you think I killed Jean?" she asked.

A smile came over his face, his expression one of sincerity and concern. He took her hand and gave it a quick squeeze. "My job is to prove to twelve people that you could never have committed this crime. The prosecution's job is to convince the jury without reasonable doubt that you're guilty. And I don't think the prosecution can prove that you killed Jean."

She couldn't hold back the grimace that wrinkled her forehead. "You haven't answered my question. Do you believe I killed Jean?"

Drew paused and sent her a reassuring lawyer smile. One that Layla knew was supposed to appease her. "Of course not. My focus is on convincing the jury that you're innocent."

Layla stared at him, still uncertain that he really believed in her innocence, but what else could she do? Yet she needed him to believe in her innocence. "I still haven't heard you say the words."

He frowned at her and sighed.

"Okay, you're innocent," he said, his face unreadable, his words lacking the conviction she so desperately wanted.

She didn't believe him, but what could she do? Her choices seemed so limited. Jail or Drew as her lawyer? The thought of jail was repugnant and would any other lawyer that the court assigned to her case believe her any more than Drew?

She sighed, hating the factors that forced her to make this decision. "All right, Drew, you can represent me. But if I'm convicted . . ."

Drew laughed. "Don't worry. I have no intention of losing this case." He sipped the coffee that Colette had brought him. "I promise that I'll do everything I can to get you acquitted. But you have to trust me."

He gazed at her, his forest-hued eyes seeming sincere, but Layla knew with an uncanny certainty that she could not put all her faith in him. And she definitely could not tell him all her secrets.

"So what now?" she asked.

"Now, we get started on my investigation to prove you didn't kill Jean."

"You know, I have a theory that there could be other women besides just the three of us. I asked the police to see if there were more wives and they ignored me."

She watched him carefully consider her words, his reaction leaving her disappointed.

"I find it hard to believe that Jean juggled three women, but four or more? I don't know how a man could keep up financially."

"Maybe he didn't support all of his wives. Maybe some of them supported him."

He sighed. "So you want me to check for other wives."

"Yes, please. It makes sense that there are others."

"Why haven't they come forward?" he asked.

"And be suspected of murder? Be ridiculed by the press? I certainly wouldn't have come forward if I'd been able to hide."

"All right, I'll do what I can, but you have to help me. We've got lots to do and little time to prepare for the trial."

She hesitated. "There is one thing I need help with immediately."

"What's that?"

"The hotel has given me until five o'clock this evening to find another place to stay. It seems they don't want an accused murderer at their hotel."

He shook his head. "Actually, that solves a problem. I intended to ask you to be my houseguest and move into my town house. Of course you'll be chaperoned by Colette and my housekeeper."

She stared at him in stunned surprise. "Absolutely not. I am not moving into your house."

"We're going to be spending a lot of time talking about this case. It will be more convenient if you're at my house."

"More convenient for you. You'll be able to watch me closely and make sure I don't run away. I'm not living under your roof. Even for a ruined widow it wouldn't be proper."

He didn't say anything but raised his brows at her. "So let's look at this situation carefully. You have no money. Cuvier Shipping is no longer going to be paying your hotel bill once you leave the St. Louis and you are being evicted. And yet you're refusing my offer to let you stay with me. Do you intend to sleep in the streets?"

Layla slammed down her hand on the table causing the dishes to clink as they jumped. She stood and walked to the window. Turning her back to Drew, she looked out at the garden below. She abhorred living without money. Since her false marriage to Jean, she had never had to worry about finances and before that, her father had taken care of her.

Once again she felt as if life had smashed her into a wall, leaving her few alternatives. To move in with Drew seemed the ultimate humiliation. The man who awakened desires she had never felt before, who was responsible for her father being cheated by Jean, who now would defend her life.

"This better not have anything to do with that kiss in the carriage," she warned him.

"Of course not. You needed comforting and we both forgot ourselves."

"Just in case you think there's the possibility of anything else between us, let me just warn you that I'm not terribly fond of men and their physical natures."

Drew nodded. "I'll keep that in mind. After last night, I would never have known."

"Well now you do." She sighed and turned from the window. She could never face him if she had to admit her distaste for the pawing she had endured from Jean.

"I'll have Colette start packing our things. We have to be out of here by five today."

"Good, I've already told my housekeeper to prepare the guest rooms." He glanced at his watch. "I'd take you over now, but I have several appointments this afternoon. I'll arrange for a wagon to pick up your trunks. Then I'll come for you before five and take you to my house. We'll sneak out the back of the hotel, to avoid the reporters waiting for you outside."

"It's rather presumptuous of you to assume I was going to agree to this, wasn't it?" she asked quietly.

He grinned. "I'm accustomed to getting my way."

"I see that."

Her comment didn't seem to bother him as he continued. "As soon as possible, we need to sit down and talk about the night of the murder. I need every detail you can possibly remember."

Layla shook her head. "I'm sick of talking about that night."

"I'll want to compare what the police have to what you tell me. Then we need to discuss other people Jean knew, people you think might have wanted to kill him." He glanced up from his writing. "We've got a lot of things to do before we go to trial."

"What happens if I'm convicted?" she asked softly, afraid of his response, but needing to know what she faced.

A tense silence filled the room. He glanced down at his hands, before he looked up and met her gaze. "They're going to ask for first-degree murder. You could hang if convicted."

She swallowed, the thought of dying frightening. She didn't want to die. Strangely enough, she wished Drew would wrap his big muscular arms around her, clasping her within the safety of his embrace and promise her that she would never hang. She had felt so safe in his arms last night that she wanted to experience that feeling again. She craved that security.

Drew stared at her, watching her respond to this newest information, not moving toward her.

"All right, I'll be your guest until after the trial," she said softly. The thought of standing on the platform of the gallows waiting for the noose to be slipped around her neck sent a shiver through her. "You are my lawyer—please remember I'm not ready to die for a crime I didn't commit."

Later that day, Drew knocked on the door of a small house set on the east side of Vacherie. A wraparound porch went around the small frame house and a swing sat beneath an awning that protected it from the late afternoon sun.

He could not help but think that the man he had hired should be loading up Layla's trunks now and soon he would escort her to his town house. He rapped again, not wanting to waste any time.

A woman cracked the door open just enough to peek out at him, her eyes wide.

"Yes, what do you want?" she asked bluntly.

Her right eye appeared to have faint bruising around the edges, though he wasn't certain because she retreated back into the shadows.

"Are you Mrs. Sycamore?" he asked.

"Who are you?" she questioned, not answering him.

"My name is Drew Soulier, I'm an attorney. I represent your husband, Bryon Sycamore," he said noticing the way her dark eyes widened at this knowledge.

"He's not with you, is he?" she asked, her voice trembling.

"No, ma'am," Drew replied.

She opened the door a little more. "Yes, I'm Mrs. Sycamore. What do you want?"

"If you don't mind I'd like to come in and talk about your situation," he said softly, trying his best to persuade her to speak to him. "Your husband came to me after he received a notice from your lawyer. I'm here on his behalf."

She opened the door and stepped outside the house,

closing the wooden portal firmly behind her. "I'll talk with you out on the porch. I don't want my children to hear what I have to say."

"All right," Drew noticed that she must have been beautiful once, but now her skin and hair looked drab. She seemed to have aged before her time.

He moved aside and she walked past him to the swing and eased down on the seat. He moved to the porch railing across from her and leaned against the wooden rail.

"Shouldn't you be talking with my lawyer?" she asked.

"Yes, and I will. But before we get into the legal wrangle of a divorce, I wanted to make sure that this is what you really want. Your husband wants you to come home and give up the idea of a permanent separation."

"I'm sure he does," she said sarcastically.

Her hands trembled in her lap and she clasped her hands together to keep them from shaking. "Why did Bryon say he wanted us back? It's not that he loves the children or me."

Drew felt taken aback for a moment. The memory of the big burly man who had sat in his office returned. Even to his eyes it was apparent the man's demeanor could be cold and harsh, but still he appeared to care for his wife the best he could.

"You'll need to ask Bryon that question. I only know he seems to genuinely miss you and the children."

A tense nervous laugh followed. "Did he mention my cooking?"

Drew cringed as he remembered the man remarking how he wanted his wife to come back and cook his meals. "Yes, he did."

"Did he tell you that we have servants for the field, but not for the house? Or that he doesn't want a plantation wife that sits and looks pretty?" she said her voice bitter.

"No, ma'am. He didn't mention any of those things.

Though he suspects you're seeing a man who travels from house to house selling goods."

She shook her head, her laugh a weird noise that almost sounded crazy. "Yes, I see the man. Once a month he comes by selling pots, pans, and silk ribbons. He's the only person besides Bryon and the children that I get a chance to talk to. Is it wrong to long for company?"

"Are you having an affair with him?" Drew bluntly asked.

The look she gave him should have sent his hair up in flames. "I have two children, a house to take care of, meals to cook, and laundry to do. When would I have time to have an affair with any man?" She shook her head. "I'm too tired from working and cleaning to spend time chasing after a no-good man. Especially when I already have one."

For a moment, Drew saw the bitterness cross her face and he knew she spoke the truth.

"Have you explained this to your husband?" he asked.

She merely shook her head. "You don't understand Bryon. He doesn't listen to reason. He hears only what he wants to and whatever you say doesn't sway him."

"Did he give you that black eye?" he asked, unable to keep from mentioning it.

The warm sunshine shimmered around them, but her dark blue eyes reflected anything but warmth.

"Are you married, Mr. Soulier?" she asked, ignoring his question.

"No. I'm not," he replied, wondering why she asked.

She gazed at him. "Go back and tell my husband that I will not be returning. I'm tired of living such a hard life. I intend to get my bed-and-board divorce."

Drew nodded.

"Tell Bryon that this time I'm serious. I will obtain a divorce and the children and I will be moving away from here just as soon as the divorce is complete."

"You're sure of this?" he questioned, knowing instinctively her answer, but wishing it could be different.

"The children and I can't continue to live this way. I'm not returning to that house to be accused every time some strange man comes around that I'm having an affair." Her voice held conviction and certainty.

Drew stood straight. "Then I won't waste any more of your time, Mrs. Sycamore. I wish you and your children the best of luck, and I'll be in touch with your attorney."

He walked across the porch and left the woman sitting in the swing. When he glanced back he watched her wipe her eyes as if she were crying. An air of hopelessness seemed to surround the young woman, who could not be a day over thirty.

How would Bryon Sycamore take the news of his wife's decision to end their marriage?

Drew pulled up in front of the modest home on the west bank of the river near the town of Gramercy. A white verandah surrounded the house, supported by white arches with oriental motifs. A small staircase led up to the house, giving it a warm cheery appearance. But no flowers graced the garden, no chairs waited on the verandah where the family could gather on cool summer evenings.

Drew walked up the staircase and knocked on the door. Bryon Sycamore yanked open the wooden portal. "I began to wonder if you'd forgotten me, Mr. Soulier."

"Good day, Mr. Sycamore. I hope you're doing well," Drew said, gazing at the beefy man, wondering if his large hand could have blackened Teresa Sycamore's eye.

"Come in," Bryon said as he held the door open for Drew. "I'd hoped Teresa would come home and we could forget this conversation, but I haven't seen or heard from her."

Drew stepped inside the house and walked into a main hallway, a parlor off to the right and what appeared to be an office to the left.

"Let's go into the library where we don't have to sit amongst the wife's pretty things," the man said, leading the way into the library.

Drew caught a brief glance of a room that hardly seemed to be filled with a woman's frills. The room seemed stark with the furniture in dark browns and muted grays. The women he knew always enjoyed colors like soft pinks, burgundy, or blues and greens. A chipped glass figurine adorned a table without a doily.

He followed Bryon Sycamore into his office. Bryon pointed to a chair, pulled close to the fireplace that occupied one corner of the room.

"Would you like a brandy?" the man offered.

"No, thanks. I can't stay long," Drew acknowledged, anxious to return to New Orleans.

Bryon seemed nervous as he tapped his foot against the hardwood floor. "So, did you see Teresa? What did she have to say?"

Drew took a deep breath knowing the news he brought would upset Bryon. "Your wife seemed surprised to see me. She gave me a message for you." He paused knowing there would be a verbal explosion. "She said, 'Tell Bryon, that this time I'm serious. I will obtain a divorce from him. The children and I intend to move away as soon as the divorce is complete.'"

The man jumped up out of his seat and began to pace the floor. "Damn her. She's going to move to her sister's in Alabama. She can't move away and take my children. I won't let her."

Bryon Sycamore slammed his fist down on a table in the room, causing a glass vase to crash to the floor and break into pieces. Drew jumped, his mind returning to the chipped figurine in the parlor. Bryon didn't seem to notice the broken vase as he continued pacing the length of the small library, his boots crunching upon the shards of glass. "I think she means it this time. I think she's really going to divorce me."

"Mr. Sycamore, there's no need to become distraught. It will take quite awhile before the bed-and-board divorce is granted."

Bryon turned from the fireplace where he stood gazing down at the charred remains of a long ago fire. "She's serious. She's not coming back."

"I have to admit she seemed determined not to return." The memory of Teresa Sycamore's pale face swam before his eyes, her blackened eye marring her tired face.

Drew wanted to ask about that bruise, but refrained. Pushing the situation could result in losing his contact with the Democratic Club. And besides, Mrs. Sycamore never admitted that her husband had hit her.

"What's my next step?" he asked.

"Have you considered filing for custody of the children?" Drew asked knowing that the court would most likely award custody to the children's father.

Bryon glanced over at Drew, his dark eyes looked wild with anger. "You mean the court would give them to me?"

Drew suddenly wondered if he should have mentioned this motion. What if Mr. Sycamore had hit his wife? "With her filing the petition for divorce and you as the children's father, the answer is yes."

"How long would that take?" he asked, eager to know.

Drew frowned. "These things take time. I'll have to file a motion with the court and it's up to the judge as to when he'll hear our case."

For a moment the man seemed to be deep in thought

and then he smiled. "Yes, file the motion and then notify her attorney, Teresa will find out my intentions and . . ."

"All right, I'll write the petition when I return to the office. After everything is filed, I'll contact her attorney and let you know what he tells me," Drew said. He stood and glanced at Mr. Sycamore, who still appeared either in deep thought or shock, he didn't know which.

The man glanced up, his eyes glazed, the depths filled with pain.

"Thank you, Mr. Soulier, for coming out to tell me the news. I don't know how my wife could have gone so wrong. But I know she won't leave the children behind. She'll be back." He shook his head. "Let me walk you to the door."

Drew followed him out the same way that he had come in. He took another quick glance at the woman's parlor and wondered how Teresa Sycamore could have created such a drab room.

"Mr. Sycamore, was your wife happy living here with you?"

"Of course. I gave her the best of everything."

Somehow his words seemed incongruous, considering the appearance of the one room Drew thought every woman he had ever known thought of as hers.

Bryon opened the door and held it for Drew. "Thanks again, Mr. Soulier. Don't worry. Teresa eventually listens to reason. It's just a matter of finding what will help her see what's important. Good day."

Drew stepped out on the porch and the man shut the door behind him. He stopped and contemplated for a moment what the man had just said and felt puzzled. From what he had seen, Mrs. Sycamore's decision was final.

A quick glance at his watch pushed all thoughts of the Sycamores from his mind. The sun would soon be setting, leaving him just enough time to get back to New

Orleans and pick up Layla. Tonight the accused beauty would spend the first of many nights beneath his roof. And he couldn't help but feel a sense of anticipation.

Layla opened the door to Jean's hotel bedroom. The image of him lying dead on the floor assaulted her anew. Somehow she had known that moment would forever change her life, but she had never imagined that she would be accused of his murder. At the time she thought he had died of natural causes, though how, she did not know.

As she thought back to that eventful day, she wondered who could have killed Jean. George, his manservant, had been devoted to him and Colette seemed devoted to her. So who could have poisoned her husband that night, other than herself?

Could someone have gained access to the suite?

She pushed the ugly thought out of her mind and tried to focus on what lay ahead of her. The room appeared scattered with clothing tossed, drawers opened, and toiletries strewn about, where the police had gone through Jean's personal possessions. Layla glanced out the door, somehow wishing she could give this task to Colette, but knowing she needed to go through Jean's things herself.

Though the thought of someone murdering Jean in this room sent a shiver down her spine and made her hurry.

She walked past where the body had lain on the floor and opened his armoire, determined to get this ugly task done once and for all. When she finished packing everything, she intended to have Jean's trunk delivered to Marian Cuvier, Jean's lawful wife. After all, everything legally belonged to Marian and Jean's children and Layla knew she wanted no souvenirs of her life with Jean.

Standing before the armoire, she gazed at his clothing, his scent still fragrant in the closet. With a shudder, she started pulling out his suits, shirts and pants, going through the pockets, keeping any coins or bills she found, feeling like a thief.

A scrap of paper fell out of one of his pockets, and with trembling hands she picked the note up, scanning it quickly. Disappointed, she tossed it in with the rest of his things. Nothing in it pertained to her.

Next she went through his drawers, packing everything into the traveling trunk she found at the bottom of the armoire.

A sense of disappointment filled her as she opened the last drawer in his chest. A few coins, his wallet, more scraps of paper and a few pieces of jewelry, including a wedding ring she had never seen before. She rummaged through the drawer searching for bits and pieces of Jean's life.

At the very back, where she could not see, her hands felt an object. She pulled a small cigar box to the front of the drawer. She opened the box and felt her blood run cold at the sight of the trinkets inside.

She found the garter she had worn at their wedding, a gold locket that held a picture of Marian Cuvier, and pair of women's silk pantalettes she did not recognize. And at the very bottom of the box lay a small book.

She picked it up and her eyes widened at the title, *Sonnets from the Portuguese, A Celebration of Love*, by Elizabeth Barrett Browning.

Jean had a book of poetry? She couldn't contain her amusement as she opened the book and read the inscription, her laughter dying in her throat.

To my Darling Jean, may Elizabeth Browning's poetry to Robert remind you of our love during the times we are apart. All my love, Blanche, Christmas 1893.

For a moment, Layla's heart didn't seem to beat and then it pounded so fiercely, she feared she would faint. Her knees buckled and she sank down onto the bed. Flipping through the pages of the book she noticed that Blanche wrote notes to Jean on the sonnets that represented their love.

Layla scoured every page, looking for any clue that would give her information about who Blanche was.

And just when she was about ready to give up, she turned the page to find stuck between two pages an envelope addressed to Jean.

With trembling fingers she pulled the parchment paper out of the envelope. Curiosity ate at her as she unfolded the letter to see a flamboyant handwriting that swept across the page.

Jean,
  For years my brother tried to warn me away from you, but I believed every lie you told me and forsook his wise counsel. All the while, you must have been laughing at how I accepted your every excuse. How gullible I was to think the love we shared was greater than any vow of matrimony, while I foolishly built my life around you, waiting for the time when you would come to me as a free man and we would begin our life together.
  Was I so blinded by my emotions not to see into your tarnished soul? I thought our love would last forever, only to find out you know nothing of the word forever. Your fickle heart is not capable of real love.
  Were the happy times we spent together with our darling daughter nothing more than a lie? So what will I tell dear Julianne about her father? Shall I speak the truth, that you lied as you professed your devotion? Shall I tell her how I suspect that there are even more women in your life than just the two of us? What do I tell her at night when she asks for her papa?

> *Though my heart is breaking, I shall never mention your name again without a curse on my lips, for you have ruined my life and left our daughter marked with the shame of her illegitimate birth. Though I moved away, hoping to spare our daughter the embarrassment, I am unable to escape the disgrace even here in Baton Rouge.*
>
> *If you should feel inclined to visit your daughter, I warn you to notify me in advance. Every member of my family harbors a violent resentment toward you. Indeed, there are times when even I feel inclined to hasten your demise. Keep trifling with people's emotions, dear Jean, and someone will make certain that you dally no more.*
>
> *Blanche*

In shock, Layla turned over the envelope, glancing at it in amazement. Here was the evidence she needed to prove that there were others who hated Jean enough to kill him.

Why hadn't the police located this piece of evidence? But then again, if they were looking to verifiy the case against her, why would they search for any additional clues?

As she had suspected, here was yet another woman that Jean was involved with. A woman who chose not to come forward. But why? Could Blanche have killed Jean?

Her letter sounded ominous enough at the end. And she had moved to Baton Rouge. She could still be living there. Layla had to find Blanche.

Layla jumped up and threw the remaining items in Jean's trunk. She slammed it shut and hurried from the room, the find revitalizing her. She had to find Blanche. Surely she knew something about Jean's life or even his death that could lead her to the murderer.

"Colette!"

Colette came to the door of Layla's bedroom. "Yes, ma'am?"

"Are you finished packing?"

"Another five minutes and I'll be done. Why?" she asked, a puzzled expression on her face. "The wagon is not due for several more hours."

"Because we're not going to Drew's town house. We're going home to Baton Rouge."

"But . . . but you can't," the maid said, her eyes wide with fright.

"Oh yes, I can."

"But Mr. Soulier arranged your bail."

"I'm coming back. But not before I find who really killed Jean. Look what I found in this book of poetry."

When Colette saw the book, her eyes widened and she gasped.

Layla watched her. "What's wrong?"

"That book. I've never seen it before and it's poetry." She shook her head. "Mr. Cuvier was hardly the type of man to read poetry."

Layla laughed. "I don't care. It's what I found inside that's going to help me. There is another woman. Someone named Blanche who lives in Baton Rouge. And we're going there to find her."

"Oh ma'am, I think you need to tell Mr. Soulier. After all, he is your attorney and he's being so kind to let us live in his house," she said, rubbing her hands together nervously.

Layla shook her head. "No. I can't trust him. Believe me, I have my reasons. I'm not telling him anything until I find Blanche. Then I'll show him my proof of another woman."

"You must trust him," Colette insisted.

Layla laughed. "No. He's only taking my case to build his law practice. I'm the only one who cares enough to find the real killer. Everyone else is convinced I killed Jean. It's up to me to prove my innocence."

"But ma'am, he'll forfeit the bail money if they find out you're not in the city."

"I didn't ask him to get me out. He chose to force me to accept him as my attorney. And I can't depend on him or anyone else to solve the death of Jean." She glanced at Colette. "If you don't want to go, you're welcome to stay here. But nothing is going to keep me from getting on the next boat to Baton Rouge."

Colette shook her head. "I'm not going to let you go by yourself. You still need someone to take care of you. Someone who gives you your sleeping draught at night. Someone who looks out for you."

Layla gave Colette a quick hug. "Thanks. If my memory serves me right the last boat leaves at two this afternoon. We've got to be packed and ready to go before that time."

"What if you sent Mr. Soulier a note saying that you had to leave town?"

"No. In fact, we're going to dress very plainly so that we can sneak out of this hotel without a mob of reporters following us."

Colette sighed. "I don't like this, but if it's what you want, then I'll go along with you."

"Drew Soulier is a smart man. He'll figure out where I went."

Layla felt a tiny bit of apprehension. And when he found her there would be hell to pay. But hopefully she would have the answer to who killed Jean by the time he arrived.

Six

At a few minutes past five, Drew hurried into the hotel. He glanced around the bustling lobby where groups of people stood chatting and knew with certainty Layla would never have waited for him here. The possibility of a reporter recognizing her was too great a risk. She would have bestowed upon the manager one of her sweet smiles and honey-talked her way into staying in the suite until Drew arrived.

He took the stairs two at a time, anxious to sneak her out of the hotel and get her settled at his home. Though he knew he shouldn't think of his client in such a way, all day he had had visions of her lying in his guest bed, her dark hair spread across the pillows. The sensual image left him eager to make it a reality.

After all, Layla DuChampe had filled his fantasies for more years than he cared to remember. The first woman to appear in his erotic dreams was Layla. And having her in his home was going to be a temptation he would have to carefully contain.

Later tonight, he intended to interview her, find out what really happened the night Jean died. For something in her story to the police seemed to be missing, some vital piece of information that he felt she hadn't revealed. He intended to seek out that missing clue.

Tomorrow he could begin his preparations for her trial. The arraignment was scheduled for next week.

When he reached her suite, he knocked on the door and waited. The seconds ticked by as he expected someone to answer the door. A minute passed and he knocked again, wondering why it would take so long for Colette or Layla to come to the door.

The silence grew longer, and like the slither of a snake, uneasiness crept up his spine. His hand shook when he raised it to the wooden door again. This time he pounded loud and hard enough to cause the door to shake, and tried the door. Locked.

Everyone on the third floor must have heard him. Frantic, he put his ear to the door and listened. Nothing.

His heart beat in triple time. Why wasn't Layla answering the door? Could she be hurt? Or had he pushed her too far this morning and she had packed her bags, determined to live a life on the run?

This morning when he left, she seemed resigned to being his guest. She seemed to have accepted his terms and willingly agreed that he be her lawyer. Either that or she was one hell of an actress and her acquiescence had all been a ruse to cover up her plans of running away.

Even so, Drew knew she had little cash in her possession, so she couldn't go far. That thought comforted him, though he worried that she lay on the other side of that door, unconscious and bleeding. Or even the unthinkable, she really was innocent and Jean's real murderer had returned to complete his destruction.

That thought sent him scurrying down the hall, racing down the stairs. Entering the lobby, he slowed his pace and took a deep calming breath, his appearance once again composed, although his thoughts were in turmoil.

He approached the registration desk. "Can you tell me if Miss DuChampe has left her suite?"

The hotel clerk looked at Drew. "She was supposed to be gone by five P.M. today."

"Yes, I'm here to pick her up," Drew acknowledged wishing the man would hurry.

The desk clerk glanced through his book. "No, sir. She has not signed out."

"I tried knocking on her door and no one answers. Could you let me in, please?"

"Let me get the manager."

The man disappeared and Drew thought the clerk's blood must flow like molasses, as slow as the man moved. Indeed, if Layla had betrayed him by running away, she had a good three to four hour head start. But where would she go with no money, no place to stay, and no family close by?

If Layla was not lying dead in her hotel suite or sitting, waiting for him at his town house, there was only one place she could have escaped to, only one place she could possibly obtain enough cash to run from a murder conviction. Baton Rouge.

The hotel manager came to the desk. Drew immediately recognized him.

"Hello." Drew's voice sounded deceivingly calm, thinking that if anyone found out about Layla's disappearance he would appear the biggest fool in New Orleans. "I came to pick up Miss DuChampe, but no one answers her door. Could you check to see if she's left yet? I may have gotten the time wrong."

"I'll accompany you to her room," the manager said. He grabbed a set of keys and came around the counter. The two of them made their way up the stairs to the suite, Drew barely containing his urgency.

Inserting the key, the manager turned the knob and pushed open the door. Drew rushed in, anxiously searching the set of rooms. The suite seemed eerily quiet. No dead bodies greeted him as he walked from room to room, his steps echoing in the suite. He could find no sign of foul play, no traces of blood, no signs of a hurried departure. The suite was empty, wiped clean of Layla's personal belongings.

A red haze of anger shimmered before his eyes. When the papers learned of her escape, his reputation would be smeared through the headlines, all hopes dashed in the black ink of the ugly headlines in the newspaper.

And he would make her wish she had stayed in jail when he found her.

Drew sighed. "I'm sure she must have meant four o'clock and I mistook it for five. She's probably waiting for me at my office. Sorry to have troubled you," he said trying not to appear too eager, yet wanting to run. Instead he casually walked out the door.

She was not dead, she was not bleeding, so she had better damn well be waiting for him at his town house or he would hunt her down and lock her up himself.

Yet some small part of him knew he would not find her waiting.

Climbing into his buggy, he snapped the whip at his horse, urging him faster as the buggy made its way down Illinois Avenue to his house. He pulled the buggy to a halt in front of the house and tethered the horse. Running up the stairs he pushed open the front door with a wham as it bounced off the wall.

"Esmeralda!"

"Yes, Mr. Soulier," she answered, coming out of the kitchen.

"Have my guests arrived?"

"Their trunks came earlier today, but I've yet to see them, sir."

He cursed and ran out of the house, leaving his servant to stare at him in bewilderment. Layla appeared to be traveling light, not bothering to drag her trunks along with her.

Drew drove his buggy as fast as he could down to the wharf where the riverboats ran.

A main shipping line ran between Baton Rouge and New Orleans. He drove the buggy to the wharf, where he jumped down, barely pausing to tie the horse, before he sprinted into the building.

Breathing heavily, he asked the clerk, "What time did the last boat to Baton Rouge leave?"

"Our last trip upriver was at two o'clock this afternoon," he replied slowly. "Why?"

"Do you remember two women traveling together? A servant and her mistress?"

He shrugged. "Several women got on the boat who could fit that description."

Drew pressed on. "One of the women is tall, with dark hair and blue eyes. She probably would have been dressed quite well." He stopped. "No. Did you have two women one of whom was lovely but dressed plainly?"

"Not that I remember. We did have a lady dressed in black from head to toe, who wore a veil covering her face. Her maid said they were going home to a funeral."

Drew tensed.

"Did you happen to hear what the woman called her maid?"

"Yes, I think she called her Colleen."

"Could it have been Colette?"

"Yes, that's the name."

Damn, she had fled home to Baton Rouge after promising him she wouldn't leave, after she agreed to let him be her lawyer. She'd led him to believe she was agreeable to him taking her case, but he would not let her get away with this deception. She'd not get far.

Darkness would soon fall, so he could not go by land, but he would be on the next boat upriver.

"What time is the first boat to Baton Rouge in the morning?"

"Our first run leaves at ten o'clock."

"I need to buy a ticket."

Drew paid for his passage and then walked away from the dock just as the sun sank in the western sky.

Anger fueled him as he drove his buggy to his office. Layla DuChampe was not going to make him the laughingstock of New Orleans. He intended to use her trial to gain the votes of the people of New Orleans, not to be made ridiculous in this city where he had worked so hard.

As soon as he found her, she would rue the day she had decided to skip town on him. They would all be on the next boat back to New Orleans and no one would be the wiser regarding her excursion.

Nobody made Drew Soulier look like a fool. Especially a twenty-five-thousand-dollar fool.

The next day, Layla brought the buggy to a halt in front of her childhood home. The late afternoon heat shimmered in the summer sky and her hands ached from the constant tug of the reins. Cicadas heralded the coming evening, their song one of anticipation.

After they arrived late yesterday, she had slept peacefully for the first time in weeks, using only a small amount of the sleeping draught. Soon she would be required to return to New Orleans and leave again the home she loved, possibly forever.

She gazed with longing at her childhood home, the house Marian now owned because of the wretched contract Drew had drawn up in favor of Jean. Bitterness at her loss filled her and she quickly pushed the feelings away. She could not think of them now, she needed to concentrate on finding Blanche, and forget the fact that her own lawyer had betrayed her.

Tired and disappointed, she had spent the day going

from the local store to the newspaper office and finally the county courthouse, asking the same questions over and over regarding Blanche and Julianne. No one remembered them.

Her only hope was a woman who wrote the society column for the local newspaper. The man at the newspaper office had told Layla that if anyone in town knew of Blanche, this woman would. Now she needed to arrange a meeting with the woman.

She climbed down from the buggy, holding onto the reins tightly, looping them over the hitching post out front of the house. She crossed the yard to the house. For all her efforts this day, she still had no information on Blanche and little time left before Drew descended on Baton Rouge and forced her to return to New Orleans.

Climbing the steps of the front porch, she noticed the sun, a golden ball, slide slowly toward the horizon in the western sky. Like the sand in an hourglass, time was slipping away.

Would Drew have gone to the police? No, he had too much pride to let anyone know she had left New Orleans. He would search her out rather than turn her in.

Opening the door, she took off her hat and hung it on the coat rack and then pulled her gloves from her hands. With a sigh, she stepped into the hallway and came face-to-face with the very man she had hoped to avoid,

Startled, she gasped. "Drew!"

Anger radiated from his tense body and his emerald eyes sparkled with fury. She took a step back.

"Hello. I thought you would arrive . . . today," she managed to say.

He stalked toward her, his jaw tense, and she took another step back.

"I knew you'd find me," she said, lamely trying to defuse his anger.

He didn't say anything, but continued to walk toward her, his steps sure, his face a hard, angry mask that gave her pause.

"Nobody makes me look like a fool," he said, his voice low and dangerous.

"I wasn't trying to make you a fool. I knew you would come after me." Her back hit the closed door. She swallowed the panic that pounded in her veins. She had never seen Drew so angry.

He grabbed her by the arm and pulled her to within inches of him. "I trusted you. I believed you when you said you wouldn't leave. Now you're eighty miles up the river from where you're supposed to be."

"Let me explain," she said, feeling his hand tight around her arm. "I wasn't running away. I had a reason to come home."

"You can give me your explanation on the boat back to New Orleans."

"No!" she cried, courage filling her. "I can't go back!"

Drew scowled and though her insides quaked, she was determined not to back down at his fury.

"At least not yet," she said.

He squeezed her arm with his hand.

"I'm not asking if you're ready, I'm telling you we're leaving, now." His voice sounded stern and merciless.

"I understand why you're angry. But I have a good reason for coming to Baton Rouge. Let me show you what I found that the police overlooked."

He didn't release her, but stared, his eyes so intense she felt like they examined her intimately, seeing right through to her soul.

"Why should I trust you?" He was so close she could smell his cologne. "I could have left you sitting in that jail. I didn't have to put up my money to arrange your release. You didn't even have the decency to leave me a note."

Layla jerked her arm from his grip, suddenly furious at his high-handed tactics. "I didn't ask you to become my personal keeper!"

"You didn't have to—my money made me your new chaperone. If you don't like it, I'm sure they still have accommodations for you at the jail."

"Did you ever consider someone other than yourself could have found the note and think I truly had run away? I have a very good reason for leaving New Orleans and returning to Baton Rouge. And you'd think, as my lawyer, that you'd at least ask me why."

"I don't give a damn about your reason. You left me to search for you, thinking you were on the run, leaving me to face the ridicule of the town and the excoriation of the court."

"Oh please. Ridicule? Do you think I'm concerned about ridicule when I could hang? When my name has been printed in every newspaper in the country?" She stalked into the library, her own anger mixed with her guilt. "If I were going to run away for good, Baton Rouge is the last place I would have gone. Give me credit for having a little more intelligence."

"How do I know you just didn't stop off here to get some cash?"

"Does it appear that I've just stopped over for cash?" Layla shook her head. "Colette wouldn't be in the kitchen preparing dinner and I wouldn't have walked in so casually this afternoon. I would have been long gone. You never would have found me if I truly were on the run."

He didn't say a word, but stared intently at her.

Frustration and anger swelled within her at his lack of interest in the new evidence she had discovered. She hated the tears she could feel brimming in her eyes almost as much as she hated Drew at this moment.

She threw up her hands in exasperation. "It doesn't

matter what I say, does it? You've made up your mind that I'm guilty and that I am running away."

Drew stared at her, his expression turning contemplative. "You should have notified me you were leaving."

"And then what? Have you stop me from leaving town? So you could tell me once again that you didn't believe there were any other women that Jean was involved with? Tell me I was on a wild goose chase to try to save my life?"

"It does seem rather preposterous that he could keep more than three women," Drew responded.

"Maybe it is."

A sense of hopelessness turned her anger into fear and a tear slipped from her eye, rolling down her cheek.

"I'm supposed to let you defend my life and you don't believe I'm innocent. Just like everyone else, you think that I killed Jean. You're using my trial to draw attention to your firm. But worst of all, you're using me like you did my father, damn you!"

"That's ridiculous," he gasped. "How did *I* use your father?"

"You helped Jean gain control of his business!" she insisted, her voice rising.

"Your father made the choice to sign that contract. I didn't force him." Drew's voice rose higher. "Frankly, you should be grateful I took your case. I didn't have to."

"Grateful?" The tears rolled faster down her cheek. "Why? Whether I live or die doesn't seem important to you. You're here to drag me back to New Orleans. You haven't even asked me what evidence brought me to Baton Rouge!"

She put her face in her hands and began to sob. "I have proof that another woman exists and you don't care."

"Show me this proof," he said in a rigid voice.

She pulled her hands away from her tear-streaked

face and hurried to the table where she had laid her reticule. Her nervous fingers fumbled with the strings holding the small purse together, until she finally managed to open it.

Layla took out the letter and handed the parchment paper to him. She had not allowed that sheet of paper out of her sight from the moment she had found it.

His eyes quickly scanned the document. "How do you know it's authentic?"

For a moment, she was stunned at him questioning the document.

"While I was cleaning out Jean's things, I found a book of poetry in a drawer full of things he collected from all his wives. Jean never read poetry. The document was hidden in the pages."

Drew said nothing, but stood, staring at the document with a disapproving expression.

"Why didn't the police find it?" he questioned.

Layla shook her head. "Oh, please. They hardly looked at anything, they were so certain of my guilt."

A knock sounded on the door, startling them both. "Are you expecting anyone?"

Layla dried her eyes and shook her head. "No."

Drew went to the door and opened it.

She moved behind Drew gazing over his shoulder to see a Baton Rouge policeman standing on the threshold. Her heart began to pound inside her chest, in a rhythm that echoed the word "doom" vibrating through her head.

If someone in New Orleans knew that she had jumped bail, Drew could save his reputation by turning her over to the police. He could look like a hero and save himself and his firm the embarrassment she had brought upon them.

"How can I help you, Officer?" Drew asked.

"Who are you?" he demanded.

"Drew Soulier, an attorney from New Orleans."

"Oh, I recognize the name from the newspapers," he said. "One of the neighbors reported seeing someone at the house. We thought we better check it out, since we know Mrs. Cuvier is in New Orleans and accused of murder. Is everything all right?"

A shiver of warning went through Layla. Drew could hand her over to the officer and she would soon find herself back on a boat headed for New Orleans, once again in the custody of the police. His reputation could be saved while she sat locked safely away to await trial.

Drew would turn her over to the police and she would never find Blanche.

He glanced back at her for a moment and then faced the policeman. "Everything is fine, Officer. Mrs. Cuvier is with me and we're doing some investigating into the death of her husband. We should be here for a few days."

They were staying here? Stunned, Layla felt a sense of relief and an urge to throw her arms around Drew. Had she misjudged him so terribly?

"All right, sir. I'll tell the neighbor not to worry."

Drew shut the door and faced Layla, his brows drawn together in a fierce frown. "If you ever disappear without my knowledge again, I will personally escort you back to jail. Until this trial is over, an invisible rope keeps us bound together. Don't think you can slip away."

Seven

Drew lay in bed, the hoots of a night owl drifting on the breeze through the open window. A cricket sang a desolate tune, calling for a mate and Drew was troubled by the melancholy sound. Lonely and restless, he had tossed and turned, unable to sleep, his mind constantly thinking of the woman down the hall.

The letter from Blanche had surprised him, though he was not convinced of the letter's relevance to the trial.

And when the officer knocked on Layla's door, the thought of handing her over to the policeman had crossed his mind, but he knew letting her sit in jail would not help the case. Not to mention the memory of her face when he had picked her up from jail the first time prevented him from turning her in. He had been angry, but not vindictive.

She stood gazing at him, wondering his intention, when all he'd wanted to do was kiss her full lips until they were both satisfied. But that would be political suicide, not to mention completely unethical. Lawyers did not seduce their clients. Even the sweet Layla, his youthful fantasy.

He needed to gain control of his wayward thoughts in order to protect himself and his dream of becoming mayor. Layla's trial was an opportunity to advance his career and further his political campaign. Yet the woman sleeping down the hall intrigued him, aroused him, and challenged him more than any other woman in years.

Unable to sleep, he arose, intent on finding the kitchen for a snack and maybe rummage through the library for some light reading. Wrapping his robe around him, he opened the door to his bedroom and quietly slipped out. Softly treading down the stairs, he noticed a light on in the library.

He halted in the doorway and gazed in surprise to see Layla sitting on the couch, her feet curled up under her, her robe tucked around her legs, reading a book. For a murderess, she seemed remarkably peaceful.

She glanced up seeing him in the doorway. "Why aren't you asleep?"

"For the same reason you're down here. Insomnia," he said.

Her dark hair, long and loose, flowed down her back, past her waist. She looked almost angelic reclining on the couch and he couldn't help but question her innocence. Could this beautiful, appealing woman be so devious as to poison her husband?

"True," she answered her voice sounding relaxed and far away. "But I took a sleeping draught and should feel drowsy soon."

"What do you take?"

She shrugged. "Something Colette buys."

Drew started to ask her if she had taken the draught the night Jean died and thought better of it. He would ask her tomorrow when they talked about the night of the murder.

He nodded. "What are you reading?"

"*Little Women*," she said, closing the book and putting it down. "Do you read much?" she asked.

"Yes, usually at night," he answered. It was strange

to stand in his nightclothes, talking in the wee hours of the morning, fighting his thoughts of kissing her lush mouth.

She glanced around the library and then back at him. "My father loved this room in the house. He spent hours in here surrounded by his maps, charts, and journals." She glanced about. "I'm glad that Blanche's letter brought me home. I know Marian has possession of the house, but I didn't think she'd mind me being here just one last time."

"No, Marian wouldn't mind," he said sympathetically.

Legal maneuverings usually didn't affect him, yet he felt sad at how much she had lost.

He walked into the room and sat down on the opposite end of the couch, wishing he could sit next to her and pull her into his arms, knowing he was safer with distance between them. She moved her legs, making room for him.

"What would you be doing now if Jean hadn't died?" he asked, trying to focus his mind on anything other than the temptation Layla presented.

Her blue eyes darkened. "That's a strange question coming from the man who has changed my life more than anyone I know."

Drew could feel the hostility building within her. He knew he could win any argument they got into, but he hadn't gotten out of bed to debate with Layla. Especially when she looked so incredibly enticing.

"Look, we could argue until the sun comes up. I know you blame me, but do we have to talk about this tonight? It's late. Could we just call a truce until morning?"

She raised her brows and yawned. "All right, until the sun rises."

"Thank you," he said and knew that soon, before the trial began, she would need to know his side and understand he had done only what his client Jean had requested.

They sat silently contemplating one another as doubts assailed him. How could a woman with such an innocent face have killed anyone? "So tell me about your life with Jean?"

She frowned. "That's not the type of discussion that leads to sleep. It makes me angry and upset, so until the sun rises that's another taboo subject. I'd rather we talked about you and your life."

He nodded. "Given the hour, fair enough. What do you want to know?"

"What happened to you after I last saw you in school?" she asked.

"I stayed in Baton Rouge until I finished twelfth grade, and then I attended Tulane University," he said, letting his eyes feast on her as she didn't appear to notice. "Now I'm considering going into politics."

"Whatever for?" she asked surprised.

He thought for a moment. "I want to bring about some positive change that will help everyone." He paused. "I don't know, it's just something I've always wanted to do."

"Louisiana politics has always been interesting," she said.

"I've always liked a challenge."

They sat there listening to the night sounds and the creaking of the old house. Layla yawned.

"Why haven't you married? Surely there must have been someone you couldn't live without?" she asked.

He shrugged. "Perhaps I'm a hopeless bachelor. I haven't found a woman I wanted to be with night and day."

In actuality, he had always compared every woman he met to her. From the first day he saw her in the schoolyard, she had always seemed so aloof, remote, and often defiant. Even today, she appeared to be a challenge he wanted to triumph over.

"Or could it be that no one you've met holds your interest for very long?" she asked.

"I do become bored very easily."

If only he could crawl inside her mind and see what lay beneath that cool exterior and see what made her laugh, what she felt passionate about, and what she loved.

He had never taken the time to understand women, but Layla had always intrigued him and now was no exception. He wanted to understand her.

"Easily bored," she said rolling her head, making him ache to press his lips on her long, slender neck.

"I see you needing someone who would give in to you and never stand up to you," she said, her dark eyes questioning.

"No. I want a woman strong in spirit, yet womanly in body and soul."

"Womanly in body and soul?" She laughed, the sound pleasant in the cozy atmosphere. "You really mean a woman with an hourglass figure."

He shrugged. "I'd be lying if I denied I like a woman with curves."

"Strong in spirit could also mean stubborn, defiant, bold or disobedient. Are you so certain this is the type of wife you want?"

"Meek women bore me."

She raised her brows and yawned again, her hand covering her mouth. "Excuse me, I think the draught is beginning to work." A frown creased her forehead. "Marriage is difficult. Most men want only agreeable, soft-spoken women, who will not stand up to them. Are you saying this because it's midnight? Perhaps we should be sleeping instead of posing rhetorical questions."

Could she feel the tension between them that he did?

"Where is the challenge if the woman I marry is fearful and subservient? I can get that from my law clerks."

Layla leaned back, closed her eyes and laughed. "So you want a challenge. So many men consider a wife to be just another piece of property. What about you, Drew? Will your wife share your life? Your possessions? Or will she be a pretty decoration to adorn your home?"

"I don't need any more decorations. I need someone who has enough gumption to fight for what she believes and love me in spite of my faults. If I ever marry, it will be for eternity."

Layla opened her eyes and glanced at him, her pupils appearing dilated. She shook her head and smiled. "Spoken like a man who has never been married. Eternity is a long time to spend with someone who makes you miserable."

"Maybe that's why I haven't married."

"What if the passion dies and she makes you so angry you want to hit her?"

"Hit a woman? I've never been that angry," said Drew.

She raised her brows. "Not even today when you found me? You weren't angry enough to want to hit me?"

"Of course not," he said, feeling nervous. He had been furious. In fact, he couldn't remember a time when he'd felt so out of control. "Did you think that I would hit you?"

"I didn't know. You did grab my arm," she said, watching him.

"I'm sorry if I frightened you. I never meant to hurt you," he said, gazing at her, wanting her to see he was sincere. "I was furious, and I grabbed you because I wanted you to stand still so that I could berate you for taking off and leaving me to face the court."

She smiled. "But I didn't leave *you*. I came here to find Blanche."

How did he respond? "And I would never have harmed you."

She nodded. "We were both wrong."

"Maybe," he admitted grudgingly. Given the way she reacted to his anger, could violence have been a part of her marriage with Jean? "Did Jean ever hit you?"

"No," she said drowsily. "I would have changed the locks on the house if he'd ever struck me."

"If Jean hadn't died, would you have spent the rest of your life with him?" Drew asked, curious. Why had she stayed if she was so unhappy with Jean?

"What else could I do? According to the church, marriage is forever, and I had no other means of support. The only means of providing a living for myself was to return to the Sacred Heart."

She sighed and turned her head, snuggling deeper into the couch. "The Mother Superior would have insisted that I resolve to remain married. Where else could I go?"

As he glanced across the small space separating them, he couldn't help but feel for the young girl who found herself trapped in a loveless marriage to a man close to her father's age. With no one to turn to for help and faced with spending a lifetime with a man she detested, would she have killed Jean?

And how could he still feel so attracted to her, while he doubted her innocence? She could be a murderess, yet he still wanted her.

"Layla?" he said, gazing at her closed eyes, wondering if she had fallen asleep.

"Hmm . . . I'm sleepy."

"I think you need to go upstairs."

"All right," she said, not moving.

He tugged on her arm. Her breathing was deep and rhythmic, and she did not move when he touched her.

"Come on, I'll help you upstairs to your room."

She didn't respond. He cupped her face and turned her toward him. "Layla, wake up."

She slept on, not stirring. He gently patted her face, trying to awaken her, but she didn't rouse.

Gazing at her small upturned nose and high cheekbones, he thought she looked so innocent, so vulnerable. Quickly, before his traitorous thoughts wandered in unacceptable directions, he stood.

He bent and scooped her up in his arms. She felt soft and light and, for a forbidden moment, he thought of carrying her into his bedroom, his bed, rather than her own. Instead, he climbed the stairs carefully, with her cradled in his arms. The smell of lilacs tempted him and he could not help but notice how her dark lashes lay against her pale cheeks, her full lips beckoning him. She looked so soft, so vulnerable, and so innocent as she slept.

He opened the door to her room and realized she did not sleep in the master suite, but rather in a smaller room decorated with memorabilia from her childhood.

Gently, he set her down on the bed. He tugged the robe from her body, unable to resist glancing at the way the nightgown underneath molded to her curves.

His fingers accidentally brushed against her full breast and he yanked his hand back, feeling like a molester. He could take advantage of her so easily, but he did not want her this way. Gazing down at her full, ripe body, he took a deep breath and reminded himself again. No, he wanted Layla to want him as much as he yearned for her.

And that was impossible.

He leaned over her bed and pulled the sheet up and over her shoulders. Reaching down, his hand brushed the hair from her cheek and he contemplated how soundly she slept. His fingers trailed across the soft fullness of her lips, down her chin, her throat, stopping when he reached her chest.

He stood, forcing himself to break the spell he was under.

With a last glance at the beautiful woman, he compelled himself to walk from the room. He would like nothing better than to pull back the coverlet of her bed and crawl in beside her.

But she slept deeply. And she was his client.

Layla made him yearn for things he had not thought of in many years. Things he had no time for. Desires he had long forgotten. The woman who had played the wanton in many of his dreams lay available before him, but he turned and walked away.

Drew gazed about the library, not quite able to put their midnight rendezvous from his mind. With the bright sunlight, the intimate setting of late night seemed more like a dream as he prepared to interview Layla.

All morning he had berated himself silently. Layla was his client and therefore, strictly off limits. Although this morning he couldn't shake the image of her in bed, her nightgown clinging to her breasts, skimming her hips in the shimmering moonlight.

He swallowed, determined to purge the image from his mind as he took a seat at her father's heavy oak desk. He glanced over at Layla. She had not said a word as she took a seat across from him.

With the daylight she had retreated back across the battle line.

"Are you all right this morning?" he asked, wondering if she remembered him touching her face.

"I'm fine," she said shyly, a slight blush tinting her cheeks. "Thank you for helping me to bed."

"You're welcome," he replied, unable to say anything more, since she obviously remembered nothing.

Drew took his notes from his bag and sharpened his pencil. She appeared tense this morning. Could she be fearful of his questions?

"I need you to be completely honest with me this morning. If I'm going to win this case, I need to know every detail, every dirty little secret that existed between you and Jean."

"All right," she answered, her blue eyes reserved and cool.

"Let's get started. We have a lot of ground to cover today and when we return to New Orleans, I'll need to meet with the other members of my defense team. They will investigate any leads I may find and verify the information you give me."

"Why do you need to authenticate what I say, if you believe I'm innocent?"

"A good attorney confirms everything that his client tells him," he said, giving her a reassuring smile, trying to put her at ease. "You may be telling the truth, but not all of my clients are so forthcoming. Also, I have to be able to prove everything to the jury and the prosecutor for you to be found not guilty. More than anything I can't have the prosecuting attorney prove my facts are wrong. So I am depending on you to be honest with me."

"All right," she replied. She sat up straighter in the chair and squared her shoulders.

He tried to watch her movements covertly as he glanced down at his list of prepared questions. "All set?"

He paused, noticing how tensely she clenched her hands in her lap.

"Yes."

"I want you to think back to the day before Jean died. Tell me everything you did from the time you got up."

Layla frowned. "I spent most of the day shopping in the French Quarter while Jean worked at the Cuvier office."

"No. I want a minute-by-minute description of your actions," Drew said. "In detail."

"All right. I slept later than ususal that morning. When I arose, Jean had already left for the day. After I ate breakfast in my room, I went with my maid to the French Quarter, where we spent the afternoon shopping."

"Can you tell me some of the stores you visited?"

"I don't remember." She paused. "We walked through the market and later had lunch at Antoine's. I came back to the hotel in the afternoon and rested until the dinner hour. Jean sent me a message telling me that he could not join me for dinner."

"Did he say why not?"

She shook her head. "No, he did not tell me his plans."

"What did you do during the evening while he was out?" Drew asked.

She hesitated, and glanced down briefly at her hands. A look of indecision crossed her face. "I ate dinner in the hotel restaurant and then came back to our suite."

"Did you eat alone?"

Her body stiffened and she avoided his eyes. Something in the way she wavered gave him cause to question her words.

She bit her bottom lip. "Yes."

"Can any of the waiters attest to your presence

there?" he asked, hoping she would tell him whatever caused that look of uncertainty on her face.

"Yes," she replied, not going into detail.

"Do you know what time Jean came home that night?"

"Yes, it was around midnight. I waited up for him," she responded, her eyes and mouth looking tense.

"Did you normally wait up for your husband?" Drew asked.

"No, but that night I wanted to speak with him and tell him I planned to return home to Baton Rouge the next morning," she said.

A pained expression crossed her face and Drew quickly made notes. What about that night upset her?

"Why? Were you leaving Jean for good?" he asked.

"No . . ." she said, her voice trailing off. "I only wanted to go home."

"How long had you been in New Orleans?"

"Three days," she responded, her eyes glazed. "When he came in, he'd been drinking. I told him of my intentions to return home and we argued about me leaving."

"What was said during the argument?" Drew watched her hesitate, remembering that night. Her blue eyes seemed distant and thoughtful, and for a moment he thought he would have to remind her of the question.

"Jean said I was a terrible wife, that I should remain with him in New Orleans for the sake of appearances. He tried to make me feel guilty for wanting to go home," she said with little emotion.

"Why were you so insistent on returning?" Drew asked.

"There seemed no reason to delay my return. He spent most of his days at the office and a lot of the evenings away. If I stayed, Jean would only want me to . . ." She swallowed and looked away.

"What did Jean want you to do?" Drew pressed, his voice calm, yet insistent. "You have to tell me."

She glared at him, pain reflected in her eyes. Drew felt a moment of regret as he pushed on.

"He wanted me in his bed. That's why he brought me to New Orleans. He thought that getting me out of the house and the city, would encourage me to let him . . ." Layla took a deep breath and shuddered. "I'm sorry, I loathed his touch."

Drew's pencil scratched against the paper as he furiously wrote notes, not looking at her. Could Layla have detested Jean's touch enough that she had ended his life so as not to endure his caresses any longer? And why did he feel glad that she had not enjoyed her supposed husband's caresses?

"So you didn't enjoy your conjugal duties. Why not?" Drew asked glancing at her.

"Do we have to talk about this?" A blush tinted her pale cheeks. "The jury doesn't need to know this."

"If you want me to save your life, then I need to know everything so that I am prepared," Drew responded kindly, understanding her embarrassment. "I have to understand your life with Jean."

She stood and walked across the room, her skirts swishing in the quietness of the office. "These are things that no one knows but me. How could the district attorney get this information?"

Drew shrugged. "People talk. The district attorney is going to dig up information that will prove to the jury that you are guilty. He has to prove you murdered Jean. He'll look at everything, just as I do. I have to be prepared to tell the jury your side. You have to trust me. I have to understand why you wanted to leave New Orleans, so that I can help the jury to understand."

She turned her back to Drew and gazed out the window. "No, I didn't enjoy Jean's touch. I felt queasy when he tried to force me to his bed." She turned from the window and faced Drew. "That's when I started putting laudanum in his evening tea. I couldn't bear his pawing anymore."

Drew once again made a note. "Did you give him laudanum the night he died?"

"Yes," she answered. "That night, I sat up waiting for Jean's return with a pot of hot tea. I knew how angry he would be at my decision to leave. I slipped in just enough laudanum to make him sleep, then I told him of my plans to return home."

She gazed out the window, her face hidden from his view, yet he could tell from her body she was upset.

"The last time I saw Jean alive, he was sleeping in the parlor in the chair where he'd dozed off. I tried to wake him, but he wouldn't budge. So I left him," she said. "The next thing I knew, Colette awoke me to tell me she'd found him dead in his bedroom."

A sudden thought sent a chill down Drew's spine and he gazed at the beautiful woman by the window. "How do you know you didn't give him an overdose?"

She took a deep breath and turned toward him, her blue eyes large, framed by her ghostly white face. "I didn't give him any more than I usually gave him."

Drew nodded, seeing that the thought distressed her. But would a guilty woman seem so concerned? Not unless Layla was an excellent actress.

"So, if Jean fell asleep in the chair, how did he get into the bedroom?"

"I don't know. I tried to wake him, but he slept soundly, so I went to bed." She paused, biting her lip. "But the detective believed Jean was poisoned."

"Yes, by cyanide," Drew answered, watching her face.

She shook her head. "I don't know anything about cyanide. I don't even know where to find the poison."

Drew said nothing, but gazed at her, his mind racing with possibilities. Who else could have killed Jean?

"Who slept in the suite that night besides yourself?"

Layla walked around the library, her hand lingering on a framed daguerrotype of a woman, before she returned to her seat. Once again her cold composure had taken over and she folded her hands demurely in her lap. She looked so sedate, so innocent, and so incredibly proper he wanted to peel the clothes from her body and find the real woman hidden beneath.

"Colette slept in a room next to mine, and George, Jean's valet, slept in a room next to Jean's. We traveled with two other servants, but they stayed on one of Jean's boats."

"Do you know their names?"

"Luke and Big John."

"Were they in the suite that night?"

"No, only George and Colette. I was the last one to bed that night."

"Can you think of any reason that Colette would have to kill Jean?" he asked.

She shook her head. "She'd only been with us for two months and I checked her references before I hired her. I released her after Jean's death, but she refused to leave. She told me that Jean had paid her through to the end of the year. So she's staying and helping me as long as I need her."

Drew frowned. Why would Colette stay with Layla, given all the publicity? Why wouldn't she take the paid time off? Perhaps she and Layla were close, even though she had only worked for the family a short time.

"I'll have someone track down Luke and Big John." He needed to talk to all of the servants. "What about George?"

"I didn't hire him, Jean did. George has been with

Jean a long time. I don't know of any reason for George to harm Jean."

Drew glanced back over his notes, certain he had missed something he wanted to discuss with her.

"Returning to the argument you had with Jean—let's go over it again, something doesn't seem right about it." Drew tapped his pencil on the desk, watching the expression on her face. "It seems to me that there should be another reason for Jean to have brought you to New Orleans than to resume conjugal relations."

She shrugged, though she clenched and unclenched her hands. "He told me that he wanted me to accompany him to New Orleans. He thought that being in the city would be a welcome change for me. I told him I didn't want to go, but he insisted. It'd been months since he'd been in my bed and I knew he would want to . . ."

Drew frowned and stared at Layla.

"What was your argument about?"

"I'm getting tired, can we stop for a moment? You're starting to repeat yourself, just like Detective Dunegan," she said, her frustration level mounting. "I realize it's important, but . . ."

"A little longer and then we'll be through for the time being. Do you need something to drink?" he said, rising from behind the desk.

"No. I'm tired of answering the same questions," she snapped.

"I do understand but, unfortunately, we have a lot of work ahead of us and I must ask you even more questions and sometimes I'll ask them three or four times," he said, watching her. She seemed nervous and fidgety, as if she wanted to get away. "Let's finish up."

She took a deep breath and nodded. "All right. I told Jean I intended to return to Baton Rouge."

"What made you decide to return?" Drew asked.

"I'd been there for three days. He wanted me to stay longer. I couldn't stand the thought of his touch again."

Drew studied her for a long moment, a frown on his face. "Tell me everything that was said in the argument. I have a hard time believing that the two of you would have been yelling at one another about the fact that you wanted to leave."

Layla took a deep breath and sighed. "When he came in that night he'd obviously had too much to drink. I asked him where he'd been and he told me it was none of my business. I offered him some tea. Eventually, he asked me what I wanted, since he knew I would never have waited up for him unless I had a reason. I told him I intended to leave in the morning and he became angry. He told me I was running back home to escape him. I agreed. I told him I liked being as far as possible from him and he grew angrier."

"Could he have been feeling the effects of the tea when you told him your intentions to leave the next morning?" Drew asked.

Layla smiled. "Definitely. When I made him the most angry, he appeared drowsy."

Drew hurriedly wrote her response to his question and then sat back and stared at Layla. He seemed perplexed. "Four people slept in that hotel suite that night. No one claims responsibility for killing Jean. Nor, appparently, has either of the servants mentioned hearing the two of you argue to the police."

Layla said nothing, but gazed at him, her eyes wide with innocence.

He sighed. This was not going to be easy. "I'll need to speak with everyone in the suite that night. Maybe they heard something that you don't remember."

She raised her brows and gave him a disdainful look.

"George and Colette were already in bed when we argued. I doubt they heard anything."

"Was the argument loud?"

For a moment she said nothing. Her silence weighed. "Yes."

He nodded. "Did he threaten you, call you names?"

"No threats. I believe at one point he called me a coldhearted bitch, but I really don't remember much, except the feeling of relief at the thought of going home."

Drew made notes. "I think I'll speak with Colette and find George when we return to New Orleans in the next few days."

It seemed strange that George, Jean's long-time servant had left and yet Colette who had been with the family for only months stayed.

He glanced up from his notes at Layla. She stared back at him, not saying a word, no longer nervous, but rather in control of the situation. He could not let the interview end just yet.

"Do you have any documents left from your father's business?"

She paused and considered Drew a moment. "There might still be some of his old records up in the attic. I know Jean brought home boxes of paper from there."

"I'd like to look at them later," Drew said, scribbling more notes.

Layla appeared exhausted and he did not have the heart to continue pressing her. "Why don't we quit for the day? We've been at it for hours."

"I've been thinking," she said, nervously biting her bottom lip. "I need to send Mrs. Gautier a note asking for some time to question her about Blanche, but if I use my name, she'll refuse to see me."

Drew nodded, realizing that what Layla said was true. "I must talk to her. What if you sent her a note and requested to see her. I hope she wouldn't recognize your name."

"All right," he agreed. "I'll pen a note to her and have it delivered this afternoon requesting an audience with her tomorrow. The two of us will visit her, but then we have to get back to New Orleans before the arraignment."

Layla smiled. "Don't worry. When we find Blanche, there will be no need for an arraignment."

Eight

After leaving Drew in the library, Layla hurried upstairs to the attic, feeling a desperate need to find anything that would proclaim her innocence. Climbing the stairs to the room on the third floor, she opened the door and walked into the darkened room. Grasping in the dark, she located the lantern that swung from a rafter and the tin of matches on the shelf below. Scratching a match ignited a small flame and she held it to the wick of the lantern. Soon light flooded the darkened room, illuminating a family's collection of outgrown treasures.

She walked over to a small window and opened it, allowing additional light to fill the room, along with a breath of fresh air to replace the smell of mothballs and dust.

She had stolen away, needing time alone to conduct her own search here before Drew missed her. Trunks lined the walls, an old dresser stood against one wall, and a portrait of her mother leaned against another.

Overwhelmed at the amount of old junk, she strode over to the wall lined with trunks and began with the first one. She lifted the lid to reveal items from her childhood. Moving on to the next one, she brushed the dust off the top and opened it to reveal items that belonged to her mother. She paused, lovingly touching her mother's silk dresses, wondering why her father had kept her things. Sifting through the clothes, she happened upon an ivory brooch her mother used to wear.

Layla clasped the brooch around her neck, intent on keeping the remembrance.

Pushing aside her desire to linger over the treasured items, she dove headfirst into the next trunk, searching all the way to the bottom for anything that would help her uncover the secret of Jean's death, not really sure what she searched for.

The interview with Drew had been long and left her feeling drained and desperate. That is why she had left and come immediately to the attic, needing some time to compose herself and search for anything that could possibly save her. She felt so helpless and she needed to do something, anything that might uncover the truth, anything that would save her the humiliating experience of a trial.

If Drew and the prosecutor found out that she had learned of the other wives the night before Jean died and how they had argued bitterly over his deceit, her life would be worth nothing.

For a moment she had been tempted to tell Drew how she had learned of Marian and Nicole the night before Jean's death. But fear paralyzed her lips, for if he doubted her innocence now, once he learned this bit of information, by no means would he ever believe she had never intentionally killed Jean.

And yet last night in the library, sitting in that cozy atmosphere, she had felt so close, so tempted to tell him everything. A part of her wanted to reach out to him and tell him the truth, but then the memory of his involvement with her father's ruination would overtake her and she withdrew from his warmth.

At the sound of footsteps she looked up to see the

very man she had been thinking of standing in the doorway.

"I wondered where you'd gone to."

"I wasn't so far away that I'd loosed the invisible rope," she chided him.

He smiled. "I'm glad to see you haven't forgotten the lesson."

"Some lessons you'd like to forget," she said sarcasm dripping from her voice.

"But you won't," he gently reminded her.

She did not respond, but instead let him ponder her reaction.

"My parents have sent us an invitation to dinner tonight," he said. "Would you care to accompany me?"

"You could go alone." She had no wish to intrude.

"They invited both of us," he said. "But I could stay here, if you'd rather."

"Oh, Drew," she said. "I'm sure they would like to spend time alone with you and not have a suspected murderess in their home."

"Nothing could be further from the truth," he insisted. "I want you to have dinner with my family."

She gazed at him in surprise. Of course, he was only inviting her out of kindness, but she appreciated the gesture.

"Then I'll go," she responded, knowing she would be nervous. She had not seen his family in years and would now become reacquainted while bearing the shame of her accusation.

"Are you certain they want me to attend?" she asked again.

"Yes," he persisted.

"All right," she replied. "Perhaps they're accustomed to entertaining murderers."

He laughed. "I assure you it's a first."

"For both of us," she said, returning her attention to the trunk in front of her.

"Have you found anything?" he asked, watching her.

"Nothing. Just some of my mother's belongings."

Drew glanced around at the boxes and trunks. "Would you like some help?"

She wanted time alone, yet this task was overwhelming. She decided not to refuse.

"That would be nice," she replied, feeling that tug of warmth when she looked at him. What was it about Drew that appealed to her? Especially since she blamed him for Jean's deception of her father.

One thing she noticed was that he listened to her. When she spoke, his eyes were on her, watching as if nothing else mattered but what she said. And often he repeated her words, letting her know he had heard her.

Drew Soulier knew how to make a woman feel special and that frightened her, for no man had ever made such an impression on her.

But did he treat all of his clients this way? Was she not the exception, but rather the norm?

"Where should I begin?" he asked, looking around at the clutter.

"Why don't you start on this trunk, beside me," she said from her position on the floor. "That way we can share the light."

"All right. The attic window is very dusty."

She nodded. "And when you're looking deep inside a trunk, you need the lamp," she said, digging once again in the trunk she was working on when he came into the attic.

Squatting down on the floor beside her, he opened another trunk. Dust motes danced in midair when he pulled out a ribbon that she had won, first place in a spelling contest. "I bested Tony Malottie for that ribbon."

"If I remember right, he never forgave you for defeating him. The boys teased him unmercifully for letting a girl trounce him at spelling."

She smiled. "You're right. He never forgave me for winning."

Drew continued through the trunk, while Layla moved to the next one.

"So far all I've found are personal mementos," she said with a sigh. "I'd like to keep some of these things, but if the worst happens, I won't need them. And I have no place to store them until I know . . ."

She trailed off, thinking how unsettled her future appeared, fear swelling within her, consuming her for a few moments, until she managed to bring it back under control.

"I'll speak with Marian. I'm sure she'll work out something for you."

"Thanks, Drew," Layla whispered and hurriedly began searching the next trunk, trying to locate anything regarding her father's business, needing to keep her hands busy and her mind occupied.

Drew moved on to another trunk, while Layla continued searching through the years of collected junk. The metal hinges on the lid creaked as he opened the wooden lid and began to search through mounds of papers.

"I think we've found what we're looking for," he said, his voice rising in excitement. He reached in and lifted out a ledger.

Layla glanced at him, watching his eyes scan the pages.

"What is it?" she asked.

"It's the accounting ledgers from your father's business. This will help me determine the reasons Jean bought him out."

"That question seems fairly obvious to me and you

should already know the answer," she said, her frustration mounting at Drew's denial of his knowledge concerning her father.

"As Jean's lawyer, I wrote the contract, but I had no idea why he wanted to buy your father's company. He didn't let me in on that secret."

She frowned at him and shook her head. "I'll believe you, when you believe I never intentionally harmed Jean."

Drew shrugged. "As I've said before, it doesn't matter what I believe and it doesn't matter that you think I swindled your father. You're stuck with me and I'm not going to waste my breath trying to convince you I only drew up the contract."

"You could have warned my father it was a bad deal," she insisted.

"My client negotiated that contract. My responsibility was to him, not your father."

"Well, you could have at least told my father that Jean was already married."

"Why? I had no reason to believe he intended to marry you. Jean didn't tell me of his plans," Drew said his voice becoming defensive. "Just as he never told you."

Could Drew be telling the truth about Jean? Did he have no knowledge of Jean's deceitful ways?

Layla stood and walked the short distance to where Drew sat. She knelt down onto the floor beside him, her skirts spreading out around her. She gave Drew a calculating glance. "Can you find 1894? That's the year Papa was forced to sell."

Drew turned the pages, scanning them quickly. "Everything seems to be in order." He frowned, a puzzled expression on his face. He turned and gazed at Layla in the semidarkness. "From what I'm seeing, your father was making money, not losing it."

STARLIGHT SURRENDER

"Then why would he sell his business?"

Layla reached over and grabbed the book, wanting to see the details with her own eyes. The ledger showed a healthy profit. "I don't understand. Why would Papa lie to me?"

"I don't know. Let's keep looking," he said.

Together they glanced through books, journals, files, everything in the trunk, searching for something that would help defend Layla.

At the very bottom of the trunk, Drew pulled out a file marked "Sale." "Look at this."

He flipped the file open and Layla leaned over his arm to see what the file held. A copy of the deceitful contract that had taken away her birthright was in the file.

Drew gazed at her, his expression stoic. Resentment flared within her at the sight of the document that had irreversibly damaged her life.

"A week after this transaction was completed, I married Jean," she said bitterly, feeling all the old resentment and anger brewing as she gazed at Drew.

His emerald gaze met and held hers. "What else is in that file?"

He glanced back at the folder, flipping through the pages one by one. "Everything appears to be in order."

At the very back a loose page lay folded flat. Drew opened the sheet of paper to reveal a note from her father to Jean.

> *I have sold you the business that I have worked hard to establish, with the understanding that you will take care of my daughter after I am gone. I want my Layla to live the kind of life she deserves. Realize that I am not a man who takes chances, especially with my loved ones. So be very good to her or pay the consequences. Though I may not be here to watch over my daughter, her god-*

father, Captain Frank Olivier, will make certain you take care of her and treat my little girl well. Make no mistake, Jean, he has my instructions and my blessing to do whatever is necessary if you mistreat her.

Anthony DuChampe

Drew turned and stared at Layla, his eyes wide. "This introduces another possibility. Perhaps Captain Frank Olivier knew about the wives and killed Jean."

Layla felt her heart hammer in her chest. She smiled, knowing her expression was not genuine. For Captain Frank, the person her father referred to, had indeed learned of the other wives. And, he had warned her the night before Jean's murder.

But she doubted Frank could have killed Jean, for he had spent the night on a boat that left at six the next morning. If she exposed him, it would be evident that she knew of the other wives the night before Jean died. And if he was not the killer, that knowledge was a risk she was not quite prepared to take just yet.

The result could have disastrous consequences for her.

Drew picked her up unexpectedly, his hands warm on her waist, as he spun her around the attic. "We have a new lead."

"Frank is out of the country on a voyage to England. He won't be back for months."

"I'm still going to investigate him," Drew said.

He put her back on the ground and she stumbled, not sure of her footing, falling against his chest. She was frightened at what her lawyer had just learned. And hoped her godfather would not return from his voyage until after the trial, for she knew Frank was not the killer.

Leaning against Drew's muscled hardness, she glanced into his emerald gaze.

The warmth beneath her hand startled her and she realized she could feel the rhythm of his heart beating beneath her palm. The breeze from the open window ceased, leaving the air hot and sticky, her breathing labored. She did not want to move. Feeling his chest hard and muscled beneath her hand, the smell of Drew filling her head, heightened her dizziness and left her heart pounding.

His large emerald eyes overflowed with passion, filling her with warmth and the need to feel his lips against her own. Afraid to move, she watched his hand reach down and touch her cheek, wiping at a smudge of dirt.

"You have dust on you," he said, his voice thick.

"So do you." She repeated his gesture, touching his cleanshaven cheek.

His arms slid around her naturally as if they belonged there, bringing her up solidly against his chest.

"I . . . oh, hell," he said, his voice rough, as his lips came crushing down on hers.

Stunned, she leaned into his kiss, his mouth warm and hot covering hers. Her knees quivered at the passion his lips evoked, causing her limbs to go weak. She clung to him, incapable of denying him as his mouth took hers by storm. Crushing her lips beneath his, his tongue tantalized her with a sensuality she had never experienced before. Trails of fire lingered wherever they touched, leaving behind a sensation that filled her with longing. Could this kiss last forever?

He cradled her face in his hands and she pressed her body in closer, wanting to feel all of him. Her back arched with a will of its own and she ached with an unknown need. She reached up and caressed the back of his head, holding him closer, wanting more, melding his mouth to her own.

What about Drew made her want more of him? She had never wanted a man before. Why this one?

He jerked back as if her lips scorched him, holding her off, putting distance between them.

"We can't," he said, his breathing loud in the semi-darkness of the attic.

He glanced at her, his eyes wild with desire, his mouth swollen and wet. Layla knew that she had never experienced a kiss quite like that in the one year of her marriage. She had never felt anything like she felt right now.

She did not say anything, her body still humming with an aching response that frustrated her. How could this man make her traitorous body come alive with need? She reached up to touch her lips and realized her own breathing was labored and fast.

"I apologize," he said.

Layla was insulted by his apology and angered at her own response to the very man who had deceived her father.

"Don't," she snapped. "Just don't touch me again."

"You're right. I should never have kissed you," he apologized and glanced toward the door. "I need to talk with Colette. Excuse me."

Before she could gather her wits to make a reasonable response, he hurried from the room. "Ran" seemed a more appropriate word.

This only confirmed that she was crazy. To let Drew Soulier kiss her until she wanted him to do far more than press their lips together could only be total insanity.

Over the last two days since he had arrived, she had enjoyed spending time with him. Last night in the library and over breakfast this morning, he was undeniably pleasant. But she could not forget he was her lawyer, the man who had placed her in this awful position to begin with. For if she had never been forced to marry Jean, she would not be here today. And if her father had never signed that terrible contract, she never would have married Jean. She had experienced one betrayal after another and somehow Drew seemed to be in the center of it all.

Drew called Colette into the library and shut the door behind her, determined to focus on his work and not on the woman he had left in the attic. Only a self-confessed coward would run when he had gotten in too deep. And kissing Layla *had* sent Drew running. Not because he was a coward, but rather because he was prudent.

Prudent? Oh no, he had run away because another moment in her arms would have found him fulfilling at least one of his fantasies about her. One very enjoyable dream of pushing her skirts up and plunging into her warm, womanly body.

Drew took a deep breath and tried to concentrate on his interview with Colette.

"Please sit down. I need to ask you some questions about the night Jean died," he said, clearing his mind of thoughts of the kiss in the attic.

Colette sank onto the same couch that Layla had occupied the night before. Drew remembered the way she had looked so beautiful, yet sad, sitting there. Unsure of her innocence, he did not want to believe she had murdered the man she thought to be her husband, yet the evidence pointed to Layla's guilt.

And kissing her only clouded his judgment more.

"To prepare for Layla's trial, I need to ask some questions about the night of Jean's death."

"Miss Layla is much too sweet to have murdered Mr. Cuvier. I don't know how he died, but after what he did to those women, his evil ways deserved to end," she offered, surprising Drew with her frankness.

"Did you kill him, Colette?" he asked in an offhand manner.

She laughed. "Why would I kill him? He was my employer. I didn't learn of his wickedness until after he died."

"How long have you worked for the Cuviers?"

"Since February. At the time of his death, I'd only been there a little over two months."

"Where did you work before?"

"The child I cared for died of yellow fever, God rest her soul."

"I'm sorry," Drew said, making a note. "Layla has your references?"

"Yes, I had worked for Mr. Hopkins previously."

He made a note to himself to check with Layla to see what she found out, eager to get to the meatier questions. "So how would you describe Jean and Layla's marriage?"

She shook her head. "Miss Layla was a saint to be putting up with that old man. He came home once every two weeks and they would spend most of the time arguing."

"What did they fight about?"

She shrugged. "It didn't matter. They'd argue over whether the sun was shining in the sky." She paused. "But late at night it really got bad."

"Why?"

"Because Mr. Cuvier was an old goat who couldn't understand why Miss Layla didn't want to share his bed."

"Did Layla tell you this?"

"Of course not, but when people are yelling, you can't help what you hear," she admitted.

"Did you know that Miss Layla put laudanum in his tea at night?"

"Yes, sir," she said. "I suggested it."

Drew made more notes. "Why would you suggest such a thing?"

"Laudanum is soothing stuff, puts a man to sleep. Mr. Cuvier obviously needed to tame some of his baser urges."

Drew carefully controlled his expression, wondering how many people Colette had used the opiate on, unbeknownst to them.

"Didn't he suspect that he was being drugged?"

"If he did, he didn't mention it to me or Miss Layla."

"How did you know how much to give him?"

"A teaspoonful seemed to do the trick," she replied matter-of-factly.

"Is it true you've also been giving Miss Layla laudanum?" he asked.

"I make sure there is always a bottle in the house. She has trouble sleeping and it helps her to relax, though lately I need to go to the store every few days so that we don't run out."

Shocked, he paused for a moment contemplating what she had just revealed to him. "Do you think that Miss Layla is addicted?"

She shrugged. "That's not for me to say. I just make sure there is always a bottle in the house."

"Did you give it to Miss Layla the night Jean died?" he asked.

"Of course. Not a night goes by that she doesn't need her sleeping medicine."

Drew jotted down more notes, while his mind assessed what she had just told him. It was certainly a possible that Layla was addicted.

"You found Mr. Cuvier's body. Tell me what happened."

"Since we'd been in New Orleans, every morning I went downstairs to get their breakfast. Usually, I arranged it all to be ready around seven, because Mr. Cuvier liked to leave and go to the office each morning." She paused. "That morning, I went downstairs and when I came back, George said Mr. Cuvier hadn't risen yet. We waited fifteen minutes and finally I knocked on the door, because I knew his breakfast would be cold and that man could be a tyrant when he didn't like something."

Drew hurriedly made notes.

"When he didn't answer, I opened the door and saw him lying on the floor. I called George, and he came into the room. Together, we checked his pulse. I awoke Miss DuChampe and told her he was dead, while George ran to get a doctor."

"Did you hear anyone come in during the night?"

"No, sir."

"But when Layla went to bed, she left Jean in the sitting room asleep in the chair. You never heard him move about or ask for help?"

"No, sir."

Drew frowned and stared at the older woman. "The night that Jean died, Layla waited up for him. Did you hear anything that night?"

She glanced down at her hands folded in her lap, then gazed back at Drew. "I went to bed early and around midnight I heard the two of them fighting. I couldn't hear all of the words, but they were having quite an argument."

"And you couldn't hear what was said?" Drew repeated, disbelief in his voice.

"He wanted her to stay in New Orleans and she was going home," she said reluctantly.

"That's all you heard?" he asked again.

She shrugged. "That was the gist of their argument."

Drew paused for emphasis before he spoke again. "Whatever you heard that night, you need to tell me so that I can shield Miss DuChampe from the prosecuting attorney. Keeping information from me is not going to protect her."

"There's nothing else to tell. They argued about her returning to Baton Rouge so quickly. Mr. Cuvier wanted her to stay in New Orleans and she was determined to return home," Colette said.

"This was Layla's first trip to New Orleans as his wife?" Drew asked, still not certain he believed Layla's explanation of why Jean had brought her to New Orleans.

She shrugged. "That's what I heard."

"That night while they were arguing, was there ever the mention of her father's business?"

"Layla asked for money and Jean told her she wouldn't get a dime," Colette said her demeanor stoic.

"Did you have any knowledge of Mr. Cuvier's other wives?"

Colette rolled her eyes. "If I had known, I would have turned him in to the law for bigamy and we wouldn't be sitting here having this conversation."

Drew couldn't hold back his smile.

"What about George?" Drew asked. "Would he have any reason to want Jean dead?"

She shook her head. "I don't know. He was Mr. Cuvier's personal manservant and he genuinely loved Mr. Jean."

Drew took a deep breath and gazed at the lady's maid. "Is there anything else you'd like to tell me? Who do you think killed Mr. Cuvier?"

"I don't rightly know. I thought it might be one of Jean's other wives—you know Marian and Nicole."

"They have good alibis," Drew told her, uncertain that he had learned anything new from Colette. "Someone killed Jean and unless I locate the killer, I fear Layla will hang for his murder."

She shook her head. "Oh, no. She won't. You're going to get her acquitted. I have faith that you can win this case."

Drew gazed at the servant and wondered. What else had happened that night that no one admitted to?

Drew pulled the buggy to a halt in front of his parents' home. On the ride over Layla sat silent, unaware that the memory of the kiss in the attic lingered in his mind.

He had been unable to resist another moment of her by his side, until finally he had given in and kissed her with all the pent-up passion he had restrained. And now that indiscretion filled the air with tension, leaving them both edgy.

He looped the buggy reins around the brake and jumped down. As he walked around the buggy to help her down, he could not help but wonder how his family would react to her. His mother would be gracious, but as to his father, he had no clue.

Reaching up, he placed his hands around her waist and lifted her to the ground. They stood close for a moment, the fragrance of gardenias surrounding them as he gazed into her blue eyes before he released her.

She had not run screaming from the attic this afternoon, though she had told him not to touch her again. In fact, she seemed to have enjoyed the passion that flowed between them until she had realized what she was doing. But still, he needed to remind himself that his behavior would be seen as unethical.

He offered his arm: She placed her hand on his forearm. He glanced down at her delicate fingers, and then looked into her face. How could he defend her if his emotions were involved? In order to do the job that would get him into the mayor's office, he could not let himself be distracted by her beauty, her grace.

Yet when she smiled at him, his resolution melted beneath the radiance of her happiness. Layla certainly deserved to be happy.

"Are you ready?" he asked.

"Yes," she said quietly. "You're certain they wanted me to attend?"

"Yes," he said, knowing he had not been completely honest with her, yet certain his family would respond graciously.

Strolling up to the house, they took the stairs that led up to the white house. Intricate white ironwork surrounded the covered verandah.

Layla glanced around. "Your house has always been one of my favorites on this block. You must have been happy here."

He smiled at her. "It was a nice place to grow up."

Drew rapped on the door and his father swung the portal open wide. "Hello, son. Good to see you."

Shaking his father's hand, he led Layla into the entrance where he presented her. "Father, you remember Miss Layla DuChampe."

"Yes, through it's been years. Good to see you again."

His mother stood inside the entryway and he reached down to kiss her cheek. "Hello, *Maman*."

"Welcome home, son. And Layla"—she held out her hands—"you've grown into a beautiful young woman."

"Thank you," Layla murmured.

His mother took her arm. "Please come in and we'll sit in the parlor until cook tells us everything is ready. I'm so glad you came with Drew to visit us tonight."

Drew walked alongside his father, down the hall to the parlor.

"How long will you be in Baton Rouge?" his father asked.

"Just a few days. I'm doing some research for the trial and need to get back as quickly as possible," Drew said, watching his mother and Layla.

"I can't imagine why you brought her to dinner," his father whispered.

Drew frowned. "I wasn't going to leave her alone."

"But your mother?"

"*Maman* seems to be handling things just fine," Drew acknowledged, his voice stern. He paused. "Don't speak of my plans to run for mayor in front of Layla. She doesn't know."

"What about your mother? What if she asks you about the mayor's race?"

Drew frowned. "We have to warn her. Take Layla out and show her the gardens, while I talk with *Maman*."

"Why is this important?" his father asked.

"I'll explain everything later," he promised.

Layla walked in front with his mother. She turned and glanced at him, her blue eyes questioning.

"Miss DuChampe, while we wait for dinner, allow me to show you our garden," his father asked.

Layla glanced at Drew and nodded. "Of course."

She placed her hand on his arm and he led her out a French door that went into the garden.

Drew smiled at his mother, who raised a brow at him. "I gather you wanted to speak with me alone?"

He laughed. "I just wanted to ask you not to say anything about me running for mayor. Layla doesn't know that's the reason I took her case and I don't want to explain it to her."

His mother frowned and shook her head. "I didn't raise my son to play such devious games with peoples' lives. You should be honest with her."

"Later, but not now. Not when I'm still trying to establish trust between the two of us," he said.

"Later, she'll find out and whatever trust you've established will be tarnished. I won't say anything, but I hope you won't hide this from her for long," she scolded. "Now let's go find your father and Layla."

Drew felt as if she had slapped his hand with a ruler, yet if Layla learned he had taken her case for the publicity, she would make his life a living hell. He had a case to prepare, and a more important battle than a skirmish with his mother to fight.

An hour later they all sat at the dinner table, spread with the dinner the Souliers' cook had prepared. The dinner passed without incident, and Drew enjoyed the company of his parents and Layla. She had responded beautifully to his parents' questions.

Gracious and kind, Layla was everything that a man could want in a woman, excepting that she was accused of murder.

Drew's father stood. "Excuse me, ladies, my son and I are going outside for a smoke. So you'll excuse us until we meet in the parlor, later."

Drew stood and followed him out the door.

Once they were outside, he handed his son a cigar. "Try one of my new Cuban cigars. I've been saving these for a special time and tonight it shall be."

"Thanks, Father," Drew said taking a match from his father and lighting his cigar.

His father drew deeply on the tobacco and released it slowly. "With all the newspaper publicity this trial is receiving, you made a very wise decision to handle Miss DuChampe's case. Joseph Hoffman, the boss of ward three, told me yesterday that your name is being discussed as a possible mayoral candidate. Seems one of your clients recommended you and they're looking for someone uncorrupted by the current scandal of the last city government."

"Ah, Mr. Sycamore, my newest client. That's great news," Drew said. His dreams were starting to become a reality. Soon he would enter his first political race. "Did Mr. Hoffman mention when they would make their decision?"

"No, they want you to attend a meeting."

"As soon as I get back to New Orleans," Drew said.

"We'll need to get the backing of several more ward bosses, but I'm working on that right now. I'm calling in a few favors and by November we should be able to announce your candidacy. Hopefully, we can make the announcement at the end of Miss DuChampe's trial."

"You've been working hard on this," Drew said, watching his father's face beam with joy.

"Of course. This is the first step on your way to being governor," his father said. "I may not have made it to the top, but I'm going to do everything I can to see that you do."

As mayor of the one of the largest southern cities, the post would start him on his way to the governor's mansion. Drew could not help feeling pressed by his father's assistance, though he was only helping him to achieve his dream.

But was it really his dream?

He pushed the thought aside. Of course it was.

"So why the secrecy about your mayoral campaign with Miss DuChampe?"

"It's not a secret, I'm just not ready to tell her. I'm not ready for her to know why I accepted her case. She doesn't quite trust me, and she would make my life hell if she learned the reason I wanted to be her attorney."

"You must have given her some reason."

"I told her I thought her case would help my firm. I

STARLIGHT SURRENDER 145

left out the part about all the newspaper coverage I'd receive because of her."

His father frowned and took a drag on his cigar. "She's a beautiful woman."

"Yes, sir, she is," Drew admitted.

"Do you think she killed her husband?"

Drew took a long drag on the cigar and blew the smoke out into the night air. "I don't know, Father. One moment I think she's innocent, but all the evidence points to her guilt even if it is circumstantial. She herself is not certain she's innocent."

"What?"

"She gave Jean laudanum in his tea at night, to keep him from coming to her bed."

His father's brows rose. "Oh, dear."

"Yet in her defense, she said she had been giving him landanum for quite some time. And he died of cyanide poisoning."

His father nodded. "She seems such a polite young woman. She has looks, grace, everything that a man needs in a wife when he's trying to build a future as a politician, except that she's been accused of murder."

Drew glanced at his father and drew on his cigar, not saying a word. His father only echoed what he'd thought earlier in the evening.

"By the time this trial is over your name will be known to every person in New Orleans. And if you get public sentiment on your side, you'll have no problem becoming the next mayor of New Orleans."

"That's why I took the trial," Drew said, though he knew there was more to his decision than a desire for publicity.

"There's only one danger in taking on such a notorious case with such a beautiful client."

"What's that, sir?" Drew asked fearing that he already knew what his father would say.

"I've watched you look at Miss DuChampe all evening. Your interest seems quite personal—and well beyond what a lawyer should have for a client. You must remain objective, my boy."

"I know the boundaries, Father," he protested, his voice sounding weak to his own ears.

"Sometimes where women are concerned, our boundaries disappear. Though I'm sure Miss DuChampe is a wonderful person, she will not help your future. This trial should boost your career, not tie you to someone who will bear the stigma of involvement in murder for the rest of her life."

Drew didn't reply for a moment. "Don't worry," he said at last. "I'll be certain I don't get involved with Layla," Drew said, feeling like a fool. His fascination with Layla was so obvious that his father had picked up on it.

"Good, son. After the trial, you could always make her your mistress."

Drew puffed on his cigar, struck by a vision of Layla in his arms as he carried her up the stairs. His mistress? She'd never agree.

Somehow the mayor's race no longer seemed as important as it once had. And the thought of never having Layla in his arms again filled him with disappointment and emptiness, for her kisses had filled a void that he had always known.

He refused to be like Jean and use her for his own sexual satisfaction. Though if he were truthful with himself, he *was* using her for his political advancement.

Yes, he was using her case to obtain publicity, but he was not using Layla. And by being her lawyer she benefited from his help. He pushed the disturbing thoughts away. They were helping each other although she did not know it.

He gazed at his father, trying not to be frustrated at

the way he liked to tell him what to do, knowing he meant well.

"I have no intention of losing this trial or falling for the beautiful charms of Miss DuChampe."

His father smiled and released a long puff of smoke. "I knew that, son. There's too much at stake here for you to succumb to such a woman."

Drew cringed. *Such a woman?*

His father could never understand how he felt about Layla DuChampe. Hell, even he didn't completely comprehend his attraction. But his father's words made him yearn for the chance to explore his attraction to Layla, rather than leave it alone. For he ached to kiss her sweet mouth and hear her laughter once again.

Nine

On the ride home, Drew sat silent, brooding over the truth of his father's words. Layla too seemed quiet as she sat on her side of the buggy, carefully avoiding his glance.

Yet how could he blame her for being displeased with him?

She blamed him for every unlucky occurrence in her life in the last two years—the sale of her father's small shipping company, the death of her father, and even her marriage to Jean. Worst of all, sometimes he could understand her misguided logic.

Yes, the contract he had negotiated for the sale of her father's company had been heavily weighted in Jean's favor, but Jean had paid him to get the best deal possible. And her father had willingly signed the agreement, without force or coercion of any kind, much to Drew's surprise.

Now Drew speculated that Jean had offered Anthony DuChampe the one thing he really wanted that he could not buy: his daughter's security. If her father had sought legal counsel, he would have been advised against the contract that Drew had drawn up.

Drew sighed in the darkness. Could he blame Jean for being attracted to the lovely Layla? After all, Drew himself had been enamored of her since his teens, and their earlier acquaintance gave him a certain sense of responsibility toward her, in part because the contract he had negotiated with her father had left her penniless.

His father's warnings came to mind once more and he glanced over at Layla. He would have to be dead not to be drawn to her.

Beautiful, strong, and more resilient than any woman he knew, Layla intrigued him. After he had kissed her this afternoon, he could hardly think of anything else for the rest of the day besides her lips, her sweet mouth, and how he wanted to do more than caress her.

An intimate relationship with his client would be a distraction he could ill afford. He had to prepare for her trial. Such an indiscretion could get his license revoked and was ethically wrong. Campaigning on honesty and integrity while conducting a secret affair with his client would hardly endear him to the voters, if they ever found out. And Layla was temptation enough to make him forget his career, his ambitions, even his determination and lose himself in sensual abandon. The image of Layla naked, her head thrown back, her eyes closed, her breathing harsh as he made love to her, held him in its grip.

He cleared his throat, determined to get his mind off the image of her, naked and vulnerable in his arms. "Did you have a good time?"

He really wanted to say, *Did you enjoy my kiss this afternoon?* but knew better than to ask.

She glanced at him in the dark. "Your mother is a lovely woman and an excellent hostess."

"What about my father?" he asked, suddenly even more curious.

"He's a man of the world and important, but he's made up his mind that I killed Jean," she said.

Drew felt a little stunned. No one could say that Layla didn't understand people. Could she, like his father, have perceived how much Drew was enthralled by her?

"Father does have a way of getting information and making a decision rather quickly," Drew said.

"A long time has passed since I've enjoyed the company of a woman at a dinner party. Your mother made me feel at ease," Layla said with a sigh. "She didn't seem to mind that her dinner guest was an accused murderess."

"Mother could entertain Judas and make him feel at ease," Drew replied. "Not to say that you're anything like Judas, she just has a way of making people feel comfortable. She's been a great asset to my father."

A tense silence filled the carriage. "They didn't invite me, did they?"

Drew glanced at her and from her perceptive gaze, he knew she realized the truth. "No."

Layla turned and looked away. "I'll never be accepted again, will I? No matter that I'm innocent, people will always remember."

"Possibly," Drew said, the need to be honest with her overwhelming him.

"I wish I could go back and change the last two years. I would have kept my father from signing your ridiculous contract," she snapped, her frustration evident.

"There's no point in blaming yourself for your father's actions," he said, calmly trying to soothe her anger.

She turned on him in the carriage and for a moment, he thought she would strike him, so much anger radiated from her. "I don't blame him. I blame Jean and I blame you. You're the man who helped Jean swindle my father."

Whatever placating response he had been about to

make died. The night breeze swept across his face, unable to cool the rage that fueled his temper.

"Layla, no one made your father sign that contract. He signed the document without seeking legal counsel. I'm not responsible for his stupidity."

"His stupidity?" she said in disbelief, her voice rising.

"You're damn right," Drew retorted. "If you are about to sign away your business, one would think he would have sought his own legal counsel. Any lawyer worth his salt would have told him the contract was one-sided," Drew said, his voice rising and falling.

She did not respond but turned away from him and gazed out the window. For the next mile there was only the sound of cicadas as they sang in the late night and the rustle of leaves from the oaks that lined the road.

Finally she spoke, her voice calm but cold. "If no one forced Papa to sign the contract and the business was doing well, why would he just give the business away?"

"I don't know. I wonder the same thing," he responded, trying to temper his anger. "Now I speculate that Jean offered to marry you, which would have fulfilled your father's need to make sure you were taken care of."

"You knew, didn't you?" she responded, her voice rising once again in anger. "You knew that Jean had other women and let him marry me."

"Like hell I did! Damn it, Layla, I handled only Jean's legal business. And he told me only what he wanted me to know. I would have told your father myself that Jean was still married, if I had known of my client's intentions. But he didn't tell me."

She sat back in stunned surprise, gazing at him, her eyes large in the dark. She didn't say anything as they continued down the road. They passed the next mile in silence.

Finally needing to somehow fill the silence with anything besides images of the two of them together entwined in one another's arms, he spoke. "I received a note from Mrs. Gautier this afternoon. She has agreed to see us tomorrow at three."

Layla turned and gripped his arm with her hand. Warmth coursed up his arm, her touch causing him to catch his breath.

"Thank God," she said, relieved. "By this time tomorrow, I could be a free woman. By this time tomorrow we could know who really killed Jean."

He nodded, not knowing what he believed any longer. The evidence pointed to Layla's guilt, but he didn't want to believe she was a murderess. For he cared about her and that frightened him.

Layla stood in the entryway of Mrs. Gautier's home, waiting nervously while her servant announced them. Pale green flowered wallpaper covered the walls of the entrance hall, with two Venetian statuettes on either side of the door. A crystal chandelier hung above them.

The fine furnishings made her uncomfortable. She had driven by the house many times, but never been inside before. And even today, she accompanied Drew uninvited.

"This way please," the servant said, motioning to them to follow her into a room dominated by a French mirror that occupied the length of a blue wall. In front of a huge window, a small piano graced the corner. The sweet smell of honeysuckle and roses filled the room, their blossoms artfully arranged in a Ming bowl atop the piano.

Mrs. Gautier stood waiting. She motioned to them like a teacher to a pupil to take a seat on the Chippendale sofa.

"Mr. Soulier, you didn't tell me you were bringing Miss DuChampe," the woman scolded him as she sat in the French chair across from them.

"I apologize, Mrs. Gautier, but Miss DuChampe insisted on seeing you and we feared you would not accept our request if I were direct."

The woman frowned. "Probably not, but now that you're here, you've piqued my interest." She motioned again to them to sit and Layla could not help but feel relieved. They were not going to be shown the door right away.

"Why on earth did you need to see me?" the woman asked Layla.

"The man at the newspaper office said that you knew everyone in Baton Rouge who was someone. I'm looking for a young woman named Blanche." Layla said. "The only information I have is that she came from a good family and moved to Baton Rouge, bringing with her a daughter named Julianne."

The woman thought for a few moments. "Yes, I knew of her. Blanche Viel lived in Baton Rouge for a short time," she said gazing at Layla, frowning.

"You said she lived here a short time. She doesn't live here anymore?"

"Why do you search her out?"

"I have reason to believe that Jean Cuvier had more than three women in his life. And I think that Blanche could be one of Jean's women."

The woman nodded, thoughtful. "That seems logical considering how promiscuous Mr. Cuvier was. I can tell you what little I know of this young woman's tragic life."

Mrs. Gautier leaned back against the cushions, settling in.

Layla felt a shiver of fear go through her. *Tragic life? What did she mean?*

Before she could ask, the woman began to tell her Blanche's tale. "Blanche moved here, a widow, to look after her elderly aunt, bringing her young daughter with her. At the time, her daughter was barely three years of age, a precious child that Blanche adored and protected fiercely."

Mrs. Gautier sighed. "Blanche kept to herself, not appearing at social functions, caring for her aunt and her daughter. Her aunt attended the church I belong to and could no longer live alone. They had been here only six months when Julianne contracted yellow fever."

Shaking her head, the older woman dabbed at the corner of her eye with her handkerchief. "It was tragic. The child lasted two weeks and then died, leaving Blanche devastated. At the funeral, a man cared for her and later when I inquired, I was told he was Blanche's older brother."

Layla couldn't help but feel for the young woman. "What happened to Miss Viel?" Layla was certain that Blanche had ended Jean's wicked life.

"Oh, dear, that's the saddest part of this tale," Mrs. Gautier paused dramatically and unease settled over Layla like a sheet. "After her daughter's death, Blanche killed herself."

For a moment Layla sat stunned, reeling from the blow. Blanche was dead?

No, it couldn't be. Blanche had murdered Jean.

"When did she die?" she asked, her voice trembling with shock, the noose suddenly swinging before her.

"Oh, she's been dead going on six months now."

"*Six months . . .*" Layla said, wanting to cry, feeling nauseated. A dead person couldn't kill. Layla had been certain that finding Blanche would culminate in finding Jean's killer.

She was going to die for a murder she had never committed.

"Miss DuChampe, are you all right? You appear so distraught. Did you know Blanche?"

The young woman had killed herself, it was so sad, so wasteful.

Drew cleared his throat, speaking for the first time since they had sat down. "Miss DuChampe was convinced that Blanche had something to do with Jean's murder."

The woman gazed at her sympathetically. "Maybe women are afraid to come forward knowing that the law will find them."

Unable to speak, her throat filled with tears, Layla merely nodded.

"What about the aunt?" Drew asked.

"She died barely a month after Blanche."

"And Blanche's brother?" Drew looked at Layla, silently staring at the flowers as she tried to recover from the revelation.

The older woman's gray head bobbed. "I couldn't say. I never met the man and only saw him briefly at Julianne's funeral."

Layla sat stunned, her hope fading like the glow of a lantern, dimming with despair.

Mrs. Gautier reached out and patted the back of Layla's hand, startling her. "Miss DuChampe, have faith. I'm sure the killer will be found and brought to justice."

Layla suppressed the urge to tell the society matron how the police had halted their investigation at her door.

Instead she smiled, feeling as if her face would crack from the strain, needing to get out of this stuffy house. She stood. "Thank you for seeing us and telling us about Blanche."

Mrs. Gauthier stood. "I'm sorry I had such disturbing news for you. I do hope Mr. Cuvier's killer is found."

"Thank you," Drew responded as he grasped Layla's elbow and helped her out the door, leaving Mrs. Gautier alone.

The same servant showed them out the front door, though Layla barely saw her.

Outside, she could not feel the warmth of the sun. An ugly shadow had engulfed her, chilling her to the bone.

Drew helped her up into the buggy and then took his own seat. With a snap of the reins, he headed back through town.

"I guess this means we'll be going back to New Orleans tomorrow," Layla said weakly.

He glanced down. "I arranged our passage on the last run of the day," he said.

She turned away from him. She had known from the day she left New Orleans that she would be forced to return. But until today, she had believed she would find the real murderer and be acquitted. Now the jury trial seemed imminent and the likelihood of hanging a real possibility.

A sob escaped as she tried to control the shivers of fear that racked her body and tears splashed down her face. She covered her face and released a torrent of tears.

Drew pulled the buggy to a halt and took her in his arms, his hand caressing her back as her tears cleansed her battered soul.

All her hopes had been pinned on this one woman— but Blance had died four months before Jean's murder, leaving Layla as the prime suspect once again.

Stars flickered in the night sky as Layla sat in the swing and gazed up at them longingly. All her hopes were crushed by the realization that Blanche Viel could not have killed Jean.

How would a jury ever believe that Layla had never intended to harm him? That all she had felt when she learned of his deceit was relief. And upon his death she had panicked, keeping from the police the fact she knew of the other women for fear they would suspect her of killing Jean in anger.

Now she only prayed they never found out that she had known of Marian and Nicole before Jean's death. The knowledge would become just one more reason for the jury to think she had truly meant him to die.

But she had never loved Jean and when she realized she was free to go, she thanked God and planned her life accordingly.

Of course they had fought the night he died, because Jean no longer had the power to force her to remain as his wife. And when she had asked for her home and money from the sale of her father's shipping company, he had laughed and said despicable things about her father, things intended to anger and punish her simultaneously.

However, fate intervened and sometimes Layla wondered if Jean had committed suicide just to avoid scandal when his multiple marriages became public knowledge. But a man like Jean would never commit suicide.

A full moon shone down from the heavens, lighting the home she loved so much, the home that no longer belonged to her. She sighed. It would not matter if they convicted her. She would no longer need any earthly possessions.

A tear trickled down her cheek, and she could not help but remember the way Drew had comforted her this afternoon while she sobbed. He had held her and patted her back while she cried over Blanche's death and the end of her hopes. Though Layla thought Blanche would be the killer they sought, she had also felt saddened by the woman's tale.

Layla's life hung in the balance. Not only would she have to face a jury trial, but the end result could be a disaster. And the thought of letting someone slip a rope around her neck in front of hundreds of witnesses terrified her.

How can I keep my composure, knowing no one will save me and that my life is over? Yet I shall claim my innocence to the very end.

She put her face in her hands and let the fear she had kept bottled up for weeks rage inside her, causing her heart to pound and her hands to shake.

Dear God, she felt so alone, so scared and defeated.

The sound of a step on the soft earth alerted her.

She glanced up from the swing and stared into Drew's concerned gaze.

"I've been looking for you," he said. "Are you all right?"

"No," she said honestly. "I'm terrified."

He moved behind her and began to push the swing in a slow, easy manner.

"I can win this case. But I need your help," he said confidently.

She tried to remind herself how much she hated him, which was becoming harder and harder as he repeatedly did nice things for her. Tonight, coming out here to try to comfort her, this afternoon in the buggy, and right now when she longed for someone to ease her troubled mind.

"I thought by coming home to Baton Rouge, I would find Jean's killer. Now the risks I've taken and what I've found out make it seem so hopeless," she admitted.

"You can't give up," he said. "I need you confident and sure of your innocence for the trial."

She laughed, the sound hysterical. "That sounds very strange coming from someone who doesn't believe in my innocence."

She trembled, her emotions flaring. "What am I saying? I'm not sure I didn't accidentally kill him. How can I convince twelve people I'm innocent, especially since I poured laudanum in his tea?"

He pulled the swing to a halt and turned the ropes until she faced him. Squatting down, he held her between his legs and looked up at her.

"You're going to look them in the eye every day, smile and say good morning," he said. "You're going to become a consummate actress who knows when to cry and dab her eyes and when to pretend that everything is good. This is your chance to convince the people of New Orleans that you were a good wife to a man that took advantage of you. We've got to prove that *you* were the injured party, not the bastard who cheated on four women. Who died from cyanide, not laudanum."

"What if I can't do it?" she whispered, not wanting to admit her weakness.

"I have no doubt you can charm the jury into believing whatever you want them to," he insisted. "You are a beautiful, resourceful woman, Layla."

She leaned her forehead on his shoulder and gathered her courage. She liked leaning on him. He felt strong, secure.

"We need to talk about where I want to be buried."

"No! There's no need for us to talk about that! You're not going to die," he insisted.

She straightened, her eyes meeting his gaze. "You don't know that," she persevered. "I need to prepare myself for the worst and right now, I don't know whom to suspect of murdering Jean. And if I killed him, then I'm prepared to die."

A shiver went through her as she thought once more of the ordeal to come.

"You can't think that way. You need to show everyone that you're certain you didn't kill him," Drew demanded.

"But what if I feel certain I'll be convicted? I'm the only one who was with him that night and the police seem to think I wanted him to die. But I didn't. I felt freed..."

She stopped, realizing she had almost blundered and told him too much about that night. She glanced into his emerald eyes and knew he had caught her slip.

He tensed and held the swing even tighter. His eyes widened and his expression became intense.

"What do you mean, you felt freed?" he asked.

She had revealed more than she intended and Drew was quick to pick up on her slip.

"I felt freed to return home to Baton Rouge," she answered. At least that was not a complete lie.

Drew stared at her in the darkness, his eyes intent on her face, studying her. The time had come to go into the house, get away from this intense man and his observant gaze.

"The mosquitoes are starting to bite. I should be going in," she said, rising from the swing, forcing him to move. They were inches apart and she took a quick breath.

"I'll go in with you," he answered, rising and taking her by the arm.

They walked across the yard, past the rose bushes and oleanders, the silence tense. They stepped up on the porch and Drew opened the door to the house.

Layla walked inside, feeling apprehensive. She had said more than she should. She had almost given away the fact that before Jean's death she had learned she was no longer his wife, determined to go home to

STARLIGHT SURRENDER

Baton Rouge and move Jean's things out of the house and him out of her life.

Drew stood in the doorway, gazing at her, a quizzical expression on his face. Uneasiness made her want to run from the room, but instead she took a deep breath and prepared a graceful exit.

"I think I'll retire for the night. It's been a tiring day," she said, intent on escaping up the stairs.

"I don't believe you," he said, watching her closely, her face illuminated by the lights indoors.

"What?" She pretended she didn't understand, trying to stall for time to come up with a good excuse.

"There's something you're hiding," he said quietly. "You're lying to me, Layla."

Ten

Fear exploded through her, and she could imagine the clang of the cell doors closing, condemning her forever. She felt trapped, pushed by the day's events, overwhelmed by what life had brought her.

"I'm lying to you?" she repeated. He didn't understand what she was going through. She took a deep breath, the air fairly sizzling as her body bristled. The truth of his words were much too close, pushing her over the edge.

"Just like I'm lying about being innocent. Just like I lied about another woman. What do you believe, Drew? That I learned of the other wives and maliciously spiked Jean's tea, intent on killing him?"

She took a deep breath, and stepped toward him. "Whose side are you on? It certainly doesn't appear that you're fighting very hard to defend my life."

"Calm down. You're overreacting."

"Overreacting!" she fairly screamed. The man could be an insensitive cad. "You bastard, I could die."

All the pressure mounted and she reached out, her open palm swinging toward his face.

Drew grabbed her hand pulling her into his arms, he held her against him, while all the anger and fear she had felt building within her poured forth and she shook with the need to hit something, anything.

She pummeled his chest with her free hand. "Damn you, Drew. I hate you."

He grabbed her fist and wrapped her arm around her back, her wrist at the small of her back, pulling her in tight against him. Her breasts were crushed against his chest and he held her there, not moving.

Shadows from the gas lamps wove an erotic dance around them.

"Now you're lying to yourself. You want to hate me, but you don't," he said, his mouth inches from her own.

"Yes, I do," she hissed.

A warm sensation grew within her, spreading like a wildfire, needy and urgent. She wrestled, trying to get away from him. Her actions only increased the friction between their bodies, rubbing her against his solidness.

"Stop fighting and help me," he demanded, and she knew he spoke of more than the trial.

His mouth lowered still farther, until they were less than an inch apart. Lust blazed from his eyes, scorching her with sensual heat.

"You want to hate me, but can't," he snarled. "Not any more than I can resist you."

She shook her head, adamant in her hatred.

"Damn it, let me show you how much you *don't* hate me."

She opened her mouth to argue, when his lips covered hers, greedy and savage, as he plundered her mouth. He backed her up against the wall, pressing into her flesh, letting her feel every hard inch of him, of his arousal.

She fought against the spiraling, inexplicable need of pure sensation that replaced all logical thought. She breathed in of his clean, masculine scent and felt intoxicated, dizzy.

Hate and love seemed intertwined and she could not

tell where one stopped and the next started. For the first time in over a year, she felt alive. Heat, hot and needy, began to build inside her and she resisted the pleasure, fighting the feelings within her.

She fought against the hunger his lips created, moving against her own, leaving her trembling. She fought until she realized she was tired of fighting everyone and everything in life and only wanted to surrender. Surrender to the passion she had always been denied. Surrender and take Drew prisoner at the same time.

Layla relaxed against him and he released her hands. With his mouth still melding her to him, she grabbed the front of his shirt in her fist and pulled on the cloth, shooting buttons across the floor, searching for his flesh.

Slipping her hand inside his shirt, she smoothed her hand across his naked skin, hot to her touch. Drew moaned deep in his throat, the noise spurring her on. With a tug, she pulled the shirt from his trousers and pushed it from his shoulders, leaving his torso bare.

Her hands roamed, feeling every inch of muscle in his shoulders and back, her fingers trailing along his flesh, delighting in the feel of him.

She had never wanted to touch a man before. She had never felt so wanton, hungry, and eager for anyone. She had never needed the comfort of joining with a man, but just his arms, holding her, would not be enough to ease the ache within her tonight.

He released her mouth and took a deep breath, his body trembling beneath her hand. "Oh hell, I'm going to regret this in the morning."

She could not contain her smile, realizing he was just as affected by this primitive feeling as she. And she needed him tonight.

"Especially when I tell you how much I still hate you," she said and skimmed her fingernails down his back.

STARLIGHT SURRENDER

He scooped her up in his arms and carried her up the stairs two at a time. When he reached her room, he pushed open the door and kicked it closed with a slam. The sound echoed through the old house.

He dropped her legs and let her body slide down his own, her hips and breasts in full contact with his torso. Her skirts bunched between them, their eyes locked in a silent battle of wills in the shadowy moonlight.

She wanted to feel his naked flesh against her own.

When her feet touched the floor, they both reached out and began to tear at the other's clothes in a hurried frenzy to reach the other's flesh. In a matter of moments, Layla felt her dress slide to the floor, along with her petticoats and chemise.

Suddenly she was naked and the cool air drifting across her bare flesh seemed to only heighten her awareness.

She tugged on his trousers, sending more buttons flying in her haste. Her blood pounded with a hungry impatience. She had never felt this sense of urgency, this need to copulate with a man. A need to feel alive.

Her hands pushed his trousers down, along with his drawers, and his erection sprang free from the constriction of clothing.

Raw, reckless need filled her and she wanted Drew now, right this instant, before another grain of sand could fall through the hourglass of her life. Before her numbered days came to an end.

Facing her, he pushed her gently backward until she felt the bed at her back. They tumbled together onto the sea of blankets, his body covering her own, his flesh against hers. She sighed, the sound more like a purr.

His mouth covered hers, his lips stroking her mouth, melding her, while his hands seem to touch her everywhere. He released her mouth and he gave her a slow, searing gaze that melted her resistance. She had never felt so alive, so aware of the heated strokes he created as his hands cupped her breasts, bringing his mouth to her nipple. He teased it with his tongue, sending sparks through her, fanning the flames of need.

She raged out of control, her hands tangled in his hair, holding his mouth prisoner over her nipple. She loved the way he suckled the swollen nub and she delighted in the sensations that undulated through her, rising and falling with heightened sensations. Flicking his warm, moist tongue across the swollen bud, she ran her fingernails down his naked back. His flesh rippled with goose bumps.

He trailed his hand down her stomach until he reached her feminine folds and his touch turned to magic, teasing her mercilessly. She clung to him, her breath suspended in her throat as pleasure she had never experienced before began to build. As he stroked her innermost core, she arched her back, reveling in the feel of his thumb caressing the bud of her desire.

Jean had never touched her there, never built the fire Drew kindled within her.

She spread her legs, eagerly anticipating, needing him inside her. He moved over her, his limbs between her own and she eagerly awaited him.

Still he continued to stroke her and the need she felt building within held her prisoner—a wanton prisoner.

"Drew, now," she cried impatiently.

"No, not yet," he said, his voice a silken whisper across her skin. He hovered above her, his rigid manhood waiting at her entrance.

She arched, rubbing against him, almost begging for him to soothe her with his entrance. She had never wanted anything so much.

"Do you still hate me?" he asked, his voice husky with need.

"What?" Passion gripped her until she could not think. How carefully he had aroused her, and now, in the moment of passion, he wanted to talk?

"Do you hate me?" he asked again.

Her earlier words returned to haunt her. She could not lie or wait a minute longer.

"No," she said, her breathing labored and she knew it was true. She did not hate him but she did not like what he had done either.

Like a wanton, she lifted her hips eager to meet his thrust, not wanting to think about what she had just revealed, but he hesitated.

"I've dreamed of this moment since I was a young man. I've fantasized about the two of us together like this for years," he said, his voice ragged with restraint.

She heard him, but her patience was at an end. The time for talking had long since passed. She reached up and gripped his chin with her fingers and pulled his mouth down to hers.

"Shut up," she said and melded her lips over his.

She lifted her hips to meet the full thrust of his arousal, her body gripping him as he entered her. In a pagan rhythm she met each thrust, her body eagerly accepting him, her cries of pleasure becoming a rising crescendo.

He plunged into her insistently, each stroke building her pleasure until she reached its peak. With a hoarse shudder, she cried out his name, the nerves in her body gathered into one explosion that left her shattered with pleasure beneath him.

Drew tensed and with one last powerful stroke, shuddered above her, reaching his own peak.

He collapsed on top of her, sweat glistening on his skin, his breathing harsh in the stillness. Minutes passed and he pulled her into his arms and curled around her.

Layla lay stunned, unable to move. Never before had she reacted so ardently, so sexually to a man. Never before had she felt such pleasure, such satisfaction and emotion.

And all of it caused by the man who had helped betray her father. She cringed inside at her lack of loyalty.

Her father was dead. She had married a man already married to another and now stood accused of murder, because of Drew.

And she could only describe their intimacy as the most pleasurable experience of her entire life. She sighed.

Dear God, what had she done? He was her lawyer. Now, he had become her lover.

Layla listened to Drew's even breathing and knew that he had fallen asleep. The clock downstairs struck twice, letting her know the night was quickly slipping away. Lying here awake for hours, her mind looking for answers as to why she had made such a huge mistake.

She had been distraught over the knowledge of Blanche's death and she'd been angry when Drew caught her slip, but that was no excuse to allow such favor to the man who'd betrayed her father. For that matter, until tonight, she had never enjoyed sexual relations. And now here she lay naked with Drew, sharing her bed, her room, her very home and reveling in an experience that should never have happened.

Tonight could be her last night in her own home. She might very well die within a few months' time. All were good reasons to seek comfort, but not in the arms of her lawyer, the very man she blamed for many of her troubles.

She sat up in bed, unable to lie beside him another minute and think of how much she enjoyed having his arms around her. For the last three hours she had tried to sleep, but her mind refused to let her. Exhausted, her body trembling, she knew she needed relief. She needed her sleeping draught. She eased off the bed, grabbed her silk robe from the hook behind the door and wrapped it around her naked body.

With her hand on the doorknob, she opened the door and quietly shut it behind her. Hurrying down the stairs to the kitchen, she went to the pantry where Colette kept her sleeping medicine.

Her hands shook as she grasped the bottle and poured out a tablespoon of the liquid relief.

"I wondered where you'd gone to," Drew's deep voice startled her, causing her heart to skip a beat.

The bottle slipped from her grasp, the cure to her insomnia shattered, spilling her dreams all over the floor.

She gasped at the sight, realizing none of it was salvageable. "Damn you!" she yelled. "Look what you've done. How am I going to sleep now?"

"Don't move," Drew cautioned. "There's broken glass on the floor. Let me get a towel and a broom to clean it up."

Layla knelt down and picked up the broken bottle, the sight of its jadded edge making her sick. She needed her sleeping draught or she would never get to sleep. She needed the peaceful dreams it brought her, she needed the drug to ease her restlessness.

"Find Colette," she insisted, fighting back the panic she could feel building. "She'll know what to do."

"There's no need to wake her. I can sweep up broken glass," he insisted.

"No!" she said, her voice rising in panic. "Get Colette."

Colette would take care of her. She would get Layla what she needed, for she always kept an extra bottle on hand. Everything would be all right once Colette arrived. The trembling would ease and the craving that gripped her would go away, because Colette would take care of her.

Drew left the room, leaving Layla standing in the kitchen; the broken glass and spilled laudanum surrounded her feet.

Soon he returned with a still drowsy Colette. In her hands she carried another bottle of the sleeping draught and Layla felt a sense of relief. Soon she'd be all right.

"Thank God you have more," Layla said, the desperation in her voice startling her. She looked at Drew and Colette, realizing how her voice must sound to the others.

"I'm distraught over everything that's happened today and I must rest. When I dropped the bottle, I feared I'd never get any sleep," she rattled on, anxious at the pity she saw in their eyes. She didn't want or need it. "Colette, just give me the bottle."

"Let me get the floor cleaned up and then I'll give you your medicine and get you settled into bed," Colette said. She glanced over at Drew, her brows raised.

"No. Give me my medicine now. Then you can clean the floor," Layla insisted, her hands trembling with need. Why did she feel so needy and dependent on the sleeping draught tonight?

Colette poured the liquid into a spoon and gave it to her while she stood amongst the broken glass on the kitchen floor.

Layla licked her lips, the syrup bittersweet, yet promising her relief.

"Is that better?" Colette asked.

"I think I need more," she said, knowing one teaspoon would not ease the craving.

"All right," Colette responded, giving her a second spoonful.

STARLIGHT SURRENDER

Though her body still quaked, Layla knew that soon she would feel better. Soon the dreams would begin. The colorful dreams that left her sated and rested, the dreams of happiness and contentment.

"Thank you, Colette," she said after swallowing the second dose. "Thank you."

Her body craved the liquid and she had been taking it only for several months. Yet the laudanum calmed her, and helped her sleep. She deserved some peace of mind.

Colette took a towel and mopped up the medicine from the floor while Drew swept the area with a broom. Layla stood trembling in her nightgown, her bare feet cold on the wood floor.

"All right, ma'am, I think you can walk across the floor without stepping on glass," Colette said. "You can go back to bed if you'd like, Mr. Drew. I'll take care of Miss Layla and get her settled back into bed."

Drew stared at Layla, not saying a word, leaving her troubled and feeling awkward. Their relationship had changed tonight and she didn't know what to do or how to act. She felt confused and unsure and she feared their rash actions had not been for the best.

"Good night," he said, his voice lacking the warmth she had heard earlier as he turned and walked out of the kitchen.

Layla watched him go, and for a moment she wanted to call him back and tell him to wait. She didn't want to return to her empty bed. But that would hardly be the smartest thing to do, considering that Colette stood beside her.

"Thank you, Colette." Her body was already relaxing. "I don't know what I would do without you."

"You're welcome, ma'am. Now let's get you into bed."

Together they climbed the stairs, walking past the

door to Drew's room. Layla paused in front of her own doorway, knowing she couldn't let Colette into the room.

"I can manage the rest, Colette. Get some sleep."

Colette's brows raised in surprise. "Good night, ma'am."

"Good night," Layla said and opened the door to her room.

She stared at her empty bed and quickly shut the door, not willing to let anyone see the rumpled sheets where they had made love, their clothes strewn about.

She didn't want to see it. Tonight had changed everything.

The next morning, Drew sat in the kitchen eating breakfast after a sleepless night. He had never enjoyed the physical act with a woman quite as much as he had last night with Layla. Yet he knew such intimacy was wrong.

For God's sake, she was his client and the consequences could be drastic.

Yet it wasn't the fact he had had the best sex of his life with his client that kept him awake. No, it was the realization that Layla was addicted to laudanum.

It was not an uncommon affliction. Since opiates were sold by every apothecary and druggist. But he needed her mind clear, her body healthy to withstand the emotional upheaval of her upcoming trial.

And he cared enough about her to fear for her physical well-being if she continued to dull her senses and ease her aches with patent elixirs.

Colette quietly appeared and began clearing his breakfast dishes from the table. They had barely spoken this morning.

"She's addicted, isn't she?" Drew finally asked. "You didn't want to tell me, yet you knew."

"Of course she's addicted," Colette responded, not looking at him. "Even Mr. Cuvier knew how much she craved the stuff."

Drew threw down his napkin and pushed away from the table. He stood and began to pace the small dining area. "Is she up this morning?"

"When I left her a few moments ago, she was dressing to come down," Colette admitted. "Will you need anything else this morning, Mr. Drew?"

"Yes, we're catching the two o'clock boat back to New Orleans. Have Layla's things ready to go."

"Yes, sir," she said and quickly disappeared.

He walked toward the library to gather his notes before he left for his appointment. There was one place he wanted to visit alone before they returned to New Orleans.

As he passed the staircase, he noticed Layla coming down. She looked sensational this morning in a soft white blouse and dark blue skirt. Her eyes were clear, though slightly red-rimmed. She appeared refreshed, the desperation he had seen the night before carefully concealed.

"Good morning," he said.

"Good morning," she returned shyly.

"Did you sleep well?" he asked.

"Very, thank you," she answered. Her hair was swept off her neck in a coiffure that made her look regal and proud. At her neck, she wore her mother's brooch.

When he glanced at her, he saw no indication that she suffered from addiction. She looked so vibrant that for a moment he doubted what he had seen in the hours before dawn.

"Have you eaten?" she asked.

"Yes, I have an early appointment this morning, so I

went ahead," he said as she reached the bottom step of the staircase. "I would have waited if I'd known you'd be down so early."

"I need to pack a few things I want to take back with me to New Orleans," she replied. "So I rose early this morning."

"I see. We're booked on the two o'clock."

She nodded. "I'll be ready."

He gazed at her, wanting to say something. "I was worried about you last night."

"Oh?" she said. "Whatever for? As you can see, I'm fine. I needed sleep."

She smiled, but he could see the fear hiding in the shadows of her eyes.

"You look absolutely lovely this morning. But last night—"

She waved away his obvious concern. "Well, all I needed was a decent night of sleep." she said with a smile. "And now I am perfectly recovered."

"You're addicted, Layla," he said softly.

Her body tensed and she scowled. "How dare you say that! You have no idea of what it's like to toss and turn for hours, wanting only to shut your mind down long enough to fall asleep."

Her eyes flashed at him angrily and she glared at him from the bottom step.

"I'm sure that's true, but your body is dependent upon the drug. Your hands trembled last night before Colette came to help," he told her in a quiet voice.

"I was exhausted," she responded, her voice rising. "You have no right to judge me or tell me what to do. I can quit anytime."

"I don't believe you," he said quietly.

"I don't care what you believe," she retorted. "It helps me and I need it."

She stood above him on the bottom step, licking her lips nervously.

"Did you use laudanum the night that Jean died?" Drew asked.

She shoved him aside and strode past him into the library. "Why does every discussion come back to Jean's murder?"

He followed her into the library. "Layla, I'm trying to defend your life. If the prosecutor finds out about your use of laudanum, he might ask how you know that you didn't kill him?"

She turned to face him, her hands clenched at her side. "That night I slept soundly for the first time in days because I took my medicine. Someone could have come into the hotel room and murdered him and I would have slept right through it."

Drew stood, watching how visibly upset she seemed at admitting that she had slept while Jean died. But was the laudanum she had given Jean been tainted with cyanide? And had Layla purposely put that cyanide in his drink and ended her husband's life?

He sighed, knowing that with every revelation his job seemed tougher, and for the first time, he doubted his ability to win this case.

"You're addicted to the laudanum, Layla. If the prosecution finds out, they will use it against you. I need you to be clearheaded and strong," he repeated and then paused, clearly seeing that his words did not seem to sway her. "I know you don't believe me. Prove to me you're not addicted by doing without it for a few nights. If you don't need it, then I won't say another word. But if you can't . . ."

"I don't need to prove that to you or anyone else. I am not addicted," she insisted in a lowered voice.

"What did Jean think of the medicine you took?" he asked.

For a moment, she stopped, stunned. "How did you know . . ." her voice trailed off. "Colette is the only person who could have told you . . ."

"Don't blame Colette. She's worried about you, just as I am," he said, wanting to touch her, reassure her.

"I am not addicted," she insisted, her voice rising once again.

"You've got to stop or it's going to kill you," he said. "Let me help you."

She turned her back on him. "I don't need your help."

He walked across the room to her, knowing he had to leave and not wanting to push her anymore at the moment for fear she would run away. He spun her around to face him. His fingers brushed a curl of hair away from her face as she watched him warily.

"We'll talk about this again when I return. Right now, I've got to leave. And I know you'll be waiting for me when I return."

She crossed her arms across her chest and frowned stubbornly. "I know, that invisible piece of rope."

He placed his fingers under her chin and tilted her face up to gaze into her blue eyes. "Yes, and this."

Knowing he should not, but unable to resist, he covered her mouth with his for a quick kiss.

The morning dew couldn't have tasted sweeter on her full lips. Sunshine bathed them with its warm glow through the windows; and the sensual attraction between them was warmer still. He quickly ended the kiss.

"I'll be back soon," he promised and walked out of the library.

Eleven

Drew snapped the buggy reins, determined to run this last errand before they caught the boat back to New Orleans. Walking away and leaving her this morning had been tougher than when he discovered she had left New Orleans. Though she kept denying her addiction, they both knew she was lying to Drew and to herself. And while he should never have kissed her this morning, he could not resist offering her some small gesture of comfort.

Only the taste of her sweet mouth had shaken him, leaving him hungry for her, knowing to continue what they had started last night would be foolish. Yet he felt more drawn to her than ever.

Quickly he reminded himself that Layla was his client. His job was to defend her, not become deeply involved with her. To do so meant putting his law practice in jeopardy, and risking the ruination of his political career. Last night he had been thinking with his body, not with his head. This morning, he regretted his spontaneous actions.

Hell, he didn't regret any of it, but today his conscience reminded him once more of his duty: To defend Layla, not seduce her.

As for her case, he needed his assessment to be clear and precise, his mind focused on her defense. He couldn't let anything slip through or Finnie, the district attorney, would bury him and Layla would hang, regardless of her guilt or innocence.

And *that* thought was something he dared not contemplate, in spite of whether or not she had killed Jean.

Yes, he had ignored his father's advice and found himself in her arms and in her bed. And the night had been more than he had expected or dreamed possible—until the moment he realized her need for her "medication." Her addiction had its talons deep in her flesh, the drug holding her in its clutches. And she did not appear to realize the seriousness of her problem.

She had been vulnerable last night and though he had not intentionally taken advantage of her, he worried that today she probably regretted her wanton response.

The gates of the Sacred Heart Convent were just ahead and he turned the buggy into the drive. He had come here after receiving a response to a hastily written letter, hoping to convince the mother superior to testify as a character witness in Layla's defense.

Pulling to a halt, he set the brake on the buggy, looped the reins around the end, and proceeded to step down. Green moss covered the old stone building, surrounded by an air of quiet solitude. As he knocked on the door, he could not help but think of Layla coming here after her mother died.

A young woman in a novitiate's habit pulled back the heavy wooden door. "How may I help you?"

"Drew Soulier, to see the mother superior," he said. "She's expecting me."

The young woman opened the door farther and he stepped into the quiet reception area. Gently, she closed the door behind him.

"Please come this way," she replied quietly and motioned to him to follow her.

Their footsteps echoed on the stone floor as she led him down a darkened hallway, the smell of incense strong, to a door where light streaked from beneath the threshold. She knocked rapidly.

"Mother, a Mr. Soulier is here to see you."

The door opened and a woman dressed in a full-length traditional black nun's habit with a white wimple framing her face gazed at him. She shook his hand, her grasp strong. "Good morning, Mr. Soulier. Please come in."

She shut the door behind him. "I must say I'm curious. Why are you inquiring about Miss DuChampe?"

Motioning to him to take a seat, she walked behind her desk and sank down into her chair.

"I'm sure you've heard that she's accused of murdering the man who called himself her husband," Drew informed her, waiting until the nun sat before he sunk down onto the hard wooden chair.

She nodded. "I'd heard the sad news."

"I'm her lawyer. I'm going to defend her. I hoped you could tell me something about Layla and her father."

The nun's eyebrows rose. "I know very little. After Layla's mother died, her father brought her to us and paid for her education. The sisters of our order run a girls' school."

"Yes, I know. I grew up in Baton Rouge," he replied, watching her expression brighten. "My parents are members of Saint Mary's Parish."

"How wonderful," the woman said, clearly warming to him as a fellow Catholic. "Layla was one of our brightest pupils. I believe she would have continued on at Sacred Heart as a teacher, if her father hadn't insisted she come home."

"When was this?"

"Not long before she married Mr. Cuvier," the nun

answered shaking her head. "I've often wondered why she married that man in such haste."

"I can answer that. She married him to save her father's business. Only Jean took over the business and her father died not long after the sale to Mr. Cuvier."

The nun frowned and pinched her lips together, her eyes narrowing. "So she lost the business, her father, and was married to a man who already had a wife. How tragic."

"Yes," Drew agreed. "I came here hoping that I could convince you to testify on Layla's behalf."

The abbess leaned back in her chair and tilted her head sideways. "Layla was always one of my favorites. I hoped she would someday join us permanently."

Drew nodded, praying he had found himself a character witness.

"Please realize I would love to help Layla, but before I agree to be a witness, there's something you need to know." Her brows drew together in a worried way.

She stood, clasping her hands nervously. The mother superior walked around the desk to the window and looked out. "Layla was very close to one of her teachers. A woman who developed the wasting disease and seemed to disappear right before our eyes."

She turned and faced Drew. "Watching Sister Elizabeth suffer was very hard for Layla. She nursed her teacher and often stayed by her side at night. One morning I went in to check on Sister Elizabeth and found her dead. Layla was sleeping in a chair beside her bed, an empty bottle of laudanum on the nightstand."

Drew frowned, filled with a sudden sense of foreboding. "What are you telling me?"

"At that point in the fatal progress of Sister Elizabeth's disease, a bottle of laudanum lasted a week. The day before, the bottle had been full. I spoke with everyone who nursed Sister Elizabeth the last day of her life, trying to determine how much of the drug she had taken—or been given. She was in excruciating pain and begging for relief. I fear that Sister Elizabeth may have received an overdose." The nun sighed and shook her head. "Whatever happened, I truly believe no malice was involved. Layla said that Sister Elizabeth was in a great deal of pain and kept demanding more medicine. And Layla, not wanting her to suffer, gave her more laudanum."

Drew sat stunned. If the prosecution learned of the nun's death, they would pounce on this incident and make the most of it in front of the jury.

"And do you believe Layla overdosed the woman?" Drew asked leaning forward in his chair, his hands clutching the armrests.

"Who is to say what happened that night? Layla loved Sister Elizabeth and would never have harmed her. I fear rather that she didn't want Elizabeth to suffer and gave her more than her body could handle. Whether or not it was intentional, I cannot say."

The mother superior clasped her hands together in front of her as if in prayer.

Though the incident appeared innocent, Finnie would twist the scenario to fit his needs, making Layla appear a murderess twice over.

Drew wanted to curse, but refrained. "What you're telling me, Mother, could send my client to the gallows. No jury will believe that she had nothing to do with her husband's death when a nun she cared for died from an overdose."

"I'm sorry. I thought it best that you were informed in case this evidence came to the attention of the prosecutor."

"Thank you, Mother, because I can tell you that Layla has not shared this information with me." He clenched his hands in frustration. Why hadn't Layla thought to tell him of someone she loved dying at her hand?

What if they had gone to trial and he had been unprepared? How could he have responded if Finnie brought the incriminating tale before the jury? Evidence like this could hang his client.

A chilling thought seized him.

"Could Layla have taken some of the laudanum for herself?" he asked, suddenly doubting her own use of it was recent.

The mother superior looked away. "I don't know. We kept it for medicinal purposes, but soon after the death of Sister Elizabeth the elixir seemed to disappear and I started locking it up."

Drew didn't know what to say. Shocked, he clenched his fists, knowing his case had just been dealt a serious blow. If the prosecutor learned about the suspicious death or Layla's laudanum use, no jury would believe her innocence.

"Does anyone else know about this?"

"Just myself and several of the other nuns who worked closely with Sister Elizabeth."

"You're right." Drew shook his head, knowing he couldn't use the abbess as a character witness after all. "I can't risk you taking the stand and answering questions that may lead in this direction. If Finnie finds out, then he'll ask you to testify and I'll ask you my questions when I cross-examine you."

"I understand," she said softly.

Defending Layla had just gotten tougher. "Is there anything else you can tell me about Miss DuChampe that will help with her defense?"

"Not really. She's a sweet child, and I find it hard to believe that she'd kill her husband or Sister Elizabeth." The abbess smiled kindly. "I'll pray for her and I'll remember you in my prayers as well, Mr. Soulier."

"Thank you, Mother." Drew stood, the need to get back to his charge overwhelming him. Too much time alone could be too much of a temptation for her. What if she took a different boat and not the one to New Orleans? "Thank you for seeing me."

Walking out the door, he could not help but feel frustrated. Once again, Layla had conveniently forgotten a vital bit of information he had to be prepared for.

He stalked out of the convent and hurried to his buggy. They were due to catch the boat to New Orleans this afternoon, but before they left town, he needed to make her realize her lack of confidence in him could get her killed.

Layla's packed satchel sat by the front door ready to go. She wandered around the house, lovingly touching all the mementos that held any meaning for her. Some of the clothes she had brought she had left behind today, and instead filled her suitcases with keepsakes she could not bear to part with.

Even if Layla lived, she wouldn't be returning here. For now, the home belonged to Jean's legal wife. A bitter taste filled her mouth. She hated Jean enough that she would have been happy to hear that he had gone straight to hell, where he belonged.

Walking into the library, she pulled one of her father's nautical books from the shelf and glanced through the pages, remembering how her father used to study these texts.

The front door opened and slammed shut.

"Layla?" Drew bellowed, his voice stern.

"In the library," she called, wondering where he had been this morning.

He rushed in, his face flushed.

"What's wrong? Did you fear that I'd run from you again?" she asked, deliberately baiting him, still upset at herself for allowing Drew into her bed, their conversation this morning still fresh.

His emerald eyes flashed with annoyance. "Does the name Sister Elizabeth mean anything to you?"

The name of her favorite teacher brought tears to her eyes. Sister Elizabeth had taught Layla literature and poetry and shown her there was strength and consolation in prayer. Layla loved her kind spirit and missed her terribly when she died.

She turned her back to Drew. He would not believe her when she told him she had forgotten the events that led to her dear friend dying. "The name means a lot to me."

He touched her shoulder and spun her around to face him. "I want to know why you so conveniently forgot to mention that she died while you were with her. And that she might have overdosed on laudanum."

"It's very difficult to die from an overdose of a medication that you're used to taking. Sister Elizabeth had been taking laudanum for pain for several months."

He stared at her and shook her head. "Don't you understand? Information like that is crucial to your defense! You should have told me!"

She gazed up at him, noticing the way his mouth seemed to tighten whenever he was angry. "I'd put the events of her death out of my mind. I didn't think to tell you."

"She died while you watched over her. The mother superior questioned how much laudanum Sister Elizabeth had been given the day she died. If the prosecution finds out about her death, they will make you out to be a coldhearted murderer who not only killed her husband, but a sick nun."

"I didn't kill her any more than I killed Jean," Layla said her voice rising along with her fear.

"It won't matter to a jury. They'll only see that this

has happened twice in your life and their doubts will disappear. You'll be convicted. You'll hang," he raged.

Layla swallowed, fear almost choking her. If she were a member of a jury, given the information regarding Sister Elizabeth, she would believe it as well.

"If there is anything else I need to know, you'd better tell me now. Has anyone else died while in your care? Whatever the district attorney might find out before I do, tell me," he insisted.

She walked across the room, trying to decide if she should tell him about the night Jean died. Should she tell Drew that she had known in advance of the other wives? She did not want him to think of her as a murderer. She wanted him to believe in her innocence and she feared this knowledge would convict her.

"No, there's nothing else," she whispered.

He stared at her. "Are you certain? The other night in the swing, you almost said something then. I must know everything, Layla."

"No, I explained that to you. There's nothing else," she exclaimed, her gaze focused on his forehead and not his eyes. She couldn't look him in the eye and tell a lie. In fact, she hated lying to him, but fear of the consequences kept her from revealing everything.

Drew shook his head. "For some reason, I don't believe you. Sooner or later, you're going to have to tell me everything, including whatever you're holding back."

She raised her head indignantly. "I've told you all I know, now leave me alone and give me a chance to say goodbye to my home."

"Not just yet," he snapped.

Layla stared at him, fearing his next words, panic keeping her immobile.

"Colette," he boomed, his deep voice seeming to rattle the windows.

She hurried around the corner. "Yes, Mr. Soulier?"

"Bring me all the bottles of laudanum you have in your possession," he demanded.

"No!" Layla screamed. "No, don't do it, Colette."

"Bring them to me now, Colette," he insisted in a voice that gave no room for compromise.

"Yes, sir," she said glancing from one to the other.

Layla took hold of her arm. "No, Colette. Don't listen to him. He can't fire you, only I can."

Colette stepped back out of her grasp. She glanced at the two of them and hurried from the room. In a few moments she returned with two bottles of the sleeping draught. Layla's hands trembled with the need to jerk the medication from her but didn't. Colette handed the bottles to Drew.

"Is this all?" he asked, more softly.

"Yes, sir," she replied, not looking in Layla's direction.

He gazed at Colette, his eyes stern and unforgiving. "We'll be staying at my home when we reach New Orleans. You are not to buy or bring laudanum into my house. Do you understand? If I find you've given any to Miss Layla, you'll be sent away."

"Yes, sir, I understand," she answered, watching him wide-eyed.

Layla knew his purpose instantly. She watched Drew turn and head toward the kitchen and quickly hurried after him.

"What are you doing with that?" she asked, her voice quivering.

"The only way to quit this stuff is to make it no longer available to you. As of today, you will no longer take any sleeping draught," he commanded, halting at the sink in the kitchen.

She watched in horror as he opened one bottle and poured it down the drain. She ran to his side and tried to stop him. "No, Drew. Please don't. I've got to have my medicine. I can't do without it. Let me wean myself slowly off it."

"No."

With despair, she watched him open the second bottle and pour that one down the drain also. Now she had nothing to get her through the night.

"Damn you! I hate you!" she cried, pummeling him with her fists. "What am I going to do? I need my sleep!"

He grabbed her fists. "You will go without, you will suffer, and then you'll be all right. It shall not be easy, but you've got to give the narcotic up."

She started to cry and sagged against him. "I can't."

"Yes, you can," he said gently. His arms went around her and he rubbed her back while she cried. "You must be alert when we go to trial. The prosecution will take advantage of any slip, and mistake."

She sobbed onto his suit jacket, not caring that her tears left wet marks on the fabric. "I hate you, Drew. I hate you for everything you've done that's affected my life."

"Someday I hope you'll see that I'm not responsible for everything bad in your life. Someday I hope you will realize that I was the only one who cared enough about you to try to stop your destructive behavior. But until that day, go right ahead and hate me."

He pulled back and glanced at her tear-streaked face.

"We leave for New Orleans in five minutes," he informed her and walked away.

She sobbed uncontrollably, overwhelmed by fear.

Yet somewhere in all of the pain of that moment, he had said he cared about her. And she wondered why.

The next day, as Drew caught up on the office work that stacked up while he was away, he could not help but think how uneventful and quiet the trip home had been.

Layla had perched on the buggy seat, her back stiff, her eyes straight ahead as they had pulled away from her home. He felt that she had shut herself away from him and a sense of sadness filled him. He had been stern, pouring away her laudanum, confronting her about her past, but there was no other way to save her.

Yet the memory of her in his arms remained with him and he wished he could experience the pleasure again, but knew holding her was impossible. For if he held her, he would covet more.

When they had arrived at his town house, he had shown her to her room. She had not come out the rest of the day, even for supper. All night long he had listened for her, half expecting her to walk the halls, unable to sleep, but he had heard nothing.

Soon her craving would begin. He dreaded the pain she would suffer and wished he could take her anguish away, but knew she must go through her own private hell before she could be restored to full health.

Eric, his law clerk, pushed open his door. "Excuse me sir, Mr. Paul Finnie is here to see you."

Damn, he wasn't prepared for a visit from the district attorney today.

"Show him in," Drew sighed, resigned to seeing his nemesis.

"Hello, Soulier," the man said cockily as he ambled into Drew's office.

"What can I do for you, Finnie?" Drew asked, not looking forward to this exchange. Had he somehow learned the truth of Drew's visit to Baton Rouge?

"I came by to see if you'd returned from your trip." He sank into a chair across from Drew's desk. "Learn anything I'd be interested in knowing while you were in Baton Rouge?"

"Absolutely nothing," Drew lied. If the district attorney wanted to know about Sister Elizabeth or even Blanche Viel, he could do his own research. He had found nothing that the law required him to share with the prosecution in the name of full disclosure.

"Shame. The trial starts in one month. And the way it looks right now, it should be short and sweet."

Drew laughed. "You have yet to prove a motive. Why would a woman without any means of support kill off the man who financially supported her? It doesn't make sense."

Finnie grinned. "Nah, she thought that with Jean dead, she'd get her father's company back."

"That's absurd. Unlike Marian Cuvier, Layla has no reason to want to run Cuvier Shipping."

"I have a witness who will testify that he heard her and Jean arguing over her father's shipping company. She wanted it back so she could leave him and Jean laughed at her." Finnie crossed his leg and rested a hand on his knee. "So you see, I have found the motive. Your client gave him laudanum to keep him from her bed. Until the night she decided that perhaps Jean needed a permanent rest."

Drew frowned and didn't reply for several moments, contemplating the other man's words. Unfortunately, his revelation did seem to fit with something Layla had said earlier.

"Who is this witness?" Drew asked, trying to appear casually interested, but not give away that Finnie had taken him by surprise.

"None other than Jean's personal servant, George. And since he traveled with Jean, he would know."

"If he always traveled with Jean then he must have known of the other wives too," Drew responded, taking the offense. "I'm going to tear his character to shreds on the witness stand. He should never have let Jean get away with what he did to those women."

"Oh no. That's the beauty of this case. Jean kept him in the dark. Said the women were his mistresses. And George knew his marriage to Marian was unhappy and understood Jean's needs. So he went along with it, not wanting to make his boss angry." The district attorney laughed. "I have to give Jean credit. The man certainly knew how to handle women."

Yes, he did it so well, he's dead, Drew thought. Disgusted at the district attorney's blatant regard for Jean, he shook his head. "All but one."

The district attorney frowned at him. "Drew, your client wanted her father's company back. George told me she blamed you and Jean for the sale. I'm here today to tell you that you may either voluntarily hand over copies of the contract or I can get a subpoena. The choice is yours."

Drew shrugged. "That's easy. Get a subpoena."

"I thought you'd say that. It's already in the works," the man sneered. "Must be diffucult, though, having a client who blames you for her troubles."

Drew shrugged and lied. "Actually, things are good."

Finnie stood, clearly not liking his response. "Well, I'm glad to hear that your case is going well. I feared this trial would be so easy there would be no challenge in defeating you."

"Don't worry, Finnie," Drew quipped with a smirk at the irritating man. "I'm up to the challenge. I can't wait to show the citizens of New Orleans that you're worthless as a lawyer."

"Not before I get the chance to show them you'd make a terrible mayor," he retaliated. "By the way, I sent a man to Baton Rouge to uncover whatever you learned while there."

"Don't bother. I'll tell you what I found. An attic

filled with papers from Anthony DuChampe's shipping company. Hardly worth the trip," Drew said casually.

"Oh well, he'll keep busy just the same," Finnie remarked. "By the way, the coroner's report is available. No really new information. Mr. Cuvier died from cyanide poisoning, though there was laudanum in his bloodstream. Just not enough to kill him."

Drew nodded, relieved that he could tell Layla she had not given her husband an overdose.

"I'll see you in one month, when I'll do my damnedest to send your client to the gallows and ruin your chances of becoming mayor."

Drew laughed. "You've got one month, Finnie, to talk dirt. But when we step into that courtroom, the gloves are off and I'll be throwing the punches."

"I can handle your hits," the district attorney retorted with a laugh and withdrew through the door.

Drew sank back down into his chair. Was anything about this case easy?

Two nights later, Drew paced the floor outside Layla's room, helplesss in the face of her agony. Inside, he could hear her vomiting the vile drug out of her system. He started to open the door when Colette stepped out, a basin in her hands.

"How is she?" he asked worriedly.

"She's very ill, sir," Colette replied, stepping around him to continue down the hall.

He could not stand being away from her while she endured the pain. He knew she would want to be alone, but the thought of her sick, with no one to comfort her, was just too unbearable.

Drew opened the door to her room. It took a minute for his eyes to adjust to the darkness.

"Layla," he whispered.

"Go away," she muttered weakly. He could see her curled in a ball lying on the bed, shivering. "I don't want you in here."

He ignored her and sat on the bed beside her. "Are you all right?"

"That's a stupid question," she answered feebly.

He laughed. "Guilty."

She trembled beneath the covers. "Give me just a little of my medicine, Drew. All I need is enough to get me through."

"I can't." He wanted to give in to her, but knew refusing her was for the best.

"Then go away and let me die," she said, angrily turning from him in the bed.

Drew reached over to another basin, filled with water, beside her bed and wrung out the cloth and gently laid it on her forehead.

"I'm not going away," he asserted. "I'm here until you're over this, so you can beg, yell, or hit me, but I'm not leaving. And don't think you can persuade me to give in, because I won't. As long as you're with me, you're not going to have laudanum."

"Have I told you today . . . how much I . . . hate you," she snarled. More tremors shook her body.

Her words stung, but how many times had she told him she hated him since the arrest? And certainly this was the drug talking as much as anything.

"Ah, there's the spirited woman I know. Keep telling me you hate me and I'll know that everything is going to be all right. That you're going to recover."

Suddenly she rose up in bed, reaching out blindly. "Basin . . . need basin."

He found one on the floor and shoved it in front of her just as she retched. The sound of her vomiting until only dry heaves convulsed her was enough to make him nauseated. But he refused to leave her. She deserved someone at her side, going through this ordeal with her and not alone.

"Leave . . ." she barely managed to whisper.

"No," he exclaimed, feeling responsible for her and knowing that he could not sleep even if he wanted to leave.

"Leave . . . at least let me have my pride," she croaked.

"To hell with your pride. I'm worried about you and I'm not going anywhere until you're resting more comfortably," he stated harshly.

She tried to push him off the bed, but she was too weak to succeed. He wrapped his arms around her and pulled her down on the bed, stretching out full length beside her. There he held her trembling body in his arms.

He ran his palm down her hair, trying to soothe her. She fit perfectly in his arms and he blocked the thoughts of just how much he liked holding her close.

"You bastard, if you wanted to help me, you'd give me some medicine. Just a little to keep me from dying."

"I can't do that, Layla. You can beg, but I'm not going to respond to that question again."

"Bastard!" she moaned.

"Yes, I am," he agreed, knowing the drug still held her in its grasp, reminding himself this was for her own good. "If you'd like some water, I'll give you a sip."

"I don't want water," she fairly yelled. "I want my medicine!"

He went back to trying to soothe her. "And I want to save your life."

She yawned, the action catching him off guard. For a moment he thought she would actually go to sleep, but then he noticed her twitching seemed to increase and suddenly she doubled over with abdominal cramps.

"Oh God," she cried. "I can't do this anymore, please Drew, give me my medicine."

The plea in her voice was not the begging need, but more of a physical cry, leaving him worried.

The urge to run out of the house and down to the nearest pharmacist and obtain what she craved tempted him, but he held fast. Instead, he rubbed her back and said nothing. If the narcotic had been in the house, he knew he would have relented, but he had purposely made sure that none of the drug was within easy reach.

Rubbing her back, he could feel her heart pounding in her chest and suddenly he feared for her life. What if her body could not take the sudden withdrawal? What if he killed her in his need to see her well?

Colette knocked on the door. "Mr. Drew, do you need anything?"

"Yes, Colette, bring us some fresh towels and a clean basin."

"Yes, sir."

He rose from the bed and stepped out in the hall. He closed the door behind him. "And send one of my servants to fetch Dr. Little."

"Yes, sir," Colette replied nervously, her eyes widening. "Is she all right?"

"I don't want to take any chances," Drew assured her.

He returned to Layla, needing to be with her.

The doctor arrived thirty minutes later, and Layla lay motionless on the bed. Her eyes were open, her breathing shallow, and she appeared drained of all strength.

The doctor checked her over carefully and then stepped out of the room with Drew.

"I think she's over the worst of it. I'm going to give her a mild herbal remedy to help her sleep, as she needs to rest. By tomorrow she should be doing better, though she will still experience occasional tremors and vomiting for the next week. You've got to get plenty of liquids into her and beef broth to keep up her strength. In ten days the drug should be out of her system, but that's not to say that the allure of the opiate will not tempt her again."

Drew shook the man's hand. "Thanks for coming, Dr. Little. My servants will show you out."

Opening the door to Layla's room, Drew glanced down at her. She lay curled on her side, her breathing even, appearing to sleep. No longer did her body tremble or shake.

"Are you going to just stand there and stare at me?" she asked abruptly.

"No, I'm going to crawl into bed beside you until you fall asleep," he assured her.

"We're not married. You shouldn't be sleeping with me," she replied, her voice weak.

"I don't give a damn," he confessed and meant it.

He crawled into bed with her and she let him wrap his arms around her and hold her. "Try to sleep. I'm here if you need me."

The feeling of her in his arms made his guilt at her pain ease a little. Staring at her, his heart swelled with tenderness.

He wanted to protect her, to watch over her, and care for her, all at the same time. Those feelings frightened him.

For if any woman could ruin him forever, Layla DuChampe could, just by him being with her. And none of that mattered with her in his arms.

Twelve

Layla felt as if someone had taken a stick and beaten her. Sore, tired, and tearful, she had only hazy memories of the last two days and the veil of pain that had surrounded her. Vaguely, she remembered Drew staying at her side through the night and she did recall the doctor's visit, which had brought welcome relief.

A knock sounded on her bedroom door and she wanted whomever it was to go away. She did not answer, hoping they would think she still slept. Facing the world when the household had witnessed her weakness seemed much too difficult a task.

The door opened. Unable to keep from looking, she glanced up to see Drew carrying a breakfast tray into her room. A bright red rose in a vase sat on the tray and that small bud radiated cheerfulness.

Layla was mortified. He had seen her last night at her worst, yet here he stood this morning bringing her a breakfast tray. Why did he treat her so kindly when she knew she had been hateful?

"Good morning," he said, gazing at her quizzically. "I'd ask you if you were feeling better, but I fear your response."

"Coward," she retorted.

He grinned.

"I brought you some breakfast."

"You can take it right back to the kitchen. I'm not hungry." The thought of food repulsed her.

"The doctor said you've got to eat and drink plenty of fluids," Drew coaxed. "Colette fixed your favorites."

"Why are you doing this?" she asked slowly, sitting up in bed, knowing this stubborn man would not leave her alone. "Is it because of the trial?"

He thought for a moment. "In part. But more than anything, no one deserves a life chained to that drug."

She felt so confused. He acted like a man who cared, yet why should he? She had nothing to offer him, yet there seemed to be a physical connection between them. But why would he care about her?

"Pretty words. As soon as this trial is over, you'll go your way and I'll hang."

"Well, you're certainly in a charming mood this morning. You should be happy to know that the doctor thinks you'll be fine. He said you may have some episodes of tremors and vomiting, but he thought the worst is behind you."

Layla sighed, a welcome feeling of relief that at least the hardest part was over. She didn't know how much more she could have taken last night. She had wanted to die, the pain had been so bad at times. But at least she would never take the drug again.

Though she knew that the lure of the opiate would always tempt her, nothing was worth the pain of withdrawal.

She owed Drew a huge debt of gratitude and that troubled her. Yet he had been by her side through the worst of her ordeal and she thought she had never known a man quite like Drew before.

"I'm sure I should apologize. I don't remember much from last night, but no doubt I wasn't the nicest person to be around," she said, unable to look at him.

Drew laughed. "You can be dreadfully cranky when you don't get what you want."

She smiled. "Please, sit down."

Drew nodded and sat down beside her on the bed. He balanced the tray on his lap. "Are you going to eat anything for me?"

Layla glanced at him, frowning. "Do I really have a choice."

"I want you to get better. I want you well," he confessed.

She gazed into his eyes and felt her breath quicken at the depth of some unrecognizable emotion there. Surely, he felt something for her and that thought gave her a warm feeling.

Reaching out her hand she stroked his face, her fingers running across his freshly shaved cheek. "Thank you so much, Drew. For everything."

"The best way to thank me is to stay on the road to recovery. Don't dwell on the past."

Layla smiled and changed the subject, suddenly wanting to please him. "What did you bring me to eat?"

He uncovered the dishes. "Colette made you *pain perdu* with fresh blueberries. She said that was your favorite."

"It is," she professed, sitting up straighter so as to take the tray from him. She took a bite and then another, suddenly ravenous. "Mmm. Delicious."

"Good. I didn't think you'd ever eat again after last night," he confessed and looked sheepishly at her. "Sorry, I won't mention it again."

She smiled feeling more relaxed. "Please."

"I do have something serious we need to discuss."

She frowned at him. "What?"

"Two days ago the district attorney came to see me. I would have spoken to you sooner, but you were unwell when I arrived home and I didn't think the time was right," he admitted, his mouth in a stern line.

"Do you think I'm ready now?" she asked, uncertain that she could handle any more bad news.

"I can't wait any longer or I wouldn't trouble you with this news. It seems that George, Jean's manservant, intends to testify against you. He heard you tell Jean you wanted your father's business back," Drew revealed.

"Is that all? I told Jean that many times when we argued. I would beg him to return my father's company to me and let me go. Or at least give me the cash from the sale."

Drew sighed.

"What's so bad about that?" she asked, not understanding his concern. "I wanted a way to support myself and after you . . ."

She didn't say anymore, not wanting to fight with him. It all seemed so useless and small in the broader scheme of things. Last night, she had thought she was dying and even today her death seemed imminent, her fate to be decided by the jury's verdict.

"The district attorney contends your motive to kill Jean was to regain control of your father's company. He's going to try to prove you believed that with Jean dead, you could take back your father's shipping company and earn yourself a living."

Oh God, what should she do now? If she told him that she knew about the other wives before Jean died, Drew could defend her against the district attorney's case. But it also opened up the speculation that she had killed him in a passionate rage. That, once she learned of the other wives, she had killed him in revenge. She just could not win.

And she could not tell him about the other wives, or that she had learned of them the night Jean died. She knew he was uncertain of her innocence and with this knowledge he would be sure that she had murdered Jean.

She closed her eyes, not strong enough to cope with everything just yet, her world spinning out of control.

"We'll talk more later," Drew said, his voice hollow and distant. "I mainly wanted to confirm that you had such a discussion, before I started trying to prove him wrong."

She opened her eyes, the spell seeming to have passed.

"My father's business was my birthright and I wanted it returned to me," she proclaimed weakly.

"Don't worry. This should be fairly easy to argue," he said, his eyes watching her carefully.

She smiled trying to reassure him. "I'm all right."

He stared at her, his eyes warm and filled with what looked like caring. "You're sure?"

"Yes."

Surely the emotion she saw in his gaze could only be pity for his client. Yet that emotion left her warm and feeling cherished, which pity certainly would not do. No, she was mistaken and would soon learn that he had felt only pity.

"I do have some good news," he said.

"What?" she asked eager for anything that could make her feel better.

"The coroner's report showed that Jean died of cyanide poisoning, not a laudanum overdose."

"Thank God," she said relieved. "Now I know I'm innocent." Layla had feared that somehow Jean had died of a laudanum overdose rather than poison. But who had given Jean cyanide?

Drew only looked at her without speaking for several seconds. "Well, I had better go. I wanted to check on you before I went to the office. The trial starts in less than a month, so I've got to spend as much time as possible preparing."

Her hand shook. "Less than a month?"

"Yes. Please rest today and try to get your strength back. I'll see you tonight," he promised. Unexpectedly he reached down and kissed her on the forehead. "Goodbye, Layla."

She sat stunned as he walked out of the bedroom. He acted like a man who cared and she realized, though she tried her best to hate him, that his kindness touched her deeply. No one had ever cared for her, comforted her or taken care of her like Drew. Not even her father.

When she tried to push him away, Drew let nothing she said deter him. How many men would have stayed with a vomiting, irrational, angry woman? And how many men would take on the case of a drug addicted woman accused of murder?

God, she had said the words. She realized her worst fears—she was an addict. But though she would always crave the opiate, she would never again take the drug. To fall under its spell again meant certain death and she had to get well. The trial started in less than a month and for some reason, she wanted to explore this attaction to Drew, for she had never felt anything like this before.

Drew watched as George Antoine walked into his office to give his deposition. The trial was less than a month away, yet this was Drew's first opportunity to interview George. The man shuffled in and took a seat in the same chair that Finnie had occupied only days ago.

"How are you, Mr. Antoine? I'm glad you could come in today."

The man grumbled, "I had no choice. Mr. Finnie, told me I had to speak with you."

Drew nodded, realizing the man's blatant attitude could make his task difficult. "That's true. I need to ask you questions since you were one of the four people in the suite that night."

Antoine raised his brows. "I've already told the police everything I know."

"Good, then the questions should be easy for you," Drew said shutting the door and taking a seat behind his desk.

The servant frowned.

"How long have you worked for Mr. Cuvier?"

"Ten years," he said tensely.

"Did you like your boss?"

George lifted his brows. "Yes. It was a good job."

"Did you know about Mr. Cuvier's other wives?"

"He told me they were his mistresses," George laughed. "I'm not stupid, especially when they call themselves Mrs. Cuvier."

Drew made notes, his pencil scratching noisily against the paper. He wanted to ask him why he had never turned Jean in to the law for bigamy, but decided to save that question for the trial.

"Tell me what you heard on the night of the murder?" Drew asked.

"When I went to bed, Mrs. Cuvier was in the sitting room of the suite, pacing. Usually she's quiet and stays in her room most of the time, but that night she was acting strange. I overheard her tell Colette to pack their bags, they were leaving the next morning. I didn't think too much of it until the next day."

George took a deep breath and looked out the open window. He returned his attention to Drew who sat patiently waiting. "Along about midnight I awoke to the two of them having a hell of a fight," he said leaning forward in his chair. "At first I couldn't hear what they were saying, but then she yelled and called him a selfish bastard. She told him she was returning to Baton Rouge and she wanted her father's business back."

"What did Jean say?"

"He just laughed at her and told her she wasn't getting anything from him."

"Was there any violence? Did they throw things or hit each other?"

"Not that I heard. The last thing I heard her say was that if he didn't give her some money, she'd tell everyone. I don't know what she intended to tell, but she was furious."

Drew's pencil scratched across the paper and he wondered what Layla intended to tell. She had not mentioned that part of the argument. Could she somehow have learned of the other wives?

George leaned back relaxing against the chair for the first time since he had arrived.

"You were in the suite that night. Did you go in to wake Jean that morning?"

"No. Unless he had an appointment, he liked to awaken by himself. Usually he was up before seven and gone to the office by eight," George said.

"So you didn't see Jean from early that morning until the morning his body was found?"

"Yes, sir."

"Where were you during the day?"

"I made sure his clothes were pressed and ran his errands. He kept me busy."

"Were you out that day?"

"Yes, sir. I ran errands for Mr. Cuvier."

"So why do you believe Miss DuChampe killed Jean?"

The man's brows rose. "Their marriage was nothing but one argument after another. The night he was murdered, she acted so strange and then later I heard her laugh and tell him she was leaving. She seemed glad to be getting away from him."

Drew stared at Jean's servant, thinking how easy it would have been for *him* to slip Jean the poison.

"You said she laughed that night, yet you also told me they argued."

"They did. It was almost as if she weren't right in the head that night. For one minute she was laughing and then the next she was demanding he return her father's shipping company or pay her for it." He shook his head. "There was definitely something wrong with her."

"But what about you, Mr. Antoine? Did you have any reason to kill Jean? You could very easily have slipped him the poison."

He rolled his eyes. "No. I didn't kill Jean. I had an easy time of it except for when he became angry. I had no reason to want him dead."

Drew leaned back and glanced at the man. "Is there anything else you want to tell me? I'm going to have a detective do a background check. Since you were in the suite that night you're just as much a suspect to me as Layla is to the police."

The man shuffled in his chair. "I didn't kill Jean Cuvier. I have nothing to hide."

"Well then, Mr. Antoine, I guess we're finished for now. If I don't see you before, I'll see you at the trial."

Two weeks passed and Layla felt stronger each day. Though her nights remained troubled, she now counted sheep or merely got up and read a book until she felt drowsy. Lack of sleep was irritating, but not enough to make her risk taking even one drop of laudanum.

Over the last few weeks, she had settled in at Drew's

town house and they had a more comfortable routine than she had shared with Jean. Every night they ate dinner together and then retired to the library, where Drew worked on the case and Layla read or crocheted.

Sometimes they sparred over the details of his strategy for the upcoming trial. Sometimes she lay awake at night half-frozen with fear, just thinking about it.

Sometimes she felt as if she had come home and that frightened her, for his domain felt too familiar, too much as if she belonged here. And yet she did not belong anywhere.

The memory of how he had soothed her lingered. When he looked at her, she could see desire shining from his eyes and the memory of that night of passion thrilled her still.

How often she thought of that night and marveled at how she had felt more with Drew than she had ever experienced in her life. She yearned to relive those incredible feelings, but fear kept her from seeking him out.

She was not free to fall in love with him. Too many obstacles blocked their path to happiness, though passion simmered just below the surface.

The biggest obstacle was her date with fate.

Esmeralda, his servant, found her sitting in the library of Drew's home.

"Mr. Soulier will not be home for dinner tonight," she announced. "I'll fix you a plate when you're hungry."

Layla frowned. "Is he working?"

"His note didn't say," Esmeralda said.

Later that night Layla watched from an upstairs window as Drew arrived home with a man Layla had never seen. She heard them enter the house and go into the library.

Layla walked out of her room, intent on going downstairs to see if she could find out the identity of the man with Drew.

She met Colette in the hall, a stack of towels in her hands. "I thought you were in bed already."

"No, I wanted to see who that gentleman with Drew is."

"Oh, that man. He's the one promising to help Mr. Drew run for mayor," Colette informed her.

"Mayor?"

"Yes, ma'am, didn't you know?" Colette exclaimed.

"Drew and his father talked politics the night we had dinner together. But I didn't have any idea he intended to enter the upcoming election."

"Oh no, ma'am. He's planning on announcing his candidacy sometime after your trial."

Layla frowned, an uneasy feeling stealing over her.

"I'll be back in a few moments to help you undress and get ready for bed," Colette promised, disappearing down the hall with her load of bath towels.

Layla walked down the stairs, her thoughts on what she had just learned. Something bothered her and she did not understand what.

As she approached the door to the library, she heard a gentleman's voice that she didn't recognize say, "This trial is going to make you very well known in New Orleans."

"Yes, I couldn't ask for a better way to get my name in front of the people of New Orleans. It was my good fortune that Miss DuChampe needed an attorney and was unable to pay," said Drew.

"Are you telling me that you took her case for little or no money?"

"Yes. The publicity I'll receive will more than pay for my time. I'll get plenty of press before I've announced my candidacy."

"And if you win, no candidate will be able to beat

you. You'll be a sure winner in the mayoral position. Especially considering our last mayor."

Layla heard Drew laugh. "Yes, I want the newspapers to print stories of how I'm working hard to save Miss DuChampe."

"So do you think she's guilty?"

There was silence. "She's my client. She can't be guilty."

Layla had heard enough. She hurried back up the stairs, her heart pounding, her fists clenched. In the last few weeks she had begun to care for Drew. With him she felt emotions she had never felt with any man. And now she had learned the truth.

Why had she ever thought that Drew Soulier, the man who cheated her father, could care for her? He cared about her, all right, but only because her trial could gain him the publicity he wanted. She meant nothing to him.

Layla lay awake reading, when she heard Drew shut the door behind his guest. Unable to sleep, she had lain awake and recalled every despicable thing she could about Drew Soulier.

With the departure of his political ally, she arose and put a robe on. Opening her bedroom door she hurried downstairs. Flinging open the door to the library, she strode into the room ready to face him down once and for all.

Drew glanced up at her from a chair, a glass of brandy in his hand.

"Oh, the lovely Miss DuChampe has decided to join me for a nightcap. And from the expression on her beautiful face, she appears to be angry."

"No, thank you," she replied stiffly, not wanting to drink any spirits.

"I can tell from the stubborn set of your chin that you're furious with me," Drew scoffed.

She laughed, the sound crisp in the quietness. "Whatever would give you that idea? You have already told me that you were taking on my case to give your law firm the attention that it needed."

"That's true," he responded calmly.

"It's not as if I ever thought that you wanted to take on my case because you believed I was innocent or cared about me."

He didn't reply, though his brows drew together in a frown. "Then what is wrong?"

"You're defending me for the publicity. And tonight I learned why." She walked across the room until she stood before him, her robe covering her body though she could feel his hungry gaze right through it, which only made her angrier.

"I have to give you credit. You've turned unpaid legal work into a winning proposition for yourself. Free publicity for your mayoral campaign." She paused, her mock smile widening. "So how can I help you, Drew? Should I wear a sign on my back in the courtroom, 'Vote for Drew Soulier, the slickest lawyer in town.' Or what about 'Slick-Dealing Drew Soulier, your next mayor.'"

"I don't think so," he said, his voice low and quiet.

"Every time I start to trust you, something happens. And I just found out you're only concerned with my case because you think it's going to carry you right on into the mayor's office."

He sat staring at her, his eyes dark with an unreadable emotion.

"You don't give a damn whether or not I live or die, only that you'll be the next mayor of New Orleans!"

At that he jumped up, his green eyes flashing, and she knew she had finally succeeded in angering him.

"If I cared only about winning the mayor's race, why in the world would I have stayed up with you all night and held you while your body sweated out the poisons you'd filled it with? Why did I follow you to Baton Rouge rather than let the police handle your disappearance? Why have I continued to put up with your nonsense about me cheating your father?"

"Because you're my lawyer," she spat back.

They stood inches apart, their bodies tense.

"You don't give a damn about me. You don't even believe I'm innocent," she hissed.

He grabbed her by the arms and hauled her up against him. "Damn it, Layla, I've tried so hard not to let you get to me. I've tried and I've failed."

He pressed his body into hers, and she could feel his erection through her gown. A tremor of excitement went through her. She didn't want to feel anything toward Drew, only to hate him.

"You're not right for me, but that doesn't seem to matter. I want you so badly, I can barely restrain myself."

His lips covered hers in a punishing kiss that took her breath away and sapped the strength from her arms as she tried to resist him. Feeling his mouth, hot and hard on hers, drained all the fight from her and left her shaking with desire. Why did this man find the empty spot in her soul and fill it with a passion for living? Why did this man seem to complete her and give her more than she had ever needed? Why this man, one whom she couldn't quite trust, yet she needed almost as much as her next breath?

His hands entwined in her loose hair, keeping her from stepping out of his embrace. Yet there was no other place she wanted to be at this moment, at this second in time, than his embrace.

His tongue lingered over her lips, caressing her with

exquisite slowness, savoring her, stoking a fire within her. She longed to give herself to him once again, but knew instinctively it was wrong. She no longer wanted to be used by a man.

Layla put her hands between them and pushed, using the last of her waning resistance to break the seal of his kiss.

Her breathing sounded harsh and ragged as she tried to muster all the anger she felt toward him. "You're my lawyer," she said angrily. "I can't stop you from using my trial to your advantage but I will not let you use me."

She turned and ran out of the library, knowing that leaving him was one of the hardest things she had ever done. For she wanted him so badly her body trembled with need. But she knew in her heart that he didn't love her and that he wanted her for all the wrong reasons.

Thirteen

Drew sat in his office, scanning the deposition from Marian Cuvier that his law clerk had taken. He was looking for anything unusual, but his mind urged him to hurry and his concentration was not on the page in front of him. He felt eager to get home to Layla, to try to mend the discord between them. Until two nights ago when Harry Luchetti from the Democratic Club visited, he had enjoyed their evenings together and the routine she brought to his home.

Dinner awaited him most evenings when he arrived. The house appeared tidy and seemed more organized. And though his servants had done a good job before she arrived, now their service seemed impeccable.

Yet, the night of Mr. Luchetti's visit, she heard the real reason he had taken her case and while he had known eventually she would learn the truth, he had not realized the extent of her anger. She made him sound like a greedy bastard. While he agreed he was using her case to get the people's attention, he was defending her at no charge. What more could the woman want?

Should he not be entitled to gain something from all the hours spent defending a woman whose innocence he wasn't even convinced of?

And yet every day her impending trial presented

more problems. Not because he could not find witnesses to defend her, but rather he felt himself becoming more entwined with her emotionally. He could not take that risk.

Layla DuChampe would forever be associated with the scandal of Jean Cuvier's murder. Not the type of wife a mayor, congressman, or even senator needed in order to rub shoulders with the social elite. And yet he found it harder and harder to resist her.

She made him feel alive. She made him more aware of being a man and she awakened feelings he had never felt before.

Last night he would have taken her right there in the library, if she hadn't stopped him. And she was right to tell him that he hadn't been hired to seduce her but rather to defend her. Though at that moment defending Layla had not even crossed his mind. He only wanted her.

Yet soon the trial would begin and Layla's fate would be decided. He glanced down at the briefs again. Could he get her acquitted and then run for mayor? Was he crazy to attempt such a feat?

And why did his mind keep returning to how Layla felt in his arms? The sound of her voice as she reached her climax that night that seemed so long ago.

The windows of his office were dark and he knew he should leave now. She would be waiting and perhaps tonight he could ease the tension he had sensed between them these last few days.

He leaned over to get the satchel he carried his papers in, when a brilliant burst of flame lit the window and a boom shattered the glass.

Something knocked the breath out of him, sending him crashing to the floor. A searing pain seemed to explode through him and he gazed down at his shoulder. His white shirt smoldered around a tattered hole where he could see blood beginning to ooze from a bullet wound.

Stunned, he realized he was shot and he lay in shock on the floor of his office, wondering if he were going to die. Fearful of standing, he dragged himself across the office floor, his shoulder leaving a trail of blood. Eric burst into the office.

"Mr. Soulier, are you all right?" he asked, looking frantically for him.

"Eric, get down," Drew insisted, trying to pull on the younger man's leg, his strength rapidly oozing out of the bullet hole. Finally the young man dropped to his knee.

"Oh my God, you've been shot!" Eric tried to stand again, but Drew grabbed his arm.

"Try to get to the light and put out that lamp," he commanded, gritting his teeth at the pain.

"Yes, sir."

Eric crawled to Drew's desk. He pulled the lamp down to the floor and quickly extinguished the flame.

Drew started to feel woozy. "I doubt the shooter is still around. The street cop would have heard that gunshot and come to investigate. But it's best not to take any chances."

"We've got to get you to a doctor," Eric blathered excitedly. "You're starting to lose a lot of blood.

Drew barely heard his law clerk. His mind focused on one question: Who would want to kill him? Who would risk shooting him and why?

In the darkness, Eric ripped off his shirt and tore one of the sleeves out. He leaned over Drew, lifted his arm and began to wrap it tightly with the sleeve of his shirt. "Until we get you to a doctor that should stop the bleeding."

The outside door to the office opened and someone entered. "Police! Is everything all right in here?"

"No," Eric called. "Mr. Soulier has been shot."

Drew felt his head start to swim and knew the loss of blood was affecting him.

The policeman stepped outside the door and blew his whistle. Drew smiled up at Eric's worried face.

"I'm going to be fine, Eric. But I don't think I'm going to be coming in to the office the next few days. You're going to have to take care of everything here."

"Mr. Soulier, please. Don't talk about work. The policeman has gone to get you a doctor."

"Just get me home," Drew muttered weakly. A sudden and terrifying thought of Layla lying hurt at his home flashed through his mind. "I need to get home to see if Layla is all right."

An hour later, Drew sat in the library of his home, where Eric had brought him, wondering where Layla could be. He had insisted on coming home only to find her absent.

Detective Dunegan stood listening while Drew tried to relate the sequence of events to the police. Dr. Little wrapped gauze around his shoulder and his armpit, after cleaning the wound. The bullet had passed straight through.

"You're a lucky man, Mr. Soulier," the detective said. "If you hadn't moved at that precise moment, I would be conducting a murder investigation."

"It wasn't my time, gentleman," Drew replied, frightened by the day's events, worried about where Layla could be at this hour. As far as he knew she never went out during the day. So where had she gone today?

The front door opened and the men all looked up to see who came through the entrance. Layla sauntered in looking as if she had been out for a stroll, her cheeks rosy, and her hat askew atop her dark hair. She pulled her hat from her head and noticed the men watching her from the library.

STARLIGHT SURRENDER

"Gentlemen?" she said.

Drew couldn't help but notice that her white gloves had smears of black on them and felt his heart slam into his chest with the missing of a beat. Could that substance be gunpowder? Could Layla have been the one who shot him?

"Where have you been?" he asked, his voice steady and firm.

She stared at the people in the library, the police, and the servants and lastly the doctor who was wrapping gauze around his wound.

"What happened?" she asked, walking into the room and removing her gloves.

"Where were you for the last two hours?" Detective Dunegan asked coolly, staring at her with an intensity Drew knew he only used on his suspects.

"I returned some of Jean's things to Marian Cuvier and then I took a stroll through the park until darkness forced me to return. Why?" She gazed at Drew. "What's happened? Why is Doctor Little wrapping gauze around your shoulder?"

"He's been shot," one of the detectives finally offered.

Layla gasped.

Fear swelled within her and she wanted to fling herself into Drew's arms and ask him if he was all right, but policemen stood watching her, making her nervous.

The doctor finished bandaging the wound and started packing up his supplies.

"Why would anyone shoot you?" she asked.

"Good question, Miss DuChampe. We were hoping you could answer that one."

She looked at the detective, startled. "What? Are you insinuating that I shot Drew?" she asked, her voice rising.

"Yes," the detective coolly replied.

"Why would I try to kill my lawyer? My trial starts in a week."

"Maybe you wanted to delay your trial a little longer. With Mr. Soulier dead, you could live several months more." The detective paused for a moment, watching her. "Or maybe Mr. Soulier has learned the truth. Maybe I should take you back to jail until you're convicted so your lawyer would be safe."

Layla felt her face flame and she pulled herself up rigidly.

"Detective, that's enough." Drew frowned at the man. "I'm still her lawyer. And I happen to agree with Layla. It would be suicide for her to try to kill me off."

The detective shrugged. "Very well. You may still be her lawyer, but I would recommend that you sleep with one eye open tonight."

"Oh!" Layla shrilled, anger radiating from her. "When we prove my innocence, I want you to remember every nasty thing you've said to me. I want you to remember that your investigation wasn't good enough to find the real killer."

The detective laughed. "Since I have no doubts regarding my investigation, I'll even offer you a public apology if Mr. Soulier can prove someone else killed Jean."

"Could we get back to your current investigation?" Drew snapped irritably. "This is starting to hurt like hell. If all of you would clear out, I can drink a brandy and go to sleep."

They turned and looked at him.

Layla went over and knelt down beside him, trying to hide her fear. "What happened? No one's told me how you were shot."

"Someone shot at me through the window in my office," Drew offered.

"Yes, and if he hadn't moved, they would have killed him," Eric informed her.

Layla felt her stomach churn as she gazed at Drew, his green eyes dull with pain. The thought of him dying frightened her for many reasons. She needed him to defend her, she needed him to house her, and oh God, she needed him here to comfort her.

"But why?" she asked, fear clutching her. "I don't understand."

"Neither do I," he said solemnly, gazing at her.

Doubts regarding her involvement shimmered in his gaze, deeply wounding her. He seemed to be wondering if she had shot him, and that hurt worst of all.

After everyone left, Drew sat in the library in his robe, drinking a brandy, trying to understand what happened tonight.

Who would want to kill him? Yes, things had been strained between him and Layla the last few days, but she certainly was no fool.

He had several other pending cases, but none of them were serious enough to warrant someone taking a shot at him.

And while running for mayor was still his goal, it was too early in the race for someone to try to prevent him from winning.

No, somehow this related back to Layla's murder trial and he needed to figure out who wanted to kill him and why.

Layla said she had gone to see Marian and then spent some time in the park. Her gloves had been dirty when she came in, but it looked more like mud than powder stains. He simply could not see her gripping a gun and pulling the trigger, but he intended to find those gloves to check them for gunpowder.

Why did he question her? If she had shot him, she would never have returned wearing the stained gloves.

In the last few days he had struggled with the fact that he had few witnesses and no other suspects. Eric had collected more information about Blanche Viel and Captain Frank Olivier, Layla's godfather. As far as Drew knew they had found nothing that would compel someone to shoot him.

Drew had interviewed George yesterday, but why would the man try to kill him? The district attorney had made it bluntly clear that George believed Layla killed Mr. Cuvier, so it would seem he would want the trial to start and for Layla to be convicted.

From now on he needed to watch his back everywhere he went.

His shoulder pained him.

Was it possible that Layla had shot him, driven by her anger and her fear, hoping to get a new lawyer to take her case?

The thought was not logical, though his doubts remained. But he would find no answers tonight—and, most likely, no rest.

A knock sounded on the door to the library and Layla peeked in.

"Are you all right?" she asked.

"It aches, but this brandy ought to help," he said. Drew took a sip from his glass while he watched her over the rim.

She came in, her nightgown covered by her robe, her hair in a long braid down her back. "I couldn't sleep for worrying about you."

"Hmm. Does that mean you did shoot me and now you feel bad, or that you didn't shoot me and you're worrying about me because you care?" he inquired with a grin.

She tensed. "I did not shoot you any more than I put poison in Jean's tea."

Drew frowned, the liquor making him feel woozy. It was easy enough to poison strong spirits. He was still uncertain of Layla's innocence in Jean's murder and now he had been shot. This case had far too many twists and turns.

"I don't think you tried to kill me," he reassured her. Though he couldn't be sure he wanted to put the incident behind him. "I would like to know who wants me dead and why."

He had never spent so much time with a woman in her nightclothes before, but with their unusual sleeping habits, one or both of them seemed to wander the house in the middle of the night. And Layla looked more tempting than ever, the way her robe clung to her womanly form.

If only he felt strong enough he would have broken his promise to himself and done more than talk of murder with her tonight.

"Drew, are you all right?" she asked him, stepping closer to him.

He shook himself, and knew the liquor dulled more than his pain. "You seemed worried about me."

"I was," she answered him honestly. She sat on the rug at his feet, her gown pooling around her. "I was so frightened. Who would do this?"

"I don't know," he said, his voice somber. He reached down and tilted her chin up to gaze into her blue eyes. "But I like hearing you say you worried about me. It makes me think you care."

"I do care about you, Drew," she admitted, her soft voice leaving tingles trailing down his spine. "You're my lawyer. You're going to defend my life."

He released her chin. He knew the words she said were true, but somehow he had hoped for more. Perhaps he was crazy to think the thoughts she evoked, but damn, he wanted her to say she cared about him for other reasons. He wanted to hear that she cared for him as a man.

Rising, he could feel the brandy had alleviated his pain and he needed sleep to cure him of these dangerous thoughts.

He started to give her a hand up, but realized his shoulder could not take the strain. "I'm going to bed. Sleep well, Layla."

Fourteen

Layla watched him lumber up the stairs, the pain in his shoulder making his gait stiffer than normal. Her heart ached with fear for him—and sadness that this vibrant man had undoubtedly been hurt because of her.

She rubbed her temples. She did not know for certain that he had been shot because of her; she was guessing. Though what other reason could there be for anyone to shoot Drew?

And seeing him with that white bandage wrapped around his smooth chest sapped the strength from her limbs and made her cringe inside with fear. She had felt wrung out since everyone left.

Had it hit three inches closer, that bullet would have ended his life.

She took a deep breath. Drew meant nothing to her. He was her lawyer, nothing more. A shiver went down her spine. God, how she wanted to believe that. She pushed the truth from her mind, not ready to face her feelings for this man, knowing it would only complicate a tense situation.

"Miss Layla, don't you think you should be getting to bed?" Colette commented, coming into the library. "You need your rest."

"I'm going, Colette. I just wanted a few minutes alone to think," she remarked, her mind still on Drew.

"That was a terribly close call for Mr. Drew today," Colette said, picking up the dirty glasses in the library.

"Yes. But who would shoot him?" Layla was determined to solve the riddle of who would want Drew dead and for what purpose.

Colette shrugged. "I haven't a clue. Maybe their purpose was to make sure you looked like a killer."

"Or to make sure I didn't have a lawyer for the trial." It was almost a relief to say her fear out loud. "The police suspect that I tried to kill him. I might as well put a rope around my neck and hang myself. It would be quicker," Layla exclaimed, still angry at the way the detective had accused her.

Colette made a clucking noise with her tongue. "Exactly. Maybe that's what the shooter wanted. Without Mr. Drew, your chances of going free wouldn't be too good."

Layla shivered. "What are you saying? That until the trial is over, I have the additional worry that something could happen to Drew?"

"It's possible, ma'am," Colette responded, staring at her mistress.

Layla sighed, feeling like another burden had been added. "Well, good night, Colette. Make sure that the doors are locked before you go to bed tonight."

"Yes, ma'am. Sleep well."

Layla glanced back at her. "Doubtful, but I'll try."

Three days later, Eric accompanied Drew on a visit to Bryon Sycamore. He had not heard from the man since he'd left for Baton Rouge, though the necessary papers had been sent to Mrs. Sycamore's attorney. A divorce in Louisiana was a slow process that could take more than a year.

Drew's shoulder injury kept him from handling the

STARLIGHT SURRENDER

tug and pull of the reins on his own, so Eric graciously agreed to drive him.

In the last few days, Drew had worked on Layla's case in his library at home, not ready to return to his office.

Eric had overseen the repair of the window in Drew's office and installed shades that could be pulled down at dusk. And to make Drew feel more at ease in the space, Eric moved Drew's desk to a new position. The police had increased their surveillance in the area, hoping to catch the shooter before he struck again.

Selection for the jury started on Monday, and Drew was anxious for the trial to begin. Layla looked more beautiful every day and her image haunted him. He could not let her die.

Eric pulled the buggy to a halt in front of the Sycamores' home. "Here we are."

Drew glanced at the house. "Come on, let's go. But let me do the talking. This man is a nervous, private type, so don't be surprised if he won't let you stay while we talk."

"All right," Eric agreed, grabbing Drew's satchel from the floor of the buggy.

Drew gingerly climbed down, trying not to put any weight on his left arm. The muscles were sore to the touch, and Dr. Little had warned him that any strenuous exercise could reopen the wound. He felt grateful it was not his right arm, his writing hand.

They walked up the steps of the porch and Eric rapped on the door.

In a few moments, the door was swung open by a boy of about ten. "What do you want?"

"Is your father at home?" Drew asked the child, surprised to see him.

"Just a minute." He slammed the door shut, but they could hear him yell, "Papa, someone is here to see you."

Drew and Eric looked at each other, questioning.

A few moments later, Bryon Sycamore opened the door. "Mr. Soulier, good to see you. Come in."

"I'd like you to meet my associate, Eric Bouchier."

"Mr. Bouchier."

They took a step into the house, where Bryon led them into his library. "You must have come for your money."

"Money?" Drew asked.

"Yes, didn't my wife's lawyer tell you? She's dropped her petition for a divorce." He lowered his voice. "I knew all it would take was to make Teresa understand that she would lose custody of the children and she'd return. And she did."

Sitting in a chair that Bryon indicated, Drew gazed at the man. "I've been out of the office quite a bit. Your wife's lawyer hadn't responded to me. This is the first I've heard that she'd canceled her petition."

Bryon shook his head and smiled. "Remember, I told you that Teresa would come around. And just as soon as her lawyer told her I intended to obtain custody of our children, she moved back home."

Drew nodded, the memory of the woman's bruised eye making him uncomfortable. "Since you didn't want the divorce, that's great news, Mr. Sycamore. Are things better between the two of you?"

He smiled. "Everything is back to normal. She's doing the housekeeping and I'm seeing to the field hands and the crops. The children are sleeping in their own beds again. There will be no more talk of divorce in this household."

Drew felt uneasy. Something did not feel right. "What about the man who kept coming around?"

He waved his hand with a laugh. "Teresa agreed not to let him come by anymore. So that's not a problem."

The image of Teresa Sycamore's bruised face and sad

eyes haunted Drew. "Do you mind if I speak with your wife a moment?"

"What for?" he asked suspiciously.

"Um, I wanted to tell her I took her suggestion regarding my niece's crying," he said quickly. He wanted to see Teresa Sycamore and make certain she was safe and well.

"I'll tell her," Bryon asserted. "She's busy hanging clothes. There were a lot of chores to be done when she got home."

"All right," Drew agreed, not knowing how else to try to see the woman without making his concern obvious. She was not his client and he really had no reason to speak with her, except some urge to make certain she was safe.

"Did Mr. Hoffman come to see you?" Bryon asked.

"Yes, he did."

"You ought to speak to the Democratic Club. We're trying to decide which candidate we're going to support now. Why don't you let me set up the time and location? That's the least I can do to help your campaign."

"Thank you, Mr. Sycamore. I appreciate your help," Drew responded, knowing if he pressed the issue of seeing Teresa Sycamore he would lose the man's support. And Bryon Sycamore was someone he wanted on his side.

"Well, I certainly am happy with how things turned out. Yes sir, I think this time she learned her lesson," Bryon boasted with a happy smile.

Drew felt uneasy, but the man had offered to support his campaign in so many ways. He needed to put Teresa Sycamore out of his mind.

He stood. "We had best be going, Mr. Sycamore. If you should ever need legal advice again—"

"I'll be certain to come and see you," he finished the sentence for Drew.

"Thanks."

"Nice to meet you, Mr. Sycamore," Eric called.

The two of them walked out the door and Bryon closed it behind them. Drew resisted the urge to try to sneak around to the back of the house and find Teresa Sycamore.

"That was odd," Eric commented.

"Yes," Drew admitted. "After talking with his wife, I didn't think that marriage had a chance in hell."

"So what changed?"

"The children. He sought custody of their children. I only wish I could speak with Mrs. Sycamore. Come on, let's go, before I decide to find her." Drew said, walking toward the buggy.

On Monday, Layla watched the two lawyers choose the twelve people who would decide her fate. At the end of the day twelve men sat in the jury box, gazing at her as if she were the evil mistress.

Layla picked at the food on her plate, moving her mashed potatoes around, her thoughts dwelling on how twelve ordinary people would come to a decision on whether she was to live or die for a crime she knew with certainty she did not commit. Now the man she had hated and blamed for the past year of her unhappy life with Jean would stand before a jury and convince these men of her innocence.

And she couldn't help but wonder if she trusted him.

Certainly he had his own personal reasons for wanting to win her trial, but did she have faith in him to keep her from hanging?

"Nervous?" Drew asked, sitting across the table from her.

She glanced up from her plate, staring into his eyes. Just one look from him made her insides ache and a sense of well-being come over her. It didn't make sense. He had helped Jean cheat her father and yet she found it harder and harder to blame him. And she no longer wanted to hate him.

Dreams of a family, a home, and everything she had never wanted with Jean occupied her mind once again. Things that she would never have if convicted of murder. Yet those were not the thoughts of a woman who did not trust her lawyer.

"Very nervous," she responded. "I keep returning to the same question: Who could have killed Jean?"

Drew paused. "That question wakes me in the middle of the night." He paused. "In the suite that night there was you, Colette, and George. George is testifying against you."

"He loved Jean. Why would the man murder him? What would be his motive?" Layla asked, instinctively answering Drew's unspoken question.

"I haven't found one. I've interviewed him. I've had my team searching into his background and so far they've found some interesting details, but nothing that says he killed Jean," Drew replied, his eyes intent upon her.

"What about Colette?" she asked, the memory of their conversation a couple of nights ago haunting her. "Did you investigate her background?"

"I mailed a letter off to her previous employer, but I've yet to hear from him. Colette said she was a nursemaid for a child who died," he added. "I couldn't find a motive for her either."

"What did the child die of?" Layla asked blindly, searching for anything that could help her.

"Yellow fever," Drew informed her. "Why?"

"I don't know. There's got to be something that

we're overlooking," she said, staring off into the distance. "I didn't kill him, so who did?"

Drew sat, quietly contemplating.

"What about the other wives? Did you check out Marian and Nicole?" she asked.

"They both have valid alibis."

"But if he died of poisoning, couldn't they have somehow planted the poison in advance?"

"Yes," he responded. "Marian is the only one of you who would have gained from his death and I don't think she did it because of the children," Drew stabbed at his food. "And Nicole loved him."

"What about his business associates?" Layla was ready to grasp at anything that could save her. "Could it have been Jean's business partner?"

"I thought about Louis Fourner, especially when I learned that he tried to sell the business out from under Marian, Jean's first wife. But then he turned around and gave her his portion, so whatever he gained with Jean's death, he relinquished."

"Still, he did try to sell Cuvier Shipping. Maybe he did it."

Drew sighed. "Actually, Jean's death hindered Louis, because Jean could have bought him out if he hadn't died."

"Then who?" Layla cried out, knowing that tomorrow the slow process of finding her guilty or innocent would begin. Fear gnawed at her insides.

"I don't know." Drew stared at her, pity reflected from his emerald gaze. "I've gone over my list of possible suspects and your name continues to rise to the top. We may never know who killed Jean."

Layla laid her napkin down and pushed her chair back from the table. She stood, unable to sit any longer. "I can't live with that. Everyone will always believe I did it and I will hang."

STARLIGHT SURRENDER

Drew sat watching her, not saying anything.

She took a deep breath, trying to control her fear. "So how do you plan to defend me?"

"I'm going to try to show that killing Jean did not benefit you in any way. When he died, you lost everything."

"But won't the jury think I didn't know about the other wives?" she asked. Maybe she should admit at last that she had learned of the other women the night before Jean's death. Yet she feared his reaction. He had insisted many times that she keep nothing back. At this point did it really matter?

"Yes," Drew said. "But if you had known of the other wives, the district attorney would be trying to prove you poisoned him in a fit of rage."

All thoughts of telling him everything vanished. She could not.

"I didn't poison anyone. I didn't kill Jean," she claimed, her voice rising.

"That's why tomorrow, I need you to cry when they mention his death. I need you to act the bereaved widow and wear a black dress. We've got to convince twelve people that, though yours was not a love match, you were smart enough to know that without Jean, you would have nothing."

Frustration mounted within her and she crossed her arms across her chest. "I don't want to die. I want my freedom. I want everyone to realize I'm innocent."

Drew stood and came around the table. He walked up behind Layla and wrapped his arms around her, pulling her to his chest. "You're not going to die. I'm going to get you acquitted."

He turned her to face him and his hand caressed the side of her face. Her knees went weak and she wrapped her arms around him. She leaned against his chest, careful not to hurt him, loving the way she felt so secure in his arms, so protected and cherished.

"Please, Drew. Please don't let them hang me. I'm not ready to die," she pleaded.

He hugged her tightly to him. "It's going to be all right, Layla. I'm not going to lose this case."

She felt him press his lips to the top of her head and she almost leaned back and let him kiss her. But she knew if she did, there would be no going back. She wanted nothing more than to find herself in his arms and in his bed, so instead she pressed her body against his, absorbing his strength, his warmth.

He was everything she wanted in a man.

As the carriage pulled up in front of the courthouse, Layla groaned. A crowd of reporters awaited them.

Drew looked at her and smiled. "Just let me do the talking."

He opened the door and stepped out of the carriage and the crowd swarmed toward him.

"Mr. Soulier," they called.

Drew took her hand and helped her to alight. He put his arm around her protectively and they began to make their way from the street into the courthouse, moving slowly through the newspapermen.

"Miss DuChampe, how do you feel?"

Layla ignored the man, her heart pounding with fear inside in her chest.

"Mr. Soulier, rumor has it you're going to run for mayor. When will you be making your announcement?"

Drew turned and smiled at the man and Layla felt like punching him. "I'm rather busy at the moment and I'm not ready to make my announcement just yet. But you'll be one of the first to hear."

STARLIGHT SURRENDER

"Will you be the Democratic Club's new candidate?"

"I can't answer that," he responded. "They may not want a trial lawyer for mayor. You know we do have the reputation of being diligent and thorough. And given our current city government, that's something they might not want."

The reporters laughed.

At the door, Drew turned and gave them a smile and waved, then followed her inside.

"No wonder you want to be a politician. You do that quite well," she said, gazing at him as they walked down the hall to the room where her life would be decided.

"I'll take that as a compliment. Thank you," he said his hand gripping her elbow.

They walked in and hurried to the table where they would spend their time in the coming days. Layla sank down upon her chair, anxious about what the day would bring. Drew took out his notes and began to scan through them, flipping pages.

"All rise. The Honorable Judge François Dimitrius presiding," the court bailiff intoned.

Every seat in the courtroom was filled as the crowd rose in unison. The door opened and a somber-looking man strode through the door, his dark robe flowing, as he took his seat behind the bench in the drab courtroom.

"You may be seated," the court bailiff informed them.

The judge leveled his steely gaze upon the two attorneys, and Layla felt her stomach do somersaults. She wanted to run screaming from the courtroom, as terror held her in its vise-like grip. Instead, she took a deep breath and released it slowly, trying to remain focused on the proceedings.

"Are we ready?" Judge Dimitrius asked.

Drew took her elbow and they stood along with the district attorney.

"Ready for the prosecution, Your Honor," District Attorney Finnie said, glancing over at the defense.

"Ready for the defense," Drew responded while Layla stood beside him, shaking.

"Good, then the prosecution may begin," the judge instructed, leaning back in his chair.

Drew and Layla took their seats, and the district attorney walked slowly toward the jury. In a gray suit, Paul Finnie appeared the ideal lawyer, all smiles. And Layla feared what he would say.

Underneath the table, Drew took her hand and gave it a quick reassuring squeeze, then released it to take notes.

Layla watched the prosecutor swagger in front of the jury and begin.

"Good morning, gentlemen of the jury. The state would like to thank you for the service you're doing your community, especially with a trial as publicized as this one. Convicting a woman of first-degree murder is not an easy task for me or for the twelve of you. The sentence for first-degree murder is death by hanging and the thought of a young woman dying such a heinous death is unthinkable."

He shook his head, his lips curved in a brief, sad smile intended to let the jury see he how he felt.

"But the state intends to prove to you that Layla DuChampe plotted to kill Jean Cuvier, whom she believed to be her lawful husband, and thereby regain her father's shipping company. She never loved Jean Cuvier and only married him at her father's insistence. And when Jean's company absorbed her father's business, she felt betrayed.

"Now Jean Cuvier was a flawed man, as you will hear, but he took Layla in, married her, and promised her father he'd take care of her when he bought the man's failing business."

He strode over in front of Layla and pointed to her. "The state intends to prove that the accused Layla DuChampe knowingly laced her husband's tea with a mixture of laudanum and cyanide, certain that Jean's shipping company would become hers and she could support herself from the proceeds, free from her older husband, the man she admitted to hating, whose very touch she loathed."

He walked back over in front of the jury. "This woman thought she could get away with murder. Who would believe that a beautiful woman, convent educated and proper, could be a coldhearted killer? But I can prove it."

Layla hung her head, feeling humiliated as shame overwhelmed her. He made her out to be so evil and calculating.

"The state intends to call one of Jean's own servants to testify that she and Mr. Cuvier fought over her wifely duties and that she begged Jean to return her father's business to her and let her go."

Drew patted her hand in a comforting gesture.

"And, last, we'll show how Miss DuChampe was shocked to learn that, at Mr. Cuvier's death, she was cheated of her hope to own Cuvier Shipping. For Mr. Cuvier's marriage to Miss DuChampe was not legal. He had a wife and two children residing here in New Orleans."

He strode back in front of the jury. "I know that as members of this jury you will pay close attention to the testimony the state will present, and in the end, you will agree that society should be rid of women who poison their husbands for money and wealth, that no one is above the law, not even Miss DuChampe."

Layla felt a hot anger rise toward the man. He'd

twisted the truth around to make her appear guilty without a shred of evidence.

Finnie took his seat, and Drew rose from his chair, without saying a word and walked before the jury.

"Good morning."

He stared at each one of them for a moment. "I'm not sure I know the Layla DuChampe that the prosecutor described, though his description of Jean Cuvier was much too polite. I'm sure you've all heard or read about Jean in the papers. Oh, he did the right thing by Layla but not in the eyes of the law. He married her when he already had not one, but two, other wives living right here in the state of Louisiana."

Drew paused for emphasis, his hands crossed behind his back.

"Bigamy is against the law, and it's morally wrong, but he kept all three of his supposed wives in residence within two hours of each other. Arrogantly, Mr. Cuvier didn't appear to worry about their feelings or their lives, because he didn't fear getting caught."

Drew walked before them, steady and sure, his every step carefully planned and Layla admired his self-confidence. "Jean had his legal first wife, Marian Cuvier, and their two children. But that wasn't enough for this man. He then married a young woman named Nicole who lived on a plantation right up the river." Drew shook his head and almost laughed. "And then along comes Anthony DuChampe, sick, with a business that Jean coveted and a daughter whose future he feared for. He was dying. And Jean smooth-talked him into selling him his business for a pittance, with the promise he'd marry his daughter and take care of her."

Like a preacher's, Drew's voice rose and fell, pausing at certain moments and rising at others. "For a man like Mr. DuChampe, that seemed like a dream come true. He could die in peace and Layla, his only child, would be taken care of."

Drew's voice grew softer. "So a marriage was made. Each party gained something the other could provide. Marriages are made this way every day. Women need husbands who can take care of them, provide for them financially, and give them children and shelter. Men need a wife, someone to care for them and run their households. Anthony DuChampe had found Layla a husband, someone who would take care of her."

Layla stared at Drew, wondering how he had read her so completely.

He paused. "But everything wasn't so wonderful in paradise. Jean liked having a much younger wife and though she didn't enjoy being with him, he wanted her the way a man wants a woman. The way a man wants his wife. So she gave him laudanum to squelch his desire."

Drew smiled at the jurors. "Why would this woman"—he pointed to Layla—"kill the very man whose support she relied on? Why would she poison the man who provided for her every need?"

Drew smiled and Layla sat amazed at his confidence, his polish. She had never seen him in the courtroom before and now she knew he was very good. If anyone could save her, it was Drew.

"Jean had many enemies. In addition to two other wives, he also kept a mistress." The crowd gasped. "He had enemies in the shipping business and even workers who didn't think much of him.

"The state has to prove without a shadow of a doubt that Miss DuChampe killed Jean Cuvier. Honestly, I don't think they can. Layla DuChampe is to be pitied. She thought she was married in the eyes of the law and of God, to a husband who would take care of her financially if not emotionally. And when she's reeling from the knowledge that she's just one of three so-called wives, the police arrest her for murder, based on circumstantial evidence."

Pacing in front of the jury, Drew continued. "The defense will present a doctor's testimony as to the difficulty of killing someone with laudanum. Cyanide leaves an easily discernible flush. Why would my client use a substance that would be so obvious?"

He stood in front of the jury. "You're about to hear testimony from both sides of this story. But in the end, if you're going to convict Layla DuChampe, you must believe in her guilt beyond all reasonable doubt. And I don't think that's possible. The woman sitting in that chair is a victim of Jean Cuvier, not the murderer the state claims her to be."

Drew walked across the quiet room and winked at her as he sat down. She felt a little more at ease, but not much.

Watching Drew, Layla realized that she had more faith and trust in him than she'd ever had before. No longer did she question whether or not he would defend her to the best of his abilities, because she saw the passionate desire to win on his face when he spoke to the jury. And that could not be faked.

Her heart swelled with a love she could no longer deny. As she watched him defend her, determined to prove to the world that she was innocent, she realized how much she cared for this man, how much she loved him.

She knew he would do his best to save her. Just as he had done his best to take care of her.

"Prosecution, you may call your first witness," the judge intoned, snapping her out of her reverie.

"The prosecution calls Marian Fournet," Paul Finnie announced.

Marian stood and slowly walked down the aisle to the

witness stand, her skirts swishing as she made her way down the crowded aisle.

Layla was shocked to learn that Jean's legal first wife had wed none other than Jean's partner.

She leaned over and whispered in Drew's ear. "She married Louis?"

"Yes, I knew Louis loved her, but I didn't know they'd married," Drew returned.

"Don't you think that's suspicious?" Layla asked.

"Trust me, no," he whispered, frowning as Marian was sworn in.

Paul approached the witness stand. "Mrs. Fournet, were you once married to Jean Cuvier?"

"Yes," she replied.

"And did you consider your marriage to be happy?"

"Not in recent years," she answered.

"And why was this so?"

She frowned. "Jean seldom spent time at home with me and the children, though in the end, I welcomed his absences."

"Did you ever suspect your husband of keeping another woman?" the prosecutor asked.

Marian's expression changed. "Yes, I feared he had another woman in his life, but didn't pursue it because of my children."

The prosecutor nodded. "Tell us what happened the morning you learned of Jean's death."

Marian related how she was asked to come to the hotel, where she found the police, along with two other young women, both claiming to be married to Jean. Layla listened carefully. The awful morning seemed so long ago.

"Did you know the women?"

"No," she responded.

"Though you were Mr. Cuvier's legal wife, did you allow them to attend the reading of Jean's will?"

"Yes, sir, I did."

"Why?"

"They believed they were married to Jean and I didn't know if my husband had provided for them in his will or not. I thought it would be better if they were present so they would have no doubts regarding my husband's wishes," she looked at Layla, her eyes dark with sadness.

"At this meeting how did the defendant act?"

"She and the other woman, Nicole, stood off by themselves."

"Did the defendant say anything at this meeting in regard to her feelings for Mr. Cuvier?"

Marian frowned. "Yes, in the course of the conversation Nicole declared her love for Jean, but Layla said she hated my husband, which shocked us."

The prosecutor walked in front of the jury, gazing at them intently. "What did Mr. Cuvier leave Miss DuChampe?"

Marian hung her head. "The will was written before her marriage to my husband. He left her nothing."

A silence filled the court as the prosecutor paused, still slowly pacing in front of the jury, letting them absorb this information.

"How would you describe Miss DuChampe's behavior when she learned she would receive nothing?"

Marian glanced at Layla apologetically. "She ran from the building, crying."

The prosecutor moved to the side of Marian so the jury could clearly see her.

"Mrs. Fournet, do you believe that Layla killed your husband?"

Drew stood up. "Objection! He's asking a non-expert witness for her opinion."

"Sustained," the judge replied.

The prosecutor smiled. "Your witness."

STARLIGHT SURRENDER

Finnie took a seat and Drew walked up to the witness stand. "Hello, Mrs. Fournet. Did you love Jean?"

Marian frowned, a sigh escaping her. "At one time, I loved him."

"What about at the time of the murder?" Drew asked.

"No. Our marriage was essentially over, though we still lived as man and wife when he was home," she acknowledged.

"Did you ever entertain thoughts of killing Mr. Cuvier?"

"Of course not."

"To your knowledge, did Miss DuChampe know about you or Nicole?"

Marian thought for a moment. "No, I think we were all shocked to learn of each other's existence that morning in the hotel."

"I'd like to ask you a few more questions regarding the reading of Jean's will."

"All right," she said.

"Is it true that because my client's father had sold his business to Jean, which included the family home, that my client lost everything of value that she owned?"

"Yes, it was tragic. Jean folded her father's business and the family home, into Cuvier Shipping. Miss DuChampe lost it all with Jean's death."

"Would you say that my client was happy to learn this news?"

"Oh, no. She was very upset. She kept repeating that she had no home, no place to go. It was quite distressing."

Drew nodded and watched the jury's response. "At this meeting, you said my client told everyone that she hated Jean." Drew acknowledged. "Have you ever said that you hated somebody when you were distraught and really didn't mean it?"

Marian smiled. "Of course. I think I even said it about Jean several times."

"You've admitted you didn't love Jean any longer. You've told us that you hated Jean at times. Did you poison your husband, Jean Cuvier?"

"Objection!" the district attorney cried, rising to his feet.

"Overruled," the judge said calmly. "I'll allow the question."

"Did you poison Jean?" Drew asked again, knowing the answer but hoping to plant doubt in the jury's mind.

"No, I did not poison Jean Cuvier," Marian replied stoically.

"But weren't you just as wronged by Jean as Nicole and Layla? Didn't you inherit all of Jean's worldly possessions?"

"Yes, but I could never kill my children's father."

"Yet, you did have more motive to kill Jean than, say, the other women?"

She paused frowning. "Maybe."

"Thank you, Your Honor, I'm finished with the witness," Drew said and returned to his chair.

"You may step down, Mrs. Fournet," the judge responded.

Fifteen

Drew awakened to the sound of pounding on the front door of his house. Who could be calling at this hour? He rose groggily from bed to glance at the clock. Four in the morning.

Wrapping his robe around his nightclothes, he hurried down the stairs. He glanced out a window to see a uniformed policeman standing outside on the steps.

He would have to talk to him. But what in hell was going on? He opened the door and frowned.

"Drew Soulier?" the uniformed man asked.

"Yes?" he questioned, wondering why the police were on his doorstep at four in the morning. "What's wrong?"

"Do you know a man named Bryon Sycamore?"

A chill ran through him and the sleep cleared from his brain. "Yes, I'm his lawyer. Why?"

"He's dead."

"What?"

"He was killed by his wife, Teresa Sycamore, early this morning," the policeman explained.

Shock racked Drew, along with a feeling of déjà vu. "How did it happen?"

"Can't tell you, sir. You need to come with me to the precinct house. You're wanted for questioning. And

Mrs. Sycamore has asked to see you," the man said. "She's in police custody."

Teresa Sycamore wanted to see him? The memory of her bruised eye haunted him. Could Bryon have tried to hurt her again?

"Of course," Drew said stepping back into the house. "Come in and wait while I change clothes, Officer."

"Thank you," he said stepping into the house.

Drew hurried upstairs, suddenly conviced that Bryon had inflicted violence on Teresa, if she had indeed killed her husband. Five minutes later he was dressed and rushing out the door with the policeman. It didn't take long for them to reach the precinct.

He walked in and saw Detective Dunegan waiting for him. "Mr. Soulier, we seem to be seeing quite a bit of each other lately."

Drew smiled, not feeling cheerful in the least. "Yes, so we are, Detective Dunegan. How was my client killed?"

"Teresa Sycamore put a bullet in him," the detective informed him shaking his head. "Their children were upstairs when she killed him."

Drew nodded, controlling his emotions. "Where are the children now?"

"They've been picked up by her mother. We have Mrs. Sycamore in custody. She admitted to killing Mr. Sycamore. Claims it was self-defense."

"Can you tell me what happened?" Drew asked.

"First you answer my questions, then I'll answer yours," the detective responded, taking a seat behind his desk. "Mrs. Sycamore told me that you had been working on a bed-and-board divorce for this couple up until the last month."

"I represented Mr. Sycamore," Drew said, pulling up the chair across from the detective. He ran his hand through his rumpled hair and preceded to tell Detective Dunegan everything he could regarding the

Sycamores' request for a divorce. He also told the detective about the fading bruise he had seen on Mrs. Sycamore's eye when he visited her.

Twenty minutes later, the detective looked up from the notes he'd been making and gave a tired sigh. "I think that's all I need for now." He leaned back in the chair. "As for what happened, Mr. Sycamore got into an argument with his wife. When he started taking swings at her with his fists, their son tried to intervene and he slammed the boy into a wall. Mrs. Sycamore went into the library, got a gun, came back, and shot him."

Drew rubbed his hand across his face, filled with regret. He'd seen the signs, but he'd essentially chosen to ignore them. He had cared about what Bryon Sycamore could do for his campaign, to his everlasting shame.

But what could he have done? Teresa Sycamore wasn't his client! He had been working with Bryon, yet instinctively he had known that there was something wrong in their home and that his client had violent tendencies.

Anything would have been better than letting Teresa Sycamore and her children suffer at the hands of Bryon once again.

"May I see Mrs. Sycamore?" It was the least he could do.

"I'll give you ten minutes with her, Counselor," the Detective promised.

He walked Drew down the hall to a room where he left him. Five minutes later a haggard, bruised Teresa Sycamore walked into the room. Her cheek was red and swollen, her blue eyes barely visible. She looked defeated with her hands cuffed, her shoulders slumped.

"Mr. Soulier," she said weakly.

"Mrs. Sycamore," he mumbled, stunned at the visible evidence of the beating she had endured, fearing that the man's huge fists had hurt her son. "How are you holding up?"

"I'm all right, though I'm worried about my children," she responded slowly.

"Did the police get a doctor for you?"

"Yes, he examined me and my son." Her voice quivered. "Thank God, he's not badly injured. But I thought . . . it's hard to talk about it."

"The police told me a little about what happened. I'd like to hear your version."

She hung her head for just a moment before she spoke. "Whenever something wasn't done the way Bryon thought it should be done, he would get angry. I learned not to argue with him, but just do what he said, but even that didn't seem to be enough. He still found reasons to hit me."

"Was that why you wanted the divorce?" Drew asked.

She barely moved her head. "Yes. I knew I needed to get my children away from him, for he thought nothing of hitting me in front of them. I knew that someday my son Martin would get the courage to defend me and . . ."

Tears fell from her swollen eyes.

Drew stared at her, his blood running cold. He couldn't help but feel some responsibility for her plight. "I'm so sorry."

She sniffed and shook her head. "Tonight he woke me from a sound sleep to march me into the kitchen because some dishes needed washing. I was going to just take the beating, but his yelling woke Martin." She stopped, her voice choking, crying again. She put her hand to her face and wiped the tears away awkwardly, the handcuffs still on. "My son . . . my son tried to stop his father and Bryon backhanded him. The smack of his hand hitting that child . . . I thought Bryon had killed him. Blood gushed from his split lip and he hit the wall hard."

She took a deep breath. "Bryon wouldn't let me go to him, told me the boy needed toughening up. Martin managed to get up and he ran back to his room. When Bryon finally thought he'd beaten me into submission, I started doing the dishes. But as soon as I could, I went into his library and found his gun."

She swallowed visibly fighting back tears. "Bryon always kept a loaded pistol in his desk. I took that gun and when I came back into the kitchen, Bryon was looking for me. Thank God, my son had returned to his room, for I couldn't shoot his father in front of him. But I had no problem pulling the trigger when Bryon started screaming at me and telling me I was too worthless to live. He reached for the gun and I shot him."

She put her face in her hands and cried, big gulping sobs coming from her. "I had no choice. He hit my son. I could not let him hurt my children. Never my sweet babies."

Drew was stunned. He'd advised Bryon Sycamore to obtain custody of his children, presuming then Teresa would return. And now his client was dead, Teresa badly beaten and their son hurt.

All because Drew needed Bryon Sycamore's help.

Intent on his political career, he'd ignored all the signs of abuse. At the moment, Drew really didn't like what he'd become.

He reached out and patted her on the shoulder, hoping to comfort her. "Mrs. Sycamore," he said gently. "Do you have a lawyer?"

"No, I can't afford one. I used all the money I'd hidden away on the divorce lawyer. I wanted that divorce so badly. But when Bryon told me he was seeking custody of the children, I knew I couldn't risk him taking them away from me. I had no choice but to stay with him, to protect my children." She sniffed, wiping away her tears.

If only he had acted at the time she might not be sitting here tonight, accused of murder. The thought of her in prison while her children grew up without their father or mother disturbed him.

"If you'll have me, I'll be your lawyer," he offered.

Her eyes opened as wide as they could in her puffy face and she stared at him in disbelief. "I can't afford to pay you."

"I'm not asking you to pay me. I want to help you," he insisted.

"But why?" she asked.

"The signs of abuse were there and I ignored them," he admitted. "I should have known from the moment I saw your yellowed eye that things were not right. I should have done something. But I didn't."

She shook her head. "What could you have done? The law doesn't give a woman much recourse when her husband likes to punch her. I'm not saying I won't accept your help, but I don't want you to feel obligated because of what happened tonight. When Bryon hit our son, he brought this on himself. Nobody abuses my children."

Drew nodded. "I advised him to seek custody of your children, knowing you would come home to him rather than risk losing your children. It's my fault to some degree that you're sitting here tonight beaten and your son hurt." He paused, looking at her shocked expression. "I wouldn't blame you at all for hating me. But I sincerely want to help you any way that I can."

She didn't reply, just stared at him sadly.

"So will you accept my offer for help?" he asked the exhausted woman.

She nodded her head and the tears ran down her swollen cheeks. "Of course I will, though I wish to God you had never advised Bryon to get custody of the children."

"I understand. But I promise you that I will do everything that I can to get you aquitted. We'll plead self-defense. I'll have a photographer come over tomorrow and take pictures of you with your permission, and your son. I want a jury to see exactly what Bryon did to you. I want to right the wrong I've done to you and your children. I want you all to be together again."

The tears streamed down her face and she nodded her head. "Thank you, Mr. Soulier."

Drew grimaced. He didn't deserve her kindness.

Later the same morning, Drew and Layla arrived at the courtroom to the usual crowd of reporters waiting. Layla couldn't help but notice that Drew seemed unusually quiet this morning. He had barely said anything to her on the ride from the house to the courtroom.

They descended from the buggy and the mass of reporters rushed at them.

"Miss DuChampe, how is the trial going?"

She ignored the question. Drew gripped her elbow and together they hurried up the steps of the courtroom.

He didn't stop to chat with the reporters or even say hello to them this morning. Since the first morning of the trial, he had always talked to them.

Layla glanced at him as they continued up the steps, hurrying into the building, leaving the newspapermen behind.

"What's wrong with you today?"

"I've got things on my mind," he acknowledged.

"Like what?"

"If I wanted to talk about them, I would," he said holding open the door to the courtroom.

"I'm sorry I asked," she said, feeling frustrated at the way he had shut himself away from her. "Why did you leave the house early this morning?"

"An urgent matter—I had to see a client," he responded.

"I suppose this is one of those things that you're not going to tell me," she said, wondering at her own sanity. She knew she loved this man, cared about him and worried about him, but he could be difficult and distant at times.

He frowned. "I don't want to discuss it."

He set his satchel down at the table they occupied in front of the judge and jury. She took a deep breath, trying to ease the tension within her.

She wanted to know more, but a courtroom full of people did not seem the appropriate place for a personal discussion.

But before she could even whisper another question the bailiff came out of the judge's chambers.

"All rise for the Honorable Judge François Dimitrius."

The packed courtroom stood in unison, the noise of shuffling feet loud in the room.

"You may be seated."

The morning passed by quickly as Layla watched the jurors listen to the different witnesses called to testify and give their knowledge of the murder. First, they heard from Detective Dunegan who told them about the discovery of Jean's body.

About to take the stand was their servant, George Antoine. She knew her character would be shredded even more, for George had never cared for her. She glanced at Drew. He gazed at her distantly, as if he didn't see her at all. Something still troubled him.

George was sworn in.

"Your name, sir?" The prosecution asked.

"George Antoine."

"And how did you know the deceased?"

"I was his servant for the last ten years."

"So you worked for Mr. Cuvier?" the prosecutor asked, strolling in front of the witness stand, as if he couldn't linger in one place for very long.

"Yes, sir."

"Tell me what happened the night Mr. Cuvier died."

"Mr. Cuvier didn't get home until late that evening. Normally Mrs. Cuvier would have been in bed, but she waited up for him."

"Did you wait up for your employer?"

"No, sir. My duties were mainly in the morning, helping him dress, preparing his clothes and keeping his room cleaned. I took care of everything so that he could concentrate on his business and his women."

"Continue, Mr. Antoine. What else happened the night Jean died?"

"About midnight, I awoke to the sound of the two of them fighting. She yelled at him, that he owed her for her father's business and Mr. Cuvier laughed at her. A little while later, I heard him yelling at her that he wouldn't give her a dime. That she was going to stay right here in New Orleans with him."

"What was her response?"

"She called him a selfish bastard."

"Did you hear anything else that night?"

"They seemed to lower their voices after that. Eventually it got quiet and I went to sleep."

"Did you see Mr. Cuvier that night?"

"No, sir, I heard them arguing, but I never actually saw him."

"Did you wake up and hear anyone else in the hotel suite that night? Any strangers? Anyone who didn't belong in the room?"

"No, sir. After they quit fighting it got real quiet."

The prosecutor nodded. "What about the next morning. When did you find out that Mr. Cuvier was dead?"

"The next morning, Colette found him in his room on the floor, dead."

"Thank you, Mr. Antoine." The prosecutor turned to Drew. "Your witness."

Drew stood up and walked across the room. For a moment he paced before the jury not saying a word, his wrists crossed behind his back. Then he turned and looked at the witness.

"Good morning, Mr. Antoine. Did you know about Mr. Cuvier's wives?" Drew asked.

"No, sir. He told me they were his mistresses."

"And you believed him?" Drew raised his brows in disbelief.

"Not really, for each one called themselves Mrs. Cuvier. But Mr. Cuvier paid my salary each month and he treated me nice."

"So you went along with Mr. Cuvier. Why didn't you tell the wives?"

"Why should I? It would only make Mr. Cuvier angry and get me fired. It was none of my business," the man said with a shrug.

"Even when it was against the law?"

George chuckled. "People break the law every day and I don't feel it's my duty to turn them in."

"So, Mr. Antoine, you have a disregard for the law and believe a man can have as many wives as he chooses?"

The man frowned and shrugged his shoulder. "Jean told me they were his mistresses and I let it go."

"Did it ever occur to you how this would affect these women and their children?"

"I'm not paid to think. I'm an employee," he responded a stubborn tilt to his chin.

Drew frowned and walked about the room.

"Did Mr. and Mrs. Cuvier fight often?"

"Yes. Usually late at night."

"Can you tell the jury what they argued about at night?"

"Most of the time I couldn't hear the actual words, but I know she didn't enjoy the physical part of marriage."

"You testified that she said he owed her for her father's business. Did they often fight about this subject?"

"Before she had accused him of tricking her father, but I never heard her demand money for the business."

"Did she often wait up for him?"

"No, sir."

"Would you describe their marriage as happy?"

"No, sir."

"Did you know Miss DuChampe's father?"

"Yes, sir."

"Why didn't you tell him that Jean Cuvier was married?"

"Not my place, sir."

"Isn't it because Anthony DuChampe, Layla's father, once fired your brother and you wanted revenge?"

"Of course not."

"Isn't that the reason you kept silent and let Miss DuChampe think she was married when indeed her vows had been nothing but a sham."

"It was none of my business," the man said again, his voice rising.

"If not informing the authorities of how Jean had deceived these women was any of your business, then why did you speak to the police regarding Miss DuChampe?" Drew asked. "Were you afraid the police might suspect you?"

"No!" the man said, irritated. "I wouldn't kill Mr. Cuvier," he insisted.

"Have you ever killed anyone?" Drew asked.

"Objection," the prosecutor shouted jumping up. "Irrelevant."

"Your Honor, I'm trying to show that Mr. Antoine could be a possible suspect. He was in the hotel suite that night."

The judge frowned. "I'll allow it."

George frowned, his face flushed with rage. "That's not fair. I was young and angry."

"Answer the question, Mr. Antoine." Drew demanded. "Have you ever killed anyone before?"

The man swallowed nervously and let out a sigh. "When I was eighteen, I accidentally killed a sailor in a bar fight."

Drew paused, letting the jurors absorb this information.

"How easy is it to obtain cyanide?" Drew asked.

"I don't know."

"Did Mr. Cuvier's shipping company happen to use cyanide for any purpose?" Drew asked.

"I wouldn't know."

"Well, I checked, Mr. Antoine and yes, his company sometimes uses cyanide to keep the warehouses free of rats. So you would have had access to the poison," Drew insisted.

George's face turned red. "A lot of people would."

"How did Mr. Cuvier treat you as an employee?"

"He took good care of me."

"He never yelled at you? He never berated you, oh, for example, when laundry wasn't done to his specifications?" Drew asked stepping in front of the witness.

"On occasion, but most of the time he was good to me."

"Now about the morning before Mr. Cuvier died—did he become upset with you?"

The witness squirmed in his chair. "He only yelled when he was irritable."

"Did Mr. Cuvier yell at you the morning before his death?" Drew insisted standing before George.

"It was understandable. He was frustrated."

"Answer the question, Mr. Antoine, did he yell at you?"

"Yes," the man answered shortly, his voice raised.

"What did you do that upset him?"

"I hadn't gotten the starch right in his shirts. He was angry because they were too stiff," George spouted, his frustration mounting.

"Did his raised voice make you angry?"

George looked at the judge. "Do I have to answer that?"

"Yes, you do, Mr. Antoine," he responded.

"I hated it when he yelled."

"So let me get this straight. You are a man who cares little for the law, with a considerable temper, and who has already taken another man's life."

"Objection!" Finnie yelled.

"Sustained! Watch your step, Counselor," the judge admonished.

"I withdraw the statement," Drew said. "The defense is finished with this witness, Your Honor."

Layla sighed with relief, feeling Drew had turned a bad situation into at least a tolerable one.

When he reached the desk, she leaned over and whispered. "Good job, Counselor."

"Who's your next witness?" the judge asked.

"The prosecution calls the city coroner, Dr. Benson."

The doctor put his hand on the Bible and was sworn in. He had first detected traces of the cyanide that killed Jean.

"Dr. Benson, tell the court what you found when you arrived at the hotel room," the prosecutor asked the witness as he paced in front of the jury.

"When I first arrived, the servant let me in and took

me to the bedroom where the body lay. Since the corpse was cold, I knew he'd been dead for several hours. At first I assumed he'd died of natural causes, but then I detected a faint bitter-almond odor, which is indicative of cyanide poisoning. Upon further investigation, I noticed that his skin appeared pinker than normal and concluded that he'd been poisoned."

"What would cause his skin to appear pinker?"

"Cyanide prevents the red blood cells from obtaining oxygen. Therefore, carbon dioxide increases in the bloodstream, which leads to loss of consciousness and asphyxiation."

"Is that the only symptom of cyanide poisoning?"

"No. Usually the victim starts to gasp for breath, then there is dizziness, headache, nausea, and vomiting before they die."

"So Jean could have suffered for hours?" the prosecutor asked.

"Hard to tell. There was also laudanum in his system. He could have been unconscious when the symptoms manifested."

"Do you have any idea how much Mr. Cuvier had been given of either laudanum or cyanide?"

"I couldn't answer that question."

The prosecutor nodded his head. "One last question, Dr. Benson. Can you describe how Miss DuChampe acted during the time you were at the hotel suite?"

"Objection," Drew called. "That calls for speculation on the part of the witness."

"I'll redirect my question, Your Honor." Paul Finnie smiled at Drew, knowing he'd been caught. "While you were there, was Miss DuChampe crying or visibly upset at the death of her supposed husband?"

"No. She seemed calm and didn't shed a tear that I saw."

"Thank you, Doctor. Your witness," the prosecutor said looking at Drew.

Drew stood and walked to the witness stand.

"The defendant has admitted to putting laudanum in her husband's tea. In fact, she often game him the drug to keep him from seeking her out for unwanted intercourse. Was the small amount she gave him each night enough to kill Jean?"

"If a person is used to taking laudanum, it's difficult to overdose. She would have had to give him a large amount."

"Could you tell from the autopsy how much laudanum Mr. Cuvier had been given?"

"I can't answer that question."

"In your opinion, Doctor, did laudanum kill Mr. Cuvier?"

"No, sir. I believe it was the cyanide."

Drew smiled. "Thank you, Doctor." He turned and looked at the judge. "No further questions, Your Honor."

The judge looked at the prosecutor. "Next witness."

Layla glanced at Drew and he gave her a reassuring look.

Her heart seemed to swell with emotion, though she was troubled. It seemed that the trial would never end. She would never be free to love him. . . .

Drew sat in the library, the light turned down low, a glass of brandy in his hand. He couldn't get the memory of Teresa Sycamore from his mind. Her bruised and haggard face haunted him. God, how he'd let her down.

Now, in the midst of Layla's trial his mind seemed splintered and unable to focus. Partly because of Bryon's murder and partly because he knew he was using Layla's trial to gain the public's attention. The Democratic Club would be announcing their candidate any day now and he intended to win their backing and become the city's newest mayor.

Layla had reason to accuse him of taking her case only for the publicity. And yes, she was right, but also he had taken her case for the opportunity to be . . .

What? To be with Layla? Their one night together was without a doubt the best sexual experience of his life, but she would never be accepted in the social circles that his career required him to seek out.

His own father had warned him not to become involved with her and yet he wanted nothing more than to find his way to her bed again, politics be damned.

Sixteen

Layla lay awake for over two hours trying to sleep, her mind going over the day's events. Tired and needing sleep, she was haunted by the coroner's testimony.

Drew had told her about the coroner's report showing that Jean had indeed died of cyanide poisoning, but still she feared the laudanum she provided had kept Jean from seeking help. And how many jurors thought that she laced his tea with more than laudanum?

More than anything, the night Jean died, she had felt a sense of relief, of freedom and an eagerness to get away the next day. Her future seemed brighter somehow than since the day she married Jean, in that false ceremony that meant nothing.

Though how could the jury continue to think she was innocent after the coroner testified she remained calm and did not shed a tear? Of course she had felt relieved Jean was out of her life, but she had also been shocked that he was dead. Either way, she had planned to leave the next day. One more day and she would have been in Baton Rouge when Jean met his untimely end.

Throwing back the covers, she gave up on sleep. With a yank she grabbed her wrapper, slipping it on over her nightgown. She opened the door and heard nothing.

Tiptoeing past Drew's room, she made her way down the stairs, determined to find a book to read. At the bottom, she turned and saw a light shining from beneath the library door.

She crossed the entryway and gave the door a slight push. Drew sat in the chair, a brandy glass in one hand, staring into the distance, a frown creasing his forehead.

"And to think I worried about waking you when I tiptoed past your room," she said, startling him.

He looked up, but didn't say anything as she walked into the room. She took a chair across from him and watched him. Preoccupied and remote, Drew sat for several minutes in silence, not saying anything.

"Am I interrupting your concentration? You've had something on your mind all day," she said, feeling disappointed. When she'd seen him down here, she'd thought . . . what? That she longed for the sense of security she felt in his arms. How once again she wanted to feel his lips on her mouth, his hands cup her breasts. To experience the sensual joy he had made her feel on that night so long ago?

To feel his naked body sliding over hers one more time.

Though she had tried to lock away those memories, each time he looked at her, she remembered some sensation of their lovemaking that night.

She stood up to leave, since he had not responded.

"No, stay," he muttered. "I'm sorry. I can't seem to get a new client off my mind."

"What is the case about?" she asked sinking back down into the chair.

He gave a frustrated laugh. "Ordinary enough at its beginning. A bed-and-board divorce of a couple with two children. Only now it's changed from a divorce to a murder trial."

"I heard someone talking in court about a murder

that happened just last night," Layla said. "Was that your client who killed her husband?"

"No, my client was the dead husband. And now since I feel partly responsible, I'm taking on the wife's case."

"But why would you feel responsible?" she asked, not understanding how he could blame himself.

"Because I ignored my better judgment." Balling his hand into a fist, he smacked it against his palm. "My client didn't tell me that he beat his wife and though I had my suspicions, I ignored my instincts and helped him file for custody of his children. So his wife, fearful of losing the children, returned. And then one night his son tried to stop him from beating his mother. He backhanded his ten-year-old boy into a wall."

"Oh no," Layla exclaimed watching an expression of pain shift across Drew's features. "Is the boy all right?"

"His lip was split and he has a slight concussion. But his mother . . ." Drew sighed, the sound heavy and filled with pain. "The mother looks like the man tried to kill her."

Layla didn't say anything, but listened to him, realizing he had carried this knowledge with him all day, brooding over his part in this tragedy.

"His wife is a quiet, gentle woman. She was determined to make sure he could never hurt her children again. She ended his life with one shot." Drew took a swig from his glass of brandy.

"And now you feel responsible."

He gazed at her, his eyes shimmering in the lamplight. "In some ways, yes."

She stood and walked over to him. Kneeling on the floor beside his chair, she put her hand on his arm. "Tell me what else you could have done."

"Layla, I know there are virtually no laws that exist to help women like her. But I don't want to believe there was nothing I could have done to help. At the very least, I could have put her and the children on a train heading out of town."

Layla paused knowing a man like Drew could not accept his powerlessness.

"Women like your client's wife have few choices. Put up with the abuse, hide from him or kill him. Sounds to me like she defended herself. I hope she doesn't die for it."

He took another sip from his brandy glass, closed his eyes and sighed. "That's not the worst. You see, her husband, my client, was a powerful member of the Democratic Club. An organization I've been wooing for quite some time, as you know."

He leaned over and put his head in his hands, still holding onto the brandy snifter. "I feel so guilty."

Surprised at the way he questioned his part in Mr. Sycamore's death, Layla felt a flash of pity for him. "We all make mistakes and you are a very ambitious man."

"Sometimes I don't know if running for mayor is my dream or my father's."

Never before had Drew opened himself up so intimately, so completely.

She sighed. "Only you can answer that."

"Do I want to curry favor with people like Bryon Sycamore? Or deal with crooked policemen and dirty politicians every day?" he asked, more to himself than to her.

She rubbed his arm to comfort him.

"The council members now in prison and the impeachment of the last mayor should warn you that New Orleans politics is not the cleanest," she said quietly.

"No, they're not. And yet part of me wants to change things for the better," he said. "But how can I make a difference when corruption is so rampant?"

She said nothing, knowing he just needed someone to listen. In the depths of his soul, Drew was a troubled

STARLIGHT SURRENDER

man who cared deeply about the choices he made and she loved him all the more for it.

"Only you can make that decision," she finally said.

"Layla, helping women like Teresa Sycamore is a much more rewarding experience than settling fights between council members and ward bosses. Didn't I go to school to practice law?" he paused for a moment. "For years I've dreamed of being mayor, but am I really seeking the office for the right reasons?"

Layla understood his confusion, hoping she could help him find his way. She wanted to comfort him, but sensed he needed someone to listen to his troubled thoughts, his doubts.

"I fear that Teresa Sycamore will not receive fair treatment down at the jail. They'll assign her case to a dishonest detective who won't care about her any more than he cares for the whore he threw in jail last week." He sighed, his frustration obvious, his voice rising, "This woman has two young children who need her with them, not locked up behind bars."

"But she did kill her husband?" Layla asked softly.

"Yes, but not many people will blame her when I show the jury pictures of the child's bruises. Of her own bruises."

Layla's heart warmed and in that moment she was glad that Drew had forced her to accept him as her lawyer. Until this moment, she had not realized the depth of his caring for his clients. Yes, he'd taken her case for the wrong reasons, but he cared about his clients, he agonized over them and she knew there was no other person she would want to represent her.

"What are you going to do to help her?" she asked, knowing instinctively that Drew could not sit by and watch this woman go to jail for the rest of her life.

"I've taken on her case and will serve as her defense attorney. I'm going down to the courthouse tomorrow and ask that the case be dismissed or the charge changed to voluntary manslaughter. When he hit her son, she had no recourse but to kill him. She'd tried leaving."

He sighed deeply, lost in thought.

After a long moment, Layla realized that Drew was gazing at her with obvious affection. "You've been sitting there listening to me for the last hour, saying very little. And you've not condemned me for my lack of action."

"You're taking steps to right what you consider is a wrong, so how can I denounce you? I don't know what you could have done to stop Bryon Sycamore from hurting his family. He could easily have replaced you as his lawyer."

He put his fingers underneath her chin. "Thank you for listening. I want to help this woman. And a long time ago I wanted to be mayor to help bring the corruption to an end. But now I doubt I could be effective enough to bring about change. And being mayor isn't worth compromising my own integrity."

She smiled and held out her hand to him. "Come to bed, Drew. It's late and we both have to be alert tomorrow in court."

He finished his brandy, set the glass down and reached out to take her hand. With his good arm he helped her rise to her feet. As his hand clasped hers, her pulse tripped and her breath caught in her throat. He looked at her, his eyes the color of green grass after a rain, with the light of passion in his gaze.

He released her hand.

"Yes, we should be getting to bed," he said though his voice did not sound convincing.

He took her arm, his hand searing her with his heat as the two of them walked through the library and out the door. With each step, Layla could feel the tension in her mounting. Nice women did not offer their beds to gentlemen they were not married to, but then nice women did not stand trial for murder with the possibility they could die soon.

When they reached the top of the stairs, Drew released her. For a moment neither one of them said anything, as they stood outside Layla's room, not touching, the air fairly singing with tension.

Finally Drew brushed a lock of hair away from her face. "Thanks for listening to me tonight. I don't think anyone has ever done that for me before."

She took his hand and brought it to her mouth, placing her lips against the tips of his fingers, she moved her mouth down his hand, kissing until she reached the center of his palm.

Drew inhaled sharply. "God, Layla."

Cupping his hand on her face, she moved her cheek against his palm letting his fingers caress her cheek. Slowly she slid his palm across her cheeks, down her throat, her chest, until his hand rested on her breast.

With a gentle squeeze, he cupped her breast, his fingers toying with her nipple.

"Are you sure?" he said, his breathing heavy, understanding her unspoken invitation.

She didn't reply. Still holding his hand, she drew him into her room and quietly shut the door.

The moment the door closed behind him, Drew pulled her into his arms. His mouth covered hers, gently at first, then more firmly until she parted her lips slightly, tasting the fine brandy on his breath.

The need to live and feel alive in Drew's embrace urged her on, as his warm mouth caressed hers. She could feel her lips opening farther to receive his kiss, her body surrendering to his. She'd longed for a man she felt attracted to, who kissed her as if she existed only for him. As if he cared about her and would all her life. And though Drew didn't love her, her love for him made up for his lack of feelings.

For in his arms, she lived a thousand happy moments and felt cherished and adored.

She had never given her heart to a man before and tonight she intended to give Drew her body, wanting to physically express what she was unable to say.

Her hands clung to the wide strength of Drew's shoulders as his intimate caresses unraveled her. His kiss enslaved her and made her his willing captive for the night.

Drew's fingers fumbled to undo the sash on her wrapper and she ended the kiss reluctantly, hurriedly completing the task for him. Shedding the wrapper, she took a step away from him, her legs bumping into the brass bed. With a last searing glance, she pulled her nightgown over her head and tossed it to the floor. Clinging to her courage, she took off her pantaloons, leaving her completely naked to his gaze.

"You're so beautiful," he whispered. "Even more than I'd dreamed."

He had dreamed of her? A shiver of anticipation went through her as his heated gaze moved over her naked flesh, leaving her trembling.

She drew back the covers of the bed farther and crawled in. Lying on her side, facing him, her head propped on her hand, she gazed at him.

"Come to bed, Drew," she said her voice husky and languid.

Quickly he untied his own robe and yanked off his nightclothes. Standing naked before her, she saw him so strong and virile and more handsome than she had ever thought a man could be. Hurriedly he crawled onto the bed beside her and she reached for him.

He pressed her back onto the sheet, his mouth covering hers, ravenous and demanding, and she marveled at the explosion of heat his kiss created. Hungrily, his mouth consumed hers, his tongue sliding over her mouth as she slid her hand through the dark hair at his nape.

Returning the fierceness of his kiss, she grasped his head, holding him to her lips, until he took hold of her hands. She needed him desperately tonight, for her tomorrows might be all too brief.

Skin to skin, he slid down her flesh, until his mouth found the tip of her breast. Lovingly he suckled the tender bud, caressing her breast, spiraling the ache growing within her. Her body arched, impatient and eager for the feel of Drew deep within her. Still he clasped her hands in his own, not letting her touch him.

"Drew," she muttered anxious. "I . . . I want to touch you."

"Not yet," he answered, his mouth nipping gently as he moved down her stomach to the juncture of her thighs. He lifted one leg, to completely expose her to his gaze. Starlight filtered into the room and Layla felt that the heat that shimmered from her face must be lighting up the darkened room.

Holding her breath, she felt his lips on the inside of her thigh, his tongue lingering as his mouth traveled over her flesh. Never had she experienced the feeling of anticipation as his mouth came closer and closer. Never had she thought that a man would . . .

"Drew . . ." she cried as he placed his lips on the very center of her. Lovingly he spread her open and caressed the utmost core of her womanhood. Shudders wracked her at the intense sensations, wresting from her a cry of pure joy.

She had never experienced such sinful pleasure, such intense delight. Gripping the sheets, she moaned, the sound loud in the darkness, as he laved the tiny nub of pleasure.

Plunging two fingers inside her, he took her over the edge of the world, sending her tumbling headlong into a thousand stars of pure sensation, until she fell back to earth, blissfully satisfied.

For a moment she lay there, stunned at the intensity of the experience, while Drew gazed at her, a smile on his face.

Half rising, he pulled himself back up beside her and held her in his arms. A sense of rightness and security filled her, easing her desperation, leaving her sated.

"Good?" he asked casually.

"Oh my," was all she could say. The experience had surpassed anything she had ever felt before. But then Drew surpassed any man she had ever known.

Tonight her intention had been to seduce him, but instead he had taken control with sensual skill.

Now it was her turn to arouse this proud man until he ached for release. Twisting around she pressed her lips against his in a quick, fiery kiss, which left him gasping. Moving her mouth down his body, she paused to trace the taut muscles of his chest, before she suckled his nipple.

His hands held her head as she kissed her way past his chest, down his torso, until she reached his erection.

She had never acted the wanton, never enjoyed a night more. And now she intended to experience something completely new.

She slid her palm along the smooth skin, and then bent her head to taste his flesh. Her tongue circled around the head, as Drew moaned, his hands winding themselves in her hair.

"Oh, Layla, you're torturing me," he moaned. "A slow exquisite torment."

She smiled and put her mouth over his sex, wanting only to give Drew a night he could never forget. A night to remember her by if the unthinkable should happen. Moving her mouth over his erection, she sucked him, taking her time to discover him in ways she had never tried before. Knowing in her heart that this could be her last chance, this could be their last time together.

"Layla," he gasped, the sound desperate and needy. Roughly he hauled her up and pushed her back against the sheets.

Parting her legs, he settled in between her thighs and buried his shaft deep within her. With a sigh, she welcomed him into her yearning body. Pleasure gathered as her body stretched, receiving him.

She had never known it could be this way between a man and a woman. She had never liked the physical act until she savored passion with Drew. She had never dreamed she would welcome a man into her bed and fall in love with him.

For love and passion were fairy tales that happened to others, never to Layla. Yet with Drew she wanted more than the fairy tale, she wanted the happily-ever-after.

As the two of them joined, sweetness filled her and she wished their union could be more than just physical. She wanted to wake every morning with Drew beside her, thankful for yet another day.

Her breath came harder and faster, until she felt her peak approaching, singeing every nerve until she cried out from the force and she clasped Drew to her.

With one last desperate plunge, Drew cried out, his body shuddering with his release. He slumped on top of her and then rolled her to the side, cradling her in his arms.

Sated, she lay content in his embrace, knowing she had never felt happier. For here she felt safe and secure, as if she had her whole life before her. Jean's death, the trial, and her possible execution seemed like a distant bad dream, not the reality she would soon face.

Contented, she clasped Drew to her, needing the warmth of his touch to chase away her fears. She only wished she had a lifetime to give, rather than just a night.

Drew lay curled around Layla, surrounding her rounded curves with his body tenderly, unable to sleep. Soft, rhythmic breathing let him know that she slept deeply and naturally. A fierce sense of protectiveness filled him, leaving him stunned and frightened. Her allure had made him throw caution to the wind and seek satisfaction in her bed.

Why would he want to defend a woman who had been addicted to laudanum and accused of murder? But he did. And lying here beside her in this bed, with his body curled around her, felt right.

A sense of belonging filled him. Tonight he had bared his soul to her and she hadn't jumped up and ran or made disparaging comments. She had listened to him patiently and never condemned his judgment. No one had ever done that for him.

If this attraction was just a simple case of lust, then why was he not sated? Together, they had created the most incredible sexual experiences of his life, but he wanted more. Mere lust would have been satisfied with once, maybe even twice.

He could not shake the thought that once again he was overlooking something important. Something he needed to know, but could not recognize.

Surely time would pass and at the end of the trial, he could put Layla into his past and move on to whatever the future brought.

In the meantime, she slept without the aid of laudanum and he could not help but smile. Since giving up the drug she seemed stronger in body and spirit.

And his mind kept returning to the way she had listened to him. When he had confessed his wrongdoing, he was certain she would berate him for being blind and stupid. He thought he had deserved her rancor, but her understanding surprised him.

Dawn brightened the room just enough for him to realize the servants would soon be rising. He glanced at Layla, not wanting to leave her, not wanting to seek his room.

He knew that soon the servants would stir and he and Layla would need to rise and get dressed for court. He ran his hand lightly across her shoulder, her silky skin soft to his touch. He longed to wake her with kisses and so much more, but knew there was no time.

Reluctantly he rose and found his nightclothes. Slipping his arms into his robe, he took one last glance at Layla, still sleeping, her dark hair spilling across her pillow.

His boyhood fantasies could never compare to the reality of the night they had shared. Yet the real world refused to go away; and either today or tomorrow he would be called upon to somehow convince twelve people, calling only two witnesses, that Layla could not have killed Jean.

Law school had never prepared him for the sort of miracle he needed right now.

Seventeen

Layla sat behind the attorney's table, waiting for the trial to begin, feeling more alive than she had in months. It was crazy when she feared death lurked only days away, but she had fallen in love. And this morning, love filled her with joy and helped her to face another day in the courtroom.

Over breakfast this morning they had teased each other playfully and she fervently wished that all her mornings would be as perfect as this one.

Though she suffered from a definite lack of sleep, she didn't feel exhausted, but happy instead for the first time in months, maybe years. She had looked forward to waking this morning, hoping to see Drew at her side.

The jury filed in, their faces somber as they took their places.

"All rise. The Honorable Judge François Dimitrius presiding," the bailiff recited.

A door opened and the judge hurried into the courtroom, his face the usual mask of seriousness. He sat down behind the bench and glanced out at the prosecutor. "Good morning, let's get started."

Paul Finnie stood. "The prosecution calls Captain Frank Olivier."

Layla gasped, the name of her godfather sending a

shock through her. Drew turned to scowl at her and she felt faint.

"I thought you told me he was out of the country and wouldn't return in time for the trial." The expression on his face was angry, his eyes narrowing suspiciously.

"He wasn't supposed to be back," she said, knowing she was in so much trouble, and that Drew would probably hate her by the time Frank's testimony was complete.

"What is he going to say?" Drew insisted in a harsh whisper.

She shook her head unable to speak.

She watched as the captain was sworn in, the memory of their last meeting sending her into near panic.

"Tell us your relationship to the defendant," the prosecutor asked the man who had been her father's closest friend.

"I'm her godfather. Her father, Anthony DuChampe, and I were close friends," he said, avoiding Layla's eyes.

"Did you recently try to communicate with the defendant by messenger?"

What? He had tried to send her a message?

"Yes, I sent her a note and asked her to meet me in Jackson Square," he replied.

"When did you write this note?"

"Yesterday. I had been out of the country for months and just returned."

"Did the defendant meet you at Jackson Square as you had requested?"

"No sir, you met me there."

The prosecutor smiled and paced in front of the jury box. "Can you identify this note?"

Frank glanced at the paper. "Yes sir, that's the note I wrote to Miss DuChampe."

Finnie walked toward Drew. "Will the record show

that I am handing exhibit one to the defense attorney for identification purposes."

Drew scanned the note. As he read, his body stiffened and then he returned the piece of paper to the prosecutor. He didn't spare her a glance, though his jaw looked ready to snap.

"If there are no objections from the defendant's counsel, I offer this into the record as exhibit one, Your Honor."

Layla watched Drew clench his fists and realized her fears regarding Frank's testimony were well-founded.

"Now that the note has been accepted as evidence, please read the note to the jury, Captain Oliver."

Layla perched on the edge of her chair, afraid that it might contain information that would warrant them entering it into evidence.

"'Dearest Layla, I have just returned from England and heard the terrible news. Please tell me that learning of Jean's other wives the night before I left did not provoke you into acting in a rash or foolish way. I want to meet with you and find out what happened. Yours, Captain Frank Olivier.'"

He folded the note and gave it back to the prosecutor. A low rumble began in the galley of the courtroom, yet Drew refused to give her a glance.

Oh God, why hadn't she told Drew she knew of the other women before now! Why had she let her fear override her common sense?

"What night did you meet with the defendant?" the prosecutor asked.

Layla couldn't bear to look at Drew, so she kept her eyes straight ahead, her back rigid, swallowing the tears that flooded her throat.

"On March twenty-ninth, we had dinner together at the St. Louis Hotel," he said. "Jean couldn't join us that night."

"That's the night Jean died?" the prosecutor pointed out.

"I didn't know that at the time, as my ship left the harbor at six the next morning."

"During this dinner, what information did you share with Miss DuChampe in regard to her marriage?"

Frank glanced apologetically at her and she could see he was reluctant to answer the question, but knew that he must.

"I'll remind you that you're under oath, Captain Olivier. I'll repeat the question in case you didn't hear me correctly," Finnie advised. "During this dinner, what information did you share with Miss DuChampe in regard to her marriage?"

Frank rubbed his hand across his brow. "I told Layla that I'd recently learned that Marian Cuvier was not dead and that Jean had married an additional woman besides herself and Marian."

People in the galley all started talking at once. The noise overwhelmed Layla and she swallowed, fighting the urge to cry.

The judge picked up his gavel and slammed it down. "Silence, or I will have the court cleared."

Layla gave a quick glance to see Drew's reaction. She could see the way his eyes darkened with no hint of warmth in them and knew his anger was fierce.

She had never intended this to happen, never believed Frank would return in time for the trial. And now her fear of the truth—that she knew of the other wives before Jean's death—seemed so small, so inconsequential.

"How did you learn this?" the prosecutor asked.

"I work on a steamer that hauls freight across the ocean. On the next to last voyage, I had a new first mate. We were talking one night and he mentioned Jean's wife, Marian." Frank took a long breath and sighed. "He told me Marian Cuvier was from his hometown. At first I thought he didn't know of her death. But when I mentioned she was dead, he told me that was impossible, he'd just seen her the week we left. When I returned home, I did some investigating. I visited Mrs. Cuvier's home and found out Marian was indeed alive. Then I followed Jean for over a week, which took me to Rosewood Plantation, where I learned there was yet another woman. I discreetly asked the servants and found out that this woman also believed he was her husband."

"When you told Miss DuChampe about her husband's additional wives, did she believe you?"

"No, not at first, but when I gave her specifics on when Jean visited each woman, she realized that was when he was away from her side and began to believe me."

"How would you describe her reaction?" the prosecutor asked.

"She went from disbelief to giddiness. She laughed and cried and kept repeating, 'I'm free. I'm really free.'"

Layla felt her heart wrench with pain. That night seemed so long ago. If she could go back, she would just leave town and never return.

"Did that last the entire evening?"

"No, eventually her happiness changed to anger."

"If she were happy to be free of Jean, why would she be angry?"

Frank glanced out at her and shook his head. She realized he felt bad for telling the district attorney their conversation.

"When she understood how Jean had bought her father's company at a fraction of the cost and knowingly cheated her, she became angry. It was obvious she

STARLIGHT SURRENDER

didn't love him, yet she was furious over his deception," Frank said quietly.

Layla put her head in her hands. Their conversation that night seemed so innocent, yet she sat accused and with every word, he pounded a nail in her coffin. While Drew sat very still and silent. Too silent.

"Did she say what her plans were?"

Frank swallowed nervously. "Yes, she intended to ask Jean to move out of her Baton Rouge home and give her money to keep her from telling his other wives until she found work."

"In other words, she intended to blackmail Jean," the prosecutor said, smiling.

Frank paused. "She wanted to recover some of what her father lost."

Layla swallowed back a sob. She had surely said the words, but she only wanted money to get herself established. And after the way he had cheated her father, didn't she deserve something to get a new start? It would not have been forever.

"Thank you, Captain Olivier." The prosecutor turned and smiled at Drew. "Your witness, Counselor."

Layla felt bad. Drew had scribbled a few notes during Frank's testimony, but he had not had any time to prepare. Usually he gave her a reassuring glance when he went before a witness, but this time, he didn't look her way.

"Captain Olivier, nice to meet you, sir," Drew paused. "You were a friend of Miss DuChampe's father?"

"Yes."

"Mr. Olivier, I wrote a contract for Jean Cuvier for the sale of Mr. DuChampe's shipping company. Would you say that Jean made a fair offer for Mr. DuChampe's business?"

"Definitely not," he responded.

"In your estimation, why did Mr. DuChampe sign the contract?" Drew asked.

"Objection, he's asking the witness to speculate," the prosecutor called.

"I can prove Mr. DuChampe's mental state, Your Honor, if I'm allowed to continue," Drew told the judge.

"Get to it quickly, Counselor."

"I'll repeat the question. Why did Mr. DuChampe sign such a bad contract?" Drew asked again

"Anthony DuChampe knew he was dying. He had been diagnosed with a blood disease that was killing him. Before he could die in peace, he needed someone to take over his business and make sure his daughter would be taken care of upon his death. And he feared Layla would never leave that convent once he died and he wanted to see her safely married."

"How did Mr. Cuvier learn of Mr. DuChampe's desire to see his daughter married?"

"The three of us had dinner the night before you presented the contract. At the dinner, Jean mentioned that he'd met Layla once when he visited Mr. DuChampe's office. At this dinner, Mr. Cuvier told my friend that his wife Marian had died of yellow fever and he was lonely. Once Jean learned that Anthony's dying wish was to see his daughter married he became adamant in his pursuit to convince Mr. DuChampe that he would make a good husband for Layla. That he would take care of her."

"At this dinner, was money mentioned in this exchange regarding the business?"

"I don't know. I left early to let them discuss the sale."

"Were you surprised when Mr. DuChampe gave you the details of the contract he'd signed?"

"Definitely. Anthony DuChampe was one of the

STARLIGHT SURRENDER

smartest men I knew. He would never have signed a contract like that, unless he had a reason."

"Objection! The witness is speculating, Your Honor."

"Sustained. Mr. Olivier, I'll have to ask you to confine your answers to facts."

"Yes, sir."

"That night at dinner did you tell Layla why her father wanted her to marry Jean?"

The captain hesitated. "No."

"Why not?"

"I didn't want her to be upset with her father."

Drew paused and considered what the captain said. "How was Mr. DuChampe's business doing at the time he decided to sell. Was he making a profit?"

Frank frowned and hesitated. "Yes, his business was doing well."

"But isn't it true that Mr. DuChampe told his daughter that the business was failing?"

"Yes. She didn't want to marry Jean and he thought this way she would agree and Jean would take care of her."

Layla sat there feeling stunned. Her father had lied to her about the business? Devastated, she dabbed at tears that coursed down her cheeks. Everything could have been avoided, if only her father had been honest with her.

And she had blamed Drew for her father's mistakes.

"When you learned that Jean had falsely married Layla, how did you feel?"

"Furious, she's my goddaughter. Her father asked me to look out for her. But I was in the middle of the Atlantic and had no way to warn her. By the time I got home, I wasn't convinced I'd be doing her a favor by warning her of Jean's other marriages."

"Why not?"

"Where would she go? How would she support herself? At least with Jean she had a roof over her head and I imagined them to be happy."

"So what changed your mind?"

"When we went to dinner, I could see that she was miserable. She told me she hated being Jean's wife and wished she'd never married him. I decided to tell her the truth except for how her father deceived her about the business." He glanced at Layla. "I didn't want her to hate her own father."

"Do you love Layla DuChampe?" Drew asked.

"Of course. She's my godchild and I feel responsible for her since her father is dead."

"Could you have felt responsible enough to have killed Jean Cuvier for ruining your goddaughter?"

"Of course not," he insisted.

"Tell the court your whereabouts on the night of March twenty-ninth. Do you have an alibi, Captain?"

"Yes, sir, I do. I was on board the *Olympiad*, the ship that I left town on early the next morning."

Layla could see Drew's shoulders sag and she knew he must feel battle weary already.

"Thank you, Captain Olivier." He glanced at the judge. "I'm finished with the witness, Your Honor," Drew said and came back to the attorney's table where he sat down.

"You may step down, Captain Olivier," the judge informed him.

An excited buzz filled the courtroom, but Layla barely heard the noise, her focus on Drew.

Fear gripped her with icy talons, as Layla glanced at Drew who stubbornly refused to meet her gaze. In the months they had been together, he had never acted like this. Never. Stone statues showed more emotion than Drew did at this moment.

"Prosecution, call your next witness," the judge instructed.

"The prosecution rests, Your Honor."

Drew took a deep breath.

The judge glanced at him. "I'm going to call a recess. Due to the Thanksgiving holidays, the court will reconvene on Monday, December second, at eight A.M."

"But that's a week, Your Honor," the prosecutor said, obviously upset. "We could be finished by Wednesday."

"But I will be out of town," the judge informed him.

Anxious, Layla glanced over at Drew, but he seemed more resigned than relieved.

The judge slammed down his gavel. "Court is dismissed."

Drew was silent. He stood and began shoving his notes into his satchel.

"Layla," Captain Frank called.

She turned and he stood on the other side of the railing. She reached out and hugged him.

"I'm so sorry. I tried to warn you, but the district attorney intercepted my note. I don't understand how he obtained it," he said releasing her from her hug.

Drew turned around and faced him, his demeanor cold.

"I don't either. Have you spoken with the person who you paid to deliver the note?" he asked in a voice not at all friendly.

"Yes, I've used the same boy for years to handle my mail. He runs errands for my sister while I'm gone. He promised to deliver the note to your home, Mr. Soulier."

Drew's brows drew together in an ugly frown.

Layla turned back to Frank. "How is your sister?"

"She's ill. I'm looking for a new caretaker for her. Her last one quit while I was away."

Layla smiled and patted him on the hand. "You'll find someone."

"I'm sorry, Layla. I fear my testimony harmed you," Frank lamented.

"It's all right, Frank, you had no choice but to answer the questions the district attorney asked. I'm sorry your note never reached me."

"Me, too," he said. "Please don't be angry at your father. He only made the agreement with Jean because he loved you and thought he was securing your future."

Layla closed her eyes as a white-hot flash of pain made her heart contract. "I'm trying, Frank, but if only he'd been honest with me, I wouldn't be in this situation."

Frank hung his head. "Sometimes fathers make mistakes."

"Layla, we must leave," Drew insisted.

She glanced at Drew and knew the trip home would be eventful, to say the least.

"I'll see you soon, Frank," Layla said and gave his hand a quick squeeze goodbye before she hurried after Drew who had already started walking toward the door.

His long strides clearly indicated his anger and she dreaded the time alone.

When she reached the front door, a crowd of reporters sat patiently waiting. "I'm in no mood to talk to them," Drew muttered and grabbed her arm. "Come on, we're going out the back."

Surprised that he would turn down a chance to talk to the reporters waiting outside, she hurried to keep up with him. She had never seen him this angry and dreaded the explosion she was certain would soon come.

They hurried out the back door of the courthouse building. Layla ran, trying to keep up with his long strides. Crossing the street Drew hailed a waiting cab.

Once inside the vehicle, Drew retreated into a corner, not saying anything. She kept waiting for the explosion of anger, but it never materialized.

Never before had she seen him this quiet. Never before had he withdrawn into himself so far that she feared she would never reach him.

"Drew, I know you're angry—" she said.

He cut her off. "Not now."

Drew surpressed the anger seething within him. How could he hold a rational conversation with her, when his entire defense had just been blown to shreds? Though he had to admit Frank's testimony hadn't proved the prosecution's claims that she had killed Jean to retain her father's business, Paul Finnie now had the necessary evidence to show that Jean's murder could have been a crime of passion. The best Drew could do was to plead guilty to a charge of second degree murder. She would keep her life, but spend most of it in prison. A hellhole for a woman.

The cab arrived in front of the house and he climbed down, his fury contained. Why in the hell had she lied to him? He had known she held something back, but had been unable to coax or force the information from her.

He bounded up the stairs of his house and held open the door, watching her walk slowly up the stairs into the house, her eyes large and worried.

"Get in the library," he commanded. Now that they were home he could speak his mind.

She glanced back at him, her eyes wary.

He had never felt so angry with a client. He had never cared so much about getting someone acquitted and yet she had never trusted him enough to tell him everything. He had never experienced a more frustrating trial or woman.

Layla stood waiting for him as he walked in and threw his satchel on a nearby chair.

She drew back her shoulders and lifted her head, like a warrior preparing for battle. "I tried to tell you several times," she stated. "At first I didn't trust you. Then I kept hoping that no one would find out that I knew about the other wives. I kept quiet for so long, I just didn't want to tell you later, because I knew you'd be angry."

Drew's restraint crumbled as he slammed the door shut to the library, causing her to jump and her eyes to widen. "You didn't know if you could trust me? Your life is at stake, Layla. Since I took your case I've been building a defense that I thought would convince the jury of your innocence. At every step you've been more hindrance than help. How many times have you not been completely honest with me? How many times have you not given me all of the information? Do you want to die?"

She took a step back. "Of course not. I was afraid. I feared that if anyone realized that I knew of Marian and Nicole they would have more reason to believe that I'd killed Jean."

"So you kept this information to yourself, hoping silence would protect you? Well, it didn't work and today I had to do some quick thinking to keep his testimony from convincing the jurors that you were indeed the killer. And I'm not certain I managed to save you in there today. For all I know, once they hear my defense, they may still send you to the gallows."

He paced across the floor, impelled by his frustration. "Damn it to hell, Layla, you haven't been honest with me from the very beginning. If you're not honest with me, how can I be certain you're innocent?"

As soon as the words were out of his mouth he wished he could recall them, but maybe the time to be completely honest with one another was upon them. He knew she hadn't planned Jean's death. He didn't believe she had even accidentally poisoned him any longer, but how could he trust her when she continually kept information from him?

She stepped toward him. "I have been honest with you, I just haven't told you everything. It's very hard to trust the man who helped swindle my father out of his business."

"Wait just a damn minute. Frank's testimony proved what I've been telling you all along. Not only did your father make a bad business deal, but he convinced you to marry a married man. Don't blame me for his bad judgment."

"Well, you still haven't proved to me that you knew nothing about Jean being married to the three of us at the same time. You don't have a clue as to who the real killer is, so don't stand there and play the injured party. I've known all along that you don't believe I'm innocent.

"If I'd known of the other wives, I would have tried to convince Jean to end the false marriages. And how can I be sure of your innocence when I keep learning new things you haven't told me?" He paused. "Next Monday I'm supposed to stand in that courtroom and defend you against the insinuations the prosecution planted in the jurors' minds. And I don't have a clue what I'm going to say."

He paused, taking a deep breath. "Damn it, Layla, when are you going to take some responsibility for what's happened in your life? When are you going to realize that you made the choice to marry Jean? I didn't force you to. Even the contract that I wrote for Jean and your father never forced you to marry that bastard. I'm sick to death of hearing how I swindled your father. But more than anything I want you to understand this—" He took a deep breath and stepped in closer to her. "If I'd known your father was looking for a husband for you, I would have asked him for your hand. No, it wouldn't have been a love match, but I could have done a much better job than that bastard Jean."

Layla's eyes widened in shock and disbelief. She stood there her mouth open, not saying a word. Then tears flooded her eyes. She turned and ran out of the room, leaving Drew, the sound of her footsteps pounding on the stairs.

Drew sank into the nearest chair, feeling a hundred years old. How could he live with himself if he lost this case? How could he watch her die? God, he knew better than to become involved with his client, yet he had not heeded the ethical caution and now he feared that both of them were lost.

Layla hurried up the stairs seeking the safety of her room. She stumbled into the room and slammed the door behind her.

Damn him! Yes, she should have told him everything from the very beginning, but she had been unable to trust him. But over the passing months, she saw the effort he had put into her case and still she remained mum about her knowledge of the other wives.

She did not want to die. In fact, she quaked at the thought of how this trial would end. She lay down on the bed and curled into a ball, letting the tears flow. Fear of how the police and Drew would interpret her knowledge of the other women had kept her silent too long.

Only recently had she begun to trust him. Had Jean's betrayal damaged her ability to believe in someone forever?

Only today had she learned the whole truth regarding her father, that even he had deceived her. She had married Jean because her father told her this marriage would save his company. She did it for her father and when he died barely a month after her marriage she had mourned both her father and her vows.

For she would never have married Jean if she thought that her father would not benefit. And he had never let on that he was dying.

According to Frank, her father had agreed to sign the contract thinking that he was benefiting her. What a twisted nightmare—one Jean had manipulated for his own good! And she had blamed Drew repeatedly for her father's actions.

Tonight Drew had said that he would have married her, if he had known her father searched for her a husband. Had he truly wanted her for his wife, before her name became sullied with scandal?

Eighteen

The next day Drew sat in the dining room, sipping the Creole coffee that he loved, hoping the strong brew would keep him awake. He had slept little the night before, worrying how he would defend Layla. He needed a miracle and he needed it now.

Yet more than anything, he was unable to sleep for thinking of Layla, seeing her face when she ran from the room. He had been hard on her, but learning she knew of the other wives had ruined everything they had had the night before. She didn't trust him, was not forthright with him, and he had never been so angry.

Damn, he wanted to save her, but he needed her help.

"Mr. Soulier," Esmeralda timidly asked. "Can I get you anything else?"

"Thank you—no," he responded absently.

"Here is yesterday's mail," she said handing him a stack of envelopes.

"Esmeralda," he called, suddenly reminded of the missing note. "Was a message delivered day before yesterday?"

"Not that I'm aware of sir. Thursday is the day I go to market. I was out most of the morning."

"Did Colette go with you?" he asked.

"No sir, she stayed behind."

"Did she mention receiving a message for Miss DuChampe?"

"No, sir. Do you want me to ask her?"

"No, Esmeralda, I will." He glanced through the mail. Captain Frank declared the boy had delivered the message to the house, but Layla had never received it—which meant that sometime after the note arrived here, it was delivered to the district attorney. Who in his household would want to harm Layla? He could think of no one.

Esmeralda had been with him for years and he had never had any problems with anything missing or going astray. Why would she send a message to the district attorney?

The only other person in the house was Colette. And she had been home and could have received the message. But why would she want to hurt Layla? She said she wanted Layla to go free. Yet she too had been in the suite the night of Jean's murder. Could he possibly have overlooked something he needed to know about Colette?

What reason would she have to kill Jean? Maybe he had spent too much time investigating George and Frank.

Drew sipped his coffee and glanced down again at the mail and the messages that Esmeralda laid before him. A name jumped out at him on one of the envelopes, causing his heart to stutter. Lying amongst the envelopes was a letter from Mrs. Nicole Viel. He ripped open the envelope and read the enclosed letter.

Dear Mr. Soulier,
　Amongst Jean's things I found something that I think could be helpful in Layla's trial. Come to Rosewood and I shall give you what I consider evidence for Layla's trial.

Mrs. Nicole Viel

For a moment Drew sat there, stunned. Nicole Rosseau Cuvier had remarried a man called Viel—the same last name as Blanche, the woman that Layla had been certain killed Jean. But Nicole had claimed to love Jean, so why would she remarry so quickly?

What could she have that could possibly be considered evidence? Did he dare get his hopes up that the proof he so badly needed to save Layla was waiting for him in Baton Rouge?

Right now his defense needed all the help he could get and if taking a trip to Baton Rouge would help, he would be on the next boat.

"Esmeralda," Drew called.

"Yes, sir," the woman said, sticking her head out of the kitchen.

"As soon as I get dressed I'm leaving for the day. Watch my guests closely and if you need any assistance, contact Eric."

"Yes, sir. When will you return?"

"I should be back late this afternoon."

He intended to catch the first boat to Baton Rouge, stay long enough to visit Nicole, and return on the next boat.

In less than thirty minutes, he was dressed and out the door. Maybe whatever Nicole had would yield nothing, but he could not ignore the lead, especially since she now had the same last name as Blanche. And not when his defense lacked the strength it so desperately needed to convince twelve jurors not to hang Layla.

Drew arrived at Rosewood. The plantation house was built in the old Creole style, with one side devoted to the men and the other to the women. Each had their own front door, with a parlor separating the two sides.

He followed the servant through the men's side of

the house into the main parlor. Nicole Viel stood waiting for him.

"Mrs. Viel, how good to see you again. You're looking much happier than the last time we met. I was pleasantly surprised when I read you'd remarried."

She smiled. "Yes. Shortly after Jean's death, I married Mr. Viel. Please have a seat."

Could the Viel she married have anything to do with Blanche Viel?

Drew took a seat on a settee and Nicole sat down in a rocking chair close by.

"How is Layla's trial going? I read in the papers that you are her lawyer," she said.

"Yes, I am. Unfortunately, the prosecution has quite a case against her," he said, his brows drawing together in a frown. "It hasn't been easy."

"Do you think she killed Jean?" Nicole asked.

"I don't know. I took this case to defend her and that's what I intend to do," he said, knowing in his heart she was innocent, but still trying to convince his lawyer's mind. "Your letter mentioned you'd found something of Jean's that I might want to see."

Nicole nodded. "Have you ever wondered if Jean married or was involved with more women than just the three of us? It's obvious the man was a womanizer, but what if there was a fourth woman? Or even a fifth?"

Drew felt his pulse start to race. Could Nicole have found more information on Blanche?

"I'd say with that many women in his life, Jean should have died of natural causes," Drew replied, trying to act as if he knew nothing, his anticipation building. "Why? Do you have reason to believe there's another woman?"

"I have a diary that indicates so," Nicole said with a smile. "When Consuelo and I went through Jean's things, we found the journal. But who the woman is, I don't know. Someone ripped out the page that likely showed her name and there are no dates. In the diary she mentions a child she bore Jean before he ended their affair."

Drew frowned. This sounded like Blanche and the last name fit. Could there be more information in the diary about her that could help him solve the murder? At this stage in the trial he needed to be the one with a surprise.

"Jean never mentioned another child to me. Of course, even as his lawyer, I'm learning things about Jean that shock me. Do you know the child's name?"

"Julianne—she died of yellow fever. There's nothing to indicate what happened to the woman. Her diary ends on an ominous note, almost as if she were contemplating suicide."

Julianne was Blanche's daughter. Nicole had located Blanche's diary. Drew suppressed his excitement but the suspense was killing him.

"May I see this diary?" Drew asked, praying that Blanche had revealed something in the book that he could tie to the murderer.

Nicole smiled. "Why don't you take it with you? You might find something I missed. I only ask that when you find this mystery woman, please tell her she's not alone. Jean hurt many women, including the three of us considered 'The Cuvier Widows.'"

Thank God, she was going to give it to him. He wanted to jump up and hug her, but he refrained.

"It may take me awhile to find out who she is, but once I know, I'll be sure to tell you," he said. He already knew Blanche was dead, but he didn't want to reveal anything until he'd read the diary. Even then he intended to keep whatever he learned quiet, not wanting to leak information to the prosecution. He had only a week to prepare before the trial reconvened. A week to save Layla's life.

"What other information did the diary give you?"

"Blanche met Jean when she was a young debutante and he convinced her he would leave his wife and marry her. From her writings I gathered that she had an older brother who disliked Jean."

Drew suddenly felt hopeful again.

"Is the brother's name in the diary?" Drew asked. "Maybe we can track her down through him."

"There were no surnames mentioned at all. Though she calls him by his christian name, I can't remember what it was. She mentions him on the last page. Let me get the diary for you."

Drew could barely contain his excitement. Could Blanche's brother be Nicole's new husband?

He needed to remain collected, obtain the diary and leave as quickly as possible. It was obvious that Nicole had no clue that this diary belonged to a Viel family member.

If Jean had ruined Mr. Viel's sister, maybe Blanche's brother killed Jean for revenge and then married Nicole for spite. Yet she appeared happy.

Nicole stood and disappeared through the dining room. In a few moments she walked back through the room to Drew with a leather-bound volume in her hand.

"Here you are," she said, handing him the journal and returning to the rocker. "I've read the entire book and I think it helped me resolve my lingering doubts. For Jean to have so many women, it wouldn't have mattered what I did. I could not have prevented his roaming any more than any of his other wives, and I can't be held responsible for Jean's cheating."

"Of course you couldn't stop Jean. You were a victim, just like the other women, Mrs. Viel." He took a deep breath, not wanting to hurt this woman, though if her husband were involved with the murder, he would return. "Jean was my client and I never knew of any of this. But I've seen the destruction his lies have caused."

Drew took a deep breath and stood. "Thank you for writing and telling me about the journal. If you should find anything else, let me know. Layla will hang if she's convicted and I must win this trial."

"Just promise me that when you find out who the woman is that wrote this journal, you'll tell me. I think she needs to understand that she's not alone," Nicole said.

"I will. Thank you again, Mrs. Viel. I must get back to New Orleans today. You may still be called as a witness at Layla's trial."

"Of course. Goodbye, Mr. Soulier," she said, and walked him to the door on the men's side of the house.

As soon as the door closed, Drew hurried down the steps, where the man who'd brought him up from the landing waited with a wagon.

"The next boat is due any minute. You should be back in New Orleans in no time," the older man said.

"Thanks," Drew jumped into the wagon, eager to be on his way. As the wagon lumbered down the road he couldn't refrain from glancing at the last page.

The name of Charles jumped at him from the page. Charles Viel, Nicole Viel? Could there be a connection?

"What is Mrs. Viel's husband's name?" he asked the servant who held the reins to the horses.

"His name is Maxim," the older gentleman replied.

"Thank you."

Relief filled Drew, yet he had to ask. "Do you know a Charles Viel?"

"No, sir. Mr. Viel only recently married our mistress."

"I understand," Drew said somewhat disappointed.

He hoped that Charles was a distant relative. Yet he did not want to hurt Nicole. She had suffered enough at Jean's hands and deserved happiness.

STARLIGHT SURRENDER

Drew settled back, holding tightly onto the diary that he hoped would lead him to the killer. As soon as he got back to the office, he would begin to investigate the Viel family and locate Charles Viel.

On the way back to the office from the river, Drew stopped and picked up Eric. With one week to pore over this diary and glean all the information they could to take to trial next Monday, they would be working around the clock.

Now as they sat in his office, Drew read bits and pieces of the diary to Eric. Somehow this little book was filled with information that he knew would lead them to the killer.

"Listen to this, Eric: '*How cruel fate is. Today, Jean informed me that our affair has outlasted its usefulness to him.*'"

"As you read, I'll write down names and we'll see all who are involved and determine from that list who could have wanted Jean dead," Eric suggested.

"Good idea," Drew said, still skimming the diary. "Egad, there's more. '*Today I buried my baby girl. After struggling for two weeks with yellow fever, she finally succumbed to the dread disease late two nights ago. My precious child passed away with only her dear uncle and myself at her bedside. Though I begged God to take me and not my dear, sweet daughter . . . Her father did not even come to see his daughter buried. Though I let him know the day and the time of her funeral, he chose not to acknowledge her.*'"

"Our Jean was a bastard. No wonder someone killed him," Eric blurted out.

Drew turned to the last page, needing to see what the final entry said. He began to read out loud. "'*Charles worries about me and I fear in the end my decision will hurt him even more than my previous behavior. If only I had listened to him in my youthful exuberance, then my life would not be in a shambles. For dear Charles warned me that Jean was married, but I foolishly believed that he would leave his wife and follow his heart. How gullible I was to believe the vows of matrimony could be so easily discarded.*

And even when Charles tried to caution me that there were other women and begged me to forget Jean and marry another, I foolishly clung to the hope that someday our love would unite us.'"

"So the first name on my list is Charles Viel, Blanche's brother. We need to investigate him," Eric said.

"Yes. If we could determine that he somehow got the poison to Jean, then our case is solved. But without a witness who saw him go into the hotel suite that night, it's going to be hard to prove."

Drew flipped back a few pages. He started reading and the name that jumped off the page at him stunned him. He jumped up, unable to sit still a moment longer.

"Oh my God, Eric. I think I just found our killer."

Shocked, Drew stood there and realized he had been wrong all this time regarding Layla's innocence.

Eric jumped up from his chair and grabbed the book from Drew's hand. He read the passage in the diary and then he grinned.

"You're right, Mr. Soulier. You've found our killer."

"Now that we've solved the murder, we have to prove how it was done."

"Break out the brandy. This calls for a drink!"

Layla knocked on the library door, needing to talk to Drew before they returned to the courtroom tomorrow.

"Come in," he called.

She opened the door and strolled in. His dark-haired head was bent over his papers as he scribbled hastily.

"It's late. You've worked every day for the last week, except for the short break you took on Thanksgiving Day. Don't you think you need to rest?" she asked. He had been so absorbed in the last week, they had barely spoken and she missed him, feeling guilty that she had created this division between them.

He smiled. "I'm almost done." He gazed at her, his eyes bright and excited. In the last week, something had changed and she wasn't certain what.

"Are you ready for tomorrow?" she asked.

He paused for a moment and glanced at her, a frown on his face. "Oh yes, I'm ready. Colette will be the first witness I call."

"I want you to know I've noticed how hard you've worked on my defense. It's my fault you had to completely redo your strategy because I wasn't honest with you, and I want to apologize," she said. "If there is some way I could pay you, I would."

He stood and walked over to her and placed his hands on her shoulder. "The last time we spoke alone we ended in a horrendous argument. I was angry and should have handled the situation better."

"No, you had a right to be angry. I was wrong. You agreed to defend me at no charge and I haven't made this easy."

He smiled. "No, you really haven't. But for now, I want you to go to bed and get a good night's rest. Don't worry about tomorrow. In the morning, I want you to wear your prettiest dress, because tomorrow is going to be the beginning of the end in a lot of ways."

"The end?" she said, apprehensive.

"Yes, the end of the trial. No matter what happens, we should know your fate soon."

"And that's supposed to help me rest?" she asked.

He kissed her on the end of her nose. "Yes, you're

supposed to show how much faith and trust you have in me and go upstairs and sleep."

"Would you be satisfied, if I say I'll try?" she asked. "I believe and I trust you're doing your best to save me. I'm just a little nervous about tomorrow."

Strangely enough she realized she meant what she said. She really did trust Drew to see that she was not convicted.

"Don't be. Everything is going to be fine," he said, smiling once more.

Nineteen

Layla sat in the grim courtroom, trying not to appear nervous as they waited for the trial to begin. For some reason an air of excitement seemed to resonate in Drew. Eric joined them at the attorney's table this morning and together the two of them hovered protectively over a mound of documents. They both seemed fidgety and occasionally would glance at each other, an excited look on their faces.

A side door opened and she watched the jurors file in, searching the face of each person, knowing that one day soon they would decide her fate.

"All rise for the Honorable Judge François Dimitrius," the bailiff announced.

A shuffling noise echoed in the packed courthouse as everyone stood.

The judge took his seat behind the bench and the crowd sank onto their benches. He gazed out at Drew, a frown on his face. "Mr. Soulier, is the defense ready?"

"Yes, Your Honor, we are. The defense calls as its first witness, Colette Malone."

Colette smiled at Layla as she passed. At breakfast this morning she admitted to being nervous, but promised to do her best to convince this jury of Layla's innocence. Layla couldn't imagine the last few months without Colette's help and friendship. She knew she would do her best.

After Colette was sworn in, she settled back in the chair.

"For the record, state your name," Drew asked, rising to cross the courtroom and stand in front of the witness stand.

"Colette Malone," she answered, her voice shaking.

"Were you in the hotel suite the night of Jean's murder?" Drew asked.

"Yes."

"How long have you worked for the Cuviers?"

"I started to work for them in February of this year," she replied.

"Who did you work for previously?" he asked.

"Mr. Hopkins," she responded. "I took care of his daughter."

Drew frowned. "I tried to find Mr. Hopkins at the address you gave me to speak with him, and all I found was an empty field, though a Mr. Hopkins did return my earlier letter."

"Maybe you wrote down the wrong address," she answered her eyes widening in surprise.

"Maybe," Drew replied. "How long have you *known* Mr. Cuvier?"

"Only since I started to work for him and Miss DuChampe last February," she said.

Drew paced in front of the witness stand, his forehead wrinkled in concentration.

"Did you ever work for a woman named Blanche Viel?" he asked, halting in front of Colette.

Layla's nerves tingled at the mention of Blanche. Why would Drew be asking Colette about Blanche?

Colette's eyes widened and for a moment she looked stunned.

"No," she answered her voice trembling.

"No?" Drew answered. "I would like to remind you that you are under oath, Miss Malone."

A scuffling noise sounded at the back of the courtroom and everyone turned to see two policemen accompanying a burly man through the door of the courtroom. They forced him to take a seat at the back of the room.

"Who is that?" Layla whispered to Eric. "I've seen him before with Colette."

Eric's eyes widened, but he shook his head. "Wait."

Layla faced Colette and noticed how large the woman's eyes appeared in her pale face.

Drew walked back to the attorney's desk and Eric handed him a leather-bound volume. He returned to the witness stand and handed the book to Colette. "Can you identify this volume for me?"

Colette gasped. "Oh my God . . ." her voice trailed off and she turned her gaze to the man at the back of the courtroom between the two police officers. "It's . . . it's Blanche's diary."

Layla gasped. Colette knew about Blanche? And when had Drew obtained her diary?

Tears welled up in Layla's eyes. She could not help herself. Instinctively she had known that Blanche was a part of the mystery of Jean's death and now her diary was being introduced as evidence. And somehow Colette was involved.

"I'd like to have this marked as exhibit two and introduced into evidence, the diary of Blanche Viel," Drew said to the judge.

Why didn't Drew tell her about this new piece of evidence?

Drew carried the diary over to the prosecutor. "Will the record show I am handing exhibit two to the prosecutor for identification purposes."

"Objection! Irrelevant," the prosecutor insisted.

"Your Honor, this diary holds pertinent information regarding Miss Colette Malone and the death of Jean Cuvier. If given the opportunity, I can show that Miss Malone knew Jean before coming to work for Miss DuChampe."

Layla's mouth fell open and the crowd in the courtroom gasped and started talking all at once.

The judge slammed his gavel. "Quiet! Quiet, now!"

After the courtroom quieted, the judge looked at Drew. "I'll allow it."

"Thank you, Your Honor."

The bailiff marked the diary with an evidence marker.

Drew approached Colette, still holding the diary. Colette gripped a handkerchief in her visibly shaking hands.

"I'll remind you once again that you are under oath, Miss Malone. Again, did you ever work for a Miss Blanche Viel?"

"Yes, I worked for her," Colette reluctantly answered.

Shock riveted Layla. When had Colette worked for Blanche? And why had she come to work for Jean?

"Did you know Jean before you came to work for him at his house?"

"Yes," she answered her eyes wide, her mouth tense.

"How did you know him?"

"He was Miss Viel's lover." Colette sighed. She glanced out at the audience and put her hand to her head as if it ached.

More chatter broke out in the courtroom and the judge frowned until the noise ceased.

"Did Blanche have any children?"

"Yes, a daughter by Mr. Cuvier, called Julianne."

Layla watched her look out at the audience again, wringing the handkerchief in her hands, fixing her gaze on a man sitting between the policemen in the back.

"Please read the marked page from Miss Viel's diary," Drew instructed.

With shaking hands, Colette took the book from Drew. "'*Dear Julianne loves her nurse, Colette, almost as much as she loves me. And a better nursemaid I could not have found for my darling daughter.*'"

She broke down into sobs, tears running down her face. Drew had to wait a moment to let her dry her eyes.

"Julianne, Jean's daughter, was your charge?"

"Yes, I loved her like she was my own little girl."

"How did Jean treat his illegitimate daughter?"

Colette bristled and she glared at Drew through watery eyes. "He abandoned her. That sweet angel loved him and he abandoned her. He stopped coming to see her, bringing her presents, or even acknowledging her. He ignored that precious child."

"What about the child's mother, Blanche? Did Jean abandon her also?"

"Blanche loved Jean. She was his mistress for over five years. She waited for him to leave his wife and marry her. Then one day he told her that he no longer loved her and he never came to see Julianne or her again. Blanche was heartbroken and Julianne kept asking for her daddy."

"What happened to Julianne?" Drew asked.

For a moment Colette held the handkerchief to her mouth, not saying a word, and Layla thought that she was not going to respond. Layla knew they were dead, but she wanted to hear what Colette knew.

"Miss Malone, you must answer," the judge finally instructed.

She raised her head, her voice weak. "Julianne contracted yellow fever. Two weeks later, she died."

Great gulping sobs came from Colette as she cried into her handkerchief.

"Did Jean attend his daughter's funeral?"

Colette raised her tear-filled eyes to Drew and the rage reflected from their depths appeared more like madness. "That bastard wouldn't even acknowledge her at her death. We buried that sweet child without her father at her graveside. He forsaked her even in death."

"What happened to Blanche?" Drew asked.

More tears ran uninterrupted down Colette's cheeks. "Less than a month after her baby died, she killed herself. She didn't think she had anything to live for after Jean's abandonment and the death of Julianne."

Layla dabbed her eyes with the tip of her own handkerchief. Blanche's tale disturbed her.

"Do you know a Charles Viel?"

Colette refused to look at Drew. "Yes, he's Blanche's older brother."

Drew walked back and forth in front of the witness stand. "Did Mr. Viel know about Jean's other women?"

"Yes, he was very protective of her and warned Miss Blanche, but she loved Jean and wouldn't listen to her brother," she admitted.

"Could you please read this passage from Blanche's diary," Drew asked.

Colette took the diary from Drew and found what he wanted her to read. "'*Charles's anger toward Jean knows no bounds. I fear what would come to pass if Jean should ever see Charles on the street. For Charles would just as soon kill Jean as to live another day. And that my dear brother should harm him would pain me deeply. For though Jean no longer loves me, I still care for him. And I would never want my brother to ruin his own life because I loved the wrong man.*'"

Colette closed the diary and handed it back to Drew.

"Do you see Charles Viel in this courtroom?"

The courtroom buzzed with chatter and the judge slammed his gavel.

"Quiet."

"Yes," she answered her eyes wide, her voice quivering.

"Could you point him out for us?"

She glanced at Drew, her eyes beseeching him. "Please . . ."

"I'll ask you again, Miss Malone, to point out Charles Viel."

She sighed. "He's the man sitting between the two policemen in the back of the court."

"Thank you," Drew said.

The crowd of people turned and glanced at Charles Viel and the judge frowned.

"Two months after Blanche's death, you accepted a position with Layla DuChampe who at the time was Jean's supposed wife. Is this true?"

"Yes."

"Why did Jean not recognize you?" Drew asked.

She shrugged. "I don't know."

"Miss Malone, do you wear a wig?"

She fidgeted on the seat and Layla could see her trying to come up with a response to the question. Finally she answered.

"Yes," she answered.

"Could you please remove the wig, so that the court can see why Jean wouldn't recognize you," Drew insisted.

With a glare, she reached up and pulled off the dark haired wig that Layla knew she wore. She always said it was because her graying hair was much too thin and Layla had never thought to doubt her.

"Mr. Cuvier never paid much attention to the servants."

Layla felt stunned at Colette's obvious deception. Since she had come to work for them, Colette had taken care of Layla. She had helped her through the crisis of Jean's death. She had managed the household to perfection. She had gone out of her way to be sympathetic to Layla's trials.

Drew paced in front of the stand, his brows drawn together in a frown.

"Why would you take a job with a man you hated? The very man you held responsible for the death of Julianne and Blanche? And why would you hide your identity?" Drew asked his voice rising. "Unless you intended to kill."

"Objection!" the prosecutor yelled.

"Overruled," the judge quickly responded.

Colette shook her head, her eyes wide with panic. She glanced at the man sitting in the gallery, fear emanating from her. "No, it's not true," she said unpersuasively. "Layla killed Jean."

Layla sat, stunned. She had considered Colette her friend and now she accused her of Jean's death.

"You gave Jean the cyanide that killed him that night," Drew said, raising his voice. "You went to work in that household, just so that you could murder Jean Cuvier."

"No . . . he killed my baby . . . it wasn't my idea . . ." she said, her panic-filled eyes searching the courtroom. "I just did what . . ."

Charles Viel stood up in court and shouted. "Shut up, Colette."

A loud boom rang out in the courtroom, causing Layla to jump, followed by screams and a scuffling sound in the back of the room.

Pandemonium broke out as the two policemen in the back grabbed the gun from Charles Viel and wrestled him to the ground.

Layla realized that the sound had been a gunshot and looked to Drew. He stood next to the witness stand, cradling Colette in his arms, her blood staining his shirt.

The judge slammed his gavel down. "Order! I say, order!"

"Find a doctor!" Drew yelled. "Quickly!"

The bailiff ran from the courtroom, while other policemen hurried in to help subdue Charles Viel. The judge tried to regain control of the courtroom by banging his gavel.

Colette grimaced in pain, a red stain spreading rapidly across her chest. "Let me die."

"No, you're not going to die," Drew insisted.

She shook her head and gasped for breath. "Hear me . . . I killed that wicked Jean, for hurting my sweet angel, Julianne. She loved her papa so . . . she would have hung on . . . she would have lived if he'd been at her side. She loved him so much and he betrayed her just like he did all the others."

Colette coughed, blood trickled from the side of her mouth, her voice weak. "That night, I awoke to hear him and Layla fighting. I realized she knew about the other women and would reveal everything. I couldn't wait any longer. I had to kill Jean that night." She paused, gasping for breath, and Layla feared she would die right then. "Later that night I found him asleep in the parlor. When I woke him, he said he had a headache. So I helped him to bed and gave him tablets tainted with cyanide. He was dead in a matter of minutes."

Layla sobbed with relief. She would not hang. Yet through her tears, she watched in horror as her servant and the woman she thought of as her friend began to fade. Her breathing became labored and blood bubbled from her lips.

"Colette, where did you get the cyanide?" Drew cradled her in his arms, her blood on his clothes.

"Charles . . . loved . . . his sister . . . and Mr. Cuvier did her wrong. Charles got the cyanide. We both wanted Jean dead. But I never intended to hurt so many . . ."

Colette gazed out at the spectators, squinting, unable to focus.

Barely breathing, she moaned, "Charles shot you—so—so Layla would need another lawyer."

Charles screamed from the back of the courtroom, his face a taut, angry mask. "Shut up, Colette!"

The judge pounded the gavel. "Quiet, Mr. Viel, or I will have you removed."

The bailiff and another man carrying a black doctor's bag burst through the door of the courtroom.

Colette smiled and her head suddenly slumped forward.

"Colette? Colette?" Drew asked.

A deep sigh seemed to escape her and she became still. The doctor rushed over to where Colette lay in Drew's arms. An eerie silence fell over the room as they watched him put his hand to her neck, searching for a pulse.

He glanced back at Drew. "She's dead."

Pandemonium broke out in the room and the judge pounded his gavel.

Drew gently eased her limp body down to the floor and stood. He walked over to where Charles Viel stood, waiting to be taken away by the policeman on either side of him. "You poisoned Jean Cuvier and shot me."

He glared at Drew. "Because of that bastard, my baby sister killed herself. Jean ruined her life and then when he no longer wanted her, he broke her heart. He deserved to die."

"Take him to jail," Drew said, shaking his head in disgust as court officers moved to put handcuffs on Charles.

The spectators in the courtroom sat stunned at the astonishing turn of events.

The bailiff and several deputies carried Colette's body out of the courtroom, behind Charles Viel.

Layla sat there astounded, trying to absorb everything that had happened in the last few minutes.

Drew strode to the front of the courtroom to stand before the bench. "Judge Dimitrius, I make a motion that Layla DuChampe be cleared of all charges in the death of Jean Cuvier."

Layla felt her heart slam into her chest.

"Granted. Jury, you are dismissed with the court's thanks," the judge muttered and then slammed down his gavel. "Court dismissed."

Free! She was free. She was cleared of murder and Drew had found the real killers.

Eric grabbed her hand. "Congratulations, Miss DuChampe."

"I'm free," she said laughing, in a state of shock. Free to live her life as she wanted. The prospect seemed both thrilling and frightening at the same time. From this time forward she was determined to make a better life. Yet her heart had already come to her first decision.

Drew walked back to the attorney's desk.

"Congratulations, Mr. Soulier, you did an excellent job," Eric acknowledged. "I'm going back to the office to take care of business. Don't forget you have an appointment this evening with the Democratic Club."

"Thanks, Eric. I'll talk with you later," Drew said.

Eric followed the noisy crowd out through the doors as the chamber emptied quickly, leaving them alone.

Layla stared at the man who had been such a challenge to her, the man she loved with all her heart. She went into his arms and he accepted her embrace.

"Thank you, Drew. I owe my life to you," she said her voice breaking. She released him. "But I have so many questions. When did you get Blanche's diary? Why didn't you tell me?"

"Last Saturday I received a note from Nicole Viel and went to Baton Rouge. Nicole gave me the book, though she didn't know whom it belonged to." He sighed. "I've wanted to tell you for the last week, but I couldn't. I feared if I told you, your behavior toward Colette could change, tipping her off. She might have run away."

Layla nodded, knowing what he said was true, but wished that he could have included her before today.

"Colette killed Jean. And all this time, I thought she was my friend."

"Until today we weren't even certain that she and Charles plotted to do this together. Sadly, they probably would have gotten away with it, if not for Blanche's diary."

"It's really over," Layla said, still in a state of shock.

Drew started packing up his papers, but paused, his hand on the satchel. His green eyes searched hers. "It's over and I owe you an apology. You are innocent, just as you said. I always wanted to believe in you, Layla, but there was so much evidence against you. And I'm a man who is accustomed to working with criminals. This time I was wrong. I'm sorry for doubting you."

She reached out and touched her hand to his cheek. "Thank you, Drew. Words aren't enough but—"

She wrapped her arms around him and gave him another hug, then stood back and stared at him. "I want you to know that I love you with all my heart. I have for quite some time." She paused. "I probably always will."

He just stared at her. "Are you saying this—because I won your case?"

She shook her head slowly. "No. I loved you long before I trusted you. But too much has happened for us to ever be together. Follow your dream, Drew, but know that you carry my love with you."

For a moment he was quiet, not reacting. She hadn't really expected any kind of answer, but she could tell he did not know how to respond.

"Mr. Soulier, the reporters are all outside waiting for you and Miss DuChampe," the court clerk shouted at him from the door. "They're threatening to bust the door down if you don't come out and talk to them."

Layla smiled. "Go on, the press is waiting for you. This is your big opportunity to tell the people of New Orleans why you should be their next mayor. I'll see you later tonight."

He frowned. "No. We need to talk."

She smiled, though inside her heart was breaking. "I insist. You need to speak with the reporters and you can't keep the men who are going to get you elected waiting at the Democratic Club. We'll talk later."

Drew stared at her and she knew he felt uncertain about leaving her. "Promise me this much, Layla—to meet tonight, alone."

"Of course," she said trying to make it easy for him.

He watched her suspiciously and she could tell he was still uncertain. But then he slowly relaxed. "Come on, let's go greet the reporters and glory in our victory."

"I'll stand in the background and let you do all the talking." She didn't want to speak with the men gathered on the steps of the courthouse. "Besides, this is your victory, not ours."

He reached down and kissed her lightly on the lips. "Thank you, Layla. For everything."

* * *

Layla watched Drew walk away from the crowd of reporters, her heart wrenching in pain as he climbed into a cab that would take him to the Democratic Club.

As soon as she arrived back at the town house, she would pack her belongings and go to a hotel for the night. Then tomorrow she would speak with Frank. She knew he needed a caretaker for his invalid sister and she would do her best for her godfather. She needed this opportunity to begin her life anew—and support herself for the first time.

She had thought of returning to the convent, but she no longer fit in that sheltered world. This was her new start, her new chance and she was determined to make her own way.

When Drew returned home tonight, it would be late and he would assume she was in bed asleep. Not until morning would he realize she had gone.

It was best if she slipped quietly away and let the world have the man she loved. He would serve the people of New Orleans well, though her own heart would be broken forever.

When she arrived at the townhome, she packed her trunk and had it carried to a waiting cab in no time. Tonight she would stay in a hotel, but tomorrow, she would go to Frank. She would never lead a life of luxury, but she would be in control of her destiny and that was what mattered most.

Now that she was free, she had her own dreams to attain.

Twenty

Later that evening at the Democratic Club, the floodtide of congratulations made Drew feel as if his mouth was in a permanent frozen smile. His mind kept returning again and again to the conversation with Layla, just before they left the courtroom.

She said she loved him. Had the excitement of the moment caused her to say those words or did she really mean them? Did he dare to hope that her love was real?

He gazed out at the men seated before him, but it was Layla's face he saw, her sweet smile, and the sound of her laughter. She was a strong woman who listened to him, yet stood up to him and she apologized when she was wrong.

Michael Ledoux, the president of the Democratic Club, stood up at the podium.

"As you may be aware," Mr. Ledoux began rather pompously, "We have been watching the murder trial of Layla Cuvier with great interest. And here today after a stunning victory that shocked the city and its citizens, is the man the Democratic Club has picked to be the next mayor of New Orleans, Drew Soulier."

Drew rose and walked to the platform, suddenly uncertain what he would say. He gazed out at the members, his mind racing, somehow feeling that this was wrong for him.

They waited expectantly while he gathered his thoughts.

"I want to thank Mr. Ledoux and the members of the Democratic Club for your nomination. It's an honor to be asked to represent the Democratic party in the next election. I can't tell you how long and hard I've worked for this nomination. My father, who is standing at the back of the room, hoped for this since I was a little boy."

Drew paused, suddenly certain that all of this was meaningless. Layla loved him and he loved her. Though he had fought the feelings, he knew with certainty that he had loved her for a long time. He looked out at the crowd of men who sat patiently waiting his acceptance. "While I'm honored that you've chosen me—unfortunately, I cannot accept."

The crowd gasped and an incredible sensation of joy filled Drew. He knew with certainty he was meant to be with Layla. He loved her, wanted to spend his life with her, wanted to grow old with nobody but Layla.

He took a deep breath. "I'm sorry if I've wasted your time tonight—and I thank you all for your faith in me."

He stepped down. At first the room was silent but then, slowly, applause began and grew louder.

Michael Ledoux approached the podium. "Well, Mr. Soulier, this is the first time we've ever had someone turn us down. But we respect your decision and we wish you the best."

Drew fumbled with the lock on his town house door, anxious to get inside and tell Layla how much he loved her. Why he hadn't known his own mind before tonight was beyond him, but once he found himself gazing out at all those pompous old fools, he'd known they weren't worth giving up a woman who loved him.

Once inside, he hurried up the stairs, taking them two at a time, anxious to find her. When he reached her door, he knocked softly. "Layla, wake up, we've got to talk."

Esmeralda came up the stairs in her housecoat. "Mr. Soulier, she's gone."

Shocked, Drew turned and stared. "What? What do you mean she's gone?"

"She packed her bags and left this evening."

"Did she say where she was going?"

"No, sir. She just left."

Drew opened the door to her room and turned on a lamp. The room was nearly empty. Everything of Layla's was gone.

A note lay on the bed.

My Dearest Love,

Thank you so much for giving me my freedom. You deserve to be happy and achieve your dreams and I don't want to hinder you in any way. So I am leaving. I have learned so much from you and I want you to know that I am determined to be responsible for the choices I make in my life from now on. Live well, be happy, and think of me now and then . . .

Layla

Drew sank to the bed, not knowing what to do, feeling as if his heart had been ripped out of his chest.

He had to find her. He loved her.

Drew had gone to the convent, to her home in Baton Rouge, looked high and low for a week, but found nothing. Layla seemed to have vanished.

Finally, in desperation, he went in search of Captain Frank Olivier, hoping he knew where Layla could be found.

Late one afternoon, he knocked on the door of the older man's home. When the captain opened the door, a grin spread across his face. "Ah, she was wrong."

"Wrong?" Drew asked.

"She told me you wouldn't come looking for her and I said you would. That if you cared for her as I thought you did, you'd show up. And here you are. You are here to ask me for her hand, aren't you?"

Drew gazed at the old man. "Yes . . . I mean, she's here?"

"She's with my sister," the captain said, opening the door wide. "Come in."

The older man laughed. "Come in and we will sit and talk. Since her papa didn't look after her the first time, I must do the honors."

Drew walked in the door and followed the captain through the house into a parlor.

"Take a seat, young man." He pulled out a chair for his guest.

Drew sat down, gritting his teeth. He had to play the captain's game in order to find out where Layla was. And he had to tell her what a fool he had been not to realize he loved her before now.

"So, do you love her?" the captain asked, coming right to the point.

"Of course I do," Drew replied. "That's why I'm here. I've been searching for her."

"Tell me *why* you love her," the captain demanded.

Drew stopped for a moment, not wanting to tip his hand. Yet he had to find Layla and if that meant confessing his love for her, he would do it.

"Because she's strong and caring and more stubborn than any woman I've ever met. She makes me laugh, she comforts me when I'm sad. And she listens to me and loves me in spite of my faults."

The older gentleman looked at him shrewdly, nodding his head. "Very good. But what happens when the ward bosses ask you to run for mayor again—and believe me, they will. What about Layla then? Will you still love her or resent her for keeping you from a brilliant career in politics?"

Drew shook his head and smiled. "I shall always love her. And if she loves me as she said, then she'll be at my side. Politicians come and go, but I want Layla at my side loving me when I'm ninety."

The captain was silent, folding his hands and assuming a waiting stance.

"Does this mean I meet with your approval?" Drew asked, not knowing what was expected of him next.

The older man nodded.

Drew cleared his throat. "Then—sir—I'd like to have your permission to ask your goddaughter to marry me."

The man laughed. "Ask her, she's standing right behind you."

Drew jumped up and turned around, while Frank softly slipped from the room.

Layla walked through the doorway, tears in her eyes, and he wondered how long she had been standing there.

Drew felt his heart hammer in his chest. She looked even more beautiful than the last time he had seen her. His eyes drank in the sight of her.

"God, I've missed you," he said knowing he meant every word. He moved toward her, his arms outstretched.

"And I've missed you," she said and they embraced, holding each other tightly.

He broke free of her arms, determined to do this

right. "I came here to ask Frank for help. I didn't know you were here."

He paused, seeing the uncertainty on her face.

"For the last week I've been searching for you, just so I could ask you to marry me. But your godfather insisted I do it right. He's given his approval," he said. "Will you have me as your husband, Layla? I promise to love you for the rest of my life. You are the only woman for me."

She put her hand to her mouth and he could see the excitement sparkle in her eyes, yet something held her back.

He dropped his voice to a whisper. "I need you, Layla, by my side. Forever."

"Drew, I—I want you to be happy—"

"Then say yes. I need your love to guide me until the day I die."

Layla reached out and took his head in her hands and pulled it toward her until his mouth met hers. She melded her lips to his as he wrapped his arms around her.

"Marry me, Layla. Marry me right now, as soon as possible."

She laughed, the sound carefree. "Yes, oh yes, I'll marry you."

"Is that the truth, the whole truth, and nothing but the truth?" he asked, still uncertain he heard her correctly.

"Stop talking like a lawyer! I need you, Drew Soulier. I need you to teach me the ways of real love. I'll wear your ring, I'll be your wife, I'll—"

Drew smiled. "I don't have a ring, but I promise I'll get you one. But I do have something else to give you."

He slipped the papers out of his pocket and handed her the envelope. Still in his arms, she glanced at him in puzzlement and then opened it.

Inside was the deed to the house in Baton Rouge. He watched as the tears welled up in her eyes.

"Oh, Drew," she cried as she wrapped her arms around him and hugged him. "I love you so much."

He smiled. "Now we can go home—to Baton Rouge. Only this time, we shall return as man and wife."

"Yes," she cried. "I want nothing more."

She snuggled up against him and Drew knew he had made the right decision. There had always been a reason he had dreamed of Layla as a young man. He had loved her even then.

About the Author

Sylvia McDaniel and her husband, Don, live in Lewisville, Texas, with their teenage son, Shane, two rotten dachshunds, Putz and Ashley, and two fish that have lived longer than all the others from the pet store. At the present time, Sylvia works for a telecom company in the Dallas/Fort Worth area.

A 2001 Booksellers Best Finalist, a 1996 Romance Writers of America Golden Heart finalist, and the 1995 President of North Texas Romance Writers of America, Sylvia is very involved with the North Texas RWA and a member of Dallas Area Romance Authors.

Romantic Suspense from
Lisa Jackson

__The Night Before
  0-8217-6936-7 $6.99US/$9.99CAN

__Cold Blooded
  0-8217-6934-0 $6.99US/$9.99CAN

__Hot Blooded
  0-8217-6841-7 $6.99US/$8.99CAN

__If She Only Knew
  0-8217-6708-9 $6.50US/$8.50CAN

__Intimacies
  0-8217-7054-3 $5.99US/$6.99CAN

__Unspoken
  0-8217-6402-0 $6.50US/$8.50CAN

__Twice Kissed
  0-8217-6038-6 $5.99US/$6.99CAN

__Whispers
  0-8217-6377-6 $5.99US/$6.99CAN

__Wishes
  0-8217-6309-1 $5.99US/$6.99CAN

Available Wherever Books Are Sold!

Visit our website at **www.kensingtonbooks.com**.

Put a Little Romance in Your Life With
Melanie George

__Devil May Care
  0-8217-7008-X $5.99US/$7.99CAN

__Handsome Devil
  0-8217-7009-8 $5.99US/$7.99CAN

__Devil's Due
  0-8217-7010-1 $5.99US/$7.99CAN

__The Mating Game
  0-8217-7120-5 $5.99US/$7.99CAN

Available Wherever Books Are Sold!

Visit our website at **www.kensingtonbooks.com**.